MAGIC IN THE MADNESS

21 *Down* IN VEGAS

STEPHEN A. HAYES

21 DOWN IN VEGAS
Copyright © 2020 **STEPHEN A. HAYES**

All rights reserved. No part of this book may be used or reproduced by any means, graphic, electronic, or mechanical, including photocopying, recording, taping or by information storage and retrieval system without the written permission of the author except in the case of brief quotations embodied in critical articles and reviews.

Stratton Press Publishing
831 N Tatnall Street Suite M #188,
Wilmington, DE 19801
www.stratton-press.com
1-888-323-7009

Because of the dynamic nature of the Internet, any web addresses or links contained in this book may have changed since publication and may no longer be valid. The views expressed in the work are solely those of the author and do not necessarily reflect the views of the publisher, and the publisher hereby disclaims any responsibility for them.

ISBN (Paperback): 978-1-64895-275-3
ISBN (Ebook): 978-1-64895-276-0

Printed in the United States of America

1ST INNING

The year was 2006 as the Las Vegas Vipers were entering their tenth season as Major League Baseball and the National League's worst failure.

From game one until present, the first decade of the team's franchise performance could easily be summarized in just one word-pathetic. While his intentions were always of the highest hopes, Vipers owner Cisco "The Dealer" Wheeler could never seem to make the fabled "Grand Plan in the Sand" work the way he had visualized it.

After nine full years of valiant effort, it was still like trying to nail Jell-O to a tree. Since 1996 and now the year 2006, the Vipers had never come close to a winning season while supporting some of the highest paid talent and free agents that money couldn't buy. Now just a couple of months into the new season, it was clearly evident that it was all over once again before it even began. As Cisco watched his team from his royal and regal perch high above Mirage Field, he sadly realized that he knew this script already too much by heart. Each year while names would change, the basic plotline of this annual manuscript of seasonal tragedy always remained all too predictable.

It was deep into June, and the Vipers' record was already at 18-39. In baseball terminology, that translated into being buried last in the cellar of the National League's Western Division. This kind of perpetual disappointment was not why the son of Nevada's largest construction family had spent over 700 million dollars of his personal and family fortune to indulge the powers that be to bring Major League Baseball to the playground of the West. It was indeed a gamble for a town that hates losing, proving Las Vegas certainly had more exciting things to do than play life-support to a failing professional sports franchise. The attendance figures sadly agreed.

The inaugural season for the Vipers had been golden. In their first eighty-one home games, Las Vegas drew over three and a half million fans into one of baseball's most plush and exotic new ballparks. Nine years later, they were well under a million. Not only was Cisco "The Dealer" Wheeler's patience running out, but so was his once-thought-of-inexhaustible bank account.

White tigers in cages and showgirls delivering beer was once again the backdrop for another typically quick-to-cool desert night as the Las Vegas Vipers took the field against the Cincinnati Reds. Pitching for the Vipers was injury-prone lefty veteran Milt Caldwell while Bronson Arroyo was the hurler of record for the Reds.

The game started off as so many before them. A walk to Ryan Freel, a single by Brandon Phillips, and then a slow curveball that bounced off the back of Adam Dunn and the table was now set. With a 2-1 count and a fastball right down the middle of the strip, Ken Griffey Junior launched one deep into the Tinsel-town night to plate four on the board before most fans had even settled into their seats.

The chorus of boos rained down hard from the stands below as Cisco Wheeler slowly reached up and begun nervously surfing through the many channels on his big-screen TV that hung from the wall in his personal luxury box. He wasn't quite sure what he was looking for, but he was hoping for a quick diversion from the grim reality that was again becoming all too painful. As he flipped through the video landscape of choices, it just so happened to be an outstanding baseball play that suddenly froze both the remote in his hand as well as his frazzled attention span. Cisco glanced and saw that the channel was now set on ESPN Sports and it was the final game of the 2006 College World Series.

The second inning unfolded as the LSU Tigers were playing the previously obscure Bentley State University Eagles for college baseball's biggest prize.

Bentley State was one of the smaller division I schools located in Portsmouth, Ohio. This team of dreams had scratched, scraped, and muscled their way into a land where no school of its size had ever been before. With enrollment of just over five thousand, Bentley State was an institution that prided itself in building character and academic achievement in all zones of their sports department. Bentley's baseball coach Keith Madison was especially instrumental in getting every ounce of grit, guts, and desire from every one of his players. Keith was also a very shrewd and crafty motivator who understood that there were no boundaries of creativity when it came to managing on the field.

As Cisco Wheeler's attention locked into the ESPN telecast, he saw Eagle center fielder Cliff Collier make a diving headlong slam into the left field wall to make an incredible over-the-shoulder catch. As Collier quickly bounced back to his feet, his laser throw easily doubled up LSU's hustling phenom Josh Raines as he attempted to scramble back to first base. As he now began to focus in on the contest with a genuine interest, Cisco's attention was suddenly diverted back to his own painful reality as the next round of cat calls erupted.

With Red's short-stop Alex Gonzales on third, Vipers' highly paid left fielder Toots Randall caught what he thought was the third out of the inning. Immediately upon snagging the ball, he casually glanced toward the crowd while grasping the eye of a well-endowed female fan. Randall then nonchalantly tossed the prize in her direction as he began trotting back to the dugout. Gonzales immediately tagged up and raced home with another Reds run. Randall looked up in disbelief at the scoreboard as it displayed that there were now only two outs.

"Hell, they can't even count to three!" Cisco Wheeler exploded as he was again forced to realize that his millions were going to a product that looked like a gaggle of over-grown Little Leaguers.

Quickly turning away from yet another major embarrassment on his home turf, Cisco once again glanced at the television screen for some peace and solace as the ESPN play-by-play team was again going wild.

"The Bentley State Eagles have just pulled off a triple steal!" relished the play by the announcers. "With bases loaded, Coach Keith Madison called for a bases-loaded green light. As all the runners were all off with the pitch, right fielder Sean Deeters dropped down what was a textbook bunt and it was a sheer beauty!"

LSU third-baseman Chuck Greenslate scooped for the ball and fired, missing John Gambill streaking for home. From his knees, he threw the ball wildly to first as it sailed over the head of LSU catcher Jerry Thompson. Two more runs crossed the plate as Bentley State now led the favored Tigers by a tally of 4-1.

Three runs on a triple steal squeeze play! Few who followed the game had ever seen such an exhibit before. The Vipers' owner continued to watch as both his interest and intrigue thickened. Cisco soon became oblivious to his own baseball misfortunes and follies as the drama of the College World Series final had become increasingly mesmerizing. Now in the fourth inning, it was the LSU right fielder Kirk Kandran that led off with a line-drive base hit to right. As a close infield summit on the mound for the Eagles finally broke up, the players returned to their respective positions. Pitcher Mitch Milhuff stood on the mound glaring toward the plate as Kandran began to take his lead off first. As quick as a fly on bad picnic food, first baseman Bombo Chadwick turned and slapped the tag on a completely astonished and embarrassed baserunner.

"You're out!" screamed the first-base umpire.

The LSU Tigers couldn't believe it! They had just become a victim of the oldest ruse in the game. It was the unheralded Bentley State Eagles that dared attempt one of the game's most underutilized tricks in the books; the hidden ball play. The dupe is where the pitcher simply slides the ball to an infielder on the mound, and he carries it back to his position and waits for the runner to leave the bag. Considered by many to be one of the cheapest of all defensive plays, it's normally the resentment of being so easily snookered that fuels the sentiment of hostility.

As the ESPN announcers again continued their cavalcade of praises for the heads up and scrappy play of the Bentley State Eagles, the Las Vegas Vipers were going down hard…again.

With the score now 9-1 in the seventh inning in favor of the Reds, the Vipers were now in the midst of a modest rally.

21 DOWN IN VEGAS

Two-on and no-outs, runners were perched on second and third as first baseman Wally Cremeans hit a screaming line drive down the left field line. As the ball disappeared into the far corner, both runners had already crossed third and were heading for home. Suddenly, the crowd roared as the third-base umpire who ran down left field line quickly threw up the out sign. It was Red's outfielder Josh Hamilton that had made a diving stab on the ball that snatched the leather just inches from touching the left field grass.

Both runners stopped as they saw Hamilton come bouncing up with the ball and fire it towards third. As the errant base runners for the Vipers attempted to retrace their steps, it was like that slow-motion dream sequence where one is running in quick sand. The throw arrived at third-base special express delivery to complete one of the most bizarre triple plays that most baseball aficionados could ever imagine. In almost every definition of the moment, this play would certainly qualify as your good old-fashioned "rally killer."

At the same time in a parallel baseball universe, even higher drama was once again unfolding. As Cisco Wheeler slowly pulled his hands away from his face, he noticed that the LSU Tigers were now coming back.

It was now the bottom of the sixth, and the score was now tied. LSU had now capitalized on Bentley State Pitcher Mitch Milhuff's tiring arm. Back to back doubles, a single, and now a triple had tied the score at four runs apiece. It was a sacrifice fly to center that pushed the go-ahead run across the plate for the Bayou Bengals.

Before Eagles Coach Keith Madison began his slow walk to the mound, the tears on Milhuff's face couldn't be hidden from the multiple camera angles. He slowly walked toward the dugout to a standing ovation. This little team from Nowhere, USA, had captured the hearts and attention of an appreciative nation for the entire tournament and was just this close to winning it all.

Cisco Wheeler's full regard was now glued exclusively to the game as Eagle's relief pitcher Jeremy Burkes got loose and finished his warm-up tosses. It was the look on Burke's face that telegraphed the next heroic story-line to the plot. In just three pitches, the task was complete. As the scoreboard displayed the stats that read LSU-5 and Bentley State4, it was the last chance for a team that had won the respect of so many and was now praying for just one more miracle.

Second baseman Brooks Snyder led off the seventh. Snyder was one of those dirty uniform curmudgeons that ran like a deer and showed no fear. He worked Tigers Pitcher Jeff Hanshaw into a full count before fouling off six-straight pitches. On the seventh pitch, he passed on a ball that was gutsy to take, but it fell in his favor. The Bentley State Eagles only hope to play-on was now standing at first.

ESPN accolades continued as the announcers compared the clash on the field to everything from David and Goliath to the movie *Hoosiers*. No sport clichés were left at the door on this one.

There were no outs as the Eagles Center Fielder Cliff Collier stood in, and he knew what he had to do; it was automatic. Problematic to the strategy of the sport, so did everybody else, including the LSU Tigers.

With the infield creeping in, Collier showed the anticipated bunt. Using a half-swing known as a "tomahawk chop," Collier put the ball into play just out of reach of the off--balance pitcher to the left side of the infield. Snyder was now off and streaking toward second. LSU's third-baseman Quinton McCauley did the only option available by picking the ball off the turf bare-handed and quickly firing it to first, nipping the speedy Collier at the bag by a half a step.

There was now one-out and the Eagles' last hope stood on second as it was "-Mr. Contact-"as he was known standing at the plate. Brooks Snyder cautiously led off second as first baseman Bombo Chadwick's job was to bring the game's score back to even. Chadwick was most certainly the "clutch" to the Vipers' offensive engine and a solid player who very seldom struck out. He led the Mid-American Conference for two years in a row with the fewest K's of any starting player. Working the count to 2 and 2, he got underneath one that he knew should have traveled much farther. Throwing down his bat in disgust, he watched a high and lazy can of corn fall into the glove of the LSU right fielder.

Once again, Cisco Wheeler's eyes were transfixed to the action from his luxury box as Sean Deeters stepped to the plate. As the ESPN field cameras slowly panned the Eagles' dugout, all bodies were now standing on the steps and adorned in frantic rally cap fashion. The players were all arm in arm and throwing as much positive energy as they could onto the field. The crowd at 1200 Mike Fahey Street in Omaha, Nebraska, was now in a certified frenzy as Deeters took the first pitch for a called strike one. Brooks Snyder continued to dance off second, clapping and screaming for the chance to join his teammates in the dugout. On the next pitch, Sean seized the moment on an outside fast-ball and swung hard. He felt he had the range, but it was a foul ball deep down the line and out of play.

With each singular event, the drama and momentum continued to build. The ESPN broadcast crew was now hoarse and losing whatever vocal stamina they had left. Often called the hitter's count with two balls, two strikes, the pitch sailed plate ward.

This time, Deeters found the seams, and like a scalded rabbit, the ball shot up the middle and fell on a short-hop into center- field. Snyder was off with the ping of the bat and knew where his last stop would have to be on this one. The ball rolled to center field quickly as the stadium erupted like the home stretch at Churchill Downs as Brooks Snyder rounded third and was heading for home.

Sensing the play would be close, he began his slide on the outside of the plate. Hearing the smack of leather meeting leather, his hand scrambled across the plate, feeling the simultaneous thud of force grinding deep into his ribs.

Both bodies crashed together and tangled into a dirt-devil of dust. It seemed like an eternity as he rolled over and lay on his back in a thick cloud of uncertainty. Snyder slowly opened his eyes and found them transfixed at the umpire's thumb level as he saw it jerk skyward. Watching in horror, he heard the two most dreaded words of the game as a runner; "You're out!"

It was over. The final score in the 2006 College World Series would forever read the LSU Tigers 5, the Bentley State University Eagles 4.

Chaos spilled onto the field from the Tigers' faithful as the story-book ending that most were rooting for was now inked into an official disappointment for the little guy. There were the typical cheers and tears as well as hind-sight's natural could-a's, would-a's, and should-a's, but there was one thing that stood alone. Any fan of the game knew and relished the taste of perhaps one the greatest sports contests that had ever been played in recent memory.

For the Bentley State Eagles, it was a relished season that few could have ever imagined. Here was a small Mid-east college team that was just a face in the crowd beating every obstacle imaginable in taking their legacy and game to the final out of college baseball's biggest reception. In a genuine and grandiose scale, the loss was pale to the effort it provided.

This truly remarkable sporting episode should have been good for a lifetime of local lore. Who could have ever imagined that this most unlikely of contingency would serve as a minor tune-up for future events yet to come. For unknown to many, it was a man who possessed an unlimited portion of passion and fervor for baseball's much storied and colorful history who had been quietly sitting back and watching this incredulous story unfold from the shadows.

The stadium's electric glow began to slowly fade into the night and history as well as the yammering post-game media finally moved out into the city of lights as two men sat alone in a dimly lit luxury suite in Las Vegas, Nevada. Both sat silent for several minutes as the one who occupied the big expensive leather chair behind the giant mahogany desk carefully gathered his own thoughts together before speaking.

"I want that team!" declared Vipers Owner Cisco "The Dealer" Wheeler.

Brandon Briggs who was general manager of the Vipers franchise looked up from his box scores for the evening and quickly shot back, "What team?"

"I want that team, damn it! The one I watched tonight. The one that lost in the College World Series, I want them here, all of them!" he sternly stated.

"Again, Cisco, you want all of whom for what?" Briggs asked in a state of virtual confusion.

"Look at your damn box score and tell me what you see… right now, please!" an extremely agitated Wheeler asked his general manager.

21 DOWN IN VEGAS

"It isn't pretty," Briggs said while clearing his throat, "but here you go. The Cincinnati Reds 14 runs, 23 hits, and no errors. The Vipers 2 runs, 6 hits, 5 errors, plus a play that will be a legendary highlight blooper from now until doomsday. What else do you want to know?"

"See, I'm tired of it…-starting today!" Wheeler shouted. "What is our damn payroll, Brandon? A hundred and ninety- million? Two-hundred million? Hell, it doesn't matter one way or the other. It's all horse-shit when you have the kind of product that we dump out there every night. All we are a glorified soup kitchen for millionaires', and it all stops today, damn it- and right now!"

Obviously, the intensity of the conversation began to escalate to what some might consider the ravings of a madman. As the owner and his general manager of baseball's worst team continued to access the dismal cards they were holding, the spirit on which their city was built began to infiltrate the evaluation process. It was time to clear the table and ask the dealer for a new hand.

The next day found the two gentlemen at it again sequestered in Wheeler's plush office overlooking the strip. In front of them was a calculator, a video-tape of the previous day's championship game, and a complete roster guide for the Bentley State University Eagles.

"Brandon, you should have seen them," Wheeler beamed. "It was baseball, man! Real baseball! It wasn't this happy horse crap we try to pawn off here every night and every season. I want to bring what I saw yesterday to our city and give fans what they truly deserve! I want to see these guys standing on the steps holding on to each other and believing totally in what they're all about!"

"As the owner of this team, you have every right to wish for anything you want, but bringing in an unheard bunch of players from some college baseball team to the Major Leagues? We're already the laughing-stock now. Believe me, Cisco; this one would give them fodder-stock for years. Think about what you're saying here, and seriously. Look, maybe we could just cherry-pick a few of their best players and start from there?" Brandon Briggs countered back in a spirit of reason.

"Let's watch the game again, and afterwards we'll talk." Cisco offered, "Not a word until after it's completely over, just promise me that."

As the two began to watch the final game again between the LSU Tigers and the Bentley State Eagles, they also silently began taking separate notes as well as scouting the roster guide. Briggs quietly figured that out of the twenty—one-player team roster, there might be only four players from the squad that could even come close to being considered for the upcoming MLB baseball draft at best.

Second Baseman Brooks Snyder was a solid fielder, and he hit for average. His senior year had him an automatic for league honors, batting .368 with a school record for doubles and 43 stolen bases. He was always clutch in the crisis.

Right-handed pitcher Mitch Milhuff had been the rock of the Eagles' pitching rotation. With a 14 and 2 record, his arm withstood a season that became extended beyond his wildest expectations. It literally seemed every big game that the Eagles needed, Milhuff was solidly there with yet another championship performance. His earned run average was a constant 2.15 and the word *walk* was foreign to his vocabulary. In almost 110 innings of work, Milhuff free-passed only 17 batters. Even as his warrior weary arm tired late in the final game, his heart could never be questioned.

Sean Deeters was best described by a sportswriter as a mosquito in a uniform. He was pesky, would never leave you alone, and seemed to bite when you least expected it. As the Eagles' golden glove right fielder, ominous things to the opposition always seemed to occur whenever he was at the plate. When he struck out, it was a local headline news story. If you needed a genuine spark for any given situation, Sean Deeters would bring the matches as well as the high-octane.

Gary "Bombo" Chadwick was the Eagles' rock-solid first baseman and a run-producing machine. He had led the conference with 27 home runs and 67 RBI's in 42 games. "Bombo" was also the kind of player you wanted at the plate when a run was considered not just an option, but a necessity.

"King Kong" Karl Smith was an anomaly of power and potential. At the age of twenty-two, he had hit a baseball over 500 feet against the Toledo Rockets which analysts proclaimed was as far as Mickey Mantle's longest career smash. As his power numbers grew, his major problem of strike-outs began to dwindle as he learned how to harness his strength in a more efficient manner. It was pretty much a given that with "Kong" at the plate, scoring opportunities were always just a plane-swat away from becoming dangerous.

As the two watched the game together in silence, they both understood what each other was feeling. What indeed went so wrong with America's pristine past-time and why couldn't it be this way again? As the post-game ended and ESPN programming quickly moved on to the Texas Hold'em finals in El Paso, the video-tape continued to play on. Shifting clock-wise in his chair from behind his desk, Cisco Wheeler once again looked at his long-time friend and general manager in the eye and again proclaimed, "I want that team."

Having placated his boss's whimsical desires for almost seven years, Brandon Briggs also had the ability to talk him off the ledge when he considered his ideas a little too bizarre. This was a classic text of one of those moments.

"You're telling me that you think you can bring that team, a bunch of college kids into this league, as is mind you, and win baseball games?" Briggs stammered.

"Yes!" Wheeler readily returned.

"Cisco, they're just college kids! If you want to start over again, we have talent in the minors who are all far more experienced than the Bentley State Eagles for Christ's sake. I'm not even sure the league would allow you to do such a thing. By the way, there is a little thing called MLB Players Union and- another annoying little agency called the NCAA, you know!-"

"So, it's my damn team, Brandon. They're my employees. If they can't do the job, then I have every right to fire them all- and I will!" Cisco blustered. "You've been with me here for most of our baseball existence, Brandon. When was the last time you saw any of our players hustle like that?"

The owner had pretty well laid it squarely all on the line, and his GM knew that any counter-response would be impossible to defend.

"I don't care whether they have Major League experience or not. Take a look around at this damn league. It's full of mediocre and over-paid whiners who think that a .500 record and a .240 batting average are totally acceptable. I'm sure you remember when we gave Eric Salmon a four-year contract for twenty-five million to go 5 and 28! I'm tired of it, Brandon. Both you and I can do something right now. Something that's absolutely never been done before. Will we be the laughingstock you ask?"

As if on cue, the *ESPN* baseball highlights from the day before kicked in live on the TV as the tape in the video machine clicked off and came to an abrupt end.

"And here's one that should have come from "*Ripley's Believe It or Not.*" A triple-play pulled off against the lowly Las Vegas Vipers by the Cincinnati Reds. Watch as the ball goes deep into the left field corner, and there's Josh Hamilton! He picks it off while both Vipers runners have already crossed the plate. Now, we've checked the *Elias Book on Baseball*, and this is the first time ever that we can find that a 7 to 3 triple-play has ever been pulled off in any league. Also, the last time we checked, those Vipers runners were still out there caught somewhere between the intersections of 'lost' and 'confused' on the base path. Incredible!"

"I think that question has just been answered, Brandon, I want that team. Now, are you going to help me, or am I going to have to be looking for a new general manager who can?"

Listening to his eccentric boss and mentor, Brandon stared at the floor before slowly preparing his answer. "OK, I have two questions, Cisco. Where the hell is Portsmouth, Ohio, and when do you want me to leave?"

2ᴺᴰ INNING

Flying into Port Columbus and then traveling eighty-seven miles south, Vipers' General Manager Brandon Briggs was actually pleasantly surprised on his arrival.

Bentley State University was a beautiful institution located directly on the Ohio River in a port town of about 20,000. Portsmouth was once a vibrant steel river settlement, but with the decline of industry like many other rust-belt cities, they were attempting to re-forge its identity after the post-war manufacturing revolution ended. Briggs found that education, and health care, and tourism had replaced the smoke stacks and the nickel plants of this former lunch—bucket town.

As he drove around, he wanted to feel all the necessary vibes before attempting to execute perhaps the most bizarre offer ever attempted in baseball history. While driving his rented Taurus toward the Third Street campus, Brandon was busy taking in the unusual floodwall artistry known locally as "The Murals." The river-front art gallery featured highly detailed panels that depicted much of the natural as well as historical highlights of the area from past to present painted by Louisiana artist Robert Dafford. As he passed one scene in particular, he slammed on the brakes in disbelief. Standing before him was a sixty-foot high painting of none other than Branch Ricky signing Jackie Robinson to his historic contract.

"*Interesting,*" he thought. "*Branch Ricky was from here? Wow, now that puts things in a whole different perspective.*"

Pondering the parallels of his mission that he had just discovered, Brandon slowly felt the tightness in his stomach begin to lessen.

As he continued to stare at the giant hand-painted mural before him, he slowly felt as if he were drawing some kind of spiritual power from what it represented. The immaculate depiction that stared down in front of him finally came into sharp focus that this just wasn't about baseball. What this stoic image represented was both daring and creative thinking in its purist form. What Branch Ricky ventured to accomplished in 1947 was to simply blaze a trail that had been previously been ostracized and ignored.

While certainly the times and circumstances were different, Brandon hit the accelerator pedal with the feeling this was a stop that had been pre-ordained to make. Rolling up to the next stop sign, he found that fate was even more succinctly spelled out for him as the brown lettering on the street sign read "Bentley State University: Left."

Call it a sixth-sense, but there's an inbreed radar that somehow leads sports people to sports people. Without any prior knowledge of the facility or even a campus map, the general manager of the Las Vegas Vipers, Brandon Briggs found himself in a complex with a hall that he knew would lead him to his prodigal calling. He finally found an office with a plate inscribed with the name of the man he was looking for.

"Hi, is Keith around?" Brandon asked the obvious student secretary at the desk.

"Well, he's teaching a class right now, but he should be done in about twenty minutes. Do you have an appointment?" she asked

"No, let's just say I'm an old friend with a lot in common. Do you mind if I just wait?

"Go right ahead," she offered. "I'm sure Keith will be happy to see you."

About a half-hour of sitting and reading through the Eagles' stats, a tall, good-looking gentleman with salt-and-pepper hair finally bounced through the door.

"Sorry I'm late Linda, any messages?"

"Yes, your wife called and Andy came home early with the flu. You need to call Bill Warnock about the baseball banquet ASAP, and this gentleman is here to see you." she casually informed him.

"I'm sorry, I don't have an appointment Keith, but I would like a few words with you if possible." Brandon Briggs began.

Sensing the encounter had something to do with his team; Keith Madison immediately pulled the trigger and threw up a quick defensive shield.

"If this has anything to do about recruiting, by law, I am not allowed to meet or even discuss scholarships for another month." he sternly responded.

"No," Brandon politely replied. "This isn't about recruiting. What I need is just a few minutes of your time, and by the way, congratulations are in order. I know I'm one in millions who you've heard say that lately, but your team's play in the series, it was certainly quite a feat."

After a quizzical glance, Keith told his secretary to hold all calls as he invited the yet to be known visitor into his office. It was a rather awkward beginning that finally put the two in front of each other in private to discuss a deal that Brandon Briggs still couldn't quite visualize, yet verbalize.

While preparing his proposal, he kept thinking back at the mural on the flood-wall and the look of confidence on the face of Branch Ricky with pen in hand. At the same time, he also gazed upon the face of a man who he knew harbored miles of character and self-respect.

Keith Madison had been a pitching prospect for the Atlanta Braves at the age of nineteen. A couple of seasons in the minors and then a torn rotator cuff, his pro career was tragically over. He went on to get his degree in teaching from the University of Kentucky and proceeded to serve as the assistant baseball coach.

When Bentley State needed a full-time coach for its then fledgling program, Keith took the job in 1987 and never looked back. Even before the Bentley State Eagles made it to the finals of the College World Series, Madison was on the radar as the kind of stand-up guy that you always wanted in your dugout. Brandon was the first to break the ice.

"Keith, again congratulations are in order on a truly magic season. The eyes of the whole nation were on you. My name is

Brandon Briggs. I'm the general manager and vice president of the Las Vegas Vipers."

"Well, thank you," Keith replied. "I'm honored to have you stop by. It has all been pretty crazy. The press has been, well, you know, over the top on the follow-up to this thing and the city is about ready to throw us a big wing-ding tomorrow night. I'm sorry it ended the way it did, but it was great fun while it lasted."

"I bet it was," Brandon responded. "I bet it was."

"Well, I'm really honored to have you drop by. Is there anything in particular that I can do for you?" Keith asked.

"That is indeed quite the question," Brandon laughingly replied. "What would you say if I told you that I was here to ask your permission to help change the landscape of Major League Baseball as we know it?"

As Brandon Briggs began doing all the talking, the Eagles' coach did all the listening. Before he began to speak, Brandon envisioned that he would probably be perceived as a wild-eyed visionary with little substance and all mega-bluster. We've all heard the world's greatest inventions and life-altering possibilities while standing around at cocktail parties.

At the time, some of those theories sounded pretty good. In a perfectly sober environment, Brandon knew that his offerings at best would be an impossible sell for a concept that was virtually unheard of. No one outside of the two principle architects of this theory knew for sure how the offer would fly outside the plush and opulent office of Cisco Wheeler. For sure, the conversation would soon be entering uncharted territory, and yes, for certain, there be dragons.

Gathering his thoughts to begin his monologue, Brandon's mind suddenly flashed back to the floodwall mural and a man sporting a confident smile, a cigar, and a massive hand-shake.

"Keith, what I'm about to ask of you has never been done before in the history of the game. All I ask is that you listen and hear what I have to say before passing judgment."

Without blinking, Keith stoically proclaimed, "The floor is yours."

"In a nutshell, Keith, the Las Vegas Vipers have sent me here to hire, not recruit, but again to hire your entire baseball team to become the nucleus of our franchise." Briggs declared. "I am coming to you first out of the respect that our organization has for everything you have done here at Bentley State."

Stunned at first, Keith slowly started to smile. "Who sent you here? Was it Doug Flynn? That ass-hole! I knew he was going to pay me back somehow for losing his tickets at the box office for the semi-finals. I must say if indeed, Mr. Briggs is it? You had me going for just a second. This is a pretty good one!"

"Well," Brandon nervously laughed. "Considering all I've been through to get here, it would have been a pretty expensive prank on the behalf of Mr. Flynn to send me all the way to Portsmouth, Ohio, just to yank your chain a little, don't you think?"

"I'm sorry!" Keith quickly uttered. "I've really had a long day, and I have to admit that I'm more than just a little lost. You say you want to hire my entire baseball team? I'm sorry, but you're going to have to do a little more explaining here."

As the two men locked serious eye contact, it was now the stand-off moment that Brandon feared might happen if his presentation seemed too extreme. All he could do now was lay all of his cards face up on the table.

"What we are willing to do, Keith, is give each one of your boys a two-year contract for the Major League minimum of $350,000 per year. Each player will then be given incentives should they excel, as we believe they will, and they will be additionally and fairly rewarded for their talents. It should also be noted that in return for the cooperation of the players…shall we say, 'suspending' their current college educations, the Las Vegas Vipers organization will pay for the remainder of each player's college degree when they decide to resume their education at whatever time they choose. We of course would also like to make a place for you too in our organization."

"Mr. Briggs, forgive me for my seemingly unappreciative stance, but my first question to you would simply be- is this even at all legal?"

"Keith, we've already explored all the legalities of such a structure move, and since this really has nothing to do with academics, we can independently hire each one of your players as we could any individual to a contract who we felt would contribute to the betterment our team. Now, Cisco Wheeler is adamant that he wants all of them, and he also wants you to be a part of our organization! I guess my question is simply, where do we go from here?"

After an awkward moment of silence, Keith Madison found himself leaning back in his chair and counting the ceiling tiles while searching the moment for the appropriate response.

"The whole team," he started. "You want to hire the entire team? I must say that I'm a bit over-loaded here. Of my twenty-one roster players, nine are seniors, six are juniors. I have five sophomores and a walk-on. Now let me get this straight again. You want all of them, every player I have, to sign a Major League Baseball contract and play for the Las Vegas Vipers? We're talking about the same team that plays in the National League Western Division I assume?"

"Yes sir, that is one and the same." Briggs answered.

"To be honest, I must say that I've never even imagined anything like that could or even be possible."

"Mr. Madison, do you believe in the concept of team?" Briggs asked.

"Of course I do," Keith Madison shot back. "I'm a coach, and that's all I believe in. You saw it for yourself what these boys accomplished this year or am I being a little too presumptuous?"

"You played in the minors, Keith." Brandon countered. "What do you think is the degree of raw talent between, let's say, a big league player and a good double-A player? Raw talent I'm asking."

"Raw talent?" Keith pondered. "It's really not that much because this game is mostly all between the ears. That is another big thing I teach my boys."

"Exactly, so what you're actually telling me is that a well-coached team with the chemistry of players who all want to win together, as a team, mind you, is really not that far removed from the field of many Major Leaguers who are playing the game today who, say…might lack those intrinsic qualities." Briggs summarized.

"I guess what you're saying kind of makes sense, but what about us? I mean, what about Bentley State University?" Madison quickly flared. "OK, you come in here and take every player I have, then what am I supposed to do for a team?"

"Good question…and we've already thought about your plight on that one." Briggs continued. "Our owner, Mr. Cisco Wheeler, is a very generous man. As a matter of record, he is far too generous at times, but he certainly wants to be fair. He has created a college scholarship fund that places well-deserving kids on many college and universities campuses across the country. He and his foundation are also very much connected to young athletes who want to play baseball at the university level. These are all good players who he someday hopes will repay the favor by wanting to play for the Vipers. He has authorized for me to give you and Bentley State University, twenty-one fully paid academic scholarships, plus a list of quality baseball talent who would love to come here and play for the Bentley State Eagles."

"Wait a minute!" Keith shot back "That is illegal! We only have so many baseball scholarships that we're allowed to give out. C'mon, the NCAA would never allow that!"

"Mr. Madison, these are not baseball scholarships. These would be general academic scholarships for students who might just like to, say, 'walk on' the team if their talent level is determined to be sufficient. Do you understand what I'm saying here?" Brandon Briggs asked.

"I think I'm hearing you." Keith politely returned. "I only have one walk-on and he certainly has no future in the game beyond where he is now. He's a great kid with perhaps the best ambassador for heads-up play I think I have ever seen. He also has a great baseball mind. That's really the only reason he's on this team, and he hardly ever plays."

"That would be Jarred Brewster?" quizzed Brandon Briggs.

"Yes, that would be Jarred." Keith replied.

Jarred Brewster's whole life simply loved the game of baseball. He was a local Portsmouth boy who grew up playing from the earliest city leagues through high school. As a rather stocky youth, Jarred either caught or played first base. He was the kind of student who loved and studied the game so much; he could often get on your nerves.

On the bench, he was constantly watching the opponent's players. He would analyze the various situations and try to get his teammates to do the same.

At the age of fourteen, Jarred broke his leg in a sledding accident and had to sit out the next season. Any evening that following summer you could always find Jarred over at Mound Park leaning up against the fence on his crutches and rooting his team on.

The next year, Jarred returned to play high school ball, but discovered a startling disappointment. He found that sitting out an entire year at the age of fifteen retarded him skill-wise and he was never really able to catch up that lost year to his peers. Jarred hung around to play on the High School Trojans as a seldom used backup catcher and a full-time cheerleader.

Coach Madison always referred to Jarred as his "talk-on" player for his ability to convince Keith to finally let him be a member of the Eagles even though his natural ability was questionable. While his playing time was indeed limited, his spirit and positive flow was always boundless as a true spiritual leader on the team.

As the conversation began to wind down, Brandon Briggs extended his offer to Keith Madison in a more definitive outline.

"Keith," he started, "I hope you realize that none of this would have ever happened without you. It is Mr. Wheeler's and my hope that you would consider becoming a part of our dream and help us with our plan to move the team and baseball's attitude in general to that next level."

"I really appreciate that, I really do." Keith started. "First of all, I do have a contract with the university as a teacher. I am the baseball coach, but that's kind of my outlet for fun. I really enjoy it. My obligation is right here and now at Bentley State University. I'm working on tenure you know, and I supposed they'll need me here. Especially if what you're proposing could actually really happen. I do thank you for your offer, but right here in Portsmouth, Ohio, this is my home."

"How do you want to do this, Keith?" asked Brandon. "Should we talk to them as a whole or individually, it's all your call."

With so much from just a short time swirling in his head, Keith Madison was still unsure that any of these proposals could actually fly. On the other hand, this was a real Major League franchise and he wanted to be fair, but careful.

"Let's see, wow!" he pondered. "My best guess is that you call a private team meeting away from the university. If you don't mind, I won't be a part of it. I can talk to the boys privately and let them know there is a person who is interested in talking to them about their services and future. That's about as far as I can really go with this. By the way, I will have to inform the university of all this first. Even if there is no way for them to stop your proposal, I will have to let them know all about your intentions."

"Quite acceptable." said Briggs. "We are clearing the way for twenty--roster spots, and there is really no need for taking Brewster since he's just a token- player anyway. I'm sure he'll understand the nature of the situation. This offer is for only the full-time squad of your team."

"Mr. Briggs, I have to warn you about something. Talking to my boys as a unit compared to sitting here and just brain-storming with me is going to be a whole lot more complicated than you realize. While to you this all might look good on paper, these kids are young, but they're also very smart. Just don't go kidding yourself that this is going to be as easy as it seems."

"I'll keep that in mind, Keith, and I thank you for your honesty." Briggs added.

"Now we're getting ready for a celebration that the city is throwing for us tomorrow night at the Ramada Inn." Keith added. "We have the banquet room already rented, so, I'll just tell the boys to meet you there, say- how about in the morning at around 11:00 a.m. if that works for you?"

"Perfect! I'm staying at the Ramada myself, so it should work out fine. Again, on behalf of myself and the Las Vegas Vipers organization, Keith, I thank you for your time and candidacy." said Briggs.

"I only want what's best for my players. Hell, if I was twenty-one again and someone offered me $700,000 to play a game that I loved, I'm sure it would have gotten my attention." Madison said with a chuckle. "I ask just one promise, Mr. Briggs. They're all great kids. Don't ever let them get embarrassed, or hurt. That's my only request."

"You have my word on it." Brandon Briggs proclaimed.

That evening as promised, Keith Madison became a phone committee of one. If he couldn't reach each one of his players in person, he then made the designated phone answerer take the responsibility of getting this urgent plea to each and every one of his boys. They were all to assemble in the banquet room of the downtown Portsmouth Ramada Inn at 11:00 a.m. for an extremely important meeting. While it was stressed that it was to be a mandatory gathering, Coach Madison would not be there. All players were urged to be courteous and kind to the special guest and speaker who would be addressing them.

"Can you believe Coach?" Brooks Snyder said as he hung up the phone.

"He's probably got us another one of those *Sports Illustrated* geeks lined up to talk about the season again. This thing just won't go away."

"Hey, pal, lighten up!" his father retorted. "You have no idea what you guys really did, and you won't know for years to come. The USA Hockey team, the '86' Mets, hell, these kind of stories only come along every so often, and you were a big part of sports history, so ya big mo, don't act so put out about it!"

"But, Dad," Snyder spouted, "We lost! And I was the guy who got thrown out at the plate, remember? I'm the guy that sent us packing with the runner-up trophy! Sure I'm proud of what we did, but even in the end, with all the honors and stories, we were still the losers!"

As the wounds began to heal, the Bentley State Eagles still had some major issues on the table. The guessing game of what could have happened had Snyder stopped at third would always be a gnawing question. Most of the Bentley State players recovered quickly, realizing that it was a great ride and they had nothing to be ashamed of. There were still a few that couldn't shake the dogma of what might have been. Brooks Snyder was one who just wouldn't let it go.

The coconut grapevine was burning up the Portsmouth night air as the shroud of mystery concerning the meeting began to spread. Players began calling players trying to see if anyone knew more than the other. The final assessment was it had to be a photo shoot of some kind before the big banquet that night. As the chatter began to subside, all twenty-one players had finally been reached and informed. Going to bed that night was just a regular routine. It would be the last for a band of baseball brothers who would learn all too quickly about destiny's unexpected curve-balls.

They say in life that 90 percent of success is just showing up. Over the past six months, the Bentley State Eagles had committed themselves to unlimited and countless hours of grueling practice and preparation like no college team before them. While they were expected to do well, no one saw or could fathom the affluence that the team would ultimately attain. As one day melted into the next, there would again be yet another open door with a most unlikely invitation. For the Bentley State Eagles, the next sojourn into the great unknown would be prefaced as "one-way only."

The team began to spill into the unoccupied Damon's banquet room of the Portsmouth, Ohio, Ramada Inn as the preparation was in the making for a celebration fit for the almost champions. Banners, press clippings, and other regalia of the season were being prepared and arranged for the six hundred-plus guests who would spill in to show their love to the team later -that evening.

Precisely at 11:00 a.m. a stranger entered through the side door and walked tentatively to the podium. As he fumbled with the volume control, there were several squeals of feedback as he nervously set up his notes to address the small, but curious audience. Brandon Briggs may have been the general manager of a Major League baseball team, but his initial impression was that of a man who was extremely nervous and really not sure of even where to begin.

"Uh, first of all, let me introduce myself." he awkwardly began. "My name is Brandon Briggs and I am the general manager of the Major League franchise, the Las Vegas Vipers."

Besides a roar of quiet, the sequence of head turning from player to player was deafening.

"I certainly appreciate everybody being here on such short notice as I do realize that we are in the midst of a festival of your achievements in the recent College World Series. Being the head of a

Major League club, I've grown to detest the phrase 'moral victory.' In watching your inspirational performances against some of the most talented universities in the country, I have temporarily rescinded my thinking on that term. What you and this university accomplished on the stage of a national arena was the pure stuff that legends are made of. While the end result came up one run short, the excess of team effort was anything less than stunning. Who would have ever thought that a college baseball team from Portsmouth, Ohio, would find ways to win over programs such as Texas, North Carolina, Stanford, Florida, and then finally giving the LSU Tigers all they could ever want. Gentleman, your execution and demonstration of the concept of 'team' is the way this game of baseball was meant to be played. For that, I applaud you all."

There was a sense of something missing in the room when Sean Deeters suddenly and impulsively blurted out, "Hey, where's Coach?"

Without missing a beat, Brandon Briggs found this the appropriate place to begin. After all, in the history of the game, there was never a pitch like the one that was now on its way to the heart of the unknown corner of the soul.

"Gentlemen, due to the delicate nature of what I am about to ask of you, Coach Madison chose not to be present. His dedication to the university and especially for each and every one of you precluded his attendance today as it could be perceived as a conflict of interest. We have both talked at great lengths, and he wanted the message that I am here to deliver to be defined in its total impact and clarity by me only. I am here to make you, the players of the Bentley State Eagles, a proposition that's unprecedented in the history of not only baseball, but all professional sports."

Stunned silence again penetrated the room as Brandon Briggs finished his unlikely opening presentation. As some of the players looked at each other in somewhat comic disbelief, he continued.

"On behalf of the Las Vegas Vipers baseball organization, we would like to extend the opportunity to hire each one of you to serve as our so to speak 'new' future. All of you who are gathered here today would become our new direction and the team who would in turn represent our new mission statement. In short, this group gathered here today as the Bentley State Eagles- would now become the new Las Vegas Vipers."

Briggs felt that he had stumbled badly in trying to convey his missive. He thought that his presentation sounded like a blithering idiot when he needed to be the most direct as he could in delivering the hook to his message. It was the Eagle's shortstop Gary Duzan that was the first to raise his hand.

"Excuse me, Mr. Briggs," he said. "Let me get this straight. You want to hire us, our entire team, the Bentley State Eagles, and plug us into the Major Leagues to replace your entire current team…the entire team? You mean that we'll all be playing baseball, but in the Major Leagues?"

"In a nut-shell, son- yes," Briggs replied. "But think about it. Do you all love this game? Would you like to continue your dream and continue playing forward your season for a couple more months?""I'm going to be painfully honest here. Baseball has lost what you guys have found. How many big leaguers do you see standing on the steps these days? How many do you see doing the little things that you all did every game in order to become the winners that you are? With your style of play and hustle, you can win anywhere because you guys are special! Let me tell you something else. Our owner has given his life and most of his money simply to experience what this game is all about. No, the fact is you didn't win the final game of the College World Series. In any sport, there is only going to be room for one winner a day, but guess what? Winners show up every day and expect nothing more than to be a winner. It's obvious that you all have something most teams don't have a clue. Now, back to your question, son, about replacing a team at the Major League level? If you show up and give the fans everything that you showed them during your run-, regardless of the score when you're finished, I guarantee you that no fan will ever go home and be disappointed or feel cheated at your effort."

"Mr. Briggs," interrupted Bombo Chadwick. "Not to be disrespectful, but I do have two questions. First of all, could we have a quick player's- only meeting, and secondly, when would all of this like happen?"

"No offense taken at all. I respect your privacy in this matter, and I want to leave it up to you to discuss it further among yourselves. I have twenty roster spots available on the team." declared Briggs. "You have your meeting and I will then discuss a timetable and all the rest of the particulars if everything is acceptable. I will just go over to the restaurant for lunch and plan to be back in about an hour."

"But, sir, we have twenty-one players." a voice from the back of the room pointed out. "If you want the whole team, one of us will be missing."

"Honestly, an offer of these complications certainly doesn't come without some minor challenges." Brandon quickly clarified. "While you all talk, I would like to take Jarred Brewster with me to lunch so we can also go over some other options in private."

A startled hush settled over the room as Jarred quickly popped up to join Brandon Briggs at the door.

"Feel free to compile a list of questions." Brandon offered. "I know we have hit you with a lot of things very quickly. I will be back in one hour to answer anything you all will need to know."

As the two closed the door behind them and the meeting began, there was no great mystery as to who was going to be the odd man out. As the impact of what was being offered to the Bentley State Eagles was now being quickly absorbed, the player's-only meeting took on a tone of unity.

"We'll be set for life! This is Major League Baseball. Think about it! I guess they'll have to put it all in writing or something." Karl Smith exclaimed.

"This is the craziest thing I've ever heard of." added Luke Shepard. "Do you all really think we're ready for this? Money or no money, this is the big-time, boys. Is it worth all that money to go out and embarrass ourselves each and every night? I don't know. Maybe it could be like the witness protection program where we can play, but they'll like let us change our names. I got dibs on 'He Hate Me.' Maybe I can use that if it's not copy-righted."

The laughter was light and forced as pitcher Mitch Milhuff began his verbal spiel.

21 DOWN IN VEGAS

"Did you hear what the man was saying? He believes in us. We all know how hard we worked and especially how much fun we had doing it. I agree! We are a team; damn it…and each one of you like a brother to me. As I walked off the mound for the last time in the biggest game of my life, why do you think I lost my shit, man? Hell, it wasn't the score. It wasn't the pressure. It really wasn't about losing. It had nothing to do with any of that stuff. All I could think about was that the best times I've ever had with my best friends, and it was all coming to an end…right now! Regardless of whether we won that game or not, it really didn't matter. All I could think about was not being out there with you guys ever again. Sorry to get so mental about it, but that's how I see it!"

"What about Jarred?" asked Eagles Center Fielder Cliff Collier?

"He's an Eagle, guys." The quick response from Bombo Chadwick was delivered.

"Yea, but right now over at Damon's, and he's being told like he's not an Eagle. Anyone here want to take a bet on that one?" snapped Deeters.

"The truth be known, we would have never got to the series without Jarred." Catcher Boone Coleman interceded. "Think how many times he scouted the plays, kept our heads in the game, and made us think. I would have never picked off that guy from Texas if Brewster hadn't pointed out he was taking too many steps from the bag. The next guy comes up and doubles. He scores, and we lose."

"Hey, this is a lifetime opportunity for us all." bellowed Chadwick." Like a lightning -bolt from heaven, we're being given financial security and a chance to look at each other's ugly mugs for a little while longer…and, we'll be playing in the fucking Major Leagues, brothers! Hoo-ha!"

The yell that erupted from the hotel banquet hall stunned the kitchen help to the point of panic. Several cooks ran into the room and witnessed twenty men with arms embraced around each other all jumping up and down in a circle on the middle of the dance floor. By all appearances, the vote had been taken and was unanimously accepted. There was just one small detail that needed to yet be worked out, amended, and passed. As the impact of the moment was beginning to sink in, the door slowly opened and in stepped Brandon Briggs...alone. As he walked backed to the podium, he sensed a feeling that this offer had aroused the group's interest.

"Well, I trust you gentlemen have had a chance to discuss our proposal." he quipped. "Where should we start? I'm sure there are many questions, I would certainly welcome anything that's on your mind."

Mitch Milhuff spoke up first. "Does any member of the team you have now have any idea that you're, like here, and presenting us with all this?"

"No, they don't." Briggs admitted. "Until we could get a commitment from all of you, we have made no public movement whatsoever toward our intentions with any members of our organization. I am operating on total trust with you all that everything discussed here, between us, stays in the most mandatory terms of privacy."

"What exactly are we going to receive if we accept your offer?" came another volley from the floor."

"It is our belief that you play as a team, you will all be rewarded as a team." Briggs began. "We are prepared to offer each of you a two-year contract at the Major League minimum of $350,000 per year. As a team, each one of you will receive an extra $3,000 apiece for every game that the Vipers win. We also understand that this project will be a major interruption to your ongoing college educations. We are also offering to pay for the remainder of your degrees at any time that you decide to go back to school and get your diplomas after your initial contracts are up. Another departure from the norm is since this is a direct hire from the team itself, we will basically be serving as your agents for the first two- years under the agreement."

"You're saying again that regardless of what happens, we each will all receive at least $700,000 over the next two years and our college will be paid for when we are ready to go back to school at a later date?" asked pitcher Jeremy Burkes who was testing out his pre-law skills.

"At least $700,000." Briggs replied. "With each of your positions will come personal incentive contracts that could pay you much more than the Major League minimum salary, but we wanted to find a uniform place to start. Payment of your college degrees will be written into the contracts as well. Those agreements will all be individually designed for each one of you. For instance, if Mr. Milhuff wins ten games, that would be an extra bonus per game. We feel satisfactory that each one of you will be pleased with what incentives we have to offer you."

"How soon would all this take place?" John Gambill anxiously inquired.

"It would begin between baseball's All-Star break coming up within the next several weeks." Briggs answered. "Our plan is to release twenty of our roster players after the last regular game on Sunday before the break. That will give us four days to get you all officially signed, some practice, and ready to play before we open the second half of the season in Pittsburgh. At this point, we plan to keep five-roster players, but we're still not sure exactly who those players will be."

"What about Jarred?" Cliff Collier suddenly blared out. "Why wasn't he here at the meeting?"

The question he knew that needed to be answered was finally at hand. As twenty- faces looked upon him for a satisfactory and honest answer, Brandon realized that in order to win them over, he couldn't stumble on this one. He took a breath and a pause as he looked the Bentley State Eagles directly in all forty of their collective eyes.

"Gentleman, while all of this so far sounds like a baseball fairy tale, there are some hardcore business issues we have to deal with here." Briggs interceded. "While I know that Jarred is a wonderful person, at the Major League level, we are dealing with a thing called roster spots. To be honest, the Vipers can't afford to give away a position to a guy who doesn't even play on the college team. I know he's a friend and a great ally, but Jarred and I had a long talk during lunch."

After a short yet awkward pause, he continued, "He agrees with me on our dilemma and he has decided that he really can't participate at the skill level we would need for him to compete."

"But, Mr. Briggs," Chadwick added, "He's a member of our team."

"I totally understand, son." Briggs answered, "But unfortunately, it's simply a decision we will have to live with in order to make this thing work. I believe that Jarred totally understands and is willing to accept it. Are there more questions?"

Restlessness now dominated the moment as the team started talking among themselves until Boone Coleman made the motion to have another private team meeting.

"Mr. Briggs," he began. "I think everything you have offered to us is truly remarkable and exciting. Your faith in us and what you think we can do as a team is inspiring. If you could just let us have just a few more moments alone…together, I think we need that to make the final decision about all of this-as a team?"

"Fair enough!" Briggs concluded. "I'll just go back down to Damon's and grab a cup of coffee and I'll see you in a few."

As he walked out the door, the conversation immediately turned to Jarred.

"It's not right!" exclaimed Sean Deeters. "I agree with Boone! If it weren't for Jarred, I can think of at least four losses we would have had and we would have never even made it to the semifinals."

"Yea, I don't get it. This guy says he wants us as a whole team, but he's taking away the one guy that knows more about this damn game than we ever will. It sucks!" added pitcher Dirty Ernie Fuller.

As one of the team leaders, Brooks Snyder took a stance. "Look guys, this is a Major League Baseball general manager. He didn't come here with this crazy idea to hire us all without a little flexibility if you know what I mean. If they need an extra roster spot, they can go figure it out for themselves. If they really want the Bentley State Eagles baseball team to save their dying franchise, I say they're going to have to do it with the whole team. Without Jarred Brewster, we are not the whole team. We all know that, it's just that simple. Are we ready to vote?"

Once again, the sound of a frat meltdown erupted from the banquet room. This time, hotel personnel let the riotous behavior continue. It was shortly after 2:00 p.m. when Brandon Briggs again made his reappearance.

"I know it has been an emotional and quite the different day for all of you and me as well. I want to say that I really appreciate your understanding on what we're trying to accomplish here. I hope we are all in agreement."

Again, Brooks Snyder became the messenger.

"Mr. Briggs, you've come a long way to our town and we certainly appreciate your unbelievable offer and we are all flattered that you feel the way you do about us. As a proud member of this baseball team, I could never image in a million years this kind of opportunity ever taking place. It's like some kind of a movie script or a book or something. I don't think anyone else here could also have ever imagined it either."

As he looked around the room, Snyder felt the penetrating eyes of his teammates as the silence again served as his cue to go ahead and deliver the epistle. Clearing his throat, he continued.

"To be honest, you had to have seen something extremely different in who we are and what we do, or else, Mr. Briggs- you would be down in Louisiana right now making this same offer to the LSU Tigers. With all respect, let me put it to you this way. As individual ball players, we're pretty good. As friends, we are even better, but I believe as a baseball team, we just might be the greatest! If you leave Jarred Brewster off this team, you're just cheating yourself out of the whole purpose of why you even came here today."

"And your point, son?" Briggs asked.

"We've taken our team vote, and it is unanimous." Snyder continued. "We're willing to accept your offer."

"That's fantastic!" Brandon Briggs exalted. "And you won't be sorry."

"But, Mr. Briggs, there is one last slight condition that was also part of that decision. If you want us as a team, well, the answer is yes. But without Jarred Brewster, we're not a team. It will have to be considered a 'no' vote for the Eagles if Jarred is not included in on the deal."

Briggs wasn't quite sure of what he was hearing and again asked him to clarify.

As several different team members explained their reasoning as to why Jarred Brewster was an integral cog to their team's success, Brandon suddenly understood why he felt like such a fish out of water.

Dealing with hearts instead of wallets was what was alien to all of his previous negotiations. In a world where money, greed, and "me" always seemed to surface first, the dynamics he was now experiencing with was indeed an anomaly. Listening intently to their all-or-nothing position, he began to slowly shift his reasoning back into their direction. While agreeing on most points of logic, Brandon had a few questions of his own.

"OK, guys, we sign a walk--on player with limited playing experience to a Major League Baseball contract." Briggs countered. "Now, we have only twenty-five roster spots. That means that we have a guy that probably will never play that just sits on the bench. Is that fair to the rest of the team?"

"For us, it is, he is one of our brosiffs and a guy that keeps our heads in the game and he's the one dude that can see huge holes in our competition." Mitch Milhuff blustered.

Brandon Briggs could again sense that the room was charged and definitely didn't want to lose it against his favor. Feeling that he was at the great divide, the last thing he wanted to do was to create a barrier just as he was trying to seal the deal.

"One of my jobs as the general manager of the Vipers is always trying to stick square- pegs in round holes." Briggs admitted. "As you men will discover, the universe of professional sports is light-years from anywhere you've ever been or seen before, but that's OK. If you can harness this enthusiasm, vision, and fire and keep it intact, I believe this team can become one for the ages at any level. I do hear and understand what you're telling me. My question to you is this. If I can figure out a way to sign Jarred Brewster as say, a non-roster player, and to find a place for him on the team in our day-to-day roles, would that be satisfactory?"

"Would he travel with us?" Cliff Collier asked. "I mean, would he be there with us in the dugout?"

"Let me put it to you this way." Briggs answered. "The Bentley State Eagles current twenty-one-man roster will be together in one of the most exciting cities on earth- and playing baseball the way it was meant to be played. If you want to take another team vote, I will be glad to leave."

"No need, sir," Brooks Snyder responded with a chuckle. "But you better hurry up and tell Jarred the news before he lands an engineering job somewhere. In the world of pencils and slide rules, he's a hot free agent!"

"OK, let's leave it at this. My promise to you is that I will offer Jarred a job with the Vipers in some sort of team capacity. It won't be a roster spot, but your man will be there, with the rest of you, as the unit that you are today!"

"If that's the case, sir, I believe we are now all in unanimous agreement," Sean Deeters echoed. "All in favor, please signify."

The slow rhythmic-clap began that soon accelerated into a thunderous roar. The ritual had become a team trademark that was a strong symbol of the team's togetherness anytime they wanted to display unity. Brandon Briggs ended the impromptu celebration with a solemn promise.

"Understand that like ourselves, we are both entering into something to my knowledge that has never been done before. There is no play-book for this one, lads. All I ask is for your trust as I also promise to give you mine. I'm sure there will be many distractions along the way of getting this thing put together in the direction of where it needs to go. There will be bigger mountains and obstacles to climb once you step out on the field with the word 'Vipers' across your chest. The Las Vegas organization and I thank you for your faith in us, and I give you my promise that we will do everything within our power to fuel your dreams and with a destination to success."

Having the verbal commitment from the team, Brandon Briggs knew that his work had now really just begun. His first task was to quickly round up Jarred and inform him that he wasn't being cast astray. Catching up with him at home, they resumed their meeting process in the family living room. Explaining to him the love of his teammates and the commitment from the Vipers, Jarred beamed at the news that his love for the game would indeed be a reality and that his guys would continue on an accelerated fast track.

With time beginning to run short on the day, Briggs informed his new team members to say absolutely nothing until he could return the following week to work on the personal contracts for each player. He also told the Eagles to get all of their personal affairs in order and be ready to join the team in Las Vegas on July 19, the week-end before baseball's All-Star break.

It was now late in the afternoon as Brandon Briggs shook each of the player's hands and then made a quick exit North on US 23 to the Columbus airport. Even though the team banquet started in less than two hours, there was one last piece of unfinished business.

Even though Coach Keith Madison had always maintained an open-door policy, he never imagined that twenty-one individuals would all try to fit through it all at the same time.

"Hey, Coach! Can we talk to you for a minute?" Bombo Chadwick asked. "We have something really important to tell you."

Looking up from his desk, he could see in the eyes of his players both the look of excitement as well as panic.

"Come on in and tell me about it." Madison offered.

That was the only cue they needed as the team all crammed into his office as for the next thirty minutes, it was like the old-fashioned Sunday morning confessional. There were tears, laughter, and an occasional stern warning. Coach Madison reinforced why he could not be a part of the decision, but lauded the players on the fact that they had become the chosen ones. He praised each member on what they personally brought to the table and encouraged them to take their gift to the highest level and succeed. As the time element began to wind down and become a factor, Keith Madison adjourned the meeting.

"I believe we have a banquet to attend in just about an hour, guys." he said. "We all better get home and slip into our monkey suits."

There was a moment of awkward quiet before Cliff Collier clumsily broke the silence. He wanted to verbalize the obvious topic that was on everyone's mind.

"Coach, what about you?" he asked. "Is there any way you could"....

"Cliffster," Keith interrupted, "I know where you're going here, and believe me, I am flattered beyond words. Let me say that the hardest thing in my life is going to watch you guys walk out that door and knowing you're never ever coming back. The fact is my life is here. Bentley State University and Portsmouth, Ohio, is my home. I have a wife, three kids, and a contract, mind you. You'll soon learn what that's all about. Another time, another place, maybe? No, you guys go make me proud and give me a good reason to visit Las Vegas a little more often. Now get the hell out of here! We got some rubber-chicken to destroy here in just a few minutes and we better not be late."

* * * * *

Over 850 fans, relatives, and community heads were in attendance for the Bentley State Eagles appreciation banquet. Ohio Governor Ted Strickland as well as former area baseball stars such as Al Oliver, Larry Hisle, and Don Gullet were also on hand as keynote speakers. After each one of the players got up to the microphone and said their piece, it was now Bentley States head baseball coach who was left to finish off the evening. Anybody who knew Keith Madison well may have detected a slight cryptic note to his accolades. While there was more than enough praise to go around for the season and his players, there also was a very subtle tone of finality in his words.

"As we wrap up this wonderful evening," he concluded, "let us not forget how rare something like this actually becomes. It's easy to adopt a wait till next year mentality, not just in baseball, but in our everyday existence. The harsh truth is the only guarantee life ever gives us is right now…the precious present. If you asked me if we are planning to do this again next year, I would have to remind each of you of this. There's an old saying that if you want to make God laugh, tell him your plans. These players…these twenty-one young men did something that I believe will probably never, ever be repeated again. As one who witnessed the drive and determination of each and every one of them, let me say you have every reason to hold them up high and carry them on your shoulders tonight. The record book will show that the Bentley State Eagles from Portsmouth, Ohio, lost the College World Series in 2006 by one run. History will prove that a most unlikely team of competitive hearts from a small Mid-western school became the biggest winners of all time. God bless you all and good night."

As the room exploded in cheers and applause, the Eagles stood and began the clap. It was an electric moment. With arms draped on each other's shoulders, the cameras rolled as the video recorders were all blinking red. Reporter Randy Yohe from WSAZ-TV in Huntington, West Virginia, sliced through the crowded pack with his cameraman in tow until he finally got to the Eagles' right fielder Sean Deeters.

"Hey, Sean! Randy Yohe from News Channel 3, can I ask you a few quick questions?"

"Sure, fire away!" Sean offered as the cameras rolled.

"Sean Deeters," Yohe began, "you've been one of the many great stories that have come from this year's near miss for a National Collegiate Baseball Championship. Where do the Bentley State Eagles go from here looking into next season?"

Deeters paused for a quick moment. "Tonight is just an unbelievable experience for us all. We're really just a bunch of brothers that love to play the game of baseball. For everybody that believed and followed us, we all just hope to work harder and make them even prouder of us in the future."

3RD INNING

The red-eye express from Columbus, Ohio, touched down at McCarran International Airport on Las Vegas at 2:30 a.m. On board was a man who spent his entire flight time on his laptop trying to make those many square pegs fit into those round- holes. As he left the terminal to flag down a taxi for the ride home, he began to have doubts about his ability to make it all work.

Nobody had ever fired an entire Major League ball team before. He knew he would have to keep five of the current players on the roster, but who would they be? What would be the ultimate impact be with the fans? Would everybody finally all just throw up their hands and look at this as a sign of self-destruction? As the cab zipped through the now quiet streets of Vegas, Brandon Briggs knew one thing for sure pertaining to his team's upcoming strategy, and that was the questions were way too many and the answers too few. This is where the phrase "sleep on it" would really come into play tonight.

The Las Vegas Vipers continued to labor in misery. While Brandon Briggs was off to meet with the Eagles, Cisco "The Dealer" Wheeler worked on a short list of the current roster worth keeping. As Wheeler crunched the numbers of all the players he had under contract, it came to just a shade over 140 million. He had seven one-year deals pending and all the rest were for multiple tenures. Once he put all the players that he was letting go on waivers, the ones who didn't get picked up by other teams would still be his lingering financial responsibility. Wheeler figured that the majority of the cut players would go unsigned due to their salaries and the fact that most were all considered poster- boys for underachievement.

Fortunately, the Vipers' three best pitchers were all signed long term. Scotty "The Golden" Arms, Brad Scarbury, and Gary Steinman had all been high-priced free agents at one time. Even though their records now reflected the overall plight of the team, they were still considered quality hurlers. As he scanned the roster sheet for who was left, he knew that catcher Doug Pouge would probably have to stay as well as utility player Terrence Kennedy. The combined salaries of those five were right at 40 million. So by letting the rest of the team go and then packing on another 8 million dollars in bottom line payroll for the Eagles, this move could possibly cost the disenfranchised owner upward close to 70 million dollars to pull it off. It was certainly a gamble, but the sports page headlines made it easier to throw the dice every day.

Las Vegas had just reeled off three straight losses to the Astros and the carnage on the field was getting worse. Current Vipers manager Tommy Leach had taken over the job on an interim basis when full-time skipper Davey Johnson finally had enough and threw up his hands at the beginning of the season and called it quits. Cisco had tried, but sadly found no managerial candidates with any credentials wanting anything to do with the Vipers' losing legacy. The underground chatter among baseball folk was that the team was cursed. The running joke was often whispered, "If you want to apply for early retirement, go and play for the Vipers."

As the door opened to Cisco Wheeler's office suite, a tired and well-traveled man slowly stepped in and slumped into the large leather recliner.

"Well, Brandon, do we have a team?" was Wheeler's first question.

"Yes, Cisco, we do." came a rather forced answer. "We have a team of young and enthusiastic kids who might create a little short-term buzz and then again may not win a game for the rest of the season."

"And why so?" snorted Wheeler as he leached forward from behind his desk.

"Cisco, these kids are good collegiate baseball players, but I'm not sure they understand the pros. All this frat stuff and all for one crap just doesn't translate into today's market." Briggs explained. "For the whole team to agree to this deal, we now have to find a spot for the walk-on kid that never plays."

"Jarred Brewster." Cisco added.

"Right, Jarred Brewster! How did you know his name?" Briggs asked.

"Brandon, sometimes I feel that you don't give me enough credit for my own love of this game. Most owners would have shit-canned you as a GM years ago. The reason you still have a job today is for three reasons. You put up with my meddling in the team's affairs, you're a good nuts-and-bolts man, and I'm loyal to you as a friend and another who also loves this game!"

As Brandon Briggs stared vacantly at his boss, Wheeler continued.

"I'm gonna be called crazy and out of my mind for what we're about to do, and guess what, Brandon, so are you. If you got as damn tired of losing as I am, maybe you could feel it too. If you want out right now, there's the door. Walk out now and you can distance yourself from all this idiocy and your name will never be mentioned and they'll be no hard feelings. For me, when I come to the park at night, I want to watch a team that I know gives a shit about winning. I want to see players disappointed when they lose. I want to see rally caps and all that, as you put it, 'college frat crap.' If that is not your idea of what winning and team spirit is all about, maybe you should go ahead and leave now because if someone doesn't do something to bring back the integrity and soul of this game, we can just shut it down right now and all go out and dig ditches!"

"Sorry, boss, it was a long flight and I didn't get much sleep," Briggs sheepishly admitted. "You're right. I spent a few unexpected minutes with Branch Ricky while I was in Portsmouth before meeting with the team, I did feel it! These kids are fresh and they're real. I always remember what you told me about the direction of professional sports the day I walked into this office. You said when you sleep in silk pajamas every night, it gets harder to get up in the morning."

"And you remembered that?" Cisco said with a smile. "Why do you think that's even relevant here?"

"Because the kids we'll be hiring sleep in burlap with baseballs under their pillows." Briggs laughed.

Over the next couple of days, Brandon Briggs, Cisco Wheeler, and a battery of team attorneys combed over all the existing contracts and started drawing up new ones. The bad news looked like the only team liability would be paying off all existing agreements that wouldn't get picked up by other teams. The good news was that there had never been a Players Union issue about firing an entire team because from at least a legal standpoint; a precedent had never been set.

Wheeler and Briggs we're preparing for damage control and decided not to let the rest of the organization in on the decision until it was time to pull the trigger. As Brandon Briggs prepared for his return to Portsmouth, Ohio, Cisco and he needed to finalize the five- roster players that they were contemplating on keeping. They also had a decision about the non-roster issue.

Both were on agreement that pitchers Gary Steinman, Brad Scarbury, and Scott Arms should stay. As bad as the team had become, these three pitchers honestly had been the victims of little field support. Starting catcher Doug Pouge had probably the best attitude considering his lot on a miserable ball club and he was a veteran catcher. He knew the pitchers well and had been a quality starter for the Cubs, the Reds, and the Marlins.

Terrance Kennedy was a versatile young player that could play both the infield and the outfield. While somewhat of an average hitter, he had turned in some dazzling glove work over his two-years with the Vipers. All five were under iron-clad contracts with the Vipers for the remainder of this season and the next several.

"How are we going to handle the Jarred Brewster thing?" Cisco asked. "You know we can't put him on the starting roster."

"I've been thinking about this," Brandon said, "and I do think that I have a great solution."

"Please enlighten me." Cisco pleaded. "This is our biggest square peg, and we need to find that pefect round hole that fits."

Looking auspiciously at his owner, Brandon Briggs needed just a quick moment to continue.

"OK, here it is, and quite simple." started Briggs, "He's a catcher and a first baseman. If we hire him exclusively as the bullpen catcher and then give him an advisory role, for instance, let him chart pitches and stuff like that, he won't need to be on the twenty-five-man roster. This way, we can keep him around, and he will still have all the other luxuries of traveling with the team."

"That should work." Cisco agreed. "I like it!"

"The rest of the team loves the kid." Brandon continued. "I have to admit that he does have an infectious personality and does know the game. If Jarred Brewster has all the same perks like everyone else, I should think that it would be both acceptable to him and to the team."

"When are you flying back to Portsmouth?" Wheeler asked.

"I'm booked to fly out in the morning at 10:00." said Brandon.

"Bring me back those contracts signed and sealed." Wheeler playfully bantered. "By the way, while you're there, stop by that flood-wall and see if Branch Ricky needs a coaching job. I think we'll probably need him."

Until the deal was reached, Keith Madison had requested not to be involved in any way, fearing repercussions from his university job. All of the private numbers and contacts for the players had been given to Brandon Briggs. It was now his total responsibility to contact the bodies and get it in writing. He had notified each player for a time to meet in his room at the Portsmouth Downtown Ramada Inn and had informed each player that they could bring a parent or a lawyer if so inclined.

Landing in Port Columbus at 5:00 p.m. Briggs quickly got his baggage and rental car and found him itching to hit Southbound 23 once again. He noted to himself that he would start meeting with players at 8:00 in the morning.

Each signing had been put on a forty-five-minute time schedule. Brandon Briggs knew that he had the biggest day in his career looming into the world known as tomorrow. As he passed a little town called Piketon, he knew it was close. Brandon Briggs just wanted to get to the Ramada Inn, register, and buckle down on a good night's sleep. After all, with the job of changing the landscape of professional sports as we knew it, a certain degree of bed-rest beforehand seemed to be in order.

The next morning started early as at 7:45 a.m. when there came a knock on room 311. As Briggs pulled it open, there stood his first appointment for the day.

"Hi, we're the Milhuffs', we're looking for a Mr. Briggs."

"Yes! Mr. and Mrs. Milhuff, I'm Brandon Briggs of the Las Vegas Vipers." he cordially delivered. "Won't you come in, please?"

Mitch Milhuff and his parents came in and took a seat around a large table that was stacked with many packets of paper. They were all in order as Brandon grabbed the one on top with Mitch's name on it. After addressing the unusual circumstances of the project at hand, Brandon got into the mechanics of the deal.

Each contract would be for two years at the Major League, minimum of $350,000 per year. All Major League benefits including retirement would also be included. As extra incentive, each player would also receive an additional $3,000 for each game the Vipers win. Brandon explained that it was Mr. Wheeler's philosophy to reward them as a team when the team excelled. Perhaps the most important contract option would be the total payment of what was left on each player's college education. It was duly noted that the Vipers understood the sacrifice that all the players were making as Cisco Wheeler was adamant about addressing it. Each contract was post-dated to take effect beginning on Monday, July 16th, at midnight.

Brandon Briggs was surprised at how quickly each player understood the mission at hand. Except for a couple of over-protective parents and extra-zealous lawyers who wanted to show off their barrister abilities, the day actually went extremely smooth. Twenty- contracts and twenty- signatures, there was now only one left to secure. The last knock on the door came with both relief and apprehension.

"Jarred, come in. It's great to see you. Did you bring your parents or any representation today?" Brandon Briggs asked as it appeared that Jarred had come alone.

"No, it's just me. My folks told me it's really all up to me, and I really don't know any lawyers to speak of."

"Well, that's not a necessity, Jarred. We just wanted all of you guys to be as prepared and informed as possible. When you get into all this legal stuff, there are often too many questions." Brandon offered.

"Naw, I'll only be a minute." Jarred began. "Mr. Briggs, you and I both know why you're offering me a spot on the team. I spent three years mostly sitting here on the bench, and I really don't feel like doing it for two more years and being thousands of miles from home. I do love the game of baseball more than life itself, but I was just lucky to be where I was with the Eagles. I'm not stupid. I know that Coach Madison pulled some strings to keep me around. After thinking this thing through, honestly, I just think I need to stay here at Bentley State and work on getting my engineering degree."

"So you don't think this is for you, eh?" Brandon started. "Well, I must say I am a little surprised. Jarred, I was told by everybody you were a fighter."

"Look, Mr. Briggs, we already had this talk once and I know these guys. I love them. They can't turn me into a charity case just to hold you hostage from signing them as a team. That's crazy!"

"Jarred, you say you love baseball more than anything else. Why not take this offer and we will work on your skills…everyday." Briggs offered.

"I know I'm not that good on the field, but I do know this game. That's where I really need to be. I love the strategy, the drama, and all the little things that go with winning. I know I'll never make it as a player, so I really think it's time for me to just kind of move on. I want you to know that I really appreciate the offer, sir, I really do."

"You say you're not a player, Jarred, but more of a 'coach', is that what you're telling me?" Brandon asked.

"It seems that way, I guess." Jarred shyly replied back.

"You have twenty friends and soul mates that all came here today because they believe in you. Twenty brothers who all put their dreams and fears on the line because they say you are as big a part of them as anything they are about to undertake. The Las Vegas Vipers are about to show the world of sports what the definition of 'team' baseball is all about, and, you can help us lead that cause. If you really think you're being asked to come along simply for as you say a 'charity ride,' don't flatter yourself. We don't give free passes to people son who don't deserve it." Brandon concluded. "Jarred, you're here and being asked because you have earned it."

After what seemed like an eternity of silence, Jarred Brewster looked up from the floor and slowly spread his infectious million-dollar grin wide across his face.

"Is that so?" he noted." "Well, you must not have checked out the box score from last night's game and seen what your pitchers did against San Diego? Seven walks? Whew! If we are going to win us some ball games now Mr. Briggs, we're definitely gonna' have to cut down on those 'free passes' now, aren't we?"

"So what do you think we ought to do to fix the situation, Coach?" Brandon good-naturedly shot back.

"Honestly, I don't give away all this valuable information stored away in my computer chip of a baseball brain for nothing." retorted Jarred," "Why don't we sit down and figure this thing out so I can legally tell you?"

The moment turned as golden as it gets as both stood up smiling ear to ear and shook hands much like a father welcoming his son into the family business. Brandon Briggs knew the character of his new bullpen catcher and coaching advisor would go a long way to cement the kind of attitude that was needed to keep things loose on the bench. It didn't take Brandon Briggs long to realize that if attitude were stats, Jarred Brewster was already a Hall of Famer.

As the two continued to chat enthusiastically about baseball in general and the challenges that lay ahead, Brandon quickly realized whatever Jarred had was extremely high octane and contagious. As the team's GM, he actually now started to get personally excited about the deal and began thinking more of that "out of the box" stuff that Cisco kept talking about. It was beginning to get late, and Brandon had an early flight back to Las Vegas in the morning. As the two headed for the door, Brandon Briggs once again thrust out his hand.

"Thank you, Jarred! It's going to be a pleasure having you on the team."

"Mr. Briggs, I do appreciate the fact that you have been honest with me from the start. I have to admit when we first met, and we, you know, talked over lunch about my situation, it was probably the low point of my life. As solid as you've been with me, I kind of felt ashamed because I knew I was lying to you."

"Lying…about what?"

"All that stuff about wanting to move on and push pencils. I really didn't mean it." he shyly admitted.

"Hey, don't worry about it. I think we're both on the same score-card now and that's what really counts so you can really use your pencil power to help us." Brandon reassured him as he walked him into the hall.

Heading toward the elevator, Jarred suddenly turned on his heels with a spontaneous after-thought, "Speaking of counts, the Vipers seriously need to work at getting ahead in theirs. That's the reason for all those free passes. I guess you also call those things walks! See you soon, boss!"

As Brandon began to clean up the suite, he knew it had been quite a day.

He felt glad that Jarred had been his last order of business. It was a nice bloom on the vine that promised he would get a quick, but peaceful nap. He had promised Cisco that he would call when everything was complete. It was now almost 11:00 p.m. Eastern time which would make it 8:00 p.m. in Las Vegas. As he turned back the bed, he remembered an old saying that bad news was always delivered in a hurry, but good news can always wait.

Brandon held off the urge to call home until he got back on the road toward the airport in the morning.

"Cisco, it's all done! We have twenty-one new faces that will soon be wearing Vipers uniforms!" Briggs reported.

"That's great, Brandon! Great news indeed! We have just about three weeks left before we can make it official. Can we keep it quiet that long?" Wheeler asked.

"I swore everybody to secrecy." Briggs promised. "What about Leach? Do you think he'll know what's going on? Managers kind of have that sixth sense, you know."

"Things in the clubhouse are bad, Brandon," Cisco Wheeler admitted. "Poor Tommy is trying to do everything he can to hold this ship together. The press has been ruthless, the fans are giving up, and I understand the players now have a pool to see who is going to be the next one to be one of Jim Rome's '*Burning Bridges.*' It's out of control!"

"I should be back into town by 9:00 tonight. Tomorrow, we can lay down our plan on how all of this is going to come together. These kids are aces, Cisco! Win or lose, I guarantee that the Las Vegas Vipers' new approach to things will be the topic of *ESPN Sports Center* for weeks, if not years to come. You can write that one down."

"Brandon, you kind of sound like you're finally buying into all of this. I hope it's not just for my sake. Remember, you are the general manager of a team that has nowhere to go but up. As much criticism as we are going to get, just remember, we can't get much worse than we are now." Wheeler reminded him.

"Cisco, you had to be with me as I talked to these kids and their parents. I guess I got a bit jaded like the rest of us tend to get. It was an unbelievable experience to actually watch these guys get excited about everything we've talked about. Guess what one topic never came up as a major issue?" Briggs asked.

"Money." Cisco Wheeler wryly answered.

"When was the last time we sat down with any player and that wasn't the first damn card flipped out on the table?" Brandon pointed out.

"I just want to make sure that you're comfortable with all this. I do own the team, but like I told you the other day, Brandon, you are the nuts and bolts that hold this leaky creaky ship all together. Just don't let us sink." Wheeler laughed.

"It's going to be fine, Cisco, and don't worry" reassured Brandon, "I did have a few doubts in the beginning, but as I left Portsmouth. I had to make one last swing past the floodwall to have a quick chat with Branch."

"So you did. What did Mr. Rickey have to tell you?" Cisco asked.

21 DOWN IN VEGAS

"He wished us luck, but said he wouldn't touch a coaching job on this team for all the gold at Harrah's."

Reading the box-scores and the summary of each game in the *Las Vegas Sun* seemed to be the same story every day except the only change were names and the numbers.

(Las Vegas) The worst team in Major League Baseball took it on the chin again for a franchise record fourteenth straight loss last night at the hands of the St. Louis Cardinals, losing 16 to 3. Viper's' starter John Welton lasted only two-thirds of an inning, giving up six runs, eleven hits, and he walked five. Vipers Manager Tommy Leach used all of his available pitchers in this charity hit-a-thon, but nobody it seemed could silence the booming lumber explosion of the Cards. Albert Pujois, Jim Edmonds, and Billy Eckstein all had four hits apiece including a grand slam from Edmonds in the third off reliever Aaron Williams. Chris Carpenter cruised into the eight, scattering three runs on five hits before handing things off to Ron Villone in the ninth who retired the team in order.

The big question now facing the Vipers franchise was how to close the floodgate of nightly failures that seemed to be spiraling out of control. General Manager Brandon Briggs spoke briefly after the loss and said, "The Vipers are certainly going through a rough time right now as it seems like we can't buy a break. We have the All-Star Game coming up in just about a week. Hopefully, we can regroup and try to salvage the second half of the season."

Team owner Cisco Wheeler was asked if there were any new signings or trades looming in the team's future. "We are always looking to improve and upgrade the quality of our team. We seem to be suffering from a lot of missed opportunities that just won't fall our way. I know Tommy is frustrated just like the rest of us. We'll just have to find what kind of help is out there and see if we can plug up some of the leaks."

Locally, the support for the once golden franchise had drastically been on the decline. Now it seemed as if almost daily. The national press was also taking swipes at the much maligned organization. *USA*

Today Sports was very up-front and with a poison-pen piled on with the woes of the Vipers.

(*USA Today*) As baseball's mid-season break approaches, the Las Vegas Vipers' lead the National League in all the wrong team categories. Those include batting (.224), pitching (6.31 era), winning percentage (.388), plus the Vipers also lead the Major League in errors with 97 after only 75 games. With a record of 25 and 50, the Las Vegas Vipers are also in contention for breaking the record of most losses in a single season held by the 1963 New York Mets at 110. Certainly not a recognized statistic, but the hapless Vipers also lead the Majors in brainless triple- plays against them so far this season with one.

While this season has certainly not been unlike all the rest before them, it does seem like the fans have certainly been more vocal this year about the lack of quality play than others. If attendance means anything, the Vipers might be only the second team in Major League history not to draw a million fans in a season.

The former Montreal Expos hold that record with 662,000 back in 2002. In a city that thrives on the virtue of winning, it would seem that decisions concerning the direction of this baseball embarrassment will need to be addressed and done so rather quickly before someone decides to pull the plug in Las Vegas and move the franchise to Montreal. If fan interest counts for anything, maybe that's where this team really belongs.

As the last week-end before baseball's All-Star Game approached, activity under the radar was quickly and quietly taking place. The last thing the Vipers needed was a heads-up in the already volatile press that a change of this magnitude was coming down.

Brandon Briggs privately farmed out the preparation of the new player's uniforms to another company as not to raise the suspicions of the wiley equipment manager.

It's a well-known fact that in any Major League club-house, the best and juiciest rumors always begin with the guys that hand out the hats and the bats.

21 DOWN IN VEGAS

Behind closed-doors, the lawyers were conducting last-minute scrutiny of the twenty current contracts that would soon be assigned to the waiver wire. As Cisco and Brandon kept the upcoming changes on the horizon exclusively to themselves, they knew another key cog in the organization was going to have to be let in on the secret.

Jack Pattie was the promotions manager of the Las Vegas Vipers. His job was to design giveaways and schedule players for all the various community functions. He had been with the Vipers from their inception and was one of the team's more passionate employees on the payroll. In their years of working together, Cisco felt like Jack could be trusted with this kind of sensitive information. He was called into Cisco's office and asked to sit down.

"Jack, we're making a few changes for the rest of the season." Cisco and Brandon began. "What we are about to do has never been done in the history of the game, and we need you now more than ever."

"I thought the changes might be me." Jack nervously laughed. "I realize that we really haven't had too much happy stuff to promote here lately."

"No, we haven't!" said Cisco, "but all that is going to change beginning immediately after the All-Star break… We're letting the team go."

"Letting the team go, go where?" Jack asked with a look of confusion.

"Any damn place they want to go. I'm tired of watching these uninspired 'check snatchers' show up every night only to live for what they're going to do after the game." Cisco snapped. "It all ends on Sunday!"

As Brandon and Cisco laid out their plan, Jack Pattie slowly realized the now grandiose scale of what his job was about to entail. There would be programs, posters, and many various giveaway nights that would all need to be changed or retooled.

Jack's biggest promotion to date was the ill-fated "Here Comes Santa Guy's Christmas in July." It was several years ago where anybody showing up at the park wearing a Santa Claus suit would qualify to win season tickets and $1,000 in Christmas cash. It just so happed that the dome was broken and the temperature that day reached a blistering 112 degrees. It couldn't have been further from the holiday spirit. Not only did the Vipers lose 15-0, but Santa's were passing out in droves from heat exhaustion and many had to be taken to local area hospitals for treatment.

Cisco and Brandon feverishly held court for over two hours as Jack nodded in agreement, finding the scenario extremely bizarre as it was exciting. As an underling who cared, Jack Pattie was also tired of losing and welcomed the change.

"One last thing, Jack," Cisco added. "These kids are going to be special, but it's going to take some time. Once the public and the fans get a taste of what they can do, that's when your job really begins. Until then, your roll is to help us diffuse the overall and general opinion that we as a Major League Baseball organization- have all lost our frigging minds!"

The code of silence that had been established between Eagles coach Keith Madison and his soon-to-be departed players had miraculously remained intact. As a baseball man and a lover of team sports, he recognized the opportunity that was being afforded his former squad. Selfishness was never a curse as Keith had given of himself tirelessly throughout his entire career to support both family and the game he loved most. Even as quirky and unbelievable as the facts he was now digesting, he put it all behind him to mask his doubts that a small college team from Southern Ohio could ever be able to perform and compete at a Major League level. If his boys believed in what they were going to be asked to do, he would be their absolute biggest and loudest supporter regardless of the unlikely outcome.

Twenty-one young souls who would soon be the new Las Vegas Vipers were having an even harder time keeping things quiet. The team had taken a general oath together that they were all preparing to attend a mid-summer baseball camp.

Keeping a lid on it wasn't easy at all. The squad continuously dealt with girlfriends, buddies, and outside family members who were all questioning the logistics of their mass exodus. To everybody's credit and integrity, the circle remained unbroken.

The team was scheduled to leave out of Port Columbus Airport in Columbus on Friday afternoon for a chartered non-stop flight to Las Vegas. On Thursday evening, a last-minute gathering at the Portsmouth Brew Pub served as an impromptu goodbye party for all the principles. With all who joined and reveled with the members of the Eagles, none could fathom the magnitude of this "baseball camp" to which these local boys were now headed. Across the country, the lack of reality was also shared from a totally different level.

Being the corporate owners of the stadium name, the Mirage Hotel was used for housing all out-of-town guests that the Las Vegas Vipers organization randomly entertained. As the week-end approached, little did the desk- clerks who were processing twenty-one luxury rooms on the ninth floor remotely understand the total magnitude of their assignments?

Viper's owner Cisco Wheeler and his general manager Brandon Briggs now knew that the ships had been launched and there was no turning back. A week-end series at home with the Nationals would culminate on Sunday evening with a mandatory team meeting as the likes of which Major League Baseball had never seen.

It was decided that Viper's manager Tommy Leach would be told about the meeting during the last- inning of the final game. It would then be important to immediately reassure him that his job was not on the line. The message would be simply worded that Cisco Wheeler and Brandon Briggs would like to have a players-and-managers gathering in the club-house immediately after the game.

It would also be tantamount that all members of the press corps be asked to leave the stadium immediately after the game with absolutely no exceptions.

As the phone rang in the dugout to begin the ninth inning, Tommy Leach was looking up and down his bench for a solution to a 7-3 deficit. Some players had already begun packing their personal bags in anticipation of getting a head start on the All-Star Break as soon as the last out was declared official. Bench coach Norm Bratchett was the first one who picked up the ringing phone.

"Tommy, it's for you!" he said, handing the extension to the manager.

"Yea, what's up?"

"Tommy, this is Cisco. Brandon and I are calling a mandatory players-and-managers meeting immediately after the game in the club-house. Don't worry, it's not about you. Your job is absolutely secure here with the Vipers." Wheeler continued, "We really want to have a few minutes alone with the players and coaches and Tommy, we're going to need your help."

"OK," Leach quizzically asked, "What do you want with me?"

"Send everybody to the clubhouse except Steinman, Scarbury, Arms, Pouge, and Kennedy." Wheeler directed. "This is very important. I want them to go to the trainer's room for a separate meeting."

"Steinman, Scarbury, Arms, Pouge, and Kennedy, send them to the trainer's office?" Leach repeated. "Something wrong with them?"

"I'll explain later, Tommy, see you after the game." The phone quickly fell silent.

Tommy's attention now turned to the dugout as the players began spilling in for the bottom of the ninth. Down by four-runs, Tommy Leach was as tired of the first half of the season as everyone else.

"OK, gentlemen, I just got a call from Cisco!" Tommy yelled at the bench. "He wants to have a quick meeting after the game."

"Damn it, Tommy! I can't hang around. I have a plane to catch." moaned left fielder Jeremy Burnside.

Several more players quickly started to vent their displeasure on being detained as Manager Tommy Leach finally lost it.

"Tell it to Cisco, ladies! I get paid by the same guy that writes your check! He calls down here and tells me he needs to see you after the game, I pass along the information. If you got some problem with that, I'm not the one to see! Do you understand?" As Leach finished, his face was blood red.

"This is really shit!" added third basemen Johnny Rice. "Mister Owner and Mister Butt-Kissing general manager both need a crash course on how to treat their players. Keeping us here to listen to all their moaning is nothing but pure bull-shit!"

Not realizing the prophet he would soon become, that lesson was to begin rather shortly as the Vipers went down in the bottom of the ninth quietly and in order.

21 DOWN IN VEGAS

The sound of cleats clacking on concrete echoed through the tunnel as twenty-five rather disgruntled ball players headed toward the locker room.

"This better not take long, I'm meeting my girlfriend in L.A. and my flight leaves in two hours." Toots Randall mumbled.

"Team meetings suck!" echoed another sentiment. "This rah-rah crap is for high school. We're shit and we know it, so let us get the hell out of here so we can go adjust our attitudes. The first round is on you!"

As all the players headed for the meeting room adjacent to the lockers, Coach Bratchett was positioned near the door to the trainer room. One by one as they walked by, he singled out and inconspicuously directed five players through the trainer's door and through the entrance.

"What's this all about, Norm?" Pitcher Gary Steinman asked.

"I can't tell you yet." Bratchett replied. "Cisco and Wheeler will be here in a few minutes to explain. Until they get here, just sit down and be glad you're not in the other room."

"What's that mean?" snapped Doug Pouge.

"I said just sit down and shut-up!" returned Bratchett's aggravated answer. "I don't know much except I think this is pretty damn serious, OK? I don't know anything more than you do, so please respect that and just do as I ask."

The room fell silent as the players slumped onto the training tables and metal chairs. Feeling bad that he had shouted at his players, Coach Norm Bratchett excused himself and left the room. In contrast, the noisy chatter from just down the hall would be short lived as the clubhouse door opened entering Vipers Owner Cisco Wheeler, General Manager Brandon Briggs, team lawyer Kobe Williams, along with team accountant Wayne Thompson. The presence of all four was a sign that this summit would certainly not be like any they had ever witnessed before.

As all four symbols of hierarchy stood before the players, Cisco Wheeler spoke.

"Gentleman, I am going to be brief and quick to the point. It has been decided that the Las Vegas Vipers need to go in a drastically different direction as a franchise. We all know the problems, and there's no reason to rehash history. As of right now, all twenty of you in the room have been placed on waivers. If you don't understand the waiver process, we have provided counsel. It's my hope that you will find opportunities with other organizations. For those of you that don't clear the waiver process, it is my intent to honor all your contracts to the letter."

"Wait a minute, you can't do that!" came an angry outburst from first baseman Wally Cremeans. "We have a thing called a Players Union!"

"You can't fire a whole team!" another protest erupted.

A plea for quiet went up as again as the room again fell silent. Cisco Wheeler continued, "I want to refrain from getting personal about our objective here. As I stated, your contracts will all be honored to the letter. You are free to pursue any and all other endeavors with your talents as perspective agents. As long as we as a team and organization live up to those responsibilities, the Players Union will be totally satisfied. I find this a very difficult thing to do as I understand that you all have families as well as other personal obligations. As I have heard you tell me so many times during contract negotiations, this is business. I stand before you today to reiterate that fact. I am also here to tell you that our business at this point is a complete and total failure. At some point, we all have to accept accountability for the product we present to the market-place. If you all sincerely understand your own philosophy that you are indeed a business, you too should also understand the issues of why we are making these changes here today."

"You son of a bitch, you ought to fire yourself and all your henchmen if you want to turn this rat's nest around!" Toots Randal snarled. "So if we go, who the hell plays the rest of the season? Our farm system is worse off than this dumpster-fire you have here!"

Cisco Wheeler made one final parting remark. "Thank you all, gentlemen. You will have an hour to remove all of your personal belongings. Mr. Williams and Mr. Thompson will be here and available to answer any of your legal or financial questions."

21 DOWN IN VEGAS

With Cisco's and Brandon's departure, fifteen uniformed security guards walked in through the door to oversee the exit process. As the door closed behind them, the catcalls and insults began to fly in unison. They both knew it wasn't going to be easy, but now a much harder and far more important message was needed to be delivered. They quickly strode down the hall and entered the trainer's room. All eyes were on the two as they walked in and greeted the five confused players and one befuddled coach.

"Guys, you're here for a very important reason." Brandon slowly began. "I don't know how to put it to you any other way except we have just released the rest of the team."

"Released the team? You mean everybody?" Scott Arms gasped.

"Yes, Scotty," Brandon Briggs clarified. "Every player who you don't see in this room is no longer a member of the Las Vegas Vipers organization. It's that plain and simple."

"If I may, can I ask you why?" utility player Terrence Kennedy asked.

"Why? Kennedy, do you seriously have to ask why?" Wheeler shot back.

Terrance Kennedy paused and then slightly chuckled. "I would assume that maybe it had something to do about the fact we kind of suck."

The bottom line in any business is to succeed. After ten years in the league, the Las Vegas Vipers had never even come close to tasting the sweet nectar of why hundreds of millions of dollars and countless hours had been invested here.

Pertaining to all the complexities dealing with the cause-and-effect rationale related to the business world, Terrence Kennedy had innocently nailed it.

The door once again opened as the Vipers coaching staff entered. They had just been informed about the mass changes and were also ordered to report to the training room. As the facility quietly filled, Cisco Wheeler again put on a brave face and again cleared his throat.

"Gentleman, we as an organization have made a statement today that to my knowledge has never been attempted in all of professional sports history. Today, we are changing everything about our team as you presently know it. With respect to Scarbury, Arms, Steinman, Pouge, and Kennedy, we are turning the page of being the laughing-stock of the league and we are doing it today! In order to stay within the law of professional and collegiate athletics, a lot of what we have been working on over the past month had to remain within these walls and the strictest parameters of the law. I do apologize for those of you who feel left out, but those are the rules that we were forced to play under. Everybody here in this room will remain as an important piece in our travels to the next level if you so choose. The coaches, Tommy, and especially you guys whom we chose to keep as a part of this team. You have my highest vote of confidence. I won't lie to you. Things are going to be different starting right now, very different. All I ask is that you search deep inside yourselves to realize and believe that there is a better way."

The cryptic remarks were beginning to make the remaining personnel in the room nervous. While not meaning to be math menses, all could count to twenty-five. There had been a lot of general and corporate verbiage, but Coach Tommy Leach couldn't hold it in any longer.

"C'mon, Cisco, cut to the chase. We got five days until our next game. What the hell is going on here?"

Cisco looked over to Brandon Briggs. The exchange of glances was all that was needed to realize it was time to go to the visual. As Brandon Wheeler reached behind the door, he removed a two-by-three foot team picture. He then nervously handed it to Cisco.

"These are the Bentley State Eagles." he exclaimed. "These young men, along with those who hopefully choose to remain with us are now the new Las Vegas Vipers. They play the game every day the way it is supposed to be played. They hustle, they run, and their enthusiasm is contagious. They will join us tomorrow morning at the stadium for our first team workout. Are there any questions?'

"A college team, you signed a college baseball team?" vented Catcher Doug Pouge. "We have minor leaguers who need to be up here, and we signed a fucking college team to play here in the Major Leagues? If you think we're the worst joke in baseball now, do you really think we're going to get any better with these guys? For Christ's sake, Cisco, this is sports suicide!"

The room again fell awkwardly silent.

"To our coaches and remaining players," Cisco continued, "Tommy has agreed to stay over during the All-Star break and help us get ready for the second half of the season. The rest of you are free to go. Lord knows you need some time away from all of this and you deserve it. Your vote of confidence and commitment will simply be your presence back here in the clubhouse here on Thursday morning."

Pausing to again scan the room to make eye-contact with all, Cisco Wheeler made one more request.

"I will ask if for any reason anybody here feels that you cannot participate in our new endeavor to simply let us know immediately. Have a wonderful break, guys, and I look forward to seeing you back here next week."

To this point, all of the high baseball drama taking place had pretty much been contained to just a couple of rooms under Mirage Field. With the press being unceremoniously asked to leave and no players immediately available after the game, the wags were all in media- purgatory. Joe Hawk of the *Las Vegas Review-Journal* knew that something highly unusual was going on. As he stood outside the press gate trying every number stored in his cell phone address book, he finally found the direct line to Cisco Wheeler's office. Figuring, "What the hell?" Hawk quickly punched it up and prayed. After a couple of rings, there came a quick answer.

"Hello, Cisco Wheeler!" Those were the words he was hoping for.

"Cisco, this is Joe Hawk from the *Review-Journal.* Can you talk to me about what's going on?" he asked.

"Not now, Joe, it's kind of busy." Cisco responded.

"Look, Cisco, we've been friends for a long time. If something is coming down, you need to have a press conference." Hawk pleaded. "You already got players carrying stuff to their cars saying that you fired the whole team. If you don't let us know what's happening here, you're not going to get a whole lot of sympathy from anyone."

After a pregnant pause, Cisco quickly addressed the issue. "OK, Joe, you can pass the word that the Vipers will hold a press conference at 7:00 tonight to be held in the media room. We're going to make a short statement then, and that's all I can tell you."

"See you at seven!" Joe said as he flipped his phone shut.

It was soon after that Brian Hilderbrand of the *Las Vegas Sun* spotted Joe Hawk still lingering at the gate.

"Any word yet, Joe?" he asked Hawk.

"Press conference at 7:00 p.m. in the war- room." Hawk shot back. "Ya know, I've got the weirdest feeling about all this. Have you ever felt like you were about to go to a friend's funeral… while he was still alive?"

"You think it's that bad?" Hilderbrand asked.

"Firing an entire Major League Baseball team? You tell me. If that's not as close to the top of the 'bad-o-meter,' as you can get, I'm not sure what else could even come close to qualify." Hawk speculated.

4ᵀᴴ INNING

The word hit the media landscape like an atomic bomb as it mushroomed through newsrooms everywhere. With a little over an hour before the official press conference, *ESPN Sports Center* broke the news featuring a live interview with Toots Randall and Dan Patrick. Randall pretty much told Patrick everything that had happened in the team meeting as he and his teammates were told they were all being put on waivers. As one might guess, his attitude was not only of surprise; but retaliation.

"I really don't understand the logic, Dan" Randall went on camera to say. "We certainly weren't playing up to our expectations, but we had some guys who can play this game. We just weren't given the right tools or the right environment to win with an organization that's never had any success. Losing breeds losing, and that's all the Vipers will ever be, losers! I feel good about my future, Dan, and I'll put it all in God's hands starting today."

Dan Patrick did counter the claim asking was it true that everybody on the team was let go. There was certainly more than just a little confusion at this point about how many players had actually been terminated.

"Toots Randall, I certainly understand your shock and disappointment at this most extraordinary of events, but are you sure it was the whole team? We at ESPN are now receiving reports that several of the players may have been asked to stay. Do you know anything about that?" Patrick quizzed.

"Far as I know, Dan, it was everybody." Randall replied. "It happened so fast that most of us thought it was a joke. We only had a few minutes to clean out our stuff and leave. I think the biggest insult was that they actually called in armed security to make sure we wouldn't walk out with all the silverware."

As Dan Patrick and Toots Randall continued their breaking story live on ESPN, other TV, radio, and newspaper crews from across the country were on scramble alert to find any way to get to Las Vegas. Within minutes, live satellite trucks from KVVU-TV (Fox), KLAS (CBS), KTNV (ABC), and KNBC (NBC) were all jockeying for position outside of Mirage Field. With the local affiliates getting in place, that meant that the national networks would also be getting feeds of the story soon. At this point, all that was known was that there were reports that an entire Major League team had been fired in Las Vegas.

In a small town in Southern, Ohio, perhaps the biggest piece of the credibility puzzle pertaining to this huge and meandering "newsberg" was quietly being prepared for launch.

Bentley State Eagles coach Keith Madison, University president Howard Morris, and University SID Jeff Perez were the only ones who knew all the facts concerning the Eagles' stealth-like departure.

In cooperation with the Vipers' wishes, they had all agreed to embargo the story until 10:00 p.m. EST to give the team a chance to issue a statement concerning the firings. They nervously waited near the computer and the fax machines, as all three openly wondered what would be the real impact once all the buttons were pushed and the official e-mails from Bentley State University were released that now made it totally official.

"Hey, come here and watch this!" second baseman Brooks Snyder shouted. "They're making this thing out to be a pretty big deal!"

It was 6:30 p.m. in Las Vegas, and the TV stations were now all prepping to air the Vipers news conference live at 7:00. All the Eagles knew at this point was that transportation was to be provided for them at 8:00 a.m. at the rear loading dock at the hotel to take them over to Mirage Field. They were not told much beyond that. As the rest of the Eagles began to gravitate into Snyder's room, the media circus that was beginning to develop was staggering. CNN was now making it their lead story. The other four major networks were also weaving it into their updated fabric as a major teaser with the standard "More to come on this breaking story!"

"So far, it's just about firing the team, right?" asked Bombo Chadwick.

"What do you mean so far?" ranted Cliff Collier. "Don't you see what's going on here, guys? Stop and think about this for just a second. What do you think is going to happen when everybody finally is told that it's us…I mean, it's all of us that's replacing all of them?"

"You don't think someone will want to kill us or anything, do you?" Gary Duzan naively blurted out.

"No, you dumb ass!" Collier shot back. "Just look! Right there! Our lives are changing forever, and we're watching it happen in front of our faces on live national TV! If they're making such a big whoop about the team that's leaving, what do you think is going to happen when they discover that it's a college baseball team from Portsmouth, Ohio, that's taking their place? Guys, I'll be honest. This is all kind of scary, can we take another vote?"

To this point, for the members of the Bentley State baseball team, it had all been a bit of a Walter Mitty dream come true. It was the Cinderella story that was written without the reality of real life actually being penciled in.

As twenty-one faces stayed glued to the harsh and unraveling developments, it became clear quite quickly that even though it was a Sunday evening, this wasn't going to be your typical slow news day.

"I want to thank you for coming on such short notice." Brandon Briggs slowly began. "I first want to say that due to the nature of today's press gathering, there will be no questions. We have a short and prepared statement that the club is ready to release.Due to some conditions of sensitivity that are still in the working process, we are not quite prepared for a full-dress conclave at this time. We will be conducting a follow-up news conference here at this same facility on Tuesday afternoon at 2:00 p.m. At that time, we will be ready to entertain all of your questions from the media."

As the cameras clicked and the ambient background noise murmured on, Brandon Briggs began reading from his hastily prepared text.

"The Las Vegas Vipers Baseball Organization has decided to embark on what we believe is to be an exciting new path. After our game today, twenty- players on the current roster were immediately put on waivers. Those names will be readily available to you in the hand out as you leave. We also have five other current roster players that are under evaluation. The reason for this change was simply to try something different. There's an old saying that goes if you do what you've always done, you'll get what you always got. Considering the very evident circumstances at hand, we all too clearly understand that nugget of wisdom. It is the intent of this organization to field a winning product. We believe that our future vision will bring to Las Vegas an exciting brand of baseball that will constitute a successful new beginning to our franchise. We will be able to tell you more about our upcoming plans at noon on Tuesday. I thank you again for coming today, and we hope to see you then."

As the tumult and the shouting of reporters began, Brandon Briggs, Cisco Wheeler, and the rest of Vipers representatives were quickly whisked away from the podium. In less than a minute, the press knew just about a little more than they did before the conference had started.

Back in suite 914 at the Mirage Hotel, twenty-one young men suddenly realized the magnitude of what was being asked of them. Most were relieved that they hadn't been personally fingered out yet as to perhaps enjoy at least one more day of precious anonymity before boarding the "crazy-train."

Elsewhere across the country, there was confusion of strategy. In a dimly lit concrete office in Portsmouth, Ohio, three figures sat in a quandary of puzzlement at the lack of reference to the master plan.

"How come they didn't mention the team at the press conference?" Madison asked. "I found that extremely odd as well. Maybe they weren't ready." President Morris added. "I think if they had wanted to make it go public, they would have done it themselves, right then. If I understand anything about how the press works, it's the facts you don't tell them that become the problem." Perez exclaimed, "Maybe we should hold back as well."

"Could be since they're our boys and I do know they wanted to give us the honors of breaking the news along with them." President Howard Morris added.

"I don't know about that," Keith Madison lamented. "It's too close to midnight on a Sunday. If we let this thing out now, of course you realize that nobody in this room gets any sleep tonight. I sense that something happened and things weren't quite right or ready. I vote that we sit on it until tomorrow."

All agreed to wait until the next day when they would be thinking fresh and could again get a handle on this rather unique and awkward assignment. Locking up the office and walking to the parking lot, the three relieved media mercenaries now hoped to get at least one more good night of quality rest before Bentley State University would become the epicenter of the sports universe. Sometimes, the only sign from day to day that one's life is about to dramatically change forever is that the sun will again slowly rise in the east.

The next morning's news headlines made no mistake that the lowly Las Vegas Vipers were quickly being programmed into America's "hot button." The reporting press found things a bit difficult to find the key people in climate control due to the timing of Major League Baseball's All-Star game to be held Tuesday in Milwaukee. As it was, the entire industry as a whole was now on the dark side of the moon. Matt Lauer was bemoaning the fact on the air that "no officials" of the Las Vegas Vipers were available to join him on "*The Today Show.*" Other news outlets were doing everything they could to bring some face-time credibility to this intriguing development.

ESPN continued to air the interview of Dan Patrick and Toots Randall. *USA Today* had a front-page story on Monday with little more than a picture of Brandon Briggs at the press conference and the prepared company line as the story. The cover page of the *Las Vegas Review-Journal* and a story by Joe Hawk became the definitive source that most of the pundits were gravitating to as the headline screamed, "Wheeler Makes Call for Entire Team; "You're Out!"

As the early morning sun began to stretch slowly above the chilly desert rocks, an unmarked bus unseemly pulled up to the rear of the Mirage Hotel. Twenty-one bodies quietly climbed aboard. Manager Tommy Leach, Cisco Wheeler, Brandon Briggs, and equipment manager Harry Stowe greeted the boys as they quickly found their seats. Bus driver Robert Eugene Ramey III finally broke the awkwardness of the moment by picking up the microphone to make a quick announcement.

"Ladies and gentlemen, we are happy to announce that we have some special celebrities on board with us this morning. Can we please hear a round of applause for the 'new' Las Vegas Vipers baseball team!"

That did it! The pent-up uncertainty that each player was holding inside suddenly purged itself into a blast of exuberance that exploded into a throng of cheers and the beginning of the patented clap.

This made it official! If the bus driver that was transporting them to the park knew the deal, it must be real. Quickly, Cisco Wheeler grabbed the microphone.

"Good morning, and welcome to the Las Vegas Vipers, gentlemen. I'm Cisco Wheeler and I own the team. I first want to thank all the hard work of my general manager, Brandon Briggs. I know that you all got a chance to know him fairly well by now as he talked to you about the opportunity of coming here and playing for our organization. I can't sugar-coat this major change we are making - it isn't going to be easy. As you may have seen on TV yesterday, we have dared to do something that no other professional sports franchise has ever done. The reason that these changes were made was simply, because of you. I watched and relished the kind of spirit and enthusiasm that you all demonstrated against LSU in the college series. At that point, I made a personal decision that this is the kind of baseball that the fans of this great game deserve to enjoy. I've been accused more often than not of having more money than brains, but the heart you left out on the field made me feel that sometimes you have to take chances that sometimes defy our traditional logic."

21 DOWN IN VEGAS

"That's all baseball really is, it's just a game of chances. More than often, those chances fail. But when an opportunity presents itself that few give little hope of succeeding, those odds under the right recipe can turn out to prove everybody wrong. When that happens, there's no greater feeling in the world.

"All I ask is that you give me the same effort I saw out there on the field against the LSU Tigers. If you do that, and regardless of the outcome of the score, I will never have to worry that I have nothing less than a team that wants to be a winner every day and will do everything in their power to be one."

The slow and then accelerating clap of the Eagles began. As if on cue, it rapidly accelerated into a crescendo as Brandon Briggs grabbed hold of the microphone.

"This is going to be exciting, guys," Brandon exclaimed. "If I may now introduce you to someone that knows this game better than anyone I've ever known, please welcome your new manager Tommy Leach!... Tommy!"

Leach quickly turned from his seat and threw a hand up in the air. As the bus slowly pulled away from the Mirage Hotel, the introductions continued.

"I feel we have a great coaching staff that certainly has the credentials to help you all get the job done." Brandon exerted. "Von Hayes is our hitting coach. Von spent most of his career with the Phillies, and if there was ever a guy who knows how to get on base and make the best of it, Von is your man. You might be familiar with our pitching coach, Tom Browning. Tom spent the majority of his career with the Reds and was one of the best finesse pitchers in the game. Tom might even show you how to throw a perfect game, so be nice to him. Our bench coach and Tommy's assistant is Norm Brachett. 'Stormin' Norman played for the Angels, Red Sox, Twins, and the Braves. Besides being a hell of a baseball man, his big claim to fame is that he was the first player ever drafted by the Seattle Pilots. They soon realized the error of their ways and quickly moved away. The sad part was that they never told Norm where they were going."

Nervous laughter filled the bus as the feeling-out period seemed to be moving along well. The awkwardness of the moment dissipated quickly as the great unknown seemed to unite all who were present. Several other coaches and key personnel were informally introduced before the bus turned off a sharp exit and headed down the ramp. All eyes had instinctively turned to the right side of the bus as the windows were now witness to a local breathtaking sight.

As magnificent as that first distant view of the Emerald City must have felt to Dorothy with the yellow bricks leading the way, this too was truly a spectacular edifice that loomed large and closing fast on the horizon. The sight that was drawing closer was truly mesmerizing. As if on cue, Brandon Briggs proudly made the definitive announcement on the speaker that separated fact from fantasy. "Gentlemen, welcome to your new home, Mirage Field, Las Vegas, Nevada!"

Monday morning broke swiftly on the campus of Bentley State University in Portsmouth, Ohio. This commonly quiet and pristine campus had suddenly been thrust into sheer media mayhem. Due to various internet reports that had begun surfacing, with the most credible coming from the internet source mlb.com, the secret was now oozing out.

It was being reported that the Bentley State Eagles had all agreed and signed contracts to replace the current Las Vegas Vipers. To accommodate the cotillion of sudden press requests for more information, it mandated a quick phone call from University President Morris to Brandon Briggs on the uncomfortable and awkward situation developing in Portsmouth. Protecting the school from any adverse publicity was paramount as it was mutually decided for the school to go ahead and hold a press conference Monday afternoon in the basketball gym at 3:00.

Wisely determined, it was decided that the only speaker for the assembly would be baseball coach Keith Madison. In a quick meeting before addressing the two hundred-plus journalists that planned to be in attendance, it was definite to simply be brief and try and explain Bentley State's position on this most unusual matter.

The general public was given limited access to the event besides family members and many of the nosey alumni that felt it was there legacy to be there.

"I want to thank all of you for your interest in coming here today." President Morris began. "From what I gather, our little team from Portsmouth, Ohio, ain't so little anymore."

Nervous and anticipated laughter permeated the gym as President Morris paused slightly before continuing.

"With a due respect to our players and the unique developments which have transpired, I wish to turn the podium over to a man I truly respect and admire. Ladies and gentlemen, may I present Bentley State University baseball coach; Keith Madison." The applause was both sincere and obligatory. As it finally died down to the mandatory level of quiet, Keith Madison spoke.

"I want to thank you for your sincere interest in something that I find a real tribute to the spirit of athletics. As a coach, you probably expect me to talk about the game and what these boys have committed to do. While I am extremely proud of them as players, I am even more proud of them as men and the kind of character that they chose to commit. When I was first and quite unexpectedly approached by the Las Vegas Vipers with their plan to embrace our college team as their own, I laughed. I laughed not in disrespect to a unit that came within a couple of runs of becoming college baseball's champions, I laughed because of the initial absurdity of such a proposal.I played pro ball and have spent my life on the diamond as a coach, a mentor, and a friend to all of my players. I also realized that I have an obligation to this university. My first fear was possible rules violation in first being approached with such a strange inquiry. I knew that I had to immediately remove myself personally from any conflict of interest. I immediately went to President Morris with all the information. After thoroughly researching the proposal, it was determined that if these players were being asked by an outside baseball organization to go to work for them, it was basically like hiring employees for a job. We immediately made the decision to steer clear of any personal involvement that could compromise our athletic program. We told the Vipers organization that if they wanted to talk to the players as individual students, there was nothing we could really do to stop them, but they could not be approached as student athletes.

"As we stand here today, I can look you all in the eyes and tell you that on behalf of Bentley State University, there were absolutely no infractions or improprieties to our college athletics program. I can also tell you that the twenty-one men who made the commitment to continue together as a team at the highest level of professional achievement is one of the most courageous and unselfish choices I have ever witnessed in the history of sports.

"Bentley State University was proud beyond words to have taken our team to the College World Series. As their coach, I will tell you straight up, we should have won that damn thing!"

That quick tension-breaking remark brought a quick flood of laughter and applause that served as an honest insertion that distanced Keith Madison from sounding too much like a talking head.

"As a fan of the sport of baseball, I hope you in the media learn to love these guys as much as I do. If they continue to play this game the way I know they can, your lives won't have a minute's peace, I promise you that—and I thank you."

Forty-five minutes eclipsed as Keith Madison answered every conceivable question that was thrown in his direction. In the archives of this quaint river town's rich sports history, this kind of total attention was all encompassing. Several reporters from Fox News fed the network with a story package that chronicled several of the local Major League players that came from the area.

They talked on camera with Al Oliver, Don Gullet, and Brandon Webb. ESPN Radio did their daily sports show live from Damon's Bar & Grill in the downtown Ramada Inn. One of Dan Patrick's more interesting guests was Ohio native and ESPN Sports personality Kirk Herbstreet. Kirk actually found the concept of hiring an entire baseball team as a unit dumbfoundedly innovative. He went on record as saying while he really didn't think it would work, he thought there was some merit in fielding a team that was already established with a certain amount of group chemistry. Most callers to the show thought that while the idea was noble, there was no way that a competitive balance could ever be attained.

In the course of twenty-four hours, over two-hundred reporters from every stretch of the universe had overturned every rock, stone, and pebble in Portsmouth, Ohio, in an attempt to up their rivals on a story that was spreading like ants underneath a kitchen sink. From interviewing local restaurant owners to tracking down friends who would talk about the players, this story just wouldn't stop running. It was still four days before they played their first game, but the Bentley State Eagles were already all the buzz of baseball.

As the unmarked bus stealthily weaved through the gates and into the stadium, a dozen or so marked and unmarked press vehicles were sprinkled about nearby. Apparently unaware that the biggest story in sports news had just passed before their noses, they continued to wait. The squeal of the breaks and a gentle jolt was the obvious sign their destination was close to journey's end. Brandon Briggs once again grabbed the microphone for final debarking instructions.

"Welcome to our final stop." Brandon joked. "Guys, our first visit will be to the clubhouse to assign your lockers, uniforms, and equipment. This will probably take the rest of the morning. We're planning on bringing in lunch at about noon, and then around 1:00 p.m. we will take the field for our first official team workout. Are there any questions?"

Pitcher Jeremy Burke threw up his hand to ask an obvious question that had yet been addressed.

"What about the other player's, sir? I mean the rest of the Vipers who are staying. When are we going to meet them, and how do they feel about us?

"That's a good question, son." Brandon paused briefly before continuing with his answer. "Being the All-Star break, we have to respect the player's right to their time off. In a quick meeting with everybody just before they left, we addressed the fact that we will plan to have a full team meeting Wednesday afternoon after they return. I'm not going to lie to you. I'm sure there will be some resentment and for certain some shared and awkward moments. Above all, you need to remember this. You guys are now professionals. I expect that you will handle yourselves in the utmost manner that goes along with that job title. The other members of this team are also professionals. When the time comes, I expect we will quickly come to an understanding and move forward. Are there any more questions? If not, please follow Tommy and Mr. Stowe, and let's get you guys looking like ball players."

The single file line procession from the players' parking entrance wound through the halls and caverns of one of baseball's most classic fields. As with everything else, when it was decided to bring Major League Baseball to the desert city, it was destined to be a sports palace. Mirage Stadium featured a collapsible dome roof for those extra cool nights and a most luxurious entertainment complex of boxes and suites that outlined the outfield fences. With seating capacity for 39,000, this baseball yard had everything you could imagine in extravagance for full-fan creature comfort. As the door to the club-house opened, the scene was surreal. Each locker already had the player's uniforms neatly hanging from each one. Around the room, the names on the back read Milhuff, Deeters, Snyder, Duzan, Gambill, Burke, and all the rest.

"OK, guys listen up!" Tommy Leach proclaimed. "Welcome to the big leagues! Find your locker and see if everything fits OK? If there's a problem, deal with it immediately; it's show-time fella's!"

While his new team was getting a whirlwind orientation to the highest level of pro sports, the news from the waiver wire wasn't good. As Cisco Wheeler sat in his office, he fielded few calls of interest from anybody for his now-released players. It appeared in a stark and humorous truth of reality that he must have made the right decision because apparently no one else wanted his team either.

Pitcher Billy Adamson was picked up by the Seattle Mariners and outfielder Louis Batista was signed by the Red Sox and then sent down to Pawtucket. Of the twenty former members of the Las Vegas Vipers, eighteen had cleared waivers and either had to sign with another team or be paid in full according to their contract. No minor league options were left on any of the remaining players, meaning the Vipers had just ten days to figure out their fate.

"I certainly thought someone would have picked up Bolander." Wheeler lamented to Briggs. "He had eleven home runs already."

"That's the problem, Cisco!" Briggs countered. "Sure, he had eleven home runs, but he also led the league in strike-outs, errors, and hitting into double plays. We are also paying him six-million dollars a year. That's a pretty expensive price tag for just eleven home runs."

"That's the problem with all these bastards, and the fan knows it!" Wheeler fired back. "That's exactly why we're doing what we're doing. Are we going to take a beating on the street and in the press? You can bet on it! Will the fans get their money's worth? I guarantee they will. The fans are as sick of seeing all this garbage as much as we are. Whether the new Vipers ever win a game all season long, it really doesn't matter now, does it? At least this organization has made a statement that will go down as a flashpoint in sports history. Our message to them is when it comes to the heart of this game, it absolutely comes first."

"Then I must ask you, Cisco, if that's true, how are we going to explain that losses are morally correct to the people who buy tickets? After all, a loss is a loss." Brandon fired back, "and that's why you're doing this."

Sitting back in his chair, Brandon Briggs knew he had hit a huge nerve, but it was a question that had to be addressed

"Brandon," Cisco retorted, "had you not asked that, you certainly wouldn't be the man I thought I had hired for this job. There are three qualities in today's work force that have tragically eroded. They are effort, desire, and pride. To me, that's the foundation for any track record of success. Do you mean to tell me that the construction workers who bust their humps all week can't recognize other people who get paid millions more and who don't bust theirs? There is a human forgiveness factor for people who try hard and fail. It's the ones who fail and show no remorse that is the ultimate insult for the ones that do. That's how our team will explain it!"

While the new Vegas Vipers were to be were safely sequestered away from the general public, the media firestorm continued to grow on the outside to unfathomable proportions. On the eve of Major Leagues Baseball's biggest mid-summer showcase, all anybody was talking about was the Las Vegas Vipers. The Vipers' lone All-Star representative had been outfielder Joey Jones, but he had excused himself after the team firing, stressing personal reasons. Facing the embarrassment of playing in the All-Star game while knowing that you didn't have a team to return to must have certainly have had its awkward side.

ESPN was like a dog with a new soup-bone on this one. Even during the Home Run Derby contest, the announcers couldn't help themselves from bringing up the "Las Vegas Massacre." While most players declined direct rhetoric on the story, several of the star players took public issue with the unorthodox move.

"This is a tough game to play." said Ken Griffey Jr. of the Cincinnati Reds. "In my opinion, I think that the management probably just over-reacted. I personally feel for all the lives that have been disrupted, and I think these college kids are going to have a rougher time because no one at this level wants to be shown up like that. There's definitely going to be a huge target on the back of this team."

Curt Shilling of the Boston Red Sox was a little more volatile toward his own contemporaries as he defended the right to hustle and play hard.

"You know, we got guys up here that once they get here, let's be honest, they coast. It's a fact." Shilling went on to say, "If a team owner gets tired of the lack of effort, he should be allowed to take drastic measures if he thinks that's what needs to be done. For me, I wish them well. I was one of those fanatics that got caught up watching the college series and I took in every game that I could. While I certainly did appreciate their style of play, I still haven't worked up the nerve yet to try the hidden-ball trick." He laughed.

Both ESPN and Fox Sports were frantically positioning themselves to televise the Friday night game featuring the Vipers at Pittsburgh. It appeared that Fox owned the rights due to their accelerated second-half coverage of the season. Once it was determined that Fox Sports got the nod, the promos began to fly. It was certainly sardonic that the cream of baseball's crop was getting ready to do battle for top honors while all of the attention was seemingly on two last place teams that were hopelessly ensconced in the cellar of their respective divisions. As in most classic human dramas, it's the element of the great unknown that always becomes that hypnotic potion of attraction. Fox had done its homework and now had a complete roster and stat sheet on each and every former Eagle player. All the secrets would soon be out.

As the players all spilled onto the field for their first afternoon workout, it was an instantaneous transition from boys to men. Jarred Brewster went down to the bull-pen with a swagger that would rival the stride of Johnny Bench as he prepared to work out the pitchers. The Eagles' starting catcher Boone Coleman was still inside the clubhouse with Tom Browning as they worked together on signs and pitch strategy. If there was one thing for certain, the Bentley State Eagles had a core of top-drawer hurlers. Mitch Milhuff, Jeremy Burkes, Andrew Shakart, "Dirty" Ernie Fuller, and Everett Carpenter all had top quality pitches that garnered them much deserved attention every time they stepped on the mound.

* * * * *

The team took batting practice as "King Kong" Karl Smith began doing what he was famous for. While only a college junior, Smith had a keen-eye and a jack-hammer attack at the plate. As the Eagles' left fielder, Smith set the all-time MAC home run record for a career playing four-years and swatting forty-seven. Some critics praised him as being too one dimensional because his average was only .241.

Others marveled at his monstrous potential and speculated what could be done if he could legitimately harness his raw talent.

Standing in the batting cage at Mirage Field, his first swing of the bat carried 435 feet of horse-hide into the left field seats. By watching the immense trajectory of his swats, it was curiously easy to see that his nick-name came honestly.

As the first workout began to take shape, so did the new Vipers line-up. In the outfield positions it would be Karl Smith in left, Cliff Collier in center, and Sean Deeters in right. The grass beyond the infield lines appeared solid. Per the starting infield look for the new Vipers, it would be John Gambill at third, Gary Duzan at short, Brooks Snyder at second, and Bombo Chadwick at first. As the regular catcher for the Eagles, Boone Coleman realized that the Vipers veteran catcher Doug Pouge was still the team's starter. Coleman took things in stride that he would probably not be the everyday choice, but relished the chance of working close at the craft he loved with a player he truly admired.

The first showcase was called at 4:00 p.m. as the players left the field and made their way into the showers. All considered it a crisp and polished session that had honestly impressed the coaches with the talent level that they were dealing with. Twenty-one exuberant and sweat-soaked carcasses now loosely spilled into the club-house where they were met by four other less disheveled bodies that were seated next to their name-plated lockers. The stall that said "Steinman" was now the only one left empty.

"Say, Skip," Scotty Arms spoke up first. "We all kind of talked it over and well, decided we really didn't have anything all that important to do for the next couple of days, so-we thought you might need us here."

Silent in his surveillance of the room, Tommy Leach seemed to choke just a bit before looking at the new Vipers and now his four returning veterans. "I'm sure the media-coverage by now warrants no official introduction of everybody here, so just let me say it's great to see you!"

"Doug, Armsey, Brad, Terry," Tommy Leach warmly addressed each of his players, "I'm glad to see you. I understand what you all must be going through and, not that I didn't think highly of you before, but you each have earned my deepest respect, and again, I thank you. Workout's tomorrow morning at 9:00."

Again, looking at each of his returning players, Tommy was more than happy to spend a little coin.

"For you guys tonight, dinner's on me so we can play a little catch-up. Reservations are at Mimmo Ferraro's for 7:00 p.m. Hope you all like Italian!"

The early return of starting catcher Doug Pouge came as an especially welcome surprise due to the excessive crop of young guns and the unusual and quick-learning curve facing the team.

Viper Pitchers Scott Arms, Brad Scarbury, along with utility player Terrence Kennedy had always tried to be good team-players, but often got caught up in the head-wind of dissent from some of their less enthusiastic contemporaries.

The whereabouts and status of starting pitcher Gary Steinman was still a mystery. He had cleaned out his locker with the rest of the released players on Sunday and had quietly disappeared without a word. A team meeting had been called for Tuesday morning at 8:00 in an attempt to unify the old guard with the new. Due to the awkwardness of the situation, Manager Tommy Leach quickly excused himself along with the four returning veterans to let the new members enjoy themselves without the peer pressure of the past. As they all stepped into Tommy's office, Doug was the first to open up and express himself.

"Skip, this is all way too insane." he blurted. "We all had to get back here because on the outside, media chaos is just unbelievable. It's absolute nuts!"

"I had over one hundred messages on my answering machine and the damn thing said on the box that it only goes up to fifty!" added Scotty Arms.

"We all got together and decided to get the hell out of the line of fire and climb back into the play-pen" Terrence Kennedy added. "It's safer here than it is out there for sure."

"First of all, guys, you don't know how happy I am to see you." Tommy reiterated. "Between us girls, this has been a hell of a ride already and we haven't even got in our seats yet. Don't think for a minute that in the beginning when all this crazy shit came down that I didn't think about telling Wheeler and Briggs where to pack it?"

"I still think this is suicide, Tommy." Catcher Doug Pouge added. "If I didn't have a family, or an iron-clad contract, my ass would be out of here faster than 'Dice Clay' on the Family Channel."

Nervous laughter filled the room briefly before Tommy consolidated his thoughts for the behalf of his four -returning veterans.

"First thing is I've never lied to you guys, and you have to believe that. I agree that this is the strangest and most challenging situation I have ever had to deal with in my over forty-plus years I've been in the game. But c'mon, you know the crap this club-house has had to deal with! We had some of the laziest sons of bitches in here that I ever saw."

Brad Scarbury tried to counter in protest, but was quickly shut down.

"Hold on for a minute!" I know some were your friends, but the reason you're here and they're not is because you want it more than they did. Let me ask you, did any of you watch these new kids play in the College World Series? They were incredible! These kids are fresh and they're all loving what they do and where they are. Try to think back and remember the days when you all used to show up four hours before a game just to be there? Get this, they're actually asking us what time they take infield and batting practice. Can you even remember the last time when you all couldn't wait to get to the ball-park? No offense, but to me, it's all pretty damn refreshing!"

"OK, Tommy, I think we hear what you're saying, but it still sounds like you're making us all out to be the bad guys, and we're not!" Terrence Kennedy vented. "Hell, Tommy, all we ever dealt with in our everyday lives around here was contract problems, what women were available after the game, and when were they going to fire you? Yea, this freshness of boyhood innocence shit is uplifting, but do you really think that hiring a college team that got some breaks is the real answer to our problems? What the hell do you all expect out of us?"

With obvious frustration starting to infiltrate the room, Tommy Leach felt it was his responsibility to put it to bed and right now.

"Here it is straight and as simple as I can give it to you." Tommy slowly began. "You have twenty new teammates. One young man will be our new bullpen catcher and assistant bench coach to Bratchett. His name is Jarred Brewster. This team was afforded the opportunity that no other group of players in the history of professional sports has ever been given. Brewster wasn't even in the plans because he never even played. All of these players took a vote and said that if he was left out, they weren't accepting our offer. These are college students for Christ's sake! Here they are with a chance to make more money than any of them may ever see in their lifetime, yet commitment to the whole precluded any individual reward. To me, guys, that's pretty fucking' strong! Now, what do I expect out of you? All I ask is acceptance…and a new spirit of adventure. That would be nice for starters."

"But, Tommy, this has never been done before." Scotty Arms argued. "The press is completely nut-zoid out there and we're the ones that are in their trigger-sights."

"Do you realize how many players would love to be in your shoes right now?" Tommy instantly shot back. "This thing here is bigger than the friggin' All-Star Game that starts in less than one hour. My advice quite honestly is to get your damn egos out of your ass and look at the big picture. Like it or not, you're going to be a part of baseball- history. Look at how many good players in the game played for bad teams and simply faded into obscurity never to be heard from again."

"Yea, but this isn't Major League Baseball, Tommy, this is just a damn publicity stunt and you know it!" Pouge shouted from his locker.

"Doug, I was here when you got called up." Leach replied. "If it weren't for a catcher named Bo Diaz, you'd have never made it here, I'm convinced of that. He believed in you and told me so many times against my own shit-judgment that you were big time. It turned out that you and he both proved me wrong."

"So, what's that got to do with anything?" Pouge again questioned.

"My point again is this." Leach answered. "Why not write your own legacy, boys, as the ones who helped to teach the Eagles how to fly. Hell, this talk show is over! I'll see you out on the field!"

5TH INNING

The Major League All-Star Game was secondary as far as the incidental chatter that went on within the broadcast booth. As hard as they tried to stay focused on the obvious event at hand, the TV announcers still couldn't stay away from baseball's biggest breaking story. During the second inning, Fox Sports announcer Thom Brennaman took time to interview Vipers' owner Cisco "The Dealer" Wheeler on a split-screen format live from Las Vegas.

"We are very lucky this evening to have Viper's' owner Cisco 'The Dealer' Wheeler here to talk about the highly unusual move of replacing an entire Major League team in mid-season. Thanks for taking time to join us tonight, Cisco." Brennaman began.

"Thank you, Thom." Cisco nervously replied.

"Let me quickly start by asking, and I guess this is the big question that's yet to really be answered, why for all practical purposes did you replace the entire team, and why the Bentley State Eagles?" Brennaman began.

"Well, Thom, in honesty, you may have answered your own question." Cisco shot back. "The Las Vegas Vipers were not a team, and we wanted to become one quickly. Our general manager Brandon Briggs and I assessed the situation and I would be less than truthful to admit it wasn't good. We lacked the key elements in almost every category to not only field a team that was competitive, but also to give the fans their money's worth." He nervously laughed and added. "Thom, you've watched us play for many years, there should be no secret that something was needed to be done."

21 DOWN IN VEGAS

"I certainly see your point, Cisco," Thom again quizzed, "but why an inexperienced college team at this level, and again, why did you choose the Bentley State Eagles?"

"Thom, again I refer to us as lacking the element known as 'team.' When I saw how hard and with the kind of passion these guys played the game in that final great game of the College World Series, I wanted to bring this kind of heart and baseball soul not only to Las Vegas, but back to Major League Baseball, period. Win or lose, we as owners as well as fans deserve this kind of effort."

"OK, you play your first game Friday night in Pittsburgh, and that's a game we here at Fox Sports will be carrying by the way. I have to ask you this. With only four days of preparation, are these guys really going to be ready to handle everything that's going to be thrown at them? I don't just mean out there on the field, but the entire media-circus that has exploded around all of this?" Brennaman asked. "Thom, these guys have been playing baseball since way back in March." Wheeler pointed out. "There's only been about a three-week break since they played for the college title, so as far as playing the game of baseball, nothing has changed for them, except they'll just keep on playing baseball and now get to use real wooden bats for a change." He chuckled.

"OK, Cisco, I thank you for your blatant honestly as we are running out of time." Brennaman warned his guest. "Quickly, your new team, or in essence the Bentley State Eagles, in your opinion, will they be able to handle all of the pressure that comes with playing this game at the Major League level?"

"It's only pressure if you make it pressure, Thom." Cisco retorted. "These are all great kids who are enthusiastic about what we've asked them to do. The thing I like best is that they lack the invisible boundaries that often plague our industry. It should be refreshing, and it certainly should be fun."

"Cisco, you're a one of a kind. I wish I had more time to ask you what you meant by that last comment, but I don't. Thank you and good luck on Friday night.'" Brennaman parted.

Thank you, Thom, and see what you can do for the National League. We need a few more runs up there." Wheeler noted.

While they had been talking, Alex Rodriquez hit a three run shot out of Miller Park in Milwaukee to put the American League on top, 4-1. While creating several poignant sound bites that were sure to be headliners for the evening's news and sports networks, Cisco Wheeler had actually handled himself quite well. When first asked to appear as a guest during the game, his initial reaction was to deny the interview. Brandon Briggs reminded him that they had been pretty much tight lipped with the press, and this might be the perfect stage and opportunity for some crucial explanations. By planting their mission-statement right there in the belly of the beast during prime-time, it certainly created the added attention to the situation much like pouring warm and gooey chocolate on a vanilla parfay.

Reaction on the media news level had already kicked into pop-status alert. Comedy Central was already running a bit called "The Las Vegas Keggers." Its premise was a bunch of college kids bringing their usual and often lampooned hijinks to professional sports. *ESPN Sports Center* had become publicly frustrated with the lack of specifics surrounding the move. While they had interviewed most of the disgruntled ex-players for all it was worth, none of the new players or management had made themselves available for comment.

While there was little or no Vipers representation in Milwaukee for the All-Star Game, that didn't keep other team owners or GM's from venting their opinion on the wholesale house cleaning. While most used the arena to criticize the team's action, there were several voices that began to emerge and actually applauding the return to accountability.

St. Louis Cardinal General Manager Walt Jocketty went on record as praising owner Cisco Wheeler for having the guts to try a different approach to the game to which he referred to as having "a deteriorating attitude with a singular mind--set."

Tuesday night's festivities followed a familiar script as the American League once again trumped the National League by a score of 11-6. The lights slowly dimmed in Milwaukee as the rest of Major League Baseball's employees headed out to indulge themselves in what was left of their precious mid-summer sabbatical.

With a couple days off still in the bank for most, a few dedicated laborers continued to toil on the clock. Wednesday morning once again started early and stayed late for a gaggle of fledgling gamers. While the veterans stayed close to themselves during much of the day, the sense that a contrived team melting point was being orchestrated.

"OK, ears-on and now!" Tommy Leach bellowed. "Good work out there today, but we got to get some things together here. Let's see, today is Wednesday? We open up Friday night in Pittsburgh. Get out of your 'uni's', go shower up, and I'll see all of you all in the players' lounge in forty-five minutes pronto."

As the team poured into the lounge and grabbed a seat, they were met by all essential team personnel, including Brandon Briggs and Cisco Wheeler. It was pretty much a given that this gathering would be the defining summit before leaving the dark side of the moon forever to once again face the light. Brandon Briggs quickly spoke up.

"First of all, I want to simply say thanks for all of your understanding and cooperation in this very delicate matter. For the ones of you who were here before the change, I know and certainly do understand how difficult all of this must feel. I just received a call from Gary Steinman this morning. Some of you may have noticed that his locker had been cleaned out. Gary told me that he went through some personal issues with everything and wasn't quite sure about his future. He called to tell me that he will be in Pittsburgh on Friday night and will be ready to play. He was emphatic that he is still a member of the Vipers. Until he shows us otherwise, Gary shall certainly still be considered a member of this team all in good standing."

"If we're going to win some games, we're going to need him" Scott Arms spoke- up from the back of the room.

"Let me take it further, Scotty. If we're going to win some games, we need all of you!" answered Wheeler. "This is not punishment we are doling out here guys. This is simply renewing the will to win. The players we chose to keep were picked on their own merit as individuals we knew could weather the storm until a better day arrived. That better-day journey starts today. This team unit who sits before us in this room I believe understands the spirit of the game. We may occasionally fail as individuals, but we shall never lose that spirit of a team! I will do everything in my power to make sure that you are protected from the onslaught of cheap shots, innuendos, and unfair criticism that we all know will come! On the other hand, if you don't play hard, if you let your ego's get in the way of your effort, if you lie down during the tough times, there is nothing that I or anybody can do to save you from that."

The room began the slow and accelerated clap until it echoed like thunder of the cinder block walls. Standing up, Brooks Snyder quickly quieted down the room to speak.

"I just want to again thank you all for the opportunity you have given us." Looking at the late arrivals, he continued, "I especially want to thank Brad, Scott, Terry, and Doug for like, not beating us up or anything or spitting on our food."

That comment brought on a welcome wave of spontaneous laughter that served as a relief- valve for the obvious set of circumstances that were present.

Sean Deeters also piled on with a comment. "They've been a great help and we appreciate their attitude. Mr. Leach, one of our biggest expenses back at school used to be for my laundry. That's one bill that Coach Madison said he never worried much about paying because he felt like it was a waste of money to wash a clean uniform. When you all start yelling at us about the size of the laundry bill up here, then, we'll all pretty much know we've been doing our job."

Sean's well-placed verbal lagniappe built further momentum as Manager Tommy Leach took the floor to outline the team's plan for their return to sports reality.

"Our flight for Pittsburgh is for tomorrow evening at 7:00. We are going to have a light workout here at the field in the morning starting at 8:00 until about noon. At 2:00 p.m., we are conducting a major press conference here at the field and it's mandatory attendance for all. We have put off the media weasels for about as long as we can, and now it's time that you guys earn your chops. Since our flight is at 7:00 p.m. we can hold this down to about an hour and then we have a great excuse to close it down. Are there any questions?" Tommy asked.

"Is there anything the press is going to ask us that we should stay away from answering?" infielder Clint McElroy inquired.

"Yea, everything, but there's nothing we can do about it!" Came Tommy's sarcastic answer. "Just be yourselves, and if they ask you something you don't know, just play dumb. The press likes naivety, it'll be OK."

Mitch Milhuff threw up a hand and was the next to speak. "We got quite a few people from Portsmouth who are coming up to Pittsburg for the weekend to watch us play. Do we like get free tickets to the game, or what?"

"Each of you as players will have six personal tickets for every away game and ten tickets for all home games. When we get to Pittsburgh, just tell Rich Norcross, he's our traveling secretary, the six names you need to have on the tickets. They will be at the will-call window on the lower plaza." Tommy also included some fatherly advice. "If I may say this, be very careful about whom you promise free tickets. I can tell you from experience that it's real easy to piss-off your family and most of your friends by choosing who gets them. My basic philosophy has always been free for family members only. If your friends really want to see you bad enough and truly are your buddies, they'll buy the damn seats."

Brad Scarbury closed out the meeting with an obvious question that had to date been avoided. "Hey, Skip, today is Wednesday, and we play Friday night, do we have a line-up card or even a rotation put together yet?"

"I wish I could say yes, Brad, but I can't." Tommy humbly admitted. "After our workout and the press conference, I will work all that out on the plane to Pittsburgh. You guys are all rested so that's not really going to be a problem of who starts Friday. My only consideration will be looking for the guys who want the ball and aren't going to be afraid to use it in a lethal and winning manner. If there no more questions, class dismissed!"

* * * * *

STEPHEN A. HAYES

"The Vipers Have Landed"
Joe Hawk
Las Vegas Review-Journal

 (Las Vegas) The shroud of mystery concerning the Las Vegas Vipers was unveiled Thursday afternoon at Mirage Field with a press conference that looked more like a sequel to "Camp O.J." Viper's team owner Cisco Wheeler along with his franchise executive's unveiled twenty new team- members who just three short weeks ago were known as the Bentley State Eagles and were the runners-up in this year's Collegiate World Series.

 In an unprecedented move that stunned Major League Baseball to the core, Wheeler released most of his players after last Sunday's regular season game in favor of a team that has never played an inning of professional baseball. Wheeler said that the reason for the move was to simply put a quality unit on the field that was already a team. When pressed by several reporters about the Eagles' lack of professional experience, Wheeler responded by saying, "We spend all of our damn time and money hiring individuals and we try to force them to play as a team. Over the years, I shudder to think at the money that I have personally spent on what were supposed to be quality free agents who never seemed to come close to paying for themselves. It was our feeling that something drastically needed to be done not only for ourselves, but for the game. Watching these boys play in the series is what team ball is all about. We realize that they have a few things they need to learn to adjust, but we are confident that they'll find it together- as a team."

 Cisco "The Dealer" Wheeler has long been known for his friendly eccentricities and flamboyant style as an owner. This move might not only be his biggest gamble to date, but also the most expensive game of 21 ever attempted in the entire history of sports.

 It's rumored that Wheeler could lose between 60 and 80 million dollars on all existing contracts. While their record would denote that the Las Vegas Vipers inherit a legacy of losing, nobody has ever accused them of not being interesting!

21 DOWN IN VEGAS

Going into their tenth year, the Vipers have never had a winning season. All twenty-one frosh players, plus the returning veterans, seemed optimistic at the massive press conference. Former Eagles first baseman Gary Chadwick expressed dismay and shock when approached initially about the project. Right Fielder Sean Deeters called it "a script straight from a Hollywood movie" while veteran pitcher Scott Arms was a little more cautious with his assessment of the move. "Sure I'm a little torn because of the situation. A lot of the guys that are my friends and are now gone, but I also realize that this is a business. I'm all in for winning and will try anything to help turn this thing around."

The four other Vipers that are being kept along with Arms include pitchers Gary Steinman, Brad Scarbury, catcher Doug Pouge, and utility man Terrence Kennedy.

"The Second Season," as the Vipers are marketing their new look maneuver begins tonight in Pittsburgh and will be televised nationally on the Fox Sports Network. Seven-game winner Zack Duke will start for the Pirates while no official lineup or starting pitcher has yet been announced for Las Vegas.

* * * * *

Bench Coach "Stormin'" Norman Bratchett was busy trying to herd all of the new faces in the right direction at PNC Park in Pittsburgh. From the airplane schedules to the hotel drills, this was a brand-new exercise in organization that had all previously been taken for granted. At the Major League level, there was almost a reverent protocol on the meticulous procedures on how to do things. Attempting to shuttle the new Vipers from Las Vegas to Pittsburgh was almost like taking twenty-one kids on a senior high field trip to Disney World. In a sense, they were all traveling to a new magic kingdom, but yet quite unaware that there were many demons and dragons along the way. It was almost 5:00 p.m. as Vipers Pitching Coach Tom Browning pulled pitcher Scott Arms aside for a private chat.

"So tell me, Scotty, and honestly, what do you think about all this? You can be solid with me. I need to hear it." he asked.

"Man, I'm not sure. Maybe it's just me. Maybe it's just not the fun like it used to be. Watching them all running around out there, whooping it up, and taking pictures and selfies of everything. I just don't know if I have that in me anymore" Arms admitted.

"If you're talking about losing, maybe that's what you're feeling" Browning continued. "These guys don't have a clue what's going on around them and you know what? I envy them! This game isn't the way it used to be when we came up, and do you know why? It's because we let all them negative bastards suck the fun right out of our souls. We drank the damn Kool-Aide and now look where we are. We're making more money than we can ever spend in a lifetime, and yet, we're all still bitchin' and complaining. You know, I haven't heard peep-one from any of these guys about what their making. Even though they're all making the minimum, hell, that's more than I would have ever made in my life-time if I hadn't got lucky enough to do this for a living."

"OK, preach, so what are you saying to me here?" Scott Arms tersely asked.

"I'm saying you're starting tonight. That's what I'm saying." Browning fired back.

"Remember when you pitched for the…what were they? The Appleton Candy Sticks in high school?" Tom Browning playfully chuckled. "What was your record?"

"I was 25-6 in four years, and they were the Admirals thank you. What's that got to do with anything?" Arms asked.

"What are you now, Scotty? Wait, I can tell you exactly. In four years with the Vipers, you are 16-32." Browning fired back. "So what happened?"

"What happened?" Arms defensively barked back, "I'm on a shit-hole team with no fielding or run support, that's what's happened!"

"Do me a favor." Tom asked, "When you're on the mound tonight, just look around at the guys around you. Then, visualize the park, the people, and the smells of Appleton High School where a young man named Scotty Arms once pitched and went 25-6 in four years. Ya know brother; you might be surprised to find that he's still around and maybe, right there where you left him."

21 DOWN IN VEGAS

It was just a few minutes until first pitch and the pageantry surrounding this quirky evening was electric. A sold-out house and an anticipatory National TV audience was waiting to get their first glimpse of what everyone in sports was yammering about. The city of Portsmouth, Ohio, had purchased over two-thousand tickets and had over ten buses headed to the games.

*****

In just one week, the Eagles' former coach Keith Madison had been on *The Today Show* with Bryant Gumbel, *Larry King Live*, and even *The View*. He had just finished talking live with a Fox reporter as he found himself seated five- rows back behind the plate.

"When was the last time you saw the Goodyear blimp flying over a damn stadium with two last place teams playing at mid-season?" hitting coach Von Hayes pointed out. "Have you ever seen anything like this in your life? This is crazy frigging incredible!"

"OK guys, we talked about it, thought about it, and now, it's time to go do it!" Manager Tommy Leach proclaimed. "Before I take the lineup card out there, remember one thing. This is still the same game that you played in both high school and college. As a matter of fact, you're all probably better than most of these hacks that we'll be facing out there tonight. If you just do what you showed everybody you can do, you'll all be fine. The lineup tonight is Snyder leading off at second, Sean Deeters batting second, playing right. Cliff Collier batting third in center field, Chadwick at first batting fourth, Gary Duzan is at shortstop batting fifth, John Gambill batting sixth is at third. Smith, you're in left field batting seventh, Pouge is behind the plate batting eighth, Arms is the only one left, and we all know where he'll be this evening. Are there any questions?"

"Hey, Skip, I was walking around out near the Pirates bullpen, and I over-heard someone say that Castillio has a slight sprain in his left knee" Jarred Brewster interrupted. "If he challenges you on a throw, don't let him fake you out. I don't think he's running too well tonight."

"Duly noted, OK, guys, let's play 'em' tough and have some fun!" Leach announced. "You all know what you can do, so go do it!"

Former Pittsburgh native and rock n' roll icon Tommy James sang the National Anthem as the lineup cards were exchanged and the Pirates lineup was announced in order.

The names of Chris Duffy, Jose Castillo, Jason Bay, Craig Wilson, Freddy Sanchez, Jeremy Burnitz, Ronny Paulino, Jack Wilson, and pitcher Zack Duke would all become trivia questions for the minutia minds of baseball fanatics for years to come. It was obvious people weren't quite sure what to expect, but by all the measurements on the events barometer, it was a "tell your grandkids special." As Zake Duke finished his final warm-up tosses, Brooks Snyder grabbed a bat and was heading for the plate.

You got the feeling that the Pittsburgh fans thought that they were taking on a Little League team as Snyder stepped to the plate as you could hear them audibly licking their chops. Duke looked at the plate and fired.

"Strike one!" came the call from umpire Ed Hurley.

Snyder again adjusted himself in the batter's box as he thought *"How do I want to be remembered with my first Major League at bat?"*

As the ball again streaked toward the plate, he got his answer, "Bunt!" He quickly laid the bat head on the ball and rolled off a masterpiece. Third Baseman Freddy Sanchez barely knew what hit him as the swifty second- baseman now stood on first with the Vipers' first hit of the "second season."

As Sean Deeters strode to the plate, in his mind, he was also thinking small- ball. Would they be ready for yet another? Sanchez was playing even at third as the first pitch flew by high and outside. Deeters knew if he saw anything outside, he could punch it to the right. He got his wish. It was a low outside fastball that Sean Deeters slowly rolled between the mound and the first base bag. As he heard his foot and the ball smack the base together, he also heard umpire Frank Pulley proclaim the end of his maiden plate endeavor into the Major Leagues. As Deeters quickly turned and looked at him, Pulley was already grinning.

"Ties don't count up here, son. You have to beat the play."

21 DOWN IN VEGAS

With Snyder on second and one away, Cliff Collier made his Major League debut with a chance to ring up some plate noise. After working Duke to a 3-2 count, Cliff got a little too ambitious under a chest-high fastball and hit one up the elevator shaft for a foul out to catcher Ronny Paulino. With two now gone and Snyder still hostage at second, clean-up hitter Gary "Bombo" Chadwick dug in.

People often quizzed Gary as to his nickname that he had carried around since grade school. As the story goes, a player by the name of "Bombo" Riviera was a prospect player for the New York Yankees. Gary loved the guy and carried his baseball card everywhere he went. He could rattle off 'Bombo's stats and Hall of Fame potential in his sleep. It earned him the same childhood nick-name and it stuck. As he now stepped to the plate for his first at bat in the "bigs," the words *fast-ball* was all he was thinking. He had decided while standing in the on-deck circle not to over-think it. Duke's first delivery was belt high and inside for a ball. His second delivery never even came close to the front doorstep.

Chadwick's hard swing met the sweet spot of the ball that exploded off the bat that launched a laser shot long and deep to left. The reaction of outfielder Jason Bay was simply a 180-degree head-turn as he watched the ball carry high over the left field fence.

The Vipers all spilled from the dugout steps onto the field like puppies being poured from a box. As Chadwick rounded third, he slowed down to relish the sight of PNC Park faithful now totally on their feet and standing in recognition of this most unexpected feat. As steel cleats finally met rubber, he now found himself officially inducted as the 'ninety-eighth' member of an elite fraternity.

Gary "Bombo" Chadwick's name would now forever be linked to Benny Ayala, Hector Luna, Jose Offerman, Jermaine Dye, Will Clark, and even pitchers Hoyt Wilhelm and Dustin Hermanson. Only ninety-seven before him had ever hit a home run in their first at bat in the Major Leagues. The Vipers' dugout was now in chaos as Chadwick dove head-first into a sea of slapping arms and shaking hands. The crowd even demanded a curtain- call as the Las Vegas Vipers had just put two on the board and over 40,000 fans on their feet in the first- inning. To get this kind of reaction in the enemy's lair was unheard of. It was a moment frozen in time as it seemed that everyone in the park with perhaps the small exception of the Pirates' dugout were being totally encased by this rare degree of high baseball drama.

Scotty "The Golden" Arms pitched camp on the mound with his friend and battery mate Doug Pouge. The surge of excitement from Chadwick's first inning blow was the kind of adrenaline rush that can elevate a good player to instant greatness. Scott Arms immediately put the glow to good use. Taking a page from the Tom Browning's "back to the basics" philosophy, he quickly disposed of Chris Duffy, Jose Castillo, and Jason Bay on two ground-outs and a fly ball to center. After one inning complete, it was the Vipers 2, and the Pirates 0.

The top of the second saw the Pirates expose their prime-time jitters as Zake Duke plunked third baseman John Gambill in the ribs to lead off the inning. That brought up Vipers' left fielder "King Kong" Karl Smith who wasted no time in trying to duplicate Chadwick's earlier heroics, only this time it was to right field. Smith muscled a deep fly-ball that Jeremy Burnitz barely got to with his back against the fence. John Gambill slowly moved toward first as if to play it safe.

Watching Burnitz closely, he waited until he caught the ball and began his throw to the cut-off man. Gambill quickly broke for second, knowing he had caught them flat-footed. It was a head-long slide as his fingers caressed the bag a split instant before the tag. This nation was once again witnessing "Eagle ball" at its best.

While Vipers' veteran catcher Doug Pouge had been outwardly and vocally skeptical of the team's unorthodox directions, he was also game savvy as it gets. In eight years as the starting catcher, he had suffered through every false promise and missed opportunity that was the Las Vegas Vipers much storied legacy.

Approaching the plate, he promised himself that he would at least give it a chance. Working Duke to a full count, Pouge swung and literally willed the next pitch just inches away from the reach of Pirate first baseman Craig Wilson as John Gambill scampered home on his short and precision single to right.

21 DOWN IN VEGAS

With the hometown Pittsburg Pirates now down by three, there were no more standing ovations for the Vipers. Zake Duke took out his frustration of the momentum by sending Scotty Arms back to the dugout on three quick pitches.

Since the recent All-Star game became a blow-out in favor of the American League, the overnight Nielsen ratings came in at its lowest in the history of the event. On this off-night telecast of a simple baseball game between two last place clubs, Fox programming gurus were rubbing their hands together as this drama continued to play out as if they had personally written it.

After the early initial excitement past the second inning, the game settled in to become a classic pitchers' duel. Scotty "The Golden" Arms kept the gold and black teetering off--balance with a dazzling assortment of pitch du jours. Zake Duke also finally found the rhythm and quickly got into his hammer-zone.

Arms seemed as if on cruise control until he got two out and one on in the eighth. Burnitz had been hot ever since Gambill smoked him in the second, and he was the kind of player that thrived on revenge. With a count of 2-2 on Jeremy Burnitz, Scotty Arms tried the heater up and away. In a game of micro-inches and precision timing, the pitch was a little less up and not that far away. On this swing, the PNC throng leaped to their feet in celebration of their own baseball family and what was now a one-run deficit.

The ball eventually landed 467 feet away in center field and was now the possession of one Kip Mayne. Scott Arms buckled it in and got Freddy Sanchez to quietly fly out to end the eighth inning. With a 3-2, lead, Manager Tommy Leach got Jeremy Burkes up and throwing in the Viper's bullpen. Burkes was a no-nonsense pitcher who simply threw strikes and challenged you to hit them.

In the top of the ninth, Terrence Kennedy pinch hit for Arms and got robbed of a rising screamer with a gazelle-like leaping move by short-stop Jack Wilson. Brooks Snyder who was two for three on the night took a called third strike as Sean Deeters hit a routine fly ball to right to end the Viper's inning. Going into the bottom of the ninth, Las Vegas held on by a run.

As the ace of the Eagles' relief unit, Burkes had a microscopic .091 era when coming in after the fifth- inning. His first pitch to first baseman Craig Wilson had eyeballs up the middle and just eluded the diving attempt by Brooks Snyder. Sensing a switch in the momentum, PNC Park began to come alive in the opposite direction as they had in the first inning. Burkes buckled down and got busy. It took four pitches to send Pirates catcher Ronny Paulino back to the bench to talk about it. Center fielder Chris Duffy was in no hurry to disguise his role as the man that was sent up there to move Wilson along. His bunt was perfect as Arms fielded it clean on the first base side of the mound and threw on to Chadwick at first.

Two outs and the tying run on second and to all in appeared that Jeremy Burkes had nothing but ice water in his veins as second baseman Vinny Castillo dug in.

Figuring that this was the first and defining game of the new Vipers debut, everybody including Burkes knew the importance of holding on and not giving into the obvious pressure. Burkes shook off the trick pitches and decided to go with the mustard that he was blessed with.

His first pitch was wide and outside. Castillo backed away from the plate and looked toward third for the sign. Burkes figured that this was really not a free-pass situation and that Vinnie was looking for something to hit. Glancing back at Wilson, Burkes rocked and fired. The crisp sound of the bat and the low trajectory of the ball quickly signaled the game would soon be tied. Wilson was off and running as "King Kong" Karl Smith fielded the scorched liner to left. With the Pirates' third base coach waving Wilson to the plate, Smith let loose with the throw most college players knew and feared. Anticipating a play at the plate, the crowd's cheers began to swell.

As Craig Wilson rounded third and sprinted home with the tying run, the throw from left field was postmarked for another destination of delivery. Vinny Castillo had rounded first base and was now heading toward second. Smith's throw was right on the bag and nailed the usual speedy Castillio by ten feet just a micro-second before Wilson's foot could cross the plate. In tandem, home plate umpire Ed Hurley immediately signaled "out" as second base umpire Mike Winters also threw up the thumb.

It was a "bang-bang" thriller to the letter and a heads-up fielding play as the new Vipers were now officially undefeated in the first game of the "second season." The win also served as postmortem of redemption for the heartache that the Eagles had been carrying since the loss to LSU. Once again, their baseball hearts beat happy. The post-game celebration that followed rivaled any seventh game exultation, and the cameras couldn't get enough of it.

"This is Thom Brennaman with the big play man here tonight, 'King Kong' Karl Smith, a great throw out there to end this game with what I must say was a stunning exclamation point! What were you thinking?"

"Well, we heard that Castillo may not have had all his wheels on tonight, so when I came up with the ball, I just kind of gambled on him thinking that I was coming to the plate. Man, he's such a great competitor, and I figured he would try to get into scoring position with the winning run, so I just thank God that my throw was there in time."

"Karl, you guys certainly didn't look intimidated out there tonight by all of this newfound drama. What can you tell the folks watching on how your lives have changed in just these three short weeks?" Brennaman asked.

"Yea, Thom…well, it's truly an amazing opportunity that Mr. Wheeler has given us. We all pretty much know each other as friends and teammates and we all believe in what each of us can do." Smith answered. "We love this game and our only regret was not winning it all in Omaha, but now, we have a different mission and I think every one of us is up for the ride."

"All the fans here tonight actually became a part of and spontaneously celebrated Chadwick's unbelievable home run. That had to be a thrill especially right here in their house!" Thom Brennaman noted.

"Oh man, we've seen him do that before, but in this park, and as full as it was…it was awesome!" Smith stammered. "We all kind of got worried about him after he hit it. Bombo left in a panic to go to the bathroom and almost never came back because he said he got lost in the tunnel or something and couldn't figure out which door to get back out onto the field."

"Your former college coach, Keith Madison was in attendance here tonight as was over two thousand Eagles supporters from your home-town of Portsmouth, Ohio." Brenneman said, "How did all of that influence help you guys out?"

"Well, having coach here was great. He's always had a kind of calming influence on us, and we all wanted him to share our big moment. Having our friends and family travel here was also great. I'm not sure we'll ever see this many friendly faces when we travel to like, Los Angeles," he joked, "but we know they're always there for us."

"Thanks, Karl, and again, congratulation on the Eagles…the Vipers…your first win of the second season." Brennaman said in closing. "I've honestly have to say that this has most certainly been one for the most interesting, if not heroic highlight reels we've seen in Major League Baseball for quite some time. Please don't go anywhere because we'll return with more from PNC Park in Pittsburgh where tonight, the Bentley State University Eagles who just three short weeks ago were playing college baseball have now assumed the role as the new Las Vegas Vipers. Tonight, it's as incredible as it gets as they win their inaugural game beating the Pittsburg Pirates at PNC Park by a final score of 3-2. We'll be back with more on the Fox Sports Television Network."

The fascination of the baseball nation to an angry revolt by a renegade team owner was reflected in the overnight Nielsen ratings. The Friday night viewing audience between the Vipers and the Pirates had out drawn Tuesday night's All-Star Game by more than eleven million viewers. Whether it was in general interest or just morbid curiosity, this had been one of the highest rated baseball telecasts in the last five years.

"Did you see those boys?" Cisco Wheeler shouted to Brandon Briggs as they sat in Cisco's hotel suite the next day. "That's the way this game needs to be played. Hell, I couldn't sleep last night. I watched the game three times in a row when I got back to my room. Those kids did everything I hoped and more. This could be it, Brandon…this could be it!"

Much like a child with a new shiny toy, the Vipers' general manager quickly realized that his boss and team owner needed a slight reality check.

"Yea, Cisco, they were great, but that's just one game." Briggs carefully injected. "I'm not trying to be negative here, but we have to remember that the Pirates are in last place. Remember, we still have to play the Giants, the Padres, the Dodgers, and the Mets. What happens when these guys face Tom Glavine for the first time? We have to be ready to deal with it."

"Brandon, if these kids play this game the way they do every day, it won't matter!" Wheeler reiterated. "Winning is achieved through effort and preparation. The fans just want their money's worth. Do you remember a player named Mark 'The Bird' Fydrych from back in the '70's?"

"Sure, he pitched for Detroit." Brandon replied.

"The fans loved him because when he was on the mound, he acted like he gave a shit. He was different, quirky, but he was fun. That's what this team can be!" Cisco offered.

"Yea, you're right, he was all that," Briggs agreed, "But don't forget, he was also a proven Major League winner. If I also remember correctly, he won something like nineteen games his rookie year. He also liked talking to ball."

"Exactly!" Wheeler erupted. "That's why you remember him today!"

The media frenzy from the previous night had finally subsided the next day with the absence of several of the circus attractions.

"I guess we're just yesterday's news. Look up there, no blimp today." Cliff Collier joked from the top of the dugout steps.

The Vipers had asked for an early workout at PNC Park in an effort to let the pitchers and the catchers work on signs, signals, and pitches. It was quickly noted by Pitching Coach Tom Browning the limited repertoire of pitches by most of the former Eagles' players. While fastballs, curve-balls, and change-ups were in place, the absence of craftier fare was a concern.

Mitch Milhuff and regular Eagle catcher Boone Coleman were both going to make their debut on Saturday night. This was going to be yet another page in this already bizarre baseball saga as it would be the first time in baseball history that both a pitcher and a catcher would make their Major League debuts together. As they both sat in the club-house going over charts and pitch strategy, Jarred walked over and sat down.

"Mitch, do you still mess around with that knuckleball? He asked.

"Knuckleball, are you crazy? I just throw that thing to screw around with you guys in batting- practice." he responded.

"I was talking to Tom about it, and he didn't even know that you could throw a knuckler." pressed Jarred.

"I don't!" retorted Mitch. "I've never thrown that thing in a real game…ever."

"Why not?" Jarred shot back. "Mitch, it's a great pitch if you use it the right way. With all this talk about you guys not having enough pitches, why not throw it as a surprise pitch or whenever you need to freak somebody out. They don't know that it's not one of your regular pitches. It might mess with their heads."

"And what the hell am I supposed to do when that son of a bitch comes fluttering in using this damn glove?" Boone Coleman added. "Do I catch it with my teeth?"

"You're missing my point! It's like the old Eephus pitch." he explained. "You just use it in select situations. Nobody ever throws it anymore and, Mitch, you have a great one. Believe me Huff, you need to think about it."

"Brewster, you're a sick man." Boone Coleman added. "That's why we like keeping you around. Tell you what, if Mitch wants to, we'll stick it in our little sack of tricks on just one condition. We keep it to ourselves, agreed?"

"Honestly, it might be fun to throw every now and then." said Mitch. "But these guys up here might get really ticked if they know we're messin' around with a knuckleball behind their backs, this is the Major Leagues. If we do this, you can't tell Browning, Von, Norman…nobody knows!"

21 DOWN IN VEGAS

Jarred smiled and noted, "I think it's great! As I always say, gentleman, it is always easier to get forgiveness than permission, but I guarantee, Mitch, that you're the guy who could pull it off."

On the massive coverage of the "new" Vipers' inaugural game on Friday, there was standing room only at PNC Park in Pittsburgh the following night for the second of the three- game series. Victor Santos would be on the mound for the Bucs while Mitch Milhuff made his Major League debut for the Vipers. At the pre-game news conference, Vipers Manager Tommy Leach warned the working press that over the next couple of weeks, the phrase "Major League debut" may get a little over-worked in their copy points.

The first seven-innings of the game was everything the fans didn't expect. Santos and Milhuff were both locked into a classic pitchers' duel scattering three innocent hits apiece with no runner advancing past second. All that changed in the top of the eight as Vipers' shortstop Gary Duzan led off with a clean single up the middle.

Third baseman John Gambill dropped back on a 2-2 pitch and then with the risk of fouling it off for an out, laid down a perfect sacrifice- bunt toward the first base bag to advance Duzan on to second. With one out, the star of last night's victory, "King Kong" Karl Smith stepped in. After watching a pair of inside pitches, he got under a belt high fastball and drove it deep to right.

From the crack, it looked like a sure dinger, but Jeremy Burnitz ran it down on the warning track as Duzan tagged and advanced to third.

There were now two-outs and a man at third as the eighth batter in the lineup, Catcher Boone Coleman sauntered up to the plate. Moving into the on-deck circle was utility player Terrence Kennedy as Coleman settled in. On the evening, Boone had gone 0-3 with a fly ball to left and two strike-outs. Coleman worked Santos to a full count before launching a rocket down the third base line and just slightly out of the diving reach of Freddy Sanchez. Coleman ended up on first as the throw from Jason Bay came back in quickly to the cut-off man. The Vipers now led 1-0 as Kennedy was suddenly called back and Milhuff was sent to the plate.

Mitch Milhuff was probably considered the Vipers' best all-round athlete. He demonstrated almost super-human strength at times when it was needed most, and Manager Tommy Leach recognized the kid's natural endurance. With a 1-0 lead, he was obviously there to pitch the ninth as he grounded out to Jose Castillo. With a genuine relief opportunity at hand, Manager Tommy Leach made the unusual call to give him a chance for a complete game.

Center fielder Chris Duffy was first up in the bottom of the ninth and quickly grounded to Brooks Snyder at second for the first out. Jose Castillo took Milhuff to a full-count before flying out routinely to Cliff Collier in Center. With two out and none on, the naturally pro Pittsburgh crowd was again split as to the allegiance they were witnessing. Nursing a one-run lead with two out, left fielder Jason Bay swung at an outside curve-ball and hit a slow chopper down the third base line. Viper's third-sacker John Gambill got to it quickly, but there would be no throw. Bay was now standing on first with the tying run, and the Pirates first baseman Craig Wilson was now at the plate.

Pitching Coach Tom Browning strolled his way to the mound for some quick words of encouragement and a breather.

"You got this one?" Browning nonchalantly asked.

"Yea, I'm fine…I'm still here" Milhuff shot back.

"Wilson likes 'em up and in the strike zone. Just don't get careless. I can probably keep you in here for one more batter, but Tommy's getting a little edgy in there." Browning reminded his young hurler. "Send him back to the dugout, and let's go find us a big steak dinner somewhere. Morton's is just down the street on Liberty Avenue, let's go!"

Tom Browning headed back to the dugout as Craig Wilson settled in. On the first pitch, Bay was headed toward second. As Wilson swung and missed, Coleman fired a seed down to Gary Duzan covering the bag. Jason Bay's hand got to the base just under the tag for a close heist that now had Pittsburg in scoring position.

The Pirates radio broadcast team suddenly felt that momentum was maybe starting to switch hats.

21 DOWN IN VEGAS

"Steve Blass here along with Larry Frattare, and I don't think I've ever seen quite a game like this. Milhuff with a 0-1 count on Wilson as he looks back at second as Jason Bay is trying to rattle the young right hander who is on the verge of pitching a complete game in his first Major League appearance.

"Milhuff deals to the plate, outside, ball-one to even the count at 1-1. Mitch Milhuff certainly looks like the reincarnation of Cy Young here tonight as he has silenced the Pirates' bats on just three hits and Jason Bay so far the only Pirate runner to reach scoring position. Milhuff sets…delivers…too far outside for ball two. You know, Karl, after watching last night's dramatic win and watching this team here tonight, there certainly seems to be a noticeable and major attitudinal difference from what we've seen in the past from this Vipers franchise. Milhuff…again to the belt… and the pitch, and there it is and there it goes! A long drive deep to left, but it's curving…twisting…foul ball!

"Foul by inches as it twists about a foot and a half to the left of the pole. He got that up into the chest of Wilson's wheel-house Larry. Whew, you don't get much closer than that as the count is now 2-2 as Milhuff as again he looks in for the sign, and the pitch. Outside and high as the count goes full.

"One has got to wonder where the pressure point is with a young man making his first professional start and facing this kind of ninth-inning pressure. Wilson is back in the box as Milhuff looks at Coleman for the sign…a full count on Craig Wilson as Mitch Milhuff once again looks, he sets…and here comes the full-house delivery from Milhuff.

"Swing and a miss, and this game is over! I do believe, and if I'm not mistaken…that was your old-fashioned, garden-variety knuckleball! Oh my, my! Mitch Milhuff has just pitched a complete game in his Major League debut by striking out Craig Wilson with a pitch that I don't think he could have hit with an ironing board! It was another superb night for the Vipers who 'knuckled' under pressure to walk away with an impressive three-hit shutout here tonight. I'm Steve Blass, and we'll be right back here with more to PNC Park on the Pittsburgh Pirates Radio Network."

It was again a euphoric post-game celebration in the visitor's clubhouse as the Vipers celebrated a sterling pitching performance from Mitch Milhuff to win their second straight. As he exhaustedly sat at his locker with a wet towel draped around his neck, he felt the presence of another person standing behind him. As Mitch turned, there stood Vipers Pitching Coach Tom Browning.

"A knuckleball?-Where the hell did you come up with a frigging knuckleball, Joe Niekro?" Browning said as he playfully feigned anger.

"Uh…well…Jarred talked me into trying it. I only did it because the way I was throwing tonight, I just thought I could get it over." Mitch lamented.

"Well, Milhuff, I got to say even pitching my perfect game and on the last pitch of that one, I would have never had the brass-balls to throw a knuckleball, but under the circumstances tonight, it was brilliant!"

"Thanks! Like I said when all of your pitches are working, you kind of feel like Rambo out there sometimes." Mitch further explained.

"Do any of your other guys know how to throw that thing?" Browning asked.

"Aw, we've all played around with it occasionally. I used to throw it at them in batting practice just to get a rise out of some of the guys. We never ever really worked on it too seriously." Mitch replied.

"We have a game tomorrow afternoon at 2:00. We're going to have a pitchers-only meeting in the bullpen at 11:00 a.m. Tell everybody it's mandatory and again, great game tonight Huff!" Browning turned and walked away.

Sports-writer's dreams of this magnitude come rare and often unexpected, much like a burglar in the night. *Pittsburgh Post-Gazette* journalist Ed Bouchette was the scribe who embraced the moment.

(Pittsburgh) The new look Las Vegas Vipers made it two wins in a row here tonight with a dazzling 1-0 win over the Pirates in front of yet another sold-out crowd at PNC Park.

21 DOWN IN VEGAS

Two stars on the night were two former Bentley State Eagles making their Major League debuts. Vipers Catcher Boone Coleman drove in the only run of the game as right--handed pitcher Mitch Milhuff scattered three hits over nine innings for the shut-out victory. Pirate starter Victor Santos went eight-innings giving up the lone run on just four hits.

Searching the *Elias Sports Almanac*, there is nowhere mentioned the last time a Major League pitcher and catcher made their MLB debuts together. The closest we could find anything about Mitch Milhuff's sterling debut, you had to go back to the date September 5, 1971. That was the first Major League appearance by the Houston Astro's J. R. Richard who beat the Giants 3-0 while tying a MLB record by striking out fifteen. There has been a play-off feel so far in this series as the fascination continues to be the unique storyline of replacing an entire Major League roster with college players. So far, the results have been interesting. There's no doubt that this scrappy squad from Bentley State University knows how to play the game, and they most definitely exude genuine enthusiasm and fun in the effort.

The real test will be how long they can sustain playing at baseball's elite level before their lack of actual experience begins to bring them back down to their much-expected perch.

6TH INNING

It was a gorgeous Sunday morning in Pittsburgh as Pitching Coach Tom Browning and the eleven Viper hurlers all huddled up in the visitor's bullpen.

"Gentlemen, we all witnessed something here yesterday that was not only a great spontaneous moment in pitching, but I also saw a weapon that we can add to our arsenal. With the lack of depth in our pitching selections, we can add one element that I guarantee will drive people bat-shit crazy. Can anyone guess what pitch that might be?" Browning asked.

As everyone began to snicker and guffaw, Scotty Arms threw up his hand and shouted, "Have they legalized the 'spitter' again?"

"OK, here's the deal." Browning continued. "How many of you little thugs remember the movie '*Rocky*', you know, where Apollo Creed can't find a worthy opponent to fight? He then says to the promoter, 'What this fight needs is a novelty.' That novelty turned out to be an unheard of fighter who rose to be a champion. Our novelty, if used correctly, is going to be a pitch that will turn all of you into champions if you trust me. Milhuff, get up here!"

Mitch Milhuff rather sheepishly got up and shuffled to the front of the pack as Tom Browning flipped him a ball.

"Share with the rest of the guys what we talked about yesterday after the game." Tom Browning instructed.

"Well, as most of you know, I had never thrown a knuckleball in a real game until yesterday." Milhuff admitted. "I guess it was out of desperation at the time and it was after Jarred's suggestion that I decided to give it a shot. So, like I told Tom here, when all of your pitches are working, I just had confidence that I could get that one over, and I did."

"Really," Browning asked. "Did anyone see the expression on Craig Wilson's face when he saw that thing come fluttering up there? I happened to be right there head- high and it was absolutely incredible! He was so completely shocked and confused. It was everything he could do just to swing the bat. What we're going to do is take a few lessons from ol' Milhuff here and make the knuckleball an honorary member of our pitching staff."

"But, Tom, you know as well as anybody it takes years to master that damn pitch," Brad Scarbury yelped while sitting in the lotus position near the mound.

"Sure it does, if you're going to use it all the time like Wakefield or the Niekros' did." Browning shot back. "What I'm talking about is every one of you learning it to use it maybe three…four times a game, and that's it. What Mitch did last night was a master-stroke, and I think we can all benefit from trying something new. After all, it's not like we're not going in that direction if you haven't looked around here lately. OK, we have about an hour. Grab a partner, and let's learn how to harness this damn thing. Mitch, show us what you got."

An hour of knuckling was first met with a high level of skepticism. Mitch Milhuff worked as a bit of a roving instructor to help each pitcher with their individual grip of the ball. There are several different ways to throw the pitch, and a lot of it is based on personal comfort to accomplish the end result. The knuckleball moves to the plate with complete absence of any spin. Having no other forces to interfere with its trajectory, it relies solely on air-currents to move it around to create a fluttering sensation. Compared to the average major league speed of eighty-nine miles an hour, the knuckleball travels at almost half that rate to further compound the matter to the hitter. Finally, at the end of the hour, it really wasn't known if anybody could throw it properly yet, but it appeared that everyone was at least having fun.

"Hey, Tom, let's have a contest to see who can be the first one to break a pane of glass with this thing." 'Dirty' Ernie Fuller shouted.

"I think I actually got one in the strike zone!" Gary Steinman hollered

"OK, guys, that's it for today." Browning barked. "We'll practice again when we get to New York. Just keep this little exercise to yourselves, and I think we can use it to our advantage. If you've looked at the schedule after today, we're gonna need everything we can get. What a bitch! Let's all get ready to play some ball."

Either the Pirates were still shell-shocked, or the Vipers actually started to believe their own press clippings after the first two games in Pittsburgh. Sunday afternoon at PNC Park was what is known in the baseball circles as "a laugher."

Veteran Viper Pitcher Brad Scarbury gave up just two- runs in eight- innings as reliever "Dirty" Ernie Fuller pitched a flawless ninth. The Vipers unloaded on the Bucs with an offensive attack that included three hits apiece from right fielder Sean Deeters, third baseman John Gambill, and center fielder Cliff Collier. As the box score showed, every position player had at least one hit as the Vipers waltzed through the Pirates by a score of 11-3.

Notable Vipers highlights included a bases clearing double by Deeters in the third and a two-run home run by catcher Doug Pougue in the sixth-inning. The remarkable statistic was this was the first "sweep" by a Viper ensemble since they took three from the Milwaukee Brewers almost four years ago. There would be no controversy on this day as to the lead story on *ESPN Baseball Tonight*.

"Hi everybody, I'm Karl Ravech and this is *Baseball Tonight*. Well, let's start here as everybody thought that Cisco Wheeler had a geranium in his cranium as he let almost his entire team go last week, only to replace them with the 'runners-up,' not the champions mind you, but the 'runners-up' in the recent College World Series. The new Las Vegas Vipers…Eagles…or whatever you want to call them ended up taking their first three this weekend in Pittsburgh. So, go ahead and break up the Vipers before we have to one day call in 'Otis Day and the Knights' to sing the national anthem!"

* * * * *

21 DOWN IN VEGAS

"Ya know, this team is only twelve out." Reserve outfielder Luke Shepard noted. "We actually picked up two- games in the standings this weekend."

As the Vipers waited at the airport for their flight to New York, this was the first reference to any mention of the "standings" that anybody could remember in casual conversation.

"What was the highest the Vipers had ever finished in a season?" asked reserve infielder Clint McElroy.

The *Elias Sports Almanac* stated for the record that in their second season of existence, the Vipers actually finished ahead of the San Diego Padres by two- games to finish next to last. As long as Las Vegas had been in the National League West Division, the word "doormat" had excessively been a common and often-used reference to the team's annual ranking. To almost every player that was now wearing a Las Vegas Vipers uniform; it was also wise to remember that any past history was now only just about three- weeks old.

As the gun-slinger division studs at this point, the field was extremely close almost halfway through the 2006 season in the National League West. It was the Padres, Diamondbacks, Rockies, Dodgers, and the Giants all within six games from the top and then the Vipers solidly owned the cellar at thirteen games out of first.

Yet another useless statistic emerged before this week-end series with the Pirates, and that was it had been almost a month since Las Vegas had even gained a game in the standings being 15 out at the All-Star break. Quietly and almost without notice, in just the last three days, they had advanced up two.

As the Viper's charter flight lifted off from Pittsburgh on its way to New York City and touchdown at La Guardia International, the normally quiet and sedate fuselage was now bubbling with excitement.

"Hey, Arms," yelled catcher Boone Coleman, "Tom Glavine just called and said he's picking up your drink tab on this flight…its unlimited!"

"Yea, tell him I can afford my own damn spirits, but I will return the favor and buy him a Metamucil on the rocks when we get there." Arms playfully responded.

Of the twenty-one newest Vipers members, only three had ever even been to New York City before. One was Cliff Collier on his high school senior field- trip. Only three years removed, it was ironic that his return would also be classified as another "field-trip" of sorts. The major difference this time would be the field would be called "center," and he would be standing in the middle of it in Shea Stadium.

"Remember, Collier," Veteran Terrence Kennedy quipped, "while you're in the outfield, please fight the temptation to stand around and count all the pretty airplanes that fly over. I know they can be a distraction."

The ribbing never quit as the looseness fueled a genuine feeling of team camaraderie that had been absent from this organization for way too long.

Was it whistling past the grave-yard, or was all the bravado and confidence that seemed to growing in place genuine? The number one Eastern Division leaders would certainly have some strong input to the answer of that question.

Not since the arrival of the Beatles in 1964 had any New York airport seen so much genuine media interest like the landing of a last place baseball team from almost three thousand miles away.

The Vipers set down on the tarmac at LaGuardia at 9:35 Sunday night and were immediately swamped with newspaper, TV, and radio requests for interviews. WNBC-TV Channel 4 and WCBS-TV Channel 2 were all waiting with live shots just outside the terminal gate. Morning radio host Elvis Duran from the Z-100 Morning Zoo was there to try and catch as many Vipers as he could for his Monday morning show. Chris Carlin from the New York's sports station 66 AM "The Fan" had been there earlier but was asked to leave after getting into a shoving match with a reporter from WCBS-TV Channel 2. It was quickly becoming competitive mayhem at an accelerated speed. As the *New York Daily News* and the *New York Post* all jockeyed for position, the door to Gate B14 opened, and one by one, out came the Vipers.

The swarm of questions in the form of shouting and screaming from all sides caught everybody off guard. Airport security quickly stepped in to try and control the rush of excitement as one of the largest and most intensive news armies on the planet began its assault. The TV stations were especially aggressive due to the time-line of getting the big story on the upcoming 11:00 p.m. segment. Fox News 5- WNYW had set up a complete temporary set and planned to do their entire 10:00 p.m. newscast live from the airport terminal.

Unprepared for the onslaught of attention, Manager Tommy Leach quickly moved into the center ring of fire.

"Sir, Jim Cerrifen from the *Daily News*. How does it feel to be managing a college team at the Major League level and do you have any plans to resign?"

Caught off guard by the question, Leach fired back with fire. "Resign! For what may I ask? Winning three games in a row? That has got to be the stupidest question I've heard yet. The Vipers organization decided to make a mid-season change of direction. That move included hiring players that were used to playing as a team as opposed to our industry's practice of hiring individuals and hoping to make one."

Sensing the spotlight, Tommy used the moment to make a definitive stand in front of his players. "As far as 'resign,' I was honored to be asked to continue and help direct these fine young men in a positive and winning fashion. "You have to be around them for only a few minutes to understand how special they really are. If you… or any other reporters want to take pot shots or questions about their ability as serious ball players, I would severely recommend reserving your judgment until you've seen them play for a while."

"Coach, Hope Edwards from Fox News 5. Your former players are now all beginning to talk. Toots Randall has mentioned that there is the possibility of a class action lawsuit from the rest of the dismissed players. Do you have any comment on that?"

"I haven't heard that one so I'll reserve comment." Tommy responded.

Standing close by, General Manager Brandon Briggs stepped in to address the inquiry further.

"If I may take that one, "Brandon spoke, "we have done nothing wrong to invoke any kind of punishment from anyone. All the contracts of our former- players will be honored, and after all, isn't that why we have them in the first place?"

A group chuckle rippled around the room on that one.

"Our decision to do what we did was predicated on only one motive; to win and win right now. I realize that this is considered by many of you and the baseball business to be a most unconventional way, but with respect to our former players, what we were doing just wasn't working."

"I'm Gary Stephens from *The Post*. How do the remaining Vipers on your squad feel about playing with former college students?"

It seemed this particular topic was the bone that everyone wanted to gnaw on. As if by divine intervention, Pitcher Scotty Arms pushed himself through and up to the cadre of microphones.

"If like I can just say this…At first, uh yea…we were all honestly kind of shocked. When they explained that a few of us had been chosen to stay on the team, we really weren't sure why they wanted to keep us.I know it's been a quick week, but after spending time with all these guys, and honestly this is no bull, our jobs have become fun again. I guess I can speak for Gary, Brad, Terry, and Doug that playing this game is mostly all just attitude. We are only on the field for about four hours every day, so, uh, there's a lot of downtime that if you're not really careful can become toxic."

As the sports-writers continued to scribble on their notepads, Arms was hoping that his ad-libs and passionate ramblings made a point!

"Not meaning to sound like a suck-up, but I think sometimes we all need an infusion of good vibes into our- lives.If any of you watched our first three games, I would hope you could see the difference in our team as much as we felt it. To answer your question, sir, there are no problems from any of us."

Tommy quickly stepped and began to lower the flaps to the "Big Top" as he explained that it was getting late. He assured everyone that the press would have their normal privileges tomorrow at the stadium. The surge began to retreat to their respective desks and newsrooms as the Vipers entourage cut a swath through the still-clamoring bodies on their way to ground -transport. Their safe-haven was a bus that sat in quiet idle, patiently waiting for its weary warriors' next stop.

The crackle and pop of the Mazda AM radio intensified as Keith Madison and Bentley State President Howard Morris passed through a small thunderstorm on their way back to Portsmouth from Pittsburgh. It seemed like the entire city had been there as most stayed for the Friday and Saturday games with all the busses rolling home on Sunday morning. Keith and Dr. Morris decided to take in the afternoon game as well and then drive themselves home afterward.

Both were still stunned not only by the three-game sweep of the Pirates, but the continued national attention that was now an avalanche of talk show radio fodder. As the two strained to listen through the intrusion of static and the clacking of windshield wipers, KDKA-AM in Pittsburgh was airing its Sunday night sports show. Charged and full of callers and opinions, it was obvious the fans couldn't get enough.

"This is 'Extra- Innings' with Charlie Harrison on KDKA. Let's go to Allentown and Victor. What's up tonight, my man?" the invite was offered.

"Thanks for taking my call, Charlie. First time caller and long-time Pirate fan. I'm just calling to say that I hate to see what's happening with the Bucs. It seems like we try so hard every year to make it happen with new players, new plans, new managers…it never seems to work. I was at all three games this weekend, and I hate to say it, but watching those kids play actually got me excited about baseball again. I know I sound like a traitor and I probably am, but it was fun to see guys play like they gave a damn. I'm just sorry it wasn't us."

"Victor, so you're saying that you are not disappointed that the Bucs lost three games to a team that was playing college baseball a month ago?" the announcer asked. "As a fan, I think I'd be pretty upset!"

"Well, Charlie, look at all the money we've spent trying to put together a winning team." the caller continued. "We've never played like one. When I saw all the energy in that dugout tonight when, I can't remember his name, the guy that hit that home run."

"You mean Chadwick" inserted Harrison.

"Thank you, Chadwick. Charlie…I was one of them that was standing up and cheering. They may never win another game, but I count myself lucky that I was there this weekend for this."

"OK, thank you, Victor. This is Charlie Harrison on KDKA Pittsburgh, and we'll be right back with more 'Extra-Innings' right after this."

After a quick burst into a Budweiser commercial, Dr. Howard Morris reached over to turn the radio down. There was a brief moment of silence before he spoke.

"I know how proud of them you must be. I can hardly believe it myself. It still feels like it's all some kind of a crazy dream." Morris observed.

"Howard, people would call me prejudice if they heard me say this in public, but these kids are no fluke. I watched them today, as I watched them every day. I saw firsthand how they played, practiced, and approached this game like no others I have ever seen before," Keith Madison pointed out.

"Remember how everybody predicted the next game would be our last in the tournament. Nobody ever gave these guys the credit they deserve until we finally played our last game and that was in the finals."

"I agree 100 percent with what you're saying, Keith. My concern is that they still have a half a season left to play. I just hope that reality isn't cruel when they start losing a few, and they will. The New York Mets on the road?" He laughed, "Wow, and we thought playing Ball State at Muncie was really something!"

"By the way," Keith continued, "I spent a few minutes with Brandon Briggs in the press booth Friday night. He wanted me to pass along that you'll be getting some new and rather interesting applications in the next few weeks. He told me personally to make sure that you look carefully at the outside curriculum interests."

"I can only guess what that means." Morris cackled.

Well, it seems like he has a lot of perspective students being funded from a certain foundation that are very interested in coming to Portsmouth to seek a higher learning experience and also play some baseball. That is, if we have room for them on the roster."

"Well, considering we have no roster," President Morris added with a touch bit of sarcasm, "They would certainly be welcome now, wouldn't they?"

The bullpen session was once again scheduled to begin at 4:00 p.m. After wandering around the outfield grass and taking in the smells of the freshly cut turf of Shea Stadium, Tom Browning was once again ready to hold court with his eleven acolytes and Mitch Milhuff on the 'art of the flutter.'

"All right, I need your attention!" Browning instructed. "Today we are going to work on spontaneous execution. What I want is for you to throw the pitch when it's called for. In other words, we are going to lawn toss until the sign is given. At that point, you throw the pitch and it better be for a strike. Mitch, Norman, and I will tell you when we want you to float it in. Now, please remember this above anything else that I tell you. The knuckleball will only be successful if it's coupled with the element of surprise. We will only use it when they least expect it. We want them to think about this damn thing in their sleep. If you can learn it to your advantage, harness it! If done right, this little bastard will turn you into the 900-pound gorilla out there on the mound, now let's get going."

As the players began to divide up into pairs, Browning made another quick addendum to his address.

"Not to get all mushy here, but I've been really proud of the guts that this pitching staff has shown. You new guys brought some balls of your own, and it's nice to see the dick- heads that I always knew could pitch bend their backs a little more and give us what we always knew was in the tank. By the way, Steinman told me that he feels like a shut-out tonight and he's never wrong. OK Rangers… power up!"

"Hey Pug, I never said that!" Gary Steinman snapped as they walked away.

"Yea, but damn…didn't it sound good hearing it in public." Browning laughed.

Whether temporary or not, the feeling of euphoria was now a ragging force in the Las Vegas main-stream. As an example of what an almost total team-change and three-wins in a row will get you, all you had to do was peruse the betting board at Harrah's. A week ago, the Vipers had been a million to 1 shot to win the World Series. The odds in just four days had fallen to a mere 300,000 to 1.

Not only were the legalized gambling establishments reflecting the giddiness of the occasion, but advanced ticket sales at Mirage Stadium had shot clear through the roof where within two- days, the Vipers' first home stand against the Giants was now an official sell-out. The last time this event occurred was almost seven-years ago on "Free Slot Machine Night" where the first 20,000 through the gate received a gratis working miniature slot machine that played on dimes. It would be the last time that a capacity crowd would ever grace the portals of Mirage Stadium, until now.

Since their inception, Ralph Hacker and former Viper Pitcher Pete Harnisch had been the play-by-play duo for the team. While trying to infuse the element of show business and entertainment into a product that barely showed a pulse at times, it had been a difficult act. Employed by the Vipers organization, Cisco Wheeler had been more than fair in letting the duo deal with the task of trying to find positive linings in a perennial rain-cloud.

While broadcasting the games on Las Vegas' official sports station, KVPR-AM, they had seen the ratings sharply decline over the last five-years. Even being as cheerful, funny, and yet as honest as they could possibly be, the city was tired of losers and turned off the broadcast in alarming numbers. In the last Arbitron rating period, KFS-AM, the "All Frank Sinatra" station had beat the Vipers' ratings in the Las Vegas radio market rankings. Now at last, "Hacker and Harnisch" would have an act they could sell and the excitement showed.

In just the one week after the change had taken place, KVPR-AM had more than tripled their entire advertising revenue for the games. Advertisers were now lining up to catch the wave of excitement and a team that all America was now wagging about.

It would just be considered cruel fate of the schedule that the team's longest road trip of the season would be directly after the All-Star Game. First Pittsburgh then New York followed by San Diego and then Los Angeles. It would be fourteen games in sixteen days before the Vipers would finally experience a place called home. In this awkward scenario, there was actually no such thing.

The only difference would be on returning to Las Vegas, they would just stay there longer than anyplace else. While the fans would be friendlier and the press would certainly be kinder, the other intangible of baseball's most brazen business decision would ultimately come into play.

For twenty-one members of the Las Vegas Vipers, there would be no real home until the end of the season.

As the pitching line-up against the Eastern Division leading Mets was being announced at Shea Stadium, the odds at Harrah's mysteriously took a bounce back up to 500,000 to 1.

Gary Steinman had signed with the Vipers as a free agent from the Cubs three- years ago. His five-year contract was one of the highest priced pitching deals ever negotiated by Cisco Wheeler. With Chicago, Steinman was considered an "innings-eater" that would consistently keep the Cubs in the game and in a position to win. While at times, he had certainly shown some super-human flashes of brilliance, he was now considered in baseball terms as an underachiever. With the apparent frustration of being on a team that was going nowhere, it seemed that apathy had most definitely taken its personal toll.

His legacy to date was thirty-million dollars over five-years and had returned a combined record of 19-29 with an era. hovering near 5.00. Heading into the second half of the season, he was actually having one of his better years posting a 5-7 record with a 4.20 era. Steinman's mound opponent for the series opener would be John Maine. For all the misgivings and excuses that had haunted his past, tonight, it seemed that Gary Steinman's name was posted in big and bold letters on that giant marquee known as fate.

"We're back on the Vipers Radio Network as Gary Steinman has shown us something tonight I don't think we've seen since he's been here, Pete." Ralph Hacker beamed in over adulated tones.

"No question on that Ralph," Harnisch responded. "Tonight, Gary is proving to everybody here at a sold-out Shea Stadium in New York that this is the guy that Cisco Wheeler and all of us thought he could be when we signed him; brilliant!Through eight and a half innings, he had allowed no runs, no hits, and is facing just three more Mets hitters in the ninth for the win."

"We still won't say it until it's a complete done deal, will we partner?" Hacker laughed in response. "John Maine has also gone the distance here tonight for the Metropolitans allowing just one-run on three-hits. It was a Brooks Snyder's single in the third, two stolen bases, and a suicide squeeze play to the letter that has plated the lone run of this ball game. Looks like the Mets' last swings will be from Carlos Delgado, David Wright, and Shawn Green as Gary Steinman has struck out nine and walked only two. That is huge, my friend."

"Delgado has whiffed three-times tonight, and I'm sure Carlos isn't happy about that." Harnisch added. "If Steinman is going to pull this one off, he will have to face the Mets murderer's row to get there."

The Shea faithful were now on their feet as Delgado dug in to face the nearly perfect Gary Steinman. The momentum had now clearly shifted as the fans realized what they were just three-outs away from witnessing. Leading the Eastern Division by four and a half games, a loss here was quite absorbable in the grand scheme of things. Both dugouts and all of Queens were now on their feet as the franchise that held the longest "no-hit" draught in Major League Baseball cheered on. They were but a half of an inning away from having it done to them by a team that in theory was only four- games old.

Carlos Delgado was labeled a "can't miss" prospect from his first season in Toronto. He had always shown the ability to be the kind of player who could get you out of a hole in a blink with his power and ability to plug himself right into the heart of the matter. His keen eye and pressure-proven savvy was always dangerous in situations such as the one that had now been scripted.

"Ball, outside." came the first pitch call from home plate umpire Ed Heilman.

Steinman could be somewhat of a nibbler around the plate as his walk-to-strike ratio had always been a little high. The forty-thousand-plus fans that were now cheering every pitch also didn't help his concentration.

"High, ball two!" Once again, Heilman called it a fastball that had sailed.

"Time!" yelled Vipers' catcher Doug Pougue as he walked out to the mound to settle his pitcher down.

"You feeling all right, Steiny? Look around at all this brother. This is quite a scene you've put us into, so what are you going to do about it?" Pougue joked in an effort to calm the waters.

"I'm fine. I just need to bring it. I can't be doin' all that fancy shit now. If it happens, it happens." Steinman softly admitted.

"You got eight of us out here brother, and we won't let it get away. Three and we're free. Let's do it!" Pouge turned and swiftly trotted back to the plate.

Delgado waited as Steinman delivered a rocket that scorched the inside corner.

"Strike one!" Came the call to the delight of crowd.

Steinman's next pitch was a horror film in slow motion as he watched an inside fast-ball float to the sweet side of the plate. He knew as soon as he threw it that this one could be a costly mistake.

"Delgado swings and sends it high and deep to right! He hit that one a ton!" Ralph Hacker's voice minced excitement with disappointment as he followed the ball's flight.

"This ball is trouble…if it stays fair it's…a foul ball! Wow! They don't call this a game of inches for nothing. Carlos Deglado just put a charge in one that scorched a spot about a half a foot wide outside of the left field foul pole, so instead of a tie ballgame, Delgado has to cue it up again. I'll take that one anytime."

With the count now at 2-2, Gary Steinman looked in for the sign. He figured Delgado might be looking for the change-up after the brigade of fastballs. He shook off the call to the surprise of Pouge.

"It's a 2-2 count on Delgado as the fans here in Flushing, New York, are all standing and rocking it away tonight." Hacker again set up the call. "Steinman looks, and delivers the breakeven pitch. Called strike three! Gary Steinman just threw a round-house curve that locked Carlos Delgado up tighter than the Statue of Liberty on a federal holiday!"

One down in the bottom of the ninth, and now David Wright steps up to do what no other Mets hitter has been able to accomplish. Wright made contact his last at bat with a ground ball to John Gambill at third. He also walked in the second and was one of only two Mets base-runners to reach first.

"David Wright steps in and as always…a good contact hitter." Pete Harnisch noted.

"You're right, Pete, when Wright swings you know that the ball is pretty much going to end up in Somewhere, USA." Hacker added. "Steinman is once again set…the pitch. It's a ground ball wide of second, Snyder fields it, up the throw…and he throws it away! Wright makes the big turn, but now throws on the brakes as the ball hit the wall behind first and then chromed right back toward the first base bag."

"That was a very tough play, Ralph." Harnisch noted. "Even with the high throw, it was questionable that they were even going to get him. We're going to have to wait and see just how unbiased this Shea Stadium scorer's table is going to be on that one."

"Well, David Wright stands on first with one out here in the ninth and all eyes are on the scoreboard as Snyder, Chadwick, Duzan, Gambill, and now Pougue are all meeting on the mound." voiced Ralph Hacker. "Quite a turn of events as this is the quietest this place has been all day."

Suddenly like cannon fire, Shea Stadium erupted to a decibel level that actually drowned out the Jets at LaGuardia. The scoreboard in center was flashing E-6.

"The Vipers and Gary Steinman sure got a break on that one!" Hacker echoed with a sigh of relief. "I certainly didn't want to play umpire until the official scorers call, but that call certainly could have gone either way."

"You're right, Ralph." echoed Harnisch. "It wasn't a given that Wright was that easy of an out at first. Had he been able to get to second, I'm pretty sure we would be looking at a hit and an error in the box-score. We can thank that thick-brick exterior here at Shea for giving us an assist on that one."

Pitching coach Tom Browning suddenly bolted from the dugout and headed toward the hill. As he approached the mound, he held out his hand.

"Steiny, let me see the ball."" Browning barked.

"You want the ball, for what? Are you taking me out?" He sarcastically asked

"No, just give it to me for a second." Browning insisted.

Gary Steinman flipped the ball to Tom Browning as he began to examine it from stitch to stitch.

"See this Gary? This damn thing is the same size it was when we started the game. When I threw mine against the Dodgers, it was right here at this exact point that I felt like I was the last man on Earth. Just tune out all the bull-shit going on and just gun your stuff. You're still pumping 93 on the jugs, so you need to just go at 'em. By the way, the real reason I'm here is because when I found myself out here against the Dodgers, I mean exactly right here at this spot, nobody dared to come out and talk to me. It was the most alone and helpless feeling I ever had in my life."

"I can relate to that." Gary replied with a smile.

"Now screw all that superstitious voodoo horse-shit about not talking about it. You are two-outs away from pitching a fucking no-hitter. Two outs to go! Just pretend it's the first- inning again and let's get the hell outta here. You can do it, brother. Let's go!"

The umpires finally broke up the summit as Tom Browning dashed back to the dugout as Shawn Green moved into the chalkbox. The crowd was once again screaming and all vertical.

Absorbing the quick pep talk that Tom Browning delivered was as welcome as a glass of cold water in the Sahara desert. The somewhat surreal atmosphere began to shrink as Steinman once again refocused on the task at hand.

Mets right fielder Shawn Green who was known for his stroke and power was next up with one out and one on and the Vipers infield was drawn in.

"Shawn Green is 0-2 today with a strikeout, a walk, and a routine fly to center. He's up now with a chance to do some damage here in the ninth." Viper's voice Ralph Hacker observed. "Steinman once again sets, and to the plate. Green shows bunt, it's a good one down the third base line. John Gambill's in on it, he picks, he fires…got him! Close play, but Gambill came up with the ball quickly as he one-handed it off the Shea Stadium turf and fired a seed to Chadwick. David Wright moves into scoring position for second baseman Jose Valentin.

Two outs with Valentin the recipient of a strikeout and a groundout to short for the day as he will hopefully represent the last man standing. Folks, listen to this Shea Stadium thunder!"

The crowd's enthusiasm level had now risen to its ultimate climax. On the Mets' noise scale, there were three settings; loud, louder, and then "game six."

For a team that had never accomplished the feat that was now just one out away, it seemed as if the Mets fans were vicariously savoring the moment through the upstart Vipers. Steinman looked in at Pouge and decided that this was the moment to completely disarm his opponent.

"Steinman looks in for the sign, he sets and…it's called strike one!" Hacker said with a laugh." Did you see that Pete? He hung the floater! We saw Mitch Milhuff throw the knuckler for the last out against the Pirates, but I've never seen Gary Steinman even attempt one before."

"I didn't even think he knew what a knuckleball was!" Harnisch added. "It must have worked because Valentin is smiling down there in the batter's box at plate umpire Ed Heilman looks like he just saw Sasquatch."

"No balls, one strike on the left-handed batter Valantin as he readies himself again as Steinman sets…and delivers. Strike- two call and Pete, Jose looks like he had never seen a fastball before. That's the kind of medicine that gets in your head after seeing a perfectly executed knuckleball. It's just like a big ol' pizza pie, but it stays with you for a while."

"You're right, Ralph" Harnisch reiterated. "It tends to take some of the steam out of the ol' boiler,"

"Its 0-2 as once again Gary Steinman is one strike away from becoming yet another charter member of baseball immortality." Hacker once again set the tone.

"The crowd again is lathered into frenzy as he looks, sets, and here comes the pitch. Valentin swings and sends a fly ball to right center. Sean Deeters is after it running…running…he dives…and it's off his glove! Now here comes Collier! He dives! Both players are down as umpire Mike Winters runs out from second. Does he have it? Does he have it? …Yes! He's got it! It appears that Cliff Collier has the ball!

"Center fielder Cliff Collier has just made one of the most unbelievable catches I have ever seen as Sean Deeters made a sensational dive and apparently deflected the ball up into the air to Collier, wait a minute. What's going on here? The umpires and crew chief are now getting together on this one as David Wright has scored what would be the tying run and Jose Valentin is now standing out on second base."

"I think they're just conferring to make sure what we think we saw really did happen, Ralph" Harnisch speculated. "It appeared from up here that the ball careened off Deeters' glove in right-center and never did touch the ground.Collier came in backing up the play from the other direction and was close enough to go for the ball while it was still in the air. There was a little bit of ice cream hanging from the cone, but it looked to me like he clearly caught it."

"Everybody is still standing around as…oh yea baby, and now here comes the call!"

Ralph's excitement was in unison with the explosion of the crowd as second base umpire Mike Winters walked over to Valentin who was still clinging to life support on second base. With a sweeping gesture of his thumb, he announced to the entire baseball nation that history was now in the books; "You're out!"

"It's a game for the ages" Ralph Hacker professed. "We are now free to say it. Gary Steinman has just thrown the first no-hitter in Las Vegas Vipers' history by blanking the New York Mets on no-runs, no-hits, and one- error. The final play of this game I'm sure will be on the same highlight reel with Fisk, the Southern Cal band, and Christian Laettner for years to come! Wow…again, Gary Steinman and the Las Vegas Vipers have just no-hit the New York Mets and with that Pete Harnisch, I don't think one person has left for the parking lot yet!"

"Ralph, if I wasn't here witnessing all of this first-hand, I think I would have a hard time believing it" Harnisch pointed out. "The one thing that is clearly evident is that by whatever insanity to logic that was used, from what we've seen so far, Cisco Wheeler has definitely bought himself a team. Watching these guys play is like watching Swan Lake at the Met! That last play of total back-up coverage by Collier was honestly something you just don't see up here anymore."

"You brought up a great point, Pete," Ralph quickly replied. "I don't think I have ever seen such instincts in ball players that genuinely anticipate each other's moves on any team that I've ever seen. In the four games we've been witness to so far, I can't remember ever seeing any of these kids out of place or lost in their positions. Today was a great example of knowing where you are on the field, and they just showed it again on the monitor, amazing! A play like that just doesn't happen by accident. Let the celebration begin!"

The on-field mayhem continued as the post-game shows as well as the fans left standing all clamored to get close to the principals on the field. Most of the Mets players who found themselves in the receiving line of humility, understood the specialty of the moment and put their pride behind them. Many stayed on the field for all the continued well wishes and requests for a quick photo to remember this night. It was an easy-feel if you truly understood the game of baseball and that spectacular freeze- frames never have to be footnoted.

In Portsmouth, Ohio, the scene at Ye Old Lantern Tavern was raucously euphoric. Many of the Bentley State students, faculty, and family members who had gathered to watch the game were now "high-fiving" around the tables as the club DJ launched into the song "Shout" by the Isley Brothers. Cliff Collier's dad was part of the celebratory gathering as Randy Yohe and the news crew from WSAZ-TV Channel 3 in Huntington just so happened to pop in after a city council meeting for a cold-one. They were all unaware of the joyous circumstances that had just transpired until it was all splashed in their faces.

Randy was quickly informed of the reason for the impromptu party and quickly assembled his videographer for a story. Cliff Collier's dad was most certainly the star of the show on this one as the cameras rolled and the action began.

"We're here at Ye Old Lantern in Portsmouth, Ohio, where we have been following the extraordinary series of events of the Bentley State University Eagles baseball team. As you probably know by now, they were recently hired as a mid-season replacement squad for the Major League Las Vegas Vipers. Tonight at Shea Stadium in New York City, two former Eagles combined on the last play of the game to preserve a no-hitter for the Vipers veteran pitcher Gary Steinman.

"I'm here with Dan Collier, the father of Las Vegas center fielder Cliff Collier. Tell us what went through your mind when you saw your son come up with the ball on that game-winning last play."

"Well, knowing Cliff the way I do and how he plays, it didn't surprise me to see him playing so close to Sean." Cliff's dad answered. "He and Sean have been in the outfield together since Little League and they always seem to watch each other's back out there. I've seen them do some pretty gritty stuff before, but nothing like tonight, I'm extremely proud with both of them."

"Four games and four wins for the Vipers, has all of this quick and sudden success surprised you at all?"

"No, not really, Randy," Dan Collier shot back. "Cliff's philosophy is that if you study the game and follow it to the letter, your odds of winning will always be pretty good. After a full day of practice, I'd come home to find him in the den, you know, studying videos of his workouts and stuff. He just loves to play that much. I think you'll find that with all of our Bentley State boys."

"Thank you Dan…Dan Collier, father of Cliff Collier, who tonight helped preserve a no-hitter as the Bentley State Eagles slash… the Las Vegas Vipers continue to roll on. From Ye Old Lantern Tavern in Portsmouth, Ohio, and for News Channel 3, I'm Randy Yohe."

Never before in anyone's memory had a four--game winning streak by a professional baseball team garnered so much press and attention. With the celebration still going on in the Shea Stadium clubhouse, the phone began ringing off the hook immediately. Producers from David Letterman, *The Tonight Show*, and *The Today Show* couldn't wait to get their hands on America's newest media darlings. As the crunch intensified, back home, the late-night cell phones were also ablaze from the women who loved them all and who knew them the best.

Carla Harris had known Cliff Collier from grade school. Their first official date together was at the age of thirteen. From that moment on, they had become virtually inseparable. Through all the high school activities, proms, and countless baseball games, Carla had been right there for Cliff and his life's passion. She often referred to herself as "the mistress" to his other love that was far from being a secret affair.

With Carla Harris's understanding and unconditional support, Cliff was able to concentrate unencumbered on his insatiable dream.

Instead of renting chick-flick movies together for the weekend, Carla would watch countless videos of the Cliff in action. Whether it was working on tweaking his already sweet -swing or looking to gain a few more steps in the outfield, game tapes always took precedent over traditional movie viewing habits whenever they were together. The fact was she was as proud of his work ethic as any soul or date-mate could ever hope for. It was a kind of given around the town that after Cliff Collier got his degree in teaching that the two would officially settle down to pursue his reverie of being a high school baseball coach. It also just-so-happened those anticipated plans took a hard left turn down a different street where the scenery was a reality that no one ever expected.

"Did you see it? Did you see the catch? Oh my god, he's all over every major TV channel that I turn to!" Carla screamed with glee into her phone.

"Hey girlfriend, you got the man tonight!" Her best friend and love interest of Eagles' left fielder Sean Deeters answered. Syleanna

Griffin was as giddy and enthusiastic about the turn of events as any ex-cheerleader could be.

"Carla, has Cliff called you yet?" she asked.

"No, I was thinking about calling him, but I think I'll wait. They're all out probably celebrating somewhere, and I don't want to be the nagging call from home if you know what I mean." She innocently laughed. "Besides, we've done pretty excellent at keeping in touch, but I do miss him though."

"Good luck sister! Say, you're getting a beep. It might be Cliff, so I'd better go. If I hear from Sean, I'll call you. Later!"

A punch of the center cell phone button instantly produced the prime subject matter as well as the star of the game.

"Hey, baby! What a night! I've really been thinking about you. Did you see what happened?" Cliff Colliers's first words gushed through the phone.

"Cliff, oh my god…you're on every TV channel I can find" Carla gleefully shrieked. "It was beautiful, baby. I'm so proud of you. I was just on the phone with Syleanna, and she's waiting on a call from Sean."

"Yea, he took off with some of the guys to get away for dinner. I'm sure he'll give her a blast here soon. I just decided to come back to the hotel room for some rest. Babe, this thing is so out of control!"

"It's like you guys are everywhere. I miss you baby, and every time I see anything about the team, my heart hurts" Carla admitted. "Are You doing OK?"

"Yea, it's like being in a wild dream honey. I love it, but I still can't believe it. Here I am, Cliff Collier, playing Major League Baseball for less than a week and I have just made a catch that everyone says is one of the greatest plays of all time…and it was a no-hitter no- less, damn!" Cliff vented. "This is just too cool, Carla."

"Well, keep playing hard and keep pinching yourself until I get there to take over." She said with a laugh. "Syleanna and I have a plan, and with a few extra sky miles on her credit card, you might see us sooner than you want to."

It was 8:00 the next morning when the hotel phone rang. Cliff hadn't slept well all night as he replayed the game and his catch over and over behind eyes that refused to close.

"Hello!" the first groggy response sputtered into the phone.

"Hey, Cliff, this is Tommy, feeling all right this morning kid?"

"Ah yea, oh, pretty good. I was just now getting up. It was pretty tough trying to get some sleep last night" he confessed. "I'm still pretty juiced-up."

"I understand" the Vipers manager quickly replied. "Look, Cliff, one thing we never quite figured on since you guys just signed directly with the team was personal agents. It is usual protocol that players book personal appearances through them. Since you don't have an agent, I guess you'll have to trust me."

"OK Tommy, so what's up?" Cliff cautiously asked, thinking he was in some kind of trouble.

"A limousine is going to pick up you and Deeters in front of the hotel today at 4:00 p.m. and take you guys over to the Ed Sullivan Theatre in Manhattan. I guess David Letterman's producer called and wants you guys to be on his show tonight to do some goofy "top-ten" list thing with him about the team or something. I'm really not quite sure what that's all about" Tommy informed his stunned center fielder. "I guess they'll tell you more about it when you get there."

"David Letterman? You say tonight? What about the game?" Cliff's flustered response caught his manager off guard.

"Look kid, they tape the show at 5:00 in the afternoon. They promised to have both you and Sean back at Shea by 6:30 p.m. The game doesn't start until 7:35 p.m. So, we're bending the rules here a little bit. I want you boys to make us proud, and by the way, just go ahead and wear your uniforms to the show" Tommy insisted.

"Wear our uniforms, on *The David Letterman Show*?" Cliff confusedly asked.

"Yea, of course!" Tommy huffed. "That's just one less thing you'll have to do when you get to the ball-park, and besides, it's good pub for the club. Just go do it and have fun."

Cliff quickly tried to dial Sean's room, but the line was busy. He figured that he was also getting the same briefing that he was quickly trying to absorb from their new agent. How boldly life continued to change for the fledgling Eagles now turned Vipers.

"If you've been keeping up with the sports headlines," David Letterman began, "you may have heard about this madman baseball owner out in Las Vegas that fired his entire team and replaced them with all college players…yes, college player's, ladies and gentlemen. The former Bentley State Eagles are now the new Las Vegas Vipers, and to be quite honest, they are doing quite well. Last night the Vipers not only no-hit our beloved Mets, but the ending of the game was a catch that has been featured on literally every TV program in existence including the cooking channel. Paul, didn't Emeril use that piece today in showing his viewers how to make his famed seven-layer salad?"

Dave's studio audience roared their approval.

"Tonight from our home office in Wahoo, Nebraska, our top ten reasons for hiring college kids to replace your current Major League team. And, to help us with the big- list here tonight, please welcome from the Las Vegas Vipers, outfielders Sean Deeters and Cliff Collier!"

Applause again erupted for the genuine surprise it was and one of the few times that David Letterman himself actually had to signal the crowd to calm down before he could proceed.

"First of all, that was indeed a spectacular play last night fellows, and I really do appreciate you both coming on the show in such short notice. I understand Leno's still trying to find your number, but he's still not quite sure what frat house you're all living in.-So- OK, it's time for our top ten reasons for hiring college kids to replace your current Major League Baseball team. Here we go…number ten!"

Cliff and Sean alternated poking fun at themselves as the pro New York audience seemed to genuinely love it.

"And the number one reason for hiring college kids to replace your current Major League baseball team?"

"You can deduct the room, our meals, and all the beer we can drink from our paychecks and we all still think we're getting a hell of a deal!" Cliff's final answer brought down the house.

"There they are, Cliff Collier and Sean Deeters of the Las Vegas Vipers, ladies and gentlemen!" Letterman announced with his trademark cackle.

"Thank you guys, and good luck. Well, not too much good luck of course, and please let the Mets get a hit just every now and then, I understand that it builds up their self-esteem. When we come back, it's Tom Hanks on the big show. Stay right there!"

The ride back to Shea Stadium was slow as the limo got caught up in typical New York rush-hour traffic. It was now 6:45 p.m. as Cliff and Sean crept their way back toward Queens.

"I feel funny about this." Cliff confided to Sean. "Tommy's rule is that he wants us at the park at 4:00 p.m. I hope he doesn't get mad. I think we're going to be late for the game."

"Yea, but don't forget, he's the one who sent us" Sean shot back. "I think we did OK, man, but shit that made me nervous."

"Me too, I think you got the funnier lines anyway, but what the hell" Cliff joked. "That place is a lot smaller than it looks on TV, and talk about cold. I still can't believe that we hung with David Letterman. By the way there, senior stud, did you notice the good-lookin' babe with the cue cards behind the camera? I think she was kind of flirting with you."

"Dream on, brother," said Sean. "I think she was just practicing on me for Tom Hanks. I'm flattered, but let's not get too ridiculous."

"You mean to tell me she'd take Forrest Gump over you?" Cliff jokingly retorted. "I've seen that look before, stag daddy, and she was trolling for more than just a damn box of chocolates."

"Shut up, you geek!" Sean burst out with a belly laugh. "I've gotta try and call Syleanna before we get to the park and let her know what time we're going to be on tonight. I hope I can take some batting practice when I get there."

The limousine arrived at the player's entrance at 7:10 p.m. as Sean Deeters and Cliff Collier bolted toward the locker room with the sickening feeling that they were in some kind of serious trouble. They finally got to the field as the Mets were finishing up their workouts. Tommy was standing on the top step as the two sprinted toward the dugout.

"Sorry we're late, Skip." Sean was the first to lament. "We didn't know that it would take us this long to get back to the park."

A long hard and stern stare from their manager slowly turned into a wide and forgiving grin.

"Guys, do you think I would send you to a function that started at five and expect you to get here any earlier? I applaud your enthusiasm, but they don't put the word 'Major' in front of 'Leagues' for no good reason" Tommy expounded.

"You guys were performing a public relations event for the club tonight. Now, if you were both holed up in some seedy strip club somewhere, and got a little lost on the time, we might have something to talk about here."

A moment of understanding was mutually reached as both Cliff and Sean felt relieved that in this case, truancy was considered a virtue.

They both trotted through the tunnel and onto the field to prepare for another old-out Shea Stadium night. On the mound for the Mets was right hander Steve Trachsel as lefty Everett Carpenter would make yet another team record-shattering Major League debut for the Vipers.

As a solid cog in the Eagles pitching rotation, Carpenter had always been one of those unpredictable hurlers who could either command feast or succumb to famine. In the quick shift of planning, it was determined that Carpenter would be the Viper's fifth starter. The hopes were that he would gobble up some early innings until the relief corps could arrive.

While Everett Carpenter possessed a wicked slider and a tricky curve-ball, the master of his control had always been the big question with the answer never really known until game- time. As a standout player for the Portsmouth High School Trojans, the quietest and shyest member of the Eagles decided to attend Bentley State University as to continue playing the sport he loved so that he could stay close to home. As he finished his warm-up tosses in the bullpen, he tried to reflect that he was totally immune to all the exaggerated attention that was surrounding him and the moment. Inside, he had never felt so alone or detached in his life.

As the teams were preparing for all the pre-game pageantry, Jarred Brewster grabbed Manager Tommy Leach at the steps of the dugout. There was a sense of urgency in his voice.

"Hey, Mr. Leach, you got a second?"

"Yea, Jarred, what's on your mind?

"I see you got Doug in there tonight instead of 'Boonie.' I feel some vibes that kind of concern me." Jarred awkwardly confronted his manager

"Vibes? What the hell are you talking about, son?" Tommy sarcastically barked

"Well, you don't know Everett like I do, sir. I think for his first start that you might think about putting 'Boonie' behind the plate. He's a great pitcher and all, but his nerves tonight are unlike I've ever seen them before. I think you might consider putting him back there for his first start. I just think he can help calm him down and stay focused. They're pretty much used to each other" Jarred attempted to explain while stumbling all over himself.

"Son, I appreciate your observation, but he doesn't know squat about these hitters. These are the New York Mets, not the Furman Purple Paladins. For Christ's sake, all he needs to throw is what Doug tells him to throw. I'd much rather has a veteran catcher out there against these guys, especially tonight!"

Sensing he may have stepped over the line, Jarred's silence was a well-lit marque to the embarrassment he felt speaking out so candidly at such a crucial moment. It was Manager Tommy Leach that felt that a further explanation was needed.

"Brewster, it's not that I can't appreciate your observations, I do. But these guys are royally pissed! Remember, we no hit them-last night. They have now become the laughingstock of every sports highlight show on the planet, and there's nothing they want more than to take our heads off right here in front of their fans and hand it back to us on a flaming shit- stick right here and tonight."

"I understand, sir, I'm sorry. I just feel it's my duty to let you know if I feel like, well…something might not be right. It's…never mind, sir. I'm totally out of line."

"Listen, Jarred" Tommy said. "You can always come to me anytime. That's why you're here, and yes, you're an important part of this team. I honestly do appreciate your thoughts, but tonight, I think Doug's the guy that needs to be in charge out there behind the plate."

Syleanna Griffin's call came at 11:15 p.m. As Carla Harris answered the phone, the shrieks at the other end were almost inaudible.

"Did you see who's going to be on *The David Letterman Show* tonight?" her overly-excited voice pulsated. "I just saw a little blurb in a commercial. It's going to be Cliff and Sean! They're going to be on the show tonight. I guess the game must be over!"

"I just got a text message about twenty minutes ago" Carla quickly answered. "I was just getting ready to call you. They said they taped the show this afternoon sometime before the game. I don't think Cliff was in a very good mood, he really didn't have too much to say."

"Wait a minute. If they taped the show this afternoon and he just sent you a text, that means the game must be over. Did you hear what they did?"

"No, he just said tonight wasn't very pretty and he would call me if it wasn't too late" Carla responded. "I know Cliff pretty well, and by the brief tone of his text, I could tell he was pissed."

"Oh well, I need to call a few more people to let them know what's going on. Call me back after the show. I don't work tomorrow and I want to know what you think." gushed Syleanna. "I still can't believe it! They showed them both reading the top ten list and everybody was making a big deal about it."

"Hey, hold on! I'm getting a beep!" Carla interrupted.

There was about a minute of stone-dead silence before Carla suddenly popped back on to see if Syleanna was still holding on.

"Syleanna, are you still there?"

"Yea, babe, what's going on?" She asked

"It was Cliff, and he's back in his room. He just wanted me to know that he and Sean's segment would be on a little after midnight."

"Back in his room, that's strange?" Syleanna giggled. "I would think being in New York City and just after being on *The David Letterman Show* that the guys would all be out somewhere tonight."

"Like I thought, he's not in a very good mood and really didn't have much time to talk. He was kind of in a funk. They lost tonight; I think something like 15-3."

The evening sports news was ablaze with highlights of a baseball team many sportscasters now began to predict were re-entering the real sports world from "fantasyland." *ESPN Sports Center* led the charge of speculation to a possible collapse after only five games.

"Perhaps 'Cinderella's' slipper has been found, cleaned, and returned all too quickly as Las Vegas Vipers starting pitcher Everett Carpenter lasted just two-innings tonight giving up nine-runs on fourteen hits against the New York Mets. His laconic welcome to the Majors included throwing a trio of home run balls to Carlos Delgado, Shawn Green, and Carlos Beltran. The lone bright spot for the Vipers was the stellar relief performance turned in by Ernie Fuller. After taking over from Carpenter in the third, Fuller went on to shut down the Mets through the eighth, allowing just one- run on four hits. After being the victim of a 'no-no' less than twenty-four hours earlier, this night definitely belonged to an element called revenge… and its name was the New York Mets."

In an out of the way steakhouse just a short drive between the hotel and the world's busiest airport, two men sat alone at a corner table absorbing not only a choice porterhouse, but their thoughts.

"Cisco, come on, you knew this would eventually happen. Hell, half the teams in the league have a night like this every night."

Brandon Briggs was trying to soften the blow as he and his mercurial boss quietly reflected on the texture of the moment.

"I don't know, Brandon, it was pretty dismal out there from the get-go." related Cisco. "The kid didn't look like anything of what we've seen him do. I hate to say it, but it was almost like he had never pitched before."

"Look, you're going to have those days. He was scared stiff. There was you, me, and everybody in the park including the Mets who could see that. Browning will help figure him out. We're going to have a meeting in the morning and talk about it." Briggs countered. "By the way, it's the old good news, bad news joke? So much for the bad news, the good news is we may have finally found ourselves a true closer. Man, I thought Fuller tonight looked like a million bucks."

"Yea, he did look good!" Cisco Wheeler agreed. "We really haven't had a stopper here since our first year when we signed Jeff Reardon. You made him cut off his beard because of our no facial hair rule, remember that?"

"Your call on that one, boss, not mine." Briggs slyly reminded his boss.

"Yea, I forgot, didn't he quit after about the first month? Anyway, don't get me wrong, Brandon. I certainly like what I've seen so far. It's just too easy to get consumed by all of this. I just feel like a kid again watching these boys play and I can't help it. I guess I'm just as guilty as anyone of getting caught up in all the hype. The problem is I'm just too much a damn fan! I exalt when they win, and like I discovered tonight, I really hurt when they lose. It can be a bitch, but I pray to God that I never lose that feeling."

"Yea…I gotcha on that one, Cisco." Brandon said as he slowly reached for the rolls. "Not to change the subject, but have you called home? I guess were in for one hell of a homecoming when we get off the road after the Dodgers series."

"Yea, I talked to promotions today and they're completely lost." Cisco Wheeler injected. "They've never dealt with anything like this. I think its best that you plan to head home pretty soon to help start coordinating everything. Apparently, Wayne Newton called yesterday afternoon and get this. Mr. Las Vegas has volunteered to sing the National Anthem for our first home game. He asked us…us! Can you imagine?"

"Wow, Frigging Wayne now wants to do the honors, how far we have come?"

Brandon chuckled. "Remember that day when we called 'Slappy' White to be an honorary team captain and he turned us down because he said that we weren't a non-profit charity?"

"If only he knew the truth, Brandon…if only he knew!" Cisco chuckled.

They both enjoyed a good belly laugh on that one as they continued to go over power- points of the much anticipated Las Vegas Vipers' return to their home city.

"Have you seen the idiot's remarks yet?" Brandon asked Cisco.

"Tommy told me some stuff yesterday. It's Toots Randall I assume you're talking about?" Wheeler deduced.

"The guy gets picked up by the Yankees, and he's not smart enough to just shut up. How much venom about the Vipers does this guy think he has in his tank to spew? The way this story is popping, all the sports shows are eating up his sound bites like ice cream in August."

"Brandon, we disrupted people's comfort zones" Wheeler confessed. "When you do that, you're wide open for all kinds of unfair criticism and cheap bull-shit. Randall was never one of us and you know it. Cashing his paycheck along with his self-proclaimed celebrity status of being a ball player was all he ever cared about or wanted. Let him talk!

We have some guys that will drown out that worthless son of a bitch because pure heart will always win out over superfluous volume."

"Quite the astute observation there, C.W." Briggs noted with a sense of agreement. "Just keep sleeping with that radio on and under your pillow, sir, I like it."

7TH INNING

The rediscovery of one's passion should be considered a rebirth of life. Brandon Briggs and Cisco Wheeler had once again fallen in lust with their first love all over again. Even though just five games into a new beginning, the turf once again smelled garden fresh and the air was dewy sweet. Even if all the attention and scrutiny that seemed so totally oppressing at times would suddenly fade away, the burst of total ecstasy was nothing short of intoxicating. Like the meeting of a new soulmate where the dynamics are often unexplainable and the surface facts are few, these two knew it could all come to an abrupt end at any minute. Their vow was not to let it slip away.

At another corner of the baseball universe, the last two patrons at Ye Old Lantern Tavern in Portsmouth, Ohio, were getting ready to close her down. The duo had worked late at the college and decided to meet for a couple of quick brews before heading home. Up to this point, the usual conversation concerning Goggle's number one search topic had been extremely quiet on the local scene. It took just a couple of Miller-Lights to change the mind-set from budgets to baseball.

"The flights are all booked, podge! Las Vegas in a week and a half is the hottest ticket in town!" Bentley State SID spokesman Jeff Perez exclaimed.

"Glad I got mine early." Keith Madison shot back. "Howard and I are going out a couple days in advance just to avoid the crowd."

"Aren't you guys doing the first pitch thing or something?" Perez inquired.

"Yea, they wanted us to do a joint thing from the mound, but we had to tell them that we are still a state-run university. I'm really not comfortable flaunting the fact that we technically sold our college team to the pros." Madison admitted. "I think that's being a little too blatant, don't you?"

"But, Keith, you and I know you went by the book." Perez said as he tried to reinforce his baseball coach's obvious guilty conscience.

"Damn it, Jeff, I love those guys too much. To be really honest here, I really haven't had a good night's sleep since this all happened. If they fail, I have twenty-one lives on my shoulders, and that's too much responsibility for one man to have to carry." Madison admitted. "This shit is honestly killing me!"

"Here's my advice and I hope you understand." Perez gently offered. "Use this opportunity for celebration, not regret. Any coach in your position would have done the same thing. You didn't break any NCAA rules. You did everything and more in your power to demonstrate that it was all done properly and with integrity in place. You know it was with the boys' best interest at heart. What more could you have done?"

"I will always wonder, Jeffrey." Keith quietly admitted. "I always prided myself in being more when they really needed me. Now that they're two-thousand miles away, I get the feeling sometimes like I sold them out. Was it me who put them in a situation they weren't ready to deal with? There's also the fact that I miss those little juvenile delinquents until it hurts."

"Keith, ease up on the guilt trip, please!" Perez said, feigning drama. "Be proud of these kids for what has happened. Too often in life, we all deal with all the constant negatives and aren't ready when a golden turd falls from the sky, brother!"

"A golden turd?" Keith said laughingly "You're probably right! I guess my problem is that I don't have a platinum commode big enough to catch one it in."

Sean Deeters had just clicked off the TV as he looked at his clock radio. It read 1:30 a.m. as he sprawled out on the bed and closed his eyes.

21 DOWN IN VEGAS

Replaying the game in his head, he still couldn't shake the onslaught. Everett Carpenter was his friend, and he knew tonight that he was hurting, Sean and Cliff tried to find him after the game, but he had quietly slipped from the clubhouse. Even though Sean had got a couple of the hits and drove in two with a double, his thoughts were on the others. As he drifted between the zones of dream state and awake, he heard what he thought was a quiet knock at the door. As he opened his eyes again, the clock read 1:50 a.m. As Sean slowly sat up in his bed, he heard it again. *What hotel service could be up at this hour he wondered?* Jumping up off the bed, he walked over to peep through the fish eye, but couldn't quite make out who it was standing there. Unlocking the safety latch, the Vipers' star right fielder slowly opened his door.

"Hi, Sean, remember me? I'm Sandy from *The David Letterman Show*. I was your floor- producer the other night." she added.

"Oh yea, the card lady!" Sean said with a bashful grin. "Yea, by the way, I really appreciated all your help. I was really nervous out there, I guess you could tell."

"No, I thought you did just fine. As a matter of fact, I was here in the area and thought I would just drop in to tell you in person what a wonderful job you did; I was impressed." She whispered.

Looking awkwardly at each other through a half-open door, she smiled and said, "May I come in?"

It seemed like an eternity of silence as Sean stood there unable to really get a handle on the early-morning encounter.

"Uh, I really should be going to bed. It's way past curfew, and, well, I guess I need to tell you that…I have a girlfriend." Sean stammered.

The dazzling beauty with auburn red hair and lips that reflected ruby-red fire again slowly smiled as she put her hand to the door.

"What's that have to do with us?" she whispered. "Let's go in, Sean. It's getting late, and you do have to get your sleep."

It was 10 on Saturday morning that Pitching coach Tom Browning checked into the locker room. The only other person present was Viper pitcher Everett Carpenter. He was slumped in front of his locker, as it was obvious that he had started to clean it out.

Wearing a combination of his uniform and street clothes, he looked like one of those loyal, but confused fans that had been poured into a sports blender.

"Interesting combination, Carpenter," Browning mused. "I don't think the commissioner will allow knit pants and Hush Puppies on the field, what's going on with that?"

"This isn't me, Tom, I'm going home. You know it, and I know it, and after yesterday, everybody else knows it too. I can't do this, man. Not at this level! I'm not going to embarrass myself when deep down, I know the truth! I just want to gather my things and get the hell out of everybody's way."

Looking long and hard at his obviously disheartened player looking like more like a bag-man from the Burroughs, he simply responded, "Are you through?" Browning asked. "I mean…from talking."

Everett Carpenter was trying to fight back the tears as Browning knew his next words could be the difference in making or breaking a young man's life.

"Yea, you got hammered out there pretty good yesterday. It's all a law of physics, you know. Up here, just like at Bentley State, an 85 mile-an-hour fast-ball with no-pepper on it seldom makes it across the plate. Carpy, we both know that wasn't you or your stuff out there yesterday." Browning softly preached.

Remaining silent, Everett Carpenter continued to stare at his feet.

"Yea, you can quit…go home…give it up, all because you had a bad day. The problem here is that if you let one piss-poor day ruin the rest of your life, then you have to wallow in the smell of it till you die! This whole thing has been quite a ride for all of us up here too in case you haven't noticed! What do you think my wife said when I had to call her and tell her that the entire team was gone and I was now a college pitching coach? Do you think maybe I felt like putting on my street skivvies, hitting the fucking bricks, and heading for home? This game up here, son, is like nothing you've ever seen before. Don't get sucked up into it on a daily basis, or yes, you will fail and fail hard! Hell, what were you, 11-4 this year? Damn it,

Everett, that's quality stuff and you didn't get there throwing batting practice pitches now, did you?"

Almost as if on cue, the next player through the door was pitcher Gary Steinman. Looking around as if he picked up on the tension, he obviously felt an uncomfortable stir in the room and started to excuse himself.

"No, Steiny, you're OK." Browning barked as he was quick to amend the intrusion. "As a matter of fact, I'm glad you're here. Mr. Carpenter and I were just having a little discussion on how you can't let emotion rule the decision-making process once you get up here to the big leagues. I think you probably know a few things about that."

It didn't take but a second for Gary Steinman to look at the forlorn image of his young teammate sitting on the bench in front of him to quickly access the situation.

"Pug, why don't you excuse us for a few minutes," Gary Steinman softly asked.

With that, Tom Browning made a quick exodus to let the two kindred souls of uncertainty go at it. As he exited the locker room, he knew that Gary was the one who could dispense the proper advice with some empathy to the matter. After all, it wasn't yet a week removed from his own personal soul-searching that he had to deal with it again.

The first pitch at Shea Stadium was at 1:10 p.m. as the Vipers had Scotty Arms back on the mound as the team looked to recover from the awful drubbing the night before. An hour before game-time, all seemed fairly back to normal. The chatter was up, the smiles were plenty, and Everett Carpenter's penny loafers and his Duck Head trousers were once again hanging neatly in his locker. With San Diego and the Dodgers on the horizon, the next nine-days could actually be the whole season.

While many were stunned and amazed at the new Vipers' fast start, there were still plenty of skeptics who were standing in line to profess their quick demise. Manager Tommy Leach had suddenly become an instant 'quote machine' in the media and he loved it.

"I never feel that I have failed," he regaled to the press. "I've just found 10,000 ways that won't work!"

Regardless of the polarized opinions, nowhere was there a more revered or anticipated coming-home party planned than the city that bore their name.

Scotty "The Golden" Arms put a quick stop to any more of the disintegration rumors by shutting out the Mets 4-0. His resurrected spirit allowed no-runs on six hits as he personally drove in three with a bases loaded double in the fifth. The old Appleton Admiral appeared to be back on his horse.

The Viper' pitching staff both young and new seemed to feed off each other's rejuvenated spirit. The phenomena of the 'knuckleball' continued to be a prime subject of media interest. The ESPN radio show of *"Mike and Mike"* started to refer to the Vipers' pitching staff as "The Knuckleheads." That name was beginning to stick and take on a life of its own.

Mitch Milhuff closed out the Mets series with seven-innings of incredible power-pitching, limiting New York to just three- runs on seven-hits. It was Vipers' left fielder "King Kong" Karl Smith that was quietly emerging as the team's "go-to" man at the plate. Three home runs and four doubles in the series started to get all the gab on the sports talk shows that maybe there was a missile plant in the making on the Vipers' roster.

Brad Scarbury and Gary Steinman both started the San Diego series in the first two games, but it was the bats of Cliff Collier, Doug Pougue, Karl Smith, and John Gambill that exploded to provide two nights of offensive fireworks and two more big wins.

The Las Vegas Vipers had now picked up three- games in the standings and were now just nine back from the Padres in the Western Division. On fire as most of the Vipers' bats had become, there was one that had gone both cold and deaf.

Sean Deeters was in the preverbal funk. He was now anchored in a 2 for 19 batting slump and had lost an obvious spark at the plate. Hitting Coach Von Hayes was tirelessly attempting to pull him out of it with extra swings in the batting cage. Others had noticed that Sean seemed a bit distracted of late and didn't seem to be quite himself. That's what happens sometimes when your game goes south.

21 DOWN IN VEGAS

The week and a half flew by at warp speed as the working staff and recharged management of the Las Vegas Vipers prepared for one of the biggest events to hit the city since the return of Elvis.

As the young Vipers continued to win on the road, each victory consummated the chaos that was building like a press-charged volcano that was scheduled for eruption all too soon in a city fueled by event celebrity.

Mirage Field had added and extra three- thousand temporary seats to accommodate the countless requests that poured in daily. It was an instantaneous buddy network of favors that were being cashed in all at once. So it seemed as if everybody wanted to be privy and witness a piece of history in the making. From the rock group Van Halen to baseball fanatic Garth Brooks, they were all set to prove that the music industry would be well represented in the avalanche for prime-time seats.

Acquiescing to his second and now third request, it was decided to let Wayne Newton sing the National Anthem for the opening game of the home stand. To a world-wide audience, what better ambassador for the city could you ask for? The media pass departments list for tickets looked like the cover credits straight out of *People Magazine*. Names like Tom Hanks, Brad Pitt, Nicholas Cage, Dennis Quaid, Julia Roberts, Steve Martin, Butterbean, Jerry Seinfeld, along with a multitude of others were all looking to get the best seat in the house. Since the resurrection of the Vipers, they were now 6-1 and heading into San Diego like a fiery asteroid looking for more dinosaurs to demolish.

Back in Portsmouth, Ohio, the cell-minutes were again burning up with many unanswered questions.

"Hey, Syleanna, have you heard from Sean tonight?" the late-night call from Carla Harris inquired.

"Not since Friday, that's three days. I...I'm really not sure what's going on." Syleanna Griffin admitted. "I know he's been in a bad hitting slump. I hear about it three times an hour every day on *ESPN Sports Radio*."

"Three days! Slump or squat, that's not like Sean not to even give you a call and check in. Have you tried calling him?" Carla quizzed.

"Yea, several times, but all I get is his voice mail. I know he knows it's me trying to reach him. I guess he's just too busy. Have you talked to Cliff?" she asked.

"Yea, we hook up every couple of days. I talked with him yesterday, and he just said that everything was hectic getting ready for the Dodgers series and then coming home to Vegas was a total crazy zoo. He sounded kind of distracted"

"Did Cliff say anything about Sean?" Syleanna nudged.

"Just that he was trying to deal with his batting problems and was working overtime with the coach. I guess that was about it." She answered.

"All this stuff, it's just happened way too fast. I feel like the love of my life has been picked up and snatched away from me. I see all of this damn attention from everywhere! TV, the papers, the internet, and I can't even get through to him on my cell or…he's ignoring me. I don't even know where to start anymore. I really do miss him."

"That does it! I got the sky miles, babe." Carla snapped. "You and I are going on a road trip. Have you ever been to LA lately?"

* * * * *

"Hey, Deeters, I think you need a rest. You just need a spot next to me so we can talk about some things. I'm letting Shepard start tonight" Manager Tommy Leach informed his young outfielder as they walked through the tunnel toward the field.

"You're benching me Skip?" Sean defensively replied.

"Son, we play 162 games a year up here in this league. I don't know how many you've played so far, but rest is not a sign of weakness." Leach retaliated. "Besides, Peavey is on the mound tonight for the Padres. He's the best I've seen come along in twenty- years, you don't need a guy like him right now the way you're going."

"Tommy, I swear I can shake it. Let me show you I can" Sean pleaded.

"Look, we have a day off tomorrow before we get to LA. We have four of the most crucial games in the history of this club. I need you to bust out of whatever brain-cramp you're in right now. We will really need you then. Think about this if you possibly can. If we win today, which honestly I don't think it will happen, it is still OK. We can then go to LA and take three out of four from the Dodgers. Not only then do we maybe get out of the cellar, but finally we will be right there in the middle of this crazy division!"

It was almost game time in sunny San Diego as Jarred Brewster tentatively caught Manager Tommy Leach in the final phases of filling out the lineup card.

"I think you're doing the right thing, Skip," Jarred Brewster blurted out.

Looking up with interrupted befuddlement, Tommy asked. "What right thing?"

"Sean needs a little rest. I think he also has some other issues that he's not dealing with very well." admitted Jarred.

"Other issues, like what?" Tommy barked, "And you better give it to me straight Brewster, this kid's a hot mess!"

"Well…woman stuff, back home with his girlfriend Syleanna." he sheepishly began. "Knowing him the way I do, Sean is by far the most grounded person and disciplined of us all. He's always been the glue that kind of glue that holds us all together. I think all of this instant attention caught him by surprise, and he may have had a weak moment back in New York and I think it's really eating at him now. For some people, a guilty conscience, I guess, is no big thing, but I know for a fact he can't deal with it right now."

"So, Brewster, what you're saying is that this young, red-blooded stud of an athlete got, shall we say… 'hormonally-challenged' on a one-night, and now he can't play the game of baseball the way he used to? Is that what you're telling me here?" Tommy sarcastically asked.

"Well, sort of Skip. It's a complicated thing, but I know that Sean feels very bad about what happened and the way he's playing. He needs some help" Jarred admitted.

"Brewster, I don't mean to be a smart ass, but I'm not Doctor Phil. What can I do to fix things? If it's between him and his girlfriend, I would think they need to talk things out. I really can't go butting inside people's personal lives. I can tell them what to do only when the uniform is on. Once they get into their 'streeties' son, they become their own managers. At that point, they need to make the decisions the best they can." Tommy lamented.

"I realize that, Tommy, but listen… anything to get his confidence a boost will help. If you need him off the bench today, he's a great secret weapon."

"How so, Brewster?" Leach asked.

"Check the numbers and you'll see that no one comes close to Sean's bunting average, he's the best! He doesn't talk about it much because it's not an especially glamorous play, but in his college career, he had a .830 bunting average. If he doesn't lay down that bunt against Florida, we go home from the series and wouldn't be here today. He's automatic, man. I just thought you needed to know."

"Thanks kid, I'll keep that in mind. Go make sure Carpenter's up."

* * * * *

Jake Peavey proved to be everything as billed plus a super-sized bag of chips. He mowed down the Vipers like ankle-high Johnson grass on a Toro-Z. The other side of the ledger was even more stunning. Everett Carpenter was matching Peavy almost pitch for pitch as both hurlers headed into the eight-inning throwing mirror image shut-outs. While Peavey had allowed three harmless singles to the Vipers, Carpenter had given up only two singles and a meaningless two-out double in the seventh inning to Khalile Green. That bared all the Padres' offensive totals so far.

Top of the eighth-inning saw more flames and smoke from Peavey. He struck out catcher Doug Pouge on three-pitches. With one out, Vipers third basemen John Gambill finally made some noise and cracked a frozen rope down the right field line and into the corner. While not a gifted runner, Gambill took the turn at second and header toward third as right fielder Brian Giles fired a laser that was right on the money.

The ball got to third baseman Kevin Kouzmanoff's glove at the exact same time as Gambill's cleats. In a cloud of dust, third base umpire Douglass Wallop started to throw up the thumb until he saw the ball had been forced- loose and was now dribbling into foul territory behind the bag.

The frantic and over-animated safe sign was now being given as Gambill was officially awarded a double and Kouzmanoff an error on the play. As Big John Gambill slowly got up and started to dust himself off third base, Vipers Manager Tommy Leach called a time-out.

"Deeters, grab a bat and go hit for Shepard." He bellowed.

Luke Shepard was already standing in the on deck circle as Sean Deeters quickly hopped up and grabbed a bat. As he headed toward the top of the dugout steps, Leach pulled him close and whispered in his ear.

"Swing away at whatever he throws you on the first pitch, but whatever you do for God's sake, don't hit it!"

"Don't hit it? What do you mean?" Deeters quickly whispered back.

"Second pitch…suicide squeeze. Get him in here, son, you can do it."

Still slightly confused, Sean Deeters strolled to the plate to dig in against one of the National League's premier hurlers. Jake Peavey stared in for the sign as Deeters prepared a phantom swing to wherever the ball might be. As Peavey delivered, Deeters leaped wildly across the plate to swing at a ball that was at least a foot outside the strike zone. Viper's' play-by-play announcers Ralph Hacker and Pete Harnisch couldn't stay away from that one.

"This kid certainly has his feet in the sand." Hacker pointed out with a sense of desperation. "Sean Deeters has been called off the bench to try to get the Vipers a lead, but I don't know what he was thinking about on that pitch, Pete. That swing was down-right embarrassing to watch, no balls and one strike."

"You know, Ralph, when you're going bad, it sometimes gets to the point where absolutely nothing you do feel's right. Deeters just seems to be in that kind of a zone right now."

"It's one out in the eight with Gambill on third for the Vipers. Pinch hitter Sean Deeters again stands in as Peavey looks in for the sign…and here comes the 0-1 pitch, and here comes John Gambill to the plate!" Hacker yelled with accelerated tone. "Deeters turns and bunts…and it's a fair ball rolling toward first! Gambill scores as Peavey fields it and fires to Gonzales for the out at first and the Vipers lead 1-0 here in the eighth! I don't believe my eyes, Pete Harnisch! How long have we been in this booth together and never…and I do mean never, have we ever seen the Las Vegas Vipers execute a suicide squeeze play like that one."

"How right you are, Ralph!" Harnisch laughed. "You could certainly sense that John Gambill wanted to get that uniform dirty all over again. He looked like a bull in Barcelona as he came charging to the plate…and he was almost there before Deeters got the bunt down." He laughingly went on to point out. "These guys are truly amazing. It's the times you think they are absolutely lost balls in high weeds when they will quickly turn in a play like that and completely prove you totally ignorant."

"Now that I look back at it, I'm not too sure that first swing by Deeters wasn't maybe a shy bit of over-acting." Ralph offered. "Even with his slump, we've never seen him look like as he did on that first pitch. It could have been a case of, look how bad I am now before I show you how good I can be."

Peavey retired Cliff Collier on a fly ball to center and Gary Duzan looked at a called strike-three. It was now the bottom of the eighth, and there were decisions to be made.

"Deeters, you stay in and go to right. Carpenter, you've done a helluva job out there today. You've thrown ninety-seven pitches, how about a fresh arm to shut these mothers down?"

Everett Carpenter looked down and kicked at the dirt and concrete as he remained silent. There is often an unspoken communication that gets the point across far more direct than verbiage of any vocabulary.

"OK, you win. Give us one more strong inning! I'm getting Fuller ready for the ninth. Carpy, get out there and bring it home! This is your game, son."

The Padres pulled Jake Peavey for pinch hitter Mike Cameron as the Vipers lefty craftily breezed through the eighth- inning, getting Cameron to ground-out to second. Padre's' short-stop Khalile

Green popped out harmlessly to first while third baseman Kevin Kouzmanoff waved at the "knuckler" for an ugly strike-out to go to the ninth. It was still a 1-0 game as Everett Carpenter came in and sullenly threw himself down at the end of the bench. He was up second to start the top of the ninth and knew his day was through.

"Carpenter, get a bat and get up there in the on-deck circle before we get written up by that son of a bitch behind the plate." Leach hollered.

Looking up, he saw Ernie Fuller sitting there on the bench wearing his warm-up jacket and a sly grin. He simply assumed that his day was done. Getting up, he walked to the bat rack and was met there by Manager Tommy Leach.

"You've pitched one hell of a game today, Carpy. Call it being in the zone, or whatever bullshit they call it now, but you deserve a chance to finish what you started. Want to go one more?" he playfully asked.

"Thanks, Tommy, I really appreciate it. You won't be sorry." Carpenter softly mumbled as he quickly and appreciatively removed his jacket.

The Vipers went one, two, three in the ninth as Everett Carpenter walked back to the mound for the ninth time as he and the Vipers still hovered to a one-run lead. The Padres had Brian Giles, Adrian Gonzolas, and Josh Beard up in order and stood as a last chance threesome to get something started.

"Carpenter has been outstanding today, giving up just three-hits against the first place Padres and a pretty fair lineup of hitters." Ralph Hacker noted. "Here in the ninth…I just wonder how much gas is still left in the old tank. 'Dirty' Ernie Fuller was up and ready to take over, but apparently, there has been a change of heart on the Vipers' bench as Carpenter now readies to face the Padres' right fielder Brian Giles to get that C and G next to his name in the book."

A he prepared for what hoped to be redemption for his abysmal debut, it now seemed almost like blasphemy to even think about throwing "trick" pitches. As Brian Giles settled into the box, Carpenter suddenly found himself in almost a Manchurian-state as he begin to carefully craft his fingers loosely around the seams of the baseball. While his intellect said no, his instincts cried yes.

Hacker again set the radio stage. "Quite a turnaround for this young man from Portsmouth, Ohio. He's just three- outs away from yet another Vipers win and a complete game for Tom Browning's staff. Giles is ready as he digs in here for the ninth. Carpenter looks for the sign…sets…and the pitch. He swings and hits it off the end of the bat. It's a dribbler toward second as Snyder gobbles it up and the throw to Chadwick, one- away!"

"There it was again, Ralph." Pete Harnisch openly chucked. "Carpenter threw the knuckleball for the first pitch and Brian Giles just couldn't lay off it. He was actually lucky to have even made contact on that one."

"Right you are, Peter. That is what's so intriguing about that pitch. It floats up there like an underhanded softball, but because it dances so much, you really just never know where it will end up." Ralph noted. "One -pitch and one-out as the 'knuckle heads' have struck again."

With a quick out in the ninth, Padres' first baseman Adrian Gonzales stepped in. His bat had been extremely quiet all day. Everett Carpenter worked Gonzales to a full-count. His next pitch was a borderline bastard pitch that was too close to the black of the plate to tell. It could go either way.

"Ball four, take your base." Home plate umpire Richard Risby decreed.

That brought up catcher Josh Beard as the Padres knew exactly what he had to do. Beard's speed was far from legendary as the Vipers infield began to inch their way in. With the territorial plate knowledge that most catchers possess, bunting sometimes becomes a natural ability. On the first pitch, Josh Beard rolled a perfect textbook example up the first base line for the second out.

Gonzales was now in scoring position with the buzz of the crowd on the up-lift as pinch- hitter Lenny Harris moved from the on-deck circle to the big dish.

"Everett Carpenter is now going to face one of the legendary pinch hitters in the game." Ralph Hacker embellished.

21 DOWN IN VEGAS

"You're so right there, Ralph." Harnisch chimed in. "This guy has been around since Methuselah, but clubs just keep picking him up for his natural ability to always get the bat on the ball. The Vipers have an honest decision here to make I would think."

"You would think now wouldn't you? Two out, one on in scoring position, and Fuller is loose, but it looks like Tommy Leach is going to stick with the date he brought to the dance for yet one more batter. One left here in the ninth to go not only for the complete game, but another Vipers' victory." Harnisch noted.

"Two down, and pinch hitter Lenny Harris at the plate as Carpenter works and fires. Strike one on the inside corner. You know, he still has lots of sting in those pitches as Harris backs out for the sign." Hacker called.

"He does, Ralph, and as long as he doesn't get too careless or impatient, he is still in control."

Harris worked the count two balls and two strikes. Everett Carpenter slowly took off his cap to wipe the salty- brine rolling down from his hot brow.

Looking around, he could see that all of his teammates were now standing together high on the steps. The sight of them clapping and rooting him on sent a well-needed jolt of express delivery into his soul. He knew now that at this point, he could not fail.

"Two balls, two strikes as Everett once again looks to Pouge for the sign. The pitch! It's a line drive up the middle and it's off Carpenter... and he's down! The ball is loose in front of the mound! From his knees, he scrambles, he fires, and...he got Harris by a half a step at first! Wow, what a play, Pete! What a play!" Ralph Hacker joined in the jubilance.

"After knocking the ball down in front of the mound, he still had the presence of mind to get to it and from his knees and throw a seed to Chadwick. The Vipers' win on an incredible play to end the game, but Everett Carpenter is still down...and I do believe that he might be hurt."

"It looked to me, Ralph, like it hit him in either the pitching hand or the lower arm as he tried to grab the ball as it as it sailed by him. This was a no-doubter –'screaming mimmy' that was headed for center field, but somehow, Carpenter got to it and then kept his head in the game enough to follow up on the throw."

"That was for sure some kind of web-gem performance, and right now, the Vipers' lefty Everett Carpenter is still down on his back as trainer Larry Starr is leaning over and working on him. At this point, we're not quite sure where the problem is." Ralph Hacker solemnly apologized.

"It's really tough to see from this vantage point to where the injury is located, but it's another dramatic finish as the Vipers hold on again to win 1-0 over the Padres. Looks to me that a bitter-sweet day belongs to a young man who was pitching like he had something here to prove. We hope whatever the problem might be isn't a serious one. While we wait for some kind of word from down on the field, we'll take this quick time-out and return to PETCO Park in San Diego for the post-game show live on the Las Vegas Vipers Radio Network."

Every day now, the after-game interviews were growing to the point of World Series importance. The novelty of the Vipers was now eating away at every sports department alive. Manager Tommy Leach finally entered the room to an almost panic-stricken cotillion of writers, reporters, and cameras.

"Tommy! Tommy! Steve Schmidt of the *Union-Tribune*! What's the injury report on Carpenter?"

"Before I answer that, I just want to say that Everett Carpenter showed us a true gut-check challenge here today." Manager Tommy Leach continued. "It was his grit and determination out there, not just for his own individual pride, but for the whole team. To answer your question, we x-rayed him here at PETCO, and it has turned up negative. For precautionary purposes, we then went ahead and sent him over to Shirley Pena Hospital so he could get some relief from the pain and a second opinion there."

"Tommy, Lee Hamilton of KBPS-TV, now that the Vipers are 9-1 on this road trip and have literally picked up five-games in the Western Division standings, what are your feelings now heading to LA?"

21 DOWN IN VEGAS

The Vipers' Manager feigned look of stun was telling as he gazed around the room as if the magnitude of the question had just hit him.

"Five-games eh, wow. We'll, a fourteen-game road trip is enough to test the most galvanized of sports teams now, isn't it? If we can just split the rest, we go home at 11-3. I personally just tell these guys that we have jobs to do, and it's listed as 'day to day.' I also tell them that if at any point we start reading our own press clippings and start taking you guys seriously, to just go ahead and prepare to watch the wheels come flying off. Next question!"

As both Cisco Wheeler and Brandon Briggs read the medical report Friday morning, they too were both relieved, but concerned.

"No breakage of bones anywhere, Cisco, but a severe sprain to the index and middle- finger muscles on his pitching hand. That generally takes some time to heal." reflected the Vipers GM. "I know the MRI came back negative, but my question now is how long we are going to be without him?"

"I talked to Tommy earlier today at the hotel." Cisco Wheeler added. "His recommendation is to go ahead and put him on the fifteen-day disabled list. When he comes off, it will be late August and we can still use him for the final month."

"Shit, Cisco," Brandon exhaled, "Carpenter finally gets it turned around and now this. We're going to have to bring somebody up from Colorado Springs. We got a kid down there that's throwing pretty good named Zeiber, Brad Zeiber. He's been a little inconsistent from what I remember looking at the sheets from last week, but he has always been a pretty solid starter. What do you think?"

"Hell, that's Tommy's call." Cisco barked. "We turned promotions and demotions over to the managers three years ago. Give him a call and see what he wants to do. The very last thing that I want to see is losing the chemistry of what we have created here. I know injuries are a part of the game, but we have to be extremely careful on this one."

If you didn't know any better you might have thought that the Oscars had moved to a Friday night in the epicenter of what's happening now. Every box seat in Dodger Stadium had filled almost two- hours before game time as the elite of the entertainment world eagerly awaited their first prime-time look at the sports phenomena that at the moment was upstaging them all.

Keanu Reeves was sitting right behind the dugout decked out in his home blue as names like Nicolson, De Niro, and Crystal were all sprinkled closely behind.

Lead vocalist for the rock group "Matchbox 20", Rob Thomas was out on the field and talking to several of the players waiting in anticipation of stepping up to sing the evenings National Anthem, KABC Radio and the legendary voice of the Dodgers Vin Scully was also fully- loaded and getting ready to deal with this most intriguing of sport novellas.

"Good evening, everybody, and welcome to Dodger Stadium. I'm Vin Scully, and tonight, we have the most unlikely of cavaliers as the Dodgers prepare to take on the new Las Vegas Vipers. By now, you all know the story line of a team that was plucked from destiny's waiver wire much like the fictitious and lovable fighter Rocky Balboa. The only difference here is that this real-life underdog is starting to make some loud and sudden noise in the Western Division baseball title chase.

"It was certainly an odds-long gamble to even think that a college baseball team could step up to this level of competition and not only survive, but thrive. So far, the house is in the hole on that wager. Either love him or hate him, the approach of Vipers owner Cisco 'The Dealer' Wheeler has certainly been the hot-button of sports and continues to captivate the imagination of people all over who have been following this most unlikely script as it seemingly writes itself yet another amazing chapter night after night."

While the LA fans continued to pack their way into Chavez Ravine, a fully loaded Boeing 737 was entering its final approach to LAX. The flight had been non-stop from Atlanta and was now making a rapid descent into the haze-mixed hue with the orange and blue pastel colors of the Pacific coast sun.

"Hey, Syleanna, wake up and put on your happy face. We're almost there."

"Oh wow…Carla, how long have I been out?"

21 DOWN IN VEGAS

"Get bright, girlfriend, because tonight you're going in for a real Major League landing!"

Two wayward travelers prepared for a surprise rendezvous of the past with the present. Coupled with the ambiguity of Sean Deeters sudden slump and lack of communication with his long-time love interest would certainly have most mystery writers scrutinizing these two events. In the everyday transcript of life, it should for sure be noted that this was just one of many mini-dramas that were being played out in both of their selected scenes.

* * * * *

"Hey, Tommy, I just heard that Brad Penny took a cortisone shot in his elbow yesterday." Jarred Brewster said as he sat down next to his manager in the dugout while Leach was in the process of filling out the lineup card.

"A cortisone shot? And where did you find out that secret little out-patient prescription of information, Dr. Brewster?" Leach sarcastically asked.

"One of the ground keepers, he didn't know I was listening, but I overheard him tell another guy the whole deal. Then I went up in the stands in my street clothes and watched him warm-up. I'm sure of it Skip, he's real slow on the accelerator tonight." Brewster bubbled.

While cortisone has long been used in sports for masking injury, if a more serious problem exists, it often will not make it better, just temporarily pain free. At first, Tommy Leach was a bit dubious about his informant's initial assessment, but then he started to think.

"If it's true, Penny is probably going to try and get loose and let his arm warm before he starts with any curves or sliders. What if I load the lineup with my best fast-ball hitters up front and see what happens?"

Vipers Manager Tommy Leach was starting to put more credence into his young sage's off-beat observations. Brewster was too much like a young puppy at times with his enthusiasm stuck in over-drive, but it was becoming clearer that he did possess a unique knack for recognizing the moment.

Tommy Leach once again scrutinized his lineup and couldn't help to think of the old phrase that "Those who can do, and those who can't, teach." Jarred Brewster's head was always in the game even though his timing was not always the best when auditioning his observations and he could sometimes come across as a bit of a pest.

Leach quickly started a new and quite unorthodox batting line-up, putting his best fast- ball hitters first. Catcher Doug Pougue who was always been in the seventh or eighth slot was now leading off. Utility player Terrance Kennedy was penciled in at second as the usual Vipers lineup now looked as if it had been determined by drawing the names from a party- hat.

Instinct now had everything to do with the opening game against the Dodgers and the local press-pundits were going to be absolutely stunned by this bizarre offensive makeover.

Unorthodox as it began, the lesson served quickly affected the Vipers manager, teaching him a lesson he had never experienced in the game. It was now OK to throw out all pre-conceived thoughts of what was considered normalcy right out the window. He had, for too many years, seen the way things had always been done and not necessarily the right way. As it is in life, too many people always expect the expected.

To change and completely come from another mind configuration is the only way to catch your opponent off-guard and unprepared. As he completed the new lineup card, the Vipers manager slyly smiled and said to himself.

"Tommy boy, what's the worst thing that can happen to you tonight? You might lose, but then again, you just might win. What the hell, you got no- guts, you get no- glory! Let's really give them something to talk about."

The Los Angeles Times
Randy Harvey

(Los Angeles) The Las Vegas Vipers feasted on Brad Penny pitching tonight as the impossible collegiate dream-team continued to roll into LA by knocking out the Dodgers early to score seven runs in the first three-innings as the Vipers erupted for a 9-2 win.

Las Vegas scored four times in the first inning as they batted around with the continued slugging of Vipers' Center Fielder "King Kong" Karl Smith. It was a bases loaded double that ended up plating three runs followed by a perfectly executed squeeze play by second baseman Brooks Snyder that caught the Dodgers napping. It was Jeff Kent who best summarized the evening's performance with his praise for the young upstart team.

"It's frustrating," Kent explained, "These guys have been here for just a little over two weeks, and they play at a confidence level that's honestly scary. We knew that Brad didn't have his best stuff early, yet they capitalized on it and took us out of the game to the point we really couldn't get back in. Being in this game as long as I have, and to be honest…I've never seen anything quite like this before!"

Both Dodgers runs scored in the seventh-inning on a Kenny Lofton two-run home run off winner Scotty Arms. "Dirty" Ernie Fuller threw two perfect innings of relief to secure the Vipers ninth victory in eleven tries.

Since the beginning of the Viper's "Second Season" which began after the All-Star break, they have picked up seven-games in the standings, but still remain in the cellar of the National League West. As the standings now show, they are only eight-games out of first which by far is the team's best showing this late in the season in the entire history of the organization.

With the last two months of the regular season campaign beginning tomorrow on August 1, many in the National League West are now looking at the standings and wondering if the best is yet to come in making this division perhaps the most interesting in all of Major League Baseball. With only eight games now separating worst from first, every game now in the NL West means something every single day.

The big question now is does a team that ended last year's season at 28.5 games out of first place even have a puncher's chance in sixty days of climbing through the maze of contenders to make this year one for the record books? The wise guys in Vegas as of today say no, giving the Vipers a 400–1 chance to climb to the top.

National League Western Division Standings
August 1, 2006

	W. L.	Pct.	GB
Padres	55–51	.519	0
Arizona	54–52	.509	1.0
Rockies	51–55	.481	4.0
LA Dodgers	51–55	.481	4.0
SF Giants	51–56	.477	4.5
LV Vipers	47–59	.463	8.0

Syleanna Griffin and Carla Harris arrived by cab at the Marriot Hotel on West Century Boulevard as the two began working on a game plan of their own. The girls quickly checked into their room and began unpacking suitcases as Syleanna was starting to get second thoughts about their spontaneous adventure.

Finally regaining her wits from the long flight to LAX, she couldn't hold in her feelings any longer.

"I don't know about this, Carla…we should have let one of them know that we were coming. I just have a real bad vibe that I know I shouldn't be feeling right now…but I do." admitted Syleanna.

"So, you haven't talked to Sean now…in how many days? Four?" Carla replied.

"C'mon, you guys have been together since high school." Carla reminded her bestie.

"Do you even realize what's going on and with him and everything right now? I couldn't even imagine being splashed on TV, the newspapers, magazines, and all the other crap that all these guys are dealing with right now. Please, just don't worry and get over it!"

"I know, but here we are, unannounced and just parachuting into all of this. I know I would feel so much better if we had at least had got together and just talked!" Syleanna continued to anguish.

21 DOWN IN VEGAS

Pulling on her Bentley State Eagles custom-tailored "E"-shirt, Carla primped in the mirror to make sure it had that elastic touch. Endowed with a magic figure that could adorn just about any fit or fashion, she was wanting to make sure that styling in LA on this special night would be straight from the book of quality hip.

"OK…the game's at 7:10 p.m. and we need to get ready and run quick." Carla said to Syleanna. "I figured out that a cab ride is about twenty- bucks from here, and we'll just have to see about tickets when we get to the ball-park. Did you bring any lip-gloss?"

Syleanna fumbled through her purse until she finally located the tiny tube of oral freshener and pulled it out as if she had just found a rabbit in a hat.

"Here, diva!" she giggled. "This is the same kind Angelina Jolie uses so if you run into her tonight, you'll both have something totally together to talk about!"

The mood began to lighten up as both Carla and Syleanna gradually began to relax and enjoy the LA experience.

Six p.m. LA time and the hotel clock showed that the game didn't start for another hour. While the atmosphere in room 210 at the LAX Marriott was starting to turn a wee more festive, Brandon Briggs and Cisco Wheeler were in another room at Chavez Ravine dealing with darker and more ponderous spirits.

"So, Brandon, have you seen the latest? It was the lead on Sports Center just a few minutes ago" Cisco Wheeler ranted. "That bastard Toots Randall has gone to the Players Union and wants to start a class action lawsuit against us? Hell, he's not only being paid in full on his over-generous contract, but he's now playing for the Yankees. That curmudgeon should count his fucking blessings and just leave us alone!"

Reflective, Brandon tried his best to placate his rather torked leader and chief as to the real element of importance.

"So what, Cisco?" Brandon countered quickly, "You know it and I know it that Randall is just a trouble-maker and a liar. If we had done something wrong, don't you think that the damn players union would have already been at our doorstep by now? He's always been a loud-mouthed idiot who should have spent more time working on his game rather than his name!"

"That's the really dark side of professional sports." Cisco huffed. "I don't even care if I go stone-cold broke doing what we did because damn it, we made this game fun again! Those kids could care less about all the bovine fecal- matter that's going on around them. It just pisses me off when I have to deal with somebody who is in it for a free ride and then turns around and spits in your face!"

Cisco Wheeler paused for a moment before his match-point comment to Brandon Briggs.

"Toots Randall is a nothing on this big picture of this game, Cisco! My best advice to you is just forgive and forget him! Why? Because nothing will annoy him any more than just forgetting him and that I promise! Write it down!"

It was now 6:15 p.m. as Carla Harris and Syleanna Griffin were finally in a cab and headed for Dodger Stadium. Their cab driver was a gabby Latino named Julio who just couldn't resist in a little spirited Q and A as to why two young and very beautiful girls were headed to the baseball game.

"So, where you girls from?" Julio politely inquired.

"We're from Ohio," Carla said. "A little town on the Ohio River called Portsmouth."

"Oh, Portsmouth, Ohio," Julio repeated. Looking back into the mirror, he seemed to connect with the T-shirt that Carla was wearing. "Wait a minute, isn't that the town where the new baseball team came from and that little college university?"

As both girls began to laugh, they could immediately tell that their hired charioteer must be in the know to the plot-line of sports' greatest developing stories.

"Yes!" Carla heartedly admitted. "We're from Bentley State University, and we flew out here to watch our guys play tonight."

"Your guys eh?" as Julio continued with his friendly banter. "You mean guys like you are fans…or does that mean guys like… your guys?"

Often, you can immediately tell when first meeting someone whether they're sincere or just being flirty. Both girls felt that the inquiries from the man behind the wheel were out of sincere interest. Since Carla started out as the spokesperson for the two, she continued the banter with a few questions of her own.

"Well, we do have a couple special interests that are on the team. My boyfriend is Cliff Collier the center fielder, and Syleanna here… she dates the left fielder, Sean Deeters. This is the first time we have had the opportunity to see them play in the Big Leagues, so we flew out as kind of a surprise."

"Aw! That is so cool!" Julio shot back. "We are about twenty-minutes from the stadium. I guess you have some pretty good seats, eh?"

"Well, I'm glad you brought that up!" Carla inserted. "We don't have any tickets yet and wondering where the best place was to get some?"

Pausing for a second, Julio froze in silence as both girls felt that sudden chill right at the point where one always knows that bad news is about to be delivered.

"You're kidding me, right! You really don't have any tickets to the game here tonight? Oh man, this game has been a sell-out for more than a week. They are going to be hard to get and…expensive!" Julio animated.

As their hearts skipped a beat, Syleanna sunk back into the cab's leather seat and renewed her funk about being there in the first place.

"See, I knew this was a bad idea," she groaned to Carla. "This whole thing is such a mess. We've come over two-thousand miles to a ballgame, and now we can't even get in?"

Julio finally broke the embarrassing silence with an alternative plan that has been used countless times over the years to gain acceptance, favor, and free tickets to professional sports everywhere; it's called memorabilia.

"Hey, I got this buddy named Ira who sells tickets at the game." Julio inserted. "He like…he doesn't work at the window, he does his selling on the streets if you know what I mean. If I can get a deal from him, do you want me to give him a quick call?"

"What kind of deal are we talking about?" Carla cautiously snapped back.

"Well, this guy is a huge sports collector because he just loves sports so much. If you know all these guys on the team, how hard would it be to get a couple of say…a few autographed balls from them…maybe a bat?"

Looking at each other, it seemed like an odd, but certainly a do-able request.

"You mean you could get us tickets to the game for just a couple of baseballs signed by the Vipers?" Carla minced. "That should be no problem."

"OK, let me call Ira and see where he is and see what we can do." Julio shot back.

As the taxi-cab continued to wind through the streets of Los Angeles toward Dodger Stadium, the driver named Julio was quickly talking in a thick Spanish accent to someone on his cell phone. Sitting in the back seat quietly, both Carla and Syleanna began to wonder what they were now getting themselves into. The last thing they both heard him say was "Vin Scully Avenue." As he quickly pressed the button to hang up button, Julio presented his proposal.

"First off all," Julio spoke, "I have been a cab driver here in LA for over twenty-two years. I would never do anything underhanded or to hurt any of my passengers. I want you to know that!"

Ominous notes for the pre-text of a proposal as Carla and Syleanna listened intensely.

"As I told you, I have a friend named Ira who has two tickets waiting for you for tonight's game. We are about five-minutes from the stadium and he is waiting for us now on Vin Scully Boulevard. He said that he will give you the tickets, and in return, you can get him a couple of autographed balls and a bat from the Vipers. As I told you, he is a big sports- nut and loves his baseball!"

"Well, that sounds incredible!" Carla said. "The only problem is that we haven't seen them in three weeks. So how would we ever be able to do this? The game starts in twenty minutes."

It was at this point that Julio the cabby looked back at the two naïve girls from Portsmouth, Ohio, who just so happened to be his passengers and said, "Because I trust you."

21 DOWN IN VEGAS

The taxi quickly turned onto the namesake road of the LA Dodgers greatest media ambassador as Julio reached into the back to hand Carla his card and phone number.

"Keep the card, ladies, and just call me whenever you get the baseballs. And if you need to go anywhere else in this town please just call me. I have everything square with Ira so just take the tickets from him and have a great time tonight." He added.

Stunned, Carla and Syleanna could hardly catch their wits on what was just laid upon them when the cab quickly slammed to a stop. Standing on the corner leading into Dodger stadium was an older-looking black man with his LA Dodgers cap on backwards. Julio quickly jumped from the cab to open the doors. It was now 6:50 p.m.

"Ira, these are the two ladies I told you about. Make sure they have a good time tonight!" Julio laughed.

With that, the man silently handed them two-tickets for a game that had not been this intensely coveted since the early days of attendance when Dodgers pitching phenom Fernando Valenzuala took to the mound.

"Thank you for allowing me to escort you ladies here tonight, and I do look forward to meeting up with you again soon!"

That said, the radio suddenly crackled with more names and addresses as Julio's attention reverted quickly to his next job. Smiling and with a quick wave, he jumped into his cab and sped away!

If there were a hole in all the craziness so far of transplanting a college baseball team into the Major Leagues; his name was Sean Deeters.

Manager Tommy Leach was becoming extremely frustrated with his left fielder at the lack of production from a kid who not only was a standout in college, but showed up on the Vipers team as a true spark plug. So far in his 68 plate appearances, Sean was batting .178 with 11 hits and 20 strike-outs. It was this from a solid hitter who had led the Mid-America Conference with the fewest whiffs of any player over his last two seasons.

Collecting 8 hits in his first 20 plate appearances for Las Vegas had Sean Deeters blistering the ball at a .400 clip. Since then, his free fall at the plate along with his confidence level in general was a big change that had become more than just a little apparent to everybody.

"I'm not going to keep running him out there if this is all we are getting." Tommy candidly admitted to his Hitting Coach Von Hayes. "I know we already turned in the lineup for tonight, but for Christ's sake, how long can we continue with him out there like this?"

Choosing his words carefully, Hayes tried to be the best diplomat he could in the manager's office ten minutes before game time,

"Tommy, he's just not focused like he was. This girlfriend issue might be it, I don't know. Believe me, I've talked to him in a million different ways, and it's almost like talking to a manikin. I say, let's just see what he does tonight or then we go ahead and make a change."

"I know we signed these guys to the Major League minimum." Tommy finally exhaled, "But that still doesn't mean we can't send them down to the minors."

"I agree totally!" Hayes responded. "We got a damn full-house out there tonight, and personally, I certainly don't want to keep Madonna waiting! It's time to hit the field."

Running from exit to exit, Carla and Syleanna finally found their ticketed entrance and dashed into the stadium. Following the directions to FD 16, the girls finally stopped and asked an usher for help.

"Yes ladies!" Came the polite response from the gentleman who took the tickets from Carla. "My name is Mark Riddlebarger, and I've been here for over thirty-years and I know exactly where these seats are, follow me."

Carla and Syleanna instantly drank in the electric atmosphere as they continued to walk. The direction was down, down, and more down, until Mr. Riddlebarger finally turned with a smile and delivered his spiel.

You're in aisle number 1 ladies, right here behind the visitor's dugout. Seats 1 and 2 are all yours for the evening unless you find me more interesting, and then we can talk." He smiled.

21 DOWN IN VEGAS

Syleanna clumsily dug through her purse and finally came up with a couple of dollars, handing them to their jovial seat guide just as the lineups for both teams were being announced.

"And playing left field and batting eighth for the Las Vegas Vipers, Sean Deeters!" echoed the official PA announcement.

"Eighth!" Syleanna's protective response erupted. "Sean isn't an eighth-hitter in the lineup. Keith always batted him either leadoff or number two. I'm sure he's not happy with that!"

It was just at that moment that Brooks Snyder strolled up the dugout steps and began looking around at the crowd. As if by some sort of premeditated providence, he casually looked over the dugout and directly into the eyes of some friends that he knew all too well.

"Carla! Syleanna! No… it's not even you guys! Holy shit! And how the hell did you all get here and, those seats!" Brooks enthused. "Cliff! Deet-Man, get your asses up here and now!"

Both Cliff Collier and Sean Deeters sprang to the steps and gazed into the faces of a much simpler time. Once hanging behind the backstop at Branch Rickey Park in Portsmouth and rooting their men on through the red Ohio dust clay, the total scene had now flipped upside down to morph into the most improbable scenario ever imagined in pro-sports history.

As other heads of the former Bentley State Eagles began to pop up to the front of the dugout and share their hometown greetings, Tommy Leach suddenly put the kibosh on the sudden impromptu reunion.

"Gentlemen, everyone on the bench now. Please!" he shouted.

Twenty-five players quickly scurried to the pine as their manager began to lay it on the line as to the magnitude of what they would be facing on this night in one of the most celebrated games they had played in to date.

"You are in Los Angeles, California, playing in the third oldest baseball park still standing. While it's been festive so far gazing at all the celebrities, these guys over there, wearing the blue hats, are not your friends! If I can take it even a little further, they hate you, and everything you have accomplished so far.

"You are now something they never dreamed you could ever be and that is called a division rival! You have beaten them once, and guess what? They would like nothing better than to destroy you right here in front of all their friends and fans. And not to diminish your celebrity status, but yes, that also includes Jack Nicholson, Tom Hanks, Vin Scully, and even God himself.

"We are eight games out of first place and they are four, do the math! If we are going to leap frog the traffic jam in front of us, we have to start right here and right now, here tonight. I want no distractions! If you guys play your game and tune out everything else, we will be seven games out at night's end. Last I saw the Cardinals' score, they have an 8-1 lead on the Padres in the seventh."

Eyeball to eyeball, Manager Tommy Leach slowly starred down each of his players to ensure the message was delivered and again received.

"Snyder, start us off tonight and let's get things going!" Leach finished with a flurry. "It's ours to take as soon as this Chris Brown guy butchers the National Anthem!"

"Shocked just a little bit, that we have surprise visitors tonight?" Cliff quickly nudged Sean Deeters.

"God am I...wow! This...I never expected them, and especially here and now. I love her so much, but..."

Sean Deeter's voice trailed as he looked down to the concrete floor as if he were ready to confess something that had been rattling around his soul like a stone in a coffee can.

"C'mon, Deets, let's put on a show tonight and let them see just how much they've been missed." Cliff quickly maneuvered the moment. "If we don't, Billy Bob Thornton and Mickey Rourke might be walking out of here with our women tonight just in case you haven't noticed who is also sitting right there in their aisle."

Frazzled by all the quick attention and fuss, Carla and Syleanna quickly settled into their seats just as the PA announcer asked everyone to rise for the traditional chorale to the country. Pop singing sensation Chris Brown no sooner belted out the words "And the home of the brave!" than the crowd exploded as the LA Dodgers burst from their dugout and onto the field.

"A little different here than Branch Rickey Park back home, eh, girlfriend?" Carla chided. "I think the biggest celebrity I ever saw at one of our games was the TV butcher guy from the Kroger grocery stores. He threw out the first pitch a couple of years ago because the university bought all their hot dogs from them."

"Oh, you mean that 'Alex the Meat Man' dude. " Syleanna giggled.

"Yea, that's him! He gave me an autographed paper hat once." Carla added.

"Nice," Syleanna sarcastically cooed.

Mitch Milhuff was the starter for the Vipers as ace Derek Lowe was on the mound for the Dodgers. Lowe was in the midst of putting together another monster season at 13-4 with a dazzling era of 2.11. Milhuff continued to be solid on the mound for the Vipers standing in at 3-0 in the much heralded 'second season" with an earned run average that was quite respectable at 2.78. Brooks Snyder was in on deck circle getting ready to lead off as a pensive Sean Deeters sat at the end of the bench in a silent stew of collection. Mulling over every brick crossed on the road to where he now found himself, he totally realized it was time to step up and deal with it and right now.

"The love of my life has traveled all the way from Portsmouth, Ohio, to watch me play ball here tonight." Sean pondered. *"These problems are all my damn-doing. It's time to face it like a man and get back to where I was before all this shit happened. I haven't been fair with Syleanna, the guys, and most important, it's time for me to get off of my-dumb ass and get out there and do what I do best!"*

His thoughts again fell back to the joy of walking up to the plate with a quick look in the stands as he had so many times before to catch the eye of his biggest fan cheering him on. It was the feeling of never wanting to let her down that he now realized was the pure motivation that drove him to his success. Sean's self-analysis continued until the plane of reality was finally broken in a rather gruff and surly manor.

"Deeters, let's go, son!" Manager Tommy Leach yelled. "It's half past ball-thirty and we need a right fielder!"

Getting up quickly, he realized that Snyder, Duzan, and Chadwick had all gone down in order.

Grabbing his glove, he bolted from the dugout and headed to his position. Fighting the resistance, Sean took a tempting glance over the dugout for just a quick second as he spied a raven-haired beauty that he knew all too well. Since those carefree days of Junior-high school, the picture was frozen in time as she was there once again standing and cheering his every running step into the outfield grass. While not yet totally exercised from the demons that lie within, Sean at least felt they had been temporarily put on hold and placed back in the box.

KVPR-AM was now by far the most listened to radio station in Las Vegas as Ralph Hacker and Pete Harnisch had been riding the Vipers' wave and had also been elevated to the status of rock stars. With all of the national exposure being pounded out every day, they were now regular sound bites on virtually every sports station in the nation. Game two against the Dodgers proved to be quite the topic involving an underachieving player who had quite an evening to remember.

"Pete, tonight we have witnessed a breakout game from a young man who honestly I had lost all faith in." Ralph Hacker confessed.

"Yea, Ralph, Sean Deeters came up here as one of the young team leaders, but as they say, he seemed to have lost his mojo somewhere along the line. Tonight however"…Harnisch said laughing, "I really don't know where to begin!

"Final score 8 to 5 tonight as the Las Vegas Vipers win again behind a monster offensive performance from right fielder Sean Deeters." Ralph proudly crooned into the headset. "Deeters ends up going four for four at the plate with a home run, two doubles, a single and five RBI's on the night. That, my friend, is not only impressive, but also considered a really good night at the office!""You ain't wrong there!" Harnisch chimed in with his excited observations. "Milhuff didn't have his best stuff, but he got the Vipers through the sixth inning holding the Dodgers to just three-runs. I sensed that every time they thought they were in position to strike back, Deeters would slam the door in their face!"

21 DOWN IN VEGAS

"It was the home run in the third, Peter, that I think set the table tonight as his two doubles, both with men aboard, plus his run scoring single in the ninth just didn't give LA any offensive breathing room." Ralph expanded. "Big nights also at the plate for Chadwick, Gambill, and Coleman have now guaranteed the Vipers at worst a split of the series before we head home."

Pete Harnisch continued to mop up the post-game fodder, "For the Dodgers, Ralph, Derek Lowe gave up six-earned runs in seven innings and credit Andre Ethier with that run scoring double in the fifth and a solo home run shot by J.D. Drew in the seventh as the Dodgers disappointed a sell-out Friday night home crowd that had certainly hoped for better things!"

"On that note," Hacker interjected, "we have picked up a game here tonight in the standings as the Cardinals beat the Padres 11-5 earlier today. Las Vegas is now only seven games out of first, two behind the Dodgers, and just a game and a half from catching the Giants and removing themselves from the cellar. Wow partner, who'd of ever thunk that!"

The Vipers clubhouse was in full-swing celebration as player jubilance mish-mashed with reporters and beat writers all trying to get a story. On this night, it was Sean Deeters' locker that was ground zero for the epicenter of media surge.

"Sean, Mark Morgan from KNBC Sports! A perfect night tonight at the plate against one of baseball's best power pitchers, what did you do different?"

Looking at the sea of microphones and camera flags being thrust into his face, Sean Deeters decided to take control of the moment.

"Whoa, guys!" he said laughingly. "I'm standing here in my underwear and I really can't breathe, let alone answer questions. If you all will just kind of stand back a little and let me put my pants on, I will be happy to talk with each and every one of you!"

It was that take charge maneuver that demonstrated the leadership skills of the Vipers star right fielder. Sean always had the ability to direct a situation using charm and diplomacy to dowse the flames of chaos and bring reason back into the room. Now fully clothed, he prepared himself for the onslaught of queries.

Returning to the KNBC reporter who had asked the first question, he smiled and began giving the Channel 2 sports department their nightly silage.

"Now, Mr. Morgan, shall we start again?" Sean began as the rest of the news-hounds let forth with an awkward chuckle.

"Same question, Sean," the reporter stated. "You had a big night out there tonight, did you do anything different?"

"I think I did." Sean admitted. "I know I was a little more relaxed at the plate, and I saw the ball well. Derek Lowe is a great pitcher, and I guess I did a lot of visualization preparation before the game. How it would feel, that kind of stuff."

"Sean! Good evening! R. J. Kaltenbach from the *LA Times*. I think you guys are proving that winning in the big leagues is not a fluke anymore. Is there any thought at this point to winning the Western Division? After tonight, you guys are only seven games out of first place."

Choosing his words carefully, Sean knew this could be a trick question as his experience in the College World Series taught him, and he didn't want to give anyone bulletin-board material. Lesson learned to be very much on the down-low when it came to your intentions or your accomplishments. He knew exactly what they were looking for and it would be the "oh shucks" route to be taken on this one.

"You know, this is all still very new to us and the guys. We've enjoyed every minute of it, and in case you haven't noticed it yet, we just love to play baseball."

That comment brought forth a spontaneous chuckle from all of the media- hounds.

"I really don't think any of us are looking that far ahead."

"Hey, Sean, Mark Harris from the *Las Vegas Sun*. Next Monday night will be the first home game that the new Vipers will play in front of a very enthusiastic crowd I'm sure. Is there anything about that that makes you the least bit nervous?"

"Well, yes, there is. I understand that Wayne Newton is going to sing the National Anthem and my mom said that if I don't get an autograph or a picture of him to not come home!" Again laughter burst forth. "I'm a little concerned about that."

The barrage of questions continued as the last reporter from KSNU-TV cleverly threw the round-house curve question of the night. As smooth and controlled as Sean had been answering the barrage of nonstop wall-to-wall questioning, this one was a seed from left field.

"Sean, quickly…the TV cameras kept showing a couple of girls behind the dugout tonight rooting you guys on. We did a little investigating and discovered that one of them is your girlfriend who flew in for the game. Do you think that had any influence on your performance here tonight?"

Stunned that this angle had even come into play, Sean was obviously unprepared for a Rico-Suave retort. After a moment of awkward silence, the Vipers star of the game finally spoke up.

"We did have friends in for tonight's game from back home, and yes…one of them is ah, a very close friend of mine. After everything the team has been through over the past month, I sometimes think the press forgets that we had lives before all this happened. To answer your question, yes…seeing people in the stands that have always been there for you…I think it gave us all an extra kick."

"If you don't mind me asking, Sean, what is her name?"

Sensing that this media circus had gotten way out of hand, Manager Tommy Leach quickly stepped in to send everyone packing.

"All right, you got what you came for! I need my team back! Thank you, thank you all for coming tonight, and I know we will see you all again real soon."

Sean sat quietly at his locker as the room quickly emptied of all the lights, camera, and action. Tommy silently came over and slid down next to him, knowing that an encouraging word was needed.

"They can be brutal, son. They just love to set you up and then go for the jugular vein. As a player and the manager of a team that, shall we say, hasn't done so well over the years, I have seen it time and time again."

Sean looked up with a little half-baked smile, relishing the fact that another human being in the room recognized his plight.

"Tommy, I don't know what to tell these guys when they get that personal." Sean softly spoke. "I can talk baseball all day long, but when they start asking all that other stuff, it just kind of rattles me. It's not that I'm ashamed of Syleanna or anything, I just don't want her to have to deal with all this."

"Do you realize Sean, that's the very first time you have ever even said her name to me?" Tommy pointed out. "I understand there's a thin-line to walk, but this is what you need to accept, Sean. Being a Major League baseball player is a privilege. It says that you have worked hard enough in life to take what you love to do to and then to the highest level. For most players. after the game is over, they can go hide in the shadows. This team can't do that!"

A silent stare into his locker was processing the pretzel-logic that his manager was passing along, knowing that there was still more to come.

"What has made you guys so special and the reason for all this damn attention from the world is the fact that you are doing something that nobody, and I do mean nobody, has ever seen before! Every guy on every big league team up here highly resents that fact of not only how you got here, but that you're winning!"

"I think that I understand that, Tommy," Sean interjected, "but where does it all go from here? "First of all," Leach continued, "The reporters and writers can't get enough of us. I would honestly have to say they are pretty much all on our side simply because they've seen it all before. Do you realize how many shitty teams and guys they have had to try and make interesting? Second, and you need to remember this, we are the good guys. That's how you and everyone else in our organization are looked upon right now with this crazy thing. We can't blow it! We are all under a microscope, and my only council to you is to continue what you're doing on and off the field, always watch your back, and expect the unexpected."

"Whew, now that's a load, Chief." Sean Deeters said with a half-cocked grin.

"Yes, it is, son. Now get the hell out of here and go let off some steam with your friends and your gal…Syleanna, is it?" Tommy Leach shot back, proving that playful sarcasm can go both ways.

"I guess the party is at the Short Stop" Dirty Ernie Fuller proclaimed as the players' cell phones were all flexing texts as to where everyone was going to meet up for the after-hours' rendezvous.

"Already got ahold of Carla and Syleanna," Cliff announced. "They have some cabbie friend they met whose going to take them over there, so they can get us all a big table. Everyone says that it's a great little hole in the wall place that's proud to be called a dive!"

It was always thought that Echo Park's Short Stop was just some hipster joint where people went to dance, get cheap drinks, play pool, and take photo-booth pics. On this night of post-game celebration, it would be the reunion post for the friends who now found themselves in an alternative reality from the life they once knew of sipping suds and playing darts at Richard Noggins Tavern back in Portsmouth, Ohio.

"So, your man did pretty good out there tonight, eh?" Julio said into the rear-view mirror as he navigated a pair of girls through the LA streets to their next destination.

"Oh my god!" Syleanna squealed. "He was fantastic! I can't believe the crowd and the way they all played. Sean looked so good out there tonight!"

"So who made that diving catch out there by the wall off of Garciapara?" Julio asked.

"That was my man, Cliff!" Carla quickly snapped. "He was showing off for me just a little bit tonight I think."

"Well, as pretty as you two are, I can see why those guys play so hard. I think I know now what the Dodgers need; better-looking girlfriends." Julio's snappy observation was met with a round of laughter as the cab suddenly stopped in front of a flashing neon sign that flashed "cocktails."

"Here we are, girls…the Short Stop! By the way, do you know when you can have those balls for me? Ira has called several times, and I just need to tell him when he can pick them up."

"Well, we will see everyone here tonight and so, does tomorrow afternoon sound OK?" Carla asked. "Cliff texted me and said that he had tickets for us from the players' allotment, so we can figure it out."

"That's fine!" Julio laughed. "I'm just honored to be the cabbie known as the transport unit for the girlfriends of the stars! Will you all be needing a ride back to the hotel? I'm on duty until 2:00 a.m."

Looking at each other, Carla and Syleanna realized that they had no car and this was a big city. All the players had a 1:00 curfew, so a quick decision was at hand.

"Yes, Julio, we'll take you up on that. We will probably need a lift, can we just call you?" Carla asked.

"Not a problem." Julio responded. "I'll just try and work this end of the city to stay close. You all have fun!"

Quickly inside the club, the set-up team of Carla and Syleanna spied a big circular leather seated table in the far corner next to a mahogany-cased telephone booth. There was another one that was directly across from it and both were empty. Quickly, Carla found the manager and informed him of the special guests that would be arriving soon. The crew on duty must have been used to impromptu celebrity gatherings as reservation signs and even ropes were quickly dispatched to mark the spot. Within several minutes as expected, the doors flew open and in came the Vipers!

Hugs, kisses, squeezes, and screams all came together as the tables quickly filled to capacity. As the taxi stand emptied outside the Short Stop Lounge, the crowd swelled to a jubilant festivity of union. What were once obscure locally known names and faces from a small town in Ohio were now of the highest sports caliber in the nation's second biggest city. Snyder, Coleman, Gambill, Collier, Duzan, Chadwick, Fuller and Milhuff were now large, loose, and living it up in the city of angels. Even the old-school dudes of Scotty Arms, Brad Scarberry, and Doug Pouge joined in for a victory brew.

While not a gin-mill dwelling individual by trade, Jarred Brewster was also there and on sight, keeping things light with a large Mountain Dew on the rocks. Jarred had been working for several days under the tutelage of Manager Tommy Leach to determine who would be the logical call-up for the Vipers since Everett Carpenter went on the fifteen-day disabled list. Life was moving way too fast.

Both Tommy and Jarred agreed that twenty-four-year-old Brad Zeiber would be their best choice from their Triple-A Colorado

Springs franchise. He was to arrive in LA on Saturday and was penciled in to start the last game of the road trip on Sunday.

While Zeiber had been a great athlete drafted straight out of high school from Bellevue, Ohio, he had struggled with his curve and his confidence during his latest stint in the minors. The talent was all there, and it was Jarred who had intently studied his tapes and methodically pleaded the case to Manager Leach for the case of bringing him into a new environment with players he knew could help make him flourish.

"So where have you been?" Syleanna hugged Sean as they sipped a Coors Light together in the furthest corner of the corner table. "I've been so proud of you, but why haven't you even called me in a week?"

"Babe, this thing is so stupid crazy that I can't even begin to explain." Sean started.

Taking another long drink, he was wondering if now was even the time to purge all of his guilt to the woman he so dearly cherished and admit to his inner angst. He quickly decided to just ease into the water.

"God, I love you so much, baby, and have missed you every single night. I guess the pressures of not even having any time off from losing the frigging college series to now have been draining me. Everywhere we go, all people are wanting is a piece of us for something, it's lunacy. I now have to wear a batting glove on my right hand just to ease the cramps of signing autographs!"

"Oh, I'm so glad you brought that up." Syleanna cleverly purred. "I need two autographed baseballs from the team to give to our cab drivers buddy. He's the one that gave us the tickets for tonight's game. Do you think that would be a problem for me?"

"Christ, Syleanna, now even you!" Sean laughed. "Naw, we can get that done tomorrow for sure. We all get great seats for family and friends, and I already got you and Carla in the players' girlfriends and wives section."

"Mickey Rourke won't be there, will he?" Syleanna cautiously inquired. "We had enough of him tonight, and he really gives me the creeps!"

"You guys were a hot topic tonight on TV, I guess." Sean disclosed. "The last reporter I had not only knew you were my girlfriend, but also made a big deal that you and Carla were friends of the 'old' team from back home."

"I had no idea that this thing had gotten so big everywhere!" Carla injected. "In Portsmouth, that's all they talk about on the radio and that morning show on MIX 99.3. The *Daily Times* now puts you all on the front page instead of the sports section."

Several hours of hometown relief quickly became a deadline as Jarred starting calling cabs to get the guys back to the hotel by 1:00 a.m. Slowly, the band of revelry disbanded as Sean and Syleanna said their goodnights. With an air-tight hug and a last warm and deep kiss, Sean couldn't hold back his emotions.

"You really don't know how great it was seeing you tonight, babe, and what a surprise! Maybe after the game tomorrow, we can get away by ourselves for a little while. I really need that right now. The game should be over by 4:00 p.m. and I should be free around 5:00 p.m. Let's do something fun!"

"Yea, I would love to!" Syleanna beamed, "Just remember that we fly out Sunday morning at 8:00 a.m."

The cab ride back to the hotel was full of giddiness from seeing old friends plus the guys that both Carla and Syleanna loved. Several rounds of the Rockies' best pure mountain water didn't hurt in enhancing the moment.

"So it sounds like you guys had a great time tonight, eh?" Julio inquired with a laugh.

"Oh, Julio, you can't believe it!" Carla shot back. "It was so great seeing everybody and that place….oh my god, they treated us all like rock stars!"

"I told you!" Julio insisted. "All of America and especially sports fans love that team because they are doing something that nobody thought could ever be done. You know my uncle used to play pro ball and was in the Angels' farm system for a while. He never made it to the big-show, but he told me that it is tough because everybody is always trying to tear everybody down trying to make it to the top.

"Once you get there, there is always somebody wanting your job and that's why it's tough to play as a team. The Vipers…the Eagles…they are just a bunch of guys that like each other and play because they love it! Everybody can see that!"

"That was very nice of you, Julio." Syleanna slightly slurred. "Thank you for sharing. We only love them because they're getting us great seats for the game tomorrow!"

As surprised laughter erupted with the trio, the cab quickly pulled up in front of the LAX Marriott Hotel.

"Hey, speaking of tickets," Julio said. "Did you girls help me out? Ira is pestering me like a hungry fly at a picnic about those balls."

"Oh, we asked them tonight and there is no problem. Are you working tomorrow?" Syleanna asked.

"Ah, tomorrow, I will be on day shift for a change. Can I pick you up and take you to the park again? It would be my honor."

"That would be great! Can you get us here at around 11:30 a.m.?" Carla asked while shoving an extra $20 bill into the hand of their new best friend.

"Sleep tight, ladies! I will see you in the manana!" said Julio as he pulled away from the hotel's porte-cochere and into the cool LA night.

8ᵀᴴ INNING

Saturday brought on another sold out Dodger Stadium crowd as the radio- sheen was a buzz on "KFWB Sports Talk." It was Charlie Stiener on the air yammering away and trying to help explain it all to the masses.

"No, it doesn't make any sense of what's going on here with this team, and really, that's the beauty of it all. Step back for just a second and as a fan of not only the Dodgers, but the game total. Isn't it refreshing that a totally screwball idea from a team that literally had nothing to lose could create this much excitement? Let's see…the Giants lose to Atlanta last night, and here you have the Vipers a mere game and a half from leaving the cellar. They're only two-games from catching the Dodgers and the rest of the log- jam in the National League West."

Laughing at himself for casually defending the enemy, Charlie Stiener did add one more thought-provoking stat to the equation.

"I know it sounds like I've switched caps here, but I'm just as stunned and amazed as everyone else considering that this whole thing for the Vipers started right after the All-Star break with the longest road trip in the Majors Leagues this year with fourteen games, and they are 10 and 2? C'mon, people, that is mind-frying amazing!"

"Hey look, it's another Ohioan here to keep the ship afloat!" Brooks Snyder playfully shouted out as Brad Zeiber, complete with bag in tow, cracked open the door and entered the visitor's clubhouse.

With a broad smile and a look of total bewilderment, Brad quickly broke the ice by asking if there were any early classes and directions to the student union.

"I think I have been to Bellevue before." Bombo Chadwick chimed in. "Isn't that the place where the entering the city and leaving the city sign is all on the same pole?"

"It's kind of like Portsmouth." Brad shot back. "Second Street is the next town over!"

As everyone stuck out their hands and welcomed the Vipers newest family addition, Jarred was also there to try and give Brad the Cliff Notes version of what was going on and make him feel a part of the club. Soon, Manager Tommy Leach entered the clubhouse and quickly whisked his young new hurler away for a more authoritative salutation to the "bigs."

"Welcome to the Vipers, Brad," Tommy started out as he slowly leaned back into his squeaky visitors manager's chair. "Looks like you were having a pretty fair season down there with the Mustangs, how's that arm feel?"

"Ah, the arm feels great sir!" Brad shot back. "I'm really thankful for this opportunity sir, and look forward to helping anyway I can!"

A lingering stare slowly mused into a smile as Manager Leach laid down the official ground rules.

"First of all, you don't work for Morgan Stanley, so suits and sirs don't apply here, just call me Tommy. Second, I really don't know what the buzz in the minors is about what's going on up here, but I can tell you that you've just stepped through the magic mirror into a baseball world like none that I've ever witnessed before… and that's for sure."

"Hey, I know!" Brad responded. "I'm just a no-name rookie call-up, and it was the hottest topic on some radio sports talk show playing in the cab ride over.. I'm here and just ready to do what I can…Tommy. I've even been working on my knuckleball!"

"Pug will be happy to hear all about that. By the way, the name Brad has a bit of a generic sound to it, and we already got one of those. Got anything better that you go by?"

"Uh…well…since I was a kid, people have called me 'Zebro.' It's kind of a nick-name." Brad bashfully admitted.

"Zebro it is!" Tommy slowly exhaled as he stood up from his chair, signifying this meeting was now adjourned.

"Let's go find Browning and a uniform that fits. We need you tomorrow, so lock and load. From everything I read in the newspaper this morning, we have yet another game to play today!"

If the sold-out Dodger Stadium had its hopes up on this day that things might be different from the last two, Gary Steinman and Catcher Doug Pouge put an instant end to that fantasy. It was almost like a throwback to the days of "The King and His Court" where you played with a pitcher, a catcher, a shortstop, and one outfielder.

Even though all nine of the Vipers were on the field, Gary Steinman's arm was a living, breathing entity of its own, scattering just four singles as he pitched his second complete game of the season blanking the Dodgers 2-0. Pouge launched a Chad Billingsley fast-ball into the right field bleachers along with "King Kong" Karl Smith aboard in the third inning to give Las Vegas all the scoring they would need on this day. Steinman struck out a career fifteen while limiting the Dodgers to a diet of routine ground-outs and a few lazy fly balls into the Chavez greenery. Now standing with an 11-2 record on the road trip, things started to take on a whole new shade of interesting.

"You put a couple of old dogs in a pen with a bunch of pups, and just watch the difference!" Cisco Wheeler beamed to his CEO as he sliced another piece of prime-rib from his plate. "I've never seen those two work together like they did out there today. It was an amazing thing to watch! What did you think, Brandon?"

While both Cisco Wheeler and Brandon Briggs wound down enjoying a quiet table at Taylors Steak House on West Eighth Street, the after-game euphoria was hard to harness.

"An incredible game today it was Cisco!" Brandon began. "I so remember when we couldn't trade either one of those guys for a shop-vac and a bag of balls. I always knew Gary had it in him, but Pouge today; wow! He's the one that I really have seen kick it into an extra gear that I wasn't sure he really had in him. The way he handles these pitchers is pure wizardry."

"You know we picked up another game? The Giants lost again, and we are now just a half game from catching them and finally getting out of the damn cellar." Cisco bragged, "Think about that for a minute?"

Smiling, Brandon Briggs was seductively cool with his answer. "I do, Cisco, every single day…I do."

Sipping slowly from his martini, the big man held his next thought close until he was able to structure his worrisome observation into words.

"Brandon, I know you realize we have had the luxury of almost a three-week road trip to test this thing out, but we go home tomorrow. I have to ask you honestly, Brandon, are we anywhere close to being ready for Monday night?'

"I think so." echoed the reassurance that his boss desperately wanted to hear. "You know it's been almost eight years since we've had a sell-out."

Looking up from a hand-scribbled checklist written on the back of a steak sauce-stained napkin, Wheeler continued to follow his notes.

"Wayne Newton's manager called me again today needing twenty tickets and I told him he could only have ten. He kind of got pissy until I told him that I had Tony Orlando already on standby. That seemed to calm him down a bit."

"What about all the freebies that I know you've been dealing with?" Briggs added. "I know Gloria has had the phone grafted to her face just answering it."

"Let's see, of course, the comp-ticket list has blown up as I knew that it would. Every damn entertainer that never cared about us before is now calling in every favor they can think of. You'll love this one. David Copperfield needed Diamond Seats because he claimed we had a special night here back in our first season where he made a player disappear!"

"Too bad, it couldn't have been Toots Randall, and it's a shame he didn't make it stick!" Briggs said with a sarcastic smile. "Access denied! Seriously, I really think we are OK. Jack Pattie has been in contact with me about every day on all things. It's really kind of nice to get a chance to worry about things like this for a change."

Sensing a small tone of relief, Brandon added his own sauce of praise to his worrisome boss. "It's gonna be a really special night, and I know it, Cisco, because you've waited a long time for this. My wish is that you of all of our people will just sit back and soak it all up. Monday night will be your time, my friend, all yours."

The cab was destined to "The Cajun House" in El Monte as the quirt conversation in the back seat was between a couple of soul-starved friends who were like sponges. Sean Deeters and Syleanna Griffin opened up honestly with views of the new world in which they were now thrust and of course the game.

"I sucked bad today, Syl." Sean admitted. "Going 0-4 is not me!"

"But you won!" came Syleanna's supportive response. "You did great! Maybe Friday night just wore you out a bit."

That attempted humor didn't carry much weight on a hitter who was supposed to be one of the offensive cogs to the machinery. Finally deciding to let it all go for a while, Sean smiled and slowly put his arm around her shoulder and was resolved to just let the moment ride.

"You're so right, babe. I just get too wrapped up in all this sometimes. It's like when I was when playing with the Eagles, but now it's a hundred times worse. By the way, I guess you can pay the ransom now."

Opening up his travel satchel, Sean showed her three-baseballs all covered in signatures of the entire Vipers team. As both shared a mutual laugh, Syleanna quickly gave Sean an exaggerated kiss on the cheek.

"I already have Julio scheduled to pick us up at the airport in the morning. I guess I can pay my debt in full before I leave."

"Hell!" shot back Sean. "You could pay off the entire national debt with these things. Do you have any idea what the asking price is on eBay for just one of them beauties? Don't be surprised if Julio and his buddy don't end up buying a small island in the Caribbean and they disappear forever!"

The cab whisked the couple up to the front door, as they casually hopped out and headed toward the rarity they both knew was so precious.

"A table for two please." Sean spoke to the lady behind the counter.

"Do you have a reservation?" she smiled and asked.

"Well, no…we've never been here before." Sean sheepishly mumbled. "We just came from the ball-park and didn't realize they were needed."

"It looks like we have an hour wait for a table for two. Can I put your name on the list?"

Rolling his eyes as he glanced at Syleanna, he knew the cab was already long-gone, and at this point, they were pretty much stranded.

"An hour? You're kidding me. Well, I guess we have no choice. The name's Deeters, Sean Deeters."

It was at that point a busboy just happened to be walking by the hostess stand and overheard the awkward exchange. Stopping in his tracks, a burst of wide-eyed enthusiasm suddenly captured the moment.

"Sean Deeters! Sean Deeters! Hey, you that dude on that baseball team that keep harshing our home boy's brother!" He laughed. "Give us some relief!'"

Turning to the lady holding the menus, the young man toned down his pitch to a loud whisper as the persuasion of favor was now fully in process.

"You got to squeeze this guy and his lady in somewhere, Britney. If you don't and he gets angry, I mean really, we ain't got no chance of winning tomorrow and you will be the one responsible for the Los Angeles Dodgers getting their butts swept by the Las Vegas Vipers. Can you live with that?"

As smiles erupted, it was a good-hearted wink to Sean and Syleanna from Hank the busboy that sealed the deal.

"Come with me." were the next words spoken as the couple followed the hostess through the packed room and up to a quiet corner table.

"Cynthia will be your server and she will be right with you. Can I get you something from the bar?"

Sean quickly threw out their beverage of choice. "A couple of Coors Lights will just fine. Thanks."

Grabbing her hands from across the table, Sean couldn't help to notice just how radiant Syleanna looked under The Cajun House's soft lighting. The past month had robbed him of so many things that he knew he had left behind. Looking into her dark hazel eyes was indeed a soul-cleansing moment as he also intuited that confession time was near. Soaking up the quiet, both lightly chatted about the day, the game, and how life as they knew it had been dramatically altered all from an eccentric millionaire's whimsical design.

"It's been tough, really tough." admitted Sean. "When we all left to come here from Portsmouth, I know some of the guys handled the change of scenery different. I know that Cliff, Mitch, Brooks, they kind of like the challenge and all the attention that's been thrown on us. It really doesn't bother them, but I'm not built like that."

"I know that, honey. This crazy thing has been tough on me too. When you ignored me for a week, I wasn't sure what was going on." Syleanna vented.

"It all kind of started after you guys were on the David Letterman show, and after that, you just disappeared on me!"

Well, I really need to talk to you about that night." Sean slowly murmured. "That wasn't one of my best evenings, and I have felt very bad about it ever since."

"Bad about what?" came Syleanna's natural response.

"This thing has bothered me to the point that I have a hard time, and I mean from concentrating on the game, this circus life of mine, and everything else! You mean the world to me Syl and I love you, but I did something in a weak moment that I am very ashamed of. I've been waiting to tell you about it so that I could just set the record clean, but I just didn't know how."

With now the full attention of Syleanna Griffin, Sean Deeters painfully went back to the night of he and Cliff's impromptu appearance on Letterman and detailed how it all fell into a happenstance situation. He painfully explained the "card lady" and how naïve he was when Cliff thought she was flirting with him. Syleanna sat silent as Sean then got to the point where she showed up at his room and came knocking on his door. After the next admission, Syleanna sternly grasped ahold of a key point of the conversation.

"You let her into your room?" The silent pause afterward was deafening.

"Honey, we just talked, and that's it! And, I felt very cheap about it, but I have been so lonely through this whole damn thing and she was being really pushy. I just needed someone to talk to, I guess." Sean countered. "I know what she came for, but I swear, we just talked and that was it!"

"So what time did she leave?" came her chippy inquiry.

"About 5:30 a.m. I guess" Sean admitted. "She knew from the beginning, nothing was going to happen between us, so we just talked about the team, New York City, and then you."

"That must have been interesting." Syleanna countered. "She must have been very impressed on hearing all about the girl back home while she was trying to make it with a member of 'America's' team."

"Come on, babe, this thing has been eating me alive and I just needed to tell you. I could have kept it a big dark secret if I wanted to, but I can't do that with you, Syl. Do I at least get any kind of points for honesty?"

Syleanna Griffin's mind was now transfixed and racing upon the admission that the only love in her life has admittedly spent close quarters with another woman. It was simply a mind-set that she couldn't determine the reason between need and desire.

As most guys know, getting attention is never the issue. How you handle that extra burst of superfluous awareness is really all that ever really matters. Being instantly exalted to national celebrity status from just a grounded small-town boy would be a wavering assignment for most, but Sean Deeters was different.

"I really don't know what to say." The silence was again broken. "Sean, I love you and have always felt that we were in my special place where others really couldn't go, but I'm not so sure now. If you let some 'pushy floosy' just knocks on your door in the middle of the night and then let her in, whether you did her or not, that still hurts!"

Damage control went from bad to worse as the evening wore on. What started out as a cherry and light atmosphere quickly turned awkward and dark as the purging of Sean's little secret wasn't accepted as he had hoped. After dinner, the plan was to spend some quiet time together, but things quickly changed.

"I'm going to call Julio and have him take me back to the Marriott." Sean heard Syleanna softly say." We have a plane to catch early in the morning, and I really don't feel like doing anything else tonight."

It's delicate times such as these that words can be turned into weapons and anger can be the driver's engine.

"Damn it, Syleanna!" Sean erupted. "So this is what I get for trying to share with you what and where my life has gone. Is that it really? So now you're just going to get up and leave? Screw me for trying to be totally honest, that's just fine!"

Standing up from the table, he quickly reached into his man pouch and deposited three signed baseballs into her purse. Guilt can often become a major force in any disagreement as it was now being used as a final foray.

"Thanks so very much for caring about me." he continued, "Take these and barter your way all the way back to Portsmouth."

With fire in his eyes and a cracking voice; Sean's final decree was delivered, "Syleanna, someday, I really do hope you can understand everything that's going on with me right now. Have a nice flight home…I'm out of here!"

With that, the Vipers' right fielder quickly turned and walked through "The Cajun House" restaurant and up to the cab stand at the front door. Climbing in, he quickly instructed the driver where to go and was then quickly whisked off into the LA night.

"You mean he just got up from the table and walked out on you, just like that?" Julio asked in astonishment.

The ride home was more of a therapy session than a LA cab fare for Syleanna Griffin and her new trusted friend as they both opened up on dissecting the events of the evening, sharing both comfort and confusion.

"I just don't understand why he would even tell me something like that, Julio. I think I would have just kept that all to myself. If he didn't do anything with her, then why get me all bitchy and involved?"

"Hey, it's crazy." Julio interrupted. "I just know that I got lots of my guy friends that I know who…well…do get around with the ladies and they would never ever open up about being with another woman like your man did tonight."

Laughingly, he tried to inject a little humor with his observation as he quickly added, "If they did, the homicide rate in this town would triple!"

Words of encouragement continued to flow from the front seat to the back until they finally pulled up in front of their destination.

"Julio, what can I say?" Syleanna began. "Thank you so much for everything you did for us this weekend and adopting me and Carla as your designated riders."

"Aww, it's been my pleasure, little girl. Now, you won't need me in the morning as the hotel has the shuttle that will pick you up right here and take you straight to the airport."

As the goodbyes continued, Syleanna suddenly remembered the precious cargo she was carrying in her purse.

"Oh…Julio, I can't forget these now, can I?"

Smiling, she reached in and handed Julio three autographed baseballs to now complete the promised deal and with that an entrusting a friendship she knew was the genuine article.

"Ah, thank you so much! Ira can now reduce his Xanax prescription to just a moderate dose." Julio chuckled. "I really appreciate this and of course your friendship. You have my card, keep it so when you come back or if you need anything, please, give me a call anytime! And your boyfriend, ah…don't worry my cuteness. Everything will work its way out. I promise you."

Giving Julio a hug, she turned and headed up the sidewalk and into the Marriott. Her mind now swirling with so much, Syleanna suddenly remembered how fragile she had felt flying into LA for the weekend. On leaving, she thought it funny how it now seemed to have been replaced with a new feeling of strength and purpose.

With less than two months before the end of baseball's regular season, the American League was being overshadowed from the developments in Las Vegas, but indeed under the radar as it had also become quite a storyboard of interest.

The heavily favored Yankees were creating some distance in the American League East while both the Twins and Athletics were fighting every night for dominant survival in their respective divisions. The Central was a dog fight with Minnesota, Detroit, and Chicago while the American League West was a two-team street fight between Oakland and the Los Angeles Angels of Anaheim.

The New York Yankees newest utility player Toots Randall quietly ended up dropping his lawsuit against the Vipers rather quickly on the advice of the Yankees CEO Brian Cashman. By changing leagues as well as not being considered an everyday player, Cashman looked at Randall's personal differences with his former team as simply that. One thing that Brian Cashman didn't tolerate or want was any superfluous team distractions and could care less of Randall's vendetta and made it verbally known.

In a closed-door meeting, he urged Randall to simply look ahead and consider the task at hand which was getting the Bronx Bombers to the World Series. The next day, in a short and prepared press release, Toots Randall thanked the staff and management of the Las Vegas Vipers for his tenure and announced that he had dropped his class action lawsuit through the Players Union. He further elaborated that his new mission statement was to now help the New York Yankees become the world champions. For anyone who knew Randall very well, they also knew that Brian Cashman was not only behind the decision, but also the formal writing.

On reading the story in the sports page, Doug Pouge laughed out loud, making the candid observation, "Toots Randall wouldn't know the difference between a mission statement and his own bank statement! I wonder if Cashman also promised to give him his lunch money every day!"

The clubhouse chatter on the final game of the road series was light and loose.

All the players were packing their gear getting ready for the chartered flight home after the final game. Sundays in Major League Baseball are always a little busier and hectic as you are either headed home or someplace else. In this case sporting an 11-2 record under the most extraordinary of circumstances was more than just a little different as the former Bentley State Eagles weren't really going home.

Cliff Collier spotted Sean Deeters sitting quietly at his locker and thought it a good time to perhaps break the ice.

"Hey, buddy, how's it going? I guess they got off OK from the airport this morning. Didn't know if you knew."

Still sitting silently in front of his locker, Sean continued to look ahead without an immediate answer.

"I know you guys had a problem last night. C'mon,-Christ, Carla and her are like sisters and what's that say about us!" Cliff Collier exclaimed.

Turning and slowly looking up to Cliff, Sean's cold stare before he spoke was something that he had never seen before in his best friend and teammate.

"If you could go back, I mean like back before all this stuff happened, would you?" he asked.

Cliff could see that there was something really big going on inside Sean's head and realized quickly that it needed to be handled with all the correct answers. Pausing before he spoke, the Viper's Center Fielder and his best friend knew this could be a flashpoint moment.

"What do you mean going back in time and what? Never doing this and saying 'no' of the opportunity to everything we're going through right now? Like, just ending up being the runner-ups in the College World Series and then what? Just go back to school and finish our degrees while we could be partying it up and drinking beer at all our old places to just sit there and talk about our past and how fucking wonderful we were. Is that seriously what you're asking me?"

After a short pause, Sean's one word answer spoke volumes, "Yea."

"Come on, buddy, get real. That's not me and…it's definitely not you. So you and Syleanna had a blow-up over that damn woman from the Letterman thing and I really do see both sides. Didn't I tell you she wanted to jump your bones and you didn't listen? So, she tracks you down and then tries to make you her new 'one-night boyfriend,' I get it! I was there, but trying to explain all of that to the love of your life is absolutely mental-illness unless you really had something to hide."

Cliff's rant stirred the ambers of fire as his best buddy rose from the ashes.

"I'm not hiding anything from anybody! I just told her the truth and tried to be honest to somebody that I trusted, and then all this shit happens!"

"Hey, I just suggest you wait until she gets home and settles down. Then you can call her and have a nice long talk about it. Until then, you got to move all this white-noise to the right side of your brain. We have another game in just about an hour in case you forgot."

They both instantly exchanged gazes that looked deep into each other's souls as Cliff Collier nodded, turned, and quietly went back to his cubicle to finish dressing. In another corner of the Dodgers visiting club-house, another young man named Brad Zeiber was preparing for the biggest day in his young life.

Pitching Coach Tom Browning was laying out the plan of attack to try and simplify and diffuse the nerves of his first time Major League starter. It was again something Browning quietly realized that he had pretty much cornered the market on this season.

"Eithier and Kemp will kill you on the high fast-ball, Zebro. Keep it low and outside on both those guys. Loney and Navarro are both suckers for a good curve."

"Garciaparra is streaky, but when he's hot, he can damn near hit anything you throw him. How's the arm feel?"

"I'm strong, Coach, just a little antsy." Zeiber admitted.

21 DOWN IN VEGAS

"Understandable, just throw to what Pogue is calling for and hit the glove." The blunt force trauma of simplification was one of Tom Browning's strengths.

"I take it you played Little League, right? He asked.

"Of course I did!" Brad laughed, feeling that a sermon would soon follow.

"Too many guys when they get here simply forget everything they ever learned. I've seen it a hundred-times." Browning pontificated. "Once you fly in a plane instead of ride in a bus, it's like all these fancy digs and conveniences freak them out. I never could understand why that happens. It's still the same damn game you've always played since you were nine-years old."

Standing up from the bench, Browning playfully flipped Brad Zeiber with his towel. As he started to leave, he suddenly stopped and turned back to ask his protégé one more question.

"Hey, I forgot to ask. Were you any good in Little League?"

"The best summer I ever spent was in Williamsport!" Brad Zeiber shot back with a grin.

"Smart-ass!"

Back in Las Vegas, the natives were restless to welcome home a team they had yet been able to see live. Since the Vipers lost their TV contract several years back, KVPR-AM was their only source, and it was on in every business and casino in town. A city that had literally forgot they had a Major League Baseball team now couldn't get enough.

The Giants were again losing on this Sunday, meaning that another win today would unlock the cellar door for the first time this late in the season, and a new occupant would now be living with the furnace and the old lawn mowers.

One individual who couldn't wait to return home was Vipers' play-by-play announcer Ralph Hacker.

"It's the bottom of the fifth and we're back with no score in the ravine as it's been a pitcher's paradise so far in the final game of this lengthy road trip, and hopefully, just five more innings until we can once again pack up and head east. Pete Harnisch, do you agree?"

"Sure do, Ralph! A win today would make it a most unbelievable tour of duty as I am truly impressed with the effort of this kid Brad Zeiber today for the Vipers. In his Major League debut, he's given up just three-hits and he has six strikeouts so far which shows me that he's really mixing up his stuff nicely."

Three up and three down brought the top of the order for Las Vegas in the sixth. Sean Deeters had gone 0-2, looking at a couple of called third strikes and now stood at the plate to try and get something going. Cliff Collier had noticed that his friend was in another zone and not a good place. Typically, Sean was a cheer leader and a bench scooter. On this day, he kept to himself and his absence of spirit was more than just evident.

"Strike-three was once again the agenizing call of fortitude. Umpire Ric Robinson rang him up with the bat still solidly resting on his shoulder. This time, Hitting Coach Von Hayes had seen enough and wasn't going to let him sit alone.

"What are you looking for out there, Sean?" Hayes asked. "That was right in your wheel house and you sat on it."

"I'm sorry, Von," Sean mumbled. "It looked like a slider."

After an awkward moment of silence, Von Hayes slapped him on the knee and got up. The unspoken word in a dugout can sometimes be the loudest voice of all.

"You'll get him next time." Von said as he turned and headed back up to the top of the stairs.

Manager Tommy Leach had a decision in the sixth-inning to either pull Brad Zeiber after a stellar performance, or let him try to nail down three more.

"Hey, kid, ya think you can give me one more?" he asked.

"One more, yea, sure Tommy…I think I can do that!"

"Get me through the sixth, and I'll have Burkes and Fuller ready to finish it off. You're showing me something out there today, Zebro. Give me three more outs now and you're off the hook for Christmas."

Ralph Hacker and Pete Harnisch threw the entire complimentary cart at the Vipers' young pitcher as he once again retuned to the mound to face Raphael Furcal, J.D. Drew, and pinch hitter Jeff Kent.

21 DOWN IN VEGAS

"What a shot in the arm this kid has been today on a team that has had a wholesale license on unexpected miracles. Today, they may have just found another one!" Ralph Hacker embellished. "Giving up just three hits on the afternoon, he now faces perhaps the Dodgers' most formidable three. The Vipers' bullpen is now busy so this is probably the last inning of work for Mr. Zebro today."

Raphael Furcal took a full count before hitting a routine ground ball to Gary Duzan at short that racked up the first out. All afternoon long, J.D. Drew had been a little too aggressive at the plate and Zeiber knew it. With a 2-2 count on one of the Dodgers' power plants, it was time for a little magic.

"Whoa, what was that?" Hacker exclaimed. "A knuckler that looked like a beach ball dancing right down the middle of Daytona, and it locked up Drew like a career felon for a called strike three!"

Pete Harnisch also added to the moment, "It obviously didn't take long for Tom Browning to inflict the "knucklehead" philosophy of the team on Zeiber, Ralph. I have no idea how long he has thrown that pitch, but I can tell you that in a clutch situation against one of the best in the business; it was perfection!"

Jeff Kent now stepped to the plate with two out and bases empty. Still a no-score game, the young kid from Belleview, Ohio, was now just one out away from doing everything that was asked of him.

"A one ball, two strike count on Kent." As again, Ralph Hacker was in the midst of setting up the moment. "There's a swing and a high fly ball to right field. Sean Deeters has it in his sights, he's under it, and…it's off his glove and now rolling to the fence in center! Kent has rounded first and is headed for second.

"Deeters is still trying to coral the ball as Kent now makes the big turn and is digging for third. The ball rebounds from the bottom of the fence and now kicks out toward left. Kent is now rounding third and headed for home. Collier picks up the ball, and here comes the throw to the plate…it's way off line, and Jeff Kent has just hit an inside the park home run on a ball misplayed by Sean Deeters in right! Unbelievable! "

"That ball just hit the top of his glove as he tried to one-hand it." Harnisch added. "I hate to say it, Ralph, but that's the first thing they teach you in Little League and that is use both hands!"

"It's one to nothing here in the bottom of the sixth, and I just have to be honest, Pete, Sean Deeters' head is not in this game today, it's clearly evident. He has looked totally lost at the plate, and that was as catchable a fly-ball that anybody could have ever asked for. Instead of an easy out that would have ended the inning, the Vipers are now down by one as Kenny Loften steps to the plate."

Catcher Doug Pouge went out to the mound to give his young hurler a little time to re-group as the buzz in the stands was still electric. Witnessing a four-base error is amazing in itself, but now the Dodgers had a 1-0 lead late in the game as umpire Ric Robinson took his mandatory "break it up" stroll to the mound.

"Just throw it where I put it, kid. You'll be OK." Pouge said as he turned and headed back to the plate.

Brad Zeiber followed the veteran's instructions to the letter and ended the sixth- inning, forcing Lofton to pop up into foul territory on the first base side. Back in the dugout, Manager Tommy Leach didn't wait long to try and find some answers.

"What the hell happened out there, Deeters? How in the shit-fire could you drop a ball like that?

"Sorry, skip…I just misjudged it." Sean sheepishly replied.

"Misjudged it? Christ! It was doing everything it could to find the pocket of your glove with a map, take a seat! Shepard, get loose, you're going in for Deeters!"

Luke Shepard jumped up and headed out to warm up his arm and replace Sean Deeters in right field. Stunned, Sean looked at his manager in disbelief. It seemed like an hour of silence before he finally heard himself ask, "Are you benching me? I mean like…right now?"

"We'll talk later." Leach shot back with a cold icy stare. "We have a game to try and win, and I want my nine best chances out there to do it."

"It's the top of the seventh, and it looks as if Sean Deeters has been pulled from the lineup as Luke Shepard is now in right field and batting in the ninth-spot. Jeremy Burkes will be out to pitch the bottom of the seventh, and he will now bat in the lead-off spot," Ralph Hacker explained. "Pete Harnisch, what do you make of that move?"

"Honestly, it looks like simple dog-house mathematics to me." Harnisch said, laughing. "Obviously, Leach had enough of what he determined was less than heads-up play from his young right fielder and did something about it. You really don't see that much anymore up here anymore. Nobody wants to get shown up during a game, but let me tell you, as a former player, I find it kind of refreshing!"

Greg Maddox had been firing aspirin tablets all day and continued to keep the Vipers guessing in the top of the seventh sitting them down in order. As Jeremy Burkes took to the mound in the bottom of the seventh, his control was instantly a problem as the first two Dodgers visited the bases on just eight-straight pitches.

"Time!" Leach bellowed from the dugout. "Pug, get out there and see what the hell's going on with him!"

As pitching coach Tom Browning trotted to the mound, he noticed the body language of one of his most reliable hurlers to be a bit distressed. Looking down at the rubber with his shoulders slumped was not the usual image he was accustomed to seeing.

"What's up, Buckles?" Browning asked. "Did they move the plate back on you today or what?"

"Naw, I'm OK. I'm just a little out of focus I guess. Seeing Sean get the hook like that and all…I've been playing ball with him since I was eleven and never ever dreamed that something like that could happen, especially to him."

Realizing that the DNA makeup of this team was like none he had ever seen before and the "together factor" was the only way they knew how to play, Tom Browning quickly switched gears from a quick ass -hewing to some Solomon-like wisdom.

"Don't worry about Sean, we'll get him fixed, I promise you that. It's these guys dressed in the blue that want to see him and us fail. Do you honestly know what they're doing right now? I can tell you because I've been there. They're all over there laughing it up right now about how some greenhorn college kid played a pop up in a run. Think about that! If you want to keep your buddies back, just do what you've always done. Bare-down and throw strikes against these bastards!"

Browning turned and left the dirt pile quickly looking back to see that Burkes was now standing erect on the hill with shoulders squared and eyeballing straight into the eyes of the enemy. It quickly appeared that his message had been received. In the booth, Ralph Hacker and Pete Harnisch were now set up to call the late-inning action on KVPR-AM.

"It's Russel Martin on first and Matt Kemp standing on second with nobody out here in the bottom of the seventh and Olmedo Saenz to the plate. One thing to note is that Saenz really can fly!"

"Right you are, Ralph. Olmedo is leading the Dodgers in stolen bases and is considered not only one of the fastest players on the team, but in all of baseball."

As if on que, the first pitch from Burkes to Saenz, he squared the head of the bat beautifully and laid down a dribbler toward third.

John Gambill quickly gets there, one handed it, and throwing off balance got the ball in the air and toward first. The thump of the cleat was a clear winner over the sound of ball meeting mitt on a very close play. Umpire Tim McClellan was throwing arms in both directions as the Dodger Stadium Crowd now sensed a total meltdown was on the way as the bases were now loaded with nobody out. Catcher Doug Pogue trotted out to the mound for a couple words of encouragement.

"Not your fault, not your fault. You put it right where I wanted it. Shake it off and let's get two. Bring it first to me if it's on the ground."

It was a 2-2 pitch that had outfielder Andre Ethier swinging a little late and under the ball, sending a sky-high pop up over second. With the infield fly rule in effect, Brooks Snyder hauled it in as it registered one out while keeping everybody in place.

"Wow, Jeremy Burkes was lucky on that one!" Ralph Hacker noted. "That was Andre's pitch to eat, and he most certainly 'Thanksgiving tabled' it on that one!"

Laughing, Pete Harnisch couldn't resist asking about his sidekick's snappy analogy on what a major holiday had to do with a flyball and lauded for interpretation.

"Peter, it's simple." Ralph stated. "Everybody knows that if your Thanksgiving Day meal is set for five, the kitchen is always crammed by four-thirty, so, in other words, he got there a little early!"

"Exactly," Harnisch retorted, "and he never got a chance to taste the giblets!"

Infielder James Loney now stepped to the plate with designs on giving the Dodgers some breathing room. Burkes seemed to have settled back into a rhythm and was throwing some hard strikes with some jump to his slider. After fouling off eight pitches in a row, Loney now held on to a 3-2 count that couldn't last forever. Again, Ralph Hacker had the call.

"Burkes is once again on the mound and toeing the rubber… he's set, and the pitch. Loney swings and sends a high fly to shallow right field. Luke Shepard is under it, and makes the 'catch…and now here comes Martin to the plate! No way! Shepard cocks and throws, it's on line, and…he's out by the proverbial country mile! What a throw from Luke Shepard to end the inning! That was as good an assist as you'll ever see, Pete!"

"Two things happened on that play." Harnisch injected. "First, it's always a liability to send a catcher on a play like that simply because of the speed factor. Second, they didn't fool Shepard for a little bit. As soon as he got the ball, he instantly fired it home and it was the proverbial seed. The Dodger blue may have gambled a bit too much on that one because he had just replaced Deeters, and I don't think they expected him to be prepared to make that kind of throw. There's gotta be some Boy Scout training in there somewhere."

While baseball drama was developing into the late Los Angeles afternoon, two tired and weary travelers where now entering the city limits of Portsmouth, Ohio. While there was plenty of in-flight gab time opportunities plus a two-hour ride home from the airport, Syleanna Griffin and Carla Harris spent most of their travel-time uncharacteristically quiet and to themselves.

Carla knew that Syleanna was hurting and chose not to engage the process. They had initially discussed the past evening's developments on Syleanna's return to the hotel room, but the re-hashing of it all again was way too tedious of a topic. Pulling up into Syleanna's driveway, Carla hopped out to help get her things out of the trunk.

"Well, girlfriend, this is where the adventure ends…for now." Carla laughed. "Three days in that crazy place and I'm ready for the home and my pajamas!"

Feigning laughter, Syleanna gathered her bags and tote as she turned to head up the sidewalk and into to the house. Looking at Carla, she couldn't hold back one last puzzling query.

"If he didn't do anything with her, why would he even tell me at all? I still can't get over all that. It's almost like he was like making a confession of some kind to me about a crime that he said he didn't commit."

"Syl, look at the circumstances…he's a guy!" Carla responded. "You've been together since grade-school. He's now on the cover of magazines, TV shows, and tabloids. Maybe he was just preparing you for what's really happening in his world now. I would just lighten up and call him after the game tonight. Work it out, sister. I'm tired and heading home to a bubble bath and an early night."

Giving each other a comforting hug, Syleanna slowly walked up the front door and past the swing where she and Sean had spent many summer nights sitting and talking about the game he so dearly loves. Turning the key and sliding through the door, bags were quickly dropped exactly where they lay.

Assessing her mood into a more leisurely direction, Syleanna grabbed the remote control and slowly stretched out on the couch to try and find something to try and take her mind off all the craziness of the past twenty-four hours. Surfing through the endless sea of channels, she finally landed on *"Entertainment Tonight."*

Listening to Mary Hart yammer on about Johnny Depp, Nicholas Cage, and Justin Timberlake started to accomplish the result of what she really wanted as a quiet fog began to settle in and her eyelids began to get heavy. All of that came to crashing halt as Syleanna Griffin was jolted back to life on Mary's final wrap-up.

21 DOWN IN VEGAS

"The Las Vegas Vipers baseball team is all the talk in sports, and tomorrow on *Entertainment Tonight,* we have an exclusive interview on "Real or Is It Rumor" with a lady who says she spent the night with one of the star players from the baseball team America can't get enough of. Don't miss that and our exclusive coverage of Brad and Angelina as Hollywood's newest power couple on "Story from Studio 4."

9TH INNING

Staring intently at the lineup card, Vipers Manager Tommy Leach was joined by another; it was Jarred Brewster. Now the top of the ninth and it was the Dodgers still leading by one as their ace and closer Jonathon Broxton had been waved in from the bullpen.

"Hey, Tommy, I got something for you." Brewster uttered.

Jarred's comment was met with stone-cold silence as Leach continued to weigh in on his late-inning options.

"I think Bombo might be your man here." Brewster again offered.

Finally turning to address his young and opinionated advisor, Leach was obviously not in the best of moods.

"What are you talking about, Brewster?" came Tommy's gruff response.

"Broxton and how he throws to hitters he's never seen, I think that Bombo would have a great shot at hitting him hard."

Still taken off guard by Jarred Brewster's odd-timing in bringing his studious knowledge to the table, Tommy Leach solidly learned early that there usually was some pretty good substance to his protégés observations.

"Why's that?" came his quick and hurried answer.

"The book on him is that he throws that rising fast-ball to the letters on players that he's never seen before. I think if you pinch-hit Chadwick here, you might be surprised to see what he can do." Brewster added. "That is for sure his pitch to hit."

21 DOWN IN VEGAS

First baseman Bombo Chadwick had been taken out of the lineup for the day for rest as utility player as Terrance Kennedy had been filling in at first. He was due up fourth in the bottom of the ninth inning behind Snyder, Shepard, and Duzan.

Jonathon Broxton was as big as a barn and really could intimidate players late in the game. He had started out the season at the Dodgers AAA level, but was quickly promoted by allowing no runs in his first eleven appearances garnering quick favor from Dodger Manager Grady Little. Coming into this game, Broxton had a stellar 2.21 era and seldom gave in with runners in scoring position.

The top of the ninth saw Vipers second baseman Brooks Snyder become one of Broxton's ninety-nine strike-outs for the season. That brought up right fielder Luke Shepard. It was his timely hit against Georgia in the College World Series that kept a last-inning rally alive for an Eagles win that stunned the Bulldogs as one of the favored teams to take it all. Luke Shepard was known for having ice water for blood anytime he stepped to the plate in a must-do situation. Running the count full, he once again lived up to the back of his baseball card.

"Broxton sets, he pitches…it's a line-drive screamer up the middle and the Vipers now have one on and one out!" Ralph Hacker again transferred his Viper excitement into the microphone. "Broxton not happy at all on that one, Pete, as now Shortstop Gary Duzan steps to the plate, and he's not fooling anybody in the house as to what he's up there to do."

Jonathon Broxton was still pissed at himself for giving Shepard such a hittable pitch and stared in hard at Russel Martin for the sign. With the pitch, Gary Duzan squared to bunt, but it was a ball low. All Dodger infielders were now on alert and playing in as Broxton's second pitch was again bunted, but foul. With a 1-1 count, "The Duz" did what he was asked and put a slow roller down and in front of the plate. Catcher Russel Martin was quick to the ball, but realized that Shepard had been off with the pitch and his only play was at first. With two-out and Luke Shepard at second, Bombo Chadwick heard his number called.

"Bombo, grab a bat and step in there for Kennedy!" Manager Tommy Leach bellowed. "And end this one quick. We have a plane to catch at 7:00 p.m. and I want to go home, hear me!"

"Two outs, one on, and Broxton going for the Dodgers save!" Hacker again lamented. "The Vipers are 11–2 on this brutal fourteen-game road trip, and even if they lose today in the final, 11–3 going home ain't too bad, Peter."

"Believe it or not, the Giants lost again today on a ninth-inning grand slam by Rich Purdy. They were up by three going in, and that has to take a toll on the guys in front of us," Harnisch added.

"Bombo Chadwick now to the plate as a pinch-hitter for Terrance Kennedy," Harnisch noted. "Chadwick has been hitting at a .288 clip since joining the Vipers and has added three home runs as well. This young man has really made a presence on this team as a leader."

Chadwick watched and reacted as Broxton tried nibbling at the corners trying to get the Vipers' first baseman to go for some garbage. Growing up, it was always the Cincinnati Reds Tony Perez that he modeled his style after to be the clutch player that he had become. As Chadwick stood solidly at the plate with a 2-2 count, Bombo watched as a fidgety Jonathon Broxton tried to put him away on a pitch that was high and straight down the middle; on this day, it didn't happen.

"Chadwick swings, and there –she- goes!" Hacker yelled. "It's long, high, and deep into the sun- decks in left center field. See ya later…it's a tater!

"Bombo Chadwick feasts on a Jonathon Broxton fast-ball and launches it deep into the ravine as the Vipers now take a 2-1 lead here in the bottom of the ninth."

Pete Harnisch was also rapturous as the entire team met for a group-scrum at home plate.

"In all my years with the Astros and all the rest of my time in professional baseball, I have never seen anything that comes close to what we have witnessed now into game fourteen! You couldn't script this excitement in a book or in a movie. Day after day these young guys just keep coming back and performing the impossible.

21 DOWN IN VEGAS

Cliff Collier is waiting to step up to the plate as Ernie Fuller is now warming up, and I assume we'll see him in the bottom of the ninth!"

Blown saves are a reliever's worst nightmare, and it was the Vipers center-fielder that assumed the wrath of Jonathon Broxton's embarrassment as he sat him down on three straight blazing pitches to end the inning.

A ninth inning crowd that had just given up a lead to his team was "Dirty Ernie" Fuller's relish and mustard. He lived for making temporary disappointment into a real and forever thing.

Fuller had the insipid personality that would laugh at the ability to make people drive home mad from the ball-yard because thinking of him and grumbling about their team as they left was an emotion that he knew that he could personally inflict upon thousands.

On this final road game of the Vipers second season, he wanted to make them suffer! It was a quick thirteen-pitch ninth-inning to Martin, Kemp, and, Furcal as it was now time to let the misery begin.

Las Vegas Review-Journal
Larry Mondello

(Las Vegas) Over the years, there have been many strange and unique acts of illusion introduced to the Las Vegas Strip, but few more anticipated than the real act of magic with the return of a baseball team that has transformed themselves from perennial losers into instant winners. Following a 2-1 comeback over the Dodgers on Sunday, the new Las Vegas Vipers featuring twenty-one ex-college players and just five of the original team have now gone 12-2 during the longest road trip in the Major Leagues this season.

With a sweep over the Dodgers and the Giants dropping three out of four to Atlanta, the LV Vipers have now closed to just seven games from the top of the National League West leading Padres, and are a half a game from climbing out of the cellar. According to Vipers Manager Tommy Leach, this team has really come together as a unit.

"At first I know, it was looked at as a gimmick and such, but these guys all know the game and how to play. I give a lot of credit to our guys that stayed with us because they have been solid in helping everybody come together and see what we're doing through different eyes. Right now, this division is really air tight separating first to last by seven-games. I'm really looking forward to coming home to Mirage Field so the hometown folks can see what we're all about."

The Vipers begin a ten-game home-stand Monday night against the Chicago Cubs. According to team promotion coordinator Jack Pattie, the three-game series is already a sellout. Las Vegas entertainment legend Wayne Newton is scheduled to sing the National Anthem with *"Field of Dreams"* star Kevin Costner set to throw out the first ball of the series.

"Entertainment Tonight. Enter-fucking-tainment Tonight! You've got to be frigging kidding me? Jesus Christ, this whole thing has gone too far!" Sean Deeters reacted to the news now being delivered by his best friend and roommate Cliff Collier.

"I got Carla's text as soon as we touched down at McCarran, and when I could turn my phone back on, there it was." Cliff explained. "I wanted to get you back here in private before I told you."

"So let me get this straight, buddy ol' bud of mine, I get pulled from a baseball game today and totally embarrassed in front of forty thousand people in LA. Now, mind you, on top of that, I am now going to get totally annihilated and humiliated on national TV tomorrow night by this bimbo that I let in my room where we did absolutely nothing?"

A quick moment of silence before Cliff could respond was deafening.

"Look, you had a bad game today. We've all had them, but a least we won," Cliff began. "You know how life is right now. Everybody wants a piece of us for something. Shit, I used to think Steven Tyler was a jerk because he was always spouting off and wanting to break up Aerosmith, now I totally understand! This thing on TV is nothing. It will be over and done before you know it. I know how you're feeling right now, hell, but if you let all this get to you, then we all lose!"

"Yea, that's really easy to for you to say, Cliffster, but right now, the two most important things in my life are gone. That's baseball and Syleanna. Right now, I don't know if I'll ever get a chance with either of them again. Tommy thinks I'm shit because I dropped a fly ball and I've probably lost my job there. Now, Syleanna and the whole world will all just think I'm just a big 'man-whore.' It's too much brother…it's just all too much!"

Mirage Stadium and its bravura image at the Corner of East St. Louis Avenue and the Maryland Parkway hadn't seen this kind of busy work since the inaugural season. Cisco Wheeler and Brandon Briggs had flown from LA early on Sunday morning to meet with all the principals involved in making sure that Monday nights "second season" home-opener would fulfill all the needs of a demanding public.

"Are we going to have enough beer, damn it? Just answer the question!"

Brandon Briggs took it on himself personally to meet with George Crumm who was the head of the stadium's sports concessions. Brandon found the vagueness of his answers frustrating.

"Well, Mr. Briggs, I think so. You're asking me about how much we need compared to how much we normally use…that's a hard one to figure out. We haven't had a sell-out crowd here in this stadium for years."

"I realize that, George." Brandon conceded. "So let's talk hot dogs. This stadium holds forty-three thousand people, so if two people ate two hot dogs apiece, would we have eighty-six thousand hot dogs in the stadium? That's all I'm asking."

"Well, yea, as long as Joey Chesnutt doesn't show up!" George answered with a grin as his attempted humor was met with stern silence. "OK, I'm sorry, now hot dogs are simple." George continued, "Really, it's all that other weird stuff we have on the menu like tilapia, tofu, and that chicken and waffle on a stick, man…now that's a hard one to figure out!"

"OK…back to beer!" Brandon's wits were beginning to fade. "Will we have enough beer in our taps, not just for tomorrow, but for all our remaining home games if we are at capacity crowd level?"

"I got a thousand kegs coming tonight and we should be up and ready by morning, so the answer is yes!" George admitted. "My usual order has been about 500 kegs a month. Lord, if we run out of beer in just one day, then I'm buying stock in AA."

Jack Pattie was still trying to get all the tickets lined up at the will-call window for the avalanche of requests for both complimentary and paid seats that were being processed. His frustration was also vented to Brandon.

"Mr. Briggs, just because some cab driver gives two people a couple of free tickets to see Louie Anderson, why do they all expect the same from us? It's been completely non-stop!"

"Look!" Brandon cautioned. "Are we going to have some hurt some feelings when it comes to the freebies? Hell yes! We have a block of gratis seats, and once they're gone, that's it. On the other hand, I have De Niro who wants twenty behind home plate and he's willing to pay $5,000 if we include food and beverage. Is he a priority? Damn straight he is! The odd thing is we have had that same offer for the last nine years, and he is the first person to ever take us up on it!"

The gift shop was another huge concern. Since this whole transition happened so quickly, old jerseys of now departed players were all put on sale at half price. Cisco Wheeler always loved people who thought out of the box, and it was a young intern named Holly Gail Hempill who had created a new look jersey design that was half Vipers/half Eagles. Unknowing the proper protocol that needed to be followed for purchasing, she unwittingly charged ahead and ordered 5,000 units in all sizes.

It was on the discovery of the arrival of 127 boxes and a $65,000 bill that young Holly was immediately ordered to Cisco Wheeler's office for an official explanation of her unauthorized purchase. After an awkward and near tearful explanation of her motivation, Cisco looked at her and uttered but one word; "Brilliant!" She was quickly given a raise and transferred as the new VP into the Concession Marketing Department.

Cisco and Brandon's offices were littered with pink sticky notes as Monday morning arrived. One read "Costner needs to know if he should wear a Viper Jersey or just a regular shirt?" Another was just scrawled with the words "Wayne still needs more tickets!" The Vipers' public relations machinery was as high in organizational chaos and at a level it had never witnessed before. Press credentials from all over the world were being requested as far away as Japan and the Nippon News Network.

"There is no way we can honor all of these requests, Cisco!" an exasperated Brandon barked to his leader and chief. "Fox Sports is coming in to televise the game for a special Monday night event. They and their affiliates have already eaten up almost half the media passes. You tell me what we should do!"

Cisco Wheeler slowly turned around in his chair with a mischievous half-smile as Brandon sensed that the answer on the way may be something he may or again may not regret putting into the court of his eccentric chief.

"Brandon, my boy, it's easy. For all in the press corps who have been with us since the start, they get priority. For the new slew of folks who legitimately want to come and find out what the Vipers organization is all about now, we will accommodate them as best we can. For the rest of the other buzzards out there who wouldn't give us the time of day, and we know damn well who they are, give them a couple of bleacher seats…and charge them double!"

The Chicago Cubs were in their 135th season of existence and considered the doormat of the National League. With Manager Dusty Baker at the helm, they were again on their way to losing close to a hundred games on the season. Pitcher Carlos Zambrano and third baseman Aramis Ramirez proved to be just a couple of the team's bright spots as the rest of the squad lacked a notable supply of everything else. The Cubs were battling the Pirates for the bottom rung in the National League Central, but on this morning, a tsunami headed toward a Monday night eruption in Las Vegas, they were about to get a taste of the high life.

"Team reports a 4:00 p.m. no excuses!" That was the hand-scrawled note that was hastily taped to the clubhouse door. Inside their offices, Tommy Leach, Tom Browning, Von Hayes, and others prepared for what would be the biggest night in the history of the franchise.

"How long have we been gone?" Leach laughed. "The last thing I remember this place was the closest thing to a morgue. Now we have security guards running everywhere. Hell, I even had to show my ID to get on the elevator!"

"So, you're telling me we now operate like a real Major League Franchise." Hayes snickered.

"Hey, I guess." Leach responded. "Pug, tell me who are we up against tonight? What are we looking at?"

"Sean Marshall! He's kind of been their workhorse this season. I know he's thrown a lot of innings already and has a pretty wicked curve-ball. When it's working, it's deadly. If it's not, just wait him out and you'll be walking all day long. We should be able to find out early if he's got his good stuff."

"What about Milhuff? Is he ready for all the shit that's gonna be raining down out there?" Leach asked. "Seriously, this rivals any game-seven that I've ever experienced, and we're still not out of the cellar. I know tonight we will for sure break the Major League record for the appearances of blimps being used in just a regular season game with a team in last place!"

On a round of nervous laughter, it was agreed that everybody just needed to roll with the flow and continue to prepare for another Vipers win.

It was now 2:30 in the afternoon as Cisco Wheeler sent in an extraordinary catered lunch down to the clubhouse for the coaching staff as a show of appreciation for all of their hard work and dedication over the last month.

"Come on people!" Tommy Leach playfully hollered. "We're eating on the old man's money, so enjoy. Just remember this moment because if we ever stop winning, your next meal just might be one of those damn chicken and waffles on a stick!"

Small towns come with big drama. Since the promotional announcement for *Entertainment Tonight*'s expose' feature was announced, that is all anybody could talk about. Texts and phone calls between all the different social strata of the Portsmouth society had but one question; are you going to be watching?

The syndicated-show aired at 7:00 p.m. on Channel 3 out of Huntington, West Virginia. As much publicity and positive press as WSAZ-TV had given the whole Bentley State Eagle story from the beginning, it was now ironic that one of their own programs was on the brink of tearing down one of its most covered principle-players.

"There's no way I'm watching it…no way!" Syleanna Griffin sniffled as she fought back the tears. "He was the one that created all this shit, and now he gets everything he deserves!"

Carla Harris had been the only person privy to Syleanna's inner feelings since Sunday night as they had spent hours together discussing this most startling development.

"You have to watch it!" Carla boldly stated. "We've been over this time and time again and you keep flip-flopping around. Everybody in this town is going to see it and you have more invested into this whole damn thing than anybody else. I know you told me you wanted to be alone tonight, but listen, Syl, I'll just come over and we can watch it together, just us. Will you at least let me do that?"

After a thoughtful pause of silence, Carla could hear a weak and worn-out response on the other end, OK"

"I'll be there at 6:00 p.m. and don't talk to anybody." Carla warned. "The *Portsmouth Daily Times* is chasing down anybody they can think of to make a comment, so just hang in there, girlfriend. Love you!"

Homes are supposed to be a sanctuary of comfort and familiarity for the dwellers who reside within them. That is the case for most unless you were a member of the former Bentley State Eagles. Since their arrival in Las Vegas, they had barely enough time to figure out how to get into the stadium and where the restrooms were before they were gone. That often cleansing effect of returning to your home-base after a grueling road trip didn't really apply since the new Vipers in reality spent more time in all the previous towns than they had in their base city. It was now 4:45 p.m. and the laughing and horseplay in the clubhouse was starting to become contagious.

Brooks Snyder and John Gambill were going at it, playing the video game "Company of Heroes." Ernie Fuller was holding court, telling anyone who would listen about his girlfriend that got arrested at the high school prom. On a stool in the corner, it was Mitch Milhuff, Jeremy Burkes, and Doug Pouge talking about the Cub batters they would be facing in a few hours. Others commiserated in the pre-game ritual of getting loose and enjoying each other's company.

The Vipers coaches were also sequestered in their offices trying to stay out of the vigilance of pageantry. Mirage Stadium had been a dumpster-fire of activity all day long with its preparations for the fans and the approaching media storm. It was now almost 5:00 p.m. as Tom Browning and Von Hayes decided to head out on to the field to check things out.

Manager Tommy Leach stayed behind to wrap up a few last minute things when he suddenly remembered that earlier in the day, Brandon Briggs had dropped off some kind of special commemorative lineup card that he wanted to use for this evening's game. Shuffling through the mountain of paper and memo's on his desk, he finally spied the prize he was looking for. Grabbing it, he stood up to see Cliff Collier standing in his doorway with a strange and puzzled look.

"What's up, Cliffster?" Leach nonchalantly asked.

"It's Sean… Skip…he's gone!"

On any given night for a Vipers game, one could easily walk up to any of the numerous ticket windows just before the game and easily purchase a ticket and be inside instantly. Here it was now just a little after 5:00 p.m. and the plaza was already choked with fans lined up at all windows clamoring to pick up their paid privilege to witness the most talked about sports phenomena on the planet.

"Are you sure everything set and ready?" Cisco warily again asked his friend and GM.

"Cisco, it is what it is." Brandon Briggs laughingly responded. "Are we going to piss off a few people tonight, yea, probably? On the other hand my friend, is this going to be the best night in your life? Absolutely! I just want you to relax, sit back for just a second, and enjoy it all, and let me tell you why!"

Slumping back into his big leather chair in his office, the wiry and original owner looked straight into Brandon Brigg's eyes and decided to let go as ordered to savor the moment.

"You've owned this team for how long, eleven years? In all of our wildest dreams and your massive disappointments, look out there for just a second, just one second. Do you see the same exact stuff that I do?"

With that said, Briggs strolled over to the curtains that overlooked the field and the dazzling Las Vegas skyline that had been pulled shut. Looking back at the desk where his boss was sitting, Brandon quickly and dramatically opened them up.

Here it was a good hour and a half from first pitch and the stands were already half-full. The Goodyear Blimp was bouncing around on the horizon as the hoard of press- representatives were all down on the field mingling with players, the coaches, and the elite representatives of the Las Vegas community.

Add to the festiveness the music and mascots all intermingling in the fun, it was certainly a most surreal site from anything that had been witnessed before in the annals of the team franchise.

Cisco Wheeler couldn't do anything except just stare. With the ghosts of his family and past finances all swelling within his mind as well as his appreciative gaze, he simply turned to Brandon in a low and cracking voice and uttered but two short words, "Thank you."

Realizing that he had hit an emotional nerve, Brandon let him relish it for a moment longer before he began addressing the real tale of the tape for this most interesting of baseball evenings.

"You know, Cisco, I look at all of this out there tonight, but I will always remember that giant painting of Branch Rickey that they had on the wall when I first went on my visit to Portsmouth. You sent me there and I swear I only did it to save my job, but something happened to me looking at that thing that planted the seed that maybe we could make this thing happen. It was your vision that created all of this. Did I think it could ever happen? Maybe I thought, but never a fart-storm in a hurricane to this degree!" Briggs laughed.

"Again, I thank you, Brandon, for standing behind me." Wheeler again spoke. "I truly believe anyone else would have just walked away. So, back to where we are for tonight?"

"All right," Brandon began, "I believe we have enough beer and concessions to get us through the home stand. We went ahead and pacified Wayne by giving him four more tickets, so he's OK. We made a custom jersey for Costner, and now he's happy. The Fox TV crew has been taken care of for the telecast. We've tripled our security on the advice of the LVPD, and Carrot Top says he now hates us on his MySpace page because we made him buy his own tickets, and at an inflated price. I can't speak for Milhuff's arm tonight, but personally, Cisco, I think we're ready for a baseball game!"

Three-hours earlier back in a small river town in Ohio, two best friends sat together talking with a bottle of wine between them. As Carla Harris figured, it might good for medicinal purposes before the evening is through. It was almost 7:00 p.m. as the dread of what they were both about to witness hurt more than the reality of what was to come.

"You know the baseball game will be on later." Carla said. "I saw a thing for it on Fox, but it doesn't come on here until after 10:00 p.m. here."

Syleanna remained quiet as she glanced at her watch while staring vaporously ahead at the TV screen.

"Did you know that Sean got pulled from the game yesterday?" Carla again mentioned trying to make conversation. "I guess he got in trouble for dropping a fly ball or something. I saw that on the ESPN baseball thing."

With that, Syleanna decided it was best to address her feelings with her closest friend the most suitable way she could.

"Carla," she started out, "after tonight, I'm losing two things that have had that have been my whole life since I was thirteen years old and you know what they are. I lived, ate, and shit baseball with the only man I ever cared about. The hours we spent on that swing out front, the things that I gave up going to all of his games, and the love that…"

Tears started to swell into her eyes as Carla stopped her there.

"Syl, it's all right. I know…remember? I have been right there with you. This whole thing with the team has not been easy for me either. Do I think that the temptations out there will ever get to Cliff? "Hell yes I do! We sit back here as the girls they left behind with all those other, shall I say opportunities that present themselves. It's a hell of a bitch thing to deal with!"

Again making eye contact and looking deep into each-other's soul, they again embraced in comfort. It was now 7:00 p.m. and that irritating theme song of the gossip guru's favorite show called *Entertainment Tonight* now concentrated the room.

"Where the hell is he?" Manager Tommy Leach said in shock.

"I don't know, Skip!" Cliff answered. "I saw him this morning back in the room, but I left early to get some laundry done and run some errands. I went back to the hotel for just a second to drop some stuff off and he wasn't there, but I didn't really think anything about it. After I got here and got settled in and stuff, I went over to his locker…and everything is gone! I tried calling and texting him, but like it all goes straight to his voicemail."

Pausing for a second to catch his thoughts, the Vipers' manager again asked the most obvious question to his center fielder.

"So, you know him better than anybody else, what's up?"

"I think you know this TV thing that's going to air tonight has really got him bothered. But to be honest, Tommy, Sean is the proudest person I've ever known. Not in any kind of obnoxious way, he just prides himself on working harder than anybody else and he is the most competitive player I know. I think he's embarrassed with everything right now. That's all I can figure!"

"You know Cliff leaving a professional baseball organization like this is grounds for dismissal." Leach offered. "You just can't go AWOL and have it be OK with everyone. Hell, we have to not only answer to the team, but to the league on this one. He can be fined, suspended, cut, or all three! Damn it, Cliff, on all nights, why didn't he just come to me first? That's what really pisses me off!"

"I'm sorry, Tommy, I came here to you as soon as I found out." Collier apologized.

"I'm not blaming you, damn it, I'm just venting to figure how we're going to handle this thing. Do me a favor; don't make a big deal about him being gone. Let me handle this. I'll just start Shepard in right to buy some time. If any of the other guys start prying, just tell them…just tell them I gave him the night off to get some rest. I'll figure out what to tell the press later."

Seven minutes deep into the show after reporting on the success of *Star Wars: The Empire Strikes Back*, an interview with Cee-Lo Green and Gnarles Barkley, along with all the Juicy details about Britney Spears' Caribbean vacation, Mary Hart was suddenly ablaze with the Vipers logo behind her as she set up her next segment.

"We all know the story by now. A losing Major League Baseball team in Las Vegas did the unthinkable by firing most of their players and replacing them with college players. Tonight, we have a lady who lost her job attempting to meet one of those players who have become the new rock stars of the baseball world. I had a chance to sit down with Sandy Brady who says she spent an intimate night with one of the Vipers players as she tells us on 'Real or Rumor' and this *Entertainment Tonight* exclusive!"

The next shot was of the two seated together in a small studio setting with Mary Hart doing the questioning.

"So, Sandy," she began, "which player did you get to know and how did it all come about?"

"Well, it was Sean Deeters." she timidly said, "We first met on the set of the *David Letterman Show* in New York when I was a floor producer there. I kind of got an immediate crush on him as he and another player were there to do a top ten list."

"Now, Sean Deeters is the Las Vegas Vipers right fielder. So, Sandy is it true that you no longer work on the *Late Show*?" came Mary's follow-up question.

"That's right, Mary. I'm no longer employed there." she said. "I was let go after it was discovered that I had made a bad decision and used private network information to find out where Sean was staying."

"So you do admit using the network as a source to gain this private material as to where Sean Deeters was staying that night?" Hart shot back.

"Yes, I did." Sandy Brady sheepishly admitted.

"As I understand it, Sandy, it was after a game that night, you decided to drop by the hotel where he was staying and that's when things happened?" asked Mary.

"Well, kind of." Sandy said, laughingly. "I have to be honest, the only reason I went over there that night was for what any woman would want with a guy she instantly got the hots for. It just all turned out so differently."

"Explain." Mary offered.

"Well, it was late and I knocked on Sean's door, and after he answered, I kind of invited myself into his room as he said that he was having trouble sleeping, so he asked me to sit down. I did offer at that point to give him a back-massage to which he instantly refused. You could tell he was still really hyped up and nervous about the game that night, so I just sat down…and we ended up talking."

Obviously bemused, Mary Hart's next question probably would have been everybody else's. "So, what did you and the Vipers Sean Deeters talk about all night?"

"Well, he was very interested as to who wrote David's lists on the show for one thing. Let's see, he was also fascinated about all of New York in general, so we talked about that and he asked me lots of questions about the city."

"Sandy," "Mary stated. "I'm not sure I'm getting all of this. A young lady who has obvious desires for a sports celebrity not only loses her job over this attraction, but is now willing to come out and discuss it publicly? There must be some other reasons why you choose to be with us and talk about all this now."

"There is, Mary." Sandy confessed. "I guess one of the big reasons for speaking out is to try and clear my name over what I did. I'm ashamed. As a working professional, I used my advantage for personal gain and got caught. I'm very sorry and embarrassed about it. I have many friends and colleagues at CBS that I can't even look in the face anymore."

"So, speaking out about this unfortunate episode, if it's helping you out in some way, how?" Mary countered.

"Yes, it's helping me, but I also wanted to use the opportunity to apologize to Sean Deeters in public for being, well, so forward. As I found out that night, he is one of the nicest and politest guys I've ever met. Lord, we need more guys like him. His told me that his girlfriend back home is the love of his life since they were like in grade school. We talked a lot about her a lot, baseball, and just fun stuff and things in general."

Mary Hart was smiling ear to ear as her final wrap-up question was presented to her guest.

"So Sandy Brady, I guess it's obviously easy to figure out which side of tonight's segment 'Real or Rumor' is about. I thank you for your candidness. Do you have any parting thoughts on your special one-night stand with a Viper?"

"I guess if I learned anything, there is still a lot of value out there in people Mary. I won't mention any names, but working with celebrities every night, there are very few who I feel are sincerely genuine. You, I'm sure would know that better than me. I just again thank Sean for teaching me a lot about him and the rest of the team on what it's like to be a part of what's happening to them right now. As you know it's a remarkable story, and I appreciate getting up close and personal to it for a short while."

"I'm Mary Hart, and coming up next on Entertainment Tonight next, David Hasselhoff gives us the inside about winning the 'Comeback Award' on VH1. The "Hoff" talks and it's all straight ahead right here on ET."

Carla Harris and Syleanna Griffin both sat in stunned silence. "That was it!" Carla expressed in disbelief, "A fluff- piece, on the Vipers' team and the insinuation that one of their players may have strayed into the world of smarm?" Reaching for her glass of wine, Carla needed an extra-big gulp.

"You mean I shaved my legs for this?" she joked. "Syl, that chick is wacked. All she wanted to do was to cry about losing her job. She didn't say anything about Sean that he didn't tell you already."

"I know." sniffled the gentle sob of a woman who felt both relief and remorse. "He told me all they did was talk. I don't know. Maybe I was just being too much a whiney- bitch about it all. Does Sean know about this?"

"I'm sure he does by now."" Carla confirmed, "I texted Cliff as soon as I saw what it was all about. The good news is that this will be on out there just about the time the game starts. Do you want to call him and give him a heads-up as to the schmooze job and ass-kissing he got on national TV?"

"No, not tonight, Carla. I'm a wreck, and I think that I'm just going to bed in a little while and deal with all of this drama tomorrow" Syleanna confessed.

The sudden ring of her phone and the multiple dings from her avalanche of texts indicated that everyone else who watched ET also wanted to check in to see how she was doing. Sliding her fingers up the side of her device, she clicked the off button on her cell phone, sending all who dared to ask on a visit to voice mail purgatory.

It was a few minutes past 7:00 p.m. in a capacity Mirage Field in Las Vegas when the unmistakable voice of Michael Buffer took to the microphone for a set up for a special night of baseball like none other.

"Ladies and gentlemen, we are honored to have you all here tonight for the first home game and the official inaugural beginning of the "second season' for your Las Vegas Vipers. Tonight, the team puts their recent 12-2 road record on the line against the Chicago Cubs. So on behalf of the staff, the management, and of course the players of the great city of Las Vegas, Let's get ready to rumble!"

With the inertia of 44,000 plus screaming fans igniting the flash, the sky above unexpectedly ripped asunder in a thunderous roar as the "Blue Angles" streaked across the sky and barrel-rolled over Mirage Field for a surprise fly-by.

"Whoa mamma! I certainly didn't see that one coming!" Vipers broadcaster Ralph Hacker exclaimed." "For this capacity crowd here tonight, there might be some serious short-whitening to do when everybody gets home! That was awesome!"

"That was a total surprise!" Pete Harnisch added. "This night continues to be full of the unexpected as now stepping out of the Vipers dugout decked out in complete Vipers gear; it's none other than Ray Kinsella. Wow, Kevin Costner is headed to the mound to throw out the first-pitch with none other than Ray Liotta who is wearing a Bentley State jersey." He playfully added, "This, Ralph, has to go down as the ultimate game of catch here tonight!"

"When you really ponder what the real field of dreams is all about, could tonight be the non-fiction adaptation of that that Phil Alden Robinson story as it has moved from an obscure Iowa cornfield to right here at Mirage Field and the city of lights?" Hacker noted.

Kevin Costner was relishing the moment to a standing ovation has he doffed his hat to the crowd while Liotta waved to the fans from behind home plate. As the frame froze on two of the most loved cinematic characters of the game, the man who built it fired a strong medium fastball to one of them who came. It wasn't quite "Shoeless" Joe Jackson, but Ray Liotta had no problem squeezing it in as Mirage Field once again detonated its approval.

Players from both dugouts spilled onto the field to get a quick picture with the duo as the two stars hung around, basking in the trice. Watching intently from the top of the dugout steps was another young man whose life could be loosely compared and shadowed to the reputation of the mythical Archibald "Moonlight" Graham. It was his favorite movie of all time, and now Jarred Brewster was just this close to it all. Gazing in awe as the actors, umpires, and the players all laughing together, Jarred quickly thought of himself, realizing that "Moonlight" had played in at least one more professional game than he had. Once again, the voice of Michael Buffer took control.

"Ladies and gentlemen, he has been the face and voice of our city for the last thirty years. We now ask you to stand up and remove your hats for a very special rendition of the National Anthem. He's known as 'The Midnight Idol,' 'Mr. Entertainment,' but we all know him best as 'Mr. Las Vegas.' Please sing along and honor our country with the beloved and world-wide entertainment legend, Wayne Newton!"

Fox Sports had never witnessed anything as bold and spectacular as the pomp and circumstance of a regular season baseball game that meant nothing in early August. Granted, the first Vipers slash Eagles game in Pittsburgh could have easily been considered just a novelty, but with almost a full month into the rest of the season and a recent record of 12-2, the casual curiosity had now shifted into full-blown obsession.

21 DOWN IN VEGAS

In attendance and honored on the field earlier in the evening had been a cadre of Bentley State University personnel who had flown out for the game.

It was a bit of a busman's holiday for some of the staff who had been treated to the gala affair, compliments of the Vipers organization as a way of saying thanks and the task of morphing the two entities even closer together. Due to a granddaughter's birthday back home in Portsmouth, Eagles coach Keith Madison couldn't make the trip, but instead sent a video clip of congratulations that was flashed up on the stadium's Jumbo-Tron.

Thom Brennaman and Steve Lyons were setting up the evening's lineup when Brenneman noticed that there was a mysterious hole in the home team's lineup.

"Batting eighth and playing right field for tonight in this first and inaugural game for the new Las Vegas Vipers will be Luke Shepard." Brennaman noted. "I asked Tommy Leach about that move and the official response as to why Sean Deeters, who has been the team's regular right fielder, is not in the lineup tonight. He simply said that his player was not available citing personal reasons. Of course I asked him what those reasons might be considering it was the Vipers' first home game since the big switch and he simply told me that he was unable to comment."

"That's really odd." Lyons added to Brennaman's comment. "I was down on the field talking to some of the players just a few minutes ago, and most of them didn't know or had just heard that Sean wasn't going to play tonight. One source who I can't reveal said he's not even here with the team. So, Thom, there is a little air of mystery to this spectacular evening of baseball here tonight."

"Even though the Chicago Cubs come into Las Vegas as the door-mat of the National League Central, they do have some explosive players." Brennaman said as he began the pre-game set-up. "When you have a Derek Lee, Aramis Ramirez, or a great young catcher like Geovany Soto, overlooking this Cubs lineup can be a mistake. The always exciting Carlos Zambrano will be on the mound tonight for the Cubbies and a young standout that has made an amazing transition from college ball to the majors, Mitch Milhuff will be on the hill for the Vipers here tonight. Our first pitch is coming up next. You're watching baseball on the Fox Sports Network."

Slowly opening her eyes, Syleanna Griffin squinted at the clock as it read 10:20 p.m.

"Did I really doze off that long?" she thought to herself. With the cobweb of dreams and reality starting to separate themselves, the sharper images of the evening began to finally return. Carla, the wine, the TV show and all of the evenings chatter were now oozing back into her memory. That was enough to make the decision to get off the couch and head to her room. Slowly standing, it was the serenity of the moment that caught Syleanna off-guard.

In the distance, she could hear the muted whistle of a train while listening to what sounded like a shower of rain on the roof. There was always gentle comfort to a quiet summer night in Portsmouth, Ohio. Perhaps it was the attraction of that peace and tranquility that lured her into walking out onto the front porch before turning in. As she opened the door, the unmistakable dewy-sweet smell of damp air swelled into her nostrils as the ratcheting sound of the cicadas also serenaded the late night vista.

August in Southern Ohio has an unmistakable quality of its own as it begins preparation of transition into the crisp and cool qualities of its next scene. Taking it all in, Syleanna slowly walked to the front of the steps when a funny sense quickly took over that said she was not alone. Slowly turning to her right, she froze at the shadowy figure sitting in the dark on the porch swing. Before she could even react, the voice she knew too well quietly broke the silence.

"Hey, babe, I'm home!"

Four blocks away and settling in on his Barcalounger fortress with remote in hand, Keith Madison had spent an incredible day celebrating his granddaughter Gwenny Vera's third birthday. As the immediate attention was now focused on the Vipers instead of the Eagles, Keith finally found time to exhale from all of the original alterations in his life. A day spent splashing in the pool transcended into a five-star cookout at his son-in-law's place with every intention to be right where he was at day's end to take in the game. Since the first series on the road in Pittsburgh, Coach Madison had purposely dodged the spotlight of his former team. Except for a few random texts and phone calls, he really hadn't had any contact with any of his former players.

The game had already started as Keith looked at the first inning stats and it wasn't good. Mitch Milhuff had walked the first three batters he faced with no-outs and Derrek Lee at the plate. Knowing the pedigree of his former Eagles' ace, he knew that walks weren't in his vocabulary. A Tom Browning visit seemed to have settled him down for a minute until a 2-2 pitch down the middle of the plate instantly turned the Las Vegas sky into a ground-to-air missile launch!

"And there she goes!" Tom Brennaman called. "You seldom throw a pitch like that ever to Derrek Lee and get away with it as the Chicago Cubs have climbed all over young Mitch Milhuff here in the first and take a 4-0 lead on a based loaded sky-jam! How 'bout' that?"

Keith sat there stunned. Looking at the multiple close-ups on Mitch that the Fox camera crew was now generating as four Cubs touched home plate, it was the image of a proud young man Keith knew from the inside out standing there alone and now looked solidly defeated.

"Oh my god, Sean!" Syleanna screeched!" "That better be you and if it isn't…what the hell are you doing sitting out here on my front porch?"

"Calm down, calm down…yes, it's me, Syl…I just got into town. I flew into Columbus, and after getting here, this is the first spot I wanted to be. I'm sorry that I didn't knock, because well, the lights were all out and I just figured you were all asleep."

After a tenuous pause, Sean made a daring offer, "Care to join me?"

With her heart racing from the initial fright, Syleanna gathered her wits in the storm of confusion and slowly sat down next to Sean on the swing. He quickly put his arm around her and pulled her close. It was immediate impulse that a long wet kiss followed before any verbiage would next be exchanged. After a moment of contemplative silence, Sean held her chin as he looked deep into her hazel eyes.

"I'm done babe," he spoke softly, "I'm here to get my old life back, and you're the first and the most important part that I came home to retrieve."

Still addled with everything that had transpired in just the last two minutes, Syleanna finally started looking for some answers.

"So why aren't you with the team?" she asked.

"I quit." Sean fired back.

You quit?" Syleanna asked again. "I don't understand, so when did all this happen? You played yesterday I thought."

"I did and I sucked, so they benched me. Then this damn hose-job was being aired on national TV tonight and I said to myself who needs this crap. I went in early this morning and packed my things and then caught the next flight I could out of there. So, here I am!"

"Did you even see the *Entertainment Tonight* piece?" she asked.

"No. I didn't want to see that hack- job." Sean reacted. "All I want you to know, Syl, is that I told you the truth at dinner, and that lying-bitch can't take any more out of me because there's nothing left!"

Suddenly feeling the vulnerability of a soul mate that had once been so strong, Syleanna felt the need to quickly respond. "She did tell the truth, babe!"

"She did what? So you saw it?" Sean reacted.

"Honey, Carla and I watched it tonight, and it was the most stupid thing in the world!" Syleanna explained. "This Sandy chick, I guess lost her job over the whole thing and that's what it was mostly about. She said you all talked about the team and stuff and she admitted to trying to jump your bones and it didn't work!"

Smiling, Sean simply asked her to "Go on."

"I don't know... They rambled on about the team and oh yea... how you thought that the David Letterman questions were all fake or something and that you had all these questions about New York."

"Oh, come on, that's it?' Sean again asked.

"No...she said that you were a gentleman or something like that and the reason why everybody loves you guys is because you all play baseball together and for all the right reasons. I don't know, it was all actually quite boring."

"Wow…so there was no trash or made-up stuff?" exclaimed Sean

"No, nothing at all," Syleanna shot back. "It was all really stupid because both Carla and I agreed it was just a chance for this bimbo to get on TV and explain why she got fired and talk about the team to get exposure. So how did you tell the team that you we're leaving?"

After an embarrassed- moment of silence, Sean said, "I didn't."

"Sean Deeters, you just left the Vipers without telling anyone? I mean, you didn't tell Cliff, Brooks, Mitch, anybody?" gasped Syleanna.

"They all know how I felt. Since yesterday, they've all been blowing up my phone with texts and voicemails. I think Tommy even tried to call me once. All this bullshit kind of exploded at once, so I took off."

"Can't you get in trouble for that?" Syleanna asked.

"Get in trouble for what? I quit." he responded.

"Carla said she saw on some sports channel that you like, dropped a fly ball or something yesterday. Is that what it's all about?" she asked.

"No…you are what it's all about! I guess getting benched and this TV thing, and then feeling like you were slipping away just got me to a point where all I wanted to do was to come back here to Portsmouth and get my life back together if I can. I think what I really discovered is that once you walk through that looking glass into a whole other world…it's hard to go back."

"So, what you're saying is you don't want to play pro-ball anymore?" she tested.

"Not the way I felt before I came here." Sean answered.

"Honey…babe…the love of my life, you know it and I know it. This job is what you were meant to do. I love you and always will. If you thought that some dumb TV show and a dropped fly ball could ever end us, maybe you weren't really paying attention since I was thirteen. It was right here on this very swing is where I learned to love you. The one thing that opened me up to you was the fact you never quit. You do remember in the seventh grade when Francis Daniels was all over me, walking me home, and hanging out here. You would not give up?"

"Yea, he was a turd." Sean laughed.

"But look who won!" she said, laughing back "It was your butt-ass that I ended up asking to the 'backward ball,' and in case you haven't noticed, you haven't left yet!"

Another full embrace with a few salty sniffles muted the chatter as she finally stopped talking and grabbed Sean's hand.

"Let's go inside, babe" she whispered. "It's been a long day."

Attempting to watch a baseball game that didn't start until 10:15 p.m. was not in Keith Madison's usual viewing schedule. Hanging in as long as he could, he finally felt himself wake up as the post-game jabber was just kicking in.

Had he known what he was missing, he could have saved himself for his Beauty Rest Mattress appointment way earlier. The final tale of the tape on the Vipers' first home appearance was not pretty as he listened intently to Thom Brennaman and the Fox Sports recap.

"I'm sure a very disappointing night for the home debut of the Las Vegas Vipers as the Cubs got out of the gate early and played pile-on, defeating the Vipers 13-2 in front of a sold-out home crowd. It was Derrek Lee's first inning grand-slam that began the rout, but honestly, Steve, the Vipers never looked like they were in the game at all tonight."

"It's rather anticlimactic, Thom," Steve Lyons added. "Milhuff lasted only two innings and the offensive output was almost non-existent for Las Vegas. While lasting seven, Zambrano didn't have his best stuff working tonight, but was still totally in control, striking out five while only walking two. Las Vegas ended up using five pitchers on the night with the only moment of brag coming in the eight on a two-run shot by Karl 'King Kong' Smith."

"Just as a casual observer to the game tonight, this was not the hustling do-or-die style of play from these guys that we've seen before" Brenneman again injected.

"As reported earlier, the Vipers were without the services of their right fielder Sean Deeters who is reported to be on a personal leave of some sort. Then again, perhaps it was the nerves of finally facing the home-town contingency, and let's face it and be honest, good teams do have bad nights. Forget the score and just focus on the good ol' eye ball test this evening. It was more than apparent that something out there was missing and a little out of sync tonight for the Vipers."

Clicking off the remote for the TV at 1:30 in the morning, Keith Madison was not only sleepy, but confused. He had missed the pregame show yet had noticed the Sean wasn't in the game. The line about not being with the team was also vexing.

"So where is Sean Deeters?"Coach Madison thought as he switched off the light and headed to the bedroom. He would have even been more astonished to discover that his answer was actually only four-streets over

"Damn it, Collier! I told you not you not to tell anyone about Deeters until after the game!" Tommy Leach bellowed from inside his office.

"I didn't say a word, Tommy! Hell, it was obvious he wasn't here! His locker is empty and everybody was coming up with their own conclusions. I tried to let it ride, but he's the leader of our team and all of a sudden, what! He just disappears? The damn vultures were all over us tonight, Tommy, and yet we couldn't say a thing? They knew something was up!" countered the Vipers center fielder.

"Calm down, it's probably my fault for not dealing with it before the game," Tommy admitted. "You saw that dog-and-pony show out there and on top of everything else, Deeters goes AWOL. How the shit am I supposed to deal with that and everything else right before game time? The old man and Briggs are calling me every ten minutes asking, "Are you ready? Is everything ready? Are the boys all ready?" It was a fucking lunatic asylum!"

Sensing that his manager was on the cusp of a meltdown, Cliff Collier tried to be encouraging as best he could.

"Tommy, I will continue to try and call him. I know he wasn't happy about being sat down yesterday and he has girlfriend issues, but let me see what I can do. Trust me. I'll see if I can make some sense of it all, Skip."

After taking a deep breath, the Vipers Manager Tommy Leach looked Cliff Collier in the eye with a forced smile.

"Thank you, Cliff! I am already late for my post-game interview. I do and always will appreciate your honesty and support. I'm telling you this bullshit now so it can be used as an official court record in my murder defense trial in case one of those wise--ass sons of bitches pushes me over the edge because of any day in my life; I will kill somebody!"

"Tommy, Mark Williams from KVPR Radio. There are a lot of rumors swirling around right now, so I want to just ask." has Sean Deeters been let go from the team?"

"No, Sean Deeters is still a member of the Las Vegas Vipers. He is on a short personal leave right now" Tommy answered.

"So his absence in the lineup tonight had nothing to do with the error he made on Sunday and being pulled from the game?"

"No!" Tommy swiftly replied.

"May I ask the nature of the leave? As you know, Major League Baseball does have protocol in place to cover all excused absences from any team?" the reporter continued. "What category does he fall into?"

"Dead aunt...next question!"

The stunning lopsided loss in the Vipers' home unveiling was certainly the water cooler topic everywhere Tuesday morning. The *Las Vegas Sun* headline read "New Vipers, Old Storyline: Hammered."

Common topics were mostly about the lack of fire and hustle from a team that brought new hope and excitement to a winning deprived city. Most of the sports writers scribed away out of temporary disappointment, it was duly noted that it was just one loss and all the excessiveness of the pre-game fete may have been a bit of a distraction factor. Lost in the jungle of rhetoric there was only one short blurb mentioned that right fielder Sean Deeters was away from the team on its "bereavement list."

Tuesday morning saw the light began to filter in through the panes of glass at 2002 Summit Street in Portsmouth, Ohio. Sean Deeters rolled over from the couch in the Griffin family room where he eventually obtained some elusive overnight rest. At this point, nobody knew that he was even back home, including his parents. The impromptu evening with Syleanna had been fulfilling, but as of this moment still incomplete. He felt entirely relieved that their relationship was solid and that the *Entertainment Tonight* piece really wasn't the scandal that he had feared.

Slowly getting his wits together, Sean finally spied before him on the coffee table the only lifeline he had between his former life and the new one: his cell phone. Picking it up, he looked at the call log to see that most of the team had been trying to call him beginning early yesterday afternoon. He also saw a missed call that morning from his Manager Tommy Leach, and two other mysterious calls from the McKinley Funeral Home.

An impasse was at hand as to what to do next. Even a three-hour time difference couldn't stand in front of Sean's first choice and next logical move.

"Where the hell are you, brother?" Cliff Collier answered in a somnolent, but serious tone.

"I came home…to Portsmouth," Sean admitted

"Portsmouth, is that where you are now?" Cliff asked.

"Yea, I got in last night late and crashed at Syleanna's house. I never even got a chance to watch the game. How did you guys do?"

"Well, it's funny you should ask because we got our asses handed to us on a flaming platter. After it was discovered you had split, then all hell broke loose with Tommy, and to be honest, man, nobody wanted to go out there and play. The Cubs beat our brains in and all in front of a sold-out crowd! It truly wasn't a fun-time."

"I'm sorry the way this all came down. After we got home late and all, I just hung around McCarron awhile and found a cheap flight to Columbus and booked it. Sunday morning I went in early, grabbed my stuff- and split."

Let me just ask this, how could you just leave us like that and absolutely tell nobody? Is life so bad out here playing Major League Baseball that you felt the need to play Casper and just leave all of us hanging?"

Realizing he had hit a nerve with his longest and closest ally, Sean froze hearing those words and suddenly felt very selfish and alone.

"I...I guess being taken out of the game Sunday bothered me more than I thought. Yea, I was having it rough with Syleanna and that TV show thing, but you know me, Cliff, I have never once backed down from anything, except this time, all this shit just came rolling in at once and buried me deeper than I've ever been before!"

There was an extended unanswered pause on the phone after that comment. Knowing each other the way they did, Sean knew that Cliff was searching to find a way to justify a legitimate response. It was awkward. Sean knew too that under the circumstances, he appreciated how stupid his comment actually sounded.

"So when are you coming back?" Cliff finally asked.

"I don't know. Syleanna and I really need to talk about some things today. I'm really not built for all of this media circus stuff. I can't believe all this crap that I keep seeing. When you find yourself on the cover of *People Magazine*, Cliffster, that's just not me, man. Hell, I remember how embarrassed I got when they put my picture on the cover of the *Tri-State Shopping Guide* back home. My mom made me sign fifty copies for all of her friends and I was totally miserable with that."

"Well yea, I can play to that because it was you that inspired us to sign up for all of this, remember? When we all met at the hotel on that weird-ass morning, we had less than a 50 percent vote to go through with all of this. Hell, Sean, I wouldn't have done it if you hadn't been so damn positive enthusiastic. You were also the one, if I remember correctly, who said leaving Jarred behind was not an option. Sean, you are one of the best baseball players and friends I have ever known. Just get your shit unbuckled and get back out here and play ball!"

"I know he's pissed, Cliff, so just go ahead and give it to me straight." Sean tensely asked, "What has Tommy said about all this?"

"To be honest, I think he's covering for your ass. I know he loves you, brother, but you are really pissing down the wrong leg on this one, so quit all this drama and just get back out here ASAP!"

"Thanks, Cliff, I really appreciate the honesty" Sean responded. "You are always the man. Let me get some things done today, and I'll call you back."

21 DOWN IN VEGAS

"I think the guys at this point all understand. We have all had to make major changes in our lives and we all understand brother what is going on here, we just need you back here. If it makes you feel better, nobody has or ever will call you a quitter…unless of course you do quit!"

Both shared an honest burst of laughter on that one as Cliff finished having his say.

"Just remember that we are all still nothing but a rag-tag band of brothers that can play this game like no team has ever done before. It took some guy that saw something nobody else could have possibly seen to put us where we are today. You have always been our soul, our leader, our chief, but never our girly man!"

Sharing another nervous laugh, Sean hung up, contemplating his next move. Talking to Cliff had been a good first step, but it was the feeling of being caught somewhere between pride and embarrassment that was generating Sean's sense of personal gridlock. After a few minutes of cleaning out the cobwebs, he decided to head down to Tim Hortons and get a croissant. Putting on his clothes, he quietly opened the front door and stepped out onto the porch. The next sight in front of him solidly froze him in his tracks.

"Hey, I thought I might find you here. I saw the car with the Michigan plates parked in front of the house and knew that no God-fearing Ohioan would do that on purpose."

Sean and his ex-manager Keith Madison were now staring each other eye to eye.

"I thought you might like to talk." Keith offered.

"Hey, Coach," Sean started. "Wow, was it really that hard to figure out where I was?"

"Well, I had a little advantage with CNN, ESPN, and of course, 'Mr. Busy Body,' Dan Patrick," Keith joked. "Have you ever noticed how much he loves inserting himself in everyone's problems? And another thing, sunshine, I hate to tell you that if you ever give up baseball and start robbing banks for a living, your career will be over real quick."

Sitting down on the porch swing was indeed the comfort zone needed for conversation as both souls who truly loved each other clumsily started to get to the real reason that both were there.

"I guess I messed up pretty big this time." Sean started.

After a moment of thought, Keith laughed and countered with a little historical rational that hit home.

"Well, we all take wrong turns in life. It's the ones who recognize it and aren't afraid to go back and ask directions to get back on course that gets them where they're going. Sean, you were always my most grounded player for basics and the fundamentals. You were also my biggest team maverick of them all."

"I just tried to play ball the best I could coach." he returned with his answer. "I didn't mean to be a problem if that's what you're saying."

"No, Sean, no, you're not getting it. Do you understand how rare it is to have a player who completely understands the essentials of the game, but still has the courage to think and compete out of the box on his own?"

"I know I played a little loose at times," he admitted. "But it was always because the other guys weren't paying attention."

"Exactly," Keith countered. "You are the only Eagle whoever stole home in the entire history of our team, and because of what?"

"Because that Dayton pitcher was more concerned about wiping his damn nose than paying attention to me on third." he quickly replied.

"Exactly! You had the guts to seize the moment and take it away. That is so special and that's the one thing you can't teach great players because most terrific players already have that instinct and, Sean, that is you!"

Feeling a little mix between honored and embarrassed, he sat with his head down for a moment before collecting the courage for guidance and asking the next obvious question.

"Coach, I know just bolting and leaving everyone behind was stupid. At the time, I felt I was losing everything and just panicked. I mean, what should I do now? Tommy called and didn't leave a voice mail so I've probably been kicked off the team."

21 DOWN IN VEGAS

"Kicked off? No, I think Tommy Leach has dealt with far worse player infractions than this. Playing the humility card and asking forgiveness might be the base path I would run down on this one. Have you talked to anyone on the team yet?" Keith asked.

"Yea, I just got done talking to Cliff before I walked out the door."

"And he said what?" Keith again questioned.

"Ah, he said the guys understood and stuff. He did tell me that they missed me and wanted me back ASAP. You can't believe anything they say because they're just a bunch of sucks." He laughed.

Smiling, Keith looked at his watch and then to the spider climbing up the web in the far right corner of the porch. After a brief moment of contemplation, he began.

"OK, it's 10:45 a.m. right now. Have you seen your parents yet?" he asked.

"No." Sean reacted.

"Have you and Syleanna talked this thing out yet?" Keith asked.

"Well, kind of, I guess. She also agrees that I need to get back with the team and knows now that I haven't been screwing around. We talked it all out after I got here last night. I still have something I need to talk to her about."

"You know I'm a coach and always have an intricate game plan for every-thing right?" That said, Sean Deeters nodded in agreement. "OK, so here is the one I have designed for you. There's a 4:10 p.m. direct flight from Columbus to Las Vegas this afternoon on Delta and you're on it! It's already paid for and you can buy me one the next time I come out. All you will have to do is confirm it at the ticket counter. If you leave Portsmouth by 1:00 this afternoon, you'll get to the airport by 3:00 p.m. and have plenty of time to check in and get rid of that damn Michigan car. Are you with me so far?"

The growing smile on Sean's face was all the answer that that Keith was looking for as he continued.

"As I figure it, that gives you about two-hours from right now to run by and see your parents and say howdy and wrap things up here with Syleanna. Your flight will get you into Vegas at 5:30 p.m local time and you should be able to join the club for the game tonight."

"That's your game plan, eh?" Sean responded. "So, it sounds pretty good, but with all of that, where does it say that you come along and help me talk to Tommy?"

"No, no, on that one. I've done everything but that, and if you've noticed over the years that most of my plans work!" Keith said as he fished in his pocket for a piece of paper with a phone number on it. "One more thing. Here, please call William McKinley at the McKinley Funeral Home. He's called me at least three-times since yesterday wanting to know something about your aunt!"

The next couple of hours for Sean Deeters was indeed living life in a blender. Shortly after Coach Madison left, Syleanna joined him to encourage everything that Keith had recommended. While cementing their bond even stronger from the time spent the night before, it was now all good. The old wooden porch swing at the Griffin homestead certainly had discovered its purpose as of late becoming the pulpit of truth.

Grabbing up his things, he next dropped a surprise visit to his parents who luckily had been spared most of the recent headlines. While his mom didn't really know that much about the *"Entertainment Tonight"* story, Sean's dad had plenty to say about the Sunday night game and was relieved that his son had no part of it, directly anyway.

As Mrs. Deeters prepared a quick homemade lunch in a sack for the road, Sean reassured everyone that his visit home while extremely short was desperately needed. Heading to his rental car, he continued to shout sendoffs to his family.

"Play hard, son." Mr. Deeters encouraged as Sean got to the end of the walk headed for the curb. "The standings in this morning's paper have you and the Giants tied for last place, both seven-games out. And tell Duzan the reason he's hitting so many grounders is that his elbow's not high enough!"

"Yea, I will. Mom, thanks for the lunch!" Sean crooned as he opened up the car door to slide in. "Now don't eat that while you're driving." she warned. "Please pull over somewhere so you don't get all distracted on the road!"

"I will, I will" Sean laughed.

21 DOWN IN VEGAS

"Drive safely, son, and good luck tonight against those Cubs. I'll be watching it on WGN, but I'll be hanging around here for a while until the phone company calls."

"The telephone company, what's that about, Dad?" Sean asked.

"It's the damn-dest thing! We've been getting all these crank phone calls about your Aunt Sally dying. We know for a fact that she's in the Caribbean on a Carnival Cruise with some of her girlfriends."

"The biggest crowd in the history of Mirage field, Cisco." Brandon Briggs sarcastically beamed. "44,378 paid and that doesn't even count the hundreds of comps we handed out. Not even 'Mr. Entertainment' himself could take us down!"

Cisco "The Dealer" Wheeler attempted to enjoy his general manager's back-handed mirth, but found it extremely arduous. His disappointment was in no way masked.

"So over 44,000 people in one evening witnessed what 10,000 fans have seen night after night for over the past decade. I am a realist, Brandon, and I knew we could lose, I just wasn't prepared or believe that we could lose that badly."

"Come on, Cisco! Think about what these kids have been under from the beginning. You know that all the pressure had to get them at some point and with all the build-up to coming home and all the expectations. I'm sure everybody out there had a severe case of the yips!" Brandon continued to reason.

"I hear you, Brandon, but something just wasn't right out there on the field last night. I felt something I had never seen before. They just looked so lifeless, both on the field and at the plate. So what is the thing with Sean Deeters?" Cisco asked. "Why is he not with the team?"

"From what Tommy said, he had to take an emergency leave for a death in his family or something. I think it was his aunt" Briggs explained.

Cisco Wheeler paused for what seemed like time spent listening to a bad sermon on Sunday morning. "Life's like a play: it's not the length, but the excellence of the acting that matters. That also applies to what we do here as a team, Brandon. Last night, we disappointed everyone who came in here with our play, effort, our attitude, and in the end; the results."

Finally realizing that he couldn't talk the obvious disappointment away, Brandon Briggs decided to simply update his boss on the agenda for the day.

"OK, well, here's what's going on tonight. Another sell-out with the usual comp scabs...they've have been taken care of. Scotty Arms is going for us tonight, Ryan Dempster for the Cubs. We have Jason Alexander, one of the guys from the *Seinfeld* TV show, he's throwing out the first pitch and Frank Marino is doing the National Anthem as Barbara Streisand."

With that last comment, Cisco Wheeler removed his glasses and slowly looked up from reading his daily reports.

"Brandon, did I hear you right? A man singing the National Anthem dressed up as Barbara Streisand...can we get sued for that?"

"No, sir! It's all actually fine. She loves it!"

Tuesday afternoons was a "two for one" margarita happy hour at the Toro Loco Mexican Restaurant in Portsmouth. It was a popular gathering spot for many who cheaply escaped into the lime and green concoction of truth, and today's list of attendees included Syleanna Griffin and Carla Harris. To say the last several days had been a bit strained for both was an understatement as the tiny booth in the back became their safe haven in the storm.

"So fill me in." Carla began. "Sean's already gone, right?"

"Yea, he left a few hours ago and he's headed back to Columbus to fly out and join the team. Keith came over to the house this morning early and unexpected and they both talked. I think that helped a lot."

"You must have freaked walking out on the porch like that and just seeing him sitting there." Carla added.

"Oh my god, my heart stopped!" laughed Syleanna. "I just woke up and thought for a minute it was a dream. When he said 'I'm back' or something like that, my head just started spinning."

As the girls continued to chat among the salsa and chips, Carla knew that Cliff and Sean had finally spoken, but was unsure of all their verbal dynamics.

Piecing together the trajectory of events from LA to the Griffin portico, there was certainly plenty to analyze. The most important piece of the equation was finally addressed by Syleanna.

"You know, Carla, Sean and I have been together since he was fifteen years old and I was thirteen, and we never had anything close to a fight until now…I swear!"

At this point, Carla just sipped on her frozen beverage with no salt and just listened.

"Even when he told me he was going to leave on this crazy thing to Las Vegas, I was OK with it. He held me last night out on the porch, and for the first time ever, I heard him cry. Then I started, and it was like some kind of giant release for both of us as he told me some things that I never ever heard from him or thought he could ever say."

"Interesting…go on." Carla quietly encouraged.

"He just told me how much he loved me and how important I was in his life for everything that he has done so far. I think it helped him to put that TV floosy thing behind him. He still doesn't think he has a job when he gets back to the team and says if he doesn't… that's OK with him."

"I can't imagine them firing Sean for just coming home for a day or two." Carla added. "So do you think he's really all right?"

Pausing for a second before answering, Syleanna's eyes began to mist up a little as it was obvious she had held back a vital piece of information.

"Well, I know that he really wants to play ball and play well if they let him back on the team. We talked about that and some of the incentives in his contract. If he does well and feels safe with his money, he finally told me that he really wants to do one thing more than anything."

"And that is?" Carla playfully shrieked.

With full-blown tears now running down the side of her lightly freckled cheek, Syleanna Griffin sputtered out her unforeseen response.

"He wants to start a family. We're getting married at Christmas."

Scotty "The Golden" Arms had been throwing the ball exceptionally well as of late and looked forward to his opportunity of hurling against the Chicago Cubs. Perfecting his knuckleball had been a priority, but Tom Browning had also helped him add some extra wicked to both his curve and his slider.

Carlos Marmol was a young Cub Hurler who had been moved into the starting rotation mid-season. While showing signs of promise, he has some rather messy control problems at times and an era of over 6.00. Gathering the team together right before 6:30 p.m. in the locker room, Manager Tommy Leach was united with Tom Browning, Von Hayes, and the rest of his coaching staff.

All in attendance could sense that the only missing person for this unified congregated summit was Jesus.

"Gentlemen, in case you're wondering, last night was by far the worst game you have all played since the beginning of this little experiment." Tommy Leach slowly looked across the room to make sure that eye contact was made to all. "I, along with our astute coaching staff, have gone over all aspects of last night's game, and I am here to tell you that out on the field, that wasn't you! Von."

Hitting Coach Von Hayes with clipboard in hand stepped out and took to the Vipers locker room floor.

"Against the Chicago Cubs, we had two errors, a balk, three-throws to the wrong bases, a lack of backup at the plate that resulted in two-runs, and a bases- loaded ground ball through the wickets at third that resulted in three-unearned runs being scored. Guys, that doesn't even address the lack of attention at the plate."

Hung heads and the sound of nervous kicking cleats helped to drown out the silence.

"Thank you, Von." Tommy continued. "As I said earlier, last night was not you! I understand all the pre-game 'entertainment' that we all had to stomach, but tonight, I want to see my team out there playing like I know they can. You guys have now had twenty- four hours to now live with all the shit they write and I can tell you… every fucking reporter feasted on what they got to slather about yesterday's massacre. Believe it or not, they are not your friends! Every one of them is just trying to outdo each other and to finally load up and trash this team, and believe me, given the opportunity, they'll sink you faster than the *Titanic*!"

Saving his best for last, Manager Tommy Leach couldn't help but to use a little reverse psychology as his exclamation point.

"Yea, you guys have a bull's-eye on your back, that's right. In case you didn't know it already, Major League Baseball is not your fan either. This is a business and it is done a certain way. When other people try to show them that maybe there are other ways of doing their business better, they don't like it. The other teams certainly aren't your fans. As overpaid and pampered individuals, they don't want to be shown up on the field by the likes of you! As I just said, the press is looking for every crack in your armor and when they find it, they will use it against you!"

As the room began to feel a bit uneasy as to where his message was going, Leach decided it was time now to bring the heavy hammer down.

"But finally, do you know who your true friends and allies really are? I mean, really? In case you don't, I'll simply remind you. It's every baseball fan who has to watch players stand at the plate and admire their long flies to the outfield.It's the runners that jog to first on an infield grounder. It's failing to go from first to third fearing an injury and pitchers who think that throwing four-innings and gone is having a good day. These are the baseball fans who really love you, and why…because they're tired of all it! That's why you are special!"

If there was a testosterone meter available at that point in the clubhouse, it would have exploded well into the red as the sound of twenty-four individuals took their manager's homily from the heart with an infusion directly into the soul.

"Get out there tonight and get back to being you! As one of the greatest champions of all time, Muhamad Ali might tell you, 'Fly like an eagle and bite like a snake! Rumble, young men, rumble!'"

Tommy and his assistants quickly left the room where there seemed to be an overall cleansing effect for the night except for the one lingering and unanswered question.

The four and a half-hour flight gave Sean plenty of time to rehearse his speech. He tried it on in every way from the "I'm sorry look" to "you don't understand me" angle. Nothing really seemed to work, so he decided to just play it by ear and roll with whatever whenever he got there.

Checking in his uniform seemed the best way he figured to preserve its cleanliness while keeping his scrub pants, hat, and cleats in his carry-on bag seemed easy. Only a few people on the flight back to Vegas seemed to know who he actually was, as he signed several autographs in the waiting area. The rest of the passengers were draped in their own personal veil of adventure and really paid him no mind.

Touchdown at McCarron International at 5:30 p.m. was as promised and delivered. Quickly doing the math in his head, Sean figured that a 6:30 p.m. arrival at Mirage Field would certainly be a gimme. After that, it was anybody's guess.

The only thing that anybody who flies know is that getting to the given destination is one thing: retrieving your luggage as planned is another. Watching all of the dwindling bags roll on by in the conveyer belt, Sean started seeing a multi-colored suit case with an American flag wrapped around the handle a few times too many. Pulling the baggage check from his pocket, he decided that someone in charge needed to figure out what was going on. The poor lady at the baggage counter was the designated truth- barer.

"Mr. Deeters, we are so sorry, but your bag was accidently marked Columbus, Georgia, and it is now in Spokane. As is our policy, you will not be charged anything extra, but it doesn't look like we will have it here until 11:30 a.m. tomorrow."

"Eleven Thirty a.m.! You've got to be kidding!" Sean shot back. "I play for the Vipers and my uniform is in that bag! Hell, I'm already late and in enough trouble as it is. Can you do something… anything?"

"We can gladly call you in the morning after your bag arrives, and one of our customer carriers will deliver it to your address, and again, Mr. Deeters, that is at no additional charge."

"I'm totally screwed," Sean thought, *"It's almost 7:00 p.m. now and first pitch is at 7:15 p.m. I guess I'll just get a cab and get there as soon as I can."* Rick Stowe was the equipment manager for the Vipers, and knowing that at least he had his pants, cleats, and cap

it shouldn't really be that much of a problem getting another jersey. Sneaking in through the back entrance, Sean finally made it to the equipment room. Standing behind the counter where Rick Stowe normally stood was a guy he had never seen before.

"Hey, how are ya doing? Where's Rick?" Sean asked.

"He's not here tonight. He had to go to a wedding. Can I help you?"

"Who are you?" Sean quickly asked.

"I'm Rick's cousin, Virgil. I fill in when he has to take off. I know who you are. You're Sean Deeters"

"Yes, I'm Sean Deeters, and I need a uniform jersey like right now. They lost mine at the airport so please get me one of my jersey tops. I'm already late for the game."

"Oh, today is Tuesday, and they have all been sent out to be dry-cleaned. I don't have any spare ones here right now."

"You don't have any? Not even one? Come on, Virgil, is it? You got to have at least one Viper Jersey back there somewhere that I can have." he bellowed in frustration.

"Let me look." Virgil Stowe replied as he stumbled off into the darkness of the supply room. While it seemed like hours, it was just a couple of minutes later that he returned with a jersey in hand.

"Thank God," Sean thought. That was until he saw the name on the back that said "Randall."

"I found this old jersey that had fallen behind one of the dryers." Virgil said. "It's the only one we have right now."

"Randall" Toots Randall…it was the name of the most hated player in the Vipers organization…and that was the only jersey in the entire clubhouse? Thinking quickly, Sean decided that he wasn't going to play tonight anyway. Perhaps he could use it figuring that all of the TV camera angles will be from the front, and if he just sits there in the dugout, nobody will even know.

"Let me have it!" he heard himself say as he walked through the supply tunnel and into the clubhouse. It was now almost 8:15 p.m. and the game was now fully in progress.

Being a player that always prided his on-field look, Sean Deeters pulled on an old scrubby pair of baseball pants along with a 'Toots

Randall' jersey. While somewhat shamed, he suddenly started to laugh at the absurdity of it all finally convincing himself that perhaps a comedic entrance for his return might be the best way to ease back into the good graces of Tommy and all of his buddies.

Nervously fixing his cap in the mirror, Sean drew one last deep breath as he turned to leave the clubhouse and enter the walkway leading into the dugout. With each step, the capacity crowd grew louder as his heart beat faster.

"The end of four, it's no score from Mirage Field as both Scott Arms and Carlos Marmol have matched each other pretty much pitch for pitch so far this evening." The voice of the Vipers Ralph Hacker explained. "Quite unlike last night when it seemed like this team couldn't even tie their own shoes properly, there is definitely a crisper and more business-like atmosphere out there."

As Sean finally got to the dugout, he looked up to see Tommy at his usual high perch standing on the steps at field level. He quickly moved left and scooted down the bench to find a hiding spot during the inning change. As much as he hated feeling like a thief sneaking back onto his own team, Sean also certainly knew the ultimate price for his actions.

While the players quietly sidled up one on one to welcomed Sean back, the coaches and Tommy seemed unaware and all too busy to notice that they had suddenly acquired an extra player. It was now the bottom of the seventh-inning when Vipers Manager Tommy Leach finally turned his head with an eye to the corner to see Sean Deeters quietly sitting there with his back against the wall. Exchanging a long hard stare, Tommy then quickly tuned forward and once again channeled his energies out onto the field.

Feeling somewhat rejected by the icy homecoming, Sean figured that his fate was pre-determined much like the 'Sword of Damocles' hanging over his head and sentence was on hold until a more appropriate time.

As inning after inning went by, not one runner on either team had yet put a dent into home plate. With base hits being wholesale the night before, the mastery of the mound was the big story emerging from Mirage Field on this given night between the lines. Even

21 DOWN IN VEGAS

play-by-play announcer Ralph Hacker had a hard time figuring this one out.

"It's the top of the fourteenth-inning with plenty of free extra baseball tonight as the Vipers and the Cubs are locked in a nada-nada tie! Pete Harnisch, how can you figure this one out?"

"Yea, Ralph, only five hits tonight, three by the Vipers and two by the Cubs. The pitching has been magnificent on both sides of the ledger. While Arms, Burkes, Leslie, and Fuller have been lights out tonight for Las Vegas, Marmol, Howry, Aardsma, and Wood haven't been too shabby either for Chicago."

"Top of the fourteenth as 'Dirty' Ernie Fuller gets set for his third-inning of work as he faces Murton, Cedeno, and Todd Walker." Hacker began. "Looking ahead to the bottom of the inning for the Vipers Tommy Leach has Gambill, Collier, and the pitchers spot up so this is probably Fullers last go round!"

Painting the corners of the plate both inside and out in the worst wicked of ways had always been a gift that Ernie Fuller possessed. When he was truly on, it was often a batter's worst nightmare to face his trademark "Bastard Pitch." It was truly an event that brought futility and disappointment to so many lives. Again, tonight was no exception. Murton and Cedeno quickly went down on strikes, and it was a weak grounder to second by Todd Walker that sent this scoreless marathon into the bottom of the fourteenth inning.

John Gambill stepped in to face Kerry Wood as few had left Mirage Field even as the clock approached midnight. The shellacking from the night before was now in the rear-view mirror as the Mirage faithful now hung on every word along with the Vipers broadcast team.

"Gambill has Wood into a full- count, and here comes the 3-2 pitch. Called strike three on the outside corner and I'm not so sure about that one, Pete."

"A very iffy call on that one for sure." Harnisch injected. "That's a pitch they've been letting go for most of the evening, so I guess the later we go, the bigger the plate gets!"

"I can't believe it, but Ernie Fuller is apparently coming back out in the top of the fifteenth-inning as he is headed to the on-deck circle," Hacker noticed. "I know both teams are a bit bench-depleted at this point, but I find this very interesting!"

Cliff Collier stepped in against Kerry Wood determined to send everybody home happy. It was on a 2-1 pitch that he got his sweet surprise and let her rip. The pitch had been just outside of Cliff's wheel-house and the fraction of a difference between whoops and whammy fell in favor of the Cubs.

"A high fly ball to right field and Collier just missed that one." Ralph Hacker exclaimed. "You can see the disappointment all over him as he knew that was the one he wanted and it got away. Two outs in the bottom of the fourteenth for the Vipers and "Dirty" Ernie Fuller to the plate."

Slowly stepping down from the top of the stairs, Manager Tommy Leach cast his gaze into the corner of the dugout.

"Deeters, grab a bat! You're hitting for Fuller!"

Looking at his manager now in stunned silence, Sean suddenly felt like the world was spinning in slow- motion as the only word that he was able to muster up was "Me?"

"How many other Deeters do I have sitting around on the bench doing nothing?' Tommy barked back. "Get up there and do something!"

"Fuller turned from the on deck circle and headed back to the dugout as little did anybody realize that baseballs version of the "crazy- train" had just pulled into Mirage Field.

"Two outs in the bottom of the fourteenth and pinch hitting for Ernie Fuller is…Toots Randall?"

The sudden dead air in the Vipers booth reflected the obvious confusion that was now settling in as Sean Deeters stepped to the plate.

"Am I missing something here, Pete? Isn't Randall still with the Yankees?" Hacker frantically asked.

"Unless they got him late today off the waiver wire or something, I certainly hadn't heard anything about this" Harnisch added.

"Well, I really don't have any stats for him up here, and he doesn't even appear on the team's roster. At any rate, its Toots Randall now stepping in to face Kerry Lee Wood with two out here in the

21 DOWN IN VEGAS

bottom of the fourteenth. If at least I do remember correctly, Randall always was a pull hitter to left and did possess some power." Hacker continued with the call as the confusion festered.

"Randall settles back into the box with a 2-2 count as Kerry Wood looks in for the sign…and the pitch!"

It was the crowd's sudden and grateful roar that shot through the Vipers' microphone before any words could actually fly through the air to describe the final ending to a very long evening of baseball in Las Vegas.

"It's a drive! Deep, deep back into right field! And way out of here! It's a walk-off home run that ends a marathon night here in the bottom of the fourteenth-inning from a player that we didn't even know was with the team,- Toots Randall!"

The greeting at home plate was a ceremony for the ages. Sean Deeters had taken aim at a Kerry Wood fastball with a swing fueled by the release of a thousand pent-up frustrations, and within in the blink of an eye and a minute before midnight, the demons had all been exorcised.

With the Mirage Field fans now in sheer pandemonium, the TV cameras were recording the post-game celebration down on the on field while the Vipers radio voices were also trying to make sense of this story-book ending. It was Pete Harnisch who finally solved the mystery.

"Ralph, I think we've all been had here just a little bit. As I look at the TV monitors, I do believe that's actually Sean Deeters who just ended this game here tonight, and for some reason, he's wearing a Toots Randall jersey!"

"Well there, Peter, as you know, ol' Toots hasn't been a big fan of us as he was one of the original Vipers let go in the house cleaning and has been pretty vocal about his former employer." Hacker speculated. "I just wonder about wearing his jersey and number tonight had any symbolic meaning except a sure fine from Major League Baseball." Laughingly, he added, "The last time I checked the rules on that, wearing false identification on the field is absolutely prohibited."

As the celebration spilled from the field and into the clubhouse, it was more than just a little evident that all was well and forgiven as far as Sean and his fellow friends and players. While pinned to his locker in sea of reporters, Deeters knew where he should be at this point and tried to gracefully bow out to get there.

With over a dozen reporters screaming out questions at the same time, Sean held up his hand and called for quiet and calm. He decided to make just one blanket statement and then exit.

"Hey, you all, I'm going to have to make this brief because some of you know I've been away a couple of days, and there are some things I need to do. I promise to answer all of your questions tomorrow. I promise…as you know, it's kind of late. I just first of all want to say it was a fastball that I was able to turn on and drive. I've been away from the cage for a few days, so it felt extra good to pop it hard. It really feels great to be back with the team, and my luggage got lost at the airport this afternoon, and that's honestly the truth on why I ended up wearing the wrong jersey tonight. Thank you all very much!"

"Why were you away from the team, Sean?"

"Do you think Randall will be upset that you wore his jersey?"

"Is Luke Shepard the Vipers' new right fielder?"

"Are you dating the girl that was on *Entertainment Tonight*?"

The questions continued to fly as Sean Deeters pushed his way through the crowd and bee-lined it to Tommy's office. Walking around the corner, he could see through the glass that his manager was standing there and alone. It was perfect timing in an otherwise imperfect day. Opening the door, Sean nodded as he sat down on the veranda across from Tommy's desk. Puffing on his usual victory cigar, he looked long and hard at his returning right fielder. Quietly sitting down behind his desk, he looked at the ceiling before finally speaking.

"That was a hell of a swat, kid. I knew Wood wanted to get out of here like we all did. I was hoping that he would become careless… and he did!"

"Tommy, I came to apologize to you and,,,' Sean paused as the words no longer flowed smoothly.

"Well, son," Tommy laughed, "You have a hell of a list of things that need to be taken care of that's for sure. I've already heard from the MLB chieftains tonight about the uniform. That's gonna cost us!"

"I know, it was stupid, but I didn't think you would put me in tonight. My bag got lost at the airport with my uniform and all of my stuff was in it." admitted Sean."

Taking another deep drag off his Corju Cubanar, Tommy then asked the next question, "So where did it all go?"

"Spokane." Sean quickly shot back.

"Spokane, Washington…home of those Spokane Indians. I actually spent a season there on my way up here. God, I loved that place." Tommy reflected.

"Great scenery and talk about restaurants, I've often thought about going back there and buying me a little place after I finally get out of this game."

The calm meandering nature of Tommy's comments caught Sean off-guard as so far it certainly wasn't the supreme ass-chewing that he expected. He again tried to breach the topic of his miscreant behavior.

"Tommy, I also want to say that I'm sorry for my attitude before I left." he confessed. "I know I should have played harder, but all this was coming down on me and I just couldn't get my head on right. It was all of that and thinking I had lost my job. It was way too much!"

"Son, sometimes you don't give ol' Tommy here the real credit he deserves. I know that you were afraid to talk to me in the dugout tonight, and that's all right. By the way and for the record, I knew you were there two minutes after you snuck in. This isn't an easy game to play even for grown men. You been doing it now for what…a month? All I ever ask from any of my players is to simply play hard and be on time, you know that. Tonight, you got one out of two!"

After a discomfited moment of awkward silence, Sean slowly started to verbalize his true feelings, but the words didn't come easily.

"I know that I wasn't a pro for what I did, but I love this game and, well, the opportunity that this organization has given me…and all of us. I know I sound like a suck up and a hack, but all I ever wanted to do is just go out there, play ball and win!"

"So let me ask. You got the girl thing worked out, so… when is the wedding?" Tommy asked with a wink.

"Christmas…hey, wait a minute! How did you know about that? Sean stammered. "Nobody knows anything about that yet?"

Smiling, Tommy picked up a list from his desk and started reading out loud. "So we're going to pay fines for wearing a wrongful jersey, probably another lawsuit against the team from dick-head Randall, and another fine for being put on the bereavement list with actually no bereavement being involved. Now I'm partially responsible for that one because I must have said something that wasn't totally factual at a press conference. That aside, I'm not sure how we are going to handle all of these infractions."

"Well, I'll pay the fines!" Sean nervously stuttered. "I mean if I messed up that bad, I'll take care of it!"

"Settle down…settle down, son, I got your back on this one." Tommy said while reaching in his top desk drawer. Digging around, he finally pulled out a Polaroid picture.

"So, you were only on the bereavement list for one day, and that was yesterday. I figured you probably would be back by today, so I went and took you off or you wouldn't have been eligible to play tonight. Are you with me so far?"

"Sean continued to stare at his manager as he nodded affirmative.

"By the rules of Major League Baseball, they will want some kind of validation of where you were on your missing day. This Jason Alexander guy was in my office earlier, funny fellow. He's on some kind of a TV series called *Seinfeld* and threw out a ball tonight. Anyway, he says this really works. When it comes time to show the proof of where you were in your darkest hour of need, he said just hand this to the Commissioner's Office."

Taking the photo from Tommy's hand, Sean stared at it as his manager as he slowly erupted into an ear-to-ear grin. It was a picture of a flower-covered casket with a handwritten cardboard sign on the lid that said, "Dead Aunt."

10ᵀᴴ INNING

"**G**ood evening everyone', and welcome to '*Baseball Tonight*.' I'm Buster Olney, and we begin with another incredible chapter of a story that could only be scripted in the 'Grand Plan in the Sand.' The Chicago Cubs and the Las Vegas Vipers were scoreless here at Mirage Field as we head into the bottom of the fourteenth- inning, two outs, and nobody on, and look who strolls out to pinch hit. Can it be? It appears to be Toots Randall?"

Olney sat back and laughed as ESPN showed the game winning video overdubbed with the confusing radio call between Ralph Hacker and Pete Harnisch

"See, not even the radio guys knew that the walk-off drive was actually right fielder Sean Deeters who had just returned to the team from a personal absence. Arriving at the ball-park late, Deeters' baseball attire was apparently shipped elsewhere, and so he grabbed the only jersey that was available thinking that he wouldn't play and later got a big surprise on that!"

"Randall who is now a member of the New York Yankees was one of the twenty players released from Las Vegas after the All-Star break and replaced by the Bentley State Eagles. The irony of this whole thing is that we checked the *Elias Book of Baseball* and discovered that during his tenure with the Vipers, Toots Randall had never hit a pinch-hit home run. We're not sure how official it will all stand up, but at least for now, he can brag that his uniform did!"

Inside the bowels of historic Yankee Stadium, the mood wasn't quite so jocular from the former Viper.

"Those bastards! They did that on purpose! I know they did that just to embarrass me!"

Randall was unraveling every conspiracy theory he could muster up as his teammates couldn't help having a little fun with his rabbit ears over this most unusual ending to the Vipers' latest win.

"Hey, Toot-Toot," chimed in Bernie Williams, "If they really wanted to make you look bad, they would have sat your ass down on three-pitches!"

The clubhouse burst into laughter as they had a much lighter tone on the situation than the principle player.

"Ain't many dudes out there, my man, who can claim that they went 0-2 in the American League and then hit a dinger in the National League all in one night, bro. That's Hall of Fame stuff!" added Robinson Cano.

Shortstop Derek Jeter also couldn't resist the avalanche of fun as he also got his two- cents' worth in.

"Hell, Toots, you got more exposure on TV tonight than you ever got with us. You might not live forever, but that damn clip will be shown on *ESPN Sports Center* for the next hundred years!'

Absent from all the good-natured ribbing, Toots Randall finally exploded in one final tirade that put an exclamation mark on his true feelings.

"Screw all you guys! You never worked for that Mickey Mouse outfit that never played me the way I should have been played. We've all been there, you know it's true. Just because I complained and stood up for myself, I got punished! Do you even know how demeaning it is at this level to be replaced by a bunch of kindergarten kids? If I ever get a chance to personally do damage to fucking Cisco Wheeler and all of his cronies, I'll be there and guarantee you all, I will be the first in line."

The room fell silent as Toots Randal slammed his locker door and headed off to the whirlpool. The Yankees knew they had hit a nerve, but never dreamed that the root had buried itself so deep. Breaking the ice, catcher George Posada finally defended their teammate's tantrum.

"Ah, leave him alone. Nobody likes to be shown up in this game. This whole Vipers bubble is getting ready to burst anyway. There's no way this thing will last with them winning like this. Breaks go both ways in this game, you know it, and they just got all theirs front-loaded."

At this point, Yankees CEO Brian Cashman walked into the clubhouse. He had obviously been listening to the locker room fracas and seamlessly continued with Posada's assessment of where his team stood. After a brief pause, he spoke.

"What George says is true fellas! The Padres, the Astros, and I believe the Dodgers will all be there in the National League. Right now, we need to concentrate on Oakland and Minnesota, and we'll be just fine. Hell, we're already eight-games over Toronto. And one last note on this Vipers thing. Yea, so they have captured lightening in a bottle, it occasionally happens."Seriously, every team in both leagues has plenty of tape on these guys. I sit in my office every day and have to hear about it. The magic will soon be over. You can accidently win some games in the dog days of summer, but once you get to post-season, we all know how tough it is. You all here and in this room are the best of the best! By playoff time, these kids you're talking about now will be back doing their homework while you all will be going after our twenty-seventh world title!"

In another locker room twenty-five hundred miles away, another message was also being delivered to a congregation of big league disciples with Manager Tommy Leach dispensing the sermon.

"OK, just a few notes, Coleman will be catching tonight in place of Pouge. Doug, you need a night of rest and thanks for being there for us yesterday. This man caught fourteen-innings last night in case you didn't notice and never once complained. In my world that is where the heart of champions live!"

The room exploded with condescending cheers and applause as Doug Pouge put his hand over his chest and feigned a heart attack. While the good-natured ribbing continued, the stern look of Tommy Leach quickly shut things down.

"We have some relatively good news on Carpy. The hand is healing nicely and if everything goes as planned, we may have him back by the second week of September. Zebro here will continue the spot in the rotation until that time arrives. That's about all I have, but I have been asked for a quick moment as I welcome a distinguished guest speaker to the floor."

Manager Tommy Leach with a wry smile looked to and nodded as Sean Deeters slowly stood up from the bench and looked about the crowded room.

"I've been a jerk! I just wanted to clear the air with all of you and apologize for all my selfish and stupid behavior. Even though we've been Vipers for a short while, we've always been Eagles. What I did was not the Eagles way. Even though I went through a rough time, I was selfish and I left my brothers behind."

Sean paused for a second as his emotions suddenly took over as tears began to trickle down his cheek. With respectful silence in the room, he struggled to continue.

"I had a long time to think about this in a short period. Yea…we came up lame the last time we played for a championship. We didn't do what we knew we could, but look at us now! I struggled awhile with all this and I know some of you did too. How does a college team like us just get plucked out of the air like we did and end up here? It's crazy! What's more insane is that I know and you know that we all belong here because we know how win! We are not a novelty! If God gave us a second chance to complete something that some near-sighted home plate umpire screwed us out of in Oklahoma City, I say let's do it!"

This time, the approbation jolted the room to its feet. Sean had finally hit the hot- button that seemingly jarred the possibility into mission compliance. This was the definitive drink from the trough that was needed. Cliff Collier, Brooks Snyder, and John Gambill all grabbed Sean with a bear hug as the rest of his teammates welcomed him back into the fold and soaked in the renewal of joy and faith in each other. As the impromptu spiritual revelry continued, Manager Tommy Leach and all of his coaches simply watched and then turned and headed for the exits.

"It's nice to hear that Cher is still filling up seats and that sixty-million dollar deal with the Colosseum at Caesars will further distance her financial statement from those gypsies, tramps, and thieves. Now let's turn to KSNV Sports with Kevin West."

"Thank you, Jerry, and just like Cher, the 'Deet' goes on for the Vipers as right- fielder Sean Deeters exploded with five hits and his second home run in two nights as the homies spanked the Cubs 11-2 at Mirage Field tonight. Brad Scarbury went eight, allowing five hits and a two-run dinger to Derrek Lee as the 'the dirt man' came on and shut 'em down in the ninth. Cub starter Rich Hill lasted 2 and 2/3 innings as the snakes struck quick and hard. Back to back doubles in the first by Brooks Snyder and Bombo Chadwick plated the first run of the game. It was then a single by Smith before the big fly by Deeters, and before you could say Donnie and Marie, it was 4-zip and the rout was on. Deeters would go on to hang four more safeties on the board and drive in 4 more runs for a total of 5 rib-eye steaks on the evening.

Also contributing to the cause with two hits each were Gary Duzan, Doug Pouge, and John Gambill. Since the All-Star break, the all new Vipers have now gone 14-3, and for the first time since, get this, 1997 are not in the cellar come August. As a matter of fact, Las Vegas is now just six-games out of first place in that extremely tight Western Division race and just a game from catching the Dodgers and the Rockies. Tomorrow is an off-day for the team before Atlanta hits town for the weekend."

The following Thursday marked the one-month anniversary of the big change within twenty-five lives. A "day off" in Major League baseball terms is a bit of a falsehood. Just because the team doesn't actually play for a day, it doesn't really mean the players are completely free to do as the wish. Perhaps a quick round of golf or a movie can be squeezed in, but overall, the responsibility of getting ready for the next day's opponent is always looming large in the headlights, especially during a pennant race.

Jarred Brewster had continued to be the silent rock of the clubhouse. As he gradually won over Tommy Leach's affection with his instincts, his work ethic was relentless. Jarred's laptop computer was always open and humming along with stats, notes, and gut-check observations that were silver bullets in the heat of battle. Instead of indulging themselves with frivolous activities on this given Thursday, it was 2:00 p.m. and the Vipers clubhouse was dark except for two stalwart occupants in the manager's office.

"I can't quite figure out these guys, Skip. They should be playing for a division title."

Looking up from his morning paper, Tommy Leach cast a quizzical stare to his busy office guest across the room.

"How you figure that, Brewster? They're sixteen games back in the East and just lost five in a row. The Mets are killing everybody over there!"

"Yea, but Atlanta's offensive numbers are actually better than the Mets. You got Jones, McCann, Larouche, and Giles with a combined batting average of .317. Andruw Jones isn't hitting for average that much, but he's on track to hit 40 home runs. Langerhans in Left is really their only weak link that I see." Jarred Brewster enumerated.

"Their pitching stinks!" Leach mumbled. "They only have two guys with an era under .300."

"Actually it's three, sir. Smoltz and Chuck James are doing OK, but they're moving Villarreal from the bullpen, and he's perhaps their best pitcher right now."

After a ponderous moment of silence, Tommy Leach asked the next logical question.

"So what are you telling me here, Einstein?"

"Well, when scored upon first, they have a hard time coming back. So far this season, they've won only .321 percent of their games when they get behind. I think a lot of it is in their heads because of the weak bullpen. If your ahead and get them past the sixth- inning, the odds drop down to .274 percent that they will comeback."

"Interesting, Jarred," Leach smiled. "So all we have to do is score early and often. How do you propose we do that little feat of magic?"

"Move Sean to bat lead-off, just for this series."

Jarred's unexpected answer got the quizzical response expected.

"Lead-off!" barked Leach, "Sean's not a lead-off hitter. He's finally found his stroke and you saw what he did last night. How can I move him from a power spot to lead-off?"

"Because Skip, he's the man that can get things happening fast and that's what you want against this team. I saw him win us three games in the tournament before the second inning. Sean is a chameleon, and he can be your best weapon anywhere you play him."

"You've put a lot of time and thought into this haven't you, Brewster." Leach snapped back.

"Not really, sir, I've just crunched the numbers. If you don't mind, I have one other little observation I would like to share."

"Rolling his eyes in an exaggerated manner, Tommy Leach laughed as he heard himself say, "Bring it on, maestro!"

"Well, I know we've used Bruce Leslie mostly as a middle-reliever so far, but he has been stretching his arm out pretty good and could actually spot-start for us if we needed him. We used him like that on the Eagles anytime we wanted to reset our rotation. He loves doing it. You might look at sticking him in against Atlanta, and I guarantee he'll give you at least six-strong innings and it will help set up the arms pretty good for the Colorado series. You might talk to Pug about that idea."

Realizing there was quite a bit of lucidity in Jarred's reasoning; Tommy slightly lowered his ceiling of irrelevance and finally acknowledged the young man for his effort.

"Jarred, most guys in my position would write you off out of their own ego and pride. You should be glad that I'm a little different. I might not always act like it, but with you, my ears are always open. You do have a gift and I recognize that. I've been in this game for thirty-five years, and you can't help it, you get a bit jaded after a while, we all do! You can't help not to have that refreshed feeling after time that you've seen it all before. That of course was before you guys came along and intercepted my life- Damn it!"

Tommy sat there looking straight ahead and into space as Jarred attempted to decipher the Vipers Manager as an endorsement of some kind. His next words were purely un-Tommy.

"We've really upset the applecart here, haven't we, kiddo?"

"Uh, yea, skip…I think we might have, uh, scattered some fruit on the floor." Jarred stammered.

"When all this first came down with you all, I was ready to quit this game. Walk away! I'd had enough. Now at night when I go to bed, Brewster, do you know what I think of? I think of all my friends out there still doing it and how sorry I feel for them. Sorry that they haven't been able to experience in a career or lifetime what I have in just six-short weeks. It is the damn-dest thing!"

At the same time and somewhere out on Lake Mead, Sean Deeters and Cliff Collier were finally getting some guy-time that didn't have anything to do with baseball. Knowing their love for fishing, Von Hayes had made a few calls and pulled in a few favors to his friends at the Lake Mead Marina. When you're playing good, it's amazing how far that will go in procuring a rental boat and some fishing tackle. As they slowly chugged by the rocky shores trolling for striped bass, conversation and conjecture came easy.

"Man, it feels good to get away from everything, only if it's for a just little while." Cliff admitted. "I almost forgot what doing nothing was all about."

Laughing as he took a swig from his Coors Light, Sean nodded in agreement as both soaked up the intense rays of the Nevada afternoon.

"Fishing on Lake Mead," Sean pondered. "I haven't held a rod since we used to have those all-night catfish tournaments down on the river at the Court Street Landing in Portsmouth. God, that seems like it was years ago."

"This whole thing has really put some distance on our treads, hasn't it?" Cliff added. "Sometimes, I still think I'm going to wake up and find myself back sitting in class and listening to Professor Hapney spewing about the right-wing pinkos taking us down."

Both Sean and Cliff had a good belly-laugh over that one. As hilarity fell to silence once again, Sean pulled his rod back and forth several times before speaking.

"Hey, Cliffster, do you think we can really do this? I mean, really?"

"Do what? Catch a striped bass? I don't know. I've never fished for one before" he answered.

"No, I mean win this thing. Hell, we're only six-games out of first. I try not to think about it, but after losing the College Series and all, and now all of this. You and I have really never talked about it." Sean admitted.

"I mean yea, at first I thought we would come out here and by now maybe be playing, maybe .500 ball and the big whoop would be over." Cliff said. "I have to admit something to ya, brother. These guys up here really don't intimidate me. I see so many mistakes they make just because they, I don't know, they just don't pay any attention to the little things. I'm all over it, brother. Do I think we can win it all you're asking me? At first maybe no, but now…hell yes I do."

"Tommy was right, you know," Sean added. "We are pissing a lot of people off. Syleanna was telling me that she was watching one of those sports shows the other day and some ex-player, she couldn't remember who, said that we were not being respectful to the league or it's players with all of our…I think he said it was our bush league enthusiasm."

"Now there's your pure 100 percent bull-hit right there!" Cliff fired back. "That's exactly what I was saying. It's so political up here that nobody wants to rock the boat, and if that means having fun and winning anyway you can, they don't like it! You know that we didn't ask for this job, we were selected…and now I think I am really beginning to understand why."

After another swig of beer, Sean laughed again at his best friend's assessment. "That's right, ol' buddy! We have finally broken into King Tut's tomb and are now learning all of the secrets and stealing all their treasure!"

"Spot on, brother!" Cliff howled, "And how much more pissed will they be when we end up stealing the Western Division hardware too?"

On that, both Sean and Cliff exchanged fist bumps to seal the deal. If not for the sudden sound of line being stripped away from a Zebco 300 reel, the baseball bravado between the two may have continued late into the Lake Mead day.

"Fish on!" Sean bellowed as Cliff quickly grabbed his pole and swiftly yanked back to set the hook.

"Damn it, Roland Martin, that's a beauty!" echoed Sean. "Don't horse him, don't horse him!"

"What the hell is that supposed to mean?" Cliff groaned as he kept his rod arched high over his head.

"I'm not sure, but I hear Bill Dance say it all the time on his TV show." Sean laughed. "I think it means just don't let the little bastard get away!"

Cliff continued to let out and retrieve line for almost twenty-minutes. As the fish began to tire and weaken, it began to give up the fight as it got closer to the boat.

"Hold on, bro! Let me get the net. Tight lines! Tight lines!" Sean exclaimed in his animated yet enthusiastic manner.

Watching the fish finally roll to the surface, both were amazed to see at least a fifteen- pound striped bass on its side and apparently ready for the fight to be finished. As Cliff pulled it closer to the boat, Sean was ready and lowered the net into the water to bring the silver beauty home.

"We got this, baby!" he shouted. As if on cue, the fish made one final unexpected run under the boat. As Cliff clumsily fumbled for the rod to tighten the line, it was the sickening sound of *"zing"* that put a sudden end to their adventure which sadly proclaimed an end of this one. The final score was; fish 1 Cliff and Sean 0.

"Damn, we had it, man! We had him right here!" Sean bemoaned. "It was right in our lap and lost it! We were that close!"

After a short and dramatic pause, Cliff and Sean embarrassing looked at each other and couldn't resist to reinforce a moment that was still plainly too painful.

"Where have we heard that one before?" Cliff solemnly reflected.

As a solid unit since getting to the big leagues, the Vipers team stats were truly amazing and often above the norm. Sports talk-show hosts couldn't get enough of the breakdowns and comparisons between the established rosters of MLB players that they knew versus a bunch of former college greenhorns. All the regulars on the Vipers had been playing well into the first eight-weeks on the "new" season. Other members of the former Eagles players who now found themselves in support roles in the world of Major League Baseball were also doing remarkably sound.

In short-inning, relief left-handed pitcher Andrew Shakart had a sterling earned run average of .097. Veteran Terrance Kennedy had worked closely with former Eagles infielders Clint McElroy, Danny Frazie, and outfielder Winston Clyde to increase their confidence and success of being a valuable utility player off the bench. Perhaps of all the quiet successes were right-handed pitcher Bruce Leslie.

On the Bentley State Eagles, Bruce had been the ultimate set-up man. While usually confined to no more than just an inning, he was a spectacular athlete that could pitch endlessly. So far in the majors, he had recorded 12 1/3 innings and not one- runner had yet crossed the plate on his watch.

Whatever Cisco "The Dealer" Wheeler visualized from his skybox on that hot and humiliating night in June, his dreams had now flourished into the hottest and most talked about sports entity on the planet. Night after night, reality began to answer the question: was it really possible that the concept of team really could trump singular athleticism.

In a city that lives on odds, the casinos chances of the Vipers making it to the play-offs went from a million to one in June to now just two-hundred to one in early September. With only three and a half weeks left of the regular season, Las Vegas was now perched to make everybody overly nervous as the three teams they had to beat loomed large and ahead on the schedule.

Beating the Atlanta Braves two out of three and then sweeping the Rockies all at home suddenly vaulted the Vipers into a true topic for the division title. The streak that first was once considered nothing but beginner's luck had now grown to such credibility and to the extent it could not be ignored.

"Here's a college baseball team, a small-college mind you, that has defied the odds to make one think completely differently about this game." Fred Hickman of *ESPN Sports Center* regaled. "Let me really put this scenario into true-grit numbers. Here is an amateur baseball team that magically made it to the big leagues who are now 19-4 as MLB professionals and are challenging for the National

League Western Division lead. The play of the Vipers right fielder Sean Deeters has been nothing but extraordinary as of late batting nearly .500 off some of the most established pitchers in the league. Pitching Coach Tom Browning has incorporated fun back into the art of throwing again with the return of the knuckleball into his pitchers arsenal.

"Watching these guys play honestly, it takes me back to the reason that I fell in love with the game in the first place. Its baseball, friends, pure and simple. Not only my opinion, but I caught up recently with baseball fanatic and comedian Bill Murray on video as he echoed his thoughts on this incredible baseball exploit."

"Oh yea, definitely baby steps, Fred, but with extremely big shoe sizes."

The much beloved actor and baseball fanatic lectured further. "I love my Cubbies, you know that, but I also love this game. If I met these Viper dudes like at a frat party somewhere, yea, I would certainly buy the first round of brewskis'. Seriously, which is really hard for me to do, these guys have really brought the joy back into my life into watching the game as just a baseball fan. I did have this wild and funny dream the other night that the Cubs will finally win the World Series. The bad news is that it won't happen until 2016! I hope I'm still alive then!"

"Bill Murray, one of my favorites." Hickman once again acknowledged. "With just a little over three weeks left in the regular season, no division in the history of divisional play has ever seen a race so close from first to worst this late in the season. With the declining play of both the Rockies and the Giants in the west, the leader-board looks quite interesting with a little over three-weeks left in the regular season, and now, here's an interesting factoid for you purists. This is the latest date in the season for any division race in all of baseball where no team has yet been mathematically eliminated. This one appears to be going right down to the wire and unquestionably one of the most interesting finishes of all time."

21 DOWN IN VEGAS

National League Western Division Standings
September 9, 2006

	W. L.	Pct.	GB
Padres	79–64	.537	-
D' Backs	78–64	.536	0.5
Dodgers	77–65	.527	1.5
Vipers	75–68	.510	4.0
Rockies	71–76	.481	8.0
Giants	71–75	.477	8.5

Back on the road, the Vipers had an unenviable task for the remainder of the season of playing Arizona, Milwaukee, and Cincinnati. The final home-stand would be between San Diego and finishing the season with the perennial favorites the LA Dodgers.

"Listen up!" Manager Tommy leach began. "We have nineteen games to play in twenty-three days. After those games are complete, you can then all go back home to Portsmouth, Ohio, or wherever because your jobs here will officially be done for the 2006 season."

That wry smile from a military delivery began to slowly emerge after a dalliance of silence.

"Unfortunately, I know you guys better than that! The press is burying you all right now because you have played an entire season of college baseball and then two months more, oh, in case you haven't noticed, in the Major Leagues! They all say you're tired, broken down, pitched-out, and don't have the strength to make it to the finish line for the precious post-season. As I look around the room I see Steinman, Carpenter, Milhuff, Arms, Scarbury, and Zebro from our pitching staff. I don't know about you, but I see some of the best arms in the league! Position players, you guys are ranked eighth overall in the National league and that's in most all of the categories that really count. That idiot who writes for the *LA Times* says our bullpen is exhausted.

"Fuller, Burkes, Shackart, Leslie, and Carpenter, you don't look overly haggard and anemic to me. So, the big question is just how many of you pussies feel you can't go another three-weeks before you need to check yourselves in for a year-long rest at the Saint Pia Zadora Golden Buckeye Retirement Community?"

Even if Tommy Leach new nothing about the art of motivational speaking, this response would have put Zig Ziegler to shame. The quick and unrestrained explosion of emotion suggesting that the Vipers' incredible mini-season was simply an anomaly or fluke cut deeply richly to the core.

As the testosterone tsunami peaked and then began to wane, Tommy had one final order of business to demonstrate his point.

"Brewster, get your ass up here and show them what you showed me!"

Jarred Brewster quickly gathered some home-made pie charts he had put together and quickly stumbled up in front of the team. As the room began to quiet down, Jarred quickly became the main focus.

"OK, here's what I have come up with," he confidently began. "We have three teams ahead of us with only nineteen to play. Fortunately, we have the three-teams we need to beat in order to move up and those would be Arizona, San Diego, and the Dodgers. If we average taking two out of three from just them and even if they continue to play .700 percent against the rest of their opponents, I think we will still be able to pick up at least three, maybe even four games in the standings. If we go just .500 against the Brewers and the Reds and I know this is all conjecture, that would put us at 9-7 from right here today with four to go against our last series against the Dodgers. At this point, if I see what I think I do, we will possibly be tied with or a game out of first place with Los Angeles and three left to play here at home."

"So, Merlin, do you also have the 'Power Ball' numbers you can also share with us!" "Dirty" Ernie Fuller shouted.

"Yea, and tell me, is Gambill ever going to get laid before the end of the season? "Karl Smith added.

As laughter filtered across the clubhouse, Tommy Leach once again took a stern stance and threw water on the humorous outburst.

21 DOWN IN VEGAS

"Look at those numbers, guys! I mean really look and study them hard. Ol' Brewster here is pretty damn close." Tommy retorted in a robust manner. "If you really want to see what you have to do here, you got a pretty clear road-map. The margin of error is the fact that the Brewers are going nowhere and the Reds are playing for a division title. I would personally be highly insulted if you only went .500 against them. If we are going anywhere, fellas, we've have got to whip the cream damn it! The Diamondbacks are stumbling, San Diego is treading water, and I too believe it's the Dodgers we really need to have in our sights. Regardless, the bottom line here it's all simple math boys, we got only nineteen-games left to move up four."

11TH INNING

Portsmouth, Ohio, was buzzing with Viper fever as the national reporters seemingly couldn't get enough of this Ohio River port town that had farmed out its college baseball team to the Major Leagues and was now being swamped with attention. A location that was previously identified with the rust belt, history past, and overall anonymity was suddenly splashed upon the headline shores in ways they could have never imagined.

Deborah Norville and the *"Today Show"* set up a mobile studio in the lobby of the downtown Ramada Inn to find local folk who would talk candidly about the most unusual sports story on the planet that was now erupting.

Jeff Albrecht, who was the owner and local business entrepreneur, had worked close with NBC to bring a live morning show broadcast to his hotel. As Jeff put everything in place for the big morning telecast, he reminded the crew that this wasn't the first time that NBC and the *"Today"* morning show had been there.

"You know that Willard Scott was here a few years ago to do a live weather broadcast from Bentley State University," he reminded the busy camera-tech.

"Oh, I wasn't working for them then," Gary Miles quickly and sarcastically responded. "I'm sure he remembers it well!"

"He should," Jeff answered. "He had sent his toupee off to be cleaned, and it never came back on time. I was actually the one that convinced Willard he didn't really need it and so he went out for the first time on camera el natural."

21 DOWN IN VEGAS

"Really," was the astonished answer from Gary Miles, "So you're the bastard that now makes me go through all those letters and emails every week to put those people on the Smucker's Jelly jars."

Caught off guard, Jeff Albrecht couldn't resist simply on asking why?

"OK, Willard is a great guy," Miles began laughing. "But they just thought since that the fake hair was now gone that anyone over a hundred would just instantly love him. So finally meet the man who gives the pleasure of making all the centurions happy every week! That is a great story!"

Both Norville and Bryant Gumball were lining up their guests when Al Roker overheard the conversation and strolled up to Jeff.

"Hey, man, don't worry about me. Let's just face it, brother, mine just ain't coming!"

"Good morning, I'm Deborah Norville on the '*Today Show*' as we come to you live from the beautiful river-town of Portsmouth, Ohio, and home of one of sport's biggest stories of the year, the Las Vegas Vipers, formerly the Bentley State Eagles. With me is the fiancé of the Vipers star outfielder Sean Deeters, Syleanna Griffin. Good morning and thanks for being here with us."

"You're welcome," her guest shyly replied

"Tell me, Syleanna, what does it feel like to see this all unfolding and especially with all of the attention now being given to Sean, your, and the rest of the team?"

"Well, it was hard at first." she lamented. "We really hadn't been away from each other since we were kids and with suddenly him being gone and all with the rest of the guys all being treated like the Back-Street Boys, there was a period of adjustment for sure." Syleanna said with a giggle.

"Sean has certainly become the heart of this team, so what about the other folks here in Portsmouth, Ohio?" she asked. "How are they handling all of this sudden fame as their ex- college team is now competing for a shot to make the Major League Playoffs and perhaps a long shot maybe, but play in the World Series?"

"I know everyone is really proud of them and especially for doing as well as they are. When they lost the college championship, it was really hard, but anyone who knows these special people understand their hearts and will to win."

"Syleanna Griffin is my guest, and by the way congratulations on your upcoming marriage to Vipers right fielder Sean Deeters, and when again is the special date?" Norville couldn't help but to ask.

"Christmas." Syleanna laughed.

"More on the '*Today Show*' coming to you live from the home of the former Bentley State Eagles and now, the Las Vegas Vipers here in Portsmouth, Ohio. We'll be right back."

During the rest of the next two hours, Bryant and Ann talked with Coach Keith Madison, University President Howard Morris, and Portsmouth Mayor Frank Gerlach on the various aspects and impacts of this first ever sports encounter.

Keith reasoned about the team's unusual chemistry and talent and reaffirmed their ability to win at any level. Howard Morris addressed the most unusual manner on how the transition was constructed and praised the Vipers organization and especially Cisco Wheeler for living up to his word on helping with scholarships and other university support.

Portsmouth Mayor Frank Gerlach expressed his thoughts on the economic impact of putting Portsmouth on the national map in such as positive manner. Ann Curry was in the chair for that one.

"Ann, what these boys have done for our city and community is beyond belief." Gerlach touted. "Our hotels are full every night from people who just want to come to Portsmouth and see what this thing is all about. Our Visitors Bureau Director Debbie Lang has now set up daily tours around the area to show people the college, the ball field where they played, and even all the pizza joints where they hung out. Our floodwall muralist Robert Dafford has been notified and is ready to set up painting the team portrait that will go up on the old Hurth Hotel as you cross the bridge and enter the city. As you know, we are the city of murals. It's all been very much fun and exciting!"

Chase Field in downtown Phoenix, Arizona, was primed and pumped as the fans gathered both inside and out for the series they knew could make or break their season.

21 DOWN IN VEGAS

While the Diamondbacks hadn't been playing their best ball as of late, they were still two up on the Vipers in the standings and only a game out of first.

Manager Bob Melvin sat in his office changing the numbers and names with his lineup like it was a Keno card. It was four-games at home with the most unlikely of late season contenders; the Las Vegas Vipers.

As Melvin continued to pencil in and then erase names, he remembered a day when having these guys at home late in the season almost certainly meant a schedule breather with wins guaranteed. For the second time in ten minutes, he found himself again erasing Stephen Drew for Craig Counsell and then dropping him from eighth to sixth in the order. It was less than two-hours to play and trying to play match-up with baseballs most unpredictable and unprecedented team proved to be quite the manager's mental challenge.

Brandon Webb had by far been the D'Backs pitching ace on the season and was in contention for the year's Cy Young Award. Coming into this Thursday night opener, he had a 14-7 record and a sparkling 3.10 era. Growing up and playing his youth baseball just a few miles upriver in Ashland, Kentucky, many baseball fans in the Portsmouth, Ohio, area knew and followed his remarkable career. After playing his college ball at the University of Kentucky, Brandon had been drafted by Arizona in the eighth-round of the 2000 Baseball Amateur Draft.

It would be soon that Brandon Webb would be taking the mound against a team whose players were just a few miles away and several years removed in age from the time that he was the star hurler at Paul Blazer High School.

"His first strike ability is insane." Jarred Brewster relayed to the Hitting Coach Von Hayes. "It's just what he does. After he gets you in the hole, he just nibbles you to pieces."

"I bet you can even give me some percentages on that one." Hayes laughed.

"Ninety-three percent strikes, first pitch, unheard of in this game." Jarred returned. "Five of his seven losses came on aggressive hitting and running wild."

"Well, bucko-O, most of the guys certainly remember who he is from all the local press back home, but I'm not sure any one of them really knows his stuff up here. I'll talk to Tommy and see what he thinks."

"Once he gets that first strike, batters are hitting .178. Get him into a two-two count or better, the averages climbs to .318."

"That's way too much math for me Brew man." Von Hayes admitted. "If you're secretly wanting me to tell everybody to swing at the first pitch, that's a little past my pay grade. Let's just see what Skip thinks. It's interesting for sure, Brewster, but I just gotta ask. Do you really stay up all night working on this kind of stuff?"

"No, only until about 3:30 am." Jarred sheepishly admitted.

KTAR-AM 620 is the hometown voice of the Diamondbacks Radio Network, and it was now late on a Thursday evening as the drive home from the ball-park was a disappointing trek for the hometown faithful.

"Back with the post-game show, this is Greg Schulte with Tom Candiotti as before a near sell-out crowd of 48, 000 the D'Backs fall to the Vipers in game one of this four- game series 8-3. It was rough for Bandon Webb early as it seemed that he could never really get his rhythm going as Las Vegas scored early and often."

"I don't know what to say about these kids who now wear a 'V' on their chest, but they certainly let Brandon know they came here to play scoring three in the first" added color commentator Tom Candiotti.

"It was second baseman Brooks Snyder and right fielder Sean Deeters who both singled in the opening frame before first pitch hitting Bombo Chadwick launched a sky-rocket into the splash pad in right." Schulte added. "That put the Vipers on the board until the second when Boone Coleman and Cliff Collier hit back to back doubles to make it 4-0. Long-ball was again in play as third baseman John Gambill quickly connected on a Brandon Webb fastball to send a souvenir chaser into the lower left field seats. That made it 6-0, and you could really tell at this point Webb's overall frustration level."

"Rightly so, Greg," Candiotti noted. "I think perhaps Brandon might have assumed, and rightly so, that as the ace of this team that

21 DOWN IN VEGAS

his stuff early was obviously disappointing as the Vipers came out swinging and once you get into that kind of a hole, it's hard to claw your way out."

"Brandon Webb gets his eighth-loss of the season as he goes five-innings, giving up seven runs on nine hits. Relievers Brandon Medders and Louis Vizcaino came on in relief and stopped the bleeding, but let's give credit to the Vipers' new young arm Brad Zeiber," Greg Schulte pointed out. "This kid pitching in only his fourth Major League start went seven- innings and gave up only one- run on four- hits. I've also gotta say that this knuckleball thing that Las Vegas is doing certainly worked in the fourth as Zeiber with two on and two outs, fluttered one in on Luis Gonzales that ended a potential rally. It was an Eric Byrnes double that scored Chad Tracy in the fifth and then up until the ninth the D'Backs bats ran silent until Orlando Hudson hit a two-out home run off Vipers reliever Jeremy Burkes with Shawn Green on board and that was all the scoring for Arizona."

"Join us again tomorrow afternoon when Claudio Vargas will be on the mound for the Diamondbacks taking on 'comeback player of the year' candidate Gary Steinman for Las Vegas for a 7:10 p.m. start. From Chase Field in Phoenix, Arizona, this is Greg Schhulte and for my partner Tom Candiote…so long, everybody!"

"We got one on the D'Backs tonight, Cisco!" Brandon Briggs beamed with a late-night call to his boss.

"Yea, but the Padres and Dodgers both won. We're still four-out." grumbled his sullen response.

"Oh, so you've been up late watching '*Baseball Tonight*' again." Brandon laughed. "I thought you told me you were going to try and get to bed earlier."

"I'll sleep plenty when I'm dead." Wheeler replied. "I've waited a lifetime to enjoy this and I'm not wasting a minute. So what's the update on Carpenter?"

"He's been lawn tossing with no pain and so we're going to send him down to Colorado Springs for a start. If all goes well there, we could have him back up here and in the rotation next week."

"What about this Zeiber kid?" Cisco shot back. "He's 3-1 and pitching lights out. Where are we going to put him?"

"Good question, but I don't have an answer for you yet. Let's see how Carpy comes along and just kick that can down the road for a little while on this one." Briggs replied.

"He really looked good tonight, Brandon. Did you see what he did to poor ol' Luis Gonzales?" Cisco chortled. "He just about corkscrewed him into the ground chasing that damn knuckler!"

"OK, Chief, it's late and I'll let you go. I'll be flying home after the weekend series, and hopefully, we'll be a little closer to where we want to be." Briggs said.

"Tell the boys I'm proud of them and keep kicking ass!" Cisco insisted. "Talk to you tomorrow!"

The locker room was loose as jokes, laughter, and snapping towels began the pre-game ritual for game two against Arizona. Gary Steinman on his return and re-dedication to the team had been the rock of the pitching rotation. Since the All-Star Break, he was 6-0 with and earned run average below one and two-complete games to his credit. With ruggedly handsome good looks akin to Clark Gable, Gary was quiet and a bit of a loner compared to the rest. As he sat in front of his locker head down in silence, he was suddenly joined by another.

"Hey, Steiny, how ya' feeling?" Tom Browning asked as he sat down beside him.

"OK, arms good…everything's fine." he responded.

"You're having a hell of a second half of the season, brother. Wow, there's nobody in the league since all this shit came down that can touch you. After all you've been through, trust me, whatever you're doing right now, just keep on keeping on. These guys need to see your light."

Still waters run deep as Gary silently nodded and then looked away. Tom Browning knew that something beyond the casual locker room chatter was at stake and pressured through with yet another question.

"I've known you since we signed you from Kansas City, third-round pick in '96. One of my best memories was the time we went back to KC and you ordered all of our meals at Arthur Bryant's Barbeque Restaurant and your personal bill was for over twenty-one hundred bucks!"

Looking up slowly, he looked Tom in the eyes with a smug half-grin before finally answering.

"Did anybody complain?" he sarcastically countered

"You know your brisket, Steiny, and that was great fun!" Browning laughed. "Everything else OK?" he asked.

After a long pause, Gary Steinman finally uttered just one word, Dad."

Pausing for a second, Tom Browning finally picked up on the message and thought long and hard before responding. It was obviously an opening to a conversation that needed continued verbiage.

"Your dad…is he OK?" asked Browning.

"Not really, tests came back that he may have a colon problem. I'm really not sure about everything or what they revealed, but Mom says at this point, it's not good." Gary admitted.

In the midst of horseplay and a casual sports atmosphere, it is always tough to really claim the moment when it comes to a serious situation, and Tom Browning suddenly felt very on the spot and a tad bit uncomfortable.

"Do you wanna talk?" Tom Browning asked.

"Naw, not now." Gary slowly answered. "Just keep him in in your prayers. I'm just trying to channel his strength into mine. He has always been my biggest fan from Little League on up, and I know how much all this means to him. I guess right now I'm kind of pitching for the both of us."

"Hey, if there's anything you need…" Browning began.

"Thanks, Pug, I really appreciate it." Steinman interrupted. "I'll let you know, I promise."

Every awkward conversation has that time you know when everything that can be said is now complete. Standing up, Tom slapped Gary on the shoulder as the universal sign of friendship and brotherhood. As he walked away, he now understood where Gary's extra-strength and focus was now being generated.

As tight as things were in the National League West, the American League race looked like it would be a photo finish in two-divisions.

It was a dual between the Twins and the Tigers in the A. L. Central with Oakland and the Angels in the West exchanging blows like two heavyweights in the late rounds. The New York Yankees were now up by ten-games in the Eastern Division and simply on cruise control just waiting to see who their first round opponent would be in the play-offs.

"Imus in the Morning' on AM- 66, 'The Fan.' It's 7:10 a.m. and with me is Warner Wolf and sports. Warner, the Yankees are headed to the World Series and we all know it, but this poser team and a bunch of college kids are still filching all the headlines. So why is it that such a big story over the most dominant baseball team in history, and may I also add with twenty-six world titles? So why are we being overshadowed by a bunch of pimple--faced losers that couldn't even win their own damn college championship title? I just don't get it."

"No, Don, you wouldn't because you really live in your own little bubble!"

Wolf clarified, "It's because these guys are exactly what the sports world doesn't want you to get or understand."

Laughing, Imus went back to his side-kick with a counter question that went straight to the soul and the kind of banter that gave Don his moniker of media irreverence.

"Warner, you've been around New York sports your whole career. You know all about the losers in this town. My god...we've had the Knicks, the Giants, the Jets, the Mets, and finally after fifteen seasons, the Yankees are finally showing us a little something. These greasy little kids who found a loop-hole on how to flunk out of college and then get paid are still catching all the press attention from you guys. Has it really gotten to the point these days that in sports you really don't have to do anything athletic on the field to get famous?"

Warner Wolf who at times could play dumb as the foil to the headstrong Don Imus, unexpectedly decided to release a diatribe of

21 DOWN IN VEGAS

his own on the fabled radio legend that is still talked about in the "Big Apple" to this day.

"Don, you know there's nobody I enjoy working with more than you. In this case though, you have just become one of the biggest idiots and fakes on the planet demonstrating to your millions of beloved listeners just how out of touch you are with not only your life, but what is going on in sports. I would hope you would really look at what you just said about 'us guys' and see just how ridiculous it makes you sound. Look at the Vipers' record, Don, look at their stats, and really, Don…you need to personally go to a ballgame occasionally and just watch how these guys play before passing judgment. The sad part is that you might even actually enjoy it!"

After an obvious pause of embarrassing silence, all that was heard next was a quick sign-off. "I'm outta here! For AM-66 Radio Sports, 'The Fan,' I'm Warner Wolf!"

"It's 'Imus in the Morning' where it's 7:13 a.m. on 'The Fan.' (Quack-quack.) I don't know who pissed in Warner's Cheerios this morning, but I do know a novelty freak-show when I see it, and that's just what this slam-sham baseball team from Las Vegas is all about. Commissioner Bud Selig should be thoroughly investigated and even impeached for ever letting this thing happen in professional sports. Delbert McClinton is coming up next to change the mood and talk about his new album release 'The Definitive Collection' and it's all right here on the 'Imus in the Morning' program on AM-66, 'The Fan', Radio Sports, New York."

As one radio host was taking the young Vipers phenomena to task, another morning duo was recapping the previous night's performance with a far more glowing mood of appreciation and accomplishment.

"It's 'Mike and Mike' on ESPN2 where the outstanding performance of last night's MLB performances has to go to the Las Vegas Vipers Gary Steinman. Golic, these things just aren't supposed to happen in real life." Mike Greenberg laughed.

"Are you referring to the now three-complete games in his last seven-starts or that a former average pitcher has now painted a big red 'S' on his chest and the hitters just can't locate the kryptonite? Wow, what a story last night in Phoenix." Mike Golic exuberated.

"Nine- innings, no- runs, two -hits, and fifteen strikeouts for Gary Steinman last night in Phoenix against the D'Backs and I think it's safe to certainly say that he has resurrected his career since the All-Star massacre as Steinman for sure has ended up one of the few lone survivors." added Greenberg.

"The Vipers Sean Deeters, now he's become quite the story too, Mike, as he went 4-5 last night raising his Major League Average now up to .318, knocking in three as Las Vegas picks up a game in that wild Western Division shoot out taking down Arizona 6-0." Mike Golic concluded. "Coming up, former boxing great and now analyst, Ray 'Boom Boom' Mancini will join us to preview the Pacquiao-Morales fight that is scheduled for later this year with 'Mike and Mike' in the morning on ESPN2."

12ᵀᴴ INNING

Back at chase field in Phoenix, a loose and confident clubhouse was preparing to wrap up the series with the Diamondbacks. As the iPods and boom boxes blared a loud mix of up-tempo tunes, Cliff Collier was all about the charging Vipers chances.

"There's nothing like a Saturday night in Arizona, baby!" Cliff shouted. "It's standing room only at the 'all-you-can-eat buffets' and an hour wait to get on a shuffleboard court, but I say tonight we demolish these 'fake- snakes' and take number three by force!"

John Gambill, Garry Duzan, and Bombo Chadwick quickly shouted in agreement as a partially clad Brooks Snyder stood up on a bench to add more force to the acceleration of emotion.

"We got to keep this thing going! I don't want to be one of those teams that all the sports channels say just faded into Bolivian! Hell, I don't even know where that place is, but the playoffs sound more fun, and I don't think you even need a passport to get there!"

"Bolivian?" Karl Smith noted.

"Forget it, he's rolling." Mitch Milhuff laughed.

Mitch Milhuff was preparing to take the hill for the Vipers and a Saturday night special against Arizona ace Miquel Batista. It was a game that purely had separation status clearly marked upon it as Las Vegas was now a half a game in back of the D'Backs and tied with the Rockies. The Vipers had picked up a half game on Colorado who hadn't played on Thursday and were now entertaining a three-game weekend series against St Louis. By winning the Friday night opener, the Vipers and Rockies were now virtually tied with a record of 76-72 and now stood just three- games out of first place in the division with the Diamondbacks at two and a half out with a record of 77-72. The first-place Padres were desperately trying to hold off the pack with a record of 79-69.

For a Major League team that had never even come close to tasting the sweet mantra of success, Las Vegas was now in the crosshairs of virtually everybody they knew from the other teams, the press, and all ex-players. The team's biggest confederate was the swelling fan base of interest for it was no more considered just blind luck that with a little over two weeks left in the Major League Baseball season; this team would take interest in the sport of baseball to a whole new echelon.

"What are we going to do if Carpenter comes back strong and we have to send Zeiber back to Colorado Springs?" Tom Browning lamented to his manager and fellow coaches. "This kid is special, and the way he's throwing right now, I don't see how we can send him down."

"If Carpenter is able to get back and pitch decent after his rehab stint, you have to remember that he's still been out for well over a month." Von Hayes added. "I agree with Tom that it might be tough immediately throwing him back in heat of things."

Looking around the room at his support group of allies, Tommy Leach slowly shook his head before responding to the potential conundrum.

"Guys, you're all forgetting our number one rule and creating a fire-storm before the match has even been struck. In this game it's a fact that you can never have enough pitching! So, if they're both reincarnations of Cy Young, we'll just have to send somebody else down, it's as easy as that. All I see right now is a calendar and it says that it's two and a half weeks until the playoffs, and we are still three-games out with seventeen left to play. So again, welcome to my nightmare!"

With the American League East virtually decided, the New York Yankees were starting to rest key players in anticipation of making a run for their twenty-seventh world title. Toots Randall found himself playing more than usual as of late, and with his cavalier attitude against his former team and natural vocal excessiveness, he had become a lightning-rod for sound bites from the local press.

21 DOWN IN VEGAS

Joel Sherman from the *New York Post* was one of the writers who was most enthralled by the connection between Toots Randall and the Vipers and couldn't help twisting the dagger a bit every time they got together. Good copy always came from difficult questions, and Joel needed a good story and knew just where to find it. It was after a Yankees win over Minnesota that he quietly stood next to Randall's locker waiting for him to return from the shower.

"Hey, Tootsie, good game today!" he barked. "Looks like your swing is in play-off form."

"Yea, I'm seeing the ball pretty good right now. I'm just getting tuned up to be used as they need me once we get into post-season."

"And you're OK with that?" Sherman jumped in. "Honestly, Toots, you were a starting left fielder for Las Vegas, and now you're a part-time player, albeit the Yankees, is that a difficult roll for you?"

Pausing for a moment before responding, Toots Randall realized that his answer needed to be as politically correct as possible.

"Yea, I'm OK with it. I think every player would like to play every day, but considering where I was. There's an old saying that says it's better to serve in heaven than to rule in hell. I'm in a much better place here in New York and happy about my role with the Yankees."

"You do realize that there is a chance you could meet your former employer at some point down the road, don't you?" Sherman coyly inserted. "How would you feel about that?"

"What are you saying…the World Series?" Randall tersely reacted.

At this point, Sherman knew that the knife had found its mark, and now he slowly smiled as the twisting began.

"Toots, you know how unpredictable this game is. What I am saying is how would you feel if by some strange coincidence you found the Yankees and the Vipers playing each other in the series this year? I mean…it could happen."

The expression on Toots Randall's face telegraphed the fact that Joel Sherman had not only hit a bull's-eye with his question, but also had his story for the next day.

"Look around this room, Joel. These are the greatest players in the game! I mean Jeter, Williams, Posada, Rodrigues, Cano, and seriously, you're asking me if that day-care operation I used to be with can compete with this?" Randall let out a belly-laugh as he tried to mimic Macaulay Culkin's face-grabbing scene in the movie *Home Alone*. "I will give them credit for being somewhat competitive playing in the weakest division in all of baseball, but when it comes to this level of skill, get real, Joel. All I can say is that when the playoffs arrive, they better all be ready to leave their toys back in the big sandbox and go home to their mothers!"

The next day's end of the world font size on the sports page was just three words: "Toys for Toots!" The story by Joel Sherman had done the deed, creating yet another global disturbance firing up everybody and all who needed yet another log on this media inferno. A quick phone call from GM Brian Cashman's office went directly to Manager Joe Torre.

"Joe, this is Brian. Have you seen the *Post* today?"

"No, I can't say that I have, what's up?" Joe Torre quizzically responded.

"You need to shut Randall down from speaking to anybody outside of this organization. I know he's got a hair up his ass about where he came from, but I will not let that stuff play here. He's a fucking bench player, and I know why Joel Sherman wants talk to him and it's just to get a stupid story like this thing that he got today." Cashman vented. "We are the New York Yankees, and trashing other teams in the press is not what we do. We do ours on the field! Take care of it, Joe!"

The receiver slammed down hard as Manager Joe Torre knew that this was a task that needed to be dealt with immediately. Summoning Toots Randall into his office, the rest of the squad knew that Torre's Italian temper was now set on high.

While not actually being able to hear the words being spoken, the thunderous rumble of noise through the wall was the only evidence anybody needed to know that an unpleasant situation was in progress.

With the sound of deafening quickly turned into mute, the door to Joe Torre's office finally opened up as a red-faced Randall left silently and headed to his locker.

21 DOWN IN VEGAS

"Hope he's got enough ass to play today." Bernie Williams laughed. "He's gonna' look extra funny out there chasing fly balls while running on his hands."

While Toots Randall was being read the riot act, others were reading the box score from the night before. In Portsmouth, Ohio, Coach Keith Madison was crunching the numbers around his Sunday morning breakfast table at his home on Woodlawn Avenue.

"Wow, seven innings of four hit ball!" he thought shaking his head. "Mitch did it again as Shackart and Fuller sealed the deal."

Totally digesting the bottom-line results was something Keith loved to do. Seeing Deeters, Snyder, and Chadwick with two hits apiece and a Cliff Collier home run all congregated in the little ink square, the 6-1 win proved that even with the early season pressure, his boys hadn't lost their desire to inspire. Now that Keith had thoroughly digested that part of the recap, the standings were his next deciphering mission.

"Tied for second place with the Dodgers, half a game ahead of Arizona." Keith pondered. "Man, this thing is just all too damn familiar."

While drifting back to the spring and early summer, the fabric of winning for the Bentley State Eagles came from challenging moments where a stutter here or a stumble there would have resulted in nothing but a good story. As he sat back and sipped his coffee, Keith again realized that this team simply knew no other way than to win. Even the final out in the College World Series was a judgment call that seriously could have gone either way. Always finding that magic door and manufacturing opportunity when you were down was a benchmark of what the Eagles did in rolling through the much more favored opponents that kept them dangerous until the end. Finishing the game synopsis from the night before, the writer included yet another zinger on the young hurlers pitch selection.

"One more than one occasion, Milhuff went with the 'knuckleball' to keep Arizona off balance. At one point, a frustrated Eric Brynes slammed his bat to the ground and broke it after a futile air-swing at a 65 mile an hour floater."

Waxing even further reminiscent, Keith suddenly felt the urge to call Sean Deeters, maybe Mitch…Brewster would certainly love to chat! After a well-thought-out moment, he quickly put his excitement into hibernation. No, this wasn't his team anymore. As proud of them as Keith Madison could be, he was now just one of the millions of fans world-wide who would just have to be content at being an enthusiastic fan!

"They're only three- games out of first place!" Syleanna Griffin screeched on the phone to her older sister. "Sean called me last night after the game and he said that they had leo-tarded the Arizona team!"

"Leo-tarded…a team!" her sister giggled. "What's that mean?"

"I guess that they moved ahead and now are closer to first place." She awkwardly answered. "I think leo-tarded has something to do with their spots or something in the standings."

"Hey, sis, I know you're high on staying up late at night watching baseball, but could the word Sean used that you're looking for be leap-frogged."

Yea! That's it! Leap-frogged!" Syleanna confusingly admitted. "They leap-frogged the Diamondbacks who were in second place, and now they're tied for third."

"That doesn't make any sense at all Syleanna!" she answered. "Are you and Carla hitting the margarita buffet again over at Toro Loco?"

"No, no, no. They were tied for third and Arizona lost, so the Vipers and the Dodgers who both won are now in third!" she attempted to explain.

"Hey, Barbie Doll, you spent far more time in home economics than math class." Her sister Lindsey laughed. "Your man is only three-games out of first and tied for second with LA, and by the way, you should also be the first person to know that the city of Portsmouth today has already lined up four busses to take people down to the ball-park for the Cincinnati series next weekend."

"Holy shit!" Syleanna screeched. "Carla and I were already going down and now the entire city has been invited too?"

"Yep! Better keep your top on over at Toby Keith's, sis," she reaffirmed, "or it might be you who gets center-stage on the next 'E' Entertainment Spotlight Special!"

Milwaukee to someone that's never been there before can sometimes be a head-scratching first impression. With the new Miller Park being one of the largest construction projects in Wisconsin history, the fans are incredibly loyal as they are Polish.

By that, they are proud blue-collar fans who love their baseball and bring their rich heritage to the park every night. If it's not "The Beer Barrel Polka" being played between innings, it's the anticipation of the legendary sausage race that pits sheer speed against foam rubber supremacy. While the Brewers managed a few minor runs to the top in the National League Central, it was a late season collapse that now had them eight- games out of first with just a handful to play. As the Reds, Cardinals, and Astros fought each night for division control, Milwaukee was firmly entrenched in fourth place and fading fast.

"It's four here and then three in the 'Nati' before we drag our poor worn-out asses back home to the desert!" Deeters joked to Cliff who was stretched out in the player's lounge.

"Yea, I can hardly move a muscle myself, buddy. These baseball games and chasing a title have really taken a toll on me." Cliff yawned in his sarcastic response. "Carla's all freaked out now about coming to Cincy this weekend. Have you heard that the Portsmouth American Legion is bringing four-buses full down to the game?"

"Syleanna told me that yesterday." Sean affirmed. "Wow, this is really turning strange. Growing up, Cliff, you and I have been Reds fans our whole lives, and now can you believe this? We are now going to play against them? This is just too funny…three games!

"We got to get through these guys first, so don't go all homie on me yet."

Cliff warned. "Fielder, Jenkins, and Lee would like nothing better than to show their folks that we don't belong here. Just remember the tourney after we beat Texas and Florida. Everybody from that point we're just licking their big ol' chops to show us the trap door to to where all the hungry alligators lived!"

"I guess up here nobody has figured out that we baseball bumpkins have finally learned how to nail the damn thing shut." Sean laughed. "Let's get out here a little early tonight to find a concessioner. I've got to find me some of that secret hot dog sauce I hear everyone talking about. Pouge was telling me that on any kind of meat, it's like nectar from the gods."

"Yea, I'm with you there. That's the stuff Joe Buck is always raving about." Cliff agreed. "I also love it here because everywhere you go and hear people talk, it reminds me of my favorite movie, "*Fargo*."

"Well, buddy," Sean laughed, "I can help you with the hot dog sauce, but if a wood chipper should suddenly show up somewhere along the way, you're on your own there bro!"

While at the this point in the season and every game crucial, all three teams at the top of the leader-board in the west held serve for the week with the Padres, Dodgers, and the Vipers, each splitting their four-game series respectively. Arizona continued to free fall out of contention, getting swept again by the Marlins.

Brad Zeiber and Scotty "The Golden" Arms threw a couple of gems against the "Brew Crew" while Mitch Milhuff became the victim of a Prince Fielder hitting clinic. In a rare default, reliever "Dirty" Ernie Fuller gave up a walk-off homer to third baseman Jeff Cirillo in the ninth with two on that would have given the Vipers a three out of four series advantage. Overall, the mood was still upbeat and positive as the young former Eagles now headed to as close to their real home as they had been during the abbreviated season: Cincinnati, Ohio.

As the chartered jet touched down at CVG, Tommy and his staff were brain-storming about their forced move of bringing Everett Carpenter back to the squad. With the play-offs now less than two weeks away, it was now decision time.

"We have till Monday, boys." Leach bemoaned. "We got to use him or lose him. He's been pretty damn impressive in his rehab, and I know he could give us a boost. If we don't do something, he won't be available to us for the playoffs and that's league rules."

"Why don't we send Winston Clyde down?" Tom Browning injected. "He hasn't really played all that much, and right now, we are a bit bench-player heavy."

21 DOWN IN VEGAS

"Chemistry, Pug, chemistry," Leach answered quickly. "We brought all these kids up as a unit, and honestly, after what they've done, I would be scared shitless at this point to break up the band. No, we have till the end of this series to figure it out, so please, any and all suggestions will be entertained."

As the crow flies, Cincinnati is one hundred miles due west of Portsmouth, Ohio. Just about anybody in the area who is a Major League Baseball fan roots for the sports' oldest professional team. It was always a rite of passage each summer to listen to Marty Brennaman and Joe Nuxhall calling the games on WNXT-AM.

Names like Rose, Bench, Perez, Morgan, Davis, Larkin, and so many others had become so much a part of the baseball landscape lore in this small river-town as the commute to the Queen City was just a mere two- hours away. The impact of the young players from Portsmouth now playing their long-standing favorite team, and childhood heroes was a definite concern during this crucial run.

On the bus ride from the downtown Westin Hotel out to Great American Ballpark, Tommy Leach took the quick ten-minute commute to address his players.

"What you guys are going to be dealing with here is a little bizarre on top of incomprehensible. I get it! Brewster has been sleeping at my doorstep trying to explain it to me for the last week. I know you guys grew up loving the Cincinnati Reds. If you go into this series as star-struck kids instead of the Major League professionals that you are, it will get ugly! This series will separate you from the boys you were to the men you are today. I also realize that the entire city of Portsmouth will be here too. That can be another huge distraction. The bottom line is we have ten games left to play, and when we get home on Monday, we will have a chance to determine our own fate. That is, if you guys do your job here so that we can be in striking distance against the Padres and the Dodgers.

Just remember, Cincinnati is fighting for a title too. They are only three-out of the Central Division, and you will be playing before 43,000 crazy people for three days. All I ask is that you stay focused, play hard, and show these sons of bitches that you're better than them. Are there any questions?"

Slowly raising his hand, Brooks Snyder had a sheepishly confused look on his face.

"Yea, Snyder, what is it?" Leach barked.

"Well, I know we are going to have distractions when we get to the ballpark, but does that also include standing on the street corner to help Pug sell his books and listen to him tell those Mr. Perfect stories to all the fans?"

The bus exploded into laughter as Tom Browning and his legacy had long been ingratiated into Reds baseball history with his perfect game he threw against the Dodgers in 1988. His free-spirit attitude added to the legacy by being the only MLB rookie pitcher to ever win twenty games, and the fact that in 1993, Tom mingled with the fans by leaving the dugout during a game with the Chicago Cubs and sat with all the bums during the game on the Waveland Avenue rooftop. That particular impromptu seat cost Browning a $1,000 fine from the commissioner.

Standing up, Tom quickly addressed the festiveness by announcing that his brother-in-law was moving on Saturday and he had already promised him that the team would be there to help transport him and his belongings in the morning since the game wasn't until later that night.

The attitude was loose and airy as the team bus finally arrived along the banks of the majestic Ohio River. One by one, the team members emerged to meet a pilgrimage many only knew previous from the ticket window to their assigned seats. Tonight, there would be no pushy usher problems what-so-ever in giving the new Las Vegas Vipers players the very best view in the house.

"Andy Furman here on WLW Sportsline as the Reds get ready tonight to take on baseballs version of the Frankenstein monster! That's right, a baseball team that's been sewn together from several different moving parts as a new life form that has somehow been miraculously breathed into a twenty-five-man roster that was as close to dead as any sports franchise in history.

"When all this craziness began right after the All-Star break, if you remember, I went stark-raving nuts right here on these very airwaves of WLW saying how ridiculous and utterly idiotic this was to the game of baseball and it should all be declared null and void at all costs. Well, I'm here tonight to eat and digest the biggest portion of crow I have ever bellied up to in my radio career because, friends…I was wrong.

"What this team from 'lost wages' has done to revitalize interest into a less than exciting and very predictable sport may and could be one of the biggest sports stories of all time. Tonight, it will be Aaron Harang on the mound for the Reds opposing Gary Steinman for the Vipers who, like the rest of these lovable freaks, has reincarnated himself from being just another face in the crowd into baseball's premier starter over the past two months. Marty and Joe are coming up next with the call right here on your home for Cincinnati Reds Baseball, WLW."

"Where's Brachett?" Tommy Leach asked, suddenly realizing that he hadn't seen his bench coach for a while. "It's less than a half-hour before game time. Has anybody seen Norm?"

"He was lying down, Skip." Bombo Chadwick answered. "Said he wasn't feeling well and was trying to shake it off. He was on the couch in the lounge."

As the players prepared to leave the dugout for their final warm-ups, Tommy went back down the tunnel to see what was going on. Checking out the club-house, he found his friend and ally, "Stormin" Norman Bratchett lying down on the couch with a cold compress on his head.

"Hey, partner, you feeling OK?" Tommy asked.

Slowly opening his eyes, the man who was his closest assistant squinted as he softly spoke. "I feel like shit, Tommy. It kind of feels like the flu is coming on, but I feel numb all up my left side. I think maybe it was all that kielbasa we ate in Milwaukee. Man, it's doing a number on me now."

Noting his ashen look and obvious lack of energy, Tommy Leach knew that a quick recovery for tonight's game was out of the question.

"OK, just stay here. I'll send Larry in to have a look at you. Von can help me out on the bench tonight. Damn it Norm! I told you too much of that spicy-greasy stuff will pickle your innards. Now you're in Cincinnati, and I'm going to have to keep you away from all that weird-ass chili shit they make here!" Leach playfully scolded.

Sporting a weak smile, the Vipers bench coach slowly lifted his hand to wave as he pulled his blanket up even tighter toward his chest. "Go kick some butts tonight, Chief. We need every one of them."

Soaking in an enthusiastic Friday night crowd as he stood at home plate with his lineup card in hand was uniquely special for Manager Tommy Leach. Along with three hundred plus fans from Portsmouth in the seats, there was a definite hometown vibe for his visiting team being so close to where all of the baseball insanity for the summer of 2006 was spawned.

A young middle school student from Portsmouth West High School named Jacob Tolliver was selected to sing the National Anthem as Randy Arnett who was the CEO of Southern Ohio Medical Center in Portsmouth was like-wise tagged to throw out the first pitch. It was a bitter-sweet night in Cincinnati where the fans of the Reds seemingly wanted to pull for the local media phenoms, but realizing at the same time that they too were also in a chase for a division title.

Among the invited guests for the evening were Syleanna Griffin and Carla Harris who were privy to the player tickets and seated right behind the visitor's dugout.

"Can you believe this?" Carla squealed. "The last time we were down here, it was with Sean and Cliff and we almost got thrown out for trying to get better seats."

"Yea, it was that old hawk-nosed guy that kept chasing us around every time we moved." Syleanna laughed. "Well, he can kiss my big old rosy-red butt tonight 'cause we ain't going nowhere!"

"The guys were so nice to surprise us with these seats." Carla added.

"I guess we are going to meet up after the game over at the Holy Grail. You know what happened the last time we were there?"

It was the sly grin from Syleanna that confirmed she remembered the now infamous table dancing incident that occurred after consuming one more Long Island ice tea than her limit during a weekend outing with the girls.

"Do you think they have possibly forgiven you yet for all that?" Carla coyly mused.

"If not, maybe another autographed baseball by Sean might take care of it." Syleanna laughed.

Since the opening of Great American Ballpark and its inaugural season in 2003, Joe Zerhusen has been the official PA announcer. His booming voice and often pro-Reds enthusiasm had made him a fan favorite often down- playing the opposition when they arrived at the plate for their required public introduction. Tonight, it was different. Joe realizing that this miracle team from just one hundred miles away deserved a better fate. Even though they would be the opposition, it would be in his full power as the stadium announcer to make each of the players from the Las Vegas Vipers feel as welcome as possible.

"Ladies and gentlemen! Tonight, we welcome a very special bunch of guys to Great American Ball Park as the former Bentley State Eagles from Portsmouth, Ohio, who now represent the Las Vegas Vipers entering tonight's three-game series against your Cincinnati Reds! Their accomplishments over the past two months have captured sports headlines around the world, and so please wish them a great Ohio homecoming here to Cincinnati!"

"Batting first and leading off and playing right field, Sean Deeters! Playing second and batting second, Brooks Snyder! Hitting third and playing short-stop, Gary Duzan! Batting fourth and playing left field, 'King Kong' Karl Smith. Batting fifth and playing first base, it's Bombo Chadwick. In center field and batting sixth, Cliff Collier. Batting seventh and playing third base, John Gambill. Doug Pouge will do the catching tonight and bat eight. And on the mound this evening and batting ninth- Gary Steinman!"

The roar of the crowd for the Vipers was almost to the fervor of the hometown Redlegs. As the Reds were now being announced, there was an eerie feeling of local camaraderie, yet also the honest truth of competition that always separates two combatants who prepared to take the field of truth on a spectacular and warm Cincinnati evening.

Inconspicuous to the sold-out crowd awaiting the first pitch was a wheel-chair-bound figure that finally inched up to the handicap section of the ball-park handicapped section.Sitting there very auspiciously was a man wearing a Vipers jersey and sporting a Bentley State Eagles cap. Ushers were there and ceremoniously trying to make the gentleman feel much a part of the evening as he finally gazed up to the young lady that that was attending his seat position.

"That's my boy out there tonight, are you a Vipers fan, my lady?" Came the soft inquiry.

"No, sir! I just work here summers to pay for my tuition. I really don't like baseball all that much, but it's a pretty good job."

"Watch my son tonight, lassie! His name is Gary Steinman, and nobody on earth can throw a baseball like that kid. I showed him when he was just eight years old the God-given talent he had inside. He's a lot like his old-man, he's always got a chip on his shoulder and got something to prove. He finally after all these years has something with it. Damn, I love that kid!"

"Thank you, Mr. Steinman. My name is Kylie, and I'll be taking care of you for the evening. From all of us here at Great American Ballpark, we certainly hope you enjoy your time tonight and here with us."

WLW Radio was blistering through the pops and crackle of the late August night sky as two of the most beloved interpreters of the sport were verbally painting the magic scenery that now lie before them.

"Marty Brennaman with Joe Nuxhall and no score here in the fourth and a game that means plenty for both teams here tonight. If the Reds win, they move two-behind St. Louis who lost this afternoon to the Cubs and the Vipers who are now three-out in the Western Division would also claim a game-up today if the Dodgers should also lose tonight against San Diego."

"Well, Marty, we've had a lot going on here tonight and off the field as well." Reds announcer Joe Nuxhall quickly interjected. "We just got word from the clubhouse that Viper's Bench Coach Norm Bratchett has been taken to Good Samaritan Hospital here in Cincinnati due to some tightness in his chest. We hear that our ol' buddy and now Vipers trainer Larry Starr has recommended that he be looked at as soon as possible and we all hope that it's just a minor affliction."

"We wish him our best, Joe!" Marty quickly added. "Stormin' Norman is truly one of the good guys in this game, and if there is a problem to deal with, Larry Starr is the best. After all, he was here with the Reds for thirty-some years, and I personally still wonder why he's not here today to be honest. I noticed earlier in the evening that Von Hayes has taken over the bench duties and now that pretty much explains it."

Disconnect between the happenings in the broadcast booth and the dug-out are often common. While the players were focusing on the game, few knew that there was a more serious concern for their bench coach and ally just a few steps away.

"Is Norm OK?" John Gambill asked, sitting next to Bombo Chadwick. "He had the flu or something. To be honest, he didn't look too good."

"Tommy sent Larry in to see him." Chadwick responded. "He'll probably give him a cortisone shot and stick him in the steamer. That's the magic bullet, you know."

"Damn, Gary is on it tonight!" Karl Smith added. "He gave up that bloop-single to Hatteberg and that's it."

"We better get our asses in gear too in case you haven't noticed, we're sitting on the nest too. Come on buddy, Harang can be had. We need this one!"

As if on cue, Brooks Snyder teed-off on a Harang slider and sent a laser-shot into the right field corner for a standup double. Two outs in the top of the fourth and Gary Duzan now stepped to the plate.

As the starting shortstop for the Vipers, "The Duz" had been certainly more than adequate in the field having made only three errors since assuming the starting role. At the plate, he was a bit streaky batting only .239, but his hits were always something that seemed to make a difference.

Standing in against Aaron Harang, Gary patiently worked him into a full- count, knowing that the next pitch should be the one to hit; his assumption was correct.

"It's a line-drive through the middle" barked Red's broadcaster Marty Brennaman. "They're sending Snyder home as Chris Denorfia cuts it off in the alley from right field and he comes up throwing, Here comes the ball, here comes Snyder to the plate…he's safe! Duzan is trying for two! And now he's going to be thrown out by a good ol' country mile from Ross to Brandon Phillips. I don't know what that young man was thinking, but that was as bad of a base running decision there as you'll ever see. In the middle of inning number four, the Vipers are the first to score as Las Vegas takes a 1-0 lead and the Reds are coming to bat."

Gary Steinman unrelenting pounded the plate as the Cincinnati Reds batters continued to come and go. Hopper, Hollingsworth, Aurillia, and the rest of the Reds finally got to witness what the others in the league had already seen since the All-Start break. It was simply total pitching domination.

As the innings continued to fly by, Manager Jerry Narron started to prepare for the ninth knowing that Aaron Harang was beginning to wear down. Reliever Todd Coffee was warming up in the bullpen as the Vipers took their swings in the top of the ninth. Bombo Chadwick and Cliff Collier both singled with one out as the Reds manager finally pulled the plug on his starter as Coffee sprinted in from left field to take over the pitching duties. It took him a mere three- pitches to entice John Gambill to ground into an inning-ending double play.

Silently, Gary Steinman walked to the mound for what he hoped would his final appearance.

Catcher Jason Larue would pinch hit for the pitcher as Narron had made a double-switch in the ninth inning trying to line up some offense. Phillips, Dunn, and Griffey were to follow.

Tommy Leach and his "hands on the knee" posture indicated unsure body language of what to expect from his most reliable arm in the ninth hanging on to a one-run lead.

"Brewster, how many pitches is Steiny up to now?" Leach asked.

"One hundred fifteen, Tommy," was his authoritative reply. "He threw 127 against Arizona, and that's the most he's thrown all season."

21 DOWN IN VEGAS

After a short pause, he added yet another quick snippet of information to his manager.

"You know his dad is here tonight." Jarred softly spoke.

With a quick jerk of the head, the Vipers manager turned to Jarred as if he had just been stung by a bee.

"He's here!" Tommy shouted. "I thought he was in the hospital and in the intensive care unit. You mean like he's here…in the ballpark…like right now?'

"He didn't want Gary to know, I guess, figuring that it would make him all nervous or something," Jarred confessed. "A friend got him out of the hospital from Indianapolis, and they brought him down just for the day. He's gotta go right back after the game."

No sooner said than the crowd at Great American Ballpark erupted as Jason Larue lifted a long fly ball to center field that just missed tying up the game as it careened off the batters-eye in center for a stand-up double. Speedster Ray Almedo quickly replaced Larue on second as the tying run was now in scoring position.

"Pug, get Fuller ready!" Leach commanded, "And quickly!"

Catcher Doug Pouge briskly trotted to the mound, giving time for his pitcher to settle down a bit and to regroup his thoughts. It was also more time to get "Dirty" Ernie Fuller lose and ready.

"You OK, Hammer?" Pouge asked

"Yea, I just got that one up too high. I'm fine, just pissed." Steinman moaned.

"All right, you got Phillips. Watch him for a bunt and keep it low."

Steinman nodded as his catcher trotted back behind the plate as Brandon Phillips now settled into the batter's box. As anticipated on the second pitch, Phillips laid down a slow- roller that hugged the first-base line. Leaping from behind the plate, Pouge fired a bullet to Bombo Chadwick that nipped the speedy Phillips by a half a step.

"One-out…and Almedo is now just ninety-feet from tying this bad boy up!" Marty Brennaman boasted. "The meat of the order is on the way for the Reds, and this might be it for Gary Steinman as Manager Tommy Leach leaves the dugout and heads slowly to the mound! Ernie Fuller also known as "The Dirt Man" has been warming up in the Vipers bullpen, and I expect we'll see a pitching change."

Eye contact was locked in as the two met on the mound with an internal battle of the wills churning deep inside.

"You've pitched a hell of a game here today, Steiny, one hell of a game. You want some help?" Leach gently offered.

"Naw, I'm OK, Skip…really." Gary shot back.

"Your pitch count concerns me a little, but if you tell me you can do it, I'll believe you." Leach offered.

After a moment of soul-searching silence, Tommy Leach looked from the brown dirt and back up and into the eyes of his star pitcher.

"You know that your dad's here today." Leach whispered.

Steinman froze for a quick second; shooting his manager the same kind of look that Tommy had given Brewster when he first gave him the news.

"My dad…is here, at the game, now?" Steinman stuttered.

Yea, they brought him up from Indianapolis and you weren't supposed to know, but I look at it this way. He's going to be proud of you no matter what the score ends up. I wasn't going to tell you, but if my old man was in the stands and was watching me pitch the way you're throwing today, I would certainly want to know about it. I apologize for telling you like this. It's probably not the best timing, but I just didn't want you to get cheated out of this kind of a memory."

Joined by another, home plate umpire Gary Stephens interjected a quick shout to get back to business as again Leach and Steinman locked eyes on the manager's retreat from the mound back to the dugout. Looking over his shoulder, he departed with one more not so subtle message.

"Get this thing over so you can go see him."

"There's a bit of a surprise, Joe, as Tommy Leach is apparently leaving Gary Steinman in the game." Brennaman expressed.

"Well, Marty, it's always a gamble when you've thrown as many pitches as he has here this afternoon, but it looks like Tommy has decided that it's his game to win or lose. Adam Dunn followed by

Junior. All we need here is a deep fly and we're all even." Joe Nuxhall pointed out. "Of course, a big-fly here, and we all go home happy!"

As the Reds big man Adam Dunn strolled to the plate, Gary Steinman couldn't help to gaze up and down into the sea of innocuous faces knowing that his life-blood and best friend was somewhere in the midst of it all and gazing down at his every move.

Adam Dunn was always a home run just waiting to happen as he stepped into the batter's box as Steinman locked onto the glove of catcher Doug Pouge.

He would later tell the press that he zoned-out at this point and really didn't remember a thing until being doused by the cooler of Gatorade. For the baseball-pure who were there on an electric sell-out night in Cincinnati, they'll never forget it.

"Dunn at the plate with one out and the tying run at third." Marty Brennaman began. "You gotta think with Dunn and Griffey both up back to back, that something good is going to happen!"

It didn't. Six-pitches later, the Vipers all spilled onto the field at Great American Ballpark as back-to-back strikeouts of Adam Dunn and Ken Griffey Jr. preserved the gem and a one-hit shut-out win for their ace, Gary Steinman.

Deep in the confines of GABP, the baseball press wags were all pinning Manager Tommy Leach to the wall.

"Andy Furman from WLW Radio, Tommy, what motivated you to keep Steinman in there instead of a fresh arm in the ninth when he was obviously out of gas and struggling at that point?"

"Out of gas?" Leached laughed, "I think that striking out both Dunn and Junior on three-pitches each proved that his octane level was a wee bit higher than you might think!"

"Hey there Tommy, Ken Broo from Channel 5. We understand Norm Brachett had a bit of a medical problem before the game. Is there anything more about that you can share with us?"

"Thank you, Ken!" Tommy started. "I just talked with Larry Starr who is with Norm right now over at Good Samaritan Hospital, and they tell me that he is still undergoing some tests, but he is resting comfortably. For those of you that don't know, our Bench Coach Norm Bratchett wasn't feeling well before the game, so we sent him over to Good Sam on the side of caution and fully expect him back with us as soon as he's feeling better."

"I'm Paul Docherty from the *Cincinnati Enquirer*. Just wondering where Gary Steinman is? Normally, the winning pitcher is required to be here for us and our post-game interviews. I'm not being nasty, just nosey?"

The room broke into a unified laughter as it was rare for the pitcher of record to be absent from the mandated after-game press conferences. As the joviality died down, Manager Tommy Leach paused for just a moment before speaking.

"I was the one that excused Gary from our little gathering here today and take full responsibility for any disappointment you might have. Gary had…I guess, I should say an unexpected meeting with a very special person. I'm going to kind of leave it at that, but knowing him and the kind of bond he holds with God and his family, I'll take the lightning-strike from you guys for him on that one. Thank you all very much!"

As the flurry of requests was still being hurled at the pulpit from the gaggle of reporters, Tommy simply stuck up his hand and walked away, ending the question-poloza in its tracks. Entering the player's tunnel from the war room, it was obvious that the look on his face masked genuine concern. Tom Browning and Von Hayes were already in his office as he opened the door.

"Where's Larry?" Leach asked.

"Still over at the hospital. I just talked to him a few minutes ago, and it might be worse than we expected." Hayes answered. "The tests are showing major blockages of his arteries in the heart."

"Shit! That's heart attack-alley." Leach responded. "Call us a cab. We better get over there now. Pug! Tell Brewster to hold down the fort and absolutely not a word about this to anybody, especially my players!"

The after-game celebration at the Holy Grail was several hundred with a mixture of disappointed locals, jubilant souls from Portsmouth, and a contingency of players and girlfriends enjoying the moment. As in most public settings concerning the Vipers and friends, the management was gracious enough to privatize the gathering from overzealous fans and the ever-present media snoops.

Even though there was certainly a celebratory glow to the assembly, this time the tone was far more business than when Carla and Syleanna partied with the guys in Los Angeles.

"This is a no-beer night for us, ladies." Sean announced with a smile. "Bring on the 'Shirley Temples' cause we promised Skip no more beer until after the series."

"Come on, guys!" Carla erupted. "You can have one! I heard Gambill say the Dodgers lost tonight, which means you're only two-games out of first place. That's awesome and incredible, and I think certainly a toast is in order."

"Nope, we're shutting it down, sister, until this thing is over. Besides, it's your turn to pick up the tab, remember?"

Cliff always had a way for sneaking in obscure facts of past pay-worthy events including the $800 bar bill from their night out in LA.

"You're getting off way too easy this time, winches!" he added.

"Seriously, we are so much being watched right now that anything we do is a frigging news headline." Bombo Chadwick chimed in. "We all took a vow to become choir-boys until the last man is out. Hell, I'm hoping not have another cold one until almost November… just saying."

"Did anyone hear from Keith?" Sean asked. "I just assumed he was coming down this weekend, but I haven't heard anything from him. Hell, with four buses of Portsmouth-ites at the game, he may have gotten lost in the crowed."

"No," Brooks Snyder shot back. "I tried calling him a couple times during the past week and just got his machine. I left a couple messages, but haven't heard back."

Lost in a quick moment of silence, catcher Boone Coleman decided to bring a reality moment to the cheery gathering.

"You know, this has got to be really hard for him. Here we are playing Major League Baseball and even challenging for a title, and he's home just cutting his grass and sitting around with his grandkids. Christ, he was everything to us until all this happened, and we just kind of took off and left him behind."

"No, Boonie, he left himself behind!" Cliff Collier quickly interjected. "If you remember the meeting, hell, he was offered a job too. You know that I love that man like a dad. Seriously, I don't think Keith is back home feeling sorry for himself. I know he follows us every day!"

Coleman again to the counter- point. "Yea, but he was such a huge part of us and almost the manager of the College World Series champions. It was some crazy order by the beard of Zeus that we all got a second chance…and he didn't!"

"Whatever, I'll call him in the morning and see what's going on." Sean Deeters said, rescuing the spiraling and awkward conversation. "Maybe we can get him down here for either tomorrow or Sunday's game!"

At another meeting taking place across town at Good Samaritan Hospital, the sense was far from buoyant. Surrounding a bed in room 410 were Tommy Leach, Tom Browning, and Von Hayes. As the doctors and nurses continued to come in and take readings and distribute medications, "Stormin" Norman Bratchett came to a sudden harsh reality that his sudden health problems weren't due to just a bad meal in Milwaukee.

"Docs are telling me that it's all finally caught up with me." he sheepishly explained. "All the good life of eating large and wherever from city to city has got me clogged up pretty good with the ticker they tell me."

"Four-blocked arteries ain't just the heartburn podge." Leach lamented. "So what are they saying; seriously."

"Looks like surgery, and pretty damn soon. I've already talked to my doctor back home and he says don't mess around and do exactly as they say. I guess I'll know something here shortly." Bratchett revealed.

A menacing silence lingered as Von Hayes was the first to address the harsh reality of it all.

"You know that you're done for the season, Norm, and you know what that means?"

21 DOWN IN VEGAS

"Yea, Bratchett slowly responded, "While you guys are feasting on that crazy Cincy Chili, I'm going to be having a four-way that's not nearly as good!"

Comic relief filtered through the room as all at least felt that while down the Vipers' much beloved bench coach wasn't totally out. "Oh by the way, Pug. I got a surprise for Zebro tomorrow and forgot to tell you."

"What's that?" Browning shot back.

"I know by Monday we have to set the post-season roster and Zeiber really thinks he is the odd-man out. He pitches tomorrow, so I scheduled Jose Mesa to make a clubhouse visit to talk to him because Zeiber is from that little town up near Cleveland and idolizes the guy."

"Does he know how to get in to the clubhouse?" Leach asked.

"Oh yea, I already got it worked out and all. He's here in Cincinnati to see a muscle specialist or something, he's cool. By the way, do you know what you're going to do by 4:00 p.m. Monday?"

"Honestly, Norm...no" Leach admitted. "Carpenter is ready to go and the reports on his rehab have been fantastic. I really don't know! The ones we got from the minors for the September call-up, you saw. Not many of those guys saw any time. We just got a 'helluva' team out there, and you can't just go screw up the chemistry a week before the playoffs. That is of course we even get in."

As a nurse quickly ran in to give Norm Brachett another drip of his meds, he looked up slowly in a twilight state and all in the room knew this would most probably be his final thought for the evening.

"If the kid does good tomorrow…go with him. He's too young and stupid to be afraid. You're going to need pitching for whoever you face…He's a fighter like…Evander Holyfield…he'll punch until the well runs dry, then you'll need to call a plumber to come…and fix it…Maybe he can fix the ceiling fan and the toilet too…"

As Norm suddenly faded to black and into a deep slumber, the three visitors in the room looked at each other simultaneously as if the question suddenly jack-hammered into their brains all at the same time. If "Stormin" Norman Bratchett was now unavailable for the rest of the season, who would now like to be the Vipers bench coach?

News had travelled fast about Norm's condition as Cisco Wheeler and Brandon Briggs were dining together at the Palazzo back in Vegas. Brandon had excused himself from the table to take the call from Tommy and on his return his face was that of a poker-player who just exposed his winning hand.

"Wow, we didn't need this." Brandon exhaled as he pulled out his seat to once again join his boss. Staring across the table, Cisco Wheeler was anticipatory that whatever the news, it wouldn't be of the welcome variety.

"Norm Bratchett is in a heart-unit in Cincinnati. He's going under the knife tomorrow for heart surgery."

"Tomorrow, For Christ's sake, what happened?" Wheeler sputtered. "This is awful!"

"Tommy just said he had chest pains earlier, and they rushed him over to a hospital, and it turned out that four of his arteries are blocked. They wanted to get it done ASAP, and so tomorrow morning is the quickest they could do it. I kind of believe we need to figure out several things here and quick."

"Has his family been told?" Cisco asked

"Yea, Tommy has taken care of that and arranged for his wife to fly out in the morning."

"You make sure that she gets put up in absolutely the best hotel there and everything she needs is at her disposal." Wheeler barked. "Norm has been with us here since the beginning, and I want everything taken care to the letter."

"Already done, now let me lay out some other things we need to think about." Pausing before asking as to not appear insulting, Briggs asked his boss a question.

"Cisco, you do know the definition of what a bench coach does, right?"

Sporting a wry smile, Wheeler wasn't going to walk into this one with blinders on so that his GM appeared to have the upper hand. Taking a sip from his water glass, he cleared his throat before answering the question.

"Well, Brandon, please correct me if I'm wrong, but the role of a bench coach is to assist their managers in the decision-making process and, at times, will relay scouting information from the team's front office to the club's players. The bench coach also typically steps in as the acting manager when, or if, the regular manager is unavailable, which is often the result of being ejected from the game. Am I close?"

"Nailed it as I knew you would," Briggs smiled. "But I really wasn't trying to be pretentious, Cisco. We have to figure out and figure out fast what to do here. Browning and Hayes are good coaches, trust me, but I'm not sure about moving one of them into that role, and especially now, Tommy needs someone who can help manage the chaos around him and the players as well!"

"Do we have anyone in the minors we can call-up? Hell, they're shutting things down next week." Wheeler asked.

"No, not really. Not at this point. After we're done, I'll call and talk to Tommy. We can hold off making some kind of a decision until the morning."

Brandon then noticed that patented "over the classes" stare that he had seen too many times during his tenure as GM from his owner. It was considered non-verbal communication at its best.

"OK, I'll also book my flight to Cincinnati, and early. I'll be there with my angel-wings on for Norman. You can count on it, sir."

A Saturday afternoon game in Cincinnati was always an event that was a day-long event. Players there by 10:30 a.m. first pitch at 1:10 p.m. and fans milling around by 8:00 a.m. With the Vipers in town and the extra added element of frenzy, the usual 10:30 p.m. players-only meeting would be a little different due to multiple levels of drama.

"Here we go!" Tommy Leach began. "Norm's surgery is scheduled for Monday morning. We need to stay focused, go out there, and do our job, and if you're of a spiritual mind and body, please pray. The early prognosis is good, so hopefully when we get home, we can all breathe a little easier. As you know, we are now only two-back from the Dodgers and tied with Padres at three-back. It doesn't matter who wins or loses because if we win, we'll still be two-down.

My guess is that we would like the Dodgers to win since we play them in a week and it would be nice to be able to control our own fate.

"Monday is the day that we must submit our playoff roster to the league. As of yet, we have made no decision on who will be on or off the roster. Carpy is done with his rehab and is scheduled to join us when we get home on Monday. As the manager of this team, I do apologize to all of our September additions who saw little time on field, but hopefully, you all have picked up the feel of what it's like to be on a very special team of champions!" Matt Belizle is on the mound for the Reds! Hope you studied the video that 'Pug' provided. Zebro is on the mound today for us! You all know your jobs, so go out there and do it, and I'll see you out on the field. Brad, I need to see you in my office for a minute!"

Rising from the bench slowly, Brad Zeiber headed toward the manager's office with a small lump in his throat and an uneasy feeling in his stomach. This might be the news he really didn't want to hear about his future, as he swallowed hard and prepared for the worst. Closing the door, it didn't look good. Pitching Coach Tom Browning was already there with a too serious look as Manager Tommy Leach hesitated before speaking.

"Here it comes." Zeiber thought.

"Brad," Tommy started, "you've been a very important member of our team since your arrival here, and both of us simply want you to know that."

"Thanks, Tommy, I appreciate that." Brad softly spoke.

"Both Pug and I have appreciated your work ethic on the mound, but there is one small problem that needs to be addressed. You come from a small town in northern Ohio called Bellevue, and you grew up a Cleveland Indians fan. How do you honestly feel about that?"

Before Brad Zeiber could muster up an answer, Tommy Leach's bad Dr. Phil impression and Tom Browning both couldn't stand it anymore. Exploding into laughter, a large body suddenly appeared from around the corner of the office. It was none other than the Tribe's legendary closer, Jose Mesa.

"Brad Zeiber…I would like for you to meet Mr. Jose Mesa." Leach bubbled. "We all know you have a ballgame today, but thought you might like to spend a little time catching up and talking about the good ol' days of Indians baseball, just don't ask him anything about game-seven!"

"Oh man, you really know how to hurt a guy." Mesa laughed. "That happened so long ago that nobody remembers anymore…I hope!"

"Take it up with this mentally scarred youth, Jose." Browning countered. "Really, thanks for coming by today. You guys have a nice chat!"

For the next hour, the Vipers young starter sat in the inner-sanctum of Great American Ballpark and soaked up stories, insights, and talked real-life ball-yard experience with the guy whose baseball card was always on top of his stack. While still technically under contract with Detroit, Mesa was on the disabled list and in town to see Dr. Timothy Kremcheck. It was on that note that Mesa also counselled the young man on his own mortality.

"We all think we be Superman!" Jose spoke in his thick Spanish accent. "Just always remember that your arm is all you got. Always pitch smart and keep throwing those knuckleballs. That save you so you can pitch into your fifties!"

Batting practice and warmups were all in session an hour before game time. Von Hayes was given the temporary roll of bench coach as Tommy sat going over his line-up card. He had inserted Terrance Kennedy at short-stop to give Gary Duzan a much deserved day off. Kennedy had quietly been the much needed mortar for the team as the veteran player coming off the bench and filling in at the seven different positions that he could play. Still lost in his contemplative haze, Leach sensed that he was being joined by another.

"Hey, Skip, what's up?" Jarred Brewster asked.

"The lineup card, Brewster." he sarcastically responded. "You know that required piece of paper that I have to turn over to the umpires before every game? It's kind of like my daily homework assignment."

"I know and I hate to bother you now, but it's kind of important." Jarred humbly pleaded. "I promise it won't take long."

Tommy had finally figured out Jarred Brewster's routine and pattern to a tee. If he ever came and wanted to talk to you at the worst possible moment, it was usually worth it.

"What is it Jarred? I really don't have much time right now."

"Well, it's about Norm. I know that right now there's a lot going on, but I wanted to throw something out at you as far as a replacement for the rest of the season. I may have an idea."

"OK, Einstein, and your suggestion is who?" Leach impatiently offered.

"Keith Madison" Jarred replied.

"Keith Madison…as our bench coach? Brewster, you're out of your mind!" Tommy started. "He's a nice guy and all, but he already has a job and the old man and him are working with the university to help re-stock their baseball program. I can think of a thousand and one reasons why that would never work."

"How about six weeks' vacation? A man can do anything he wants on his own time, can't he? This is the dead-zone for college baseball and who knows this team and the game any better than Keith? Besides yourself, of course." Jarred quickly added.

The added attempt at humor didn't slow down the immediate reaction from the Vipers manager.

"Jarred, I do appreciate your out-of-the-box thinking, but this late in the season and all, I don't see how an outsider could come close to coming in here and hit the ground running. We have less than two weeks left in the season and still don't even know if we are going to make the play-offs."

"Just one last thing," Jarred began, "I know Keith would never say anything, but I know he took it hard when we lost to LSU because he was the one that sent Snyder home on that final play. He won't let it go that he made that mistake. Nobody else on the team ever felt that way, but I know Keith plays it over and over in his mind. Now you have his team here with a second chance to play for a title, and he's on the outside looking in. I think if you could just make it work, it would pay huge dividends for the guys, our chances to play on, and for you! That's all I got, Skip."

Absorbing the thought, Tommy Leach sat silent, letting the words of Jarred sink in. In a sense, it all made a certain amount of pretzel logic. Often-times in the face of multi-tasks and time restraints, we all take the easy way out by not wanting to add even more to our already full plates. Turning to his pesky protégé, the Vipers manager smiled as he heard himself say, "Thanks Jarred, I'll think about it."

The sell-out crowd at Great American Ballpark had little to cheer about on a gorgeous Saturday afternoon as the Vipers utility man Terrence Kennedy suddenly turned into the reincarnation of Babe Ruth. With already a run in the first, Kennedy blasted a bases loaded Matt Belisle fast-ball deep into the second deck in left field for a grand-slam giving Las Vegas a 5-0 lead. In the fourth inning with Deeters on second, Kennedy once again connected to deposit another two-run dinger into the sun deck in right. Two home runs and six runs batted in and he wasn't done yet.

With the Vipers using the Reds for batting practice, Kennedy came to the plate in the seventh-inning with two-outs and two-on to once again send a David Weathers slow curve-ball into the batter's eye in dead straight center field. The one-man wrecking crew of Terrence Kennedy now had three-homers for the day and nine RBI's as the Reds had been kept off the board with just four-scattered singles from Brad Zeiber. The Vipers radio crew of Hacker and Harnisch were literally jumping through their microphones.

"Who could have ever in their wildest dreams, Pete, ever seen this one coming?"

Hacker beamed. "A blowout here in Cincinnati as the Vipers lead now lead 11-0 after eight as Terrence Kennedy might have a chance to come up in the ninth and make Vipers history."

"That's right, Ralph," Harnisch added. "It was the Vipers inaugural season back in 1996 when Terry Pendleton hit three in a game, and that has only happened once in their ten-year history. It was a great afternoon of pitching for young Brad Zeiber as Bruce Leslie is warming up and will handle the bottom of the ninth. In case you're wondering, Kennedy is up fourth in the inning, so somebody needs to get on to give him a chance to do what only sixteen players before him have ever done in the history of the game: four home runs!"

"The last time it happened I believe it was the Dodger's Shawn Green a few years ago in Milwaukee." "Hacker added. "He had a monster day if I recall going 6-6 with four round-trippers. That's the last time, and only again, the sixteenth time that a player has taken four out in a single nine-inning game."

Right-handed reliever Gary Majewski was brought in to mop-up the final inning for the Reds as Collier, Chadwick, Pouge, and Kennedy were all due up in the top of the ninth. While some of the 43,000 plus crowd decided to finally call it a day, surprisingly many were still on hand to watch the former Bentley State Eagles perform yet another marvel.

Cliff Collier led off the ninth over- anxious at the first pitch and sent a lazy can of corn to left for the first out. Bombo Chadwick then sent a screaming line drive to right that Jay Bruce barely held onto has he slammed into the fence for out number two. As Terrence Kennedy moved to the on-deck circle, fans were now on their feet as the allegiance to the hometown Reds had now decisively shifted. The Viper's catcher Doug Pouge patiently worked Majewski to a 3-2 count while fouling off six- straight full count pitches.

"Majewski will try yet again as Pouge settles deep into the batter's box."

Hacker called, "Here's the set…the pitch…just outside and ball-four as Doug Pouge draws a two-out walk and now here comes Terrence Kennedy once again! Already with three home runs and nine RBI's on the day, there's no doubt about what he'll be trying to do here."

As the Cincinnati fans cheered, he stepped up to the plate, knowing that this wasn't one of those team moments to help win a ballgame. That contest was over, and he apprehended this moment and the feat that everyone including himself was asked to do. Terrence Kennedy suddenly realized that sometimes it's OK to be selfish.

"Majewski looks at LaRue for the sign…and the pitch. Strike one on the outside corner!" Ralph Hacker again relishing the call. "If this young man's nervous, he certainly doesn't show it. He again steps in with a one strike count as Majewski brings it to the plate. Swing and a miss and that was a fifty-six foot fast-ball straight in the dirt!"

"Exactly," Harnisch confirmed, "Terry got a little over-anxious on that one, and you could tell by the swing it was all from the heels."

Hacker again took a deep breath as he again prepared to bring home the bravado.

"Terrence Kennedy back in the box facing a 0-2 count from the Reds Gary Majewski. Again the look…and here comes the pitch. Swung on…and a laser shot to right! The only question is will it be high enough…and…it is! Terrence Kennedy has just hit his fourth home run into the third row of the right field sun deck here in the ninth as the Vipers now take a 13-0 lead and what a day for one Terrence Kennedy…wow! Four home runs, eleven- runs batted in, and TK now becomes only the seventeenth player ever to take the grand- tour four times in a single game. This is just too unbelievable!"

It now became a race for all media outlets to seize this storybook sports moment and cash it in for ratings gold. *Good Morning America* had their A-game producers on the hunt for a live studio hookup in the morning.

Both ABC and CBS also had calls into people as ESPN's Baseball Tonight may have accidently been the big winner simply staying with a now national audience they inherited from their Cincinnati affiliate. As cameras rolled and George Grande recapped the stunning action, the last three outs for the Reds were barely discernable. This baseball night took on a whole different aroma for the simple reasons of drama, accomplishment, and it was the Las Vegas Vipers.

In certain situations with permission and proper credit, TV networks can be accommodating to other competing outlets especially during rare and flashpoint moments. As the word quickly spread, more and more affiliates joined the growing celebration at Great American Ballpark in Cincinnati to be a part of the post-game show and share the infused celebration live.

"This is Jim Day as this post-game show has never, and I say never has been bigger than this evening, and what we've witnessed tonight. With me is Las Vegas Vipers Terrence Kennedy, and tonight,

Terrence, you joined an exclusive fraternity of only sixteen others who have ever done what you accomplished. How does it feel?"

"Well, thanks...man, I really don't know what to say." Kennedy laughed.

"I've never done a show like this in an enemy's ball-park if you know what I mean, and I just hope nobody waxes me."

Laughing back, Jim Day tried to make him feel at ease with the multiple-rush of emotions obviously at play.

"No, no...win or lose, Cincinnati just loves good baseball, Terrence, and you certainly gave them that here tonight."

"Well, again thanks." Kennedy stumbled. "I'm just amazed and grateful for what our management has done to turn this thing around for us. These guys inspire me every day when I watch how they play and their love of this game; it truly is a blessing for me. I'm really not really a homerun hitter, but tonight, I was just seeing the ball real good and I just got lucky with some pitches that I could drive."

Jim Day once again dealing with a live TV audience suddenly looked off camera and was caught with yet another surprise as he was handed a card.

"Terrence, your fourth home run of the night was to right field. Everyone here knew what you were trying to do, right?" Day asked.

"If you're asking me was I trying to hit a home run...I was actually given the bunt sign and went against Skip's orders." Kennedy joked. "No, I knew what was at stake, but honestly, I was just looking for a pitch that I could get a solid swing at because I knew if I could just connect with one, well, it might have a chance of getting out of here."

As the camera panned back, a young boy stood next to the on-field announcer with his baseball glove and smiling from ear to ear.

"Terrence Kennedy," Jim Day once again began, "we have a young man here that would like to give you something. This is fifteen-year-old Ryan Gennett and he snagged your fourth home run out in the right field bleachers, on the fly I might add...and would like to give it to you right now!"

21 DOWN IN VEGAS

As the scene played out, the crowd swelled to the occasion as the youngster handed Terrence Kennedy a souvenir that would be destined to reside at the Baseball Hall of Fame in Cooperstown. The two looked at each other as Terrence took the ball from Ryan and then extended his hand. As they both beamed and shook on it, this would be the pop-media TV clip deemed worthy to be seen around the world!

Proving again the fact that grand moments at their best are fleeting, the Reds and Vipers had yet one more meeting before the final home stand in Las Vegas. Scotty "The Golden" Arms would take the hill on Sunday afternoon for the series finale facing Kyle Lohse.

As much as the previous day had been an offensive showcase for Las Vegas, the Vipers bats at been shut down through seven innings against the crafty Lohse who had allowed just two singles and an infield hit. A Brandon Phillips two-run homer on a high fastball from Scotty Arms in the fourth inning was the difference as the Vipers prepared to bat in the eighth.

Brooks Snyder led off the inning with a sharp single up the middle with Sean Deeters then drawing a quick four-pitch walk. While pitching superbly so far, Kyle Lohse had a reputation for having the wheels fall off quickly. Reds Manager Jerry Narron decided at this point to go to his bull-pen and bring in reliever Jason Standridge, With two on and none out, Strandridge struck out John Gambill and Bombo Chadwick in order as only "King Kong" Karl Smith stood in his way of shutting down the only real scoring opportunity the Vipers had seen all day.

"Every third pitch he throws is a curve-ball." Jarred Brewster whispered to Karl Smith as he grabbed his bat in the dugout.

"And how do you figure that?" Smith asked.

"I've been counting." Brewster replied. "Gambill went down on six-pitches and Bombo on seven, and every third one was a curve-ball. Math is a very important component for an engineering degree, so you're going to have to trust me on this."

"Every third pitch a curve?" Smith musingly again asked.

"Yep, every third one." Jarred replied.

"Two-on and two-out here in the seventh!" Ralph Hacker began as the pro Cincinnati crowd started making some noise. "For the last two days, I had sensed some kindred togetherness from the crowd here in Cincy for our Vipers, but after taking the first two games from the Reds who are also in the hunt for a division title, I sense maybe today the honeymoon might be on hold!"

"I think you're right." Pete Harnisch said laughingly. "With both teams' now only two- games out of their divisions, every one now looms large!'

"Jason Standridge looks in and gets the sign." Hacker began, "Strike one down the middle as Smith watched that Linda Ronstadt special ring him up!"

Harnisch was quick to finish the joke, adding, "You mean the ol' blew by you…I'm guessing."

"Standridge is firing aspirin tablets out there as he again sets… fires…swing and a foul ball behind home plate. Karl Smith now in a deep hole with no- balls, two- strikes, and ducks on the pond" Ralph Hacker explained.

Stepping back from the plate after calling a time-out, Karl Smith knew he had one more chance to get it right. Quickly glancing toward the dugout, his eye caught Jarred Brewster's standing on the top step. Jarred was simply smiling and nodding.

Smith quickly again settled into the batter's box as Jason Standridge gazed in to Jason LaRue to end the encounter quickly.

"The 'Kong' man is again and ready in the box as the runners lead." Hacker began. "Standridge to the belt, the pitch…it's a high fly ball to deep right- center field! Griffey is going back to the wall… he leaps…it's gone! A three-run blast from 'King Kong' Karl Smith and the Vipers now take a 3-2 lead here in the top of the seventh."

"I believe Smith feasted on a good old-fashioned round-house curve-ball, Ralph." Harnisch added. "It was a good pitch to throw, but the 'Kingster' was all about that one!"

The Las Vegas dugout was electric as Smith entered the cha-os-zone. Pushing his way through the pile of high- fives and chest-bumps, he finally caught up with Jarred at the far end of the bench.

With a less than joyous expression, he stared down his friend with a long pause before speaking.

"OK, you gooney twerp," he playfully roared. "Does that now qualify me to be an engineer too!"

Both breaking out into monster smiles, they grabbed each other and both shared what they knew was another special seat in a most unbelievable ride.

Tommy quickly called the bullpen to get Fuller and Leslie up and throwing. It was moments like this that the Vipers' manager knew couldn't be wasted. The last score showed the Padres were losing again, 5-3. If that stood up coupled with a Viper win today, it would have them both dead-even at just two games out of first of the division-leading Dodgers.

It was a lead-off single to Reds third baseman Edwin Encarnacion to begin the bottom of the eighth that prompted Leach to make the slow stroll to the mound to make a pitching change. Reliever Bruce Leslie was called in to relieve Scotty "The Golden" Arms who was obviously physically drained. Leslie had been an efficient setup man and a guy you could always count on to throw strikes. It took only two-pitches before Todd Hollandsworth grounded to short for an easy 6-4-3 double-play.

On the next pitch, outfielder Norris Hopper tapped one back to the mound to finish off the inning.

"Three pitches…three outs!" yelled Leach. "Throw like that and you'll be pitching up here until you're a hundred! Top of the ninth and one more to go, guys! Let's add on and shut em' down!"

The Reds called on Bill Bray who had been part of a controversial trade with the Washington Nationals to help bolster the Reds relief corp. It was earlier in the season that Cincinnati had traded Austin Kerns and All-Star shortstop Felipe Lopez to the Nats which proved to be a highly unpopular move. For the Reds on this given day, Bray had no problem easily dispensing Gambill, Duzan, and Pouge to bring on the bottom of the ninth with the Vipers clinging to a 3-2 lead.

"Bottom of the ninth here in Cincinnati and here we go!" Hacker again bellowed into the microphone as Rich Aurillia stepped to the plate. After fouling off a couple of Ernie Fuller fastballs, he got locked up on a slider and was then asked to take a seat. First Baseman Scott Hatteberg drew the count even before lifting a long and lazy fly to right for out number two. It was at this point, Fuller began to get too fancy nibbling at the corner of the plate resulting in a walk to Chris Denorfia. With two out and one on, Doug Pouge quickly called time to claim a visit to the mound.

"Come on, Dirt! This game has gone on long enough!" Pouge barked.

"I know, I just wanted to keep it in the park and didn't want to give him anything." Fuller sighed.

"Right, you don't have to worry about Freel hitting it out. Just throw strikes MO Jamba and let's get this thing done. It's all bueno!" the Viper's catcher added.

"Pouge is headed back from the mound and Ryan Freel now steps to the plate," Ralph Hacker expounded. "Freel one of those pesky hitters who subscribes to the 'hittem' where they ain't' theory. He's 1-3 on the afternoon as he settles in against Fuller. The Vipers lead by one as here's the pitch…strike one on the outside corner. Fuller has really been the go-to guy for this team as most hitters in the league I don't think have figured him out!"

"I hear that a lot." Pete Harnisch added. "He has that Rambo-like attitude that says I fear of nothing. I think batters are more than just a little intimidated."

"I see that." Hacker injected. "Fuller to the stretch…and the pitch. Freel swings and there goes a soft liner over second on a hop and a base hit to right field. Deeters gets to the ball and here comes Denorfia rounding second and heading for third! Deeters throw is up and on line! Here comes Denorfia and here comes the ball…he is…out! What a bang-bang play, but the throw was perfect and so was the out call from third base umpire Hunter Wendelstedt and this game is over! Vipers win, but third baseman John Gambill is still down on the ground, Pete, Did he get a cleat?"

"The replay looks like the ball was slightly to the outfield side of the bag, and when he tuned he might have twisted his ankle. In order to apply the tag it was a bit of an awkward turn, but it looks like he's in some pain for sure." Harnisch added.

"The final out of the game comes on a spectacular laser shot-throw from Sean Deeters to John Gambill and you can bring out the big broom here and now in Cincinnati. Final score the Vipers 3 and the Reds 2. I'm Ralph Hacker and we'll be back with the post-game wrap -up right here on the Las Vegas Vipers Radio Network!"

Less than an hour after high jubilation, the mood in the trainer's room had now turned grim. Surrounded by Larry Starr, Tommy Leach, Von Hayes, and Tom Browning, the news wasn't good for third baseman John Gambill.

"It's worse than I thought." Viper's trainer Larry Starr was forced to admit.

"I'm afraid, John, that we have several ligaments here that have separated from the bone. In these cases, it's sometimes worse than a break because the muscle tissue has to all re-heal back and on to the bone. How's the pain?"

Submitting to a forced emotion of silence, Gambill finally admitted it was about as bad as he had ever felt. The swelling was also evidence of the diagnosis nobody wanted to accept.

"Shit, Larry! We have a week left in the regular season, and I have to have my play-off roster in by midnight tonight to the Commissioner. If I put him on the disabled list, that's fifteen days and that won't fly. Is there any way we can just list him day to day so he can be back up and ready to play again in a week?"

"Tommy, I know how you feel and especially you, John." Starr sympathized. "To be bluntly honest, unless the MLB suddenly allows players the use of crutches on the field, I'm afraid Gambill's season is over."

It was in the vortex of stunned silence that all were searching for the next plausible response that could remotely reflect the delicacy of the truth.

"That's OK." John Gambill softly replied. "I know where I am on this. The one thing Keith always taught us is sometimes things just happen. Hell, we won the game, didn't we? If that ball would have whizzed by me and he had scored, I would be feeling much more harsh about it all, seriously. Tommy, do what you have to do."

Watching boys become men within an instant is an adhering quality that has no boundaries. It was decided that John Gambill would boot up and join the team on the return journey to Las Vegas instead of staying back in Cincinnati for more tests.

Starr arranged an ambulance to meet the plane at CVG for the 8:30 p.m. departure time. Between there and midnight, critical decisions were on a mandatory timeline for the Eagles turned Vipers.

Two-games out of first with seven left to play, a bench coach missing, a post-season roster yet to be submitted, and, who would be the Las Vegas Vipers new third baseman? The clock was ticking.

"I'm John Anderson and this is *ESPN Sports Center*. Your big story on this Sunday night is the season ending injury of Las Vegas Vipers third baseman John Gambill on the final play of this game-winner against the Reds today. Watch this play as the Reds Chris Denorfia tries to take third on a shallow liner to right. Shot down at high speed here as right fielder Sean Deeters fires a seed, but the move to apply the tag? Oooh, that's going to leave a mark! Torn ligaments and a season-ending injury for a guy that was having a remarkable run promoted only in July from the college ranks to the Majors.

"Gambill was batting .259 with solid power numbers and only two-errors in ninety-six chances. The good news for Las Vegas heading into the last week of the regular season is they are now in a dead-heat with San Diego and both just two- games behind the division leading Dodgers."More bad news for the Vipers also just in as ESPN has also learned that they have lost bench coach 'Stormin' Norman Bratchett for the rest of the season. Bratchett who fell ill at the ballpark was taken to a local Cincinnati hospital where he was diagnosed with an undisclosed heart ailment and will undergo surgery tomorrow morning. Norman, we all here at ESPN still remember that golf tourney you joined us for back in the '80's. Even though you were barred from ever attending it anymore, we still love ya, buddy, and hope you get well soon! Coming up next: Have Tom Brady and Bill

Bilichick finally come to the end of the road and their winning ways? *ESPN Sports Center* will continue after this."

As the charter jet lifted off from CVG for the return flight to McCarron, the players and staff were all lost in their own worlds of thought. Had the loss of one of their most solid performers doomed their fate? Players congregated around John Gambill who was placed in the back, so he could elevate his foot with words and jokes of encouragement. Towards the front of the Boeing 757, there was a summit of thought and decision from the coaching staff and especially Manager Tommy Leach.

"I guess that last play made our decision easy, Pug." Leach admitted to pitching coach Tom Browning. "We keep Zebro and activate Carpenter. I know that makes us pitching heavy, but I don't see what else we can do at this point."

"I know, Tommy, but if we can win this thing and make it into the play-offs, whew…we just lost our third baseman and a guy with a stick. Maybe we ought to look at bringing up Jamison from Colorado. You got a third base ready guy who hit .300 this year." Browning injected.

"In the minors, Pug…in the minors." Leach added. "Naw, you can't throw a kid like that in this thing. Shit, Clint McElroy might be able to handle it. Every time he's filled in for Gambill, he's shown us some pretty good stuff."

Sitting in the seat behind Tommy Leach and listening intently, Jarred Brewster slowly got up and moved one up the aisle to get sit next to his manager.

"Tommy, I couldn't help listening, and if I may offer a suggestion?" Jarred began. "Gary Duzan plays a hell of a third base. I mean he could step in and play it like he stole it. Then, you could let Kennedy play short and still have a pretty good bat in there every day. I mean, we don't have much time with a week and all, but I think it would work."

"Brewster, how come nobody ever told me that Duzan could play third?" Leach asked with an incredulous tone.

"I guess nobody ever asked!" Jarred fired back.

After a moment of ponderous silence, Von Hayes was the first to test the uncertain temperature of the water.

"He's a great athlete, Tommy. He's a damn good shortstop. I don't see why he couldn't play third if we needed him. We know what Kennedy can do, and maybe he's getting hot at the right time. Four-dingers in a game after all is pretty frigging smoking!"

"All right, I'll take it under advisement" Leach barked. "When we land, I have to fax this damn post-season lineup to the Commissioner's office and it has to be there by midnight. So are we are all in agreement here, Carpenter and Zeiber will round out our twenty-five?"

"I'm in!" Browning responded.

"Make that two, Chief." Hayes added.

With a sarcastic look to the seat next to him, Tommy Leach couldn't help but to have a little fun with the wide-eyed Jarred who wasn't really sure if he was part of the brain-trust or not.

"So, Brewster, anything you would like to add?" Leach slowly asked.

"No, I think that's great. Carpenter will be a fresh arm, and after we get to the play-offs, I know that we'll all be glad to have him."

With the final vote, both Tom Browning and Von Hayes quickly excused themselves to go back to the end of the plane and spend a little buddy-time with their ailing third baseman. Again breaking the silence, Jarred approached a topic that he and his manager had previously engaged.

"Hey, Tommy, have you given anymore thought to what we kind of touched on in your office? You know, about Keith maybe filling in for Norm."

"Let me tell you something, Brewster. Do you have any idea at all of the degree of bull-shit I'm dealing with right now? Do you have any kind of a clue?"

"Yes, I do." Jarred strongly answered. " I'm really not trying to put any more fecal matter on your plate, Tommy, I just sometimes see things and want to share them with you, that's all."

"I know I'm going to sound unappreciative about this, Brewster, but the biggest thing you can do right now to help me is just stay out of my way until tomorrow at 1:00 p.m. Oh, there is something you can do! Make sure all players, coaches, support personnel be in the clubhouse promptly then and here as well; no excuses. Now please just leave and allow me to rot in my own private hell with a little dignity here…thank you!"

Flashing him a forgiveness grin, Jarred understood the gravity his manager was facing and slowly removed himself from the seat and back to his laptop to start, composing a memo for the next day's meeting.

13TH INNING

With the many plates still up in the air bearing down on the final week of the regular MLB season, it was determined that Vipers Team Trainer Larry Starr would stay back in LA as official team comfort for the scheduled Monday morning heart surgery for 'Stormin' Norman Bratchett. Bedlam was breaking loose in Las Vegas as Brandon Briggs quickly decided that his guidance to an over excitable team owner was the place he needed to be. Walking into Cisco Wheeler's office at 8:00 on a Sunday night proved his gut-check correct.

"Seven-games to go, and have you ever seen anything like this in your life? Right here, Brandon, and a chance for our first division title!" Cisco Wheeler exclaimed. "I showed those bastards it can be done!"

"Slow down, Cisco. I know you're excited, but we have a lot of work ahead of us, and it all begins right now." warned his GM.

On top of all the Las Vipers organization had gone through to this point, add the fact that the league was now allowing select teams to begin selling tickets to the post-season on the Monday before the end of regular play. That meant along with seven sell-out home games for the Vipers, fans were also jockeying to witness the teams very first post-season appearance on the big stage with the demand for access at unfathomable levels.

"So now, Wayne Newton wants to sing three National Anthems during our home-stand? Absolutely not!" Cisco Wheeler barked. "He's just doing it for free tickets, and by the way, we are not going to allow ourselves any comps this week to any of the show business weasels, my orders!"

"Cisco, settle down here for just a minute!" Brandon chuckled. "It's all under control. Jack Pattie has done an excellent job anticipating all of this and everything is now in place. Wayne Newton will get one night and no comps, I promise!

Everybody in the ticket office is more than ready for the crunch, and I promise you, we will not run out of food, beer, or national attention! If there was ever a great week for you to celebrate your vision, this is it. Please, Cisco, just sit back and enjoy it!"

Comforting words always have a delayed reaction at times for sinking in.

Leaning back into his big leather chair, Cisco Wheeler finally captured the elusive character of calm. After taking a puff of his ever-present cigar, Cisco smiled slightly before looking at Brandon before he finally verbalized his thoughts.

"I know I'm looked at as a bastard around here at times, I realize that. Brandon, all I ever wanted in life when I was young was to become a major league baseball player myself and to live that incredible dream. I remember going to bed at night and listening to the broadcasts under my pillow of the New York Giants…the Yankees… the Dodgers, all of them from Hodges, Campanella, and Mantle, they were all my idols growing up and I wanted to be them. You've been around me long enough and know how much I love this game. It's been only through, well, let's just say…the financial privilege of my family…that I have had a chance to attempt and recapture my youth for that one last time. That's all I ever wanted. One shot, Brandon, that's it. I guess I thirsted for that perfect last dance to prove that while growing up and in love with something, that I just wasn't totally blind and wrong about my feelings!"

Brandon Briggs looked at his boss and realized that to interrupt him now would be akin to asking Knute Rockne where the clean towels were being kept during his legendary address. He continued to stand, stare, and listen.

"These past seven weeks have given me a sentiment that I really can't describe." Cisco went on. "Watching those kids hustle every night and them lifting the others up to see what they can achieve is the romance that this game is all about. When you've been a loser like us for as long as we have, you learn to take what you can as good things will find other places to land. I don't know if we will win this thing or not, Brandon, but I have finally learned whoever that son of a bitch who coined the phrase it's not whether you win or lose that counts, probably lost!"

Laughter from both Bandon Briggs and Cisco Wheeler accented a very honest straight-from-the-heart diatribe. As the Vipers' owner slowly returned to reality, both he and his GM solidly knew and anticipated that this upcoming one-week would unquestionably be the most challenging in their professional careers. Coming attractions always cast shadows.

In an attempt to escape the smothering press corps that awaited them back home, the chartered team flight back to Las Vegas got permission to land on an adjacent runway used for shuttling employees to the mysterious Area 51 job site.

With a hundred or so TV, radio, and newspaper representatives all gathered in the main terminal, the announcement that alternative plans had been made for the Vipers arrival was met to the same reaction as "Elvis has already left the building."

Once off the plane, the team was quickly shuttled back to the Mirage Hotel for an evening's rest and a chance to stay focused on the upcoming task at hand.

The local evening news reflected the bitter disappointment of being duped and left standing at the altar.

"For KLAS-TV News Channel 8, I'm George Knapp. Tonight the excitement and homecoming for our Las Vegas Vipers looked like another David Copperfield stunt at McCarron International as the team decided to bypass the usual protocol and completely disappear from the media throng gathered there to celebrate their incredible season. As a reporter who knows a little bit on how our airport works, arrangements were apparently made to land and de-plane using the privatized runway that's used to transport military personnel. That's the same runway I've reported on many times that escorts high level security out to Area 51 and other locations not privy to us garden variety work-a-day citizens. My question to Cisco 'The Dealer' Wheeler is why all the mystery? Two months ago, you would have killed for this kind of attention your ball club is now getting. Instead of embracing it tonight and letting myself and the many other journalists just do our jobs, you decided to disappear faster than a watermelon at the hands of Gallagher."

"Listen to that bull-shit!" Sean Deeters huffed while hitting the TV remote button to off. "Can you believe it? Just because we wanted to get home and get ready for this week, that clown is dissing us. Man, he's supposed to be on our side!"

"So, bro, it goes to show when you got your own TV station and you believe you have been shat upon, you are free to shat on anything you want." Cliff Collier added. "Don't let it get to you. I guess Briggs has already put out some kind of response to get them off our backs. By the way, I talked to Carla and I guess her and Syleanna found some dirt-cheap air fare and might be coming out again this weekend."

"Yea, she said they are thinking about it. I don't know." Sean lamented, "I would love to see her, but I am clearing out the cranium to just play ball right now. I mean, think about it, Cliffster. Two months ago, we were the dark horse in the college tournament, and now we have a chance to win a Major League Baseball division title. Doesn't all of that seem just a little too whack-a-doodle to you?"

"I guess it's pretty stupid." Cliff laughing responded. "But really, nobody but us really knew how good we were except for Wheeler and he just so happened to have enough money to prove it. So 1:00 a.m. comes too quickly, Deetman. Sorry to close down the party here, but I'm fading to black!"

As both said their good nights, the room went dark knowing that Monday morning would be the next stop on their journey through the looking glass and the challenges ahead.

The *Las Vegas-Review Journal* was the apologetic delivery system first thing in the morning as a letter written by Vipers GM Brandon Briggs explaining the team's reasoning for bypassing the usual media circus on the return flight from Cincinnati.

According to the short and brief statement, the team decided to "forgo any meeting with the public out of respect for their ally and Bench Coach Norm Bratchett who they unfortunately had to leave behind."

While sounding somewhat like a company line, any media outlet with any degree of conscience couldn't be too hard about putting thoughts of a critically ill employee first. While there was some lingering skepticism to the explanation, it seemed to diffuse the tempest in the teapot.

Ten-thirty a.m. at Mirage Field and players were filing in and getting ready for the final week of the regular season, knowing that continuing to win plus a little luck, all had to be on their side. Now two-games back of the first place Dodgers and tied with the Padres, the Vipers needed to take two out of three in order to have a chance into the final four games with LA. Anything less could have the Vipers mathematically eliminated before the much anticipated showdown.

Normally, daily team meetings were rather light and loose. As the clock struck 11:00 a.m. at Mirage Field, Manager Tommy Leach and his coaches walked in and immediately projected a decorum of urgency.

"OK, listen up! A lot of things have happened over the past twenty-four hours, and I appreciate each and every one of you for handling it like the men that you are! Sweeping the Reds in your own backyard proved to me that this is truly a team of destiny."

As several players started to celebrate their manager's remarks, Leach held up his hand for quiet.

"Before we go any farther, I just got off the phone with Larry Starr. Norm went into surgery this morning at 6:00 a.m. Cincinnati time and just came out about a half hour ago. They had to clean out four blocked arteries, but the good news is that all the doctors say the surgery was a complete success and we should have our bench coach back by spring training."

At this intersection moment of good news and relief, Tommy didn't even try and restrain the joyous thunder that resounded through the clubhouse. As he let the crescendo naturally wane, he once again took domination of the flow.

"Guys, we have just one week to get it right or we all go home. A bench coach for any baseball team is not a luxury, but a necessity. With everything that 'Pug' and Von have to control within their duties, we can't afford to not to be up to full-staff especially now. I have taken it under my authority to bring in some interim help for the remainder of this season, and I would like to introduce you to him at this time."

As if on cue, the door to Manager Tommy Leach's office slowly opened and out stepped a figure that many in the room already knew and loved all too well; it was Keith Madison.

The brief moment of silence of trying to decipher joke from reality quickly erupted as it was clear that the man who taught the Eagles how to fly was once again back in the flock.

The hugs, handshakes, and high-fives were infectious as the outrageousness of the moment finally settled in and about the room. Again, it was Tommy that restored the order.

"As our new interim bench coach, Keith, is there anything that you might like to say or address to our…and your former squad?"

Wearing a sly grin, Keith approached this moment as he had done so many others in the past with a room full of souls that entwined with his own.

"Well, first of all and as you know, I am so damn proud of what this team and what you have accomplished, Tommy. To say I haven't followed you all and every day from afar would be a huge disservice and a bold-faced lie! Before we go any further, I have to also say that it was Tommy himself who called me at home Saturday night and asked me if I would be interested in taking on this unusual assignment. And in case you're wondering and I know you are, I have taken a month sabbatical leave from the university as my vacation consultant Mr. Jarred Brewster here has constantly reminded me how much stockpiled time I still had left."

As the giddiness of the moment settled in, the business of Keith Madison wanted to make a very important statement to the group.

"Guys, it's very important for you to know that as honored as I am to be here, Tommy Leach is your manager and leader. I am simply here to help him and do what I can to support him and be another tool for a person who in my opinion is Major League Baseball's Manager of the Year."

With that, the floodgates of cheers were on again as the players now collectively started chanting "Tommy…Tommy…Tommy!"

It was hard even for the man whose name they were exulting to not get caught up even a little bit in the honest and impromptu celebration at such a time. Smiling, he again held up his hand as an attempt to regain command of the room.

"Thank you…thank you, heathens…and, Keith, I do appreciate those kind words. It's nice to have you on board with us and I sincerely enjoyed our chat Saturday and thank you for accepting our offer so quickly and under such crazy circumstances.Keith and I and the rest of the coaches will be getting together here shortly to plan our fast and furious game plan. One thing I can tell you is that we are playing a one-week season. That's it! As you now know with Gambill out, Carpenter as well as Zebro have both been activated and added to the roster that will take us into the post-season. By adding 'Carpy' it gives us a chance to rest all of our arms for another day."Everett will start game-one tonight. I haven't completely made up my mind yet, but we are working out Duzan today at third. If both he and we feel this is the thing to do, 'Duz' will move to third and Kennedy will take over shortstop. Quoting a line from one my favorite singers Mr. Jerry Reed, *we have a long way to go, and a short time to get there!* Let's roll!"

As the formality of the gathering quickly dissipated, Keith Madison hung back for a few minutes surrounded by his ex-players to further explain his more than surprising and sudden appearance in Las Vegas.

"God, Keith, unbelievable!" Mitch Milhuff roared. "Man, this is such a blow-monkey moment! What happened?"

As the questions came rapid-fire and all morphed into one, Keith Madison finally stepped back in an attempt to make some sense of it all.

"OK, guys, gentlemen, I hope it doesn't come as a big surprise, but Tommy and I have talked a few times since you all got here. When he needed a little extra personal advice on handling any one of you, and I hope, Deeters, that you're not listening, he might call and fill me in a bit. That's really what makes this guy so special because he always does his homework and he sincerely cares about you all."

As the laughs and good-natured snickering filtered through, it was Cliff Collier who finally managed the scene- shift the best.

"Coach, the only reason we've all been on this crazy train is because of you. You taught us how to play like we do and it's only right that you'll be here for whatever happens next. I just hope your wife and kids understand that you blew their Kings Island vacation for a really good reason!"

Again, nervous laughter filled the air as Keith again smiled and fired back with a subliminal message of his arrival.

"You'll have to check with Brewster on that one." Madison chortled. "He's the keeper of all my vacation days and master of my temporary universe. Look, we've all been here in this position before. I love you guys, and all I can say is I have always believed in your abilities as players, but more importantly as men. I'll see you out there on the field!"

Knowing the pressure-pot of excitement el Grande, Everett Carpenter had his usual worrisome moments trying to understand why he was selected for starting a most crucial series with everything on the line. His arm felt fine and his rehab assignments had all been strong, but getting back into the flow as an everyday arm wasn't back into his head yet.

Tom Browning and he finally caught up during a rare quiet moment and had a serious talk about the scope of his assignment.

"Pug, I thought when they kept me on the roster that I was just going to be in the bullpen. What's Tommy thinking starting me out of the gate?" he anxiously asked.

"I can tell you exactly why you're starting, and it's brilliant!" Browning answered. "So don't get torked-off by me telling you this, 'Carpy', but you're the sacrificial lamb!"

"The what?" he curiously asked. "What the hell does that mean?"

"Look, and please don't take offense to what I'm about to tell you, but right now if it were to happen, you're an expendable loss." Browning explained.

"You'll have to do better than that!" Carpenter shot back.

"OK, here's the deal. We are two-games back and have had no days off to rest anybody. Milhuff, Steinman, Arms, Scarbury, and Zeiber absolutely need an extra day of rest right now if we are going to win this thing. If you pull us through tonight, it will be a huge bonus. If you don't because you just came back off the DL, all that means is you've made the pitching staff stronger, and you now have a game under your belt heading off into the play-offs."

"No, wait a minute. Losing is always a bitch thing! If you're telling me I'm going out there tonight and everybody expects me to lose, you're screwed!" Carpenter angrily retorted.

"Come on, Everett, that's not what I'm saying. I truly hate bringing up sports analogies, I hate them, but Muhamad Ali gave away four-rounds and lost them all on purpose to George Foreman so that he could come back and have enough gas in the tank to knock him out and win the heavyweight title. All Tommy is asking is that you go out tonight and do your absolute best. A win would be wonderful, but a loss won't kill us. We have a hell of a pitching staff, maybe the best I've ever seen and that includes you. The rest of these sleeping beauties in the league haven't really caught up to us yet, and for the real element of surprise, we all need to be totally rested, and especially right now. Just understand Everett that there is method to the madness and just give us your best out there tonight. That's all we will ever ask, and we all know you will bring it!"

"Welcome to *'ESPN Sports Center day Night,'* I'm Buster Olney. It was a mysterious roster move by the Las Vegas Vipers that may have eliminated them from the play-offs as Manager Tommy Leach started left-handed pitcher Everett Carpenter against the Padres after just coming off the DL. Carpenter pitched into the fifth, allowing four- runs on seven hits, but it was this Mike Piazza two-run shot to right that sealed the deal as Woody Williams kept the Vipers at bay, scattering five hits over seven innings. It was a two- run blast in the third by Karl 'King Kong' Smith that accounted for all the Vipers' runs as the final at Mirage field was San Diego 5, Las Vegas 2.

"Other Western Division action had the Dodgers doubling up on Philly 6-3 and they now stay two ahead of San Diego and three-games in front of Las Vegas with just six left to play.In the NL Central Division, the Cardinals now hold a four-game lead over Cincinnati as the Mets finally clinched their Eastern Division title this past weekend with a sweep over the Marlins. While in the American League, it seemed like an eternity since the Yankees made it official and now hold a sixteen-game lead in the AL East over Toronto. The only real race now left in the AL is between Minnesota and Detroit where the Twins maintain just a mere one-game lead over the Tigers. Oakland is a five-game advantage over the Anaheim and could clinch it all tonight with a win over Cleveland coupled with an Angels loss to Boston.

"In the Wildcard race, it will be the loser in the AL Central as the runner up between Detroit and Minnesota who will be there. For the National League, the Phillies have their spot already secured with the second best record in the NL East. If I may, back to the Vipers mystique for just a moment. As the Cinderella team that as it appears most of the country seems to be pulling for, I must say as a reporter for a network that prides itself in fusing sports and entertainment together that this may be the number one headline of the century. You have a college baseball team, with no previous professional experience, suddenly thrown into the Major Leagues and somehow finds a way and a will to win. By no means am I being critical because this has been great fun, but as we now get ready for the play-offs, it's time to face reality to understand why teams pay big money for big talent and survive long past the regular season. It's my opinion that you are now witnessing that very fine thread between flash and substance.

"Don't misunderstand me. It's been a great run and, believe me, quite the riveting story-board of drama every day that I've come to work, but with six- games left and now three- games out, I say let's get ready for some real honest post-season baseball as it's more than just obvious that this glass slipper may be cracked beyond repair!"

Losing at any level for a championship mentality never mixes well. The sound of cleats scuffing to the concrete floor and the low level mumblings in the Vipers' club-house were muted testimony to the evening's results. As the players sullenly headed toward their lockers, Keith Madison had already planted himself in front of the one that read 'Carpenter.' As the two made eye-contact, it was almost a mirror image of a time before. As they both silently sat down, Keith extended his hand to the player he knew all too well and who was hurting.

"Good game out there tonight, Everett. Your stuff looked really good." he began. "Tommy had me doing the charts, and so overall I have to say your pitches were all working pretty well."

"C'mon, Keith, that's bullshit, they lit me up. You know it and everybody who watched the game saw it. I sucked! I just didn't have it! You don't have to say this crap just to make me feel better, I can take it."

Keith Madison was not just a great baseball mind. His skill-set of getting every ounce of effort from his players was always the honest and select approach of being a master communicator

"Look, 'Carpy,' Remember when you thought you really got rocked by Texas in the tournament? Same thing tonight. Five, maybe six bad pitches out of what…eighty-two…that's it! Everett, you're a hell of a pitcher and that's why everybody wanted you back and especially this week. Honestly, you could have been Nolan Ryan out there tonight, but hell's bells, kid…we only scored two! Nobody up here is going to win by only denting the dish twice. It just wasn't our night out there tonight!"

As the words sank in, Carpenter continued to sit and stew refusing to make eye-contact with his mentor, knowing that his words reflected the hurting truth.

"Just understand where we are in this thing. I agree totally with Tommy that if we are at least two-out when the Dodgers hit town, our fate is in our own hands. I know it hurts to lose, but look what you've gained by being back on the hill tonight and that will help us down the road, I promise!"

Slowly looking up from the floor, Everett Carpenter once again looked at his ex-coach in the eye and slowly smiled.

"So I guess that curve-ball that didn't curve to Piazza was one that went on the bad side of your list?" Carpenter mused.

"Well, honestly, I think a knuckleball right there might have been the way to go." Keith chuckled.

With an awkward moment now diffused, the two lightly chatted for a few more minutes before Keith got up to join Tommy and the rest of the coaches at the post-game press conference.

"Standing room only last night, Cisco, it was officially our biggest crowd ever at the Mirage: 47,892." Brandon Briggs briefed his boss as they met in his office for early morning coffee and to compare notes. Silence along with a sour pale of expected disappointment was also present in the room. Brandon let the good financial update linger well, knowing that observation alone wouldn't be enough to turn the tide of emotion that his owner was feeling. Finally looking up from his list of notes and shaking his head, Cisco "The Dealer" Wheeler let his thoughts be known.

"Why the hell was Carpenter in this game? I understand the back-handed logic that Tommy explained last night, but shit, Brandon, we're now in a fucking hole!"

Pondering for the proper response, Briggs decided to paint the positives as he saw them.

"Look, if it were a three--game series, I totally understand." he began. "We now have six and all the arms are rested. Bruce Leslie pitched a hell of a relief stint and he only gave up one-run the rest of the way, so the bullpen also got a break last night. Right now, Cisco, we need to look at the big picture!"

"Three-out and six to play, that's a hell of a mountain to climb, Brandon! We could be out of it before the Dodgers even get here and I don't even want to think about that!" Wheeler continued. "And would someone tell frigging Wayne Newton that we do appreciate him, but no more free tickets! Damn! That's the first thing I got when I turned on my answering machine this morning!"

"Don't worry,' Brandon laughed. "Some guy named Rascal Flatts is singing the Anthem tonight, and to my knowledge, he'll only need one."

"Where were our bats last night?" Cisco quickly changed directions. "Damn it, only two- runs on five- hits. That's not us!"

"Right, it wasn't, but it happens. Let's give some credit when it's due." His GM countered. "Williams was on fire last night, Cisco, and remember that the Padres are fighting for this thing too. But did you notice how smooth our infield transition worked? Wow, Duzan made a couple of great grabs at third, and I think we both kind of forgot how good Kennedy's defense is at short. I know it was tough to lose Gambill, but I really think we may have improved ourselves a bit out there on the left side of the infield!"

"Who's starting today?" Wheeler asked

"Steinman's on the mound today, Zebro tomorrow." Briggs justify replied.

"Did I hear we had a problem last night with the fireworks?' Cisco barked.

"Oh, you mean on Smith's home run?" Brandon explained. "It seems like we had a bit of a delayed reaction from the pyro-tech people for some reason and the fireworks actually didn't go off until after the next batter, and that was when Chadwick struck out."

"So, we actually sent up fireworks after one of our own players struck out?" Wheeler quizzed.

Pausing for the awkward response, Brandon Briggs delivered the news best he possibly could. "Yes, sir, it was an accident, but we did."

"We have to get that fixed immediately Brandon! Fireworks? After one of our own players strikes out? I don't think I'm over-reacting here, but personally, I think that might send out a totally wrong message to the other team!"

The campus at Bentley State University in Portsmouth, Ohio, was now adorned with every motivational sign and substance that they could muster. Watch parties had been scheduled each night in the Rhodes Athletic Center to bring the town and the college together for this most unusual of sporting experiences.

Even the 10:30 p.m. start-times didn't defer hundreds of fans from showing up to watch the games on a huge jumbo-Tron TV system that had been donated by local businessman Rich Fraley from 'Rich TV and Home Center.'

Other resident merchants also chipped in providing music, food, and contests before the games to help add to the occasion as the reality of what lie ahead was starting to take on a manic form.

Syleanna Griffin and Carla Harris had now become fixtures in the media machinery for interview requests now that their relationship with Sean Deeters and Cliff Collier had finally been revealed. As the "Do or Die" week for the Vipers began to pick up steam, calls from all over the country were pouring in. *"Regis and Kathy Lee," "Ellen," "The Tonight Show with Jay Leno"* and yes, even *The David Letterman Show* was again knocking at the door for a desperate bid to grab a piece of the dream. While flattered, the girls simply decided to not accept any of the tempting invitations as to keep their minds focused and their options open.

"I can't believe that the *David Letterman* people wanted you on his show." Carla laughed as her and Syleanna sat eating lunch at the Market Street Café. "You know they saw that *Entertainment Tonight* thing. What were they going to have you do? Maybe it's a top ten list of reasons to fire your cue-card bimbo!"

"The funniest to me was the phone call we got from "*The View*," added Syleanna. "I just for some reason don't think I could hold my water sitting there and blabbing baseball with Barbara Walters, Meredith Vieira, and Star Jones."

"Well, so what are we going to do?' Carla asked. "Are we going to go out to Vegas or not?"

"I don't know, Sean's being real funny about us being there. I personally don't want to do anything to make him feel uncomfortable, and besides, we got ourselves involved in all these 'rah-rah' things here. Maybe we just wait, and if they move on, we can catch them later."

"I'm just so glad Keith is with them now. Isn't that strange how all that went down?" Carla pointed out. "And oh my god, all so quickly."

"I just ran into his wife at Kroger yesterday and we talked about all that." said Syleanna. "According to her, he said no at first because of his position with the university. I guess he finally made some phone calls, and President Morris said that if he used his own vacation time that he could do anything he wanted to with it and there would be no problem. I guess he also got her blessing and he hopped on a plane the next morning from Columbus and headed to Vegas."

"Keith is such a great guy" Carla added. "I just hope having him there can help do this thing. I know Cliff was like so totally stunned when he was first introduced that he said he darn near shit himself. His words, not mine!"

While sharing a good old-fashioned girly- laugh moment on that one, a gentleman suddenly and without warning approached the table and introduced himself.

"Excuse me ladies, I'm Bruce Smith of the *Columbus Dispatch*, but you can just call me 'Smitty.' Do you mind if I sit down and have a few words with you about what's going on here in Portsmouth? You know, about the team."

Looking at each other, they had become quite accustomed to the art of interruption by the press. Before they even had a chance to give an answer, the sound of another chair being pulled up and across the hardwood floor to their table was the unspoken sign that lunch had now become a three-some.

Sitting in front of his locker, Gary Steinman was quietly pulling on his socks as Tommy Leach momentarily stopped by to inject a burst of positive energy.

"Go get em' today, Steiney! Just give them your usual stuff and we'll be just fine."

Looking up, Gary nodded in his usual aloof manner and then again looked down to button up his jersey. As Tommy slapped him on the shoulder and started to move on, he noticed a little different body language than usual. Stopping again in his tracks, he doubled back and then sat down next to his star pitcher.

"By the way, maybe none of my business, but wondering how your dad has been doing." he gently inquired.

21 DOWN IN VEGAS

"Ah…about the same." Gary's forced reply sounded. "He's hanging on, and that's about it. I know he'll be watching today … from his bed"

Trying to explain further, he then stalled in his tracks as his manager immediately knew that he had hit the wall of any more casual conversation. As the verbal pause started to transcend into that zone between done and awkward, Tommy suddenly slapped him on the knee and hopped up. "See ya out there, kid!"

"Welcome to *ESPN Sports Center*, I'm Matt Barrie as tonight our lead as it has been for almost two-months now is the incredible story that just won't go away from Las Vegas. Eight- innings of two-hit baseball from Gary Steinman and an arsenal of offense lifting the Vipers over the Padres 11-0 tonight in a bounce-back win that Las Vegas definitely needed to stay alive in that oh so tight NL Western Division chase.

"Here, the Vipers score three in the first as David Wells hangs a slider to 'King Kong' Karl Smith, and wow…they're still looking for that one out in the weeds. In the second, two on and none out, Boomer to the plate and look at Sean Deeters with a perfect drag bunt to load the bases. Terrence Kennedy up next and you've got to watch this…a screaming line drive off Donnie Osmond's teeth and the center field sign of one of the most popular shows on the Strip and a three-run double. Looks like Marie will have to do all the singing tonight!Pitcher Gary Steinman was finally pulled after eight with the Vipers up seven-zip, and they're not done yet. Pinch hitter Luke Shepard now up with the bases full strikes four of a kind with long grand- salami to left to seal the deal. Final: Vipers, eleven, the Padres nada!"

The Vipers clubhouse was already a blaze on the lopsided win alone as the celebration was about to erupted to a much towering level. It was Jarred Brewster who dashed into the room and delivered the news.

"Philadelphia just scored two in the ninth to take down the Dodgers 4-3!"

That announcement meant much more than just gaining a single- game. It now meant that the Vipers were somewhat in control of their own destiny when Los Angeles rolled into town Thursday night for the final four games of the season. The other order of business was now taking care of the Padres who were now in a virtual tie now two-back from LA and five left to play. San Diego would leave Las Vegas after an afternoon contest on Wednesday to end their regular season with four games in Atlanta.

Sequestered back in the manager's office, the coaches and Tommy Leach were again plotting their course into uncharted waters. Tom Browning was up and at it again, explaining the pitching rotation from this point on.

"Zebro tomorrow, then Milhuff, Arms, Scarbury, and then Steiny to close things out. I think that's pretty strong."

"What about Carpenter, Pug? How are we going to use him?" Tommy asked.

"At least through this week, I figured either long relief or late innings. I hope it doesn't come to that, but it's always nice to have an extra wing if needed."

"What about the Dodgers rotation? Pretty well set?' Tommy quizzed again.

"Yea, I don't think we'll see any surprises. It looks like Lowe, Penny, Sele, and Tomko in that order. They're starting Maddox tomorrow, so it looks like we'll miss him." Browning noted.

"A great 'pick me up' win tonight, fellas! Nice to see the guys spanking the ball around a little bit." Leach added. "Larry's due back on the overnight 'red-eye' and says Norm is doing great. I guess he's already trying to order tacos from the hospital cafeteria if that tells you anything. Keith, I know there has been a lot to digest here in a short amount of time, if there's anything you want to ask, please feel free."

"Thanks, Tommy, but not really. Just hanging around the guys again has been great and you all have made me feel more than welcome. I really do appreciate it. I kind of understand my role, and if I can help move a muscle memory or two and help these guys boost the flow of how they scraped to get to the finals, I'm certainly fine with that."

Glancing at his watch, Manager Tommy Leach knew it was now time to switch gears and get to the postgame news party. Before he got up, he shot an appreciative glance to the newest member of his staff.

"You're a class act, Keith, and I again, I thank you for being up here with us. OK, the wolves are waiting, let's get out there and let 'em' rip a little more meat from our poor brittle bones!"

The "Thunder Dome" as it was now being referenced, was now closed as 117 degree heat beat down on a Las Vegas Wednesday that was normally packed with tourists and excitable game players. This day was different. Radios in all the business's and the cabs running to and from the airport to the strip were all super-glued to KVPR-AM. On contact to any who suddenly realized it was the game and heard Ralph Hacker's voice describing the event at hand, the next question was always the same: "What's the score?"

"It's another standing room only crowd here at Mirage Field as the young man affectionately known as 'Zebro' has given the Vipers what they desperately needed so far this afternoon." Hacker described, "Brad Zeiber has really kept the Padres off-balance with an assortment of pitches as we head in to the eighth inning up 4-1."

"You're right about him mixing it up today, Ralph." Pete Harnisch added, "Except for that solo homer from Dave Roberts in the second, it's been quite the pitch de jour this afternoon from a young man that's been very impressive since his call-up from Colorado Springs. I do believe I've even seen that knuckler float by a time or two as well."

"It gets into their heads for sure!" Ralph added. "I was talking to shall I say an un-named hitting coach here recently who totally admitted that the Vipers' ability to use that thing as the weapon it has become is now quite the buzz in all the club-houses. Now, when you get them yammering about it like that, you know it causes skull-trouble at the plate."

Per textbook, Viper baseball Brad Zeiber disposed of Adrian Gonzales, Brian Giles, and Will Venable in order with "Dirty" Ernie Fuller coming in and slamming the book shut in the ninth. As the final-four games of the regular season were now at hand, Las Vegas was clearly where Manager Tommy Leach wanted them to be.

"First of all, that was a hell of a series! You all are playing like the champions you are!" Tommy began as he purposely quieted down the noisy post-game after-glow. "You are all doing all the little things to win, and these are what make you all special. Kennedy with the fake pick-off move at second that nailed Cameron, Collier throwing behind the runner at first, and Pouge calling a pitch-out to third base! That's brilliant stuff! Now, I see you all are in here celebrating tonight so I guess I'm going to have to be the bastard that's going to flicker the lights and say 'the party's over.' Whooping it up is all well and good, as long as you realize you haven't won a damn thing yet! One ballgame today? Yes! And that's one more step that gets us closer to our goal, but we're not there yet, fellows!"

As the room remained silent, Manager Tommy Leach delivered the epilogue for the next step and the path required for his team's final journey where no team such as this had ever gone before.

"Was it really just two months ago that I was told that I would be inheriting a new team for the rest of the season?" He laughed. "And a college team at that, wow. You were all here, I believe, and perhaps remember how it was. Four-days to fit uniforms, assign lockers, deal with all the media shit, and then we were expected to go out there and win baseball games? Hell, we had fucking blimps in Pittsburgh, riots in New York, and then when we finally make it home for our first game here, there's tired old Mickey Rourke out there in the stands trying to hustle all your girlfriends."

While indeed soaking in a serious point, a few titters and light-laughs of remembrance broke through to slightly soften the oration. Tommy knew at this point that his window of opportunity was now open for his message as he now hoped to galvanize the flash.

"We are masters of our own universe, gentlemen, because we and we alone are now in complete control of our own fate. If we just continue to do what we do, and that's win, ain't nobody gonna' stop us now! If we continue to win, the Padres can't catch us. If we continue to win, we will not only catch, but overtake the Dodgers, and if we continue to win, the National League West is ours! Do that and then we'll really have something to celebrate Sunday night. It's all your decision and yours alone to make, guys. Have a great night!"

21 DOWN IN VEGAS

Tommy spun on his heels and quickly exited the stage toward the office as his once swaggering band of youth absorbed the missive delivered. As conversations resumed, there was definitely a much more serious tone of business that suddenly and decisively permeated the room.

"Welcome to *ESPN Sports Center Thursday,* and I'm Ryan Field. So, it's all down to the last series of regular season baseball in the NL West this weekend as the showdown that clearly all of sports will be watching is about to happen. With just four games to go, the LA Dodgers and the Las Vegas Vipers will anti-up this weekend to see who is the 'Best in the West!'

"Last night, Las Vegas got a stellar pitching performance from Brad Zeiber as the Vipers shut down the slumping Padres 4-1 to capture second place alone and are now just two-games out with four left to play. The Vipers jumped out early on Clay Hensley as Bombo Chadwick rocked a two-out double to right scoring Sean Deeters and Gary Duzan in the first and that makes it two-nothing, Vipers.

"Here in the second Zeiber hangs a curve-ball to Dave Roberts that becomes an instant souvenir, but for the Padres, it would be their lone-run on the afternoon. Later in the seventh, it's one on and 'King Kong' Karl Smith to the plate as this one goes high and deep joining the Mirage cacti-garden over the right field fence and it's another win for Las Vegas.

"If I may say, this month of baseball has perhaps been the most enjoyable for me and perhaps for you too if you like the world of unpredictable. Just three short weeks ago, it looked like Arizona and San Diego would be slugging it out at the end, but how things have changed. The Dodgers got hot, others not, and the Vipers kept winning and a division that was once as close as a colony of *E. coli* on room temperature beef has finally defined itself.

"Heading into the last weekend of play, here are your standings in the NL West and don't forget that we will have complete highlights and coverage right here and when it happens on *ESPN Sports Center!*"

STEPHEN A. HAYES

National league Western Division Standings
9/25/06

Team	W	L	Standing
Dodgers	88	70	-
Vipers	86	72	2.0
Padres	85	73	3.0
D' Backs	82	76	6.0
Giants	78	81	10.5
Rockies	76	83	12.5

Even when the Vipers were the easy pickings of the league, there was always a big buzz when the Dodgers rolled into town. Interstate 15 between the two cities was always extra heavy as the four-hour drive carried fanatic Dodger blue fans to "Glitter Gulch" for a chance to play as well as support one of Major League Baseball's most storied franchises. On this last weekend in September of 2006, it was miles beyond outrageous as the moment you hit the famous sign that read "Welcome to Fabulous Las Vegas, Nevada," you had now officially entered the "Bozo -zone."

"This is Tim Smile in the NEWS4 chopper flying high in the sky over Las Vegas as our viewers back in LA can clearly see the pilgrimage of Dodger fans on I-15 streaming in for tonight's first game at Mirage Field between the Dodgers and the Vipers. To kind of demonstrate just how crazy this weekend is going to be, we are now showing you the secondary parking lot which was seldom ever used here at the ballpark. It is now totally filled with news trucks and media outlets from all around the country.

"I understand we even have a news team from London, England, set up to cover this series which most likely will determine the Western Division champs. By the way, guys, if you're looking to find a cheap hotel room in Las Vegas this weekend and you don't already have a reservation, good luck. I just heard that any remaining rooms within thirty miles are going between a thousand and fifteen hundred dollars a night. More coming up during our six- o'clock report, from NEWS4 live in the sky from Las Vegas…I'm Tim Smile, and now back to you, Kelly!"

"Thanks Tim, and as you could see, they're getting ready to rumble tonight in Las Vegas and don't forget that our pre-game coverage for the game begins at 7:00 p.m. right here on KNBC. I'm Kelly Lange, and coming up next on 'Live at 5' we meet LA's oldest Dodger fan!"

There was a loose, yet confident atmosphere in the Vipers clubhouse as Bench Coach Keith Madison sat down next to his starting pitcher for the evening.

"Kind of feels a little like that Florida game tonight, eh?" Keith spoke. "You had ice-water flowing in your veins that night, remember, partner?"

Mitch Milhuff smiled as he looked over into the face of comfort and a true ally. It was Keith that could always seem to get the best out of him in any situation as both knew what cards lay on the table tonight.

"Yea, everybody thought Florida was going to take it all, even in the semi-finals, didn't they? I still say that was my biggest win of all-time coach." Milhuff admitted.

"Naw, tonight's going to be your biggest win of all time." Keith playfully responded. "And more after that…arm feeling sturdy?"

"Yea, real solid. Brewster has had me going over his damn flash card system again on the batters. He makes me feel like I'm back in class!" Mitch laughed.

"Don't worry, just go out there and be Mitch Milhuff tonight," added Keith, "and don't be afraid to give them the knuckler a few times either. You have them looking for it every time they come up, so just give it to them when they least expect it."

"Gotcha, coach…thanks!"

As all the analysts and the media posse were giving the Las Vegas Vipers a mere "puncher's chance" of taking down the Dodgers in this must-win series, back home at the Rhodes Athletic Center on the campus of Bentley State University, the crowd gathered were witnessing that good old fashioned home-cooking .

"Holy shit," Jesse Johnson screamed. "He's now struck out nine, and we're only in the fifth-inning! Is that the same ol' damn Mitch Milhuff I used to play 'quarter bounce' with over at Buffalo Wild Wings?"

Others in the packed arena watched the telecast with unbridled enthusiasm as the Dodgers continued to send player after player to the plate with nothing for their efforts except a frustrated stroll back to the dugout. In the often pre-scripted ledger of sports and the anticipation of what should occur on any given night, this one so far was a complete impromptu surprise. Even the great Vin Scully had a time of absorbing this Thursday night's development on the field.

"A fairytale dream lies in a young man's arm tonight as the purple and orange hues of a hot desert day slowly disappear along with the Dodgers offense so far here in our first of four in Las Vegas. Derek Lowe has been reliably solid for the Dodgers except for that two-run blast back in the second by the Viper's Terrance Kennedy. Heading into the top of the seventh inning it will be Drew, Betemit, and Lofton to again face Milhuff who to this point has allowed no-runs and only two meaningless singles.

"Scanning another sold-out crowd here at "The Mirage" the crowd could now solidly feel the inner- strength and energy as it related to the heart and soul of the participants and their performance on the field when it came down to old fashion 'crunch-time,"

From the top of the stairs, both Keith and Tommy watched the escalation of pride and effort that Mitch Milhuff now seemed to own as the Dodgers were again retired in order.

"Two-more innings, guys! Just six more at bats and we're outta here!" Sean Deeters echoed as the Vipers again spilled into the dugout. A quick inventory of emotion by Keith Madison saw his once pack of over-animated college kids now handling themselves as the men they were asked to be.

Knowing that two-runs against the Dodgers could evaporate at any point, Keith quizzed Tommy on Gary Duzan.

"'Duz' has really come to own third base." Keith observed. "He's actually a little more mobile and faster than Gambill. Have you ever bunted him?"

"You mean for a hit? Naw…just to sacrifice." Leach said

"He might surprise you. We tried it a couple of times in the tournament and we caught them flat on their heels. You might just file that one away."

"Ralph Hacker, along with Pete Harnisch here as Gary Duzan leads off the bottom of the seventh and, Pete, Again I must say that Milhuff has been throwing the proverbial aspirin tablets out there tonight."

"Mitch has been nothing short of amazing to this point." Harnisch beamed. "He's thrown 74 pitches, 62 for strikes, and has only been behind the count on a batter twice. I can honestly say that this is the best we have seen him throw so far in the past couple of months since this whole crazy thing started."

"Here's the first pitch to Duzan from Dodgers reliever Joe Beimel. It's a called strike down the middle as the Vipers third basemen hopes to get on and paint some more insurance runs up there on the big board."

With the ebb and flow of emotion that the game of baseball possesses, there are those rare times that not only the fans, but the opposing team can also sense the reality of futility. On those humanly magic moments of physical command, even a two-run lead can be one too many. As it turned out on this given day that was certainly the case. Mitch Milhuff dutifully enjoyed his assigned task to completion by not only setting the next six Dodgers down in order, but also striking out the side in the ninth-inning. As pinch-hitter Sandy Alomar feebly swung and missed at the final pitch; the thunder rolled!

Slumped over at his locker with a towel over his sweat-soaked head, Mitch Miluff's right-ear was being chewed off by Jarred Brewster.

"Ninety-nine pitches, Mitch! Ninety-nine, brother! You were on fire out there like I've never seen you before. Guess how many curve-balls you threw?"

With a slow smile of antagonistic appreciation, Mitch slowly looked at Jarred before he spoke. "Can we talk about this a little later, bro? I have just ten minutes to shower and get to the press room."

"Well yea, I just wanted to give you some stats while you were still fresh, but we can do it later if you want." Jarred fired back." What time do you want to get together?"

Standing up and heading to the showers, Mitch looked back over his shoulder at the over-energetic Jarred. "My people will call your people!" He laughed. "And by the way…eleven!"

"Eleven what?" Jarred yelled back.

"Curve-balls, ya little bastard!" Milhuff animatedly shouted, "Curve-balls!"

Striding briskly into his bosses quarters, Brandon Briggs quickly blurted out the death-nail news. "Hot off the press Cisco, San Diego just got routed by Atlanta. They're not totally gone yet, but on life support for sure!"

Spinning back around to the front of his desk while being absorbed in his big leather chair, Cisco Wheeler was holding a copy of the sports page and was especially keyed into the baseball standings.

"So, they're three-games back with three left to play, another loss by the Padres or a win by the Dodgers takes them out for good now, doesn't it?" he confidently noted.

With a broadening smile, the Vipers GM couldn't resist a good-natured dig at his friend and owner who had now turned into a human 24-hour sports channel.

"By the way, I think the Vipers won today also. I wonder where that puts them in the standings, Cisco?"

Quickly slamming the paper down on the table, Cisco 'The Dealer" Wheeler stood up with child-like enthusiasm and a smile wider than Hoover Dam.

"This is what I have lived my whole life for Brandon!" he exulted "Those kids! Those magnificent kids who have defied every rule in the book! This has got to be the greatest sports story ever, and I mean in any form of athletic competition.Did you see that media-circus in our war room today? Christ, Mitch Milhuff just threw the game of his life and the fucking press just kept hammering him with all those stupid questions! Were you nervous? Can you do it again if you make the playoffs? Why didn't you throw the knuckleball more often?"

"I thought he handled it extremely well." Brandon added.

21 DOWN IN VEGAS

"Hell yes, he did…and all the rest of them as well. I think they have all handled this with so much class and grace it's almost super-natural. Except for that little meltdown episode we had with Deeters at the beginning, this team has done exactly what I envisioned it could do, Brandon, and that is simply to be a team of stand-up winners."

"Deeters certainly turned his ship around in a hurry. He's leading us in almost every offensive category right now, and Tommy tells me he has really taken a big role in keeping this clubhouse loose and focused."

Pausing transitorily, both men absorbed the special moment like inhaling expensive perfume permeating from the décolletage of a beautiful woman. Sweet moments are always fleeting, and knowing that there was more work to be done, Brandon Briggs took it upon himself to snap back to the reality of the day.

"OK, Cisco, where are we for tomorrow night? Everything in place?"

"Hell no!" Wheeler bellowed. "This place is nuts! I still have to find twenty extra tickets for the cast of *Glee* and the Oak Ridge Boys want to sit in the dugout after they sing the National Anthem. The one with the big deep voice, you know, the om-papa-mow-mow guy."

"You mean Richard Sterban?" Brandon interjected.

"Yea, him! He loves baseball, and I guess he knows Karl Smith's mother from being in some fan club and she told him it would be all right for him to sit in the dugout with her son. Christ, Brandon! That's just the tip of the shit-berg that I'm dealing with right now!"

While impossible not to laugh at Cisco's animated frustration, Brandon Briggs knew that a swift reality check was needed

"OK, quickly. Let's look at the numbers. We are one- game out with three to play. We need to sweep them to take the division, we both know that. If we lose just one, that means our best shot is a tie and they will take it because they have more division wins against us. We got Scotty Arms and they got Aaron Sele for tomorrow night. He's a big right-hander who can pitch lights out, or he can have some trouble finding the plate. Scotty has been solid and pitching the best ball of his career now, and I know how bad he wants it. I think we're in a good place now to catch them!"

"I hear Toots Randall has been making the rounds again." Wheeler lamented. "Why doesn't that noisy bastard just shut-up and pay attention to his own turd- pile? He was on Dan Patrick's show again the other day spouting off about that little league team in Vegas!"

"Forget him, Cisco," Briggs pleaded. "The Yankees have had this thing wrapped up since July, and they all have too much time on their hands. We really need to get ready for what happens if we take this thing!"

"And we will!" Wheeler blustered. "I've already got it figured out. Let's see…Detroit and the Twins are still in it for the AL Central, but the loser will be the wildcard and it's Oakland in the West! For us it's the Cardinals in the Central, the Mets in the East, and Philly is in as the Wildcard. I think that I am correct."

"Right!" Brandon added. "So if…I mean…when we get in, that means we will go to St. Louis since the Mets have the best record in the National League and that's where Philadelphia will go."

"So when did baseball standings become calculus?" Wheeler huffed.

Sensing that it was time to exit stage right, Brandon walked to the door and as he turned, paused with a final reflection. "Hey, boss, you know the Oak Ridge Boys got their start in Christian Gospel music, so it might not be a bad idea to have a few professional prayer warriors on the bench for tomorrow night's game…just a thought!"

At the Market Street Cafe in Portsmouth, Ohio, the travel-wheels were once again turning. Syleanna Griffin and Carla Harris were at odds late in the evening of a Thursday night as to what they should do for the weekend. The Rhodes Athletic Center on the Bentley State Campus was again packed for the first game with the Dodgers and the next three-games had literally been sold out. As the two discussed potential scenarios, the options were mind-boggling.

"Look, Carla, *Good Morning America* said they would fly us out and put us up if we agreed to do the interview with them after this is all over. I got the guy's number, and he said he could have us on a plane within a few hours. I think we should go!"

"Wait a minute, you hooch!" Carla shot back to Syleanna. "I thought that you were the one that didn't want to put any extra pressure on Sean. What about all that has to be done here and this town is going frigging stark-crazy! Besides, Cliff wouldn't be so happy if I just popped in either. He is so wired right now, and I certainly wouldn't want to distract him."

"Everything is already done, Carla. Jennifer Shakart has taken over the busy-work that needs to be done at the university over the next few days. You know what a planner she is. This could be the biggest thing ever in both of our lives. I just don't want to miss it! What if we didn't tell them we were coming and just stayed out of the way?"

"You think somebody here wouldn't spill the beans? Get real." Carla teased.

"No, we don't tell a soul!" Syleanna affirmed. "Look it's Thursday night. The game doesn't start tomorrow night until 10:10 pm. Las Vegas time, I could get packed in an hour…two hours tops. I'll even drive us to Columbus."

Contemplation was a moment of sipping- silence as both Carla and Syleanna took a slow and ponderous taste from their green tea. With her hazel-brown eyes now firmly fixed to the face of her best friend Carla, it was Syleanna who fired the one-word question across the bow.

"Well?"

"So you're sure you have that guy's number, right?" Carla asked.

14TH INNING

Thursday slowly faded into Friday in Las Vegas as Tommy Leach was suddenly awakened by the phone ringing. Looking over at the clock on his dresser, the time read 3:30 a.m. As he groggily fumbled to pick up the receiver, he couldn't help to realize that good news is never delivered at this time in the morning.

"Hello." he heard himself say.

There was a pause on the other end of the phone as he could hear light sobbing before the conversation began. On the other end of the line was a very distressed Gary Steinman.

"Skip…this is Gary. Sorry to call you like this, but… I lost my dad tonight."

"Oh, Gary, I'm so sad to hear that. I thought he was doing better the last time we talked."

"He was I don't know…I guess everything just finally caught up with him. They called me about twenty-minutes ago from the hospital. I have a flight out of here at 7:00 a.m. to Indianapolis."

"Don't you worry about a thing, Gary, I hate this for you. Just go do whatever you have to do. I have Carpenter who can pitch Sunday so don't even worry about that! Take care of this first, believe me, everything here will be fine!"

"I hate leaving you like this, Tommy. It's tearing me apart, but he is all I ever had and I need to get there."

"God be with you Gary. I'll pass along our prayers to the team this morning. Everything here will be OK. All I ask is for you to please travel safe."

"Thank you, Tommy, I appreciate it. I'll stay in touch." as the phone fell-silent.

Pondering yet another unexpected major challenge, the Vipers manager slumped back into his pile of rumbled covers. In times like this, it's easy to get caught up in the cross-hairs of empathy versus selfishness. As he lay in the dark, his thoughts teetered between the hurt of a quiet rock-solid kid that he had developed a genuine love for and the question of who would now pitch perhaps the biggest game in Las Vegas Vipers history come Sunday. After a quick- prayer, the momentum switch was easy.

The mandatory 4:00 p.m. meeting was much quieter than usual as the twenty-four participants awaited the arrival of Tommy Leach. Bench Coach Keith Madison was trying his best not to answer any questions that he felt unappropriated or out of his jurisdiction. At the strike of 4:00 p.m, Manager Tommy Leach briskly entered the room.

"First of all, guys, you will notice that one of your brothers isn't with us here today. We have a Viper who is hurting. As you all know, Gary Steinman's dad was not in good health and overnight he passed away. I got the call that nobody wants to get early this morning, and Gary is now off to Indianapolis to take care of what I know has to be some very hard arrangements.. I simply ask that all your energy of thoughts and prayers be with him during this very tough time. I know Gary was set to pitch Sunday, but we cannot honestly look that far ahead. We can't even look past today, because one more loss… and our season will end on the Lord's-day. I won't make this meeting much longer because I want all of you to take a little extra- time for yourselves and look deep inside for the answers we must solve to play-on.

"We have Scotty on the hill today who has definitely been golden as of late and living up to his nickname. The last time Sele pitched, the Padres ended his day in the fourth-inning. Go out there today, guys, and do what you do, that's it.

If you just play like you have been doing it since the day you got here, this is the day we can officially say that we finally catch these wankers!"

The release of pent-up tension was explosive as the tapestry of emotions that cascaded across the clubhouse. Players were now cheering, some crying, others internally set themselves to meet the challenge of taking it a day at a time. With a nod from Tommy to Keith Madison and Tom Browning, it was Keith that put his hand on Everett Carpenters' shoulder and guided him out of the fracas. All four men then quietly slipped away and entered the lair of the Vipers' manager office; the door slowly shut.

It was an extremely busy day at McCarron International Airport as sports crews, fans, and the world converged for the biggest baseball weekend in the history of the city. Even the pilot couldn't resist some half-witted attempts of humor on descent while welcoming his passengers in for the landing.

"This is your captain speaking, and in case you don't know, our team, the Las Vegas Vipers are playing for a division baseball title this weekend. By the way, you can always tell the difference between a Dodger fan and our engine. Our engine will stop whining when we get to the gate!"

A chorus of cheers mixed with boos rained out as the levity of the moment captured the reaction of all passengers who were about to de-plane into the ground-swell of media attention.

"I thought that was pretty clever." Carla remarked. "I didn't think they could say stuff like that on the airline speaker you know. I just thought it was for like serious stuff."

"So thanks for flying with us and we're really glad that we aren't crashing would have be better?" Syleanna laughed. "C'mon, you ditz, we got to figure us out what to do here. CBS is picking us up in a limo, thank you, and then taking us to The Mirage. We still need to find some tickets for the game, that's the only thing Andre couldn't do."

"Oh, Andre, he's the guy you called to set this thing up" Carla remarked." "Well, it's almost 4:00 p.m. now. We land and get to the room and then just head to the ballpark I guess, right?"

"With no tickets…again…and on this game!" Syleanna moaned. "Think again, girlfriend. We will have to figure something out quick because the last I heard, the cheap seats were over $300 apiece."

21 DOWN IN VEGAS

"This is *Baseball Tonight,* and I'm Steve Phillips with some breaking news on this Friday as we prepare for a monumental game tonight between the Los Angeles Dodgers and the Las Vegas Vipers. It was reported late this afternoon that Las Vegas pitching-ace Gary Steinman has left the team on bereavement leave due to the passing of his father. Apparently, team officials were notified early this morning of the situation and no other details are readily available. Steinman was scheduled to pitch on Sunday as the Vipers need to win the next three- games to capture the NL Western Division. From an analytical situation, this could be devastating news as Steinman had certainly been the 'go-to' guy whenever they needed a big win. Since the All-Star break this past July, he has been nothing short of Superman going 11-1 with a blistering era of .091.

"Knowing that the Vipers need a sweep this weekend to win the division, it's pure speculation as to who could or would be called on to go Sunday for such a big game. With Scotty 'The Golden' Arms pitching tonight and Brad Scarbury on Saturday, many questions are now on the table. Of the available options you have, a few long relievers like Burkes, Leslie, or Shackart that could give you a spot start or would they actually bring back Brad Zeiber on just three days' rest? Another possibility might be lefty Everett Carpenter who just recently came off the DL and has pitched only once in a not so impressive performance last week against San Diego.

"Wow, to say that excitement is missing from Major League Baseball on this final weekend would be like saying 'King Kong' was just another garden variety monkey. I'm Steve Phillips inviting you to stay tuned as we will be back with all the stats, highlights, and action after the game right here with *Baseball Tonight!* on ESPN."

Upstairs at Mirage field in the office of Cisco Wheeler, Brandon Briggs, Tommy Leach, and a worrisome owner cautiously compared notes. While a certain giddiness of the moment was present, the three had to address the reality that their ace was missing in action.

"Seriously, Tommy," Brandon asked, "how are the guys taking this, knowing they have to win out here?"

"I think they're OK. It was a bit of a shock and bad timing for sure, but thankfully, they seem resilient and are trying to help figure it out."

"Hell, Tommy!" Cisco retorted. "These are the Los Angeles Dodgers, and I'm sure they think they got it figured out too. His name is Maddux. If they lose today, they know that they got him and we have…somebody!"

"We have options," Tommy shot back, "and that's the one thing they won't know until tomorrow."

Manager Tommy Leach again quickly stated. "We could throw Zebro out there on three days' rest, but honestly, how much has this kid got left in his tank? We could start Leslie and see how far he could go as all the sports idiots are predicting, and of course, we also have Carpenter."

A slight pregnant pause erupted before Brandon Briggs cleared his throat to add his thoughts on the matter.

"Tommy, do you really think starting Everett in a game of this magnitude is the right thing to do at this point. He's been on the DL, and on top of that, he's been spanked around pretty good, even when he was healthy."

"Well, Brandon, that's all in God's master plan, and to be honest, he really hasn't shared that with me as of yet. As soon as he does, you'll be the first to know!"

Looking up from his daily sheet, owner Cisco Wheeler dialed back into the conversation from scanning sales reports, vendor activity, and the usual landslide of minutia that comes from running a Major League Baseball team.

"Massive attention needed here please!" Cisco began, "Let's not lose fact that we win three and we play on. If we don't, people are going to simply say we were a fluke or gimmick, and it was a hell of a sports story. Then, as most of these things do, we will just fade away into a damn trivia-book never to be heard from again. You don't choose the year to win, it chooses you! Never lose sight of what these guys have done. Is it beyond the boundaries of believability? We need to right now let them know what we're talking about in this office never happened. We all need to get our asses in full-gear, and despite what little grass-fire we're dealing with at the moment, let them know that the Las Vegas Vipers can't possibly be stopped. Are we all on the same page on that one?"

Slightly shamed by the owner can sometimes be a good thing. As all nodded their approval, Cisco suddenly threw up his hands as if he were prepared for a momentous afterthought.

"And who is this Daniel Powter guy and why is he singing our National Anthem tonight? It says his claim to fame is a song called 'Bad Day.' Christ, what kind of message is that to our fans? I'll never understand who comes up with this happy-horse-shit!"

Checking into the Mirage Hotel late in the afternoon was pure traveler gridlock. Carla and Syleanna slowly stood in line as they slowly creeped toward the overworked and understaffed counter.

Finally, the desk clerk spoke those magic words, "Hi, welcome to the Mirage Hotel, My name is Sharma. How can I help you?'

As the girls quickly explained their reservation, it was quickly determined that all the paper-work was in order. Going through the mandatory Q and A from house-keeping to where the ice machines were located, Sharma Brown, the head desk clerk, handled it all. As they got their room- key and prepared to depart, Sharma suddenly looked at her computer screen again.

"Oh, which one of you is Carla Harris?" she asked.

"That's me." Carla responded with a surprised look

"You have a phone message when you get to your room. It came in a little earlier today so we went ahead and saved it for you."

"Oh thanks," Carla responded, wondering who even knew they were coming. It was to say the least that her interest was definitely peaked.

Getting to their room, both girls slung their baggage onto the bed as Carla quickly moved toward the flashing red-button. Hitting the famed number nine for messages, she intently listened for the tell-tale beep to find out who knew their big secret. As the message began, the animated look on her face to Syleanna indicated that they had been busted in a most bizarre manner.

"Hey, Carla, this is Julio, your cabbie in LA. Remember me? Hey, you won't believe this, but I was driving this dude from CBS that I haul around all the time and we were talking about the game last night as I was taking him to the airport. He mentioned that he had hooked up a couple of players' girlfriends from the Vipers to the Mirage for the game tonight and I just figured it was you. Give me a call when you get in if you need tickets or a ride to the game. I'm in town and would love to hook up with you guys again. If you lost my number, it's 555-353-6409. Hope to talk to you soon!"

"That was Julio, you know, the cab driver from LA!" Carla screamed. "You know, the one that we got us in the game the first time we tried this crazy stunt. Give me that pen and paper on the desk. I'm calling him back!"

With the afternoon shadows were creeping toward 5:30 p.m. at Mirage field, Dodger's Manager Grady Little was trying to instill some steam with his guys in the visitor's clubhouse. As the men in blue all gathered round, the LA Dodgers manager was on task with the message to be delivered.

"We only have to win one and were in, easy task, eh? I've heard some of you guys talking as if we've already won this thing. Let me tell you a little something. When I was out of baseball for a while and farming cotton down in North Carolina, I had a whole lot of time to think about this game. When you're growing and picking cotton balls every day, nothing ever really changes. It's actually quite boring. The thing that I missed most about what we do was the element that anything and everything could and will happen out there!

"You know me, I'm not a scream and holler person. Everyone in this room are professionals and I respect that. I know some of you think it was cool because I got that little thing in '*Bull Durham*,' but I'm here to tell you boys, this is a real team we're playing, and is not a movie script.

"If you simply look at what this small-college club has done since they became the Vipers, it shatters anything we previously thought about this game. That said, are we a better team than them? Do we have more talent? Have we been here before? I think you all know the answer to those questions."

Thickening up on the attitude, the Dodger players began to respond in unison to the pep being provided by their leader. Gutchecks are never a bad thing heading into attack as J. D. Drew added his own mantra to the message.

"We can do this thing, guys! In the minors, we were about to win the Carolina League Title and our manager told us to walk with the Lord. I told him I would rather walk with the bases loaded!"

With the lame attempt at hijacking a poignant situation, the smirks and cackles from his teammates was the expected reaction which brought further rejoinder to the room. Calling for quiet, the Dodgers manager obviously had a parting shot for his players.

"By the way, one quick thing I did learn about my time away from this game." Grady Little inserted in closing. "If you don't pick those damn little cotton balls on time, if you miss the very short opportunity to get those little bastards, they will hang around and turn to stink before you know it. We all understand what we have to do here tonight I believe, so, let's go out there and do our jobs!"

Las Vegas traffic on Interstate 10 to "The Strip" rivaled Los Angeles at its worst as gridlock to Mirage Field played the table of late arrivals who had been leaving the casinos. As the jumbled jungle of junkery slowly moved toward its destination, a blue 1999 Camry was entangled in the mess and full of spirited chatter.

"I bet you guys never thought you would see me again, right?" the smiling driver exuded to his two passengers seated in the back. "I knew it had to be you two after talking to Mr. Kinosian about flying you out here. He didn't say your names exactly, but I just figured you wouldn't want to miss your men in action!"

"We're really glad you saved our numbers, Julio." Carla added. "Like the last time, we just did this on the fly, and again, our guys don't even know that we're in town."

"Man, they really shook up the snow globe!" Julio beamed. "Since I met you, I have really been following what this team is all about. You know I'm a die-hard Dodger fan, but your guys are doing something that's never been done ever in all of sports! You got to love all this!"

"We are!" Syleanna quickly chirped. "Our town has gone batshit crazy over all of this, and just like this interview thing, the world has moved in right there on our doorstep. It's really impossible to get away!"

"I got all that" Julio added. "Now, Carla, you said that you don't have any tickets for the game tonight, right?"

Slowly smiling, Carla Harris could feel the setup coming on this one. "I told you that when I called you back, remember?"

"Oh yea, I remember now, temporary magnesia," Julio joked, "I'm just messing with you, but I need for you to do me another favor."

"I smell more baseballs, Julio…am I correct?" Carla shot back.

"Yes…and a bat, if that isn't asking too much?" he playfully responded.

"Hey, Julio, we're just a couple of poor college girls, we're not a sporting goods store!" Syleanna added.

"I know, I know, but remember, Ira? He got you those really good seats the last time you were here. We'll, he's done it again for all of us for the series. I'm not going to lie to you. Vipers stuff is the number one thing on EBay these days, and if you can help us out just a little, that would help…help…well…defray costs I guess you could say. "

"Is that even legal?" Carla naively asked.

"Oh yea! A couple of signed balls and a bat is all we would need to take care of our 'expenses' and of course the wonderful transportation and genuine customer service you are experiencing this weekend!" came the laughing response from a gentleman whose spirit and warmth certainly was contagious.

"Wait "till" you see these tickets, sisters! We got you right there in celebrity row with all the famous people, you're gonna love them!"

"You mean, we have to sit there and dodge Mickey Rourke's droll again?" Carla chuckled. "Sorry, but you'll need to pay us for that experience.""

The final notes of Daniel Powter's rendition of "The Star-Spangled Banner" burst into exuberant cheers as the Las Vegas Vipers took the field.

Tommy Leach had kept his lineup pretty much intact from the beginning, but tonight catcher Boone Coleman was starting in place of Doug Pouge behind the plate. According to the Vipers manager, it was the freshness factor for the rookie that came into consideration,

21 DOWN IN VEGAS

plus the option of holding Pouge back for some bench strength later on if needed. Finishing his warm-up tosses, Scotty Arms turned on the mound while rubbing up the ball as lead-off hitter Kenny Lofton settled into the batter's box.

Casual baseball fans can almost get a glimpse into a pitcher's performance on his first hurl of the game. On that theory, Lofton watched a sizzling fastball right down the middle for a called first strike and the tempo was now set.

It would take Scotty "The Golden" Arms just thirteen-pitches to dispose of Lofton on strikes, Rafael Furcal on a ground- out and Jeff Kent to an infield pop-up.

Aaron Sele took his place to see what he could do with the team that had captured the hearts of so many people that had put their lives on hold to witness the impossible dream. The story-line of the Vipers rivaled "The Miracle on Ice" in 1980 with the one huge factor: this wasn't hockey, this was baseball!

Many in America became temporary hockey fans while the Olympic odyssey of Herb Brooks' team of destiny unfolded on the ice and deservedly so. Hard-knock baseball aficionados have been witness since the professional beginning of the game in 1869 and few if any chronicles of this proportion had ever been seen.

Of course, you had your instant game heroes over the years that instantly ingrained themselves into the sport forever. Teams were a bit different because late-season success usually at the end depended on unprecedented failure.

You could certainly pin-point those teams that opened up a crevasse of opportunity to a surprise guest into post-season play. There was the 1952 Brooklyn Dodgers, the 1964 Phillies, and who could forget the 1995 Angels in the lock-out year that provided an eleven-game tumble late in August only to get thumped 9-1 in a one-game playoff and allow the Seattle Mariners a chance to play on.

The Western Division in 2006 of the National League was indeed different. All the teams had been very close all season long except the Las Vegas Vipers who slowly took their two months of provided playing time and stunning the critics night after night to eventually ascend to the position at hand. Three games to win, three games to go, and Sean Deeters steps to the plate.

The 11:00 p.m. news on KTNV-TV 13 exploded from the screen as anchors Kelly Swaine and Bob Murphy pounced on the latest breaking chronicle.

"The team who's mantra is 'refuse to lose' did it again in front of a sold-out Mirage field faithful tonight as the Vipers beat the rival Los Angeles Dodgers 5-3 to stay alive in the Western Division Pennant chase!" Kelly Swain proclaimed. "It was a pitcher's duel for most of the game until the Vipers broke things open in the bottom of the seventh with four runs off Dodgers starter Aaron Sele. The Dodgers who scored two in the bottom of the second on a J. D. Drew double held on until the fifth when 'King Kong' Karl Smith got the Vipers on the board with a long home run to center that pulled the Vipers to within one. Vipers Manager Tommy Leach talks about the Vipers big win tonight!"

Manager Tommy Leach, Scotty Arms, and Sean Deeters were collectively seated in front of the MLB media backdrop at the post-game press conference as the Vipers skipper purposely tried to down-play the critical win for his team.

"It was a great game for sure as Scotty kept us in it and it never hurts to get a bases-loaded double from this guy." He casually put his arm around Deeters' neck. "The Dodgers are a great team. They got on the board early when Drew got one down the line past Duzan, but we were fine. Smith picked us up with his long- fly and there was never any panic. Everybody just did their jobs out there tonight. We all know what we have to do and our post-season right now is simply day to day."

"The Vipers and Dodgers are in a virtual tie for first place in the standings with two- games left to go." Swayne continued. "If the season were to end that way, the Dodgers would win the division and move on due to the tie-breaker rule which says the team with the most victories head to head in the division would be declared the winner and that would be Los Angeles. We'll have more on the Vipers' big win tonight when we get to sports, but right now, Bob

Murphy brings you up-to-date on the other big stories of the day on KTNV-TV 13."

A solemn festiveness was the best description of the clubhouse as the Vipers began to discard their super-hero uniforms to slip quietly into the Las Vegas evening for dinner and relaxation. A few hours to tune out all the white noise of celebratory chaos from virtually every angle of existence was but a barren retreat. As players grouped up and disappeared, the light in Tommy's office was still burning bright with some hard decisions yet to be made.

With the manager were Tom Browning, Von Hayes, Keith Madison, and Jarred Brewster. The topic was what to do in the next forty-eight hours.

"So we pitch Scarbury tomorrow and we win, the biggest game of the season would then be Sunday and who do we have?" Tom Browning lamented. "They come back with Maddux and we're cooked!"

An awkward silence filtered through the room until Jarred through up an idea that had some sustained merit.

"I've been watching these guys, Skip. I've been watching them throw, using the gun, when they didn't realize it. I think Carpenter is better ready than you think he is. Why not spot start him tomorrow with a ready bull-pen and then we can save Scarbury until Sunday? That's just a thought."

Keith Madison slightly nodded as he absorbed the possibility and paused to group his thoughts together before he spoke.

"I've known the kid since he was fifteen years old, and trust me, there's no better competitor than Everett Carpenter. True, he can sometimes be erratic times on the mound, but I've also seen more than not flashes of brilliance. I also understand pitchers as I'm sure Tom here knows as well.

In a sense, I like Jarred's suggestion, but I know how pitchers prepare. My fear would be to get Brad out of his usual work rhythm and perhaps lose the momentum we got going."

"Valid thought, Keith," Leach quickly reacted. "While Brewster here has a great thought, and I tend to stick to the game plan because without a win tomorrow, it won't really matter much come Sunday.

Look, we got a strong and healthy bull-pen, and if Carpenter crashes early, we will just need to be prepared. Burke, Leslie, Fuller, and even Zebro can come in if needed."

"I agree too, Skip!" Von Hayes added. "Maddux isn't the same Maddux of old. By the way, the old man called from upstairs a few minutes ago. We better have four more seats in the dugout tomorrow for the game; we're going to have guests."

The Pepper Mill Restaurant and Lounge in Las Vegas has long been a late night hang-out for entertainers and extended party-goers as great food and a laid-back atmosphere extends to a pleasant vibe in an often hectic setting. It was 11:45 p.m. as a table for three became open, and Carla, Syleanna, and Julio all slide into the purple polyester booths.

"Your boys were rockin' it tonight, ladies!" Julio expounded. "Man, that Sean can spank it! When he first hit that thing, I thought he had a grand-salami, but that damn fence got in the way!"

Laughing at his quirky exuberance, Carla and Syleanna quickly perused the menu as both hadn't eaten since they left Port Columbus earlier in the day.

"I still can't shake the feeling that we're doing something wrong." Carla lamented. "I know Sean and Cliff really wouldn't really mind if they knew we were here, but I know everything they're dealing with. Just our little world circling their planet is totally bazoo."

"Here's what I would do if I were you, ladies." Julio inserted. "Just wait this thing out until Sunday and deal with it then. I got the tickets for the next two days and my ride is yours. I told Ira he has to wait on the balls and bats and he's fine with that."

"Ah, Julio, that was *a* bat, as in singular, meaning just one." Syleanna was quick to clarify.

"Oh yea, A bat!...what was I thinking?" Julio laughed. "You know in school, math was not my best subject!"

"Right!" said Carla, "Next thing the media will pick up on is our black market operation of signed Vipers crap and that will be splattered all over *Entertainment Tonight*. Wouldn't Mary Hart have fun with that one?"

21 DOWN IN VEGAS

"Seriously, have you talked to your guys since you've been out here?" Julio inquired.

"Just texts," Carla answered. "With their travel schedule and all the other time zones and schedules, we find that's the best way to stay in touch. We normally talk on Sunday nights and catch up."

Suddenly from nowhere, a lady dressed in flashy frills with a camera appeared at the table.

"Welcome to the Pepper Mill, folks, would you like to have a picture?"

Looking at each other, the first impulse was to say no and finish the risotto, but Syleanna was the first to speak up.

"That will be $15 for three." she answered.

"Oh what the hell," Julio responded, "It's not often a guy like me has a date with two beautiful femininas. I'll pick this one up, ladies. Go ahead and shoot!"

As always in perfect pitch- harmony, the four-voices and icons of country music hit the last stanza of their song with the same force as the streaking Blue Angels overhead.

"And the home…of the Brave!"

As the sold-out crowd again exploded, the Oak Ridge Boys turned and waved at the crowd as they sauntered over to the Vipers' dugout. As they reached the top step, Tommy Leach was there to greet them and thrust out his hand.

"Great job, guys! We have a spot for all of you right down here on the end of the bench. It might get a little crazy this afternoon, but we know you love the game and it's a pleasure having you."

Richard Sterban was the first to thank the Viper's manager for the privy opportunity of sitting on the pine.

"It's certainly a pleasure and a privilege for us as great baseball fans. We have been following your success with keen interest from the beginning and it's a great story. It will be such a thrill to see it like this."

"You're welcome, Richard." Tommy shot back. "We already know that Joe Bonsall is from Philly, so if we do get that far in this thing, I guess he knows that he might have to sit in another dugout."

Duane Allen, William Lee Golden, and all erupted with laughter on that one as it was once again- time to get down to business. Tommy headed out to home plate with the line-up card as the ground crew was putting the finishing touches on the baselines. With yet another day and the season again on the line for the Las Vegas Vipers, it was time to play ball!

For the first three innings, it was more than evident Brad Scarbury didn't have his best stuff. Nomar Garciaparra lead- off the game with a double, stole third, and scored on a past-ball. In the second, Scarbury hung a slider to Jeff Kent with Kenny Lofton on base and the tale of the tape was a 478 foot home run to right. The third inning consisted of a walk to J. D. Drew, a hit batsman, and a blistering single by Rafael Furcal up the middle that plated another score. At the end of three, the LA Dodgers had a 4-0 lead over the Vipers who to this point had scratched out just a single by Gary Duzan from Bret Tomko.

As Brad Scarbury headed toward the mound in the fourth, Tommy leach picked up the phone to the bull-pen. In a business-like tone, he gave his orders.

"Get Burkes and Zebro loose."

In a game where emotion and physicality collide, it's never a given on any day that reliability will be there on command. Brad Scarbury had been one of the most reliable mounds men over the past couple months for the Vipers, but his leash was now as tight as it would get. Four runs down to a team like the LA Dodgers playing for their baseball lives can seem like a hundred.

With Tom Browning standing next to Tommy's steps, Leach was thinking out loud. "If we can get him through this inning, I'm going with Zebro in the fifth. I think I can get three strong innings out of him."

"Yea, Tommy, but the way Tomko's painting those corners, we need to start getting some hits. Browning responded. "He's a good pitcher, but today, he's the best I've ever seen him ever. We have to do something to slow him down."

A ground-out, a strike-out, and then a stupendous running catch by Cliff Collier off the bat of Andre Eithier closed out the top

21 DOWN IN VEGAS

of the fourth with no more damage. Scarbury was due up fifth and plans were already being formulated on what to do. Manager Tommy Leach was verbal.

"Come on everybody, be patient! Let's get some back this inning. It's Collier, Duzan, Chadwick, Pougue, and Scarbury. Let's go!"

How often have you ever seen the player that makes the last dazzling play in the field the first up in the inning? Cliff Collier picked up his bat and strode to the plate with one purpose in mind. He was going to get on anyway he could. Tomko had been throwing inside to the right-handed batters and Cliff had a funny stance where he extended his leg. Banking on that first pitch to being low and inside, he decided to extend it out just a little more.

"Take your base!" yelled home plate Umpire Terry Craft.

By design, Cliff let the ball nip him on the shin to get a free pass to open up the bottom of the fourth inning.

"All right, Cliffster! We'll take them anyway they give them to us!" Sean Deeters echoed.

With Cliff Collier dancing off first, Gary Duzan picked up his second hit of the day flaring one into no-man's land in right field putting runners on first and second with no outs. Bombo Chadwick took Tomko full-count as he tried to bring the Vipers back to within one as he swung for the fences. His efforts resulted in a mighty slow-trickler to second that got him out at first, but advanced both the runners into scoring position.

Baseball wheels were rolling as Tommy Leach was about to throw the dice. With his pitcher visibly on deck and his catcher at the plate, he was hoping to catch the Dodgers asleep at the wheel with them figuring a bunt wouldn't be in order until the next batter; they were wrong.

"KVPR-AM and Ralph Hacker here in the bottom of the fourth with runners on second and third and just one out. It looks like Tommy Leach is still going with Brad Scarbury who is standing in the on deck circle. There's no indication of a pinch-hitter yet as Doug Pouge now steps in. Tomko has cruised for the first three, but has run into a truffle of turbulence here in the fourth. Tomko sets…

to the plate…a big swing and a big miss from Pouge as there was no surprise as to where he wanted to deposit that one.

"This can be a cagy game, Ralph." Pete Harnisch added, "But sometimes just like that… everybody in the park knows what you're going to do."

"Tomko back on the mound," Hacker continued. "A long look in and the sign…the pitch, and here comes Collier to the plate! It's a suicide squeeze as Pouge gets it down in front of the plate, Russell Martin's up with it as he tries for third and he threw it away! The ball is rolling down the left field line. Collier scores, Duzan scores, and Pouge is safe and standing on second! Wow, just like that the Vipers create some offense and have now cut the deficit in half!"

As the dugout was now alive with a much needed relief, Tommy Leach had a quick decision to make. Should he go against his gut and leave Scarbury in for another inning or make the change now? Sometimes, you make the call on a situation and at other times, the situation calls on you. Two runs in, one out, runner in scoring position, and down by two in the fourth. Leach responded.

"Frazie, grab a stick!" he barked.

Brad Scarburys' day was over as he turned from the on-deck circle and headed back to the bench. Danny Frazie was now putting on the batting helmet and heading toward the plate. Even though he didn't have his best stuff on this given day, the Scarbury decoy of staying in the game was a subtle move that proved to be integral.

"It's a 4-2 Dodgers lead here in the bottom of the fourth," Ralph Hacker again setting the table on the Vipers Radio Network. "Danny Frazie comes off the bench as a part-time player with a .247 average to see what he can do against a highly effective Bret Tomko."

With Doug Pouge firmly planted on second, Frazie worked Tomko hard by fouling off multiple pitches to now run the count full. The anticipation of the next pitch had the Mirage Field crowd on its feet.

"Frazie is wearing Tomko out as he has thrown sixteen pitches to the pesky Vipers utility man. Again, it's 3-2 to Frazie as Bret Tomko sets…and to the plate!"

21 DOWN IN VEGAS

Sound is an important quality in any sport, but certain nuances can let a fan know instantly whether or not success has been achieved. The singing crack of the bat on this ball let everyone who had ears know that Danny Frazie had hit this pitch on the proverbial screws.

"It's a line- drive up the middle and...oh... it hits the rubber on the pitcher's mound and now... the ball is slowly rolling toward the first base line! Garciaparra picks it up in foul territory...and here comes Pogue to the plate with the throw! ...and he's out! Martin applies the tag and now here's Frazie and he's trying for second and the throw from Martin to to Kent...out at second, wow, now there's a double play I can honestly say, I've never ever witnessed before."

Ralph Hacker was stunned as a promising Viper rally suddenly turned into a Little League nightmare. His side-kick Pete Harnisch attempted to help sort it out.

"I don't know if I've ever seen anything quite like that one before myself, Ralph. Whew, on a line drive the ball clearly hit the rubber on the pitching mound and then, it ricocheted between home- plate and first. Frazie was safe, but Pouge decided to cash-in on the confusion and tried to score. Garciaparra's throw was right on target to Russel Martin for the out there and then, I guess Frazie thought he could take second and like you said, it was a bad choice as a bizarre double-play has taken them out of a promising inning."

"Pete, in all my years of doing this, I don't believe I have ever seen such a weird play and there's still some confusion on the field." Hacker continued. "The Vipers bench looks absolutely stunned as home-plate umpire Terry Craft and several other members of the 'blue crew' have gathered together, but the Dodgers have left the field and it appears the game will continue."

Turmoil was unleashed in the Las Vegas dugout as Jarred Brewster was trying to get the attention of anyone who would listen.

"It's a foul ball! It's a foul ball!" he kept yelling.

While everyone was trying to dissect the uncanny turn of events, Tommy, Keith, and Leach were huddled together, as Jarred was relentless in his observation that the play in question was indeed a foul ball. Finally with his animated manner, he caught Tommy's ear.

"I swear, Skip," Jarred emphatically pleaded, "I can't remember the exact number of the rule, but the ball never crossed the bases before going foul. It's a foul ball! You need to play this game under protest!"

After a long look, his demeanor quickly changed as the Vipers manager decided to go out and have a talk with the umpiring crew. As the search for a plausible explanation of what just happened seemed to go nowhere, the play was determined to stand as the Dodgers were now getting ready to bat.

Brad Zeiber's number was called as he trotted in from the bullpen to take over in the top of the fifth as the P.A. announcer had more to say than just who was now on the mound for the Vipers.

"Ladies and gentlemen, under section 4.19 of the rules of Major League Baseball, we have just been informed that the Las Vegas Vipers are playing this game under protest."

A roar went up from the crowd as the young kid known as "Zebro" finished his warm-up pitches. Even Richard Sterban of the Oak Ridge Boys who had been a part-owner of the Nashville Sounds knew the rule that apparently the umps had forgot as he discussed it with Keith Madison.

"We had that very same thing happen to us once against the New Orleans Zephyrs, but there the umps got it right. Since the ball never went past the first- base bag that was for sure a foul ball!"

"The damn-dest thing I've ever witnessed." Keith admitted. "This will be a test for sure!"

As the game of baseball is designed to do, the moment swiftly changed to a new scene. The intensity of the new hurler on the hill for the Vipers was more than evident as Martin, Eithier, and Furcal all experienced brief stints of attempted optimism before being silently returned to the dugout.

Bret Tomko seemed to have re-focused himself after the fifth-inning specter of controversy and also quietly retired the Vipers in order. It was now getting late. Down by two runs in the sixth inning, the massive sold-out crowd at Mirage Field could suddenly sense the urgency demanded for the most improbable of all story-lines to continue.

21 DOWN IN VEGAS

As he had done so many times before, Sean Deeters lead off the bottom of the seventh with a frozen-rope line drive off the right field wall. Both Carla and Syleanna jumped to their feet sending a freshly purchased beer from their next-seat neighbor three-rows deep. While awkward at best, nobody seemed to mind as First Baseman Bombo Chadwick quickly followed with another clean single shot up the middle.

"Deeters scores and the Vipers have now have pulled to within one!" Ralph Hacker elated. "Chadwick on first with none-out and here comes the Vipers second baseman Brooks Snyder."

Snyder laid down a clean bunt down the first base line and Chadwick easily glided over to second with the potential tying run with just one out. It was at this point that Dodgers' manager Grady Little went to the bullpen as the call went to their closer Jonathon Broxton.

"They're bringing in their big man early, Ralph," Pete Harnisch observed. "Here we are in the seventh, and you now have a guy in there that you normally only see in the ninth. This to me proves that the Dodgers are pulling out all their stops right here and now!"

Jonathon Broxton began the 2006 season with the Dodgers Triple-A affiliate and after allowing no runs in 11 appearances with 18 strikeouts, he was called up on May 1 to become Grady Little's primary setup man, and the team's backup closer. He was elevated to main closer midseason as he held batters to a .159 batting average with runners in scoring position, and held right-handed batters to a .196 batting average. He was a force late in a game.

"I think your observation has merit, Pete." Hacker recoiled. "They might be playing defense a little early here with Duzan and Collier due up next in that order. We know he can throw smoke, but there's still two more innings after this which is two more innings he hasn't done yet this season."

As advertised, Jonathon Broxton struck out Gary Duzan on just three pitches as Cliff Collier weakly grounded out to first. End of seven, it was the Dodgers 4. the Vipers 3.

"You got another one in you, Zebro?" Tom Browning asked.

"Yea, sure…I got this one." Brad Zeiber fired back quickly.

"I got Fuller ready for the ninth, just pin 'em' back and hold them sons of bitches!" Browning growled. "I got a feeling about this one!"

The top of the eighth- inning saw Kenny Lofton fly out to center and J. D. Drew line-out to third before a scratch single by Jeff Kent. Brad Zeiber put the proverbial explanation point on his efforts by striking out Garciaparra on three- pitches.

"It's Kennedy, Pougue, and…McElroy, you're batting for Zebro. Let's get it done!" Manager Tommy Leach snapped.

That was the perfect order in the eighth- inning as Jonathon Broxton once again took the mound. It was the bottom of the order for the Vipers, but the ever precious ninth brought up the top of the order. As he entered his second inning of work, it was evident that Jonathon Broxton had worn off his first wave of pure adrenaline. It took thirteen- pitches to finally get Terrence Kennedy to fly out to left field. Doug Pougue was even peskier as he fouled off eight- straight full-count pitches before hitting one deep to right on the warning track. Two outs brought up reserve- infielder Clint McElroy.

Clinton Bernard McElroy had been a perfect complement player for the Bentley State Eagles squad as he was known as "Mr. Be There." Never flashy or overly noticeable, Clint was just the kind of player that every team needed to tuck-point the starting talent and offer a stealth-like approach to the game. He was sometimes never noticed until needed; and today was one of those days.

"Broxton has struggled a bit here in the eighth." Ralph Hacker again with the call on the Vipers Radio Network. "McElroy has seen limited duty so far in this abbreviated season, but he can get the bat on the ball if needed. Again, Broxton to the stretch…the 2-2 pitch. And thar she blows! A long, long sky- drive deep to center…and… its cactus food! What a swat that was! A pinch-hit home run has just tied this game at 4 apiece! Wow!"

Pete Harnisch was also dumbfounded. "Too incredible, Ralph, as this is the first home run this young man has hit in either level of play this season and it could not have come at a more needed opportunity."Bedlam was now running amok with extra security being quickly ushered onto the field as the fans kept demanding curtain call after curtain call for the Viper's newest hero. Reserve infielder Clint McElroy had just carved his name into the wall of baseball immortality, but only for the moment. Dodger Manager Grady Little had walked to the mound to calm down his over-extended reliever as inside the Vipers' dugout, the wheels were also turning.

"Browning! I want Carpenter up with Fuller, now!" Leach yelled.

"I got Fuller and Burkes, why Carpenter?" Browning quizzed. "We are going to need him tomorrow! What are you thinking here, Tommy?'

"We just learned a valuable lesson that got us back into this thing. I'm not gonna fuck it up now. Get 'em' ready!"

Moments of euphoria generally do have an expiration date and this one faded fast as lead-off hitter Sean Deeters struck out swinging to a visibly pissed-off Jonathon Broxton.

"Top of the ninth and what do we have here?" quizzed Ralph Hacker.

"Tomorrow's scheduled starter Everett Carpenter is now on the mound for the Vipers. Quite an unusual move if you ask me, but Manager Tommy Leach must know something as Grady Little's team comes to bat here in top of the ninth all tied at four."

"Carpenter's a bit of a surprise, but if you look at his work since he's been back off the disabled list, he's had some decent outings. We saw his replacement earlier Brad Zeiber come in and give the Vipers that needed energy boost earlier, but now it gets interesting as Everett Carpenter will try to keep the Dodgers off the board."

As the intensity magnified, so did the innings. Eric Gagne entered the game in the bottom of the ninth for the Dodgers and it was game on. The only difference is that both pitchers were throwing their best stuff. Gagne was hitting the corners of the plate like he invented them as Everett Carpenter mixed fast-ball, off speed, and the 'Nasty Knuckler' to no-hit the Dodgers through the top of the thirteenth- inning.

"Just when you thought it might settle down a bit, Peter?" Ralph Hacker said in a slap-happy demeanor. "Here we are in the bottom of the thirteenth- inning tied at four with a game being played under protest and the Dodgers and the Vipers locked in a season-ending death match. Who could write something like this? Quite a scenario, eh?"

The top of the thirteenth brought in Dodger relief pitcher Olmedo Saenz as Greg Gagne's tour of duty was almost flawless, giving up just an infield hit to Gary Duzan. The bottom of the thirteenth for the Vipers would be Brooks Snyder, Doug Pouge, a pinch hitter for Carpenter, and then Sean Deeters at the top. The longer this game continued, the escalation of madness was now percolating to an explosive boiling point.

As Brooks Snyder stepped up to the plate, it was almost evident from all who were watching his body language that he wasn't going to take no for an answer. Working Saenz to a full count, he finally got the gift that he was looking for.

"Snyder swings and there's a line drive into left to open up the bottom of the thirteenth, and everybody in the Mirage is now solidly planted on their feet! That's going to bring up an interesting decision here for Leach. Do you bunt Pouge or let him swing away?" asked Hacker. "His power numbers are far better than his bunting stats, but you just got to be careful about staying away from the double-play here."

Pouge was patient at the plate, but slightly missed his pitch, sending a high fly to Kenny Lofton in Center. Now it was up to pinch-hitter Jack Tackett whose adroitness with the bat laid down the perfect sacrifice bunt to advance Snyder to second. Two outs with the winning run now standing on second base, and now slowly making his was to the plate was Sean Deeters.

With the decibel level in Mirage Field now that of a departing space shuttle, Brooks Snyder was quietly taken over by something very eerie. It was that sudden realization that yes, you've been here in this exact frame before. As his lead-off second widened, his total concentration was now and only on Sean Deeter's bat for the moment he knew was coming, and it came.

"Deeters swings and there's a flair into short center field, and… this ball is going to drop! They tried to stop Snyder at third, but he's rounded the bag and he's headed for home, and here is Lofton's throw to Russel Martin."

Sensing the play would be close, he began his slide on the outside of the plate. Hearing the smack of leather meeting leather, his hand scrambled across the plate feeling the simultaneous thud of force grinding into his ribs. Both bodies crashed together and tangled into a dirt-devil of dust. It seemed like an eternity as he rolled over and lay on his back in a thick cloud of uncertainty. As Brooks Snyder slowly opened his eyes, he found them transfixed at the umpire's hands as they were wildly waving into the air side to side as he heard the two most joyous words of the game as a runner; "Runner's safe!"

"It's over!" Ralph Hacker ecstatically screamed into the microphone. "It's over! this perhaps the greatest one-game ending that I have ever witnessed with money on the line and what a finish here at The Mirage! "Brooks Snyder literally wills in the winning run in the bottom of the thirteenth-inning and the Vipers…those incredible Eagles slash Vipers are still alive to play for one more day. You can't make this stuff up!"

Inside the club-house, the Vipers celebrated hard. With iPod and boom-boxes again blaring as they were living for the precious present, if only temporarily, while suspending any thought that tomorrow might ever come.A small corner bench near his locker sat an almost invisible Brooks Snyder with his former coach Keith Madison. Both had just survived the hailstorm of emotion on the field and the colossal euphoria of great deeds done. As tears streamed down the young second baseman's cheek, Keith new exactly what the act of redemption was all about as he wrapped his arm around his shoulder.

"You know you ran that stop- sign, don't ya?" Keith said. "If I remember correctly, I believe that I gave you the green light against LSU."

"Man…that was the wildest feeling ever, Coach" Brooks spoke softly while gently sniffing back the tears.

"I swear as soon as I saw the ball leave Sean's bat, it was like changing a TV channel, and there I was back in Omaha again. I could hear my cleats in the dirt, but it all seemed to be in slow motion. As

I got to third, all I remember is looking back to see Lofton field the ball and that was it. Then, everything went black until I opened my eyes laying there in the dirt...and the nightmare I have seen in my mind every day that replays itself over and over...it was finally gone."

"Congratulations, Brooksie," Keith hurried. "A great game and I am so proud of you, let's talk later. Right now, you got a press conference waiting on you upstairs."

In the Vipers media room, it was the crunch known as the post-game "yak- attack" where Manager Tommy Leach, Everett Carpenter, Brooks Snyder, and Sean Deeters were all in attendance."

"Tommy, Ray Fannin from KKSS in Silver Springs, can you explain the decision of putting your starting pitcher for tomorrow's game in as a reliever today?"

"Yea, it's easy." Tommy explained. "We lose today, we go home tomorrow. You saw what they did by bringing in Broxton early. I knew Carpy was well-rested and they really hadn't seen him much, and I have to be honest to say after we tied it in the eighth with McElroy here, I was playing for extra-innings. I had my relievers ready if I needed them, but fortunately, they are now all rested too!"

That brought a thunderous chuckle from the swarm of reporters who continued to pour on every aspect and query of yet another miraculous Vipers win.

"Question up front here for Tommy, Doug Saint Carter from KTRH, Houston. Were you aware at first of the ruling on that play the umpires missed on the foul- ball call? Is that why you played the game under protest?"

"We'll yea, it really doesn't matter now, but I'm sure that you duly noted, that whole missed debacle took us out of an inning. I really don't know how they would have handled had we lost, I'm just damn glad that I don't have to worry about it now!"

15ᵀᴴ INNING

ESPN was all over the potential for disaster had the Las Vegas Vipers lost the crucial game- three with the Dodgers. With a panel of experts, they turned *Saturday Night Sport Center* into the Warren Commission of baseball trying to evaluate the potential imbroglio it could have caused. Karl Ravech was the most informed and seemed to have done his homework

"That play that occurred in the fourth- inning was, and I state, a foul ball! How Major League umps could have blown that is ridiculous. True, it doesn't happen very often, but it is stated plainly in the rule book and had the Vipers lost…I'm confident we would be playing part of game three again tomorrow."

"Karl," injected Kenny Mayne, "That was under the jurisdiction of an umpire's decision and umpire's decision are not reversible under protest!"

"You are wrong, Kenny Mayne!" Ravech raved on. "That was a rule that was missed on the field. Hey, I got it right here, and it all means yes, there could have been another game. This is straight from the MLB rule book, OK, it's all right here! And it says, 'Managers can protest a game when they allege that the umpires have misapplied the rules. The umpires must be notified of the protest at the time the play in question occurs and before the next pitch or attempted play begins.' That indeed happened, right? No protests are permitted on judgment calls by the umpires, and as you just heard, that wasn't a judgment call. That my friend was an iron-clad rule and it was missed!"

The beauty of a classic sports moment is that every element of execution is always up for discussion long after the play has faded to black. The Ali phantom punch over Sonny Liston, Steve Bartman, and the interference call in the 2003 Playoffs, the Immaculate Reception, the US/Soviet Gold Medal game in 1972, all of these and many others lived on infinitum fueled simply by the mystique of the great unknown.

While many were debating a moot point on a Saturday night in Las Vegas, George Knapp of KLAS-TV took the initiative to put together a split-screen TV production together of Brooks Snyder and his two identical plays at the plate.

"This is why you have to love sports. Hi, everyone, I'm George Knapp and this is *Vipers Roundup*. I hope you know by now that our Vipers are now but one win away from cashing in on any kind of honors since their inception and that would be of course the Major League Baseball Western Division Title for 2006.

"By now, you would have to have lived in a cave or been in a coma not to know the story of this team and their mid-season adjustment by team owner Cisco 'The Dealer' Wheeler. It was his fascination of a small-college team from Portsmouth, Ohio, named the Bentley State Eagles that was just one play away from at least tying and going on to win the College World Series back in June.

"Many may have never seen that final last play at the plate with Brooks Snyder against the LSU Tigers that was almost identical to the winning play this afternoon at Mirage field. Ironically, it was also Sean Deeters who got both hits with two- outs and Snyder on second that set up both scampers to the plate. Let's take a look."

It was uncannily breath taking to watch the stop-action, slow motion frames of the "two" Brooks Snyders' in almost identical mirror-image sequences of each other, until the collisions at home plate. Aside from the different uniforms, it was almost the same play exactly step for step, but with two different endings. After showing it several times, it was back to the narrative of George Knapp.

"There you have it, history repeated, but this time, Las Vegas got the right call. Not to be stirring up any more controversy here, but let's leave by taking another quick look at that play against LSU.

21 DOWN IN VEGAS

As we drop it down into our super slo-mo setting, watch Brooks Snyder's hand as he crosses the plate. Does he get it there just before the LSU catcher? Certainly looks like it a little bit now, doesn't it? Thanks for joining us tonight on *Viper Roundup* on KLAS-TV, I'm George Knapp.

"Las Vegas and the rest of the sports world continued its non-stop revelry of the Vipers who now held a one-game lead in the National League West standings with one left to play while the biggest answer to the most cumbersome question of them all was still yet unanswered: who's going to pitch Sunday?

"God, I hope we didn't screw the pooch today using Carpenter." Manager Tommy Leach lamented. "We really didn't have a choice as it turned out."

"Naw, we did the right thing, Skip. I'm not sure we would be here worrying about tomorrow if you hadn't" Tom Browning added.

The Vipers brain-trust of Leach, Browning, Hayes, Madison, and Brewster had once again sequestered themselves in the bowels of Mirage Field to try and figure it out for just one more time.

"I thought Carpy had his best stuff ever today" Jarred declared. "It was like his knuckleball had a brain."

Awkward silence again filled the room until Von Hayes quietly broke the still.

"Maddux, just that name scares the shit out of me, guys, and we have him tomorrow with everything on the line."

"No, Von, we shouldn't be scared, we have been doubted since we started this thing back in July," Tommy Leach surrendered. "The main battle is to make people realize that doubt is important. Doubt is good! It's the 'don't know' answer box the one you should check more often than we do, and not be cared about it. Even the greatest minds don't know everything!"

It was the silence of Keith Madison that finally got the attention from Tommy.

"Keith, congratulations again! You saw your boy exorcise those demons today and that had to make you feel mighty fine. That was a hell of an effort out there from Carpenter just when we needed it the most."

"I think it makes life more interesting when we always have things to prove." Keith smiled. "Yea, I think Everett learned maybe tonight that the journey isn't so much about becoming something, it's maybe more about shedding everything that really wasn't you to begin with. I'm proud of him, you bet! So, are open for some thoughts about tomorrow?"

"The floor is yours." Tommy said with a hand-sweeping gesture.

"By the way, the call today was pure genius." Keith began. "It's a game we had no choice really, and had we gone with Fuller and Burkes as we probably would have had to do, where would we have now been. That would have left us with three-arms on the shelf on the last day of the season and two of them relievers.If you're open to something a little different, here's what I think might work."

Keith Madison had total command and attention of his peers.

"OK, Tommy, you kind of gave it away today at the post-game press conference. We have two-fresh arms in Fuller and Burkes. Let's throw in Leslie and build the perfect Frankenstein pitching machine. By design, I mind you."

"You mean, we take three of our relievers and use them as starters? That's what you're saying?" Tom Browning quizzed.

"That's exactly what I'm saying" Keith confirmed. "First of all, the Dodgers wouldn't be ready for such a thing. We let them go three- innings each and move Andrew Shackart into the closer role if we need a fourth. I think we can have them so confused and off-guard, we might be able to get into their heads a bit."

Looking about the room and examining the body language, Tommy needed to hear more from his minions on this one. "Pug, what do you think?"

"I'm not sure," Tom Browning responded. "I know we do that kind of stuff in spring training, but damn, this is the last game of the season. Maybe we can get some innings out of Milhuff. I know he'd go for us on just a few days' rest."

"I kind of like the idea if you ask me." Von Hayes blurted out.

"Hell, Tommy, all that stuff that you blurted out a minute ago about doubt, I think they're all sitting over the right now in the Dodgers clubhouse and figuring they have us up shit- creek without a paddle and doubting that we can pull this thing off. If we do something like that and even if we were to lose the game, they could never say we didn't go down gambling!"

"If I can add just something," Jarred spoke up, "I really respect all of you guys and your opinions, like, look at where you've taken us. We are now at the doorstep of baseball immortality, and we've done it by breaking all the rules. Why stop now? I think a three-pitcher rotation for one day and completely unexpected is an incredible thought. I would start Bruce, use Jeremy in the middle, and then come back with "Dirty Ernie." To me, that's solid!"

"Baseball immortality? Come on kid, you got to quite listening to all that Dan Patrick bullshit," Browning sarcastically chuckled.

"All right, we all got to be here at 9:00 in the morning, so let's get the guys in here first thing and build this damn pitching-monster" Tommy agreed. "If I remember correctly, Von, and I believe I do, I also recalled saying that even the greatest minds don't know everything. By God on this one, I hope I'm wrong! There's nothing quite like Las Vegas sense on a Saturday night. Add on to that the biggest sports story on the planet and its fanatics who were now buzzing up and down everywhere from the strip and onto Freemont Street, the scene was surreal. Sitting in the Golden Nugget and soaking it all in were Carla, Syleanna, and Julio where the emotions were truly mixed."

"I feel so awful, "Syleanna whined, "Sean thinks I'm back in Portsmouth and here we are all sitting together in the same city and he doesn't have a clue!"

"Back up now…who was the one that wanted us to sneak out here and not make any waves?" Carla shot back. "Cliff thinks I'm back at the Brew Pub by now in Portsmouth and watching it on TV! C'mon, you Huss, look at what we are able to do by standing back and out of the way. Someday, we will all have a great laugh about it."

"Ladies, ladies, ladies…guilt has no room for a night like tonight and especially in this city." Julio empathized. "Your boys won! What a great time in your life. Wow, ease up and realize that no matter what ever happens this story will forever be told. Your man got the winning hit too! He's amazing, really!"

Like a classic old movie with a romantic plotline, Syleanna let that last comment soak in as the laughs, music, and ambient sounds all faded away to a vision of once again her being back on the playground of Grant Middle- School.

The total attention was to a young boy absorbed in nothing more than swinging a baseball bat. Sitting in the stands behind the screen near home plate was a young enamored soul, trying everything from making eye contact, flipping her hair, to even a resort of fake stretching to reveal her already over-developed female protuberances; nothing worked. She finally decided to hang around until after practice to make an "accidental" run-in with the object of her teenage desires,

After the awkwardness of breaking the ice, the smiles had it from go. It was Sean's genuine fun-loving ear-to-ear grin with the Jessica Alba lips of Syleanna that ensured that this staged spontaneous moment really didn't take long to create some honest interest.

Their first kiss came as they sat on her front porch as Sean was reciting the one hundred best hitters in Major League history. Feigning interest, it was finally somewhere between Pete Rose and Joe DiMaggio that she finally stopped him cold in his tracks to include a future nominee; Sean Deeters.

At that point, she couldn't hold her raging hormones back anymore. At that point, all the superfluous baseball chatter was also put on hold.

Their passion, yet honesty were cemented from the beginning. Sean Deeters revealed to Syleanna Griffin early that she would always be his mistress to his first love of baseball. She in turn agreed to accept that role, knowing that every great performer needed to have that one element of support in their life who wasn't intimidated by accepting that position.

Screaming zip-line participants whizzed by overhead as the reality of the freaks and fun of Freemont Street slowly came edging back as Carla and Julio were discussing Sunday's plans at the ballpark.

"I heard this is going to be the most watched sporting event tomorrow since some woman played some dude in a tennis match back in the '70's." Julio proclaimed. "I wasn't around then, but man,

I grew up with the Dodgers and I know what this thing is really all about!"

"OK, Julio," Carla challenged while sipping on her mojito. "Spill it, brother, where is your head really? What's your story, you know ours, we want to hear yours!"

"OK ladies, this isn't just drunk talk now, it's time to hear all about me." Julio began. "We all grow up with our dreams, right? Well, I wanted to be either a cast member on *"The Fresh Prince of Bel-Aire,"* or a zone-busting shooting guard for the Lakers. As you can see, I am neither."

Both Carla and Syleanna remained respectfully silent as he continued.

"All I am ladies is a self-employed cab driver from LA and my best years have all been wasted. I can't tell you how many times, Kobe Bryant and I took a fast break down court or I was dancing with Carlton and Will Smith, but it was only a dream. We all dream! The question is really how many of us work that machinery it takes to really make it all happen? You, ladies, are in that dream right now and it still going on."

Looking at each other, the girls had that look of partial remorse and some understanding with the resolution this just might be a crazy person on a rant.

"Julio!" Carla interjected, "I understand what you're saying, but what's all that have to do with us here…right now?"

After a blank stare that eventually broke into a slow smile, Julio leaned back on his stool and looked both Carla and Syleanna directly in the eyes.

"OK, your two guys who are on the verge of making the most unbelievable thing happen in sports history…and that could be tomorrow. Right now you are sitting here with a nobody cab driver tonight instead of being with them!"

"But Julio!" Carla began before she was instantly interrupted.

"No, wait until I'm finished!" Julio asked. "My dream is watching my favorite team since I was just a little bastard to win tomorrow. Instead, I want to see this story continue for my dream too."Both you say you are staying out of their way to let them concentrate on the game and all that silly bullshit. If you both mean as much to these guys as you say you do, and with everything they will be facing tomorrow, all this texting crap and weekly phone calls can only go so far."

"So, what are you really saying here, Julio?" Syleanna snapped back.

"Hey, call them tonight and tell them you are here! Tell them you are going to be at the game tomorrow nine- rows back from their dugout. You just got into town as a surprise and found the friendliest cab driver in town that put you on the tickets and a ride to the game. So what's that gonna do? If you lose tomorrow, my first own personal dream lives on. If you win, we all win… and imagine the ride after that?"

With both Carla and Syleanna suddenly stunned at their new-found friend's sage-like advice, they both took another sip of their drink before responding.

"Maybe we have been too careful about all this." Carla admitted. "Cliff and Sean never really ever told us not to be here, we both just tried to stay out of the way."

"If you think that they might lose because you're here, that's completely stupid! And you two are getting married at Christmas!" Julio laughed as he pointed a finger at Syleanna. "So he wouldn't want his own fiancé to be there on the biggest day of his life? Ay carumba!"

Epiphanies occur at times you least expect as the three continued to chatter about Carla and Syleanna's new game plan. Texting the guys they were in town and letting them know they would be there tomorrow with a chance to touch base by phone if they weren't too busy should be the way to go. As the last round was being delivered, Carla spontaneously toasted Julio for his verbal bravery.

"To you, Julio!" As all three raised their glasses. "To be kind of blunt about it, I don't know too many guys who would have talked to us like you did. I've got to say you have balls!"

That brought forth a hearty-laugh from all as they all tinked their glasses together and took a swill. Afterward, Julio looked at both Carla and Syleanna with his pointed response.

"Thanks, ladies, I didn't want to be over the top, but you deserve to share this moment not only with yourselves, but with your guys." He paused for just a second, feigning a look of disappointment. "Now as far as having balls, I have none…or a bat either. So, I recommend we start working on that before Ira makes me repossess those tickets for the game tomorrow!"

Julio's playful demeanor cemented the moment with another round of laughter as the night was quickly fading to an end and a trip back to Caesar's Palace was just minutes away.

ESPN Sports Center was again on fire with all and everything about the final showdown on Sunday. Jay Harris was loading stats, scenarios, and opinions into the fire- belly of the drama train, knowing all too well that might possibly be the most anticipated audience watch in MLB history.

"One game…just one game to go for the Las Vegas Vipers or the Bentley State Eagles to win the MLB Western Division. They have honestly defied all odds to be where they are, and who could deny the story-book finish that is now less than fourteen hours away? His name is Greg Maddux. These are the kind of situations that Maddux feasts on. You can just go ahead and chalk this one up tomorrow as a post-game start, considering it's one or done.

If I had to choose just one pitcher from all the rest to be on the hill for me in this kind of game, it would be Greg Maddux."

Video then rolled with Greg Maddux over the years from his first appearance with the Cubs in 1989 to chronicle his incredible post-season record appearing in 9 division titles, 8 championship contests, and 3 World Series. While his overall post-records pitching showed 11 wins and 14 loses, Maddux always kept his teams in contention. The video tribute on the scoreboard came to its conclusion as Jay Harris once again appeared on screen.

"That's who the Las Vegas Vipers will be facing tomorrow at Mirage Field with first pitch slated for 1:10 pct. As for the Vipers, It's that little known guy that occasionally pops up who has meandered around both leagues for decades. He goes by the initials of TBA. It was first rumored that Everett Carpenter could get the start with Gary Steinman away on the bereavement list, but with his five-innings of work today, that scenario is highly unlikely. Coming up next on *ESPN Sports Center*, how are the odds-makers handicapping this one? We'll return with the latest numbers right after this, stay tuned!"

The sun began its dawdling ascent over the chilly desert peaks as sports history was about to make a new high watermark in the much storied and sports legacy of the Las Vegas record books.

There was New Year's Eve in 1967 when Evil Knievel left his body in bits and pieces attempting to jump the fountains at Caesar's Palace on ABC's "Wide World of Sports." Next to those big turbines at Hoover Dam, is there anything that can generate electricity like a big fight night in Las Vegas? Names like Ali, Haggler, Holmes, Forman, Hearns, Castillio, Holyfield, Tyson, and many others were cause for the strip to stand still on their given night of spectacle.

For ten days every December, Las Vegas still takes great pride in being called a "cow town." The National Finals Rodeo moved from Oklahoma City to the Thomas and Mack Center in 1985, explaining why local tourism officials no longer worry about filling hotel rooms or whiskey glasses during what used to be considered a slow time of the year.

In the ultimate pecking order of commanding the world's attention, it was now a single baseball game that suddenly vaulted its place onto the highest echelon of consequence.

It was now 7:00 a.m. as cops, bread trucks, and taxis from the airport were the prime movers on Interstate 15 plus add to the count one manager of the Las Vegas Vipers. As Tommy Leach pulled into his parking spot and the under-belly of Mirage Field, he realized that whatever happened out there today, the next time he stepped back into his 2004 Dodge Durango; his life would forever be changed. He pondered that stunning thought for a second before slowly heading toward the bright green door that denoted "Employee Entrance Only."

Being the first one in the office he casually glanced down to see the red light on his phone was blinking. Knowing that the possibilities on this one could be staggering, Tommy sat down in his chair and pushed the button that denoted 9.

21 DOWN IN VEGAS

"Hey, Tommy, this is Brandon. Look, I know you got your hands full and especially today, but Cisco wants to come down and say a little something to the guys before the game. Look, I know…I tried to talk him out of it, but he insists on it. Let me know a time we can come down and I promise to help make it quick. Thanks!"

Leach took a deep breath now adding a pep-talk from the owner on his list of chores to get done, notwithstanding creating a starting pitcher from thin-air for the biggest game of his life. One by one, the arrival of Browning, Madison, Hayes, and Jarred all trickled in to add some creature comfort to the abyss of the great unknown.

"OK, so before we bring them in here and give them our plan, are we sure this is what we want to do?" the Vipers' manager asked. "We all have to be on board with this or it's a recipe for disaster."

Glancing around at the body language of the main principals, all seemed to share optimism that this quick-strike stealth delivery would work.

"I personally think they'll love the opportunity to do something this crazy and out of the box." Keith Madison offered. "I know all three like they were my own and I never ever saw them back down to a challenge."

"Really, Skip, I'm a little more worried about getting some runs off Maddux," Tom Browning added. "You better have these guys juiced up and believe they can hit that son of a bitch or it won't matter who's out there for us."

"I got this one!" the Vipers hitting coach fired back. "I had a four-hit day off him in Atlanta back in '97'…I got the code to unlock the hitting machine."

"All right, get Leslie, Fuller, Burkes, and Shackart all in here at 9:00 a.m. so give me a few minutes. Right now, I have a lineup card to get done and I'm sure we have a few of our friends in blue across the way are licking their chops to get a chance to see it."

"Good morning, Las Vegas, its Dan Swartzman on AM- 920 KBAD and this is *Sunday Morning Sports Talk*. It's just after eleven and the most talked about and perhaps puzzling secret in baseball is now out. Personally, I'm more than just a little stunned at this one as Manager Tommy Leach has released his lineup card for the Vipers today and a relief pitcher, Bruce Leslie, is listed as the starter!"

Feigned silence for effect mixed in with the ambient crackle of the AM airways was a ploy the host was obviously using to make a point.

"Let's see, Bruce Leslie has made sixteen appearances for the Vipers and all in relief. The longest stint he has ever gone was against the Reds last month when he pitched two and a third innings of relief. Leslie of course is one of the former Bentley State Eagles, but this is madness! His earned run average isn't bad at .310, but hauling him out here today to face the Dodgers and Greg Maddux for the Western Division Title is just all too puzzling. You know me! There's no bigger fan of what has happened this season to our little ball club out here in the middle of the desert. Sorry to be such a downer on such a big day, but honestly folks, I just don't have the energy to like this too much today!"

The inside of Grady Little's mind was also trying to decipher the convoluted message that had recently been transmitted to the media. As the manager of the Dodgers, for sure his job was to have to know the make-up of the twenty-five man squad he was facing alas, he could only know names and numbers. Unfortunately they never provided much statistics on the strength of the heart.

All that he could make out of this unwary lineup call was that the Vipers had run out of starting pitchers and figured that this lesser known reliever could go as long as he was able. That move had to have a bit of a consoling thought for Grady's Little knowing that your guy had been out there in these kinds of games and status situations twenty-times before.

It was an hour before first pitch, and the Viper' club-house was now diligent in preparing for a game like none other in the sport before. Surprisingly, the attitude was loose as Cliff Collier ran over to Sean and flashed him his phone.

"I know…they're here." he responded with grin. "I got the text from them at two- in the morning. Said they got a red-eye out of Columbus and couldn't refuse."

21 DOWN IN VEGAS

"You know, I'm glad damn it!" Cliff responded. "Since we started this whole thing, it's like we've been in the government 'Witness Protection Program.' They want to promote us as much as they want to protect us. I'm not saying this is a 'dig-me' moment, but I now know what The Beatles must have gone through; this is absolutely nuts!"

"The girls have been great!" Sean instantly responded. "I can't blame them for staying away because we've been living inside this crazy parallel universe. "I always knew we were a good baseball team, and truthfully, I have never experienced togetherness like us. I love us guys! It's everybody else that's always guessing what we're doing and nobody…I mean nobody ever knows!"

"Bingo, brother!" Cliff toughened. "As much as I love this game and what's going on right now, it would be great to be back at Mound Park in Portsmouth and just play for fun again."

"Hell no, it wouldn't, you moron!" Sean laughed. "We were only fourteen years old, the outfield fences were 200 feet, and you never hit my fast-ball past the pitcher's mound anyway. Besides, all the dads walked their pretty daughter's home and all we ever got stuck with was a grape snow-cone…and that's only if we won!"

It was 12:30 p.m. as the Dodgers were finishing up batting practice; the Vipers locker room was standing-man only. As the elevator opened up, both Brandon Briggs and Cisco Wheeler briskly walked out into the clubhouse. Brandon quickly shushed the commotion and did the introduction.

"OK, guys, this is what you have worked now for over the past two and a half months. Let's not get stupid, we all know now how unique we have become. As I stand here, I see a vision. Not mine…it belongs to the gentleman I am standing with who would like to say just a few words today. This is your owner, Cisco Wheeler!"

A cinematic classic clip couldn't have captured a more perfect setting than an obviously nervous employer about ready to address his employees.

The moment of silence was deafening as Cisco "The Dealer" Wheeler slowly looked about the room to all the faces that were once nothing but images of fantasy that were impacted into baseball lore.

"I'm not here to be wordy." Cisco began. "In my ten years of owning this team, I've really never really had this opportunity to ever say what I feel."

The nervous laughter and genuine quality of the moment allowed both players and the coaches to recognize the importance of the circumstance.

"I know that Brandon here is the guy that I ordered to do the impossible. He drove to Portsmouth, Ohio, and allowed me to hire my vision of what many have called pure insanity…to simply prove a fact that we have so long since forgotten. That is like childhood, dreams last forever."

While at first it appeared to be a little bit of an awkward time to deliver such a speech of this magnitude, he was the owner and the room was all his.

"I know we're all busy and thanks for allowing me to stop by for a minute and just want to thank you all. This time is now all yours!" Cisco bellowed in a fiery bravado. "It is more important now to remember that great teams will always be remembered for individual achievement. How many of your personal idols were players growing up? I know you had many, but then you had your own favorite team. I had one team for too many years, gentlemen, and that team turned out to be my greatest disappointment. That was a fact until about two and a half months ago. Brandon understands that when we decided to do this kind of change, my friends, family, and most importantly, my accountant all said that I was the craziest son of-a- bitch on this planet. Why? because I simply dared to believe in something that I saw with my very own eyes.

Watching you guys do what you did to almost win the College World Series wasn't just a fluke. I as well as you all knew that.

"Great moments like that, whether it be in sport or any other special capacity, don't just happen by accident. They happen because people sacrifice and prepare. You all left your souls out there trying to win that final game and that's the only thing that I ever wanted to see in my team. Some still think I'm just an eccentric old-coot with too much time and money, but I can now say that I have seen it, felt it, and certainly now believe it!

21 DOWN IN VEGAS

"Thank you for showing me every day that if you can envision it…see it…you can do it! You fellows are rewriting the history books every single day when you step out on that field and yet another chapter begins with another great Vipers win today. Good luck, men…and I will forever be indebted for your time and effort!"

Not knowing what to expect after such a passionate discourse, the slow to faster acceleration of clapping once again began. Brandon and Cisco both stood with arms now extended upward as they turned and together made a quick-stride off to the elevator. The in-house frenzy continued for a couple more minutes until real-time veracity took over and Tommy decided to move it all to another place with a brief and definitive declaration: "Let's go guys! It's showtime!"

In comparison to all the other glitz and glamour associated with the final home game in the series, this one from the beginning had much more of a business atmosphere to it. Mike Maddux and Bruce Leslie warmed up as the standing room crowd, vendors, players, and dreamers who had followed this storybook fantasy realized that today was the intersection of "Termination or Continuation."

Before the game, Cliff and Sean and come out onto the field to glance behind the dugout to see where Carla and Syleanna were seated. After a couple of playful waves, they both stepped back inside for manager Tommy Leach's final discourse before taking the field.

"Not much to say here really. We have all worked our asses off every day to be here. As Keith told you earlier, there is no such thing as luck. It's the preparation that we all have done to the point of infimum that will give us the edge against any opponent and especially the Dodgers who think they have us on the ropes. You know our game-play and you also know what it takes to get to these guys. Let's do it one more time and get ready to head to St. Louis!"

The crowd noise was thunderous as eight-bodies sprinted from the dugout to assume their designated positions. The throng continued to stand with an ovation that was fortitude and gratitude mixed into a mosh-pile of respect. All knew the story by heart added the incredible travels of this team of resurrection after they were again written off in June.

Greg Maddux was a freak of nature when it came to pitching. Not physically gifted in the way we think of athletes, but between the ears, he was a virtuoso. Wasting time and energy were two things that Maddux loathed. He was known for working quick, throwing strikes, and not getting over 100 pitches too often. There's even a stat named after him called, 'The Maddux'. That's reserved for when a pitcher throws a shutout with fewer than 100 pitches. Some of the shortest games in Major League history have a "W" beside his name when he was out there on the hill working.

Viper's right-handed reliever Bruce Leslie was momentarily the talk of the entire sports universe as he was now set to welcome Dodgers center-fielder Kenny Lofton to the plate. While getting ready to deliver the first pitch, Leslie's thoughts now swished through his brain on how he had accepted this bizarre assignment with close-mouthed trepidation. As part of the Bentley State Eagles Vipers triple-headed relief force inclusive of Jeremy Burkes and "Dirty Ernie" Fuller, the truth being that Leslie hadn't started a game since his junior year in high school. Play-by-play announcer Ralph Hacker and Pete Harnisch were there for the tale of the tape.

"A tough first-inning for young Bruce Leslie giving up two on a Garciaparra walk and then a Jeff Kent home run to right and the Vipers find themselves in a hole early!" Hacker proclaimed. "You get a feel that with Maddux on the mound, the Dodgers have no fear."

"I get that sense too, Ralph," Harnisch added. "Especially knowing the experience of Leslie, I do understand the unique move here from the Vipers, but that still doesn't compensate for skill in these unique circumstances."

"It's the bottom of the first and Maddux will face the top of the Vipers order." Hacker noted, "Still a lot of baseball to be played here at the Mirage on the final day of regular season on KVPR-AM."

Thirteen-pitches were deployed by Greg Maddux in the bottom of the first to easily send Deeters, Snyder, and Chadwick back to the bench. A pop-up, a ground-out, and a called third strike was all he needed to quickly bring the Dodgers back to their quarters with bats in hand. As Rafael Furcal stepped up, Tommy Leach and Keith Madison were staring hard onto the field. Down by two this early against a bona fide punch-out pitcher had their steadfast attention. All that focus was quickly disrupted from a voice emanating from the shadows of the Vipers' tunnel.

"Hey Skip, I'm here if you need me."

Turning around, it took Leach a full-second to focus his eyes and disbelief on the apparition that had just suddenly appeared; it was Gary Steinman in full uniform.

"Sorry for getting here late. Uh…my plane got delayed leaving Indy. I just got here from the airport."

Stunned, yet remorseful for everything he knew his star-pitcher had endured over the past four days, Tommy struggled on how to handle things.

"Gary, you know you weren't expected back," he began. "I know it's been tough and your dad…"

"No, it's OK," Steinman interrupted.

Reaching into his pocket, he pulled out an envelope that had obviously seen a great deal of travel. Showing it to both Tommy and Keith, he quietly spoke again.

"When I got home, my brother gave this to me. It's a letter from Dad that he wrote to me the day before he died. I can let you read it later if you want to, but it basically says…that I'm supposed to be here."

As if on cue, it was the crack of the bat and a crisp line-drive single up the middle off the bat of Furcal. Looking into his eyes that seemed like an eternity, Leach could only muster up three words,*" Are you ready?'*

The simple nod from Gary Steinman told him everything that he needed to know.

"OK, Steiny, take the tunnel out to the bullpen and start warming up. I don't want to bring any attention to yourself until you get there. Get "Pug" on the phone. I need to tell him we now have a new game plan."

Keith Madison was instrumental to quiet down and maintain the buzz from the other players in the dugout who had just witnessed the return of their prodigal son. It was now imperative to keep the

Dodgers off the score-board and, in turn, maintain their false sense of security for just a wee bit longer.

"There's no- sugar- coating this one, Pete, Bruce Leslie is struggling here in the top of the second." Hacker defined. "That lead-off single by Furcal and hitting J.D. Drew have really put the Vipers in a hole here early with none- out and Andre Eithier now steps to the plate."

Pete Harnisch also echoed his feelings of concern. "Leslie is now up to thirty-eight pitches and it's only the second-inning with nobody out. You don't have to be a math-mensa to realize he can't continue this way. It looks from here like Tom Browning already has arms up in the bullpen. Can you see those numbers?"

Straining to see through the screen of the right field area that harbored the Viper's pitching crew, Hacker finally zeroed in on a number that looked like a pure phantasm.

"It's…number 16, How can that be?" He stumbled with incredulous dis-belief.

"Gary Steinman who was on bereavement leave is apparently back and now warming up in the Vipers bullpen. Did you know anything about this? As far as we knew, he was gone throughout the play-offs, but now, apparently not! I guess the big question here is simply where did he come from?"

"I know he wasn't in the clubhouse earlier, Ralph, when I was doing my pre-game interviews with Tommy." Harnisch answered with a slight laugh. "I know if I had seen him and there wasn't a word said!"

Meanwhile on the field, things were going from bad to worse. Bruce Leslie had just walked outfielder Andre Eithier to load the bases. Pitcher Greg Maddux was due up next as Tommy Leach made a slow march to the mound. With the infield also gathered in and round, his manager was short and to the point.

"I'm proud of you, Bruce." Leach said to his young pitcher as he reached for the ball. "You got a hell of a lot of guts to come out here and do what we asked of you today. Keep your head high son; you have proved you're a true champion."

21 DOWN IN VEGAS

The Mirage Field crowd was kind, giving young Bruce Leslie a thankful ovation as he slowly headed toward the dugout. That appreciative jangle quickly accelerated into ear-splitting thunder as the 46,000 plus witnessed number 16 with towel still draped over his shoulder staunchly leaving the bullpen and heading for work.

"That's him for sure!" Ralph Hacker beamed. "Gary Steinman who many have said should get the Cy Young award this season or the MVP is here and now headed to the mound to take over the pitching duties in a relief- role and a pitcher's worst nightmare!"

After his eight freebie throws to the plate, Gary Steinman was now ready. Most humans would find this kind of a situation as intimidating as it gets, but ol' number 16 was a rarity. Few could match the Greg Maddux pitch-management style, but it took only three-throws from Steinman to give 'Mad Dog' Maddux a taste of his own bone to sit him down. It took just another three pitches to force Nomar Garciaparra to slap into an inning-ending double play. With the Viper crowd almost drowning out the announcers, Hacker and Harnisch couldn't believe their eyes as they screamed over the appreciative voluble.

"Incredible! Have you ever witnessed anything as '*Cool Hand Luke*' as that?" Ralph Hacker teased. "Gary Steinman on just six-pitches gets out of a bases-loaded jam and will you look at the inside of that Vipers' dugout! Its mass- hysteria in there and a whole lot of gratitude is going on! "

The TV cameras were now bouncing from all angles, showing the mobbing love-fest the Vipers were bestowing upon their returning warrior. Bruce Leslie was one of the first to come up and give Steinman a bear- hug of appreciation. The look on the Dodgers faces were also telling. Panning across the LA bench, the cameras caught rolling eyes, deadpan looks, and the slight grins of some of the players who realized they may have just been royally bamboozled.

Vin Scully was one who couldn't resist his epic vocalization that there may have been a sniper on the grassy knoll.

"Here in the city that likes to throw the cards around occasionally, we may have just seen a little hoo-doo chicanery on the part of the Las Vegas Vipers as their 'disappearing ace' was suddenly pulled from the bottom of the deck and is now on the table for everyone to see. The simple question that I have, folks, is why an inexperienced young man like Bruce Leslie would start this game if not just as just a decoy if the Vipers were going to bring in Steinman anyway. So just remember that the most beautiful experience we have is the mysterious moment, because without it, life would be very dull indeed if everything was pre-known." Scully said with a wry-chuckle "OK. Here now to lead off the bottom of the second is the Vipers left fielder, Karl Smith."

With the resurgence of having their pitching ace back on the mound, the Vipers now had to attack offensively against another hurler who could paint the corners of the plate second only to Rembrandt.

Karl Smith had spent the past week watching videos of Maddux pitch and after hours of tireless viewing thought he might have discovered a small clue to perhaps penetrating the armor. Karl eventually realized that Maddux got frustrated if you slowed the game down on him. The key to his success was letting him keep you off-balance with quick pitches, so down by two- runs in the third, it was time to experiment.

"King Kong" Karl Smith is getting his money's worth here as with another full- count as Maddux sets…again fires. A swing and another foul, and this one down the right field line. It's been a thirteen-pitch appearance so far for Karl Smith and that's as many pitches as Maddux threw in the entire first- inning." Ralph Hacker chortled.

"If you watch closely, Ralph, Smith is moving around the batter's box and not allowing him to pitch to that same spot every time." Harnisch injected. "This has been a good at-bat for the Vipers clean-up hitter." Ralph Hacker once again set the stage.

"Maddux is again ready with the 3-2 pitch…he sets…and now Smith steps out of the box yet again as Umpire Charlie Reliford calls time…and now, Pete, you can start to see the frustration on the face of Greg Maddux as Smith is once again adjusting his batting gloves as Maddux kicks the dirt. A little harder too, I would have to say." Harnisch humorously added.

21 DOWN IN VEGAS

"Pitch number fourteen is about ready to be sent on its way to the plate as again as Greg Maddux now sets, delivers, and this swing is going to make it a one-run game!"

Pandemonium erupted as "King Kong" Karl Smith had patiently waited on an inside slider that was now being deposited twenty-one rows back in the "Sinatra Center Field Pavilion." As the *ESPN "Web Gem"* star of so many other spectacular out-field grabs, Kenny Lofton was now just one of the spectators who was witness to this dramatic send-off except for one small exception; he wasn't cheering.

Great pitchers and competitors always adjust to the moment. As Karl Smith jogged the bases in his home run trot, Greg Maddux was looking deep into his glove and everywhere else getting ready for the next challenge. If there was ever a pitcher in the history of the game who used selective-amnesia to clear the air and move on, it would be this particular mound trooper of the day.

The thrill of a dramatic flash is short-lived. The cheers finally settled down to the will of a great competitor who disposed of his next three aggressors in order. After three- innings in the game heard round the world, it was the Dodgers 2, and the Vipers 1.

The next four-innings saw Gary Steinman match Greg Maddox almost pitch for pitch as the afternoon shadows at Mirage Field started to grow long and the time short. Entering the bottom of the eighth- inning, neither pitcher had surrendered a hit, and the only baserunner was allowed by Maddux was on a Gary Duzan walk in the sixth. A sense of urgency was now permeating the Vipers dugout.

"Let's go, guys! We need some knocks!" Manager Tommy Leach bellowed.

"Grab your kryptonite if you got it, and let's send Superman packing! Kennedy, Pougue, and Steinman…it's time to do some damage!"

There are times that unexpected levity in a dire situation is exactly what's needed. Tommy Leach with his bend, but never break demeanor was the anchor of patience and solitude that infused confidence and diffused panic at times of critical mass. For it was now that everybody in the Vipers' dugout knew what they were up against and were again being tested.

Taking his manager up on his challenge, veteran shortstop Terrance Kennedy suddenly became Lex Luthor by pounding a long line-drive off the left field wall for a stand-up double. With none out and a man in scoring position, catcher Doug Pouge got his chance to make Vipers baseball lore to the verbal excitement of Ralph Hacker.

"Kennedy leads off second as Jeff Kent is trying to keep him close. Maddux being very deliberate now with his pitches as I have never seen this place as flat-out rocking as it is right now. Everybody is on their feet as Pougue settles back in as Greg Maddux comes to the plate with the 2-1 pitch…swung on…and a line-drive over the out-stretched glove of Kent into left field! Eithier charges and is up with the ball, here comes the throw and here comes Kennedy to the plate… He's in there! And this game is tied!"

"It could have been a little closer, Ralph, but it looked like Eithier double pumped the ball before he threw it." Pete Harnisch explained.

"On a throw like that, quickness is as important as accuracy and Kennedy had plenty of room to slide away from the tag."

Swarming high-fives and transformation to the rally caps was the jubilance of the Vipers dugout except for one. Gary Steinman with bat in hand was locked into the eyes of his manager.

"I want to finish this, Skip. Let me do it." Steinman quietly asked.

"We need a run, Steiny, before you can do that" Leach responded. "You've done a hell of a job for us, but I have Fuller up now and we need a run. I'm going to hit Shepard."

At times when you've known that you made the wrong decision, pride often pre-empts the reversal of doing the right thing. Manager Tommy Leach knew by looking into the eyes of his pitching ace that it was no longer by the book or by the numbers. The eyes are the window to the soul, and Tommy Leach was now witness to life's most intangible force.

"Let me finish it, Skip, please. I give you my personal guarantee."

"There are no guarantees in this game, Gary, you know that." Leach responded.

21 DOWN IN VEGAS

Reaching into his back pocket, Steinman once again pulled out the crumpled envelope Leach had seen before as he held it up.

"I got you're guarantee right here…in writing."

Before either could respond, Umpire Charlie Reliford was standing at the dugout steps and he wasn't happy.

"Leach! I need a batter and I need one now!" he barked.

"Get him down to second, Steiny," Tommy said.

With the game now tied, the Dodger blue faithful knew that Greg Maddux was most likely facing his last batter. Eric Gagne was warming up as pitcher Gary Steinman stepped to the plate. All 48,000 in the stands including both dugouts and all nine players on the field knew exactly what was coming next.

"Steinman squares to bunt…and it's a beauty!" Ralph Hacker beamed. "Right down the first-base line as Garciaparra has no option but to throw it to Maddux covering and the go-ahead run is standing on second with one out."

At this point, the mechanics of strategy began to spin off the grid. Doug Pouge was replaced at second by pinch-runner Luke Shepard. Greg Maddux day was done with Grady Little waving in Eric Gagne from the bullpen. While all the changes were being put into place, Sean Deeters kneeled in the on-deck circle and casually looked up on the giant screen to see the love of his life in a 40 by 40 foot close-shot image. Smiling and waving were Syleanna and Carla on the Jumbo-Tron scoreboard with the caption "Viperlicious."

Sean couldn't help to smile watching Syleanna and Carla exude themselves with their rare brand of enthusiasm as he suddenly flashed back to the days in the McKinley School playground in Portsmouth.

It was here that he first got the bravery to talk to Syleanna through the old rusted-out chain-link fence as she always wished him well as he strolled to the plate while playing for the Roosevelt Rough Riders. Mind-muscle doesn't lie as Sean also knew why she was watching, which gave him every reason to find a way to excel.

As he stood up to prepare his swings, Sean again found himself at the age of fifteen with the mind-set to do whatever it took to keep this dream alive. Another glance at the scoreboard was all he needed. Patience at the plate had always been one of Sean Deeters' strong points. Eric Gagne was trying to get him to commit to pitches that weren't to his liking. Finally on a 2-2 count, Deeters connected. Again it was KVPR-AM and Ralph Hacker with the call.

"It's a ground ball deep in the hole at short! Furcal backhands... looks at third, and now there's no way that he's going to get Deeters and all hands are safe as the Vipers now have runners on the corners with just one out! Raphael Furcal knew his only play might be at third, but Shepard with a great lead-off off second was gone with the crack of the bat!"

Crossing first base without a throw, it was then turning around back to the bag that Sean again glanced up to the big screen where his 40 by 40 foot fiancé was clapping and cheering him on as again, he did not disappoint.

At this point, the Vipers dugout had sprung alive with the movement of hope and impending opportunity. To the Dodgers, it must have felt very still and empty, much like the eye of a hurricane which moves unceremoniously dull in the surrounding hullabaloo and that brings up 'King Kong' Karl Smith with two on and two out looking for that one pitch he knew could make him the hero; he finally got it.

"Snyder swings and it's a high fly ball into shallow right! J. D. Drew comes running in and gets a bead on it...two outs!" Vin Scully exclaimed. "This young man from what I've seen doesn't miss many like that, but fortunately for the Dodgers, he got under it just enough and that brings up the Vipers three-hole hitter with two- outs, "King Kong" Karl Smith.Many have asked how Smith came to that unusual moniker. The word has it that as a kid, he hit a home run in senior ball that hit a lady square in her chest and actually knocked her off the top of the stands in the outfield. Fortunately, she wasn't hurt, but from that day on, his power skills were likened to the beast-like aptitude and strength of one of the cinema's most famous and recognizable primates. Standing in batting .316 with sixteen home runs, he had certainly become one of the primary power- plants of this Vipers offense during this abbreviated season.

"Well, it looks like the wheels are again spinning as Grady Little is going to his bullpen and once again calling on old reliable

Jonathon Broxton to face Smith here in the bottom of the eight. I'm Vin Scully, and we'll be right back after this break in the action on your home for Dodgers baseball!"

"Hey, Coach!" Jarred leaned over to Keith Madison. "Does this look familiar?"

Jarred was referring to the play-off game against the Texas Longhorns where Shepard was on third and Sean was on first.

After surveying the situation, Keith Madison knew exactly what Jarred was referencing. He was refereeing to a base-running play that had kept the Eagles in the semi-finals of the college World Series and the scenario here at hand was identical.

"Yea, but we can't do that here, Jarred. Not with Karl at the plate." Keith reacted. "You can't take the bat out of his hands right now."

"Why not, they're bringing in Broxton to pitch to him. They wouldn't have a clue. At least mention it to Tommy." Jarred appealed. "Come on Keith, they're not even thinking about it!"

With that, Keith slowly got up and then quickly moved over to where the Vipers manager was standing. After a brief conversation between the two, Leach signaled to his third base coach Von Hayes who in turn signaled first base coach Ron Peters. As Broxton tossed his final warm-up pitches and unbeknownst to all, a stealth and silent operation was now underway. The inter-workings and complicity of Major League Baseball signals rival anything seen on the planet including the wind-talkers of the Navajo Indians Nation who helped the United States win World War II.

"It's been quite an inning already as the Vipers have tied it up here in the eight with two- away and now runners at first and third." Ralph Hacker recapped.

"Sean Deeters dancing off first and getting the attention of Broxton as he throws over to keep him honest. It's Smith at the plate as Broxton looks, stares, and another throw to first as Deeters dives back."

To any baseball purist, it was obvious that the ploy was to try and get Deeters down to second, but the Dodgers playing on the road with their ace reliever on the mound were not looking to give up anything with everything on the line. After a quick called strike to Smith, Broxton was again ready.

"Big Jonathon Broxton sets as Sean Deeters leads off first. He's set…and yet another throw over…and they have him picked off! Now here comes Shepard to the plate! Garciappara has the ball and Deeters is just walking back toward second as Nomar turns, fires, and Shepard scores easily as the Vipers now take the lead! They now have Sean Deeters in a rundown as Jeff Kent finally puts the tag on him for the final and third out of the inning, but not before a daring play that I feel caught the Dodgers asleep at the wheel! Can you believe it?"

"Talk about the element of surprise, wow!" Harnisch chuckled. "As Jonathon Broxton threw to first base yet again, Sean Deeters stood there and acted as if he were picked off. It was that split-second of hesitation were Garciapara froze as Shepard broke with the throw and was well on his way to the plate. That was not only gutsy, but all about timing to a tee! Unbelievable!"

"It's 3-2 as we go to the top of the ninth with the Las Vegas Vipers now just three-outs away from winning the National League Western Division Title! This is Ralph Hacker along with Pete Harnisch and you're listening to the Vipers Radio Network on KVPR-AM!"

All eyes were now on Gary Steinman as he stood on the mound. Could this fairy tale finally come to an end without someone either breaking a glass slipper or turning into a pumpkin? Kenny Lofton, Jeff Kent, and J. D. Drew were far from ugly step-sisters, but their bats pleaded one more shot at turning the Vipers' dream into a nightmare.

Steinman was all business as he continued to throw strikes in the 95 mph zone. It took only four-pitches to send Lofton back to the bench bat in hand with two-outs to go. Jeff Kent ran the count full before swinging at a slider down and low for out number two. The Viper Nation was on their feet as J. D. Drew now positioned himself at the plate for the Dodgers' last gasp of hope. With two quick strikes, it was now down to a final pitch.

"Steinman looks in as Boone Coleman flashes the sign. He now sets; he's ready, and the pitch! It's a high fly ball straight away center field! Cliff Colliers moving in…under it, and…he drops it! Cliff Collier had that ball all the way, and all of a sudden, its two-outs and now J. D. Drew is standing on second. What about them apples? Wow!" Ralph Hacker anguished.

"That is the first error that Cliff Collier has made in center field, Ralph, since he got here." Harnisch added. "He's been like a fielding machine out there, and what an unfortunate time to get that first big 'E' on the scorecard."

Steinman quietly shook off the masque as the 48,000 stunned fans again rose to their feet. Facing Russel Martin, Steinman now had trouble locating the plate as the Dodger catcher quickly got a free-pass to first base on just five- pitches.

With "Dirty" Ernie Fuller still loose in the bullpen, it was time for Manager Tommy Leach to face some hard and fast decisions. Walking slowly to the mound is always the perfect body language indicating that seldom good things are being delivered.

"I got Fuller up and ready, Steiny." Leach calmly offered. "You've done more than I could ever imagine. Let's call it a day."

"Still feel good, Skip" Steinman answered. "Let me finish it out. I'd tell you if I didn't have it, but I do, and want this more than you'll ever know. Trust me on this one."

"You know they're sending Cruz up here next to pinch hit and then you got Garciaparra." Leach added. "You know he wants nothing more than to get back up here for a chance to make-up play on his scroogie, and that's one guy I wouldn't want to see."

"I know." Steinman added.

"Gary, you've never lied to me and you've always been solid and given me your best. I supposed I would know if you were hosing me or not, but that's not why I'm leaving you in."

Puzzled, Gary looked at his manager as if he didn't quite understand.

"So, you're letting me stay Skip? Thanks!" he added.

Smiling, Tommy Leach stepped back for his return trip to the dugout, and as he looked back, he patted down his rear hip pocket. "Did you forget, Gary? You gave me a guarantee, and it's in writing, remember? Bring it on home, Steiny!"

"I'm extremely surprised at that move, or lack of." Ralph Hacker expressed. "Tommy is leaving Steinman in the ballgame even though Fuller seems ready. I honestly don't understand this one, Pete!"

"Yea, in reality, he's already won this game, but his pitch count is still pretty good at just 87 pitches" Harnisch echoed, "If it were me, I would have made the move just to get a fresh arm in there, but that's why they're down there and were up here!"

"Jose Cruz is batting just .245 but always a dangerous hitter in these kinds of circumstances." Hacker explained. "He's not the player he once was in the prime of his career, but understandably, he has been through the fire many times over his long career and is always a threat."

Gary Steinman again went to work Jose Cruz as he fouled off several good pitches to put him in a hole at one ball and two strikes. Ralph Hacker again set up the moment.

"Steinman is ready now with the set to Cruz, the pitch, and Cruz swings and there's a dribbler down the third base line! Duzan charges, picks up, and throws…not in time! Jose Cruz topped that ball in the worst possible place and hop-scotched it down the third base line into no-man's land, and now we have the bases loaded, two outs, and here comes Nomar Garciapparra!"

Pete Harnisch was again right there with the stats. "He's the one guy you really don't want to see right now, Ralph. Batting .303, Nomar leads the team in hits, doubles, and is tied with J. D. Drew for homers on the team with 20. For whatever reason, Manager Tommy Leach is going to do or die with Gary Steinman, as there's no movement in either the dugout or the Vipers bullpen."

"The outfield is straightaway as Garciapparra settles in." Hacker noted. "It was his indecisiveness in the eight that gave the Vipers the go-ahead run and now here in the ninth…he's got the hammer! Steinman looks in, he sets…fastball on the outside corner for strike one. The Mirage crowd is now all on their feet as these are those frozen–frames of pure drama that everyone will remember for a lifetime and are being taken right here and now at the corner of Mirage and Meredith Streets.

21 DOWN IN VEGAS

"A ball outside…and the count stands at one apiece. Garciapparra has not had a great series here, but his overall body of work since he came here from Boston is most impressive. Steinman looks in to get the sign and again delivers. He swings and it's a long drive high and deep down the right field line, twisting, curving…foul! Wow…that was close!"

"Yea Ralph," Harnisch again added. "I really never though it would stay fair, but he spanked it hard and didn't miss that one by much."

"Ball-two as Nomar lays off one on the outside corner." Hacker cautiously noted, "The infield is playing regular depth as Steinman again gets his sign from the young Boone Coleman who came in to do the catching duties for Pouge in the eight. Here's the stretch…the pitch…it's high, ball three, and now we have maxed out the meter as far as it can go. The Vipers cling to a one-run lead here in the top of the ninth with the Western Division title in the balance. Boone Coleman has called time and has now heads out to the mound to talk it over with today's surprise starter Gary Steinman. A quick check between the two and Coleman is back behind the plate.

"You now can't even hear yourself think here at Mirage Field as for what we're all witnessing, nothing like this has really ever happened in the arena of sport. The noise is deafening as all Vipers' players are now standing together with locked arms on the steps of the dugout with rally-caps in place. It's a surreal scene with a full count now to Dodgers first baseman Nomar Garciaparra as Gary Steinman again sets, he looks into Coleman…and the pitch!

"Swing and a miss!…and the Vipers win!! The Vipers win! Gary Steinman threw the 'knuckler' right down Broadway and past Garciapparra to open the door to the big-dance for the Las Vegas Vipers, who have just won the National League League West title!

The Vipers have won a game for the ages, winning it here 3-2 over the Los Angeles Dodgers. Oh- my- my folks, and here come the Vipers!"

"Of all the knuckleballs we've seen from these guys this season, that was the absolute best!" Pete Harnisch regaled. "It looked like

Garciaparra was trying to hit a wasp with a switch as Gary Steinman obviously saved his best for last!"

With now hundreds of fans spilling onto the lush grass at Mirage Field, it was the media frenzy who was desperately trying to position themselves with anybody they could find. ESPN's Steve Levy was one of the first to dive into a scrum of Vipers players in the sea of emotional madness. "Sean Deeters! Sean Deeters! Can I talk to you for a moment?"

Barely able to hear, Levy grabbed his interview by the scruff of the jersey and pulled him close. Leaning in as strong to Deeters as possible, he knew his decibel level better be on par with the other 48,000 around him.

"Sean! Two and a half months ago you were just a college student at Bentley State University in Portsmouth, Ohio. Look around at all this! Can you give me your thoughts of this most impossible miracle that you and your team-mates have just created?"

Smiling from ear to ear, Sean leaned into the microphone and stumbled for his thoughts.

"It's amazing! I mean…totally unbelievable! These guys are like no other brothers in any sport!" he gushed. "After we lost on that final play in Omaha, I think we all felt like we left something out there on the field to prove. I thank Mr. Wheeler and Mr. Briggs who saw something in us and god decided to give us all a second chance! I'd like to say hi to my fiancé Syleanna who always gives me the spark to play my hardest!" Looking behind him, he started to laugh as he was being pulled away by Brooks Snyder. "Just don't be too hard on my buddy Cliff…he really doesn't want to take extra fielding practice tonight shagging balls in the outfield!"

"Thanks, Sean! Sean Deeters who was obviously having a little fun referring to that dropped ball in the ninth-inning. Tommy Leach! Manager of the Western Division Champions, come here! Tommy! How does it feel to pull off a feat like this that many said was impossible!"

"Wow, Steve! I'm numb! I really don't want to come off here as one of those overworked sports clichés, but I am totally in awe of these guys. We all know what happened in mid-summer and the merciless hammering that this organization took for daring to do something different. I've been in the game now for thirty-nine years in every single level and I've never…I mean honestly never…seen a bunch who could play like these guys!"

Another closed-quarter's chamber of Mirage Field there were tears flowing with no shame from an eighty- two year old man.

"By god, they did it! Brandon! Those kids just won the first title this club has ever seen!"

Sniffing back the tears as he rambled on, Cisco Wheeler was now letting everything out with his closest ally and CEO Brandon Briggs.

"My ex-wives, my kids, my sainted mother, and even my dad always thought me stupid because I was a dreamer!I know you really didn't buy into this either, Brandon, but at least you listened. You could have walked out that god-damn door the minute after I told you what I wanted to do and got a job with any team out there doing something, you didn't!"

Reaching out to shake his hand, Cisco totally broke down and then quickly embraced him in a bear man-hug. With tears streaming down his cheek, he held him close for a couple of seconds before softly whispering two words into his ear.

"Thank you!"

"This is Randy Yohe live on WSAZ- News Channel 3 in Portsmouth on the campus of Bentley State University where the former team of players here known as the Eagles, have just swept the Los Angeles Dodgers in four-games to win the National League Western Division Title!As you can see behind me and the massive celebration from all the students at the Rhodes Athletic Center, it's off the charts as this community has just witnessed both collegiate and Major League history. In case you may have forgot, the storyline started here last July when Las Vegas Vipers owner Cisco 'The Dealer' Wheeler sent his GM Brandon Briggs here to Portsmouth to hire this team, the Bentley State Eagles, to replace his existing team at the All-Star break. I'm here now with the University President Howard Morris and just anxious to get your thoughts on all of this!"

Shaking his head with a slow smile of disbelief, he gathered his thoughts on live local TV.

"Randy…I have to say I'm so totally split down the middle right now on all of this. I am so proud of our guys and what they have achieved, but I do remember when it all first happened and I was as scared as a rabbit trying to cross the interstate."

"How so?" Yohe instinctively asked.

"The last thing that I ever wanted was to see were these guys get hurt or be embarrassed. We had just come up short in the college World Series, and honestly, I was not for it. The one thing you learn in academia is to question first and decide later. I must say tonight, watching this game, that I am a new fan of not being afraid to break some of the existing rules. We all here are at Bentley State and the whole city of Portsmouth, Ohio, are extremely proud of our boys and what they accomplished tonight and we're all looking forward to the play-offs."

"Thank you, President Morris" Yohe added. "As it turns out, the Vipers will now travel to St. Louis beginning this Wednesday night to take on the Central Division champs, the Cardinals."

Making a dramatic pause of looking down and then back up into the camera, it was obvious that this reporter wanted to make a point.

"So many firsts in all of this and a story that most people thought could only be concocted in some crazy book will now continue forward.A college baseball team from a small mid-western town is now playing in the Major Leagues after only two and a half months and is winning. As a reporter over the last thirty years, I have covered some pretty remarkable stories, but I truly have to say that this by far…is the biggest of them all! I'm Randy Yohe, and we'll have more coverage coming up in sports, but right now, it's back to you in the studio!"

"Those fucking bastards! The Dodgers are on the take!" Toots Randall screamed as he watched the multi-layered celebration of his former team's win now taking over on all of the sports channels from the Yankees clubhouse.

21 DOWN IN VEGAS

"Settle down, Toots," Derek Jeter exclaimed. "What those guys did today was totally amazing. It's great for the game. You're just pissed-off because they didn't want you!"

Sitting in the Yankee clubhouse, Randall stared daggers at the star-shortstop as Derek maintained an aggravating smirk in his direction.

"Right! Talk to Cashman about that, Captain." Randall countered. "You mean that I would rather be back there than here with this team? C'mon, letting me go was the best thing that ever happened in my career. You know better than anyone that you can't really ever get over that first girl who gave you some attention that just suddenly walked away from you, no matter how fuggly she was."

"Well," Jeter began with a pause, "since that's really never happened to me, I guess I'll just have to take your word for it, bro." He laughed. "We all know it's a great story, but we have a lot of work to do here. Since you already invoked his name, I would just mute myself from having the 'Cashman' hear anything about any of your outside opinions, been there, done that. We just need you to get ready for the play-offs!"

The post-season press conference was minus the usual locker room celebration.

Manager Tommy Leach nixed any champagne or any alcohol usage, feeling that it was inappropriate celebration to be televised around the world. He kept the locker room sacred as all players were now in the direct-fire of the media arsenal. George Knapp was one of the first reporters to step up.

"My question is for Manager Leach. Why did you hide Steinman from the lineup today? Was that a planned strategy?"

Looking around at the press corps, Tommy thought carefully about his words while trying to make some sense of a rather convoluted situation.

"Gary has just lost his father, George, and had been on bereavement leave. While it was only a 48- hour furlough, he was told to take as much time as needed. I hope you understand when that happens, it becomes a sensitive situation and supersedes any other directive from our club. We had an alternative plan for our rotation today, but

Gary came back to us early and requested that we use him if needed. As it turned out…we did…and he pitched a hell of a game."

"Thank you. I'm Jack O'Shea from the *Kansas City Star*. There's a rumor going around that certain girlfriends of some of the Vipers players are now using autographs and other memorabilia to make extra money. Can you address that?"

Staring coldly through the reporter, Tommy Leach coldly and sternly shut him down.

"Who let the *National Enquirer* in here?" Next!"

The questions and rehash continued until it was decisively time to pull the plug and let everyone go their own ways. Vipers Media Relations spokesperson Andy Glockner finally took the last question as the manager and team left the podium. With the MLB regular season now at its official end, Tommy and his staff were slowly realizing that there was much more time-sensitive work to be done. Back in the clubhouse, Tommy quieted everybody down to make a final discourse for the night.

"This is the first time we have all been here together, guys, since the end of the game and I thank you for all we've had to put up with including the fans and the press. You are the National League Western Division champs, and I thirst to say how proud of you all I am today."

The room was exceptionally quiet as the Vipers manager continued.

"You have all given of yourselves to arrive at a level few of you even knew had in you. As your manager, I thought that I saw you grow up in front of my eyes, but in fact, it was the opposite, you were already there. To be honest, it was me that really had to make that adjustment. In life, it's always the great unknown that tests the spirit, and that said, you have all conquered the first obstacle. We all have a lot of work to do getting ready for St. Louis. All I ask from you is to embrace this kindred piece of time and celebrate safely. If by chance, you do choose to stay up a little later than usual tonight, I will still need you all back here tomorrow morning at 11:00 so that we can go over our travel-plans. You're all dismissed except Collier! Grab your glove, Cliffster, we got some late-night shagging to do!"

As the room exploded into tension-relief laughter, Leach winked at Cliff as he and his coaches now headed toward Tommy's office. Getting to the door, there was one extra-body bringing up the rear. Standing there alone was Gary Steinman.

"Can I see you for a minute, Tommy?" he asked. "I won't be long."

Looking at his coaches, they all simply nodded, letting him know that they understood the moment. As the two entered the manager's lair, Gary again softly spoke.

"I just wanted to thank you for keeping your trust in me out there today. It meant a lot."

"Well, Steiny, I know your DNA pretty well. You showed us the heart of a champion once again, and in my mind, you were the best-bet to get it done, and you did." Leach replied.

A long awkward pause ensued as Gary reached inside his pocket to again pull out the tattered envelope that he had showed him before. Holding it close for a second, he slowly handed it to his manager.

"After I got back to Indianapolis, my uncle picked me up at the airport." Gary explained. "We didn't talk for the longest time. I really didn't have any words to share because all I could think about was Dad and the fact that my best friend and number one fan was gone. Just before we got home, he handed me this. I just wanted you to read it, Skip."

Carefully, Tommy removed the crumpled letter from its envelope and embraced the contents.

To my son Gary,

By the time you read this, I will be gone to my next great adventure. Since my illness son, I have tried to stay out of your way so you could do what you love to do. Watching you play baseball growing up was my biggest joy in life. Just waiting for you to come home after your ballgames to just sit on the back-porch and talk are my greatest memories.

When you came to me all discouraged this summer and we talked about you quitting the team after all the changes, I knew that really wasn't you. After we sorted things out, I saw you go back to be a part of something that kept me going. While the doctors here had me on life-support, you and the Vipers were truly my only reasons for hanging in there.

Coming to watch you pitch, I realized that would be my last time to ever see the classy kid that I raised do what he was born to do. You are a winner son! As you read this, please realize that my spirit has now been set free from all the pain. I don't want you to spend precious time here dealing with me. What I truly want is for you to get back to your teammates and do what we both know you have to do.

God has touched you Gary, and now both of us can watch you help complete a miracle. I will love you son, forever and forever, amen.

Dad

Absorbing the impact of the words he just read, Leach realized the power of the message as it related to his grieving star. Looking up, he slowly handed it back to Gary with a gentle smile.

"That's a hell of an insurance policy, Steiny," he spoke. "I understand how much he meant to you. I appreciate you sharing it with me."

Silence once again ruled the decorum as Steinman and Leach knew words were at a loss for the true meaning of the encounter. As Gary stood up and gently returned the letter into his hip pocket, his manager could now see the track-mark of tears running down his face.

"He was my whole world. He always believed in me and so did you today. There was no way I was going to let either one of you down."

Giving him a manly shoulder-hug, Tommy knew at this point he had to be running on fumes. "Go get some rest kid. You've had an extra-long day today and just know how proud both of us are of you. That was a super-human effort what you did out there today, and without it, I'm afraid we'd all be heading home in the morning."

21 DOWN IN VEGAS

Sundays are usually a slow information day for any news outlet, except the fact that a professional game that had been around for 138 years, had just made history. The overflow of interest from just the sports world was enormous. NBC, CBS, and ABC were all doing live reports and running special inserts from Las Vegas. The print-media was also setting up for the mother of all headlines to capture the spirit of the accomplishment. *USA Today* went to press early so they could be one of the firsts on the street on Monday. Their header in the boldest of fonts screamed "The Kids Kick Ass!" was indeed a bit of an attention-getter.

Elsewhere, *ESPN Sports Center* was not only praising the Vipers, but also setting up the next round of play.

"Good evening, everybody, I'm Rece Davis, and this is *ESPN Sunday Night Sports Center* and to dream the impossible dream. Elvis Presley was once famous for that one in the Las Vegas desert long before the Vipers proved that scenario is indeed not just a reverie, but a reality by knocking off the Dodgers in a four-game must-win sweep to capture the NL Western Division title on the last day of the regular season.

"It was a monster-pitching performance by the Vipers ace Gary Steinman who stunned both the capacity home crowd and the Dodgers by unexpectedly coming off bereavement leave early where he had been away and dealing with the passing of his father. Las Vegas overcame an early two-nothing deficit to pick up one in the third and create two more in the eighth to hold on and win the division by one-game.

"Had the Vipers tied for the division, the Dodgers would have been given the nod for post-season honors due to head to head wins of the season being in their favor in the decisive tie-breaker rule. We'll have much more on the Vipers coming up in our next segment, but for now, the post-season is set, and I for one who at times can feel a little jaded about these things, now feel like a five-year old kid again who just found his first ball-glove under the Christmas tree!"

"In the National League, the first round of play-offs games begin on Wednesday as Las Vegas travels to St. Louis to play the

Cardinals and the wildcard Phillies will head to the 'Big Apple' to tangle with the Mets.

American League play will get underway on Thursday with the Central Division champs Detroit traveling to take on the Western winning 'A's' in Oakland while the Twins, who by losing today to the Tigers become the AL wildcard representative, they head to the Bronx to take on the Yankees. It's Major League Baseball's 'second season" and be sure and watch ESPN for all your local start- times and much more as the road to the fall classic begins here!

Stay tuned! Neil Everett has more on the stunning turnaround from worst to first of the Las Vegas Vipers coming up next right here on *ESPN's Sunday Night Sports Center*!"

16TH INNING

The Pepper Mill Restaurant was again the chosen location for the reunion of old friends on a celebratory occasion.

"A table for eight please" Cliff Collier asked the hostess.

"Follow me," She offered as Cliff, Carla, Sean, Syleanna, Karl Smith, Gary Duzan, Brad Zeiber, and Brooks Snyder all traipsed a path to a table that was partially closed off from the rest of the dining room which allowed everyone to talk unencumbered.

"I'm still stunned." Gary Duzan began. "Did we really beat the Los Angeles Dodgers in four-straight? It's almost like having one of those freaky out-of-body experiences and I'm up there in the corner looking down and just watching us."

"C'mon 'Duz', you kicked ass man after John went down," Sean added. "I mean, with all respects to 'the Gambler', you played third like you invented it, brother!"

"Did you hear all those insane questions at the post-game interview? Damn, do those things ever get old?" Brooks Snyder laughed. "You girls were even brought up in some stupid thing about something."

"Us!" Carla shrieked. "You're shitting us, Snyder. Why would anyone want to know anything about us? That's stupid!"

"Ah, some guy just said something about player's girlfriends selling our memorabilia or something," Karl Smith inserted. "Tommy pretty well shut that clown down."

"Is that when he was talking about the *National Enquirer*?" Sean asked. "Yea, I remember now, he was acting like he had some kind of a big story or something."

"Hey, speaking of that, we need a few balls and a bat signed by the team for Julio," Syleanna remembered. "He got us the tickets for the game and has been so really nice about it."

"Julio…you mean that cabbie from LA who got you tickets the last time we were out there?" Sean quizzed. "We had to sign him some balls then. What's he doing here?"

"He's just a fan, babe, he's harmless. Julio came to watch the Dodgers and still had our number and called. Seriously, without him, we would have never gotten in, would we Carla?"

"I mean, he not only gave us tickets, but got us to the games too." Carla reacted. "It's no big thing! He and a buddy just wanted to have some balls and a bat signed by the team. He wanted more bats, but I told him he could only have one!"

As Sophie approached the table to take their orders, the conversation quickly changed to beers, nachos, burgers, and fries. Few in the well-known Las Vegas establishment realized that the special guests that were being catered to were in reality hiding from the world.

"I love this place!" Luke Shepard endorsed" "We could come here after any ballgames, and it was never a big deal. Ikea, Sophie, or the owner would just hide us away and let us relax! In this town, it's rare to be able to do that."

After the orders were taken, Sean quickly went back to the previous topic of conversation.

"So, about these balls and bats? What are we expected to do?" he asked.

"Julio knew it would be crazy and all, but said that if you could sign them and then we could just leave them at the hotel and that would be fine."

After a ponderous moment of silence, Cliff Collier took a big swig out of his Coors Light before offering a final thought on the matter.

"Honey, I realize everybody wants a little something from us and especially right now, but we've never really talked to the Vipers on how to handle this. Yea, we give autographs out to the kids and all and other people who ask, but signing bats and balls is like team-sanctioned stuff, I just don't know"

21 DOWN IN VEGAS

"If it's going to be a problem, we can just give him some money" Carla shot back. "That guy from *Good Morning America* who flew us out here didn't have a clue on what to do about tickets…and neither did we."

"It's OK…Calm down" Sean intervened. "A few balls and a bat won't be a problem! We can do that tomorrow morning before we leave and you girls don't fly out until 2:00 p.m. I can have someone drop them off tomorrow morning after our team meeting. By the way, it's National Fiancé Day today, and after our delicious dinner, I had planned perhaps to spend a little quieter evening celebrating the holiday if you please"

Reaching over to pull her near, he gave her the kind of kiss one delivers on really wanting to be alone. In mixed company, that never seems to happen as the next event of conversation was delivered to the troupe.

"I think, Sean, you might be glossing over the biggest problem that we might have here." Brad Zeiber suddenly spoke.

As all eyes at the table quickly locked onto the intense young rookie, his eyes and demeanor suddenly projected a dark cloud.

"You say we have to sign a bat…and some balls?" he quizzically asked.

Syleanna decided to take this one to clarify the circumstances of the barter arrangement.

"That's all, Brad!" she said in a huff. "A bat and a few balls, that's all we promised them!"

"Well, I'm still a little worried," Zebro responded. "I think most of us can handle that kind of an autograph assignment, but what happens when we give one here to Cliffster here…and drops it?"

There's nothing like a little ill-placed wit to get the party started. From this point on, it was a celebration of friends and teammates enjoying a life-time moment as it would be all too soon and in just a few hours before the next chapter would begin to be story-boarded and their future again ready to be written.

Catching up on the fly was the order of circumstance with Sean and Syleanna along with Cliff and Carla getting some much needed private- time together if only for a few hours. While the Vipers rested, the world was ramping- up for a baseball playoff event that few post-seasons had ever seen. In retro-scan, there was plenty of history that would forever be defined as lore to be used as ingredients for the anticipation created.

From the walk-off homers of Bill Mazaroski, Kirk Gibson, and Joe Carter to Don Larsen's perfect game, they are all stand-alone memories that seem to never lose their timeless sheen.

In what other sport can you just mention "game-six" to bring a smile to any New- Yorker's face? When Edger Renteria lined a ninth-inning single to bring a World Series Championship to Miami over Cleveland in 1997, that's why we love the game of baseball. The Marlins were only in their fifth year of existence, but defied all the odds by even being there, yet winning it all in such stage-setting drama.

For these and many other colorful expectations awaited a small-college baseball team suddenly turned pro. As the clock turned 11:00 on Monday morning, it was the clubhouse at Mirage Field where final instructions were now being dispensed.

"OK, time to get down to business!" Tommy Leach began. "For some of you that perhaps over-celebrated last night, I apologize for speaking a little louder than usual this morning, but I need for all of you to totally understand what's going on here!"

A smatter of nervous chuckles and accusatory glances made their way around the room as Tommy purposely paused to let the message set the table for his next verbal communique that was headed for uncharted waters.

"It's not been twelve- hours since you guys shocked the frigging world of what you have done here in Las Vegas, and there's nobody any more proud of you than me!"

Understandably that brought forth a round of enthusiasm as Tommy Leach withstood the unintentional call for praise before raising his hand again to speak.

"I thank you, but this is not about me, it's all about you. This team has earned the right to swag a bit because you all have earned it, flat-out! Enjoy this moment, but let me put it into everyday perspective. How many guys have we here that went to your high school prom? May I see a show of hands?"

It was unanimous.

"Look at it like this. You wanted to take the most beautiful girl in your school to the prom, but so did every other guy. You worked hard every day schmoozing her in the halls, getting to like and trust you, working on that perfect time to finally ask the question, knowing there was a hundred other guys out there doing the same thing. You put in all the overtime, you did all the prep work, and at that precise moment you ask her, and she said yes!

"After that, there's that period of exotic anticipation where you rent your tux, buy the flowers, borrow your best friend's stud car, and then it's here; the night of the prom!As you walk up the steps with the corsage, maybe a little nervous, you knock on the door. You hear those footsteps inside as you're standing there, and suddenly the door opens and you are now looking at the most beautiful girl you've ever seen. You gaze at her for a few seconds before you realize that it's you she is going to be spending the rest of the evening with, but also with all the other guys you beat out doing it. So, gentlemen…that is where you all are right now! Standing on the front porch looking at that gorgeous lady and ready to go to that big dance, and you've earned every right to go!

It's how you handle yourself from this point on that will determine how long your evening lasts, and in the end, whether or not you even take her home."

That fanciful analogy brought smiles to the team's faces as most were young enough and could easily relate,

"The Cardinals haven't made any official announcement yet, but in a five-game series, you can pretty well guess they're going with their big-three. If I were Tony La Russa, it would be Carpenter Wednesday, Marquis Thursday, and Suppan on Saturday. I'd think if it went into Sunday, you're talking either Mark Mulder or Jeff Weaver.

"Now, for a short series, here is the pitching rotation for us. Mitch will throw on Wednesday and Scotty on Thursday. We will go with Steiny on Saturday. I'm saving him until then for two reasons. If we are going for a split or even maybe taking the series, that's the arm I want out there. Scarbury is in for game-four on Sunday.

"Mind you again this is a five-game series, and we are going with a four-man rotation. I'm saving Carpy and Zebro for long-relief. Fuller, Burke, Leslie, and Shackart will all be available for short-relief. Should there be a game- five on Tuesday; 'Big Mitch' is our man."

Hurriedly glancing at his watch, Leach was feeling the pinch for time himself as he went over the itinerary for the next twenty-four hours.

"The bus will leave here at 2:00 p.m. and our flight leaves at 4:30 p.m. See George Crumm for your tickets along with your other information in your packets. We check in tonight at the Four Seasons at Lumiere, your vouchers should all be there with your tickets. We will have our team transportation waiting at 10:30 in the morning to take us over to Busch and our workout time will be from noon until 3 p.m. After that, we have press conferences, an MLB promo to shoot of some kind, and then it's back to the hotel at 6:00 p.m. for dinner, any questions?"

Sustaining amazing quiet, the guys seemed to have absorbed an army's worth of data with no apparent overload as Sean sheepishly raised his hand.

"Yea, Deeters, what is it?" Leach asked.

"Would it be a problem if I borrowed a few balls and a bat? I'll pay for them if I have to. It would be a big favor to me."

Looking quizzically at his star right fielder, he decided to have some fun at his expense.

"First of all, Sean, thanks for asking. Most ball players just steal all the stuff when we're not looking. I don't think I've ever had anybody ever ask before. Secondly, yea, I will put this on your bill. Balls, what? Ten bucks apiece, bats…now you're getting into high dollar. Game-used bats go in the gift shop for at least a hundred and fifty. So five balls and a bat, I'd say a couple hundred should cover it."

Looking rather sheepish, Sean nodded and said, "OK, who do I pay?"

"You pay me of course. I am the manager of all including this domain along with its people and all the equipment. I'll just go ahead

21 DOWN IN VEGAS

and put it on your tab, but if you can muster me up three-hits or better Wednesday night, we just might have to consider your account paid in full!"

Still not sure he was kidding or not, Sean Deeters politely nodded and simply said, "Thanks, Skip."

"If you need me, I'll be in my office with the coaches. Let's do it, guys! The glass- slipper still fits and this pumpkin is now officially headed to St. Louis!"

Touching down at Saint Louis Lambert International, the scene was eerily reminiscent of the first time the Vipers landed at home. Finally getting inside the terminal at around 6:00 p.m., three major television stations were set up to do live- shots during the six o'clock news.

KDSK, KTVI, and KDNL-TV all had their reporter's set-up outside the gate and ready to go. KMOX and KGNU radio also had their nightly sports talk-shows emanating from a make-shift studio.

Exiting the plane it was the usual team bombardment of trite questions and media positioning that the Vipers had now grown used to. Tommy again took the bullet for his players standing back to body-block the surging press while his boys quickly exited toward ground transportation.

"I'm Melanie Moon on KTVI TV-2 coming to you live from Lambert Field as the Las Vegas Vipers have just landed and the fanfare and excitement here is quite honestly hard to believe. In one of the truly great stories in all of sports, the Vipers have won the National League Western Division title and will now play our hometown Cardinals beginning Wednesday at 7:00 p.m. I talked with the Vipers Manager Tommy Leach just seconds ago, and this is what he had to say."

As the big-smiling blonde looked into her camera, there was a slight hesitation before the video-tape hit the screen and the face of the Las Vegas skipper.

"It's great to be playing extra- baseball. I'm not going to lie to you about that. Being from Southern Ohio, most of my boys grew up eithers Reds or Cardinals fans, and for sure, it's a thrill for them to be here to display their talents to such a baseball-rich city as Saint

Louis. As I have tried to hammer it into them in just the, really, three months we've all been together, to be the best, you have to beat the best. We certainly look forward to playing some great games here against a legendary baseball franchise."

Feeling confident that he said all the right things, the live-shot now went quickly back to the airport concourse to wrap-up the first of many other television interviews.

"The first round of the National League Division Series starts on Wednesday night as Chris Carpenter will be the starting pitcher for St. Louis to oppose Vipers right-hander Mitch Milhuff. Earlier this afternoon, I caught up with the Cardinal's Manager Tony La Russa and got his thoughts on this bombshell match-up."

"Well…I guess I am as surprised as everyone else on what this team has accomplished. Playing baseball at this level isn't easy, and when this all came down this past summer, I had my doubts, but no…I saw it first-hand on the field plus night after night watching the scoreboard and all the highlights. These guys have certainly earned the right to be here. It should be a good match-up between our players and theirs. I'm looking forward to it!"

"Don't forget that the Channel 2 'Fan Van' will also be at both home games with plenty of free Cardinal fun for the entire family. For KTVI-TV live at Saint Louis Lambert International, I'm Melanie Moon."

As the baseball essayists began their usual sojourn to bury the underachievers, the Las Vegas Vipers cleared the air with an offensive memo on Wednesday night. Before Chris Carpenter could get out of the third-inning, he had given up six-runs on twelve hits and a throwing error on perennial All-Star Jim Edmonds.

Viper starter Mitch Milhuff kept the birds at a distance allowing only five scattered-hits and a mound performance that certainly took the home-town air out of Busch Stadium.

"Not the kind of evening we were rooting for so far, right, Mike Shannon?"

That offered up by the Cardinals first-year radio voice John Rooney throwing up some thought to his legendary sidekick.

"Let me be honest!" Shannon offered. "These guys came out here with an offensive mind-set tonight! Deeters drives home the first run with a spanking-screamer for a double to left, and from that point Chris, it looked totally out of sorts with his pitch-selection tonight."

"You're right Spike!" Rooney re-enforced his thought. "These Vipers have shown a noticeable edge of confidence that I'm not sure the Cardinals were quite ready for to be honest; but you do get this for perspective. It was four-months ago to the date that this exact team played an afternoon game with William and Mary… and they won, but it's always a given when you field nine against two, you're really expected to prevail!"

"When you start telling those old-jokes this early, John, it's never a good-sign." Shannon sarcastically responded.

It was KMOX radio announcer Doug Mc Elvien that was the messenger on this given night of delivering the sporting news that no Cardinal fan wanted to hear.

"I was once involved in a radio prank when I was working in Louisville, Kentucky, and another announcer who took my job in Lexington went on the air to request the song 'I'm Sorry' for me and told listeners to call up and request it to my afternoon radio show. As you might understand, I was a bit bitter then, but today I feel like calling it in myself on the effort of one of Major League Baseball's elite teams!

"In case you're just joining us the final score tonight, it was the Vipers 11, the Cardinals 2. Homers by Smith, Kennedy, and Chadwick gave Las Vegas the fire-power they needed to score early and often as Sean Deeters and Terrance Kennedy both collected three- hits apiece. Up by nine in the ninth, reliever Bruce Leslie came on to close out the best of three series in order.

"Game two is tomorrow afternoon at 3:00 with John Marquis on the mound for St. Louis and Scotty 'The Golden' Arms will be hurling for the Vipers. Hear all the action right here on your number one home for Cardinals Baseball, 1120 AM- KMOX, St. Louis!"

The National League day-game was far from a slugfest at Shea Stadium as the Phillies Jon Lieber out-lasted the Mets Tom Glavine in a grinder. It was all tied up 1-1 in the eighth inning until a Ryan Howard solo shot made the difference as the favored New York Mets fell 2-1. The ESPN pundits were all on it as Peter Gammons brought everyone up-to-date.

"It was day one of the National League Division Series as the surging Las Vegas Vipers continued to be all business and went to the trough faster than a weight-watchers convention given a free day-off at "Pappy's Barbeque!"

"Twelve runs on nineteen hits, and if you're a Cardinal fan, you have to be somewhat concerned of losing the first one at home like this. As the sun rises over the arch in the morning, it will be a new day as Scott Arms for the Vipers and Jason Marquis for the Cardinals will face off in game- two of this best of five series.

"Another stunner for the day has got to be those 'wildcard Phillies' who stole the first one at home from New York in a classic pitchers throw-down. Tied 1-1 in the eighth, it was a Ryan Howard solo- dinger that broke the tie as Philadelphia wins 2-1 takes game one.

"Tomorrow, it's the American League Division Series beginning from New York as the Yankees host the Wildcard Twins starting at 2:00 p.m. It will be Randy Johnson on the mound for the Yanks as Johan Santana will counter for Minnesota, and later in the day, Detroit will be at Oakland for the nightcap with the 'A's' Barry Zito on the mound and he'll be opposed by the Tiger's Justin Verlander.

"It's really rare to have two teams from the same city playing here this time of year, but if you truly love New York baseball, you can actually take in the Mets and the Yankees both in the same day. I honestly think that the last time that ever happened, Central Park was considered the burbs."

New York Radio was on fire as one of the city's elite was stirring it as usual.

"This is the 'Imus in the Morning' program on WNBC, and I'm Don Imus. With me is Brian Cashman, CEO of your New York Yankees. So, Brian, you've had this thing wrapped up since spring training, I mean, what's it gonna feel like going out there and finally playing baseball that means something!"

21 DOWN IN VEGAS

On the phone from his office in Yankee stadium, Cashman chuckled to gather his thoughts before answering radio's number one agitator.

"Thank you, Don, for easing me into the deep water here this morning." Cashman responded.

"Hell!" Imus retorted. "You guys haven't really had to work up a sweat this season and look where you are! Does that at all worry you?'

"It's not been as easy as your painting it, Don. No, we've had a good season and all of our guys know what we have to do. Minnesota is a young hungry team, and we just need to go out there and play great baseball like we've doing and I think we'll be just fine."

"What are your thoughts on that circus tent from Las Vegas? I mean, do you honestly think there's any way they can really get past this first round? It's a freak show! You know that…and they're ruining the game! "

Sensing the set-up from Imus, Cashman wasn't going to bite on something that had turned into such a lightning-rod of positive publicity just to become a news-cut on all the networks.

"Don, what these guys did this year was pretty remarkable. I give a lot of credit to Cisco Wheeler for taking a chance. It has to be the feel-good story of sports this year or maybe forever. I'm just going to focus on us and hope we can bring another World Championship to this great city. That's really all I have to say."

After a long pause, Imus said, "That why I love you, Brian, you're just a big lovable non-committal wiener! Good luck with them Twinkies!"

"Thank you Don," Brian Cashman again said, laughing. "You know it's always a divine pleasure being on your show, and somehow it always changes my life!" "Coming up next, Warner Wolf handicaps the Mets chances in the play-offs. Next hour, it's Delbert McClinton on the 'Imus in the Morning' program with some new stuff off of his latest album '*Wake Up Baby*.'(Quack, quack.) We'll be right back!"

In Portsmouth, Ohio, local radio station MIX 99.3 orchestrated a promotion called "A Day-Off for the Play-Off," urging local business owners to close early and join a community-wide party starting at 11:00 a.m. for the 3.00 pm. First-pitch.

The stately Vern Riffe Center for the Arts on the Campus of Bentley State was designated to host the soiree with free food, music, and the game to be televised on the giant screen inside this fine art and music venue.

Local morning show voice Hobie Harrison finagled Portsmouth Mayor Frank Gerlach to make the proclamation on his MIX 99.3 morning show.

"Thank you, Hobie," he began. "As the mayor of Portsmouth, I can't begin to tell you what this means to me and our city. To turn on the TV, the radio, or pick up a newspaper and see the level of excitement that these boys have created, not only on a national level, but on a worldwide scale it is truly incredible. Just yesterday, I got calls for interviews from London, Melbourne, Australia, and New Zealand."

"That's pretty far-fetched stuff, Mayor." Hobie inserted, "I guess Mule Town, Ohio, can't be far behind!"

Sharing a laugh on that one, the morning-host wanted to keep the mayor on point. "So, Mayor Gerlach, tell us what we're cooking up for today"

OK…since it is a day-game today for the Vipers, we have created a promotion that we are calling 'A Day-Off for the Play-Off," and I am declaring it a legal holiday in Portsmouth. I urge everyone to skip work or school under no penalty of the law and come and celebrate with us starting at 11:00 this morning at the Vern Riffe Center, and let's win another one against the Cardinals!"

The fifteen-hundred plus in attendance certainly had again something to celebrate as the Vipers' Scotty Arms continued to roll keeping the previously hot Cardinal bats in neutral striking out thirteen on the day including Yadier Molina and Albert Pujos three-times.

The Vipers took the Division Series matinee with a solid 5-1 win. It was a lone Jim Edmunds home run in the ninth-inning off reliever "Dirty Ernie" Fuller that was the only highlight of the Cardinals offense.

Faced now with a day off to think about it and a trip to Las Vegas, Cards Manager Tony LaRussa was visibly upset at the post-game news conference.

21 DOWN IN VEGAS

"Am I disappointed? You're really asking me that question? Hell yes!" LaRussa shot back to perhaps the most under-thought inquiry for the occasion.

After a long pause and a look that could melt mercury, Tony LaRussa translated his inner-most thoughts into his own fiery rhetoric.

"I thought this team was prepared. I thought this team was ready to show their hometown fans how Cardinal baseball is supposed to be played. Well, I guess I was wrong."

"Mark C. Harris, Tony, from the *Kansas City Star*. The Cardinals only had five- hits through the eighth-inning off of Arms. Did the Vipers pitching catch you off-guard at all today?"

"What do you mean off-guard?" LaRussa angrily shot back. "These guys see this kind of pitching every day! They are the best of what they do. They've seen this kind of pitching since spring training. Today we just didn't do what we are supposed to do, plain and simple."

"Hey, Tony, Rick Mayne from KMOV Channel 4. You're down two- games and now heading into their house on Saturday. Just wondering in your own mind what you have to do now to turn things around?"

Again the look of Cardinals Manager Tony LaRussa flashed repugnance to the level of depth he was being forced to admonish.

"Mr. Mayne…first of all, if I knew that answer, do you really think I would stand up here and tell you! It's just simple mathematics, and I think that most everyone here in this room can count to three. That's all I have to say."

With that being the final question, the Cardinal's manager got up and briskly headed for the exit, leaving a stunned press corps behind to mull over the stifling awkwardness. On this given day, there was no escape- hatch from the volatility and major frustration left lingering in the bowels and rafters of Busch Stadium.

In other parts of the sporting universe, the ambiance wasn't quite as sullen.

"Shit, brother! One more to go and we're moving- on!" Sean Deeters regaled to his best buddy Cliff as they left the shower and headed to their lockers.

"You were Clarence Carter out there today my man, Strokin'!" Sean continued talking to Cliff. "That was one of the hardest doubles I've ever seen you hit. At first, I thought it was headed out and through that frigging arch!"

Laughing, Cliff acknowledged the compliment with his own sarcastic spin.

"I thought so too until the top those right field stands got in the way. By the way you pimp-stick, you got yourself a nice little bonus out there today as well!"

"Bonus! What you talking about, Willis?" Sean shot back.

"How many hits did you get? Did I count three?" Cliff quizzed.

"Yea, Three." Sean smiled.

"Well then, you, my friend, are now the proud owner of four-balls and one bat courtesy of the Las Vegas Vipers…now paid in full!

Suddenly remembering the promise Tommy made to him earlier, he again beamed from ear to ear.

"Yea, that's right! Looks like the house lost big on that one!' Sean realized. "Maybe Saturday I can go for some batting donuts and an old pine-tar rag!"

Unlike the last journey home, this time McCarren International Airport was packed with the anticipation of their returning heroes and there was no place to hide. Fans, reporters, and the never-ending press were all jockeying for position as flight 14713 from St. Louis eased up to the gate at almost midnight, the crew made a rare exception and afforded the Vipers manager the occasion to address his team on the microphone.

"This is your manager speaking!" Tommy Leach began to the cheers and whistles from the plane's passengers. "I know the last time we did this drill, it was to keep you guys focused and to avoid as much of the distractions that you will soon step into. Tonight, it's different. Tonight, it's all yours because you've earned it!As we get off of this plane soon, all of us will be pulled in a million different directions. We will get scattered apart, so listen up. The team- shuttle will

21 DOWN IN VEGAS

meet you at ground transfer and will leave at 1:00 a.m. You all need to be at the field no later than 2:00 tomorrow afternoon. With all the attention waiting for you out there, all I ask is that you represent this team with the kind of attitude and class that you've shown from the beginning. Now, please return your damn chairs in their upright position and let's get the hell out of here!"

Genuine applause and raucous ovations burst loose as the cabin lights quickly flickered on and that defining *'ding'* sounded as the Vipers players and coaches got out of the seats prepared to leave their safe-haven and step into the fan-frenzy of the great unknown.

"Ron Franklin here with *ESPN Baseball Tonight* as division play-off baseball got off to a full-slate on Thursday as both leagues were in action. In the National League, it was Las Vegas with the power pitching of Scotty "The Golden" Arms and the hitting of Sean Deeters and Cliff Collier that shut down the Cardinals 5-1 as the Vipers now take a 2-0 series lead as game three now moves on to Las Vegas. In other action, the Phillies also go up 2-0 in their best of five series over the Mets as Chase Utley broke up a 3-3 tie in the top of the ninth by driving in David Bell with a double off of reliever Chad Bradford. "The National League Series will resume on Saturday with the Mets taking on the Phillies at 4:00 p.m. with the Vipers and the Cardinals first pitch set and ready for 8:00 p.m.

"In the American League, it was home runs by Alex Rodrigues and Jorge Posada along with Randy Johnson shutting out the Twins 6-0 as the Yankees take game-one at home while in Oakland, Jason Kendall collected three hits including a grand-slam to lift the A's over the Tigers 9-3. "The American League Division Series will continue tomorrow with the Twins at New York starting at 3:00 p.m. with Detroit at Oakland-Alameda County Stadium and the first pitch at 7:10 p.m. Again, join us for all of the Division Series action right here on ESPN."

As the Mets and the Cards were on the brink of elimination after only two days in the first-round of Division Series play, Philadelphia was already looking ahead to the real-life "Rocky" adventure that seemed to be brewing in their window of destiny. In a sports-rich city made famous for producing the cinema's most heralded underdog, the analogies just could not be stopped. Philadelphia radio sports-patriot Tony Bruno was all about it.

"Coming next Tuesday, could the baseball version of these cities most storied sports fantasies actually become a reality? Tony Bruno here beaming to you from high in the sky on XM Satellite Radio and the *Sporting News Network*. As a Philly native and one who cut his radio-chops in the "City of Brotherly Sports", for all, I am truly excited about this potential first round set-up that would be for the National League title. Go ahead and call your hometown Philly's the favorite! Go ahead and chant 'Creed, Creed, Creed,' but then look who could be the unheard of street-fighter that suddenly gets thrust into the world- arena? Does a matchup like that sound familiar?

"I must say that the reception the Las Vegas Vipers experienced on returning home last night was just a just *Star Wars* episode away from Rocky Balboa's smelly two-room dive down on 1818 TusculumStreet. When over a hundred of your local police and security personnel are at the airport just to welcome you home, now that's a global sign that your neighbors did a little more than just pick up your papers and hide the key."Coming up, I have the latest exclusive interview with Charlie Manuel and his candid thoughts on your play-off Phillies right here the *Sporting News Network*!"

Mega-bustling for Saturday's game-three at Mirage Field was the equivalent of herding mice. Tickets for the game sold out in twelve minutes after they were put on sale, and the mounting pressure had categorically festered all the way to the mountain-top.

"So, Cisco, getting tired of all those freebie requests yet?" Brandon Briggs chided his boss as they got ready for the biggest game in the history of Mirage Field.

"Not now, Brandon, please!" Wheeler responded. "I know you're trying to keep me calm, but those god-damn ticket requests are driving me crazy!On top of that, there's this reporter from some rag who keeps calling to tell me that we are involved in a black-marketing scam of some sort with Vipers' merchandise. I don't need this shit… and especially today!"

"They're coming at us from all angles." Briggs reinforced. "This is called success, my friend. Cisco, I know you've worked for this all your life, but there are absolutely no guarantees that there wouldn't be a little pain in the buttocks getting here."

Pausing while rummaging through his cluttered desk, the Vipers owner acted as if he hadn't heard a word from his staunchest friend and ally. Finally faster that a hornet with road-rage, the prize was found and exalted.

"Here they are, finally!" Wheeler exhumed an envelope and hoisted it into the air. "Six tickets for Donald Trump! I thought for sure I'd lost these bastards."

"So you got all that excited over tickets just for him?" laughed Briggs. "I know he's one of your business cronies and all, but come on, boss, he's not the president!"

You could feel the tightness in the Cardinals dugout as the Vipers burst onto the field to the usual thunderous explosion. The press conference after game- two was a license for the press to take Tony LaRussa's remarks to the media wood-shed and give further prominence of what would now have to be a miraculous turn-around.

The late afternoon sun started its crescent decent over the loud and raucous Mirage Field as the man who willed his talents to the zenith stood strong on the mound, rubbing the ball for the Vipers. Gary Steinman and and Tom Browning had spent most of the morning talking over each hitter and visualizing the different pitch scenarios. With names like Molina, Eckstein, Edumonds, Pujols, and Rolen, there was little room for error, especially knowing they were now a wounded animal fighting to stay alive.

The Vipers crowd stood as after only sixteen pitches, Steinman was headed back toward the dugout after disposing of the inning in order.

"Snyder! Get us going, Brooksie!" Karl Smith roared. "Wait on your pitches, guys, let's go!"

Jeff Suppan finished his warmup tosses as the energy in the Vipers quarters was definitely super-charged and contagious. Several of the Cardinal players had taken public the issues of their manager calling them out in the press for the lack of fire.

Center Fielder Jim Edmonds had been especially vocal that his team had not been caught sleeping at the wheel. Proper credentials were given by him to the stellar level of play of the Vipers with the side-bar that St. Louis was a proven championship caliber team they should never be counted out. Feeding from the fuel of wanton desire, Brooks Snyder was determined not to let the fans' thirst linger for long. The two hardest tests on the spiritual road is patience to wait for the perfect moment and the courage not to be disappointed for what it might encounter. Working Jeff Suppan to a full-count early, Snyder's perfect moment was a change-up on the inside corner of the plate.

"Snyder swings and there it goes!" Ralph Hacker roared. "That's high and deep to left and the Vipers quickly put the venom to the Cardinals, taking a 1-0 lead here in the first with a lead-off dinger!" Pete Harnisch was elated as well, praising his well-placed solitude.

"There was no doubt about that one and with all the different looks that Snyder was seeing, you knew it would be just a matter of time before he saw what he wanted. With all respects to Suppan, it reminded me of a batting practice pitch. We sometimes would throw one like that to a batter after a lot of pitches more out of frustration than anything. Sometimes, it works, sometimes it don't. That one was a definite 'don't.'"

The hit parade continued in the first as Las Vegas scored four while batting around. While Brooks Snyder dug in for his second serving of the inning, it was at this point the Cardinals manager had seen enough.

"Here comes LaRussa and that's all for Jeff Suppan as Adam Wainwright is now being brought in with four-runs on the board, two outs, and bases loaded here in just the first-inning. Ralph Hacker here with Pete Harnisch, and I'm as shocked as anyone else Pete, that this team just kind of picked up where it left off."

"And especially all they have been through with the global crunch that has followed them everywhere. I know just trying to get through the airport the other night, it was wall to wall. If you remember, we were to be on the team bus by 1:00 a.m. and it didn't end pulling out until 2:30 in the morning. How these guys can handle all of that and continue to play baseball like this is simply amazing!"

21 DOWN IN VEGAS

With a sense of urgency, Adam Wainright got Brooks Snyder on a pop-up to second and mercifully ended the first-inning. With a 4-0 lead and the Viper's ace throwing on this given day, while it was still early, it would be too late for damage control. Saint Louis radio announcer Mike Shannon shared the lament of the Cardinal Nation with two-outs and Albert Pujols at the plate.

"After that horrendous start in the first, Adam Wainright has come on to pitch a masterless six and a third- innings with Isringhauser in for the last two. Nobody is up throwing in the Cardinals bullpen right now, but the real story today is the total dominance of a pitcher who may just be having the best half-year in this games history. Gary Steinman has thrown only 89 pitches and now faces Pujols here in the ninth with two-out and none-on. He is set to deliver…the pitch…a swing and a miss by Pujols and there's your ball game!"- Mike Shannon draped the stunning conclusion with a moment of stunned silence watching the on-field celebration before continuing. "Gotta be honest here, folks, I don't think anyone quite expected this kind of a termination to another great season as with a heavy heart, some major disappointment, and after just three games; it's a sad fact that the Cardinals are now going home to roost!"

For those who reveled late watching the aftermath of the game, it was former KMOX announcer and NBC commentator Bob Costas who was summoned onto the scene to give the final eulogy.

"Call it what you want. Some in my profession like to use words like *destiny*, *blind- luck*, perhaps a *puncher's chance*, for through the propensity of sport, there has always been a true fascination for creating a written depiction for the totally unexpected. Based on what I've seen here in the last few days, this is the most unusual set of circumstances. I'm not really sure there is an appropriate word or phrase that can accurately designate the true faith of what we are witnessing here with baseball in the city of Las Vegas.

"I can't say I've seen them all, but certainly plenty to establish the fabric that defines winners from losers. Much has been written and seen from these twenty-one ex-college players from a university and a small-town scarce from this nation's radar. The five remaining veterans should also be recognized for having the ability to not walk out on what seemed to be at the time one of the murkiest of moments, but instead, they chose to stay and play.

"The Las Vegas Vipers have just beaten the St. Louis Cardinals 4-0 to sweep the reigning National League Champions and be the first team to clinch a spot for the Major League Championship Series. Collectively, these players, who are making only the league minimum with some contract incentives I might add, are at least earning collectively 6,700,000.

"The remaining five veteran players according to the records we resourced from the Major League Players Association reveal that they are making in the financial neighborhood of around 19,000,000 which brings the Vipers' entire payroll to near or about $27,000,000. That brings us to the most stunning precipice of fact that this team has just swept an established perennial champion who garners a team payroll of $165,000,000. To put it in even a more stunning comparison, the total cost of the Las Vegas Vipers entire labor force is close to or equivalent of Barry Bond's salary alone!

"When I see instances like this as it pertains to sport, I can't help but to think of the mighty ocean. It can be calm or still, rough and unpredictable, but in the end, it's always beautiful. I'm Bob Costas from Mirage Field in Las Vegas. Goodnight, everybody."

With a few days to themselves to now think and regroup, the first round of the NL playoffs became anticlimactic as all were now waiting to see who the Vipers would play for the National League title. The Mets down two- games to none travelled to Philly where they finally busted out of their funk, taking game three at Citizens Park behind a home run barrage from Carlos Delgato, David Wright, and Carlos Beltran. In game four, Philadelphia returned the favor behind eight innings of five-hit pitching by Brett Meyers and a four-hit attack from Ryan Howard including two home- runs that put an exclamation point on the other 58 he had hit during the regular season.

The National League Division Series was now set as the Las Vegas Vipers would square off against the wild-card winner Philadelphia to play in baseball's most storied vitrine.

21 DOWN IN VEGAS

In the American League, the Yankees cut down Minnesota's chances like a hot knife through butter. Between the collective New York starting pitching of Randy Johnson, Chien Ming-Wang and Mike Mussina, the Twins were only able to muster up five- runs in the total series for a three-game sweep that left most baseball pundits discussing the 2006 team in the same breath as the '56' Bronx Bombers.

While the Pesky Detroit Tigers took Oakland to the fifth game of the series, it was Esteban Loaiza that silenced the Tigers' bats with a two-hit performance to shut out Detroit 2-0 at Comerica Park and move on to the next level of taking on the super-charged Yankees for the American League title.

With a story that too many thought too good to be true, there was a small chink in the "feel good" armor that was about ready to develop. The LA Police Department had been conducting a sting operation over the past several months on a local black-market operation that was using sports memorabilia to finance illegal gambling in the area. There had been a recent raid at several local storage units with hundreds of items seized from every avenue of the sports world. Among them some autographed balls and bats from the Las Vegas Vipers. In a press release, Los Angeles Police Chief Charlie Beck wanted to be extremely careful not to condemn the teams or individuals whose product was involved, but at the same time, there were many questions on how these people had procured the items in question. In a story that should have been lost in the daily shuffle of robberies and domestic disturbances, the press couldn't let this one pass for one pure and simple reason: The name Las Vegas Vipers was involved..

KCAL-TV9 Kent Shocknek was one of the first to break the story in Los Angeles.

"In a South Central LA neighborhood, several storage units license to the name of Ira Bell were confiscated early yesterday containing millions of dollars worth of high profile sports memorabilia that were allegedly to have been used to finance illegal sports gambling in the greater Los Angeles area.It's unspecific at this time where the money was targeted, but authorities are saying that the confiscated items is a 'who's who' collection of sports collectables including all Los Angeles sports franchises and even the new Las Vegas Vipers are represented in the haul.

"With a prepared press release, LA Police Chief Charles Beck said that a complete inventory would soon be assembled as this investigation continues on how professional sports is being used in the most illegal of ways. My big question if, true, is simply how does a team whose players are barely three- months' old to the Major Leagues also get involved in something like this? There are many questions to be answered, and we will keep you updated here on KCAL-TV 9 as the developments progress. I'm Kent Shockneck reporting."

As baseball euphoria continued to saturate Las Vegas and preparation for the arrival from Philadelphia, the office and business of Cisco "The Dealer" Wheeler was comparable to the control tower at McCarron International.

"No, Wayne Newton cannot sing the National Anthem again!" Wheeler angrily screamed into his phone to his agent. "You know it and I know it, that he's only doing it for free-tickets. Christ, Bernie, he almost owns the whole damn town, why can't he just buy a fucking ticket?"

"Mr. Wheeler, Donald Trump is on the phone again and this time says that he desperately needs to speak to you." his secretary interrupted.

"Tell him I'll call him back," Wheeler barked. "He's another one that's getting on my last nerve. I wish I could just build a wall around him and all these other idiots that all want something for nothing!"

As Brandon Briggs walked in wearing a half-cocked smile, he couldn't help but to needle his boss for just an instant.

"Think of that. I can remember a time when he wouldn't even take your calls, Cisco," Briggs casually spoke, "and all you wanted to do was to give his hotel guests half-price admission to our games. Maybe he's calling to take you up on that offer now!"

"Not funny, Brandon, not funny!" his boss replied in frustration. "We got two days until we play the next biggest game in our history. Over ten years I've spent telling everybody 'yes,' and now I am crashing here, learning to use the word 'no,' it's not easy!"

21 DOWN IN VEGAS

Sensing his exasperation, Brandon Briggs quickly turned on the common-sense shield of demeanor that he was known for in order to restore the sanity of the situation.

"Hey, Cisco, before you self-combust and implode into a green puff of sludge, just remember what Albert Einstein said, be careful for what you wish for, because it could come true."

"He didn't say that, I think that was Shecky Green!" Wheeler retorted. "I remember hearing him use that when he was doing his lame act over at the Sands."

A few days' down time also came to the New York Yankees after their sweep of the Twins. One thing the Big Apple press corps never needs is idle time between major sporting events. Every nook, crevice, and corner of story possibilities became harvested for fill-time narratives.

WNBC Radio agitator Don Imus was again on his game, booking Toots Randall on his "Imus in the Morning" program.

"Tootsie, your former team seems to be playing pretty good without you, do you think you may have been the problem or what?" Imus playfully began the interview.

"Let it be known that Toots Randall has never hung up on a radio legend and will continue that streak despite your cruel and inappropriate sense of humor." He laughed.

"Seriously," Imus continued, "you've come here to a pretty good situation as I once heard you say it was like being given a free subway token from hell to heaven, and now there's the possibility you may have to play with the devil again. How do you feel about that?'

"Look, Don, I love you and know you're just trying to get me in trouble again with the brass. I love being a Yankee, and all my past is behind me as I can now say that I wish the best for my former team."

"You know that's bovine fecal- matter, Toots!" Imus laughed. "But I do get it, so just let me say good luck against the 'A's this weekend.

"That's kind of you Don. We have great fans here in New York and I look forward to moving on for them to bring home some more glorious hardware for you to brag about on your award-winning show and MSNBC."

"That's nice," Imus continued. "By the way, I saw that sports clip again of you that Warner Wolf keeps wearing me out with about every other day. Play hard, Toots, but always be sure there are three-outs before you start pimping balls to the hookers in the stands! Will you do that for me?" (Quack, quack.) (Click.)

"We must have lost Toots Randall for some reason, but, we'll be back with Big and Rich right here on the 'Imus in the Morning' program on WNBC!"

In an empty Mirage Field, the pods of players were dutifully going through the motions of working out, but their minds were all buzzing from the next room they were all about to enter together. It was midafternoon when Tommy Leach finally called a halt to the action and pulled everybody into the dugout for a team meeting.

"I gotta say we've not had the luxury of having an open-air gathering like this in quite some time." he playfully quipped as he looked around at the emptiness of the great Mirage structure. "Before we take the next step in our journey, I just wanted us all to get together and talk. You know what we've all been against in not only getting here, but keeping our sanity, Chadwick, you're up first, tell us what you're feeling!"

The Vipers big first baseman looked stunned as he leaned back on the pine. On gathering his thoughts, he flashed that big smile as he looked up and down the home bunker.

"Well to be honest, to me, it's how fast this all has moved along." Bombo shared. "Christ, it seems like yesterday that we played our first game of the year against Kent State, and now we're here playing the Philadelphia Phillies. I just know that as a player, the big thing I've noticed is that it's still the same game. I know these guys up here are better, but since we got here…so are we!"

During the next half-hour, the Viper's bench was like the sports talk show that all of the talking-heads would have loved to have had access to. Sean Deeters, Cliff Collier, Mitch Milhuff, Gary Duzan, Terrance Kennedy, and even the quiet one, Gary Steinman, all aired their innermost thoughts of this most incredible journey. While some teams who are playing badly have meetings to clean the air, this was a much needed assembly to halt time for just an instant to

21 DOWN IN VEGAS

enjoy the moment and the accomplishments of a most remarkable band of brothers.

Between the games, press conferences, and all the white-noise interference that comes with a feat such as this, personal communication often suffers in simply trying to maintain the chaos. Looseness, smiles, and confident calm were now at hand at the end when Manager Tommy Leach called upon Bench Coach Keith Madison to wrap up the impromptu rally session.

With one foot on the upper step, Keith paused as he looked up and down to each and every one of the players. You could hear the breath enter his chest cavity as he began his oration.

"Kent State…they had us in the seventh if you remember, Chadwick. It was Snyder, Collier, and I believe you, Coleman, who had to bail us out in our last at bat on that one." Madison opened up. "Yep, it seems like yesterday for sure especially when Brandon Briggs entered my office in what I was sure was a practical joke. I still think that I might just suddenly wake up and find my head on a pillow back home in Portsmouth, Ohio." He paused again. "I will make this short. Aside from watching first from afar and now being a part of all of this, I absolutely would like to specifically thank Terrence, Doug, Scotty, Brad, and Gary for your talent, understanding, and all of all your influences. "Watching as I did up until the last month, it is much more than evident that you all walked through the fire together for a reason. I knew the heart and talent that was coming to Las Vegas from Bentley State. What I didn't know was all the other intangibles it takes to continue to win at this level. "Looking here at all of you now…and together as one, I am sincerely humbled of you for allowing me to share the ride with you. "For Tommy, the staff, and again to all the vets, I again just thank you again for not giving up on these guys when it was so easy and being the solid people, players, and inspiration that you have been for helping the Eagles to fly!"

An explosion of joyous relief ensued as the bench began to bubble with true anticipation of hosting the Philadelphia Phillies for game one of the NL Championship Series. Manager Tommy Leach had purposely waited until the announcement of Charlie Manuel's starters before releasing his rotation. After his decision, it was seconds before ESPN and all of the networks burst forward with the anticipated news.

"In the very first home playoff game in the history of Las Vegas, Manager Tommy Leach released his starting rotation and I have to admit that I'm more than a little stunned." Steve Lyons feverishly burst forward with the news.

"In game one, it will be Cole Hamels against Scotty Arms, in game two, his matchup will be Mitch Milhuff facing Brett Myers, and a real stunner here is that Gary Steinman won't go until game three against Jamie Moyer. I guess the thought process here as the last series, so after two games at home and it shifts to Philly, you will have your ace on the mound on the road. As you know, Philadelphia can be a snake-pit for visiting teams, and on paper, there seems to be quite a bit of confidence that the Vipers will win at least one at home. On the other hand, the Phillies are a play-in team as I compare them both relatively the same. It's almost like we have two wild card opponents going at each other in final series for the flag. It will be maximum curiosity for sure! You're watching *ESPN Sports Center* and I'm Steve Lyons."

The influx of ticket requests coming through Bentley State's pipeline was staggering. In a town of 20,000, both University President Howard Morris and Sports Information Director Jeff Perez had at least 30,000 inquiries on passes for the series. At Port Columbus International, Delta had to put fifteen extra-planes in service with direct flights. Among two who had the in-rows to acquire authorized permits for the first game were Carla Harris and Syleanna Griffin. They randomly packed to catch their evening flight to Vegas, but Carla couldn't help but to bring up the curious story she had heard on CNN.

"Isn't that wild about all that sports stuff? I mean, who could ever think that an autographed ball and bat was against the law?"

"Got me!" Syleanna answered. "All I know is that we didn't do anything wrong having the guys sign that stuff. We didn't get any money, just tickets."

"I know, but why are they making such a big deal out of it? Carla continued. "Between all that Enron crap and Paul McCartney's divorce, you'd think the damn press could find something else to trash more than just a signed baseball and some bats! It's stupid."

"Forget about it." Syleanna replied. "We have all these other bitches that need our help in getting to Vegas, our flight tonight is all full of the girlfriends and groupies. I just found out that crazy lady with the frizzy hair who has been after Brooks Snyder forever is now on our plane. That should be a circus!"

"Better hurry, senorita winch, our ride will be here in ten minutes!" Carla shot back. "We gotta move!"

The Vipers were all standing along the first base line as the group Nickleback sang an acapella version of the National Anthem. With 44,576 fans also upright, it was the last event before the first ceremonial pitch to ignite the fuse that was to be bona fide baseball frenzy. Completion of the last note was done by Chad Kroeger as the crowd roared their approval. Walking back to the dugout "King Kong" Karl Smith elbowed Everett Carpenter with a question.

"Why does everybody hate those guys so much? Listen to the response they're getting."

"Might be the song selection, Karl, that one's been around a little longer than 'Rockstar,' I think" Carpenter sarcastically replied.

"Yea, good point."

The Las Vegas line had the Vipers a 7-5 favorite to win it all, but many of the experts were picking the Phillies based on their toughness of schedule and overall offensive weaponry. The National League Eastern Division in 2006 was considered the home of the heavyweights. Names like Carlos Beltran, Brian McCann, Andruw Jones, Alfonso Soriano, plus Ryan Howard and Chase Utley were all part of the pistons that powered the engine labelled 'The Beast of the East."

On the field, camera crews had surrounded the honorary pitcher for the night who had just served up the first throw plate-bound; it was businessman Donald Trump.

"It's an incredible night tonight. Unbelievable! I just threw a perfect strike to that catcher Doug Pouge, it was a beauty!" As the Donald spoke, the cameras kept rolling. "I would like to thank my very good and close friend, Cisco Wheeler, who put a lot of faith and his own money mind you, into creating this incredible team that everyone has fallen in love with, including myself. I would just like to say thank you to the Las Vegas Vipers for making baseball great again!"

Game one of the NL Championship Series was everything billed and more as Scotty "The Golden" Arms kept the Phillies off-balance with a junk-yard assortment of curveballs, sliders, and even the dreaded knuckler as the Vipers got on the board early.

Cole Hammels struggled through six innings surrendering doubles to Deeters, Duzan, and Chadwick for scores, but it was the big blow by Karl Smith in the sixth with Collier on board that barely missed the giant slot machine in center-field that put Las Vegas up 5-1.

Ryan Howard, Jimmy Rollins, and Chase Utley all seemed out of rhythm, trying to figure out the pitch code for the night.

After seven-innings, Manager Tommy Leach let his relief corps take it to the house as Jeremy Burkes pitched a perfect eighth. "Dirty Ernie" Fuller's only mistake was a hanging curveball to Ryan Howard in the ninth that this time boinked the fifty-foot Marie Osmond likeness almost square on her nose to join Donny as two of the most abused brother-sister acts in any Major League Baseball park. The final score: Vipers 6. Phillies 2.

KNTV's news ace Katelyn Marie waded into the mob to interview Scotty Arms, the 5'2" blonde reporter was tenacious in her attempt to get the story first.

"Scotty, you really had the Phillies baffled tonight. What was working for you?"

"Well…everything really," he responded, "I know how aggressive they can be at the plate, so I just tried to keep them guessing."

"You threw the knuckleball to Ryan Howard, I believe in the seventh-inning, and he didn't seem too happy about it. Did you notice that?"

"Yea, I did!" Scotty Arms laughingly responded. "As Tom Browning told us when we all learned to throw it, guys in this league don't like to be shown up very much, it's a frustrating thing to hit if you throw it right. As long as we get the out, I'm OK with it."

"What about that long home-run by Smith?" Katelyn Marie asked. "Many are saying that might be the longest in the history of Mirage Field!"

"I feel kind of bad for Karl because that sign says if you hit it, you win a million dollars, and I know he's getting a little light on pocket change right now" Arms jabbed. "I think at that point it gave us all a jolt that we could really take control of the game… and we did."

"Thank you, Scotty Arms, and the best of luck to you in the series!"

"Thank you." Arms politely responded.

"Game one of the National League Championship Series goes to the Vipers tonight 6-2 behind a stellar pitching performance by Scotty "The Golden" Arms. Reporting live from inside Mirage Field, I'm Katelyn Marie for KNTV-Action News 13."

Thursday night's home-sequel between Mitch Milhuff and Brett Myers had a completely different texture as the Phillies got on the board first and stayed there.

Baffled the night before, Ryan Howard and Jimmy Rollins both homered in the first- inning, staking Philadelphia to a 3-0 lead. Milhuff had control problems getting the ball where he wanted it, and after four-innings his night was done. Relievers Bruce Leslie, Clark Carson, Andrew Shackart, and Everett Carpenter were used in the proverbial "mop up roll" as the Phillies cruised to a 9-2 win over the Vipers.

The post-game show on KVPR-AM reflected the mood of the loss and perhaps an Achilles heel of the hometown favorites.

"Ralph Hacker along with Pete Harnisch, and tonight, we may have seen a glimpse into a very long season for some of the Vipers, Pete."

"I hope you're wrong, Ralph, but in the respect that people don't realize how long these young men have been playing baseball. Honestly, tonight, Milhuff just looked tired."

Harnisch countered, "They have a day off before playing again Saturday in Philly. I just hope that all the wear and tear of playing basically two-seasons, literally, doesn't hit the wall now. I know we aren't the only ones with these concerns."

"Good point, Peter" Hacker admitted "If you think about everything these kids have done, not even considering losing the College World Series by one run in late June, then just three- weeks later, they're up here and facing the best of the best in the Major Leagues? It's truly a super-human feat of not just athletic stamina, but emotional fortitude as well."

"That's it from Mirage Field tonight as again we will be back on the air Saturday night from Philadelphia for game-three of the National League Championship series. For Pete Harnisch, I'm Ralph Hacker on the voice of the Vipers, KVPR. So long everybody!"

The early morning flight from McCarron International to Philadelphia gave everybody a chance to absorb and dissect the day before. Cliff Collier and Sean Detters sat side by side lamenting the short time they had to spend with not only their girlfriends, but the hometown folk in general.

"This ain't right, man." Sean vented. "Everybody came so far, and we didn't spend twenty- minutes with them. I've told you this before, but I feel like we're in a damn federal prison!"

"We are pal, remember!" Cliff casually retorted. "It's called the 'Penal Institution of Fame' and our parole date won't be until sometime late in October, or it could be as early as next week!"

"Come on, you know what I'm saying. You saw Carla for what, thirty- minutes max? And that was at that damned Peppermill Restaurant with people everywhere and all that neon lighting. It makes me dizzy and who can get romantic about that!" Sean animatedly asked.

"Whoa, bro! I know that vibe, my brother of raging hormones, it's all of us, man. When we signed up for this, there was no clause that I saw in any of our contracts for conjugal visits. We're all kind of like on our own there buddy-bud." Cliff laughed.

Realizing that his best friend could always diffuse complicated issues with his humor, a smile slowly spread on Sean's face as he felt the decline from his preface of frustration.

21 DOWN IN VEGAS

"I know it, you know it, and we're both unbelievably lucky to be doing this. Last night was tough, man. Meyers had both of our numbers, so I'll just let it go, and besides, I've been going over Moyer's stats. If we're patient, we can wait him out."

"Kind of what you've been doing with Syleanna, huh, my little horny-toad brother. There's a lesson there, I think," Cliff again chimed.

"Can you just let it go? Really, please!" Sean playfully shouted.

If there were ever transference of energy and spirit from one location to another, Citizens Bank Park in Philadelphia was ground-zero for the arrival of the perceived biggest baseball event to hit the city of brotherly love.

Into its third season, nobody could recall this amount of raw demand for attendance.

Abandoning the famed Veterans Stadium in 2003, the Philadelphia Phillies left behind a legacy of two-Division Series, six-League Championship titles, and three-World Series appearances. Philadelphia's brightest moment came in 1980 when they beat Kansas City in six- games to become baseball's reigning World Champs. This is the year the city hungered for its first taste of the high life in its new digs, and everybody was there to be a part of it.

Pulling out all the stops, the city paraded out every favorite son they could find to create an all Philadelphia extravaganza, from Chubby Checker singing the National Anthem to Sylvester Stallone throwing out the first pitch, they even had Will Smith making a shameless fan surge from the PA booth for "The men in…the men in…the men in red!"

Destiny is a hard train to derail and so is personal will. On this given night in Philadelphia, Gary Steinman knew what his mission was all about and literally again took fate into his own hands. After eight- innings and just eighty-nine pitches, the supercharged offense of Philadelphia could muster up only a couple of hits. One was a scratch single up the middle by outfielder Shane Victorino, the other a bloop single to right by catcher Carlos Ruiz. The Vipers took Sean

Deeters and Cliff Collier's scouting reports to task and waited at the plate for their pitches.

Tolerance from the toll of swinging at bad deliveries netted five-walks from Jamie Moyer coupled with some extreme timely hitting from Chadwick, Snyder and Smith. The results were seven runs on the board for Las Vegas with "Dirty Ernie" Fuller throwing a perfect ninth to seal the deal. After the game, Phillies Manager Charlie Manuel was eloquent and truthful at the post-game interview.

"Hey, guys, they hit and we didn't. Really not much to say about that. I thought Steinman pitched one of the better games against us that we've seen all year. You could just tell watching him on the mound that he was all business tonight. I think Jamie had some control problems at times and that kept him into some trouble, but hell, it's just one game. We play another one tomorrow!"

Youngster Brad Zeiber got the Vipers call for the mound in game-four as the Phillies countered with lefty Randy Wolf. Pitching into his eighth season, Wolf was a promising arm that ended up on the disabled list frequently after the 2003 season. That was the year that he posted a career best 16-10 record with a 4.23 .era.

Up the road and to the right a piece, the pin-stripes were showing no mercy on the green and gold. Behind Randy Johnson and Mike Mussina, the Yankees put on a hitting- clinic in the first two-games at home, scoring 21 runs and allowing just 3.

With 12-1 and 9-2 wins respectively at home, the long plane ride to Oakland looked more like just a minor inconvenience before handing over the AL championship hardware to New York. Johnny Damon, Alex Rodrigues, Jorge Posada, and Derek Jeter had been especially toxic at the plate recording three-hit games in each of the two. Robinson Cano had also gone deep in both games making the "A's" frontline starters look more like batting practice hurlers.

Game three in Oakland was set to start later in the day with the Yankees Chien-Ming Wang opposing lefty Barry Zito.

High atop the Four Seasons Hotel from the luxury suite, Cisco "The Dealer" Wheeler and Brandon Briggs were beginning the day with eggs benedict and coffee prepared by hotel award-winning chef

Greg Vernick while Brandon casually scanned the morning headlines of the *Philadelphia Enquirer*.

"Looks like we are going to play the Yanks, don't it?" Brandon said.

"Don't say that…please!" Wheeler barked. "I hate that we have to sit around here all day and stew in all this media-garbage about every microscopic detail of what these idiots think is going to happen, and now you're joining them!"

"Hey, hey, Cisco, calm down," Briggs offered with a smile, "I was just making a comment, that's all."

"Yea, but you'll jinx us with that horse-shit. We got two more to win before we can say that. I wish we could just play the damn game today and move on!"

Sensing his boss's edginess on the matter, Brandon attempted to talk him off the ledge with a little word of comfort.

"You better stay away from that coffee, boss. As tight as your wound up right now…you just might explode." He laughed.

After a contemplative minute of silence, Wheeler seemed to have gathered his wits as he was the next up to speak.

"Tell me, Brandon, honestly, Milhuff didn't have it! I've never seen him pitch like that and I'm concerned. Do you think he's hit the wall?"

"Cisco, these are boys out there, not machines. We've all been spoiled not just a little bit on how good these guys have played. Seriously, who could have ever imagined that this would have ever worked at all? You remember all the things the press were saying when you did this. You were voted the absolute craziest person on the planet! Even I was also a bit skeptical until I saw the complete package of what they could do on a baseball field. We have also been extremely lucky on injuries to boot. Cisco, as I've told you, time and time again, relax, soak it in, and just enjoy the ride. Also just relish the fact that you have now definitely been expunged and freed from the reputation of being the craziest person on the planet! That job now belongs to Mel Gibson!"

"I guess you're right, Brandon," Wheeler admitted with a deep sigh. "I'm sorry I get all wound up like this, but those guys are trying to give me a dream that I've lived for my whole life, and for the first time in a long time, I really do care about the players."

"There's certainly a lot out there to love, Cisco." Brandon shot back, really not quite understanding his cryptic comment.

"You know, you've been around this place long enough with all of those over-paid pansies that were going to turn us around with that damn Toots Randall being the worst. It really steams my ass that there is a possibility of that no-talent and classless curmudgeon playing against us in the World Series!"

"Now...wait a minute, Cisco!" Brandon shot back. "You shouldn't say something like that, that's totally wrong!"

"And why the hell not!" Wheeler bristled.

Pausing for a short and needed moment, Brandon delivered the coup de grace, "Hey, you might jinx the team!"

While the Championship Series in both leagues continued, it was more than clear that the "team of destiny" was on a collision course to meet up with the "team of dynasty." On back-to-back nights, the Vipers fought the hostility and fervor of the Phillies faithful with crafty pitching, timely hitting, and a little luck.

As the World watched with a 3-2 count in the bottom of the ninth and two-outs, it was "Dirty Ernie" Fuller who delivered the final death-blow with a 67 mph pitch that fluttered by a transfixed Ryan Howard and the party was on!

With more than just a few Vipers fans in attendance to witness history, the dugout emptied and the field blossomed into the usual scrum of celebration on the infield of Citizens Bank Park. NBC had set a record for mobile camera crews ready to secure the moment and one of the networks' best baseball personalities was ready to go.

"This is Jon Miller and with me is Scotty Arms who I'm sure feels pretty 'golden' right now. Scotty, you came in today with just four days' rest, but you kept this team in it until the end which was in no way bitter!"

Wow...this, I mean is something that...is kind of beyond me right now!"

Arms laughingly stuttered. "I knew if I could keep it close, we would have a chance. We never give up. Yesterday, Karl had the big bat going, and today our guys capitalized on that error by Howard, but yea! It's all good!"

"I have to ask this question!" Miller fired. "Was there ever any doubt when the guys arrived here in the Major Leagues from Portsmouth, Ohio, in the third- week of July that you didn't belong here?"

"Well, Jon, as I hope you remember, I was here," Arms joked, "but to answer your question, no! Baseball players get baseball players, and it really didn't take long for all of us to realize while this was certainly a different approach to creating this team, I think everyone pretty much saw the potential, and when you start winning together, it kind of all takes care of itself."

Handing off the scene, Jon Miller playfully sent things inside. "My partner Joe Morgan is now live in the Vipers clubhouse, don't get too wet, my buddy!"

Standing next to Manager Tommy Leach was former Reds great and HOF member Joe Morgan. In the background, players were being showered with bottles of a bubbly beverage.

"Thanks, Jon, I'm here with Tommy Leach surrounded by twenty-five guys who have reached that impossible dream and the man who helped lead the surge; congratulations Tommy Leach!"

"Joe, as I stand here getting soaked from all directions, I must say thanks to Cisco Wheeler, our owner. When he first came up with all of this, I know there were a lot of doubters, maybe myself a little, but these guys here are truly special and are all winners and I think they proved it yet again here tonight."

As if on cue, Sean Deeters and Karl Smith collectively poured a bottle over each one's head live on camera. Laughingly, Morgan stood there drenched in his Armani suit as he addressed the contents.

"The normal choice of beverage for a celebration such as this is usually champagne," Morgan chortled, "but tonight, it's a little different, tell everybody who might be wondering what are we taking our ceremonial shower with!"

"It's Fresca, Joe, a refreshing soft drink that the guys like, and this is what they chose for their party tonight."

"That's a little different! I have to admit when I was with the Reds when we won our back-to-back championships we used something a wee bit stronger!"

"Well, nothing against something with a little octane in it, but our guys know there's a lot of kids out there watching right now and they didn't want to get too out of line, if you know what I mean."

"Classy stuff! Thank you, Tommy Leach. Now let's go back upstairs where Jon Miller is standing by with owner Cisco Wheeler and Vipers CEO Brandon Briggs, Jon!"

The collapse of the Phillies in their own house was the outrage of fans who tuned their wrath to the ones who understood it the most. "Sports Radio 94, WIP, you're on the air with Angelo Cataldi as we go to Roxborough-Manayunk and Jon Barstow, good morning, John, what's up?"

"Don't hold me back, brother, I am as upset and pissed as I've ever been, I think maybe in my whole life!"

"And I can't imagine why," Cataldi laughed, "Don't tell me it's your hometown baseball team?"

"You got the player that is probably going to be the MVP playing like an NVG. That stands for Not Very Good. Angelo, they stink!"

"Ryan Howard, I'm guessing you're referring to there. He had his struggles at the plate. So, Gary, it doesn't sound like you are handling this very well at all."

"Game-four, we had it, man! How can you blow a 3-1 lead in the eighth when you got Lieber on the mound and some kid from BFE, who's only been with the team for a month. Manuel keeps Lieber in there to pitch to that gorilla guy, Smith, he's only their best home-run hitter and what does he do, he jacks it into Camden with a grand-slam! Why the hell didn't he bring in Gordon or Geary? That's why you have relief pitchers for, Angelo!"

"I get your point, Jon, you're dwelling on the 5-3 loss in game four, but I thought last night's game was the one that was in the bag, but then you had that dropped ball in the seventh by Burrell that kept the inning alive." Cataldi added.

21 DOWN IN VEGAS

"Christ, how can a guy who hit 29 home runs and almost 100 -RBIs on the season, drop a can of corn like that with two-outs and let two-runs score. My nine year old kid could have caught that damn thing!"

Angelo Cataldi continued to try and placate his more than fanatic caller with some credible baseball observations.

"If you noticed, John, there were two outs when I believe Snyder hit that fly ball to Burrell in left. Did you notice that both Vipers runners were cranked up at top speed and never stopped? You never see that kind of hustle in the Major Leagues anymore. I'm sorry, but most players in a situation like that start heading to the dugout."

"Lazy bums! That's all they are these days. I do have to give those kids credit. They were fun to watch and they came to play baseball. The Phillies should be ashamed that they don't play hard like that. Howard was so locked up at the plate that I think he's going to have to go see a shrink after that knuckleball thing!"

"Well, Jon, we have other callers on the line and have to move on, but I thank you for joining us this morning. I'm Angelo Cataldi and you're listening to all Philadelphia sports on WIP-Sports Radio 94."

Later in the day it was a mirror- image of chatter on all the West Coast sports stations. It was no secret that the New York Yankees would be the team to beat, but no one including the Oakland 'A's' were able to find the magic decoder ring to explain how to do it. Unlike the sandpaper-rough crowd in Philadelphia, it looked and sounded like most bay-view fans didn't really hold out much hope anyway. Swept in four, there's not much wiggle-room for sympathy or excuses.

17ᵀᴴ INNING

"The Home of 'A's baseball on 1550 KCYC, I'm Steve Bitker along with Vince Cotroneo and Vince, It certainly has been a frustrating five –days, I must admit. It's always nice to find a silver lining in a dark cloud, but the problem here was that it never stopped raining so you could even look up."

"Losing three out of four of your games by double digit scores simply means you weren't built for this kind of post-season adventure." Vince Cotroneo added. "I mean seriously, the "A's' pitching was awful to the point that what was Ken Macha supposed to do? He used everybody I believe on the roster who could pitch and it still didn't make any difference."

"With all respect to Billy Beane, he's great getting to the play-offs, but as you alluded to, Vince, there's a higher step that this team just can't seem to take."

"It's always tough to lose, but always fun being here playing baseball with your partner." Cotroneo added.

"You too, Vince, thanks so much and as always look forward to next season. Steve Bitker here again to recap the Oakland 'A's' as they lose to the Yankees today by a score of 13-5 to capture the American League Championship for the twenty-seventh time in their history sweeping Oakland in four.

"With that, the 2006 World Series is now set as the little team that could, will! The Las Vegas Vipers and Champions of the National League take on the Bronx Bombers from New York beginning this Saturday night. It's a series that I believe will garner more than just a little casual interest from a team that has seemingly broken and re-written almost every rule you can imagine for this game. It should be one for the ages.

"For Vince Cotroneo and myself, we thank you for following Oakland Athletics baseball all season long right here on your home for the best bay sports coverage on 1550-KCYC."_

In Portsmouth, Ohio, the usual small-town coconut pipeline of local news and information suddenly roared into a gear that had not been tested since the 1937 flood.

The *Portsmouth Daily Times* had published an everyday morning newspaper beginning back in 1887, but on Wednesday, October 18th, they published a special afternoon edition featuring headline size font last used when Pearl Harbor was bombed in 1941. *"Eagles Land In World Series!"* was now being screamed from the street corners all over the town.

Local radio station WNXT-AM had somehow acquired the tapes to the playoff games called from KVPR Radio in Las Vegas and were now playing them all back to back in sequence.

News reporters Sam McKibbin and Mistie Cook had stayed at the station for the past twenty-four hours straight breaking down sound-clip interviews from the players' families and friends for inserts into the games.

Chip Maillet of WIOI-AM 1010 set up a live open microphone kiosk on the downtown Roy Rogers Esplanade to let anybody who wanted to stop by express their thoughts and tributes.

While the city had not been a stranger to the national spotlight during the past few months, the floodgates exploded with regional TV stations as well as all the networks being called into action to find any different angle or style-points they could in reporting this most improbable scenario.

Holding back on their latest edition, *"Time Magazine"* suddenly released its latest creation featuring a split-cover photo of the Eagles and the Vipers with the words "Dream It!"

In conjunction with an afternoon press conference scheduled on the campus of Bentley State University, a spontaneous rally of students and supporters had erupted to the point where the college opened the doors to the Rhodes Athletic Center early so that the public could be there to be a part of the 3:30 p.m. forum.

Hosted by MIX 99.3's morning voice Hobie Harrison, over 3,000 fans filled the capacity Rhodes auditorium to drink from the cup of unstoppable praise and accomplishment. Followed by University President Howard Morris, the dais of speakers included S.I.D. Jeff Perez, Former Major Leaguer and Portsmouth resident Al Oliver, Reds super-scout Gene Bennett, and as a surprise guest driving down from Cincinnati was Hall of Fame Announcer Marty Brennaman.

Stepping to the microphone with grin from ear to ear, Marty looked around at the pulsating multitude gathered together and after a long pause, uttered the words; "Unbelievable!" With that thunderous decibel level rose to somewhere between the Rolling Stones firing "Start Me Up," live to the landing of a Boeing 747 on the parking lot. He let the moment linger on until slowly waning away before speaking.

"You all might be wondering why I'm here standing in front of you today. When Gene Bennett called me this morning and asked if I was available and the first thing I said was 'what the hell would they want me there for?' He then explained that Portsmouth, the fans, and especially the players of Bentley State University were all Reds fans first. That said, it made sense for me to run down here from Cincinnati to share my love and joy with you all and help put it in perspective on what an elite accomplishment we all got a chance to witness this season."

Another tumultuous crescendo swelled across the hall as Marty truly captured the moment. Fifteen minutes later, Marty knew it was time to ignite the room.

"I talked to Keith Madison late last night to offer him my congratulations, and we talked for about ten minutes. I can honestly say that he and everyone else is so fired up and ready for the final challenge."So vividly I remember talking to my dear friend and colleague Joe Nuxhall in the booth when the Vipers played the Reds just about a month ago in Cincinnati."I can remember telling him, and this is while the Reds were still in the hunt, mind you, I remember saying how much like a veteran club these guys looked and how professional they carried themselves. Like everyone else I admit that I was a skeptic at first, I used my own criteria of just watching them play and I could instantly tell that these guys are so differently special!"

The moment was at hand for Marty to do what he did best and light the fuse.

"Again, I thank Gene Bennett for inviting me down here today to share with all of you this very special moment that's being generated here in Portsmouth and at Bentley State University. So as a National League guy myself, and on behalf of the Reds and the rest of the league, there's really nothing more left to say guys except…bring on them Damn Yankee's!"

On that final decree, the crowd was firmly on its feet and *ESPN Sports Center* had their opening clip for the night!

As the celebration continued in Portsmouth, the *New York Times* headline for the next day sent mild-shock waves across the eve of one of sport's biggest events when it declared, "Vipers Insiders Linked to Gambling Scandal!" The story was written by James Risen and Eric Lichtblau and chronicled the ongoing Los Angeles Police investigation into professional sports memorabilia being used for an illegal gambling sting.

According to the story, the names of Carla Harris and Syleanna Griffin had been found among the muck-pile of notes that had been intercepted during the warehouse raids. No formal charges had been filed against anyone to date, but the uncanny timing of this breaking story, just two-days before the beginning of the World Series, was highly suspicious.

Overall, the details of the investigation were still very benign, but with the investigative release of some of the names of where the merchandise came from, it had now become a matter of public record.

"This story is pure horse 100 percent horse-shit!" Sean Deeters screamed across the room to Cliff Collier. "All we did was sign a few balls and a bat, which I paid for by the way, and gave them to the girls to just take care of their tickets with that scalper dude."

Arriving in New York only the night before, both players as well as the team were now able to bask in the never-so-polite slant of the sinister press.

Relaxing on his king bed at the Grand Hyatt and watching TV, Cliff seemed coolly unconcerned about all the hub-bub.

"Come on, Sean, the girls aren't not supposed to be here until Saturday. This thing will have blown over by then. It's just this city is trying to stick things in our heads that don't exist!

It's just mind-games or how you so classically put it…it's bovine fecal-matter."

"I said horse-shit! but we can handle it!" Deeters declared. "We've put up with all this press- garbage since the day we got here, but they don't deserve this! I can tell you now with all of the fan crush and diffused drama they've had to deal with just being our girlfriends, and soon my wife, there's a ton of stuff that we don't even know about."

"So when someone finally writes the book about what really went on behind the scenes during the year the Vipers stole the pennant, they'll have it nailed!" Cliff laughed.

"Right, I can't wait until we don't have to deal with all this crap and Tommy in the mornings too." Sean muttered. "I love the guy, but meetings are for bankers, not ball-players."

The Vipers right fielder's prophecy couldn't have been more on target as early Thursday; the team had their first visitation at the address of the most revered sports arena on the planet located at 1 E.161 Street, the Bronx, New York, New York. Formal to be certain, but most of the locals simply knew it as just Yankee Stadium.

"Here we are, girls! You are now all standing in the holy grail of what this game is all about." Leach began. "Walk around, check it out, spend a few personal moments knowing that you'll be walking in the same patches of grass and dirt of Ruth, Gehrig, DiMaggio, to mention a few. These hallowed walls of baseball purity are also the former home and name-sake of one of our own here today, that would be Bombo Rivera!"

21 DOWN IN VEGAS

Points offered was a definite and much needed ice-breaker for the team that drew playful stabs and barbs to one of the quiet, but good-natured leaders of the team.

"Bombo was a god!" Chadwick declared. "Don't ever forget it!"

Waiting on the trice to settle, Tommy suddenly put on his serious side.

"Listen up! We as the visiting team have the facility here today until 2:00 p.m. Tomorrow morning, we will meet here again and that's before media day which starts at 1:00 in the afternoon. This is a mandatory meeting where every press idiot will be here, so just be prepared. Following that I will need everybody in the conference room at 4:00 at the hotel. I think that's about it. Right now, you are all free to roam the cabin until our practice starts at 11:00 out the field. Sean and Cliff, come with me."

Walking briskly behind their manager on route to a quick right and then a left turn into a small room titled "Visitors' Manager," they all quickly sat down where they all found a seat.

"Look, guys, I didn't address this thing in the group because I personally don't believe it's any big thing. The other side of the coin is that we have to deal with it, so tell me exactly what went on here with all this memorabilia crap!'

"Syleanna and Carla met these guys in LA. when we were playing there and they gave them some tickets, and in return, we signed a couple of autographed balls and bats! That's about it." Sean explained.

"Skip, we've done this dozens of times for friends and charity and stuff." Cliff added. "This story in the paper makes no sense and makes them sound like a bunch of hoodlums or criminals or something!"

As the exasperation level between the two began to accelerate, Leach forcibly regained the room with his verbal tone.

"Look, I'm not mad!" he explained. "I'm just pissed-off that something as stupid as this has simply become an issue. As for you, us, and the rest of our fans get ready for the most important moment in our lives. I've already talked to Cisco and Brandon and they have been on the phone with the commissioner already today trying to smooth things out. It's just the timing right now couldn't have been worse!"

"So what's going to happen?" Sean cautiously asked.

"First of all, there have been no charges filed against anyone." Tommy explained. "Second, every sports team on the planet is allegedly represented in this hall of fame 'storage unit'...including the Yankees. My gut feeling is at best, it will take years to figure out how they got all this stuff and where it came from. Knowing the mental mind- fuck of this game, I truly believe this is just a grand-plan designed for distraction to keep you all from doing our job."

"So, what about Carla and Syleanna? Cliff huffed. "What's the deal with them? Are they even allowed to come to the games or what?"

"I can't answer that question...yet" Tommy replied. "Let's get past all this phantom voo-doo chicanery first and see what happens."

Surprisingly, media day at Yankee Stadium experienced very little questioning from reporters on the latest chronicle. Most of the buzz focused on how a small ex-college team felt about playing in the house of the most successful Major League monolith in history and the biggest show-case on the planet. Television and newspaper scribes scrambled and squeezed their way into every position for an effort to laud the perfect question.

"Mike Downey from the *Chicago Tribune*. My question is for Manager Tommy Leach. Tommy, let me be the first to say I am one of the most stunned sports columnists in America standing here today addressing you and the team's accomplishments. It is truly a remarkable story. I would simply like to know was there ever a point during all of this that you honestly felt you had just been designated as the new captain of the *Titanic*?"

"If you're referring to the beginning when all the changes were first made, sure, there were a lot of questions." Leach replied. "Something of this magnitude had never been done before. Fortunately the game of baseball is still the game of baseball. The only thing that changes is the guys inside the uniforms. Once we all got to see the quality of the players coming in and what they could do on the field, I knew instantly the ship would stay afloat, and to contradict your earlier reference about the *Titanic*, as you can see, we did made it to New York."

Sarcastic groans and off-handed titters reacted to the room on that one. As the managers, players, and personnel for both teams continued to cruise from station to station, Cisco Wheeler and Brandon Briggs were having their own private confab upstairs.

"Selig says that there's really no basis for any of this and he too is highly pissed it's even an issue." Briggs declared Cisco.

"These are the best boys I've ever seen, Brandon, and why does this even have a shit-shingle of relevance to anything!" Wheeler blustered.

"Look, Cisco, Bud Selig is also a lawyer and he said that just because you provided the 'evidence,' that in no way indicts you on how it is to be used. Anybody can sell or trade something to anybody as long as it's legal, and to my knowledge, baseballs and bats have not yet been declared as official contraband."

"So what is he going to do about it?" Wheeler brashly asked.

"He told me he has been in contact with the D.A. in Los Angeles and that he plans to issue some kind of statement within the next twenty-four hours to address it. He by the way also feels this is nothing more than a ruse by the Yankees to throw interference in the way of the series toward us and he's completely not happy with it at all!"

"Well, join Sargent Pepper and the entire fucking lonely hearts club band, Bud!" Cisco exclaimed,

"Looks like we could all use a little refresher course of anger management today." Branden Briggs lightly chuckled.

"I don't need anger management! Wheeler added. "I just need people to stop pissing me off!

The pilgrimage to the "Big Apple" from Portsmouth, Ohio, had already begun for game -one of the World Series on Saturday. Friday morning Market Street Café was the meeting place and travel-headquarters for Carla, Syleanna, and others as discussion ensued over a delicious egg and ham wrap with lattes: there were a lot of questions also on the menu.

"I talked to Sean last night and he said several of the reporters have already tried to talk to him about us and this whole thing and he wasn't happy at all," Syleanna revealed. "He said he wasn't sure what is going to happen."

"Look, I was the one who blabbed to that jerk from the paper." Carla shot back. "He started out like he was interviewing me about the team and then here come all these questions on how we got our tickets for the Dodger games. Before I knew it, I was a guest star on *LA Law!* I'm really sorry I was so honest."

"I don't know what to do," Syleanna admitted. "We are supposed to fly out tonight, and you know we'll be instant targets for the press. Just look how it is now with *Regis and Kelly* practically here on our own doorstep." She laughed.

The reference was to the popular TV morning show setting up and broadcasting live the day before from the popular downtown eatery.

Both Carla and Syleanna had both been asked to appear, but refused to avoid any embarrassing questions.

"So…OK…what are we going to do here, sis?" Carla asked, "We got plane tickets, we got real authorized passes for both games from the university, we can't just stop now!"

After a long pause of silence, Syleanna looked up from her wrap with a crooked but playful smile.

"Did you talked to Cliff about it?" she cautiously muttered.

"Hey, the guys want us there, babe! It's their party and they want us to crash it! Screw the press! If we don't do this, we will regret it for the rest of our lives. Just always remember, it's always easier to get forgiveness than permission!"

"You're right, to hell with it!" the usually soft-spoken Syleanna suddenly retorted. "We've been in deeper ditches of shit than this before, and we've always been able to climb out smelling like a gallon of Ezra!"

"See, that's the attitude of the Syl that I know and love!" Carla chirped. "I'll get the check on this one, and you can catch me up tonight for relaxing dinner in New York City!"

18TH INNING

"This is a special edition of *Baseball Tonight on ESPN*, and I'm Chris Berman on the eve of perhaps the most anticipated meeting of any two teams ever to meet in the Fall Classic! Good evening, everyone, as we are live at Yankee Stadium for this special look at a matchup that few knew could ever have happened as the genetically altered Las Vegas Vipers are now set to take on the 'Cranky' Yankees for all the marbles.

"First and breaking news is a statement from Baseball Commissioner Bud Selig on the ongoing investigation into the 'ticket-gate' story that broke several days ago in the *New York Times*. According to Selig, there is no course of illegal behavior that has been proven from any of the parties who may have, willing or unwilling, donated to or sold items to the alleged gambling-ring in Los Angeles revolving around professionally signed sports items and memorabilia. According to Selig, who talked with the authorities, He reported that every, I repeat, every professional team including boxing, Olympic sports, and many others are all represented in this makeshift 'Hall of Shame.' Those again are Bud Selig's words.

"The commissioner also mentioned that he wasn't pleased with the slanted journalism of the *New York Times* as it pertained to several of the Viper' girlfriends who allegedly traded some signed balls and bats for tickets. Selig also noted that until or if there are any charges to be filed in the case, Major League Baseball will not get involved in any way. So, that's the latest on that and as I've said many times, part-time information and full-time opinions can be dangerous.

"Back to the real epicenter of the joyous juice, the pitching matchups are now set and in place for the Vipers and the Yanks and so here…here…here we go! Tomorrow night, it's two-aces at the same time, Randy Johnson goes for the Yankees while Gary 'What a Fine' Steinman hurls for the Vipers. Game two, it's Mike Mussina versus Scotty "The Golden" Arms. In game three in Las Vegas on Tuesday night it will match Chien-Ming Wang against Mitch Milhuff, and game four Wednesday afternoon has Brad Zeiber scheduled to go against Jaret Wright. That surprises me a little that Brad Scarbury isn't in that slot, but holding back a proven strong starter in a series like this might be an just an insurance policy brokered by Manager Tommy Leach.

"Talking to my friend and the Vipers Hitting Coach Von 'Purple' Hayes, he feels strong that the Las Vegas bats are ready for the challenge against the Yankees pitching corps who are throwing potentially two Hall of Famers in the series with Johnson and Mussina.

"And of course the newest edition to the Berman 'nickname' Hall of Fame for the 2006 World Series is the Vipers "King Kong" Karl Smith. Even though I wasn't the one who came up with that one, Karl, you are now officially enshrined with Juan 'Going' Going' Gonzales, Burt 'Be Home' Blyleven, and Mike 'Enough' Aldrete, congratulations!

"I'm Chris Berman live from Yankee Stadium in New York and you're watching a special edition of *ESPN's Baseball Tonight*! When we return, our panel of know-it-alls will be Dave Winfield, Jim Palmer, Johnny Bench, and Whitey Herzog to discuss the match-up of the 'Knocks in the Bronx'. We'll be right back!"

Inside the bowels of Yankee stadium anticipation was at an apex as outside on the sweet and watered turf, the shadows were growing longer. The clocks hands stood transfixed at 5:30 p.m. as Von Hayes, Keith Madison, Jarred Brewster, Tom Browning, and the rest promptly corralled all of the principals involved for a final shakedown. This time, Manager Tommy Leach didn't need to quiet down the room as you could hear the proverbial pin-stripe drop.

21 DOWN IN VEGAS

"All right, here we go, history is now at hand for all of you to write. The good thing about all of this is that you can choose the outcome of the script. They say that history is written by the winners, which is absolutely true!" Tommy Leach began. "I didn't stay up all night thinking of some kind of corny bull-shit speech to try and inspire and get the most out of you. You guys have already given that to me since the day we met!

"In a few minutes, we will walk through this tunnel together as a team and out onto the field to play the New York Yankees. You all right here, in is this very small and antiquated locker room, and guess what? You are feeling the same moment and experiencing the very same emotions that this games greatest immortals also shared.

"Right now, think about it. Stan Musial, Jackie Robinson, Pete Rose, Mike Schmidt, Dwight Gooden, and not to get too historical here, but our Right Fielder Sean Deeters is going to be playing in the very spot that Babe Ruth patrolled for fifteen-years. Collier here will be filling in for DiMaggio, Chadwick for Lou Gehrig. The fact is that while all of this is pretty much amazing, the fact stands that you all have earned this right to be here…today…right now!"

With nervous noise now beginning to ascend, Tommy Leach ended with a cascading directive.

"You've already proved that you are the best in the National League, now let's get out there tonight and show everybody on this big blue marble that you are the best in the entire world!"

"Where's all that fucking noise coming from?" Derek Jeter annoyingly asked Joe Torre.

"Beats me, sounds like it's down the hall, but in this old creaky place, who knows!"

As all the players took to the field for warmups, the garnish to the stretches, the running, and batting practice, then came a special reverberation from the PA speakers high above Yankee Stadium; it was the legendary voice of Bob Shepard.

With an intonation that sounded like he came from perhaps an out of the way European country, there was arguably no more distinctive declaration of New York sports authenticity than he.

During his career, Bob Sheppard had announced more than 4,500 Yankees baseball games on the PA over a period of 56 years, including 22 pennant-winning seasons and 13 World Series championships; he called 121 consecutive postseason contests, 62 games in 22 World Series, and six no-hitters, including three perfect games.

For more than a half-century, Shepard was the voice of the New York Giants football games, encompassing nine conference championships, three NFL titles (1956, 1986, 1990), and the game often called "the greatest football game ever played." That isolated event was the classic 1958 championship loss to the Baltimore Colts.

Sheppard's smooth and distinctive baritone delivery with his precise and consistent elocution became the iconic aural symbols of both the old Yankee Stadium and the Giants Stadium as well.

Reggie Jackson famously nicknamed him "The Voice of God," and it was the Red Sox right fielder Carl Yastrzemski who once said, "You're not in the big leagues until Bob Sheppard announces your name."

"Look around at this place!" Gary Duzan casually mentioned while fielding grounders. "This ain't no Omaha!"

"Hey, brother, think about it!" second baseman Brooks Snyder shot back. "Three months ago, we were chowing down in that 'Boiler Room' place in Nebraska before we played LSU and now look, last night it was dinner last night at 'Mickey Mantle's. That's will always be a scrapbook moment in my trophy case."

With the rest of the Vipers taking their final throws and swings, it was the Yankees play-by-play announcers that were setting up the final showdown of the 2006 baseball season.

"Well, here we are and good evening from historic Yankee Stadium in New York, I'm John Sterling along with Suzyn Waldman, and I have to honestly say since 1889, that's the year I began my career here with this team, I've never seen a more sincere, or should I say most anticipated showdown between two Major League teams perhaps in the history of this sport."

"Total agreement here, John," Suzyn added. "What I find unusual is people and fans who haven't followed sports in years are all about what's been happening with this team from Las

Vegas.""Agreed 100 percent Suzyn." Sterling continued. "By now, most know that the Vipers' most unorthodox method of revamping their team in mid-season was by literally hiring a small baseball college team from Portsmouth, Ohio, on a whim from Las Vegas baseball owner Cisco Wheeler. Honestly at that time, most of us in this sport, including myself, thought he had gone completely off the rails and I'm not talking about just a little bit either. This was the kind of crazy you were never warned about because no one even knew that this level even existed! Now that he's been exonerated from that rap, here we go!"

"John, fighting hard and almost winning the national college title, three months earlier, they have earned the right to be here not only winning the National League title, but now playing here against the Yankees for baseball's biggest prize." Waldman again expressed.

Praising the competition was always a bit dicey in your own house, but in this case, the little extra- relish to the mustard was well-deserved as John Sterling wrapped up the accolades.

"Witnessing many classic moments from this perch, I am not in the predicting business, but I will say this. The next scheduled seven-games in my opinion could possibly be the best sports theater and a showdown for the ages of which we've never seen before!"

Scanning the crowd, it was the most complex mixture of human beings you could imagine. Hard-core Yankee fans, movie stars, entertainers, plus the small-town fervor of the Bentley State faithful were now all thrown together as one. A sign brought and hung by local Portsmouth businessman Tim Wagner showed a picture of the Vipers' left fielder Karl "King Kong" Smith standing on top of the Empire State Building holding a bat, swatting away at the faces of several Yankee foes.

Nearly indescribable was the complexity of the setting when Bob Shepard once again called for a reverent gathering of respect.

"Ladies and gentleman, welcome to Yankee Stadium for game-one of the 2006 World Series as the City of New York welcomes all fans of baseball and a special salute to the accomplishments of the national League Champions, the Las Vegas Vipers!"

That dictum was met with a surprisingly hardy roar of applause, figuring the fact that it was from within the enemies' lair.

"I now ask you to remove your hats as our national anthem will be performed by a gentleman who was born here in the heart of the Bronx and has represented our great city with honor and pride. Over the years, his records have sold millions worldwide while he has always maintained that New York state of mind. Please welcome singer/songwriter, Billy Joel."

Stepping up to the microphone, Joel fought a standing ovation before dutifully breaking into the first lines of "Oh say can you see?"

On completion, Billy Joel couldn't help but to then show some hometown allegiance meant to fire up the crowd as he enthusiastically proclaimed, "I love you, New York! Go Yankees!" That response got the walls of old Yankee Stadium rattling at a Jericho-like magnitude!

Bob Shepard next spoke into the microphone to announce the lineups. The names that had slowly become known to all over three-short months were now being heralded as the best to step onto the turf. Names like Snyder, Deeters, Smith, Collier, Chadwick, Kennedy, Duzan, and Pouge were now step in place with Rodrigues, Jeter, Williams, Posada, and Cano. The lineup cards had been exchanged at home plate which now left but one thing left to do: "Play ball!"

Again doing what he had done more than any other public address announcer in the history sports, the distinct tones of Bob Shepard would now forever be a part of the record.

"Batting lead-off for the Las Vegas Vipers, second base, Brooks Snyder."

"Come on, Brooksie, get us going!" Sean Deeters yelled from the on-deck circle. Randy Johnson had now completed his warmup pitches and that little undefinable zone between "I'm ready and now here it comes" was now in place. Looking into Posada for the sign, Snyder's only instinct was first pitch down the middle, and he was right.

"Johnson's first pitch, swung on and a line drive up the middle into center field, and just like that, the Vipers have broken up Randy Johnson's bid for a no-hitter!" Radio play-by-play announcer Ralph

21 DOWN IN VEGAS

Hacker laughed. "It looked like Johnson was just trying to set the tone for the game with a first-pitch strike and Snyder guessed right."

On the bench, Jarred Brewster plopped down next to Tommy Leach with a suggestion.

"Skip, Johnson has trouble when he gets scored on first. I ran the numbers and you have a 64 percent chance of winning if he pitches from behind in the score. I would surprise them and let Sean bunt him over."

Manager Tommy Leach had been used to hearing Jarred's backhanded logic since jump and had slowly gotten used to his accuracy in most observations that he brought to the table.

"Have him bunt, now?" Leach countered.

"Yes, did you see how flustered Johnson looked after that first-pitch? They wouldn't be expecting it, just saying"

"One on and no-outs here in the first and that brings up Sean Deeters to the plate. Deeters has had a great season as a Viper, batting .310 with twenty-doubles and has been clutch when the team needs runs." Hacker continued. "Johnson glances over to Snyder off- first, now looks, and fires!Deeters to squares to bunt, and he lays down a dandy rolling towards the front of the mound. Johnsons' running, up with it and his only play will be at first. Wow…I don't think anybody saw that coming. A sacrifice bunt in just the first- inning, and after just two-pitches, the Vipers now have a runner in scoring position."

That's kind of been the Vipers way, Ralph, doing the expected when you least expect it" Pete Harnisch observed. "It's obvious that against this future Hall of Famer that small-ball might be a wise decision."

It took eleven-pitches for Vipers Center Fielder Cliff Collier to finally ground-out to Yankee second- baseman Robinson Cano, but that brought "King Kong" Karl Smith to the plate with Brooks Snyder now standing on third.

"Look at that guy in center field!" TV analyst Joe Buck laughed. "I've seen a lot of crazy signs in this place, but kudos to creativity on that one. 'Kong' as he is referred to by his teammates, now steps in as the Vipers first inning continues."

Randy Johnson had a certain look when he wasn't happy on the mound, and that appearance was evident as Karl Smith dug into the squares. Standing six- foot, nine- inches tall, his walking around behind the mound and rubbing the ball was never a good sign to the batter. Again stepping onto the rubber, Johnson now faced the Las Vegas Vipers biggest long—ball threat and he knew it.

Since coming up to the Major Leagues, Karl Smith was perhaps the biggest student in re-inventing his game. In college, he was the team's "crusher" and he knew it. In the Major Leagues, he had learned to ease the pressure on himself and just go with the pitches. This was a huge plus for him for being able to keep his batting average high while still putting some sting on the ball. Ralph Hacker was again making the call for KVPR radio.

"It's a 2-2 count on Smith as again Johnson sets on the rubber. Karl has shown some pretty good resolve at the plate as here comes the pitch. Swung on and it's a soft-liner to right *over* the outstretched glove of Robinson Cano and Las Vegas draws first-blood as Brooks Snyder scampers home, and the Vipers now lead the Yanks 1-0 here in the first!

The NBC-TV cameras were once again focused in on a jumping Tim Wagner holding his "Kong" sign in center field and Joe Buck played it to the zenith.

"There's one happy man!" Buck laughed as the camera moved in for the close-up with the sign of the Vipers left fielder swatting the Yanks from up high and above. As the camera shot moved to the mound, color analyst Tim McCarver had the next best line.

"And there's one 'not so happy man,' Joe, as Randy Johnson has given up a Texas League flair-single and he don't like it! The one thing you have to respect about this guy on the mound, and that is, you always know where you stand with him."

Gathering his wits, Randy Johnson needed only three-pitches against the Vipers first baseman Bombo Chadwick to make a statement and bring his team in from the field to the dugout.

"Play strong! Hold 'em!" Keith Madison shouted from his perch on the steps as the Vipers moved into their respective positions. Since the game was being played under the American League rules, out-

21 DOWN IN VEGAS

fielder Luke Shepard would assume the designated hitting duties for the Vipers as Jason Giambi would DH for the Yanks.

What makes the theatre of sport so hypnotic and mesmerizing is always the unexpected. In an arena that is so amped up on expectations, the true human element of spirit is the beauty of derailing what many fans and followers of any given game have already imagined in their heads. Until this year, the name Gary Steinman had simply been a face in the crowd. Considered by many a decent Major League pitcher, he could go either way on any given day.

Clive Gammon of *Sports Illustrated* once said of Steinman, "This guy has all the physical tools you could ever ask for, but you have to wonder about the most important organ; his heart. I have seen many players with far less talent take their careers much further down the road. My frustration is simply watching a guy who sometimes acts as if he doesn't want to even be there…and pitches like it.On the other hand, when he's inspired, he can be the best there ever was. With all respects to Roy Hobbs, it's really all up to Gary Steinman as to the path that he chooses to follow."

"Now batting leadoff for your New York Yankees and playing center field, Johnny Damon!" Bob Shepard's words were again met with instant approval as Steinman readied himself for the biggest baseball challenge he had ever faced.

You can often tell by the first couple of pitches of any ballgame which way the rest of the day will follow. Nine-pitches into this mega-monitored Saturday night classic, Steinman had disposed of Damon, Derek Jeter, and Bobby Abreu in order. A ground-out, pop fly, and down on strikes was now in the record book as again the Vipers returned for the top of the second inning.

While rally chatter was always a staple of dugout jargon, Gary Steinman silently slipped into the corner to be by himself. His teammates all knew simply to leave him alone as his ritual was accepted and respected, knowing that still waters run deep.

For the next two hours, the fans at Yankee Stadium witnessed an array of futility from batters from both teams. While low-scoring contests are usually not a fan favorite, Joe Buck and Tim Mc Carver were both duly impressed with the effort.

"Who knew that a scratch hit and a run in the first inning would be the only score to stand up so far tonight, Tim, these guys are both on fire!" Buck gushed.

"Right you are, Joe, and the thing that amazes me," McCarver continued, "is that here we are in the top of the eighth- inning, and since the first, no batter has advanced past first-base. You had a single by Shefield in the fourth and an infield hit by Jeter in the sixth, but that's been it for the Yankees. The Vipers got a hit by Deeters in the fourth- inning and a walk to Gary Duzan in the seventh, and besides that, it's been a pretty empty night of running the base-paths for everybody."

Gary Steinman had thrown just seventy-four pitches as he faced the bottom of the Yankees lineup in the eight-inning. Leading by one with six-batters to go, the Vipers at this point looked unstoppable.

Steinman ran the count even to Hedeki Matsui before a fly ball to right and Sean Deeters quickly put him away. Jose Posada had come up empty all night and continued his struggles at the plate whiffing on three-pitches. That brought to the plate Robinson Cano.

"Two out here in the bottom of the eight and the Yankees second-sacker again steps in 0-3 on the night grounding out twice and being retired on an infield fly."

Ralph Hacker and Pete Harnisch on KVPR struggled to contain their inner- enthusiasm, but both secretly knew the possibility of what might be.

Steinman worked Cano into a one-ball, two-strike count before the unthinkable erupted.

"Gary Steinman working at a fast pace and again ready to deliver to Cano, the pitch…it's a line drive OFF of Steinman. The ball rolls toward second as its' picked up by Snyder, the throw…Cano is out at first, but Steinman is down Pete! Oh my lord, that wicked line-drive looked like it hit him flush in the face!"

"He is hurt Ralph." Harnisch confirmed, "I can already see there's blood coming from his left eye, and that was a horrible thing to see!"

"Gary Steinman is still motionless lying on the mound as the trainers from both teams and teammates as well are all surrounding him. The ball coming off the bat of Cano appeared to hit him somewhere on the upper-left cheek." Hacker explained. "This is such a horrible thing to witness as this young man was pitching perhaps the best game of his life. Manager Tommy Leach, his staff, and his players are all standing around him. This is really hard to watch. Everybody is looking for what, if any movement that might be going on!"

The FOX-TV crew was equally as stunned at what they had just witnessed, and the replays were immediately cancelled until clarification of his condition could be determined. Expressing his deep concern, you could easily see that Joe Buck was shaken.

"The unthinkable has happened here tonight, Tim, and all of our prayers go out that Gary Steinman that he isn't as seriously hurt as it appears and that he will be all right."

A stunned and silent Yankee stadium crowd suddenly started to spring to life once again as it was evident that Gary Steinman was now in the midst of standing up. Once erect and appearing to be standing on his own feet, the crowd followed suit.

"There's something we all held our breaths to see!" Ralph Hacker beamed with relief. "Gary Steinman is finally up and surrounded by Vipers trainer Larry Starr and teammates, but he is apparently standing on his own!"

"They still have that towel over his left eye, and by the looks of it, there had to be some kind of cut or abrasion as it's pretty much covered in red." Pete Harnisch inserted. "By all appearances, he looks alert and is talking to everyone, and by the grace of god, we are all happy to see that!"

"Gary Steinman is now walking off the mound and listen to that incredible standing ovation, folks, as everyone here in the Bronx including all the Yankee players are paying respects to a wounded warrior here tonight!"

"You talk about class," Harnisch echoed, "Robinson Cano just went over and hugged the guy before he slipped into the walkway to the locker room. That is a true showing of what this game is all about as class is not being noticed, but it's about being remembered. That's a scene there that will be shared and should be for the ages!" Ralph Hacker knew it was time for a break in the action.

"We'll keep our ears open for a medical report as soon as we hear anything we will most certainly pass it along, but for now, it looks like 'Dirty' Ernie Fuller' is warming up in Vipers bullpen and we will expect to see him shortly. You're listening to Vipers World Series Baseball on KVPR-AM, Las Vegas"

The Vipers top of the ninth-inning was Terrence Kennedy, Doug Pouge, and Luke Shepard as a pall of obvious concern was wafting through the Vipers dugout. Gary Steinman had been taken from the stadium by ambulance to Calvary Hospital in the heart of the Bronx and no word had yet been released on his condition.

After eight strong innings and a major delay, Manager Joe Torre opted to remove Randy Johnson in favor of legendary right-handed closer Mariano Rivera. It didn't take long for "The Sandman" to do his job as the bottom of the Viper lineup went down in quick order.

Anticipation of the Yankee fans was now at a desperate level in the bottom of the ninth- inning to somehow, anyhow, create their team to victory. "Dirty" Ernie Fuller would be facing the top of the order as Johnny Damon now settled in to a thunderous soundscape. And like he had done so many times in his career, when it came to a clutch hit, Damon took a fuller- fastball for a ride.

"There's a deep fly to center off the bat of Johnny Damon as Collier is in full pursuit and…it's off the wall! Cliff Collier gets it and fires a seed back to the infield to Snyder at second and Damon is in there! Great fielding by Collier on that one or it could have easily been a triple!" Joe Buck described. "All right, is it Yankee magic- time here in the ninth? Derek Jeter now steps to the plate with a huge opportunity on the line. Jeter has gone 1-3 and now looks to even things up or even turn- off the lights here at Yankee stadium."

"Fuller nibbled on the corners until the count was full. The next pitch would be the biggest opportunity for the Yankees yet. Ernie Fuller looks, he's set…and to the plate and Jeter swings and sends this one deep down the line to right, it's in the corner!"

The collective groans from the 48,000 fans could be heard all the way to Flushing before the TV announcers knew what happened.

Sean Deeters came running with the ball high in hand, then quickly throwing it back to second just an eye-lash instant before Damon got back.

"What a play by Sean Deeters!" Buck exhorted. "That ball left our camera angle of sight, but look now at Sean Deeters as he slides into the wall to make that catch in foul territory. Wow, you don't see that happen often here very often in this ballpark!"

With Damon now back on second, Bobby Abreu took his turn *out at the plate* to change history.

Abreu was a new-comer to the Yanks coming over at the end of July at the trading deadline from the Phillies along with Cory Lidle for lefthander Matt Smith and prospects. Since wearing the pin-stripes for just a couple of months, he had been a major cog in their continued dominance.

Against the crafty Fuller, all Abreu knew was he liked to paint the corners of the strike- zone. Holding back on a 2-2 count, he thought he had the pitch to hit; almost.

Reaching for and outside fastball, Bobby Abreu slapped a slow grounder directly to Gary Duzan at short. Throwing quickly to first, Abreu beat the play by a step as Damon running on contact was now just ninety feet from tying the game at third. One out, bottom of the ninth, as Yankee Stadium was now all standing including Alex Rodrigues at the plate. Tom Browning quickly pranced to the mound for a full-summit meeting between him, Fuller, and the team.

"OK, Dirt…whatever you do, we got to keep in in the park, got it?" Browning barked." "You throw a knuckler to him, he knows it, and it will be in Queens, we don't want that."He's smart and he has watched the films. Guys in the outfield bring them in to play medium depth. We can give up one, but don't let this son of a bitch take it away from you. Do we all understand?"

"We got ya, Pug…no worries!" Snyder answered.

"Do it, guys, it's all yours to win! Let's go!"

Trotting back to the dugout, the entire Yankee nation was on red alert for something good to happen. Fuller was careful to the power-laden right-handed hitter nibbling again low to the corners at the right side of the plate. Ralph Hacker was again setting up the most important at-bat in Vipers baseball history to date.

"It's a 1-2 count to A-Rod and you can tell he's looking for something to drive grab ahold of here. Fuller looks hard for the sign to Pouge, he's set, ready, and the pitch!"

The crowd reaction could be heard bursting through the woofers and tweeters on radios a split-second before Ralph could call the shot."

"Rodriguez hits it high and deep to left! It's going to stay in the ballpark, but Johnny Damon is halfway home already. Karl Smith is under it, he has it, as Damon is now back at third …and now he's going to try and score! Here comes the ball, here comes Damon, and he's…out at the plate and the Vipers' win! Vipers' win!"

This crowd is stunned as Johnny Damon is nailed at the plate on a perfect throw from "King Kong" Karl Smith and the Vipers win on a thriller! Wow, that throw by Smith was right on the money as Doug Pouge applies a textbook tag, and you can't have much more excitement than that! The Las Vegas Vipers have just won game- one of the 2006 World Series! Incredible!"

"My question, Ralph, is what was Johnny Damon doing?" Pete Harnisch questioned. "You have to believe that maybe he forgot how many outs there were. Why didn't he just tag and run? He could have walked home from third!"

"Not sure on that one myself, Peter, but I know for sure it was an inning for the ages. Your game-totals for tonight is one-run, three-hits for the Vipers. No-runs, three-hits for the Yankees as Gary Steinman is the winning pitcher and Randy Johnson takes the loss for the Yanks. The "Dirt Man," Ernie Fuller comes in and pitches the ninth and picks up the save.

"We hope to have some news on Gary Steinman who got hit by a ball in the face in the eighth-inning, and while looked horrific, he did walk off the field on his own power as we understand he was taken to a local hospital for observation and I know all of our prayers go out for him tonight.

We'll be back with the Vipers post-game show right after this on KVPR and the Las Vegas Vipers Baseball Radio Network!"

21 DOWN IN VEGAS

The tale of two post-game press conferences couldn't have been any more diverse as Manager Tommy Leach stood with Karl Smith, Ernie Fuller, Cliff Collier, and Brooks Snyder. All questions were centered on their missing hero of the night.

"Let me get this out of the way!" Leach started. "I just talked with Calvary Hospital and all X-rays came back negative. Gary Steinman is now resting comfortably from what I understand. He did have a laceration under his left-eye that required several stiches, but aside from that, he will apparently be wearing a pretty big shiner for a while. So, that's all that I can give you on Gary's condition, and any other questions about it will be ignored."

"Dan Mcknight from the *New York Post* here. Does that mean that Steinman could lose his next start in the rotation?"

"Next!" Leach bellowed.

"Hey, I used to play for the Yankees and I'm an intelligent man!" Mcknight yelled back.

"No you didn't…and no you aren't! Next!" Tommy again yelled.

In the adjoining media room, the questioning to Manager Joe Torre was a little more sensitive bordering on "hardball harsh." Because of the magnitude of the series, there were far more news organizations permitted than just the usual beat-writers.

"Joe, Carl Ackerman from the *Toronto Sun*. It looks like you had the game tied in the ninth. Could you explain the Damon thing a little clearer?"

"What Damon thing?" Torre responded. "He got thrown out at the plate. You saw, I saw it, so what's to explain?

"C'mon, Joe," Ackerman laughed. "There had to been a reason why Johnny was half-way home when Smith caught the ball?"

"I guess you'll have to ask him and he's not here, next question?"

"Ben Spicer here from the *Scioto Voice*. Mr. Torre, I first want to thank you for letting me in with my credentials. I'm from Portsmouth, Ohio, and my question is had you ever heard of our town before the Bentley State Eagles became the Vipers?"

As the light-heartedness of the question caused a murmur of laughter from the rest of the room, Joe Torre answered the query with all respect from the young reporter.

"To answer your question, son, yes…I have heard of Portsmouth. Names like Al Oliver, Larry Hisle, Don Gullet who technically was a Kentuckian, but played for this organization, and another good friend of mine is Gene Bennett. Yes, I have heard of your hometown."

To break the tension in the room a bit more and to even interject a small dollop of humor, Torre added onto his thought.

"Just because I was born in the Italian Bronx here in New York City, people don't think I ever get around. Yes, I've been to towns like Portsmouth where the Motel 6 only sleeps 4!"

After the brief interlude of levity, the press went back on attack mode turning the Yankee manager back into his surly-self.

The Vipers clubhouse was far more somber than it should have been following the opening round win of the World Series. In the manager's office, there was a cluster of activity as Tommy Leach ordered no one to leave until they had a quick post-game meeting. The feeling between high and low was a substance of hard feeling for the young as well as the veteran players to grasp. Finally, Tommy and the staff made a quick exit to address the team.

"First of all, I want to thank Reverend John Gowdy from Temple Baptist Church in Portsmouth for sending us a direct prayer of thought for Gary this evening via the internet. His words were perfectly chosen and spoke as comfort for Gary as we all hope for a safe and speedy recovery. It is posted on the bulletin board for all of you to read. As of my last check about twenty- minutes ago to Calvary Hospital, Gary is alert, talking to the doctors of what I understand, but they are keeping him over-night for observation. Keep him in your own thoughts and prayers please."

There was a short pause before Leach continued which was rare for his fiery personality.

"You guys played one hell of a game out there tonight, I'm proud of every one of you" he began. "I always try and give credit where credit is due, but tonight our own star of the game is Jarred Brewster. He was the major factor on his advice that we went for the sacrifice in the first inning. I want to thank him publicly in front of you all for the little things that he pulls together that we sometimes may not see. Again, thank you Jarred!"

A spontaneous cheer erupted along with assorted brotherly catcalls roasting a brother they dearly loved. Finally, it was Tommy's stern look that brought the room back to silence and critical mass.

"You got your schedule for tomorrow? Everybody needs to be here no later than 3 p.m. Scotty, you have your charts, and all I ask is that you all understand that if we can win here tomorrow night, we may not have to come back again, and I hope you understand what that means. Curfew is tonight strictly at midnight and I'll be spot-checking. If you want to play tomorrow, you will be in your quarters on time. Again, this is all yours to win gentlemen. Rest up and I'll see you all tomorrow."

Cliff and Sean had decided to meet up with Syleanna and Carla at the hotel bar just to have a snack and chat before bed. On arrival, the girls had a table complete with Mylar balloons with the words "Kickin' Ass" pasted on them.

Staring at first in disbelief, both Sean and Cliff both broke out in laughter at seeing their girlfriends with a table decorated like it was a six-year-old biker's birthday party.

"Don't say anything!" Carla laughed. "We got them from some guy on the street that was a Yankee fan. He was so pissed-off after the game that he just gave them to us!"

"How's Gary?" Syleanna quickly asked. "That was so awful out there tonight!"

"Tommy says he's OK." Sean replied. "No broken bones, but standing there over him, I couldn't believe that he could even get up and walk away like he did. I guess they're keeping him overnight at the hospital, but he's gonna have the black-eye from hell for sure."

Sliding into the leather sofas, both Cliff and Sean melted into the arms of the ladies who had been so patient and understanding on this whole journey down the yellow-brick road. Catching their breath while enjoying a few Coors Light drafts and a plate of ultimate nachos, Carla suddenly got rather excited.

"Oh, I forgot to tell you that the latest word is that the Yankees have been the biggest contributors to this memorabilia thing from a big story I read in the *USA Today*."

"Really," Cliff replied, "tell me more."

"Well, all it really said was that most every team had stuff in this warehouse, but the New York Yankees were the biggest suppliers of everything, including bats, balls, and even some uniforms from games and some of the Yankees biggest stars."

"Really, no wonder that story died on the vine so quickly." Sean reflected.

"That's really freakin' strange if it's true, because that would be so easy to track down you would think."

"No news is good news, but what the hell!" Sean bemused. "In our little world, all I knows is we's got us another game with those big, bad behemoths tomorrow. Pretty cool throwing out that big ol' over-priced sausage at the plate tonight, eh, Cliffster?"

As the girls giggled and went on about that, Cliff Collier suddenly talked about Smith's accuracy of the throw.

"You know, they made this big deal about Damon coming back to the bag and all. I was right there and saw it happen. Karl gunned him down by at least five feet, and I'm sorry, he's not the speedy Johnny Damon of old. My man just locked, loaded, and flat out nailed him!"

"To 'King Kong' Karl!" Cliff responded, holding up his beer glass high in the air. With all celebrating the toast with laughter and revelry, Sean suddenly felt a weird presence as he slowly took a glance over his left shoulder. Sitting there in a booth with a sullen look and glassy stair and all by himself was none other than the former "Encino Man" himself, Johnny Damon. Obviously lost in his own thoughts, he seemed to be oblivious to the corruptive company he was sharing just two tables away.

Forgetting that some of the Yankee players also share the same hotel, it was a unanimous choice that this party be better celebrated upstairs in private-quarters.

The morning headline in the *New York Post* read "Lost and Homeless" as the front page was a giant blowup of Johnny Damon trying to score and the play at the plate. On the voice of New York Sports AM 66-WFAN, the Sunday morning call-in show was again proving how merciless the Yankees fans can be.

21 DOWN IN VEGAS

"It's Ed Randall and *Sunday Morning Sports Talk* and you know where we're going this morning. The lines are already full as we head out to Queens and Jeff Bodine. Good morning Jeff, you're on the FAN."

"Ain't nothin' friggin' good about it this morning, Ed. I got just one question for ya, and all I want is a truthful answer."

"I pride myself in being a truthful person, Jeff," Chuckled the legendary radio host, "Lay it on me, brother!"

"Why is Joe Torre actin' like it's no big deal that Damon lost us that game yesterday? I saw it, you saw it, is that all he can come up with at the friggin' press conference? Christ, Ed, you or I could have easily scored on that damn play. At least he could have been honest and said something like he screwed up! Why try to just act like nuttin' stupid happened out there that cost us the game!"

"An honest answer you want, so let me attempt to immerse you in my own beacon of the truth." Ed Randall cordially responded.

"Jeff, we both share the passion of the New York Yankees, and first of all, Joe Torre is just protecting his player, that's all. He's not going to scold or trash him in the press, so let's move on from that. What I saw out there yesterday was simply a bit of honest confusion. When the ball left the bat, I honestly thought that A-Rod had a won the game with a walk-off home run. I also think for a split-second, that Johnny Damon also thought 'game-over.'"If you watch the replay, and I mean watch it closely, you can see Johnny's face as he mouths the words, 'He did it!' Now, I don't think it was him not knowing how many outs there were as to his brief excitement that he thought that the Yanks won!"With that, yes, I think he was too cavalier on the base-path before he realized the ball was going to be caught, but at that point, he had no choice but to try and score. And as we all know by now, that really didn't work out to well for him now, did it? So, there it is Jeff from Queens. I hope I didn't over-radiate you with my articulated honesty."

"Yea, I thought Rodrigues had got a hold of it too, Ed, but still, a heads-up guy in a game like that shouldn't ever let his enthusiasm turn him into a dumb-ass! Sorry, but that's how I feel about it!"

"Johnny Damon is a great player, and yes, Jeff, we all have our lucid moments at times and who knows, today's another day and Mr. Damon just might be our guiding light. Thanks again for your call as we have many more to get to this morning and thanks for joining us on New York's 24-hour sports station, WFAN."

"The smell of this place is so unique. I can't really put my finger on it." Vipers reserve infielder Clint McElroy noticed. "It smells like something between mashed potatoes and Brut cologne."

"Could still be the Babe's jockstrap!" catcher Boone Coleman shot back while tying on his spikes. "He was here for a lot of years."

"I ran into this guy in the lobby of the hotel that said the right-field bleachers were designed by the same company that built our football stadium back home. I think he said his name was Paul O'Neill!" John Gambill added. "Imagine Spartan Stadium in Portsmouth and Yankee Stadium in New York coming from the same mother…pretty cool actually!"

As the Vipers players once again assembled for their pre-game ritual, the outside sports world was again going nutzoid. It was just past 5:00 in the afternoon and already the police had intercepted a guy in a Spiderman suit trying to scale the outside stadium wall and a hang-glider who tried his best to land in center-field. Both were intercepted and landed in the Vernon C. Bain Center more commonly called, "The Boat."

New York native singer/song-writer 50 Cent was set to sing the National Anthem for game-two of the series as actor Al Pacino, who was a close friend of the Steinbrenner family, was also selected to fire the first pitch. It had to be worth the price of admission alone simply to hear the ninety-year old Bob Shepard in his velvet manner and dulcet tones articulate to the field one of rap music's biggest draws.

You could tell the New York crowd was hungry and restless for a win as Mike Mussina showed nothing but a shut-down demeanor in his warm-up tosses. With Scotty, "The Golden" Arms also zeroing in against all the orbital distractions as the time had now arrived to stop all the sideshows and again take it to the turf! The first three-innings were flawless for both pitchers. Mussina and Arms had picked up where their counterparts had ended in game one, both retiring the first nine they faced in order.

That was until the bottom of the fourth inning when the Yankee bats sprung to life. Johnny Damon led off the inning with a double off the right field wall as Derek Jeter quickly singled him home. Arms then walked both Abreu and A-Rod to load the bases. Pitching coach Tom Browning called time and traipsed to the mound to settle his normally solid pitcher down.

"You OK, Scotty?" Browning asked. "Looks like you're over-throwing a little."

"I know…just a little more ramped up than usual" he whispered from behind his glove. "My pitches are not really going where I want them right now."

"Look, just take a deep breath a go back to the basics. Get Giambi to hit it on the ground. He runs like he's got a piano on his back. A double-play here and you're one- away from leaving the inning behind. We're only down one. Don't let those pin-stripes get into your head."

"Got it!" Arms said with a nod as the meeting quickly disbanded and everyone returned to their positions. Looking down from behind home plate was Yankee's announcer John Sterling who had seen this kind of Bronx moments begin to brew many times over.

"Bases are loaded here in the fourth, no outs, and here come the 'Giambino' who lives for the kind of situations just like this. Again tonight batting DH, Jason is looking for his first hit in the series as Scotty Arms steps back on the mound. He stares into Pogue for the sign, the pitch…it's high, ball one."

The New York crowd was now turning up the decibel level in the Bronx as Scotty Arms was again frozen to deliver.

"Again the look, he sets, and Arms to the plate. Giambi swings, ooh, baby. This one is a no-bout a doubter! This ball is crushed… high and deep to left and Jason Giambi has just cleaned the table with his eleventh career grand-slam and the Yankees bust it wide-open here in the fourth to take a 5-0 lead over the Vipers!"

Manager Tommy Leach had seen enough and started the slow walk to the mound. In his mind, it wasn't going to be a pleasant experience to let one of his best pitchers labor any further in the abyss of failure to which Tommy knew Scotty Arms loathed.

Reaching the circle of raised loam is always an awkward moment, but the universal handing over of the ball and a traditional pat on the tush is really all you can do.

"It looks like lefty Everett Carpenter will be taking over on the hill for Las Vegas." John Sterling proclaimed. "Carpenter was one of the starters for the Bentley State Eagles when he arrived in July with the rest of the team, but it was an injury to his pitching hand that sidelined him soon after he got here and he was never able to really break into this Vipers rotation. Carpenter has, to this point, been mostly used in spot relief appearances and since coming off the disabled list hasn't really pitched all that much. Carpenter's official stats are seventeen and a third innings, giving up eight- earned runs with a record of one and one plus a save. Still, none out here in the bottom of the fourth inning as Gary Shefield steps to the plate."

The music swelled to a crescendo as the brand-marked "da-da-da-da" set the table for another dramatic ESPN update.

"Welcome to *Sunday Night Sports Center,* I'm Fred Hickman. You knew it was only a matter of time before the bats of the New York Yankees would once again do what they've done all season long, and tonight was the night!

"Behind some home-cooked taters, the Yanks beat the Las Vegas Vipers 8-3 to even the World Series at a game apiece. Bottom of the fourth as Damon lights up Scotty Arms with a double. Next, Derek Jeter fires a frozen-rope up the middle to plate the first run of the game. Jason Giambi now with bases loaded, and 'boom goes the dynamite!' The 'Giambino' cashes in a full-house on Las Vegas and the Yankees are rolling 5-0.

"Top of the sixth as the Vipers are trying to make it interesting against Mussina with Sean Deeters on second, Cliff Collier shoots one into the gap in right for the Vipers first score. Bombo Chadwick here at the plate and he goes long-yard deep into statue-land to make it 5-3, but that's all the Vipers would cash in on for this night.

"We now flash to the bottom of the eighth as it's Bobby Abreu with Johnny Damon and Toots Randall on board for an 'NSYNC moment as it's 'Bye, Bye, Bye.' Abreu lights up Andrew Shackart and sends this baseball deep into the New York skyline to make it 8-3 and watch Randall as he rounds third doing a little base-pointing into the Vegas dugout and clapping along with some jaw-action on the side. Randall apparently is showing no love for his former employer. Final tonight, it was the Yanks over the Vipers 8-3.

"One bright spot for Las Vegas was lefty Everett Carpenter who came on in the fourth with no-outs and pitched five strong innings of middle-relief, allowing just two-hits and walked one. It's a travel-day off tomorrow before the series resumes and that will be Tuesday night at Mirage Field in Las Vegas!"

Conversation was candid on a private jet somewhere between La Guardia and McCarron airports the conversation was all over the board between Cisco Wheeler and his GM.

"You got to be happy with a split there." Brandon Briggs reflected. "Behind Boston, they have the best home record in all of baseball."

"I just hope we can win three at home so we don't have to come back to this rat-hole." Wheeler huffed. "They just need to tear down that antique monument to Ruth and finally realize, he's not coming back."

"It was good to see Carpenter throwing the ball well. This was really his first test under pressure. I was impressed" Briggs added.

Acting as if he wasn't listening, Cisco Wheeler looked off into the distance in a state of muse before changing the subject.

"Gary, did you get an update on him?" Cisco asked. "He's flying back with the team, but when we get home, we're sending him over to Elite Medical Center for a second opinion." Brandon explained. "Everything checked out fine in New York, but I'll feel safer having our own people take a look at him."

"Such a great kid. I don't know where we would have ended up without him." Cisco lamented.

"Honestly, not here!" Briggs shot back. "He has been the backbone of this team ever since the change, which makes you think. Gary's been with us for several years and all we knew was that he had potential, but it wasn't until we pulled the trigger on this that the real Gary Steinman finally showed up."

"The kids." Wheeler answered, "it was the kids, I'm telling you. I saw that sitting in my box and watching them on TV. Just like I got hooked by them in June! Their play is infectious, and it makes everybody better, except for that fucking Toots Randall!"

Brandon had been waiting for this topic to emerge ever since they fastened their seat belts.

"Incredibly un-classy, I'm sure the Yankees couldn't have been happy with all of that."

"Yea, but the idiots on all the sports-talk channels and TV won't quit talking about it or showing it. I ask you, Brandon, if you can tell me, why do all the jerks and social nitwits get all the publicity these days? I don't get it!"

"That's just the way this business is wired" Brandon admitted. "Controversy sells, and just like wrestling, you need your good guys and the bad. If Bud Selig ever steps down, I'm not so sure that Vince McMann wouldn't be a good fit to replace him as commissioner. You do know who he is, right?"

"That wrestling guy!" Wheeler blustered back, "He's another son of a bitch who is on the request list for free tickets…just like all those other slackers."

"I might seriously consider taking care of him Cisco, but only if he brings Maryse Ouelett with him." Briggs jabbed back.

"What does he do?" Wheeler shot back.

After a brief pause, Brandon slowly grinned and muttered, "Oh nothing boss, just another one of those…slackers."

The so-called "off-day" in Las Vegas was anything but that as Tommy Leach herded his team into and through the media-hoops at the airport during the late night hours as he had done so many times before. Coaches and crew were instructed to be at Mirage Field Tuesday morning at 9:00 a.m. Team arrival would be at 3:00 in the afternoon. All cylinders of the first World Series game to ever be played in Nevada seemed to be stroking along rather smoothly.

21 DOWN IN VEGAS

Unlike New York City with its limited choice of diversions in the barrios, the world was now here and soaking up every entertainment venue from gambling to gala.

Country music legend Garth Brooks had announced his "retirement" at the beginning of the new millennium, but has signed on to do some periodic acoustic shows as part of a limited residency in Vegas. Being a huge baseball fanatic, he had called Cisco Wheeler personally during the play-offs to offer his services of singing the National Anthem should the Vipers make it to the World Series. With so much going on, Cisco politely thanked him at the time and moved on. That long-forgotten offer was suddenly resurrected when Cisco returned to his office early Tuesday morning and began listening to his voice mails.

"Hello, Mr. Wheeler, this is Garth Brooks and I'm just checking in to see if you still need me to sing the National Anthem for you during the Vipers home-stand. I know you're an awfully busy guy, but I would be honored to be able to be a part of such a great story as what you all have written. By the way, I'll pay for my own tickets, and this would all be for free. I'm over here at the Wynn Casino and I happen to be off on Tuesday night if you need me. My number is 770-7000. Thanks!"

"You know we have only until noon today to make the decision." Manager Tommy Leach disclosed to his staff deep inside the Mirage Field bunker. "That's in three- hours."

"You mean what to do with Gary?" Tom Browning quizzed.

"Yep, if we want to bring in another player or put him on the D.L. Post-season rules are a little different." Leach explained. "We can only bring in another player within forty-eight hours after the day of the injury or we lose that option."

"Then we are down to a twenty-four-man roster." Keith Madison added.

"Exactly, so what are we going to do?" Tommy asked.

"Well, Elite went ahead and admitted him this morning for observation." Von Hayes informed the circle. "Apparently, the swelling is still pretty severe around the left eye. My question is simply who could we bring in now and make a difference at this point? Everyone in the minors is either playing winter ball or has gone home."

"That Terry Hatton guy if I remember who finished up pretty strong down in Colorado Springs, he might be an option. From last reports at the end of the season, he was one mean son of a bitch to hit!" Leach recalled.

Jarred as usual waited until he had heard all sides before putting in his well-placed opinion into play.

"If I could say, I'm not sure making a change now would be a good thing. The guys are really upset at what happened to Gary, and I think it might inspire them even more knowing that they're all now playing for him." Jarred observed. "If you cut him from the roster now to just like bring in another player, I think it might be a bad sign for the rest of the team."

"There's only a maximum of four games left." Browning added. "I kind of agree with Jarred on that one as we just go with who we got. Besides, Steiny still may be able to pitch."

"Not in game-five, and that is still a problem we have to figure out!" Tommy added. "So, OK guys, it's time to vote. Do we all agree to do nothing by noon and keep Gary on the roster?"

Unanimously, the Vipers brain-trust decided to go with the flow and keep Gary Steinman on the team's active roster. Mitch Milhuff was scheduled to open the Las Vegas series on Tuesday night with Brad Zeiber on the mound for Wednesday, but that still didn't diminish the looming specter of who indeed would be the Vipers starter for game five.

"What a performance by the legendary Garth Brooks here tonight and singing the National Anthem." Vipers' announcer Ralph Hacker elated. "That all came as a bit of a surprise to everybody today because at last word, Mr. Vegas himself, Wayne Newton, was supposed to again have delivered the traditional homage."

"There must have been a scheduling conflict of some sort." Pete Harnisch inserted. "It was great to see Garth back at it again. You know he loves this game."

"True, it was just a few years ago, Garth actually went to spring training with the Padres if I remember correctly." Ralph recalled. "I'm sort of glad that didn't work out because I do love his music. Well, we are just a couple of minutes away from the start of game-three as Mitch Milhuff versus the Yankees Chien-Ming Wang. I'm Ralph Hacker along with my side-kick Pete Harnisch and you're listening to Vipers baseball live on KVPR-AM and world-wide on the Las Vegas Vipers Radio Network."

For the next several days, the city of Las Vegas had never experienced the pandemonium that this World Series showdown had generated. The t-shirt industry imploded to a level never seen before as at almost every step along "The Strip" there was a huckster and a deal. The Yankees, the Vipers, and perhaps the best-selling shirt of all were a mash-up of the Bentley State and Las Vegas logos that simply said, "Fly like the Eagles."

Morning show host Hobie Harrison took his show live to Harrah's on MIX 99.3 and was given permission to broadcast from the lobby. It was a chance for all the Portsmouth, Ohio, fans to stop by and share their love from one of Las Vegas's most legendary hotels.

"I thought I was living the dream." Harrison admitted on the air, "but when you can sit here, talk to the fans, and suddenly have 'Carrot Top' just stop by and out of the blue for an impromptu five-minute chat, that's Xanadu!"

Yankees fans were also there in force, taking over several watering holes and putting their brand on them. Bourbon Street Sports Bar and the Bacon Bar were two in particular. Yet with all the pomp and circumstance, the Vipers fans were equally territorial and weren't out to give-up their home turf easily.

19TH INNING

KLAS-TV and long-time reporter George Knapp hit the 11:00 p.m. news with the euphoria-meter pinned deep into the red.

"The Las Vegas Vipers are now just one game away from what many at first believed was the most impossible dream. I'm George Knapp, and as long as I've been in this town, perhaps behind the Bob Lazar interviews, this may absolutely be the most unbelievable chronicle that I've ever witnessed as a news journalist as yes… the Vipers do it again and totally stun the New York Yankees for the second night in a row 5-1 here at Mirage Field. Brad Zeiber who was a late season call-up from Colorado Springs allowed only four- hits and no-runs over eight innings as Yankees starter Jarred Wright gave up a lead-off home run to Brooks Snyder in the first inning…and as we hear from tonight's star pitcher, it was at that point the Vipers never looked back.

"I really can't really explain it, wow. I just felt really comfortable out there tonight and was able to do everything I wanted with my pitches. Doug, as always, he called a great game for me from behind the plate, and the guys really picked us up big-time and these fans… man, are they incredible. If there is anybody that gets us fired up to play hard, they always become our Monster Energy drink for sure!"

"That was Brad Zeiber on his astonishing command tonight on the mound for the Vipers. He's only twenty-two years old from a small town in Northern Ohio, and get this, he didn't even begin playing baseball until his senior year in high school. Last night, it was Mitch Milhuff hand-cuffing the Bombers to a 4-2 win, and now coupled with the victory yesterday and again tonight, your Las Vegas

Vipers 'slash' the Bentley State Eagles are now just one-game away from winning it all. There's plenty more on the way this evening, so plan to get 'Viper Hyper' with us and more highlights and interviews from Mirage Field as again the Vipers beat the Yankees 5-1. For KLAS-TV live in Las Vegas, I'm George Knapp."

"One more and we are home stag-daddy!" Gary Duzan shouted as he flipped his towel toward Karl Smith as they headed toward the shower. "Kong bonged another one tonight and sent another little kid home happy!"

Duzan was making reference to the two- run tape-measure blast by Smith in the third- inning that put Las Vegas up by three.

"Hey, if they want to throw me breaking balls that don't break, I'll take 'em' all night long, just lay'em down and smakem' yakem!"

The mirth was contagious as it should be throughout the Vipers den. They had simply gone through the New York Yankees pitching staff with reckless abandon and had shown no fear. Except for Mussina in game-two, great pitching and timely hitting was the key formula for success so far.

As the Vipers testosterone-laden celebration continued, a more serious confab was in progress three doors down.

"Great game…just great, great game tonight!" Tommy Leach repeated. "I am so proud of them, damn! We got to bring this home, fellas. We gotta decide and pretty damn quickly who's gonna take the ball tomorrow. Rules say that we have until 10:00 in the morning to figure it out."

"I think we can come back with Arms." Tom Browning suggested. "Hell, he is chomping at the bit to get back out there. He's turned into our Robo-Pitcher!"

"Maybe, but if there's a game six…that's where I would want him." Leach countered. "At that point, he would have five-day's rest, only four if we cut him short a day."

"Carpy might be an idea, Skip" Jarred added. "Look, he pitched five-innings on Sunday, why not run him out there tomorrow just to see how far he can go."

"Maybe, but with Gary out, I was holding back Scarbury for emergency relief, but hell, this is an emergency isn't it?"

"With the schedule as it is and the travel days, you can go with a four-man rotation and get away with it." Keith Madison interjected. "I think Scarbury would work out fine. You've got Carpenter if we need him, and the bullpen is pretty well rested."

"Thanks, Keith, I think that might be our best answer!" Tommy paused and pondered. "At best, it's a three-game season, but I want it to end tomorrow. Pug, go get Brad and get him ready to go. One other thing. I still want to wait until the deadline tomorrow to make the announcement. I know it will drive those Yankee sons of a bitch's Bonkers like it did the Dodgers and any distraction like that is working for us!"

Back in Portsmouth on the campus of Bentley State University, those that stayed in town continued the non-stop vigil of support for this most incredible sports feat in the making. Ducking the publicity- bus was a hard act to perfect, especially if you were the girlfriend and fiancé of two of the team's biggest stars. Carla Harris and Syleanna Griffin were like rock luminaries when it came to slipping in and out of all the public places un-noticed.

One spot they couldn't slither out of was on Tuesday afternoon when three FBI agents showed up on Carla's front doorsteps to ask for a meeting. While nice, they were firm that it was very important that they talk to both girls together about the ongoing memorabilia investigation. Quickly calling Syleanna, they agreed to sit down and tell their story in Carla Harris's living room.

Never tipping their hand on where they were really going, the FBI questioning all seemed to surround the circumstances of why the exchange of tickets for sports souvenirs with the girls was conducted. Playing the innocent card, they simply told them what had happened without mentioning names.

"We flew in late to Los Angeles, didn't have any tickets, and this cab driver gave us some if we could have a few balls and a bat autographed for a friend." Carla explained. "I told him that it would take a day or so to get them and before we left town, I just left them at the front desk at the hotel. That's about it!"

As the questioning continued, it was becoming more obvious to the agents that the two girls they were grilling certainly couldn't be the ring- leaders of some kind of nefarious inner-circle of the "Momento Mafia." After about an hour of poignant questioning, the process was complete.

"We appreciate your time, ladies, and all the information." the tall one offered.

"We are just tracking down leads and your names were a part of the seized items that we confiscated in LA, so we had an obligation to come and get your story."

"OK, so, we're like not in any trouble or anything?' Syleanna's voice quivered.

"No, ma'am, you and Miss Harris are simply persons of interest as we continue our investigation, but I have to say your comments here today are a part of our official records as they were taken under oath."

"So where did all of the stuff come from?" Carla innocently asked.

"We're not at liberty to address anything about the case at this time." the agent responded.

"Well, like how then did *USA Today* have this big story I read the other day saying like the Yankees had the most of it? They didn't mention us by name, but said like some girlfriends of the players were all involved. I know they meant us."

"All I can tell you, Miss Harris is that any newspaper reporting you might read has nothing to do with the Federal Bureau of Investigation." Glancing a semi-smile to both girls, he attempted to defuse the edgy-tension, "When it comes to these kinds of cases, ladies; our printed word is the only one that really matters."

Because of the sensitive situation, the girls had both decided to stay home and not put themselves into any unwanted scrutiny with the team. Carla quickly texted Cliff to tell him of their session with the Feds and it seemed to all go down smooth and easy. Syleanna was also relieved realizing that she now wouldn't have to watch her fiancé play baseball from the activity room at the Scioto County Jail.

Game-five of the World Series was to be shown on a giant theater screen inside the fifteen-hundred seat center for the arts on the campus of Bentley State University. It was open to the public on reserve that everyone brings a canned good that would go to the local Salvation Army. Local musician Steve Free was going to play on stage for a social- hour before coverage of the game at 8:30 p.m.

The media crunch was the most spectacular segment of the evening as all of the national press wanted to be on hand to witness history in the making. Perhaps one of the funniest moments occurred when one of the Bentley State students stonewalled Katy Couric at the door from entering the auditorium because she didn't have the proper ID.

"I'm sorry, I can't let you in unless you have a canned good" she was told.

Looking stunned, Katy quickly pulled out her CBS credentials and thrust them upon her barrier.

"I'm Katie Couric and I'm here to cover the game tonight." her reply was with a slight hint of agitation.

"I'm sorry ma'am, I was strictly told that nobody gets in here tonight without a canned good," the steadfast student responded." My director, Carl Daehler gave me strict orders, and I have to obey them."

"Look, young lady, I've been to Beirut, Lebanon, Russia, and China, I've never had a problem getting in those places. I will not have a problem getting into this place tonight!"

After an embarrassing moment of silence, the student looked at the now livid reporter and was perplexed as now what to do; her response was priceless.

"Well, I hope you didn't go to all those places in a row because without a can of baked beans, your streak just might be over!"

Turning and storming away, Katie Couric simply became a casualty of small-town propriety and eventually made her way into the festivities with her minions.

Feeling the relief of uncertainty after meeting with the FBI agents earlier in the afternoon, Carla and Syleanna decided to grab a couple super-sized cans of the Jolly Green Giant and head down to the university. The wear of the past three months was beginning to take its toll as Syleanna secretly prayed that it could all be over with tonight. From the last game of the College World Series to the fifth-

21 DOWN IN VEGAS

game of the MLB version, it was certainly excitement extraordinaire beyond expectations. Truth being on all counts, these were just two chicks that couldn't wait for the official end of the season.

Every great live sports moment has that special apex that fans will never forget. Anticipated or not, they are quilt- patches frozen in time. There was the Willie Mays over-the-shoulder catch off the bat of the Indians Vic Wertz in the '54 series. Derek Jeter's flip-throw at the plate to nail current teammate Jason Giambi in the 2002 series. And who could ever forget a wobbly-legged Kirk Gibson stumbling to the plate in 1988 to hit the most improbable of home- runs ever off of Dennis Eckersley to steal game-one for the Dodgers against the Oakland A's.

Another immortal flash was now in the incubator and about to be hatched as spot-starter Brad Scarbury had thrown eight-remarkable innings as the Vipers lead New York 2-1 heading into the ninth.

Back to back doubles in the fourth from Terrence Kennedy and Doug Pouge, plus an added single from Luke Shepard accounted for the only two runs of the games for the Vipers against Randy Johnson. In the fifth, it was a triple by Matsui and a sacrifice fly from Jorge Posada to finally bring home a run for the Yankees.

With two-outs and the baseball world now collectively standing on their feet, short-stop Derek Jeter worked reliever "Dirty" Ernie Fuller to a full count. The Las Vegas Vipers' were now just one strike away from creating the greatest sports upset in all of sports history.

"Fuller is on the back of the mound," Ralph Hacker announced. "Scarbury allowing just three hits over eight- innings to the Yanks in simply an outstanding performance here tonight. Ernie Fuller in relief is now set…ready to the plate, its high, ball- four, and the Yankee's captain now trots down to first base with two-out and Alex Rodrigues is coming to the plate."

Tom Browning quickly called time and jogged out to the mound to offer some comfort to his closer in this crucial cross-roads situation. In homes, on radios, at sports bars everywhere, real time suddenly had switched gears into agonizing slow-mo as every angle of the instant was dutifully being absorbed

Joe Buck and Tim McCarver were again waxing poetic on the preface of team immortality until a 2-2 count on A-Rod quickly switched everything back to a stark and jolting reality.

"Rodrigues swings…and there she goes!" Buck swelled. "A-Rod waited on what appeared that trademark 'knuckleball' and he crushed it high and deep to center field as the Yankees now take a 3-2 lead over the Vipers here in the ninth! Wow!'

"Problem is that it was a knuckler, that didn't knuckle," McCarver added. "When I played, that thing was known as the 'eephus pitch' because it comes in slower than a week in jail."

"This Mirage Field crowd is simply stunned!" Joe Buck continued. "One strike away from ending it all here tonight and the air has absolutely been sucked out of the dry, desert landscape. Las Vegas will have a another shot coming up in the bottom of the ninth, but a town that lives on the odds will not be in favor of this one."

With Jason Giambi grounding out to second, that set-up baseball's ultimate closer and the most feared name in the game with it all on the line. Mariano Rivera entered the game with his 1.80 era along with his twelve- years of triumph along with 413 saves.

Facing the heart of the Vipers order, it took but a fleeting moment for an anguished squad of believers to hear those words from Joe Buck that again harshened their dreams to veracity: "And now, we are headed back to New York!"

"You live by it, you die by it." Tommy leach shot back at a reporter who questioned him on the knuckleball to A-Rod. "If he'd have swung and missed, it wouldn't even be an issue now, would it?"

The post-game press conference more than mirrored the frustration felt by a unit of warriors who had come as close to winning the ultimate prize as you could get.

"Sure, we're disappointed in the outcome of tonight's game. I can't lie to you about that!" Leach continued answering to the press. "To win it in front of our home-house would have been this team's ultimate goal, but that's not the way it worked out."

Relentlessly, the press corps railed away at the evening's failure until Leach finally decided on the last word.

21 DOWN IN VEGAS

"If I could remind everyone, we are still up three games to two, I believe. We will take a day-off to travel back to New York tomorrow, I believe that's how it works, and then we will then play again on Saturday night. Safe travels to you all and we will see you there!"

With that, the Vipers post-game gathering came to an end. On the Yankees side, the assembling didn't want the evening to die. Joe Torre, A-Rod, Derek Jeter and Rivera were all at the pin-stripe dais in joyous splendor.

"Alex, we're you guessing on the pitch or did you just react to it?" the next question arrived.

"To be honest, I was a little stunned to see it, but it was so slow, I had time to adjust and just zero in on it because it kind of made batting- practice pitches look fast!"

"So, Joe," you're taking this thing back to New York, what are your feelings about escaping tonight here with a win and heading home?"

"First of all, this is a good ball club we played tonight." The Yankee Manager began. "Honestly, we are very lucky to be standing here with the opportunity to play on. The big guy here bailed us out, and I guess that's why we keep him around." The crowd chortled as Torre continued. "We are…and always will be Yankee proud. As our team proved tonight, we will never give up. There are still two games left for us to win, and we will do everything in our power to make that happen. Thank you all, and see you fellas in New York on Saturday!"

Fifteen hundred utterly decimated faithful slowly left the Bentley State auditorium following the game. Amid the lingering reporters trying to capture the sagging moment, most just wanted to slink by all the paparazzi and get home to grieve in private; two of those multitude were Carla and Syleanna.

"God, that sucks, we had it!" Carla anguished as they headed toward their car. "And why do they have to keep putting those stupid cameras in front of everybody's faces?"

"I know it's awful!" Syleanna agreed. "They kept showing Cliff over and over again just standing out there after the home- run: that's so mean!"

As the girls walked down Chillicothe Street, they quickly decided to duck into the Port City Café for a beer.

"Well, I've made a decision tonight!' Carla confessed over her Coors Light. "It's time to become a whore!"

Flashing that certain kind of quizzical look that only two best friends can share, Syleanna thirsted to hear more and Carla was ripe for the fixins."

"You remember the guy from CBS that I promised the interview to? Well, he told me that anytime I ever needed anything else to just give him a call. Now that we have all that other shit out of the way with the autographs and all, I'm completely ready to do something mad and stupid, and I believe you are too!"

"What now may I ask my most evil influence?" Syleanna grinned.

"Simple, we're going back to New York!"

"Like by Saturday, day after tomorrow? Who do you think you are, Sabrina the damn teenage witch?" Syleanna responded.

"No, here's the plan, it's simple." Carla explained. "I'll call him up first thing in the morning and promise an exclusive interview only, and I mean only, if we get tickets and a hotel room for the weekend. You know he can do it! Our guys need us and they need us there now. The TV people also need us, so…let's just use the opportunity that has been made available for us and get the hell out of here!"

"ENE, it's the 'everybody needs everybody rule!" Syleanna giggled. "I think that I know you all too well my evil twin sister, and I'll start packing as soon as I get home."

Friday moved quickly with the transference once again of global scenery from Las Vegas back to New York. Teams, the press, and fans were again on the move. One stationary item was Vipers' ace Gary Steinman. He had been held over at the hospital for what they had called retinal bleeding behind his left eye, and they had been reluctant to release him back to the Vipers.

"I can see fine!" a frustrated Steinman blurted out to his doctors. "I need out of here to catch a plane with the team! We leave for New York at 1:30 p.m."

"Mr. Steinman, I know how you feel, but your team doctor told us specifically that he didn't want you released until we felt that everything was safe, and at this point, we're still not sure." the doctor lamented.

"Look, I feel fine! I can see fine, it doesn't even hurt. So I got a black-eye!"

Gary pleaded, "Nobody ever died of a black-eye that I ever heard of. Really, just let me go and I'll be fine!"

"I wish it were that simple, but I'll tell you what. We can take another x-ray this afternoon, and if it all comes back negative, maybe we can let you go at that time. Right now, there is nothing that I can do until then."

"But I have a plane to catch! Can't we do it now?"

"I'm afraid not. I will go ahead and put you into scheduling right now and our next open window won't be until around 3:00 this afternoon. After that, Mr. Steinman, we will know much more!"

"Hell, this isn't a prison and there's nothing stopping me from just walking out of here right now if I wanted to!"

Giving his obstinate patient a glaring look, the doctor coyly replied, "You are correct, but if you want to pitch baseball Mr. Steinman, there's a little thing you might need, and it's called a medical clearance!"

"It's Friday on the "Imus in the Morning Program" on WNBC. (Quack-quack.) Charles McCord has rounded up one of my favorite guests, and if I remember right, the last time he was here, he actually hung up on me. Live this morning from the New York Yankees, it's the outspoken super-sub Toots Randall. Good morning, Toots!"

"I think it was just one of those quirky bad phone connections, Don!" Randell chuckled. "I would never hang up on a radio legend!"

"If NBC had anything to do with it, they probably hadn't paid the phone bill." Imus quipped. "Anyway, you guys are back in this thing. Be honest, did they give you a little bit of a scare?"

"Not really," admitted Randall. "When you have a team with this kind of talent, it will over-ride luck eventually. I knew it was only a matter of time before the Yankees bats came alive and the breaks started falling our way."

"I have to ask. Did you have a nice reunion dinner while you were out there in Vegas with your former boss? At least you could have given them all a nice fruit basket or something for sending you here to New York." Imus teased.

"No, everything was very cordial, and by that I mean, I really didn't come into direct contact with anybody who was responsible for the re-mastering my destiny. It was all fine and I was happy with that."

"Toots Randall is my guest." Imus continued. "So, if you would have run into Cisco Wheeler, say in an elevator or something, what would have you said to him? C'mon and be honest."

"Don, I probably would have smiled and just said hello Mr. Wheeler, it's nice to see you again, and the best of luck to you and all of the team."

"I thought we were going to have an honest moment here." Imus countered.

"We are having an extremely honest interlude, Don because I know that Mr. Cashman happens to be a big fan of your show. You're not getting me again!"

"Two tickets to New York, ball game, hotel accommodations, and a $600 gift card for dinner, tell me, do I know how to get things done!" Carla playfully boasted over the phone to her bestie, Syleanna.

"You strumpet! How can you sleep at night?" Syleanna laughed.

"Don't be turning all Nancy Grace on me, mamma, because we are both going to have to be guests on the CBS morning show on Monday morning. That's the deal."

"Both of us?" No!" Syleanna reacted. "So what do we have to do?'

"I talked with Charlie Perry from CBS this morning and win or lose the World Series is over on Sunday. So Monday morning, we pay the piper.He got real excited that we wanted to come so he picked up our air fare and everything else we need to stay until Tuesday. On Monday morning, they're picking us up at the hotel and taking us to *The Early Show* and I guess were going to be interviewed by Hannah Storm. At least that's what he told me over the phone!"

"Do the guys know we're coming?" asked Syleanna

21 DOWN IN VEGAS

"Yes, I texted Cliff a little while ago. So, get your shit together girlfriend because we're gonna' be 'whoring it up' in the Big Apple tonight." Carla jokingly laughed. "We fly out of Columbus at 6:30 p.m. so I'll drop by and get you this afternoon at 3:00!"

"I know Ernie's taking it pretty hard, Skip" Jarred Brewster mentioned to Tommy Leach as they sat together on the tarmac at McCarron International.

"Not an easy thing to live with" Leach responded. "A strike, a pop up, a ground ball to someone, if that had happened; we wouldn't be sitting here right now. It's all part of the game kid. He'll get over it."

"I think Scotty is ready. He and I have been really going over stats and the video and he's about as quietly cool as I've ever seen him." Jarred offered.

"Scotty's a rock, he'll be fine. We just have to go back there and do what we've been doing every day since the third week of July and we will have nothing to fear." Tommy once again offered. "I just get so sick and tired of the damn press always trying to twist and make issues out of everything" Leach confessed.

"Then I get a call from some bozo this morning saying that he's heard we've cut Steinman from the roster. For Christ's sake, he's in the hospital with a serious eye injury. Don't these nosey bastards have any common sense?"

Sensing that Tommy was a bit agitated himself, Jarred decided to go back to his magazine and let the accelerating boil back off to just a slow-simmer. After all, it was going to be a long flight and he would have plenty chances to chatter away at 35,000 feet.

"I dread going back to that soul-vacant city," Cisco Wheeler huffed as he and Brandon once again boarded his private Bombardier 300 Challenger headed for New York.

"Cisco, had we been swept in four, you would have relished the opportunity!"

Brandon reminded his boss, "Look, this is what we played for since you made this previously unheard of move. I know you hate coffee, so I'm not going to even tell you to stop and smell it, but at least smell something that makes you happy."

An awkward moment of silence drowned out the jet engines preparing for their final take-off.

"Brandon, I grew up with everything any child could ever imagine. As long as I could remember, I wanted for nothing! When I fell in love with this game at the age of ten, my parents actually hired chaperones to escort me to my Little League games to ensure my safety. Unfortunately when your family had the kind of wealth we had, everybody's eyes were always on you. All I ever wanted to be was just like Joey Babcock. His parents were always at the games, they never stood out, and he was able to be the player I always wanted to be." Faltering for a moment with words, Brandon knew Cisco was struggling. "My whole life is now these kids. Screw all the money and all the crap that goes with it! There are now twenty-five versions of me out there…and it scares me!"

Pausing before answering, Brandon was carefully trying to decipher Cisco's guarded rant before reacting.

"And why does that scare you if I may ask?" Brandon quietly asked.

"Because…I want twenty-five Joey Babcock's out there to prove that good kids with natural talent can also make it to the top!"

Slumping back into his seat, Brandon felt that an emotional volcano had just purged itself of the many fallen-angels that were perhaps trapped inside. Realizing that their discussion was now over, he slapped his boss on the knee with the only thing he could think of to close the revealing passion "Don't worry Cisco, the Joey's will all be there, I promise."

"It's game-six of the 2006 Worlds Series! Good evening everybody, I'm Jeanne Zelasko for your continuing Fox Sports coverage, and tonight it's do or die for the Hometown Yankees as Mike Mussino will take the mound against Scotty 'The Golden' Arms for Las Vegas. It was a two-run ninth inning home run by Alex Rodrigues in game-five Thursday that brought he series back home to the Bronx. Today I had a chance to catch up with some of the principals earlier today."

"Anytime you play from behind in a series, it's really rough." Johnny Damon admitted. "These guys are honestly off the charts because nobody has ever seen this kind of baseball before like this in an extended series. Our luxury has been getting to know them a little better each game that we play."

"I also talked with Keith Madison, Bench Coach of the Vipers and who was the college manager of the Bentley State Eagles, on witnessing the transition of a team he coached in college and now to this extraordinary level, he said this!"

"Well, Jeanne, honestly nobody back at the end of our run in college baseball could ever have imagined something of this caliber! It was a unique idea for sure, but being asked to be a part of it was great! These guys that I initially coached are playing a game that was invented back in 1869 with extremely few logistical changes over all those many years. I'm just proud that the way we taught them how to play the game at Bentley State is still applicable even at this high-level. It's a true testimony from these guys that team sports is forever!"

"So tonight, we shall see just how this continuing spectacle plays itself through as in just a few minutes, Joe Buck and Tim McCarver will bring you game-six of the 2006 World Series from Yankee Stadium. For Fox Sport live, I'm Jeanne Zelasko!"

New York Bronx native singer/songwriter Henry Gross was called upon to sing the National Anthem for the electric night ahead. As a founding member of the group Sha Na Na, he also had national success with the hit-song "Shannon" in 1976 and was acclaimed for other great tunes and albums in his career. As a big New York baseball fan, Henry knew several of the Yankee players and as he was getting ready to head to the field microphone, Bernie Williams couldn't resist making reference to one of Henry's other songs that had charted success.

"Hey Henry Gross," Bernie yelled, "instead of doing that thing we hear before every damn ballgame, help us out man and sing 'One More Tomorrow!' We might need it!"

"Scotty, I just heard some clubhouse scuttlebutt about Sheffield's left knee. It might be a little tender, and it's hard to extend to those outside pitches!"

"Thanks Jarred, really, you're always there for me and I appreciate it!" Arms responded. "Now give me something juicy about the other eight and I'll really feel good about all this."

For seven innings, Mike Mussina and Scotty Arms battled as brilliantly as two mound warriors could ever throw. The standing-room-only crowd at Yankee Stadium was in stride with the "choosing to stand only patrons" in a contest that was as electric as any before it. Diving stops, dramatic catches, and perfect pitches were all a part of the canvas that was being painted of sports at its very highest level.

"Its two-outs here in the bottom of the eight and no-score with Jason Giambi on first via the first walk of the night by Arms." Vipers radio host Ralph Hacker reported. "That brings up Gary Sheffield who has had a tough time at the plate tonight going 0-3. Still no score as Scotty Arms continues to pound the ball to the outside corner."

"It's not real obvious, Ralph, but he seems to me that Sheffield is favoring that left knee just a little." Pete Harnisch added. "There wasn't anything on him with the medical report tonight it's just the good ol' eyeball test."

"Two outs here in the eight as Arms readies, step onto the rubber, and here's the 2-1 pitch. It's a ground ball to the right and under the glove of Snyder into right field. Giambi is rounding second on his way to third. Sean Deeters is up with the ball and now...fires it back to first as Gary Sheffield took a long turn...and now he's having trouble getting back! The tag is down...and Sheffield is out at first!"

"It's that knee Ralph! He over-extended himself rounding first, never figuring that Deeters' throw was coming back in that direction, and he was just hung out there like dead-man walking!" Harnisch added.

Hacker chimed in next with the tale of the tape, "Heading into the ninth here in New York, it's the Yankees and Vipers all tied up at nothing apiece!"

"Burkes is ready! Pitching Coach Tom Browning reported to Tommy as he informed his reliever that he was the next man up. "Go get 'em,' Jeremy! We also have a double-switch in the line-up with McElroy taking over third base."

21 DOWN IN VEGAS

The Yankees also went with a fresh arm as Kyle Farnsworth took over the mound in the ninth for the Yanks to face Deeters, Collier, and Smith. Joe Torre obviously waiting on his behemoth stopper in Rivera should the Yankees get the lead, there were no promises. After the night before, when it looked like it was over and iced, nobody at this point felt confident in making any predictions.

Farnsworth had little trouble disposing of the Viper trio in order as the 6'4" right- hander who had a reputation of being a bit on the scrappy side seemed to have his house in order on this given night.

Listed for an official capacity of 57,545, Bob Shepard had just announced that this was the largest capacity crowd ever to witness a World Series game in the history of Yankee Stadium. Adding in the additional 8,000 standing-room-only tickets that were sold the capacity was swelled to nearly 66,000 as everyone was trying to out-shout the other.

"We've had boxing matches, Olympic Games, everything from pro football and even the Reverend Billy Graham, "Joe Buck reminisced, "but I have never, and I do mean never, have ever heard it as loud as it is here tonight as we go to the bottom of the ninth!"

Flash bulbs were popping with each pitch now as Jeremy Burkes faced Hideki Matsui leading off the ninth. "Godzilla" as he was called by his teammates, worked Burkes to a full- count before lofting a Texas league single to left. Jose Posada only needed one- pitch to lay down the perfect bunt up the first base line to move Matsui on over to second.

"Here's a head- scratcher for you as Joe Torre is apparently is taking down Robinson Cano for a pinch- hitter here in the ninth with one on and one out!" The Yankees John Sterling announced. "Former Viper Toots Randall is now headed to the plate, and I can only guess what this is all about!"

"I'm sure there might be some physiological warfare going on right now" Suzyn Waldman added. "High theatrics with a chance for a former player to scorn his old team? You betcha, and here's his chance!"

"Since coming over to New York in the mid-July house cleaning in Las Vegas Randall has been used mainly as a bat off the bench and an occasional pinch-runner, "Sterling added, "but as Suzyn just alluded to, this might be all about timing."

As Matsui led off second, Jeremy Burkes worked his pitches to the outside corner of the plate. With a 2-1 count on Toots Randall, he left one just a little too tempting toward the inside corner.

"Randall swings and it's in there and it's a line drive to left!" John Sterling screamed. "Matsui is on his way to third and they're giving him the green light. Smith is up with the ball! Here comes the throw…and here comes Matsui to the plate…it's gonna be close and…he's in there! Matsui scores and the Yankees win! Yankees win! It's on a pinch-hit single from Toots Randall and Hideki Matsui running from the crack of the bat just gets under the throw from Karl Smith in left field as 'Godzilla' out-runs 'Kong' for the victory herein game six! How bout that?"

"Only here at Yankee Stadium in New York can these things happen and we are all tied up now at three-games apiece…and yes…Cinderella…we are taking this ball to game -seven!"

Next day the morning headline in the *New York Post* proudly read, "Randall a Hand-Full!" as it showed him thrusting out an open hand toward Jeremy Burke as he was rounding first with the winning hit. Play-by-play announcer Ralph Hacker was offended by the gesture in his post-game wrap-up.

"Tonight the Vipers lose 1-0 on a simply outstanding pitching performance by Scotty 'The Golden' Arms. He and Mike Mussina battled again as they did in game-two right down to the wire. It was all settled in ninth-inning relief where Kyle Farnsworth looked unhittable setting the Vipers down in order. Normally a set-up reliever, Jeremy Burkes was kind of in the Twilight Zone being called into the closers roll and pitched well, but tonight; just not well enough.

It was former Viper Toots Randall who in a daring move by Yankee Manager Joe Torre sent Randall to the plate to pinch-hit the winning run home with one-out in the bottom of the ninth.

"If I can just editorialize here for a moment, the gesture that Randall made after his game-winning hit in my opinion was totally uncalled for. It's a matter of public record that after being cut with the rest of the former Vipers this summer, his personal vendetta against

21 DOWN IN VEGAS

this club has never stopped. His non-stop venom toward his former team and management has far exceeded anything from any of the other former teammates. Also in just simple observation, if you were cut and then lucky enough to catch on with a team and the legacy of the New York Yankees couldn't you just let it go? At any rate, it was a with pitcher's bonanza here tonight as again the score, it was the New York Yankees 1, the Las Vegas Vipers 0. I'm Ralph Hacker and we'll be right back on KVPR-AM and the Vipers Radio Network."

In a closed door meeting in the locker room after the game, it was a very disheartened crew of players that Manager Tommy Leach was forced to address.

"Great game tonight Armsy, you deserved to win." he started. "When you allow these guys three- hits in eight-innings, you're doing something special!"

"Jeremy, it was just one of those things. Players get hits, and unfortunately tonight it was by a flaming ass-hole! I really didn't think Farnsworth could throw like he did, and I was honestly saving 'Dirt' until we got to the lead, but that didn't happen."

After a long pause of awkward silence, it was Sean Deeters who final spoke up both strong and solid.

"OK, so what's the fuck? We have them just where we want them!"

Tommy looked quizzically and smiled, knowing the veracity of his players and let them pump their own air back into the room.

"How many times have we been on the line this season?" Brooks Snyder declared. "The more pressure there is on us, the more pressure-er we take it! That's the Vipers way!" he yelled.

Suddenly, the laughter spilled forth in realizing that the Vipers second baseman was now making up words, but the point was received.

For the next twenty-minutes the Las Vegas brothers rejuvenated themselves by group therapy in getting ready for the second biggest game in their lives.

"They are still going with Wang." Tommy threw out in the coaches meeting late Saturday night after the players had all dispersed. "Is Milhuff ready for what's laying ahead, do you think?"

"Yea, he's had ice-water in his veins ever since he got here." Tom Browning replied. "He's definitely rested and ready to go I think! I love that kid."

"Well, at least we got some well-rested arms in Zebro, Leslie, and Carpenter." Leach reflected. "Make a short list of those three unless we need 'em 'tomorrow."

"Is there any word at all on Steinman?" Tommy asked.

"I got a text from him yesterday, and all it said was 'good' Tom Browning reported. "As we know he's always been a guy of few words, and texts, so I'm guessing his eye- treatment is going well."

"OK, it's the usual report time tomorrow for the players and for all of us!" Tommy concluded. "I don't know about you, but Billy's Bar is still open and right across the street and for the record, I'm tired, pissed off, but the first round is on me for everybody!"

Within two minutes, the visitors' clubhouse at Yankee Stadium went totally dark.

"It felt great!" Toots Randall exalted as he was being interviewed by WNBC-TV Channel 4. "We're all motivated to seek revenge. If an injustice has been committed, then the only way to restore balance in the moral universe is for the wrong-doers to pay for what they've done. I think that I did that tonight and can't lie to you, it feels pretty good!"

While the desire for revenge is often motivated by spite, bitterness, and an over-bloated ego, Toots Randall continued regaling well into the night about his game-winning accomplishment and to all who would listen.

While a city celebrated, a Delta red-eye special landed at 2:30 a.m. at JFK International Airport. Among the eighty-seven incoming passengers from the long overnight flight, one of them in particular was also in pursuit of seeking justice of a different kind.

It was now early morning Sunday as everything that began with a little college team from Portsmouth, Ohio, in the earliest of spring would on this given day be forever enshrined in the annals of time under the file titled "game- seven." Like mile-markers in time and forever frozen,, the memories of these one-game lessons of finality remain steadfastly alive as well as eternal.

21 DOWN IN VEGAS

In 1952, Brooklyn loaded the bases with just one out in the bottom of the seventh, looking to finally dethrone the Yankees after World Series losses in 1947 and 1949. But Duke Snider and Jackie Robinson popped out to end the threat, and the Dodgers' rallying cry was born: "Wait 'til next year." The final score was Yankees 4, Dodgers 2.

While overshadowed by the classic 'game six' that preceded it, game seven in 1986 was a nail-biter in its own right. The Red Sox jumped out to a 3-0 lead, but the Mets rallied with three of their own in the sixth. It was Ray Knight that greeted reliever Calvin Schiraldi with a go-ahead homer the next inning that sent Shea Stadium into history with the final Mets 8, Red Sox 5.

The 1991 Series between the Twins and Braves had it all. Three games went into extra innings, four ended via walk-off, and five were decided in a team's final at-bat. So, naturally, game-seven featured arguably the most heroic pitching performance in World Series history and that was 10 shutout innings from the Braves Jack Morris: Twins 1, Braves 0.

Ironically enough, perhaps one of the greatest game-sevens in history wouldn't have been without some dramatic support from a player from the hometown of Bentley State University.

The final game of the 1960 World Series between the Yankees and the Pirates was perhaps the best ever. The Pirates decided to stack their lineup with left-handed hitters in game- seven against the Yankees starter Bob Turley. Pirates Manager Danny Murtaugh even benched his first baseman Dick Stuart who was the team's leading home run hitter for thirty-five year-old backup player, Rocky Nelson.

Nelson, a Portsmouth, Ohio, native had spent most of the 1950s smashing home runs in the minor leagues after failing an initial big league trial. The unorthodox move paid off big when he hit a two-out, two-run homer to right in the second to give the Pirates a 2-0 lead.

It was a see-saw battle until the top of the ninth when the Yankees scored two to tie the game at 9 runs apiece as the end came from just about the unlikeliest source imaginable. Bill Mazeroski had hit just 11 homers in 151 games that season, but his "no hands" magic at second base was mythical. The underdog, blue-collar Pirates hung with the heavily favored Yankees in a game that saw four lead changes of course until he ended it in the ninth-inning with the dinger heard round the world. Final score Pirates 10, Yankees 9.

Through all the minutia and clutter of any great achievement, there sometimes comes a moment that derives its own interpretation of importance. One of those moments was about to happen.

20TH INNING

As Manager Tommy Leach and his coaches sat together piecing together the day's strategy together, a large shadow slowly moved into the room. Oblivious at first, it was Jarred who finally looked up and saw the hovering figure now lingering in the door well.

"Gary!" Jarred blurted out. "Man, it's great to see you!"

With that, everybody's focus was now on the Vipers re-appearing ace who supporting a rather robust black eye.

"Hey, guys, sorry I'm late. I couldn't get a flight out of Vegas until 10 last night." he apologetically mumbled.

Still at a loss for words, Tommy did his best to cobble together a thought as it came out rather awkward. "Gary, I really wasn't expecting to see you here…today, uh, fellows, would you excuse us here for a few?"

With that, everyone hopped up and headed toward the door. Browning gave Gary a big hug as he was the last out while closing the door.

"Sit down!" Leach offered. "It's good to see you. How's that eye doing?"

"Na, I'd rather stand, I've been sitting on that damn plane all night."

Silence again fell across the coach's quarters: it was obvious that Gary Steinman was there for a reason.

"Skip, I'll be honest and just get to the point…I want to pitch today."

Taken aback by this most unusual request, Tommy sat back in his chair to give him a little more time to dissect the moment before finally responding.

"Gary, the last time we spoke, you were still admitted to the hospital and you weren't even sure when you would be released. Pug said he got a text and all you said was 'good.' He just assumed that you were doing all right."

Reaching into his back pocket, Gary pulled out a pink piece of paper and handed it to his manager.

"Here, this is my medical release. They gave it to me yesterday."

Quickly scanning the medically official document, it did appear that Elite Medical had indeed found Gary Steinman clearance to assume all normal work duties. Even though it appeared in compliance, it certainly didn't specify pitching the seventh- game of the 2006 World Series.

"You still have quit a shiner there, bud, what's up about that?" Tommy asked.

"No problem, I know it don't look too good, but I can see fine, and all the bleeding has stopped. I feel great, Tommy. I just want a chance to do what I know that I can do, that's all."

"Look, I have Milhuff going out there today. He's been going over all the charts with Jarred...he's ready, I can't take him down now."

"The hell with charts, I know, but I missed my start because of this." Gary said while slowly pointing to his left eye "I'm not going to stand here and tell me you owe me this, but you do! I'm rested, I feel great...and I can't miss on this Skip, I promise!"

"How 'bout we do this. We'll put you in line for first wave of relief?" Tommy countered. "You go through Browning, and if we get to that point, we'll get you in there if we need you."

"C'mon, Tommy, I'm not a damn relief pitcher. When I get out there, you get everything inside me and more. That's just the way I'm built, you know that better than anyone." Steinman countered.

Leach could sense a certain anger level beginning to build and wanted to shut it down before it escalated.

21 DOWN IN VEGAS

"OK, Gary, I understand, but to be fair to Mitch, I want you in the bullpen at 5:00 p.m. to workout with Pug for twenty- minutes. By that, I'm not saying that I have changed my mind at all. As you well know, Gary, we are a team first. To be fair, I will take all this into consideration because as you well know, win or lose, we all go home tomorrow."

Taking a quick breather, Gary looked long at hard at his manager before gradually responding to the proposal.

"If that's the best you can give me Skip, I'll take it. I'm also here to remind you that without me this season, well…you know as well as me where we'd be. I just want the ball tonight. You won't be sorry."

"Thanks Gary, let's work through this thing together if we can. It's certainly great having you back with us, and I sincerely mean that. One other thing, call it divine intervention or what, but I made a major mistake in filling your paperwork with the commissioner and your bereavement listing actually expired yesterday at midnight." Tommy slyly admitted, "I never was much on pushing around papers ya know."

Pausing again before over-reacting, Gary turned it down a notch to obviously show respect for his manager. In his slow southern Ohio drawl, he finally said everything that he came to present.

"I appreciate that Skip, but just let me go out there tonight and let me return the favor!"

"The term 'come to Jesus meetings,' has long been an over-used acronym for inherent gatherings of perceived importance. Two-hours before game-seven of the World Series most certainly quantified for such a particular assembly. The coaching staff, plus Mitch Milhuff, all jammed themselves into the cinder-block office at Yankee Stadium to make a major decision.

"Guys, we all have the biggest and most honest decision we have ever had to make as a baseball franchise here, and we have just ten minutes to get it done." Tommy began.

"Mitch, since you joined this team you have been nothing but the 'Rock of Gibraltar' to us. The decision that has come to our attention is completely in your hands."

Showing a bit of uneasiness, Milihuff threw up his hands very quickly to stop the flow of the superfluous verbiage.

"I'm fine if you want 'Steiny' to start tonight, he deserves it!" Mitch emphatically declared.

Stunned that he was unable to deliver his version of the Herb Brooks speech that he had hurriedly rehearsed for the occasion, Manager Tommy Leach knew when to stop and let his star pitcher continue.

"I just love what I and the rest of these guys came here to do, and that's just play ball and win. Hell, we all took the offer initially because after losing to LSU, we suddenly had a chance to keep us all together. Ask me did I ever expect that even we as a team would ever be here in the seventh-game of the World Series?"

The room was dead silent as all eyes were on a true warrior for what the game of baseball is all about.

"If any one player on our team deserves to be out there tonight, it's Gary who's most definitely the one that got us here. I'll do whatever you need me to do Tommy, but my vote is for the player who should be the CY Young and the MVP winner do what he does. I say let him loose Tommy, so we can win this damn thing and go home!"

Not only a sense of relief, but a renewed cause of resolve rippled through the room as Von Hayes, Tom Browning, Keith Madison, Jarred Brewster, and Tommy Leach all felt the unencumbered bond was to now move on with a critical call at no penalty to a valued teammate.

As the first-pitch was being thrown out by former New York City Fireman Bob Beckwith, the crowd was somewhat oblivious to a major change on the field. All eyes were on Beckwith as he took the mound to celebrate the occasion.

This hero was at ground-zero as it was still smoldered just days after the 9/11 attacks and is best remembered as President George W. Bush stood with a bullhorn in one hand and his arm around him on the other, instantly making Beckwith an iconic image of the nation's strength and resilience in the wake of the terrorist attacks.

"Yankee Stadium has never been so vibrant tonight as the finale of this most unusual baseball season draws to its final conclusion.

21 DOWN IN VEGAS

"Good evening, everyone, I'm Joe Buck along with Tim McCarver, and just when you think you've seen every dodge, twist, and curve, here comes another bombshell here tonight as the Vipers starting pitcher Mitch Milhuff has been scratched for the hero of game one; Gary Steinman!"

"A total and unexpected move here by the Las Vegas Vipers Joe, as at last report, Steinman was still in the hospital after that unforgiving line drive off his head in game-one of the series." McCarver added. "All reports seemed to imply that he wouldn't be back for the rest of the series, but there he is, warming up as tonight's starting pitcher for game-seven."

"There's no escaping the camera angles tonight either Tim, as it's more than quite evident that Gary Steinman's black-eye of courage certainly won't go unnoticed!"

"No it won't!" McCarver laughed. "But as I've always heard from my dad, a bright-eye indicates curiosity, a black-eye…maybe a little too much!"

"There's no doubt about what this player means to the Vipers as he is certainly a Cy Young as well as a MVB candidate, but most importantly, he has been their ace, their heart, and most importantly, their go-to guy in games just like this. Coming up next, it's the New York Yankees and the Las Vegas Vipers in game- seven of the Fall Classic here on Fox Sports!"

"Sean said to be careful whatever we do because the camera guys all know where we are sitting." Syleanna nervously chattered as she squirmed in her seat. "He said he knows that we are going to be a target tonight."

"I think if they come to us, I'll just flip my top off and show them the sisters!" Carla laughed. "I ran into Kirk Donges and Dave Stone getting a beer and both of them told me to make Portsmouth proud!"

"Can you believe all the people we know here from our little ol' town?" Syleanna reacted. "I feel that there more people here than watching me at 'Dirty Butts' on a Friday night."

"I hope this Gary thing works out." Carla lamented. "Cliff told me that some of the guys feel that maybe Mitch got a bit of a raw deal being taken down tonight."

"Yea, but you know how this game works. Being the 'ball-bitches' as long as we have…they have more drama out there than we ever had at any good day at the salon." Syleanna laughed..

"Then here we go sister! To our guys, the team, and an end to all this craziness and just one more win for our men…and home we go!"

With that toast, Carla and Syleanna clinked together their plastic beer-cups in sweet harmony.

"I kind of like being a woman in a man's world, ya know?" Carla added. "After all, men can't wear dresses, but we can sometimes still wear the pants!"

Bob Shepard announced the starting lineups as the almost 70,000 screaming fans in attendance from every sector of society knew for certain that whatever they witnessed tonight, it would forever carry them through their earthly existence.

Prestigious to the sport was tonight's umpiring crew that had Terry Craft behind home plate, Joe West was at first base, Mike Winters would guard the second sack with Randy Marsh at third. Down the lines, Tim Mc Leland was in right with Alfonso Marquez guarding the left field line. In a game with this magnitude of importance, it was certainly the cream of the crop when it came to the men in blue that called them as they seen them.

"All right guys, short and to the point! By now we all know who we are and what we gotta do. Wang is tough, but if you're patient, and look for your pitches to hit- they'll be there." Leach reaffirmed. "Let's go out there tonight and make sure that all the breaks belong to us!"

With the Yankees were now sprinting onto the field, Brooks Snyder slowly headed to the plate. It was Joe Buck and Tim McCarver for Fox TV, John Sterling and Suzyn Waldman for the Yankees, along with the voices of Ralph Hacker and Pete Harnich representing the Vipers radio network, there were certainly plenty of orations to paint the canvas of consequences on this very special night in New York.

21 DOWN IN VEGAS

"Hello everybody, I'm Ralph Hacker here on a night that will define baseball greatness! By now, we all know the curious storyline, but an improbable saga that has developed over the past three-months is not just a baseball story anymore. Through global technology, tonight's game will literally be seen and heard around the globe. The attraction: a worldwide chronicle to a bunch of college kids that suddenly went pro and now are facing the best baseball team on the planet!"

Pete Harnisch was always the spot-on guy who could nail a liquid moment into a thoughtful ground of solidarity.

"Right Ralph, and as of tonight for whatever reason, Manager Tommy Leach has yanked his starting pitcher at the very last moment for a guy that honestly…we weren't even sure was here!"

Hacker chuckled off the observation, but suddenly grasped that reality was now in place and it was all now all set for the record.

"Snyder will lead off the first-inning against the Yankee's Chien-Ming Wang as it was an astonishing end to the National Anthem expertly done by Kelly Clarkson here tonight. She got that last little high- note off just in time before the legendary Blue Angels added the extra 'umph' to the city with an incredible fly-over crescendo!"

The carpe diem moment had now officially arrived. Brooks Snyder was staring down the barrel of the Yankees timeless pitching lore as Wang let go of the first pitch of the game. Fox Sports announcer Joe Buck was all over this one.

"Snyder swings…it's a ground ball to and…under the diving stab of Derek Jeter, and just like that, the Vipers are open for business."

Sean Deeters could be quite the chameleon to the opposing team through his total unpredictability. Here was a player with power who was built for banging doubles all day long and who could also lay down a bunt so fine that the rules committee would have serious grounds for declaring it illegal. This time, Tommy called for the sure thing.

"Deeters squares to bunt…it's down, and it's a slow- roller toward first! Buck screamed. "Shefield has it and flips to Wang who beats Deeters to the bag for the out, but a perfectly executed sacrifice by the Vipers as they take a small-ball chapter from game-one, and now it's one out, one on, and Cliff Collier to the plate"

Cliff hung in there as Wang threw sliders, curves, fastballs, and change-ups.

On the thirteenth pitch, he got under one just a little late under the hands of Collier that sent a lazy fly ball to Center Field.

"The power-plant, Karl 'King Kong" Smith now steps up to the plate, two- out and Sean Deeters standing on second. This is a great opportunity for Las Vegas to draw first blood," Buck said.

Finally working Chein-Ming Wang to a full count, Karl Smith found the pitch to hit.

"Smith sends one long and hard to left! Matsui is going back ... and plays it off the wall as Snyder is on his way home! Here comes the relay- throw from Jeter to the plate and he's safe! No! now they're saying that he's out!Home plate umpire Terry Craft looked like he was ready to call him safe, but now is emphatically waving the out sign, and I really don't know why! It certainly looked from here, Tim, that Snyder had beaten the throw and crossed the plate just ahead of the ball, and now...here comes Vipers Manager Tommy Leach from the dugout, and he is 100% percent steam- broiled!"

"What the hell are you looking at Terry?" Leach screamed. "His foot was across the damn plate before the tag! They could see that from the fucking space shuttle!"

"Not the way I saw it, Tommy, he got the ball down before his shoe crossed over the plate." Craft coolly reacted.

"There's no way! No way! Are you watching the same game I am? Ask your crew! C'mon, Terry, this is the World Series, man! You can't cheat me out of a run here!"

At any level of officiating, there are several words one should avoid especially as the banter becomes heated, and the Vipers manager just used one of them.

"I'll pretend only once that I didn't hear that!" Craft said with his feathers now firmly ruffled. "I'm giving you just one more warning Leach, and that is to get your ass back in the dugout right now so we can get this game over before Christmas. He's out and I stand by my call."

21 DOWN IN VEGAS

Tommy continued to press the boundaries of who gets the last word until while face to face, he finally verbalized just one too many insults over the line.

"At least you've taught me something about the animal world, Craft, because until now, I thought only horses slept while standing up!"

With that, Terry Craft had heard all he cared to hear as he defiantly pointed to his tormentor's chest and then threw up the thumb.

"You're out of here, Tommy, Take a hike!"

"You've got to be kidding me!" Joe Buck parlayed in disbelief, "Home plate umpire Terry Craft has just thrown the Vipers Manager Tommy Leach out of this game! Unbelievable! It's the seventh-game of the World Series, and he's still out there trying to get his money's worth! Oh my, Tim, just when you thought you couldn't get any wackier with all this, here ya go. This is indeed one of the more bizarre turn of events that I've ever witnessed!"

"I don't know what he must have said to get that kind of mustard slapped on him, Joe, but the Yankee Stadium crowd is also giving him the famous cheer that this borough is given credit for inventing!" Tim McCarver chuckled.

"The Vipers manager has finally left the field as the Las Vegas brain-trust are now huddled together in the dugout, and it looks like Bench Coach Keith Madison with clipboard firmly in hand will now be handling the managerial duties for the rest of the night." Buck continued. "This just compounds times-two the craziness as if you will remember, it was Madison who was the coach of the Bentley State Eagles during their run in the College World Series just a few short months ago before they became the new Vipers, and by now, we all know that story! So now he's back as the manager again in perhaps the biggest baseball game of all time. Wow, how's that for your good ol' country-coincidence?"

With all the temporary chaos surrounding the ejection of Leach, a lone and focused figure slowly strode to the mound to begin his eight warm-up tosses. Gary Steinman had been named the new starting pitcher less than an hour before game-time, and that too added just another unexplained sideshow to the already blustering atmosphere. John Sterling was one who was most puzzled to see him and couldn't help but to wonder aloud from the Yankees broadcast booth.

"It's been a wild-one so far and we've just played a half an inning here in New York. The Vipers manager will now get the best seat the clubhouse has to offer as another big change for Las Vegas is that the announced starting pitcher Mitch Milhuff has now apparently been taken down for the veteran Gary Steinman."

Resetting the stage and explaining the changes, Sterling was like many that thought that the eye-injury in the first game of the series was disabling enough to end any chance of seeing Steinman again in the post-season. As the Yankees prepared to bat in the bottom of the first, he still had his doubts.

"I don't know what the medical report on Steinman's injury is because that information is obviously in the HIPA files of Major League Baseball, but I can tell you I personally don't know how this guy can even see out of that left-eye as he faces Damon, Jeter, and Abreu to start off the bottom of the first!"

Jarred Brewster stood by Madison as he was quickly assembling his new duties while trying to get a handle on the state of affairs.

"I was watching him real close out there in the bullpen Keith. It looked like he was throwing as good as I've ever seen him."

Ignoring the impromptu pitching report for just a second, Keith Madison was overwhelmed cram-coursing information. Realizing suddenly that he had just been addressed, he finally turned to Jarred with a response.

"Uh, thanks Jarred. Look, here's where I need your help tonight. You have to be my second set of eyes starting now. Charting pitches, taking care of the bench, that's where I really need you right now. Just like you always do, just keep your head in the game for me."

"You got it!" smiled Jarred while quickly reaching for the clip-board, "No worries, you just do your thing and let's take home some hardware!"

If there was any doubt about his ability to throw a baseball on this given night, ten- pitches is all it took for Gary Steinman to sit the Yankee's lead-off trio down in order.

"If I hadn't seen it, I wouldn't have believed it as Gary Steinman strikes out the side here in the bottom of the first!" Viper's announcer Ralph Hacker proclaimed. "Wow, ten- pitches with one being a foul ball, that's what I call maximum pitch efficiency."

"That foul-ball by Jeter almost snuck in under his bat." Pete Harnisch added. "But every pitch was in the strike zone and as the record indicates, that's rather unhittable."

"No score after one as Chadwick, Kennedy, and Duzan are scheduled up here in the top of the second. In case you're just tuning in, Tommy Leach was thrown out of the game in the bottom of the first-inning disputing a play at the plate. The Vipers' Bench Coach Keith Madison is now the interim-manager for the rest of this game. It's not like he's new to this position, Peter." Hacker railed.

"The Bentley State Eagles were the smallest team ever to make it to the college finals, and yea, Keith was their man as they were beaten, I believe by LSU on a final play at the plate?"

"You are correct!" Hacker affirmed to his sidekick as Karl Smith stepped in to take his first-swats against Chein-Ming Wang.

Patience at the plate drew a leadoff walk for first baseman Bombo Chadwick as Gary Duzan followed up with a crisp single to left. Vipers' catcher Doug Pouge tried to drop down a bunt to move both the runners into scoring position, but was nicked on the wrist as he tried to pull away from an inside pitch to load the bases for the Vipers.

Pitching Coach for the Yankees Ron Guidry took a quick- trot out to the mound to try and settle his normally steady ace as a feel of early restlessness began to waft among the New York faithful.

Terrence Kennedy had been a bench player on a bad team until the infusion of the Bentley State Eagles. Making the decision to stay and step up was like a magic transformation for a player that was considered just a good player with potential. Since taking over the shortstop duties in August, his batting average climbed to a solid .291 with a fielding average that was pristine. Only three errors marred his total attempts that put him right alongside Omar Vasquel, Dereck Jeter, and Jose Reyes.

"Guidry is now back to the dugout and has for sure said his piece," assured Joe Buck as Wang now stared into Jorge Posada for the sign. Running the count even at 2-2, Kennedy waited on a pitch that he hoped would come as FedEx couldn't have delivered it any sweeter."

"Kennedy swings and there's a long drive to right! Abreu is on the warning track and it's …off the wall! Chadwick scores, Duzan scores, here comes Pouge to the plate as the throw is cut-off by Jeter, and Terrence Kennedy has just cleared the bases with a double and the Vipers now lead the Yankees 3-0 here in the top of the second and still…nobody out!"

"Wang had been teasing him on the corners with those fastballs, and you had the feeling he just might have known that change-up was coming." Tim McCarver added.

After a brief meeting on the hill with Jeter, Rodrigues, Shefield, and Posada, Chein-Ming Wang went back to work getting DH Luke Shepard to groundout to short keeping Kennedy at second. Back to the top of the order, it was second baseman Brooks Snyder that hit a screaming liner over second that Derek Jeter somehow snagged for the third out of the inning. The Yankees had salvaged the onslaught; but it was damage done.

"Keep your heads up, two-innings down, seven to go, keep them off the boards!" Interim- Manager Keith Madison shouted his encouragement. "Winners never look back!"

Watching his players sprint back out on the field suddenly forced a familiar flashback to Omaha, Nebraska, when he knew that his team could and would win the collegiate title. Perhaps it's an impression only one can get when you know deep down in the burrows of your soul that you are supposed to accomplish something and are totally shocked if you don't. Keith Madison was now immersed in the glow that this time; the ending had to be different. Wrestling with the incubus of our personal failures, whether deserved or not, it is always the quality core of difference from winning or just giving up.

In Portsmouth, Ohio, every sports bar and tavern had suddenly erupted into unstoppable celebratory behavior witnessing now a three-run lead against the Yankees. At the Portsmouth Brewing Company, owner Steve Mault offered a round of free drinks for every inning the Yankees didn't score.

Scott Schmidt who pioneered the first Buffalo Wild Wings to the area was giving away a free chicken- wing for every run that the Vipers scored. So far, he was three in the hole to every patron, but he really didn't seem to care.

ESPN's Erin Andrews was live on the campus in the student union center of Bentley State offering periodic updates as Rich Fraley of Rich TV and Home Center had again installed ten big-screen TV's for the students to join together for the game. Local notable memorabilia collector Johnny Carpenter was also on hand with a display of his vintage baseball mementos including an autographed ball from Babe Ruth.

Local jeweler Rick Morgan was the first to yell at Johnny with a light-hearted, but heeded- warning.

"Hey Johnny, I hope you didn't get that thing from those guys in LA. or you just might have some 'splainin' to do!"

Overall, the atmosphere was beyond mirthful as Gary Steinman headed into the bottom of the second.

"Hey, boss, Wang's up to thirty-seven pitches already and that's only in two-innings. Just once he has he done that this year and it was against Oakland and then he was knocked out after four." Jarred Brewster dutifully reported to Keith Madison.

"OK Jarred, who's Torres' 'go-to-guy' up next?" Madison casually asked.

"Mike Myers or Scott Proctor, probably Myers because except for Rivera, the other guys in the bullpen give up too many runs. Farnsworth would be their last choice in a game like this I would think, Meyers is the man."

"Start breaking him down for me Jarred, I agree, that we won't see Wang into the sixth-inning." As most flash-point moments in sports go, the highlights are exactly that.

Gary Steinman was an emotionless robot on the mound, mowing down batter after batter in an almost surgical procession. At the end of five-innings, he had thrown a total of sixty-three pitches and allowed just one infield hit to Johnny Damon who beat out a questionable call at first. Chein-Ming Wang continued to labor, walking several Vipers and giving up a couple of benign hits along the way he continued to pitch out of any serious trouble. At the end of five-innings, the score remained the same.

"We might just be witnessing one of the greatest pitching performances in World Series baseball history here tonight!" Joe Buck admitted. "Watching a guy who, and let's face it, got beaned in the head just a little over a week ago and tonight is as masterful out there as any pitcher that I have ever seen."

"The one thing that I personally can't look away from honestly is that left eye." Tim McCarver added. "As I sit here in the booth, and I'm sure our TV audience can't help but to also notice that huge patch of purple and black."

"I agree Tim," Buck inserted, "But it ain't on the outside here that counts tonight. It may not look pretty, but inside, this guy so far is a well-oiled mean and lean pitching- machine."

The Vipers teased another run in the top of the sixth as Sean Deters lead off with a line-drive double past Johnny Damon that went to the wall. As predicted, that was the end of the line for Chien-Ming Wang.

"It looks like Joe Torre has seen enough." John Sterling announced. "Wang had thrown 103 pitches, but was laboring out there through five-plus innings. It looks like Joe is calling to the bullpen to bring in the submarine captain, Mike Meyers."

A rarity on any pitching staff, Myers was a lefty reliever who was deemed a "submarine pitcher" because he threw the ball with his arm at or below his shoulder rather than above.

When he was with the Tigers, it was Baseball Hall of Famer Al Kaline, then a broadcaster with the team that suggested that Myers experiment with the unorthodox style of delivery.

Moving over from the dugout rail, Jarred leaned into Keith Madison's ear. "He's here just to hold serve until Proctor is ready."

"How so?" Keith asked. "What do you see going on?"

21 DOWN IN VEGAS

"They can't afford to give up any more runs, he's not a long-reliever. This, and maybe the seventh, and that's it for him." Jarred responded.

"Well, you've nailed it so far Brewster." Madison noted. "But we really need to get Sean in here. You can never have enough runs against the Yankees."

Mike Meyers did exactly what Joe Torre hoped he would do as Cliff Collier grounded out from third to first, keeping Deeters at second. "King Kong" Karl Smith just missed his pitch on a high fastball and got under it for an infield pop-up. Bombo Chadwick then ended the threat by going down on strikes and that left the Vipers right-fielder stranded at second-base.

Matsui, Posada, and Cano were now up to face Steinman in the bottom of the sixth as the Yankee Stadium crowd began to sense the proper degree of urgency that was due. Three runs down and just twelve- outs away. That was the dip-stick of reality for the trailing Yanks against a baseball heart that looked like it was made out of tungsten and steel.

"Steinman has been stellar here tonight!" Ralph Hacker noted from the Vipers' radio booth. "I keep wondering though, Pete, about that eye. You would know better than anyone, but when pitching injured like that, does it really take you away from you're overall game?"

"It certainly can, but it's all a level of endurance!" Harnisch responded. "I once pitched with a cracked rib for three-innings that I got while sliding into home when I was playing for Houston. I never even knew what happened until the next day. To answer your question truthfully, it's all on a case by case basis!"

The Jumbo-Tron also used this pitching break to highlight both Carla and Syleanna sitting together in the stands. No fuss was made, but looking up, it was extremely awkward to hide from an eighty-foot head!

"Holy shit, that's us, winch!" Carla squealed as she pointed at the screen!

"I really could have just spent a little more time on my 'Peachy' or on my Lindsey Lohan stuff…this isn't right!. If I only knew I would be that big, maybe I would have taken a little better care of myself." Syleanna admitted.

The television crew also picked up on the camera shot using it as a bumper as they returned from a commercial break on Fox. Joe Buck couldn't resist a little extra commentary on the two beauties that he had been cued were Vipers devotees.

"Sitting and I'm sure enjoying what they're witnessing here so far tonight are the girlfriend and fiancé of a couple of the Vipers' players. I believe the one on the left is Carla Harris who is the significant other of center-fielder Cliff Collier and the other is Syleanna Griffin who is the fiancé of right-fielder Sean Deeters. I'm sure they would be the first to admit this has been quite the special experience to live through this summer. The two have obviously traveled a bit watching their guys play for two major baseball championship titles in just several months."

Yankee Stadium was beginning to get nervous as once again, Gary Steinman took to the mound in the bottom of the fifth-inning as he continued to pound the plate with aerodynamic achievement. Hideki Matsui was a four-pitch strike-out casualty as Jorge Posada flew softly to right. Proven time and time again with the game of baseball that reinforces its charm is the fact that change can come at any given moment.

"One ball, two strikes on the Yankees second baseman Robinson Cano." John Sterling verbally posted as Cano once again stepped back into the batters' box.

"What this young man has accomplished in only his second season is truly amazing and ending up with a .342 batting average. He's 0-1 here tonight as Steinman looks into Pouge for the sign… he sets, and the pitch. Swung on and a deep drive to right and down the line! If it stays fair…and it does…and it's home run for Robinson Cano and the Yankees finally get on the board!"

"It looked to me like he hung a slider that Robinson just went with and that has been the only mistake we've seen tonight from Gary Steinman." Yanks radio voice Suzyn Waldman added. "Hopefully, we'll see some more!"

21 DOWN IN VEGAS

Staring into the outfield from the back of the mound, Gary Steinman gathered his wits to face lead-off hitter Johnny Damon. The score now 3-1, he knew facing the Yankee hitters for the third time around would be a more daunting task. After working Damon to a full-count, he sent the slider that previously didn't to the out-side corner of the plate. This time, it found its mark.

"Strike three, you're out!" home plate umpire Terry Craft barked, and through some disapproving glances from the Yankees center-fielder, he reluctantly headed back to the dugout.

"At the end of six, it's all in the books: the Vipers 3, the Yankees 1" Sterling dutifully reported. "We'll be back with more on the New York Yankees Radio Network!"

"You OK out there, Steiny?" Pitching Coach Tom Browning asked as he plopped down at the end of the bench."

"Yea…I'm fine." Gary quietly responded. "He just got me on a bad pitch."

"How's the eye holding up?"

"It's OK…it hurts a little still, but it's all right." Steinman said.

Understanding that his pitcher was in a rare zone, he was respective not being too intrusive with any extra conversation, Browning slapped him on the leg as he got up. His final words of encouragement were brief.

"Bring it home, brother, but don't forget you got a lot of help in here if you need it. Don't be afraid to ask, OK?"

Steinman just nodded as he threw the towel over his head and gathered his thoughts for heading out again in the seventh inning.

21ST INNING

Few sporting events in the history of the planet actually were riveting enough to actually stop it. There were the 1937 Olympics when Jesse Owen upstaged Adolf Hitler and the Germans by winning the gold medal. There was the first Muhamad Ali versus Joe Frazier fight in 1971 between two undefeated heavyweights, the 1980 USA Hockey win over the Soviet Union, and even the manufactured battle of the sexes tennis match between Bobby Riggs and Billie Jean King from the Astrodome in 1973 garnered enough attention to affect our big blue marble from spinning on its axis at a thousand miles an hour.

Three-innings of baseball would next define another one of the most historic accounts of "fan-demonium" ever witnessed. Since the invention of the World Wide Web in 1990, information was much more readily available on anything and everything. The seventh game of the World Series was accessible virtually in any country by computer savvy consumers as well as the most number of TV outlets internationally making this one single game: the most viewed and followed in the history of sport.

Steinman was again a rock on the mound as the home run to Cano seemed to have awakened the fire of desire. Vipers radio announcers Ralph Hacker and Pete Harnisch also sensed that something spiritually may have transcended.

"Steinman is throwing now and as hard as I think he was in the first-inning," Hacker reported. "He just struck out Derek Jeter and now three-strikes Bobby Abreu. That brings up A-Rod with two-outs and nobody on in the bottom of the seventh."

21 DOWN IN VEGAS

Pete Harnisch as an ex-pitcher threw some philosophy stew on the moment that was unfolding.

"I agree, Ralph, that Steinman is using his one mistake as a bit of a motivator here as we get into the late innings. Unless you've done it at this level, people don't really understand what an emotional role the pitcher has. Sure, he has his teammates to back him up on the field, but that mound is always a lonely place no matter how you're throwing the ball because whatever happens, it's all about you."

"I totally understand that as Rodriguez who is 0-2 steps in. First pitch he looks at a ball outside. We have just received an unusual communiqué from Vipers Manager Tommy Leach who has sent to us a telegram, if you can believe that, to Gary Steinman praising him on his great outing here tonight and encourages him to keep it up! Strike one to A-Rod."

"Harnisch laughing all the way explained the move. "According to Major League Baseball, if you get thrown out of a game, you can have no contact with your players or personnel on the field. Leach has figured out that by sending us an old-fashioned telegram, he can get around the rules. Good creative thinking on his part!"

"Well maybe," Hacker mused, "the commissioner will have the final say on that one. Here comes the 1-1 pitch to A-Rod…a swing and it's popped up high over third! It's in play and in fair territory as Gary Duzan slides under it, he has it, and that's all for the Yankees here in the seventh. As we go into the top of the eighth-inning, it's still the Vipers 3, Yankees 1."

"Gary has thrown eighty-four pitches, Skip, sixty-eight for strikes, sixteen for balls. He's on track for a complete the game if he continues doing what he's doing."

"I know, Jarred, but we have to start looking at relief." Madison admitted. "Remember what happened in that Stanford game when Milhuff was cruising along just fine? If we hadn't fired up Fuller and Burkes in the bullpen, there's no way we would have been ready for that. We're not going to let it happen again here!"

It was the distinctive voice of Bob Shepard that once again breezed across the loudspeaker as a part of the Yankee Stadium montage of chatter where the fan- buzz in the stands had intensified and become noticeably more desperate. "With a change in the lineup and now pitching for the New York Yankees, Scott Proctor."

As Jarred had surmised earlier, the Yankees right-handed set-up man would try to hold serve until the ninth before the arrival of "The Sandman," Mariano Rivera.

Until then, the Vipers would continue to stun the sports world holding on to a 3-1 lead sending their heart of the batting order to the plate in the top of the eight with Deeters, Collier, and Smith. Before Sean Deeters stepped out on the dugout steps, Keith Madison quickly called the squad together.

"Listen up! You're about to play the hardest two-innings of baseball in a place where no lead is ever safe. Let's play this game as you have always shown me you can do. We need more runs, so guys, do your job now is to go out there and get it! Let's go!"

Far from any classic locker-room spiel you choose, Keith deferred simply knowing the caliber of grit his teams had always shown and the ability to give every effort to do what was needed. As if on cue, Sean Deeters slapped a base hit between Jeter and Rodrigues and the Vipers were off and running. Another sacrifice bunt by Cliff Collier sent his best friend to second base as "Kong" strolled to the plate.

"Karl Smith now stands in as Proctor toes the rubber," Ralph Hacker again explained. "A base hit here certainly would be welcome to give the Vipers a little more breathing room here in the eighth."

Noticing that A-Rod was playing him extra deep and guarding the left-field line, Smith knew he was waiting for him to swing away. This time, he would do what few ever expected a power-hitter to do in this kind of situation.

"Proctor is now ready with the 2-1 pitch. It's on the way as Smith squares to bunt, and yes, it's a beauty down the third-base line. Rodrigues has got to hurry! He bare-hands the ball and the throw… not in time! As Karl 'King Kong' Smith catches everybody off guard, and now the Vipers have them on the corner and just one out!"

Ralph Hacker's excitement burst through the radio speakers with the impact of a lightning bolt from Zeus as the Yankees pitching-coach Ron Guidry headed to the mound.

21 DOWN IN VEGAS

The Vipers had a series of verbal signs that Madison had put into place using college names that called for select plays. Each scenario was extracted from an event that happened during a previous game with each team.

As Guidry was trying to settle down his pitcher, Keith Madison quietly sent out the word "Marshall"- two" for his third and first base coaches to be relay onto the runners. The "two" simply stood for the count the play would be executed.

Ron Guidry returned to the dugout while Scott Proctor walked around the mound, rubbing up the ball as Bombo Chadwick stepped in. From the television booth, Joe Buck and Tim Mc Carver were also wailing on the moves as well as the angst of this New York crowd.

"I'm totally shocked that Joe Torre didn't go get Rivera right now." Buck offered. "You're down two- runs here in the eighth-inning and you have a scoring threat from the Vipers, I just don't get it!"

"I can say this." McCarver added. "This Yankee Stadium crowd is on the brink of despair at this point, and it won't take much more to get their 'doomsday clock' a ticking."

"Bombo Chadwick is at the plate and he takes the first pitch for strike one…right down the middle" Buck noted. "Deeters holding slightly off the third base bag and Smith a few steps off first as Scott Proctor again sets, he pitches, and there goes Smith! He's off and headed toward second as Posada is up and throwing! It's a double steal, and now here comes Deeters to the plate! Cano puts the tag on Smith and now he's coming to the plate! Cano puts the tag on Smith and now he comes up and throwing! Deeters slides… and he's in there!…And what a gutsy way to manufacture a run. Wow…we've seen that kind of play several times, but this was a full bore 'sacrifice-steal' based on nothing but impeccable timing! That's a play you know they've had to practice time and time again to get it right, but the Vipers give up an out to score a run and now go up 4-1 here over the Yankees in the top of the eighth. Fueled by nothing but hustle on that one and this crowd is not shy in letting all who care to know that they aren't happy!"

"And now here comes Joe Torre from the dugout, and I think we all know what's coming next." McCarver winced.

"Joe Buck with Tim McCarver and its World Series excitement here in Gotham City as the Las Vegas Vipers have now taken a 4-1 lead over the New York Yankees in the eighth-inning of game-seven of the 2006 World Series… we'll be right back after this!"

Mariano Rivera was all business as he ascended to the mound while Scott Proctor walked off to a smattering of Bronx- boos.

On completion of his warm-up pitches, the Vipers third- baseman Gary Duzan would receive the wrath of a hurler who's reputation was turning off the lights quickly. After just three pitches, the top of the eighth- inning suddenly went dark.

Taking the field briskly, the Vipers players knew they were just six-outs away from proving the impossible. Gary Steinman slowly walked out again to the mound as Keith Madison couldn't honestly help to wonder how much his pitcher really had left in the tank. Bernie Williams and Jose Posada were next in line as Steinman now faced the crowd's pleading form of excitement to begin what would truly be an incredible rally. After just five- pitches, they had at least a small start.

"Ball-four to Bernie Williams and that's the first walk of the day for Gary Steinman as the Yankees have the lead-off hitter on here in the bottom of the eighth!"

Yankees announcer John Sterling had witnessed his team's late-inning heroics many times over as his excitement level was definitely on the rise. While facing Jose Posada there was even more optimism than ever growing the 'House that Ruth Built.'

"Steinman with a 2-2 count to Jose Posada, and the pitch… there's a line-drive in the gap between right and center! It will go all the way to the wall as Williams comes around to score, and just like that, the Yankees are down by just two with nobody out here in the eight!"

Gary Steinman stood on the mound staring down at the dirt before finally making a hand motion to the Vipers dugout. Keith, Tom, and Trainer Larry Starr quickly headed out as all could tell this visit probably wouldn't be pleasant.

"I can't see." Gary softly spoke his concerned assembly. "It started last inning, but I thought I could pitch through it."

"The left- eye, is that the one you're talking about?" Starr asked.

"Naw, it's both of them. I couldn't see out of the left one since the second. My right eye is now acting funny…I just can't go any further." He reluctantly admitted.

As the crowd on the mound now swelled to players, coaches, plus a trainer, Umpire Terry Craft finally intervened to break up the growing gathering.

"I've got an injury here, Terry." Keith Madison spoke. "I'm going to have to bring in someone else, he can't see."

"OK, all I ask is that you hurry it up. This is seventh game of the World Series in case you haven't noticed." Craft wryly replied.

Leaving the mound and slowly walking back to the visiting dugout, the Yankee fans, even at the stage of disappointment, showed their gratitude for a great effort by giving Gary an appreciative ovation. Even John Sterling was a bit in shock.

"Apparently, that's going to be it for starter Gary Steinman here tonight," Sterling noted, "but what a wonderful gesture as the best-educated baseball fans in America show their warm appreciation for an extraordinary pitching performance here tonight!"

Tipping his hat to the crowd, the following close-up camera shot exposed a telling single stream of water trickling down the right cheek of the now departing pitcher's face. Along with trainer Larry Starr, he made a sudden and quick exit through the visitors' dugout and into the clubhouse.

Taking a page from the Yankees playbook, Keith Madison called for his usual ninth-inning closer "Dirty" Ernie Fuller to take over an inning earlier than usual in the bottom of the eight.

On the season since coming from the Eagles, Fuller had been the Vipers true number -one "stopper." but for just a few stumbles along the way, had always shown the grit that you want in a guy that can't wait to get the ball in crucial situations.

"An unusual encounter here," Joe Buck informed his massive TV audience.

"Ernie Fuller, nicknamed 'The Dirt Man,' now enters the game and is allowed as much time to warm-up as needed. Interim-Manager Keith Madison already had him up in the eight-inning doing some throwing with Jeremy Burkes, but he will now take over with one-run in and Johnny Damon now standing out on second."

Fuller finally indicated that he was ready to play. Pinch-hitter Bubba Crosby would be the first to greet the new pitcher as he was fishing for a first-pitch strike that he could hit. Swinging away, he hit a long looping fly ball to center-field that Cliff Collier easily corralled for the first out of the inning. A third of the way home Miguel Cairo next sent a high bounding hopper over second that Gary Duzan slickly-fielded and the throw just barely nipped the Yankee's speedster at first. Posada moved over to third on the play as the Vipers were standing tough with an out left to go.

"Two outs, let's go, Vipers!" Brooks Snyder brashly yelled as Alex Rodrigues came to the plate. Catcher Doug Pouge ran to the mound for a quick word with his pitcher to make sure they were all on the same page. Bouncing back behind the plate, they were ready. Taking the count full, Vipers announcer Ralph Hacker was ready to bring the inning to an end.

"Fuller has to be careful with first baseman Andy Phillips now at the plate as he is an excellent clutch hitter" he proceeded. "Two-outs and Posada on second for New York. He sets, and the 3-2 pitch is on the way. Phillips swings and sends a ground ball down the line... and through the glove of Bombo Chadwick! Posada will score...and the Yankees have turned this into a one-run game!"

"I hate even saying this, Ralph, but that was an almost identical recreation of the Billy Buckner ground ball from the '86' series. Chadwick had the play at first, but it snuck under his legs and his glove" Pete Harnich added. "I'm sure that one will go down as an error."

"It's 4-3 here in the bottom of the eight as Jason Giambi now steps in. He will represent both the tying as well as the go-ahead run!"

Carefully pitching to Giambi's weak right side, Fuller enticed him to hit a soft- grounder to third-base that ended the inning.

"We have eight in the books here at Yankee Stadium in New York as the Vipers hang on by one as we head into the ninth. I'm Ralph Hacker along with Pete Harnisch, and you're listening to the Las Vegas Vipers Radio Network!"

21 DOWN IN VEGAS

Because of the overwhelming physical sense to the crowd, Brian Cashman went overboard to hire as much security as possible. Regardless of the outcome of this evening's contest, Yankee management knew its audience infinite and fiery passion they carried for the team. Along with over two-hundred of New York's finest included, the team hiring three -extra private security companies, plus fifty off-duty fire fighters to maintain the crowd safety.

As Mariano Rivera exercised his warm-up tosses, Bob Shepard made yet another one of his most important and sternest announcements of the evening.

"Ladies and gentleman, may we remind all of you attending here tonight that leaving your seats at any time to go onto the field of Yankee Stadium is in strict violation of the New York City law. Any patron attempting to do so will be immediately apprehended by the Yankees security, arrested, and prosecuted to the highest level of the law. From all of the New York Yankees management, we want everyone to have a safe evening, and we all appreciate your kind attention."

"Last swings kiddos!" Keith Madison blithely announced in the dugout. "We need more, but this is the inning you all know better than anybody else. History is not always a friend, but the power you all have within you can change it. Tonight is what makes you the ultimate author."

Since the sport of baseball was invented in 1869, there would be few to argue that there was a better relief pitcher in the entire game than the one that the Las Vegas Vipers were now facing. Given it was now into the ninth inning of the most viewed sporting event to date, Mario Rivera was not simply on display to just get a few outs, but also to rally his troops to victory.

Channeling skill over will, the top of the Yankees ninth- inning simply added to Rivera's already accepted Hall of Fame legacy as he struck out both Terrance Kennedy and Doug Pouge before allowing a harmless throwing out of DH Luke Shepard at first on a weak chopper back to the pitcher. The 2006 World Series was now down to just three- precious outs.

"Three- outs to go here in New York City and Tim McCarver," Joe Buck asked. "With all respects to my dad who saw so many of these classic games in his career, I can't remember another series that even comes close to what we're all been witnessing here tonight!"

"Anytime you're talking about thrown-out managers, blind-pitchers, and fan-standing ovations for the enemy and it's all in just one game, you're right Joe!" McCarver laughingly noted. "You can say that's pretty much a ball- game that has everything!"

Ralph Hacker and Pete Harnisch were probably at this juncture the most amazed spectators in the house. Ralph started the bottom of the inning, bearing loose a little of his broadcasting soul.

"Three-outs away from a world championship and I can remember so clearly that day in July when Cisco Wheeler made the big announcement, and I knew that I was headed for the drive through at Jack-in-the-Box." He laughed. "Who knew what great players and future- vision came out of that one single decision? Holding on to a 3-2 lead, Gary Shefield will lead off the bottom of the ninth- inning followed by Hideki Matsui and Robinson Cano."

"Looks like Fuller is now ready as Gary Sheffield steps in!" Harnisch added.

"It's truly electric!' Hacker agreed, "Yankee Stadium is now firmly on its feet as every patron in the house is looking to a higher place and fervently trying to will home this win!"

Shefield worked Fuller to a 3-2 count before awkwardly lunging at ball-four that hit in the dirt a foot before the plate. Hacker's jubilance was now penetrating.

"One out and it looks like Joe Torre will be taking down Matsui for Melky Cabrera to pinch hit. Cabrera has been little used here in the post-season due to a tight ham-string he suffered in the last week of regular play, but Joe Torre thought enough of his accomplishments to keep him here on the roster."

"Fuller now sets, and the pitch…it's a line-drive…off the arm of Ernie Fuller! The ball scoots toward third as Duzan picks it up and they'll be no-throw and Cabrera is now standing on first- base with the tying run!"

Immediately, the full consortium of Vipers representatives again headed to the mound as "Dirty" Ernie Fuller was bent over and in obvious pain. Keith was the first to get there and ask how he felt.

21 DOWN IN VEGAS

Grimacing while holding his arm, he looked up at his coach who had also been his history teacher back at Bentley State.

"Hey Keith, remember that horse-shit you taught us in school when Gandhi got shot and was assassinated? He said something like 'Hey, Ram' or something like that?" Fuller said.

"Yea, that's what's in the book," Keith quizzically replied. "What's that got to do with this?"

"Looking his friend and mentor in the eye he quickly added, "He couldn't have said that. It would have been more like, 'Hey, mother-fucker that hurts!"

Recognizing the levity coming from his number-one reliever, the concern was now could he continue?

"Where did he get you, Dirt?" Madison asked.

"On the shoulder muscle, I think I'm going to be OK." he quickly answered. "I need to throw a few."

The mound congregation grew by one as umpire Terry Craft again strode to the mound to recognize the official filing of a potential injury.

"Jesus Palomino Madison, are we going to do this again?"

"You saw the shot! Give him a chance to work it off, Terry!" Madison volleyed back. "Nobody's going to leave and your wife's probably taping your favorite TV shows, so you won't be missing anything!"

Realizing he may have been a little too blustery on that one, Terry Craft simply feigned a sarcastic smile as he walked back toward home plate. Meanwhile "Dirty" Ernie Fuller continued to throw, simply to see if he could continue.

"Fuller took the blunt-force blow of the line-drive by Cabrera," Joe Buck commented while the cameras captured the replay. "It looks like it caught him square on his pitching shoulder, but he is now nodding 'yes' to everybody. It looks like interim-Manager Keith Madison is going to go ahead and leave him in."

"This kid is tough!" Tim McCarver added. "He will not back down, and that's what many of the established hitters have all finally quietly realized that a guy who was throwing college ball in the spring can and will get you out here!"

Robinson Cano who was a Yankee fixture in the big-play moments for New York during the regular season was now standing at the plate as play continued. Waiting out the verdict of Ernie Fuller's arm, Cano found out quickly and it took only four-pitches.

"Ball-four, take your base! Terry Craft bellowed as Keith Madison had quickly seen enough.

"Not your fault, Dirt," Madison said, greeting him at the mound. "You gave all you had as always."

"Handing over the ball, "Dirty" Ernie Fuller headed toward the dugout as all the Vipers were now standing on the steps and welcoming their brother home. In the bullpen, Jeremy Burkes, Mitch Milhuff, and Everett Carpenter had all been up and been throwing. Looking deep into his soul, he methodically tapped his left arm bring in the lest-used Carpenter into a pressure-cooker situation. He called Browning as his choice was now officially into the scorer's book. At his arrival to the mound, the meeting of the two would not be long.

"Carpy, you're the right man for right now!" Keith confessed. You've done this for us a hundred times. Get me two- outs and let's go home!"

Noise perhaps being a game-changing factor in previous contests at the world's most famous stadium, this night it had to be the pinnacle of support as Everett Carpenter assumed the duties assigned. Again, Joe Buck and Tim McCarver hovered over the action.

"Back to the top of the order and Johnny Damon now stands in with runners aboard on first and second," Buck announced. "Big-drama here in the Bronx tonight as the Yankees fight back against the ex-Bentley State College Eagles!"

No media member could be a participant on this extraordinary night and not know and understand the history of what this franchise was all about.

There was of course Reggie Jackson who hit three-home runs all on the first pitch in game six of the 1977 World Series that helped the Yankees win their first- title in fifteen years. Then Aaron Boone's eleventh-inning bomb in 2003 that will and always will define what is melodramatic post-season play the Yankees way.

21 DOWN IN VEGAS

Inside Everett Carpenter's mind was a maze of emotions of what he could do as a pitcher in a situation such as this. Lack of work over the past few weeks was his first concern, but to know Keith Madison saw something strong enough inside of himself for this opportunity wired him up to maximum velocity to get the job done.

Working Damon into a 1-2 count, he decided to throw the pitch that no batter was ever really ready for. Again, Joe Buck called the action.

"Johnny Damon looks out to the mound as Carpenter now sets…and here comes the delivery! Strike three! The 'knuckle-heads' strike pay-dirt with a flutter-by that literally froze Damon up like a DQ blizzard on a Saturday night as the New York Yankees are now down to their last- out here in the ninth!"

"You know they've been throwing that as a regular repertoire from all of their pitchers," Tim McCarver added, "We just witnessed how deadly that thing can be when it's thrown right and well-placed."

"High-octane palaver is now at its best as the captain, Derek Jeter now steps to the plate, and you know this standing Yankee crowd wouldn't want it any other way as they are now literally imposing their own Yankee will onto the field!" Buck continued "This is what makes this game so special!"

Since he was twenty-years old and first put on his number "2" jersey in 1995, Derek Jeter had been the much needed missing link to a Yankee team that had seen some darker days. Eleven-years deep into his career, he had upheld time and time again that when the money was on the line, he was the guy who could put it in the bank.

Standing at the plate with Cabrera on second and Cano on first, the giant number "2" that stood above the number of outs in the game was daunting. KVPR Radio's Ralph Hacker was there to paint the audio delineation.

"It's two-out, two- on, and the Vipers leading by one here in the bottom of the ninth. Carpenter is ready…and the pitch! Ball one, outside. Jeter is one of the more patient batters you'll find in the game. His numbers always reflect that he's that kind of hitter that looks very carefully for his pitch."

Another ball, and this time it was on the inside of the plate as that turned the decibel level up another notch as all the concrete and steel that had been in place since 1923 was now physically vibrating.

"Carpenter behind two- balls, no- strikes, and again delivers! Strike on the outside corner as Jeter has yet to remove the bat from his shoulder." Ralph delivered.

Jeter took a full- swipe at the next pitch sending it deep down the left-field line clearly in foul- ball territory. With the count of 2-2, Everett Carpenter just missed low and the count now was full. Behind the microphone, you could again hear the pitch of anxiety from Ralph Hacker.

"Who could have ever imagined this, honestly friends? After these months, all these games, all the Vipers magic moments and it would all intersect here with a full-count in the bottom of the ninth, two outs, and the great Derek Jeter at the plate. Carpenter again stands in, he gets the sign from Pouge, and here comes the 3-2 pitch! Swung on and a foul at the plate! And it looks like that one caught Jeter on the foot!"

"It certainly did Ralph." Pete Harnisch chimed in. "That ball went straight down off the bat and got him square on the ankle-bone I think. He's trying to walk it off, but you can tell that one left some hurt on it!"

"Joe Torre, the Yankees trainer and several others are out now trying to give the Yankees' captain some assistance." Hacker explained. "We've seen those kinds of injuries a bunch up here and they never seem to go away easily. We'll take a quick time-out and be right back on KVPR and the Las Vegas Vipers Baseball Radio Network."

After several minutes of unplanned commercial fodder, the voice of Ralph Hacker once again emerged.

"Derek Jeter is walking gingerly back down the first base line and appears to be OK. Torre and his posse have all returned to the dugout, so here we go as we get back to baseball as Derek Jeter, gingerly I might add, gets back to the batter's-box with a full- count.

Carpenter rubbing the ball hard as he toes the rubber as Jeter is now set as once again Doug Pouge flashes the sign. Carpenter's set… and here's the pitch…its high! Ball-four as Derek Jeter has walked to load the bases and that will bring up the Yankees right-fielder Bobby Abreu."

"I don't think they're going to let Jeter run, Ralph. He's still being bothered a whole bunch by that foot, and instead of heading down to first, he's still kind of standing at the plate. Derek is moving and now he's slowly walking over toward the Yankees dugout." Harnisch noted. "Yankee manager Joe Torre I believe may be calling for a pinch-runner here."

"They are indeed," Hacker cackled. "Coming into run for Derek Jeter is none other than our old friend Toots Randall. Of course, who can't remember the former Viper who was let go with the rest of the team at the All-Star break? He did invoke some personal revenge last night with the game winning pinch hit in game-six. So now, ol' Tootsie is once again on the field with his replacement team now running for Jeter at first! How ironic is that?"

If there were ever a time one could sense that total pop-culture devotion was being absorbed by just one majestic happening, this singular moment certainly just might qualify for attention-domination.

As *Sports Illustrated* author Tom Verducci wrote on the issue that the Bentley State Eagles-Vipers appeared on its cover, "The fascination with this team is that it represents each and every one of us as we all struggle through life. Winning and losing is simply a part of our everyday DNA. It's the micro struggles in between that really complete the total picture. We all fantasize about breaking away toward greatness of accomplishing the unexpected. These guys are all living proof that it can be done as they have certainly proved that there is the temptation to give in, to give up, and then do what it takes to keep going."

A spontaneous visit to the mound by Doug Pouge with Carpenter, Snyder, Chadwick, and Duzan was brief, but to the point.

"Everybody! Head in the game! Play at the easiest base. Hold 'em and we're out of here. Throw strikes, Carpy, Let's go!" barked the Vipers catcher.

Returning to their respective positions, it was the roar that is the Yankee Stadium crowd soundly cascading through the Bronx late-night air as Bobby Abreu now took his stance in history. Even a couple of guys who had seen it all, Joe Buck and Tim McCarver, both seemed awestruck of this anticipatory confluence.

"Here we go!" Joe Buck began. "You certainly couldn't write a script of this caliber of excitement happening right here, right now in New York City. Two- outs with the bases loaded, and little- used Vipers Pitcher Everett Carpenter is now pitching to one of the real Yankee bangers, Bobby Abreu. Bobby started out the season with the Phillies, but since coming over to the Yanks has really upped his game batting .330 with a whopping on base percentage of .419. "Carpenter is now ready, he sets, and his first pitch is a strike right down the middle!"

"This lefty-lefty matchup is really intriguing." McCarver added. "Abreu has really had a little more success with lefty's coming from this side of the plate."

"Carpenter fidgets on the mound as he once again stares into Doug Pouge for the sign. The 0-1 pitch is on the way! Swung on and fouled away!" Buck reported. "At this point Carpenter looks like he's all business out there as Abreu steps away from the plate."

"I can't help but to notice," Tim McCarver interjected. "It looks like Randall is upset over at first as it appears to be jawing at someone."

The close-up camera angle seemed to agree with his observation as the Yankees pinch- runner appearing to be talking to someone on the field.

"Who knows?" Buck responded. "It's the heat of the moment in one of the greatest World Series moments that I can ever remember as Carpenter is again ready, and here comes the 1-1 delivery…a ball, low…as Abreu held back and now the count is 1-2."I want you to look at these dugouts for both teams. Who can remember the last time you saw the the Yankees wearing 'rally hats' and the Vipers' are all hanging on the steps arms linked together as something is going to have to break here soon.Pouge threw down the fingers for the sign as Everett Carpenter looked in and then slowly nodded. With Bobby Abreu locked into his hitting- stance, one could almost feel that this just might be the defining moment."

21 DOWN IN VEGAS

"Carpenter is again ready with the 2-1 delivery." teased Buck. "Abreu swings and it's a ground-ball up the middle! Snyder coming over from second and dives…and it's 'Off' his glove and the ball rolls into short center- field! Cabrera will score! Here comes Cano rounding third and he scores! And that's it! Here in the bottom of the ninth the New York Yankees have come back and won their twenty-eighth World Championship against the Las Vegas Vipers! Oh-my my, can you believe it? …What an ending!"

"After that ball hit off of Snyder's glove, it just rolled into 'no-man's land' a good thirty- feet from Collier who had no chance of even getting to it." McCarver added.

As if in slow- motion, the Yankees were bursting from the dugout, massive security was now rushing in keeping fans off the field, and Jarred Brewster sat transfixed in the dugout witnessing three things.

His team now dejectedly leaving the field, the ball which rolled about thirty-feet behind the second base bag was still lying there, and Toots Randall was standing between first and second base with arms in the air screaming at the stands.

Quickly, Jarred pounced from the dugout as Cliff Collier slowly jogged in from center- field.

"Get the ball! Get the ball! Get the ball!" he repeatedly screamed as Cliff finally acknowledged his desperate plea. Picking it up as he again started jogging in again as Jarred could be heard in panic-mode and screaming, "Touch second-base! Touch second- base! Touch second base!"

As a non-player, Jarred understood that there would be severe penalties if he himself stepped out onto the playing field. Looking again to his right the Yankees were all hugging and jumping in a rolling scrum Randall was still standing between first and second- base and seemed totally oblivious to the chaos.

Finally as Cliff got into voice distance from the thunder of the Yankee crowd, he slightly understood what Jarred was all excited about and stepped on the second- base bag with the ball in tow. At this point, the entire team thrust aside their bitter disappointment of losing to try and understand what all the unscripted confusion from Jarred was all about.

"Cliff! Stay on second! Don't move! Stay right there! Don't move!" Shrugging his shoulders, the rest of the team was now more than curious to what was going on and remained on the field together as the Yankees celebration continued. Maneuvering through the melee, Jarred finally got Keith Madison's attention.

"Keith, don't let the umpires get away. Go get them now! We won!"

Taking into consideration that all of the controlled bewilderment was now happening in the blink of an eye in real time, the Vipers interim-manager was again looking for a clear explanation of what Jarred Brewster was saying.

"Keith, get the umpires together now! Randall never touched second base! It's a force out…and we won!"

Looking out upon the now accelerating celebration on the Yankees field and turf, Keith Madison sprinted from the dugout to grab the first umpire he could find. That would be the first base umpire Joe West.

"Joe, I need you guys back here pronto! You've got to make a call!"

Looking at Madison as if he had just stepped out of a spaceship, Joe West simply asked, "What call…the game is over!"

"Randall never touched second base, it's force-out!" Madison replied pointing to the Yankees pinch-runner that had since stripped off his jersey and had now given it to a fan.

Looking around, West saw Cliff Collier standing on second, the Yankee players were all oblivious to any potential problems highlighted with a bare-chested Toots Randall slapping hands with fans along the first base line, and the Vipers players all still celebrating on the field.

"Stay here," West abruptly ordered, "I'll go get everybody else."

Upstairs in the Fox broadcast booth, Buck and McCarver were also extremely confused by the mixed-euphoria of what they were witnessing.

21 DOWN IN VEGAS

"The game is apparently over and the Yankees have won, but as our cameras are showing you now, there is something else going on down on the field." Buck observed. "The Vipers' players are all still out on the field as it appears the umpiring crew is now being called back out to discuss something. I know it's a rule of thumb to get the 'blue- crew' off the field as soon as possible after a game like tonight, but something is definitely going on!"

"I'm thinking it might have something to do with missing home- plate," Tim McCarver added. "I've watched the replay, and it looked like both Cabrera and Cano both touched the dish; "What we're seeing here at this moment is very bizarre."

"Yes it is Timmy, and you can feel the Yankee celebration throttling down here a bit as security is doing everything to keep the fans off the field, and even some of the Yankee players have now stopped the party out of curiosity. We're going to keep it here live until we get some kind of validation as to what's actually going on."

Standing between home-plate and the third-base now was the entire umpiring crew of Craft, West, Winters, McClelland, Marquez, and Marsh. Yankees field presence was Joe Torre, Ron Guidry of the Yankees also strolled up as Jarred Brewster, Keith Madison, Tom Browning, and Von Hayes all faced the judges in the baseball court of law.

"OK, let's get this figured out and go home, Madison!" Terry Craft proclaimed.

"So what you're saying is that it was a force- out at second, and the play never was completed. That's your grounds here, right?"

"Hell yes! That's exactly what I'm saying. You saw it too if you look right over there because he's still not doing it! Randall never touched second base!" Keith then pointed over beyond the first base line." My guy picked up the ball, and as you can plainly see, he is now standing there with the ball on second base: game over!"

Just the ponderous quality of something occurring of this magnitude in the seventh- game of the World Series, and especially in New York, was completely unfathomable to the six individuals who were now held accountable for such a decision.

"OK, everyone away, we're going to talk this thing over" Craft gruffly ordered.

"All six members of the umpiring crew have now moved down behind home plate and we still have no idea what's going on." Joe Buck tried to explain. "I can certainly tell you that the change in atmosphere here in the confines of Yankee Stadium has seen a dramatic turnaround as within just a couple of minutes this place has gone from sheer jubilation to almost a morbid sense of happiness. It's a very hard feeling to explain."

Tim McCarver also threw in his thoughts on the timeline of events as to the end of the game as he saw it.

"As I sit here, Joe, it's been almost five-minutes ago that the Yankees won their twenty-eighth World Title. Since then, we have seen the expected celebration, and now, it's obvious there is some kind of confusion on the field. The umpires are being brought back out and the Vipers' Center fielder Cliff Collier is still standing on second base with the ball. I personally don't see this turning out good for the home team."

"Well noted," Buck continued. "On that observation, there is an extra- swarm of security that is now moving toward the Vipers dugout as Collier has just left the second base bag to join the rest of his teammates inside of the dugout. As you might expect, nobody has left the premises here as it finally looks like this lengthy discussion may be coming to an end."

Unnoticed to most of the Yankee fans, the Vipers were quickly ushered from the field through the tunnel under intense safekeeping as all the Yankee players were still out and meandering about on the field. Breaking from the pack was Crew Chief Randy Marsh now had the job of walking up the first base line with a purpose.

With all eyes and ears of the world upon him, Marsh briskly walked up to the bare-chested Toots Randall and threw up a thumb.

"You're out! The force-out at second-base is enforced and the game is over. The Las Vegas Vipers win 4-3!"

Dazed and still confused of what they just witnessed, the Yankee fans began raining anything they could find onto the field as a quantified explanation had still not been given. Even if Bob Shepard could elucidate it over the PA, nobody could hear it. Yankee Stadium was in lockdown mode and had now exploded into pure bedlam.

"You have got to be kidding me?" Joe Buck retorted, "Joe Torre and his crew are in disbelief as this game has now officially been overturned, I do believe. The umpiring crew is surrounded by security and is now leaving the field. Manager Joe Torre is now beyond livid and I just pray for people's safety here tonight because we have just witnessed something that I don't believe has ever happened to any degree in professional sports!"

Caught up in all the pandemonium were Carla and Syleanna as their instincts told them that this was not the place to celebrate the Vipers' apparent victory. The pro-New York crowd was understandably terse and getting more volatile by the minute.

Not having a planned escape route of this proportion, the two understood the potential danger and started easing their way toward the tunnel that said "Exit," sensing a safe-haven from the storm. Zipping up their jackets as to not expose their enemy support on their shirts was also done as a safety measure.

"We still don't really have a clear or definitive understanding of what the ruling is, so we're going to take a quick time-out here and try and figure it out. It's Joe Buck with Tim McCarver and we're coming to you live from a very volatile and confused Yankee Stadium on the Fox Sports Network!"

The longer that the Yankee players all lingered on the field, the murkier the moment became. Finally, security insisted that the players now move within the confines of the clubhouse so they could attempt to empty the stadium safely. After an extended break, Joe and Tim retuned to finally explain the unbelievable turn of events.

"We are back at a quickly depleted Yankee Stadium as we finally have some resolve in what happened here tonight in game-seven of the 2006 World Series. It all resulted in an apparent early celebration from the Yankees pinch-runner Toots Randall." Buck began, "As an ex-player, would you like to explain it further Tim McCarver?"

"Sure, first of all, I wasn't totally blindsided by what happened out there, Joe, but I was waiting to hear what the official ruling would be. Toots Randall was ruled out for the third- out of the inning simply because he didn't complete the play on a force-out situation. Here is the rule and how it's stated. *Force plays are constituted where a runner on base is required to advance to the next base because a batter becomes a runner through a hit or a base on balls. If a runner is on first and a batter hits a single, that runner is legally required to advance to second base because the batter himself has become a runner. If not, it's then a force out.* Randall decided to start celebrating early and didn't advance to second to complete the play. The Vipers realized that error, called them on it, and…it cost them the game!"

"Wow," Joe Buck exclaimed, "this has got to not only go down hard with the Yankee nation, but Toots Randall as well. Not to be cruel, but I would think that he may have just roller-skated himself for enshrinement into the 'Bone-Head Hall of Fame.' I can't even imagine!"

"Actually Joe, this isn't the first time that something like this has happened in Major League Baseball." McCarver added. "If you go back to 1908, there was a player named Fred Merkle who played for the New York Giants and the same thing was called. Of course, it was a regular season game, but the Giants ended losing to the Cubs by one- game that year, so it did make a difference."

Breaking from the usual winning tradition, the Las Vegas Vipers quickly requested to all media that no live- coverage of any kind be shot in the clubhouse.

Tommy Leach was concerned of team safety as well as the sensitivity to the fans' emotion for the unusual end of the game. While the clubhouse seemed to be more like a bunker, that didn't stop the Vipers from finally cutting loose!

"Jarred! Jarred! Jarred!" The guys all chanted as they hoisted their Brainiac-charged teammate high above their heads.

Surrounded by the privacy of their own celebration, tears were shed, laughs were shared, and total team honesty was being expunged on the conclusion of what many will say was perhaps the greatest sports story of all time.

With arm draped over Keith Madison's shoulder, Tommy Leach was humbled to let everybody know that this man pushed all the right buttons to bring home a world championship to Las Vegas. Looking at Everett Carpenter, Leach toasted him as well.

"Carpy, this man saw something inside of you tonight that I probably wouldn't have seen! I know it wasn't easy for you with the injuries, plus at times I know you doubted yourself. Tonight, my man, you proved to yourself, to us, and to everybody in the world that you have the heart of a champion!"

The room exploded with gratitude as Sean Deeters noticed there was one of their brothers who was missing,

"Hey, where's Gary?" He asked.

With Keith, Tommy, Browning, and Hayes all falling silent, it was Tom Browning who was chosen by his peers to solemnly break the news.

"We didn't think that it was appropriate to tell you all during the game, but the sad news is…he died."

As the gasps and immediate silence gripped the room, Browning's lower-lip began to quiver. Looking at the broom closet to his left, he knew it was time to let loosen the love for the team's MVP.

"But, while the Yankees hope he stays dead, he just so happens to be here with us tonight. Please welcome, Gary Steinman!"

As the door clumsily opened up, the chants about the room begun. "Steiny, Steiny, Steiny!"

Cliff Collier quickly held court standing on a table as he began what would be an impromptu testimonial to their ace pitcher.

"As we all know, Gary is not much for words. He always lets his pitching do his talking for him. I think I speak for everybody here. Gary, in case you don't know it, and you are the one person on this team we have always looked up to. Even with your dad's health, you were always there for us. After you got drilled, you shouldn't have even been out there on the mound for us, but you were. Who cares what anybody else says…Gary Steinman, I believe it's a unanimous vote that you are the Vipers and Major League Baseball's VIP! Long live Gary!"

Opposite to the fact that Gary Steinman had just been temporarily interned in a broom closet, he was now totally revived from the living- dead and with a rare appreciative gesture of his teammates.

"Um...first of all, thanks...I never wanted to trouble you all with my problems. I just wanted to play baseball. That's all I guess I ever wanted to do, really. It's been a tough year for me, losing my dad and all. I know sometimes...I probably maybe didn't show it...but thanks to my coaches for understanding...ah...that's really about it. I just want to say thanks again for sticking with me during all this and allowing me to become a part of the greatest ball team in history."

As the cheers began, Tom Browning threw up his hand to add an additional log on the fire.

"In case you didn't know it, and you should, 'Steiny' here pitched almost eight- complete innings with one-eye. Just file that one away for a guy who loves what he does!"

The famed slow to accelerating hand-clap begun as the Eagles 'slash' Vipers realized that on this date in baseball history, they had indeed accomplished something that no- team before or perhaps after will ever create again.

The inter-belly of Yankee Stadium was almost like a war-zone. Carla Harris and Syleanna Griffin hung close to each other to simply find a way out. To say it was an inimical environment reminded both of an angry ocean that couldn't be tamed. Carla suddenly thought of a favorite quote she once read from the author of *"Jaws,"* Peter Benchley.

"The ocean is the only potentially hostile environment on the planet into which we tend to venture without thinking about the animals that live there, how they behave, how they support themselves, and how they perceive us. I know of no one who would set off into the jungles of Malaysia armed only with a bathing suit, a tube of suntan lotion, and a book, and yet that's precisely how we approach the oceans," yet tonight, it was Yankee Stadium in New York City that turned unpredictably turbulent.

Finally making their way out into the landscape outside it was totally gridlocked and streaming with mega-mad New Yorkers as the limo that brought them there was nowhere in sight. Making it to the corner of E. 161 First Street, the duo now felt completely helpless until they heard a voice somewhere in the massive sea of traffic calling their names from a rolled down window.

21 DOWN IN VEGAS

"Hey, Carla! Hey Syleanna! Hey… over here!"

Looking quickly around, they spotted a face looking out of the passenger's window and motioning them in their direction.

"Julio?" Carla screamed. "Is that you?"

Approaching the car, both girls were totally stunned to see their cabbie friend and felonious ticket scalper offering them a ride in the deepest, darkest confines of New York City; they instantly froze.

"Get in! Get in quick! I'll take you to the hotel!" he insisted. Looking at each other, both found themselves scurrying quickly into the backseat of a 2005 luxury town car. Partially relieved and a bit skeptical of their newest fate sliding into the posh leather interior, while placating this strange turn of events they were both in search of answers.

"Julio? What are you doing here in New York? This is the wildest thing I've ever seen!" Carla screamed. "This place is like that damn escape movie with Kurt Russell! God, it's ugly out there."

Laughing out loud, Julio turned to look at the ladies that he had just acquired.

"Hey man! No worries, now it's party-time for you ladies! Your guys are now the World Champions! What a game!"

"Julio, what happened? We still don't know!" Syleanna pleaded. "They lost, but how did they end up winning? I don't get it!"

"It was our buddy, Toots Randall, he fucked up really, really big-time tonight by not touching second-base," he started to explain. "It's a rule ladies…he was supposed to do something he didn't do, but then it started the gala maybe just a little early. He's also now in even more trouble than you even want to know!"

Feeling like they were talking to a person in a foreign language, Carla decided to take control of the Lincoln town car conversation as they maneuvered through the Bronx traffic.

"This is way too weird Julio!" she blurted out! "This is the third damn city we have seen you in. I'm really not buying this at all! So, you want us to believe that this is all you do? You just drive around in a cab stalking people?"

"OK, I really can't believe I saw you here, man…this has got to be fate." Julio began. "But since we are all here together, I do have something to confess. I am not really a full-time cab driver."

Not really feeling overly refreshed by that candid admission, Syleanna offered the next obvious question. "OK, then what are you?"

Pausing for a moment to create a manufactured dramatic moment, he reached into his pocket to hand them a leather-bound cache. Turning back he handed it to Syleanna to expose his real identity. "I'm also an undercover cop."

Letting the message sink-in, Carla was the first to respond. "No-way! You can't be! You're the one that got us in all that screwy trouble by making us give you all those balls and bats for the tickets…no, Julio, that's bullshit!"

With the car radio now playing on AM-660 WNBC Radio, Yankees announcer John Sterling was reporting some ground-breaking news. Without saying a word, Julio slowly turned up the volume.

"Perhaps one of the most stunning turn of developments in New York sports history has happened here tonight as the Yankees were deprived of their twenty-eighth World Championship by a player who put his own selfish interests before the team. It has now just been reported by the *New York Times* that Toots Randall has not only been dismissed from the club, but was not even allowed to re-enter the Yankees clubhouse after the game."

"Wow, man! That's some heavy hammer, man!" Julio commented.

"It has also been reported that owner George Steinbrenner was so distraught and furious that he ordered all of Randall's personal possessions to be removed from his locker and put immediately out into the hall with instructions given to security guards to immediately escort him and all his things to his car."

Trying to gather his thoughts, Sterling was obviously in a meltdown moment as he attempted to explain or even make any kind of sense to the devastating set of circumstances.

"In a further, but still yet unconfirmed story, Los Angeles authorities are now saying that the name Toots Randall has been identified as a major person of interest in selling massive amounts of unauthorized Yankees memorabilia to the now infamous sports-gambling ring in LA. Needless to say folks, this has all turned into a very dark night here in New York City as Suzyn and I will be back with more right here on 660 The Fan: WNBC Radio, New York."

Silence dominated the ride as again Julio looked back at his passengers. "That was me. I was the set-up man to help figure out where all this stuff was coming from."

"So why did we get in all that trouble?" Carla asked.

No, no, no, no…you guys were never in trouble. Actually, you were all kind of a big part of helping us pin down Ira. It was Randall that we all knew was out there cabbaging the Yankees stuff, we just couldn't prove it. So, I used you guys to help get me into the underbelly of the loot, and tonight, we get him…and, you guys win the World Series…it doesn't get any better than that!"

Letting everything sink in as they motored back to the Mid-Town Hilton, Carla and Syleanna began to believe that maybe their incredible journey through the looking glass may soon be coming to an exit. After a long night of celebrating with the team at the hotel, the morning came way too quickly as the limo arrived to take the girls to *The Early Show* at CBS for their last obligated -duty.

Hanna Storm took them through everything from the Eagles to the Vipers, the scandal to the surprising series-end, and even chatted about the wedding plans for Sean and Syleanna. As the floor manager was giving her the wrap-up sign for the last question, Hanna looked directly at Carla and Syleanna and asked. "We are almost out of time, ladies, but quickly I must ask, what do you think both Sean and Cliff and all the other girls behind the team's challenges felt your part was in accomplishing this incredible feat?"

Looking at each other and knowing they had to answer fast, Syleanna quipped, "Lots of unspoken love, we all kind of just stayed out of their way, but they knew our support was there."

"Carla, you have fifteen seconds, same question." Hanna asked.

Beaming ear to ear with a smirkish, but yet playful smile, Carla Harris looked directly into camera-three.

"Well, Hannah, the way I see it is that none of us ever really stood behind our men at all, they all knew we were there, all right there next to them!"

Back in Portsmouth, Ohio, it was an early morning radio voice that navigated through the celebration on WNXT-FM. His voice was far worse for wear, but the local flavor of an international aftermath was now as raw as it was real.

"We did it! We really did it people!" MIX 99.3's Hobie Harrison rejoiced with strained vocal chords. "Like you, I haven't slept at all. It has been such a great night! Replaying the games, being out there along with you, it's hard to put all this into words. Damn, I am so proud of our guys and I know you are too! I think it might be time to just shut-up and let one of the greatest tunes of all time really do our talking. This one is for all of Bentley State, the Vipers, and for all of you out there that made it really happen!"

The D.J. went silent as it was the familiar guitar-riffs of the Steve Miller Band that brought chills to the listening audience who instantly felt the connection and emotion to the true course of an incredible flight into the impossible.

"Time keeps on slippin', slippin', slippin' into the future. I want to fly like an eagle, to the sea, fly like an eagle, let my spirit carry me, I want to fly like an eagle, till I'm free…oh, Lord, through the revolution!"

In the year 2006, the Bentley State Eagles proved to the world that all dreams are crazy…until they come true."

22ᴺᴰ INNING

Post-Log

With-in a week after the 2006 World Series was over, Toots Randall was officially charged with being a major accomplice in the ongoing sports memorabilia scandal. He was eventually charged with felonious theft and conspiracy. Cab driver and undercover police officer Julio Rodrigues would become a star witness in the case as Randall ended up being sentenced to eighteen-months in the Albion Correctional Facility in New York and would never play professional baseball again. The Yankees owner George Steinbrenner tried to appeal the World Series loss to the MLB hierarchy, but was unanimously over-ruled

The Las Vegas Vipers players all immediately hit the talk show circuits into the fall and then on November 27th they traveled to the White House to meet with President George W. Bush. Upon regaling the players with his own baseball days at Yale, he publically lamented, "Hey, where were all you guys when I owned the Rangers?"

On December 23rd, 2006, there was another Vipers reunion at the Mirage Hotel in Las Vegas where Cisco "The Dealer" Wheeler threw a wedding like none other for Sean Deeters and Syleanna Griffin. While calling in all past favors and surprising the newlyweds, it was the heart-wrenching performance of "Just a Gigolo" by Wayne Newton who brought down the reception as he agreed to perform live and for free as long as he could get good complimentary seats to all of the Vipers home-games.

Norm Bratchett's four-way bypass was a total success, but his doctors warned him heavily about returning to work following the life-changing medical event. He finally decided that a healthier lifestyle was his new path, and on New Year's Eve of 2006, he informed the Vipers that he would be officially "retired."

Once regaled as Las Vegas's biggest loser, Cisco Wheeler turned the tables on his reputation by pulling off the biggest come from behind odds upsets in all of sports- betting history. While his passion for the game of baseball is what drove him, Cisco was no stranger to the 'wise guys' and their ways. Perhaps just a helpless romantic offering of the sport, nobody can really explain the $100 ticket that he purchased in early June when the Vipers were at a million to 1 to win it all. Local Las Vegas charities began to immediately taste the fruits of his generosity. Both Cisco and Brandon Briggs were awarded the Major League Executives of the Year Awards for 2006

Pitcher Gary Steinman not only won the Cy Young award for 2006, but also the MVP for the season. That had only been done by a miniscule few as he joined the names of Bob Gibson, Don Newcombe, Sandy Koufax, Roger Clemens, Denny McClain, Rollie Fingers, Dennis Eckersley, and Willie Hernandez. League Rookie of the Year in 2006 was Sean Deeters as it was also a landslide and unanimous win for Tommy Leach as the National League Manager of the Year.

The city of Portsmouth, Ohio, was now forever changed. It was immediately put on the map as a destination location by the "Travel Channel" for all interested in absorbing the actual feel of the entire Bentley State experience. Local merchants began offering reality packages to come and participate in the small-town climate that lay birth to a legend. Artist Robert Dafford created a mega-mural of the team at the cities entrance as thousands came to soak up the hospitable locality that was splashed upon an all-watching world and would become legend for years.

Bentley State University also dedicated a new wing and an Eagles museum to the event that was generously contributed by an unnamed donor. They also received over 150 applications from prospective students from across the country and expressing interest in attending the university and most were interested in becoming "walk-on" baseball players.

Keith Madison returned to his cozy little home at 2202 Woodlawn Avenue in Portsmouth, Ohio, with the feeling of unfinished business somewhat resolved. Realizing that he had scratched a very important itch in his life, he was well-placed in knowing that they tend to return sometimes without warning. Living it day to day, he was totally satisfied with the storybook ending of his adventure; at least for now.

There's an old saying that if you accomplish a great feat once, its luck. If you can do it twice, it's skill. Old sayings have that shelf-life of longevity for a reason, and it's because they're mostly on-point. For the Bentley State Eagles, turned the Las Vegas Vipers and who captured lightning in a bottle during the summer of 2006, sports experts, fans, and most people in general couldn't help but to debate as to whether this episode of theater could ever reprise itself again.

Always debatable, but never for sure, there's that familiar axiom that generally falls under the headline-banner of pure fan love and speculation. While often overused for sure, it at least brings comfort and hope that further success is as close as just another season away; "Wait till' next year!"

CPSIA information can be obtained
at www.ICGtesting.com
Printed in the USA
BVHW030446270223
659227BV00003BA/618